The Wapshot Chronicle
The Wapshot Scandal

John Cheever

The Wapshot Chronicle

The Wapshot Scandal

Harper & Row, Publishers
New York, Hagerstown, San Francisco, London

Six parts of *The Wapshot Scandal* have appeared in *The New Yorker* and one in *Esquire* and the author is grateful to the editors for their permission to reprint.

THE WAPSHOT CHRONICLE: Copyright 1954, 1956, 1957 by John Cheever. THE WAPSHOT SCANDAL: Copyright © 1959, 1961, 1962, 1963, 1964 by John Cheever. All rights reserved. Printed in the United States of America. No part of this book may be used or reproduced in any manner whatsoever without written permission except in the case of brief quotations embodied in critical articles and reviews. For information address Harper & Row, Publishers, Inc., 10 East 53rd Street, New York, N.Y. 10022. Published simultaneously in Canada by Fitzhenry & Whiteside Limited, Toronto.

FIRST EDITION

Library of Congress Cataloging in Publication Data
Cheever, John.
    The Wapshot chronicle, the Wapshot scandal.
    I. Cheever, John. The Wapshot scandal. 1979.
II. Title.
PZ3.C3983Wap 1979   [PS3505.H6428]   813'.5'2
79-1806
ISBN 0-06-010741-3

79 80 81 82 83 10 9 8 7 6 5 4 3 2 1

Contents

PUBLISHER'S NOTE

Although *The Wapshot Chronicle* and *The Wapshot Scandal* have been continually in print since they were published—the first in 1957 and the second in 1964—they have for some time been unavailable in hardcover and have never previously been published in one volume. Here then, for those readers who have caught up with John Cheever's marvelous inventions only in the past twenty years, is the complete story of the Wapshot inheritance, the incomparable portrait of an American family and a classic of American fiction.

The Wapshot Chronicle

To M with love:
and with best wishes to practically
everybody else I know

Part One

1

St. Botolphs was an old place, an old river town. It had been an inland port in the great days of the Massachusetts sailing fleets and now it was left with a factory that manufactured table silver and a few other small industries. The natives did not consider that it had diminished much in size or importance, but the long roster of the Civil War dead, bolted to the cannon on the green, was a reminder of how populous the village had been in the 1860's. St. Botolphs would never muster as many soldiers again. The green was shaded by a few great elms and loosely enclosed by a square of store fronts. The Cartwright Block, which made the western wall of the square, had along the front of its second story a row of lancet windows, as delicate and reproachful as the windows of a church. Behind these windows were the offices of the Eastern Star, Dr. Bulstrode the dentist, the telephone company and the insurance agent. The smells of these offices—the smell of dental preparations, floor oil, spittoons and coal gas—mingled in the downstairs hallway like an aroma of the past. In a drilling autumn rain, in a world of much change, the green at St. Botolphs conveyed an impression of unusual permanence. On Independence Day in the morning, when the parade had begun to form, the place looked prosperous and festive.

The two Wapshot boys—Moses and Coverly—sat on a lawn on Water Street watching the floats arrive. The parade mixed spiritual and commercial themes freely and near the Spirit of '76 was an old delivery wagon with a sign saying: GET YOUR FRESH FISH FROM MR. HIRAM. The wheels of the wagon, the wheels of every vehicle in the parade were decorated with red, white and blue crepe paper and there was bunting everywhere. The front of the Cartwright Block was festooned with bunting. It hung in folds over the front of the bank and floated from all the trucks and wagons.

The Wapshot boys had been up since four; they were sleepy and sitting in the hot sun they seemed to have outlived the holiday. Moses had burned his hand on a salute. Coverly had lost his eyebrows in another explosion. They lived on a farm two miles below the village and had canoed upriver before dawn when the night air made the water of the river feel tepid as it rose around the canoe paddle and over their hands. They had forced a window of Christ Church as they always did and had rung the bell, waking a thousand songbirds, many villagers and every dog within the town limits including the Pluzinskis' bloodhound miles away on Hill Street. "It's only the Wapshot boys." Moses had heard a voice from the dark window of the parsonage. "Git back to sleep." Coverly was sixteen or seventeen then—fair like his brother but long necked and with a ministerial dip to his head and a bad habit of cracking his knuckles. He had an alert and a sentimental mind and worried about the health of Mr. Hiram's cart horse and looked sadly at the inmates of the Sailor's Home—fifteen or twenty very old men who sat on benches in a truck and looked unconscionably tired. Moses was in college and in the last year he had reached the summit of his physical maturity and had emerged with the gift of judicious and tranquil self-admiration. Now, at ten o'clock, the boys sat on the grass waiting for their mother to take her place on the Woman's Club float.

Mrs. Wapshot had founded the Woman's Club in St. Botolphs and this moment was commemorated in the parade each year. Coverly could not remember a Fourth of July when his mother had not appeared in her role as founder. The float was simple. An Oriental rug was spread over the floor of a truck or wagon. The six or seven charter members sat in folding chairs, facing the rear of the truck. Mrs. Wapshot stood at a lectern, wearing a hat, sipping now and then from a glass of water, smiling sadly at the charter members or at some old friend she recognized along the route. Thus above the heads of the crowd, jarred a little by the motion of the truck or wagon, exactly like those religious images that are carried through the streets of Boston's north end in the autumn to quiet great storms at sea, Mrs. Wapshot appeared each year to her friends and neighbors, and it was fitting that she should be drawn through the streets for there was no one in the village who had had more of a hand in its enlightenment. It was she who had organized a committee to raise money for a new parish house for Christ Church. It was she who had raised a fund for the granite horse trough at the corner and who, when the horse trough became obsolete, had had it planted with geraniums and petunias. The new high school on the hill, the new firehouse, the new traffic lights, the war memorial—yes, yes—even the clean public toilets in the railroad station by the river were the fruit of Mrs. Wapshot's genius. She must have been gratified as she traveled through the square.

Mr. Wapshot—Captain Leander—was not around. He was at the helm of the S.S. *Topaze*, taking her down the river to the bay. He took the old launch out on every fine morning in the summer, stopping at Travertine to meet the train from Boston and then going across the bay to Nangasakit, where there were a white beach and an amusement park. He had been many things in his life; he had been a partner in the table-silver company and had legacies from relations, but nothing much had stuck to his fingers and three years ago Cousin Honora had arranged for him to have the captaincy of the *Topaze* to keep him out of mischief. The work suited him. The *Topaze* seemed to be his creation; she seemed to mirror his taste for romance and nonsense, his love of the seaside girls and the long, foolish, brine-smelling summer days. She had a sixty-foot water line, an old Harley engine with a single screw and enough room in her cabin and on her decks for forty passengers. She was an unseaworthy hulk that moved—Leander said so himself—like real estate, her decks packed with school children, whores, Sisters of Mercy and other tourists, her wake sown with hard-boiled-egg shells and sandwich papers and her bones shaking so wildly at each change of speed that the paint flaked off her hull. But the voyage seemed to Leander, from his place at the helm, glorious and sad. The timbers of the old launch seemed held together by the brilliance and transitoriness of summer and she smelled of summery refuse—sneakers, towels, bathing suits and the cheap fragrant matchboard of old bathhouses. Down the bay she went over water that was sometimes the violet color of an eye to where the land wind brought aboard the music of the merry-go-round and where you could see the distant shore of Nangasakit—the scrim of nonsensical rides, paper lanterns, fried food and music that breasted the Atlantic in such a fragile jumble that it seemed like the rim of flotsam, the starfish and orange skins that came up on the waves. "Tie me to the mast, Perimedes," Leander used to shout when he heard the merry-go-round. He did not mind missing his wife's appearance in the parade.

There were some delays about the commencement of the parade that morning. These seemed to center around the Woman's Club float. One of the charter members came up the street to ask Moses and Coverly if they knew where their mother was. They said they hadn't been home since dawn. They were beginning to worry when Mrs. Wapshot appeared suddenly in the doorway of Moody's drugstore and took her place. The Grand Marshal blew his whistle, the drummer with his head in a bloody bandage played a measure and the fifes and drums began to squeal, discharging a dozen pigeons from the roof of the Cartwright Block. A little wind came off the river, bringing into the square the dark, raw smell of mud. The parade picked up its scattered bones and moved.

The fire-department volunteers had been up until midnight, washing and polishing the gear of the Niagara Hose Company. They seemed proud of their work, but under some enjoinder to appear serious. The fire truck was followed by old Mr. Starbuck, who sat in an open car wearing the uniform of the G.A.R., although it was well known that he had never had anything to do with the Civil War. Next came the Historical Society float where a direct—an authenticated—descendant of Priscilla Alden sweated under a heavy wig. She was followed by a truckful of light-hearted girls from the table-silver company who scattered coupons into the crowd. Then came Mrs. Wapshot, standing at her lectern, a woman of forty whose fine skin and clear features could be counted among her organizational gifts. She was beautiful but when she tasted the water from the glass on her lectern she smiled sadly as if it were bitter for, in spite of her civic zeal, she had a taste for melancholy—for the smell of orange rinds and wood smoke—that was extraordinary. She was more admired among the ladies than the men and the essence of her beauty may have been disenchantment (Leander had deceived her) but she had brought all the resources of her sex to his infidelity and had been rewarded with such an air of wronged nobility and luminous vision that some of her advocates sighed as she passed through the square as if they saw in her face a life passing by.

Then some hoodlum—it must have been one of the foreigners who lived across the river—set off a firecracker under the rump of Mr. Pincher's old mare and she bolted. In recalling this disaster much later the people of St. Botolphs would recall its fortunate aspects. They would say how providential it had been that none of the women and children who lined the route of the parade had been trampled. The float had been only a few feet from the junction of Water and Hill streets and the horse took off hell for leather in this directon with old Mr. Pincher shouting whoaa, whoaa. The first marchers had their backs to the accident and while they could hear the cries of excitement and the noise of hoofs they did not guess the magnitude of the disaster and the fifes went on squealing. Mr. Starbuck went on bowing to the left and the right, the girls from the table-silver company went on scattering coupons into the crowd. As the wagon heaved up Hill Street Sarah Wapshot's lectern could be seen to go over and with it her water pitcher and glass; but none of the ladies of the Woman's Club was cowardly or foolish and they took a firm hold on some nonportable part of the wagon and trusted in the Lord. Hill Street was then a dirt road and that being a dry summer the horse's hoofs beat up such a pillar of dust that in a few minutes the float was gone.

2

The Harcourts and the Wheelwrights, the Coffins and the Slaters, the Lowells and the Cabots and the Sedgewicks and the Kimballs—yes, even the Kimballs—have all had their family histories investigated and published and now we come to the Wapshots, who would not want to be considered without some reference to their past. A cousin by marriage had had the name traced back to its Norman beginnings—Vaincre-Chaud. The declension from Vaincre-Chaud through Fanshaw, Wapeshaw, Wapshafftes, Wapshottes and Wapshot had been found in Northumberland and Dorsetshire parish records. In St. Botolphs it was given the catarrhal pronunciation "Warpshart." The branch of the family that concerns us was founded by Ezekiel Wapshot, who emigrated from England aboard the *Arbella* in 1630. Ezekiel settled in Boston, where he taught Latin, Greek, and Hebrew and gave lessons on the flute. He was offered a post in the Royal Government but he judiciously refused, establishing a family tradition of thoughtful regret that would—three hundred years later—chaff Leander and his sons. Someone wrote of Ezekiel that he "abominated periwigs and had the welfare of the Commonwealth always upon his conscience." Ezekiel begat David, Micabah and Aaron. Cotton Mather spoke the eulogy at Ezekiel's grave.

David begat Lorenzo, John, Abadiah and Stephen. Stephen begat Alpheus and Nestor. Nestor—a leftenant in the war with England—was tendered a decoration by General Washington which he declined. This was in the tradition established by Ezekiel and while these regrets sprang in part from a candid assessment of the man's self-knowledge there was also some Yankee shrewdness here, for to be conspicuous—to be a hero—might entail some untoward financial responsibilities. No man of the family had ever accepted an honor and in upholding this tradition of unworthiness the ladies of the family had so enlarged it that when they dined out they merely picked at their food, feeling that to refuse the sandwiches at tea or the chicken on Sunday— to refuse anything—was a mark of character. The ladies were always hungry when they left the dinner table but their sense of purpose was always refreshed. In their own bailiwick, of course, they ate like wolves.

Nestor begat Lafayette, Theophilus, Darcy and James. James was captain of the first *Topaze* and later a "merchant" in the trade with the West Indies. He begat three sons and four daughters but Benjamin is the only one that concerns us here. Benjamin married Elizabeth Merserve and begat Thaddeus and Lorenzo. Elizabeth died when Benjamin was seventy. He then married Mary Hale and begat Aaron and Ebenezer. In St. Botolphs the two sets of children were known as "first crop" and "second crop."

Benjamin prospered and was responsible for most of the additions to the house on River Street. Among his relics were a phrenological chart and a portrait. In the phrenological chart the circumference of his head was given as twenty-three and one-half inches "from the occipital spinalis to individuality." He measured six and one-half inches from the "orifice of his ear to benevolence." His brain was calculated to be unusually large. Among his largest propensities were amativeness, excitability and self-esteem. He was moderately secretive and showed no signs of marvelousness, piety and veneration. In the portrait he appeared with yellow sideburns and very small blue eyes, but his descendants, studying the picture and trying to divine what, buried beneath the hair ornaments, the man had been, always came away with an impression of harshness and dishonesty—an uneasy feeling that was increased by the conviction that Benjamin would have detested his descendants in their gabardine suits. The force of mutual disapproval in the portrait was so great that it was kept in the attic. Benjamin had not been painted in the uniform of a captain. Far from it. He appeared in a yellow velvet cap, trimmed with fur, and a loose green velvet gown or bathrobe as if he, bred on that shinbone coast and weaned on beans and codfish, had translated himself into some mandarin or hawk-nosed Renaissance prince, tossing bones to the mastiffs, jewels to the whores, and swilling wine out of golden goblets with his codpiece busting its velvet bows.

Along with the phrenological paper and the portrait were the family journals, for all the Wapshots were copious journalists. There was hardly a man of the family who had doctored a sick horse or bought a sailboat or heard, late at night, the noise of rain on the roof without making a record of these facts. They chronicled the changes in the wind, the arrival and departure of ships, the price of tea and jute and the death of kings. They urged themselves to improve their minds and they reproached themselves for idleness, sloth, lewdness, stupidity and drunkenness, for St. Botolphs had been a lively port where they danced until dawn and where there was always plenty of rum to drink. The attic was a fitting place for these papers, for this barny summit of the house—as big as a hayloft—with its trunks and oars and tillers and torn sails and broken furniture and crooked chimneys and hornets and wasps and obsolete lamps spread out at one's feet like the ruins of a vanished civilization and with an extraordinary spiciness in the air as if some eighteenth-century Wapshot, drinking Madeira and eating nuts on a sunny beach and thinking about the passing of the season, had tried to capture the heat and light in a flask or hamper and had released his treasure in the attic, for here was the smell of summer without its vitality; here seemed to be the lights and sounds of a summer preserved.

Benjamin was remembered in the village—unjustly, to be sure—for an incident that took place on his return from Ceylon in the second *Topaze*. His son Lorenzo gave a good account of this in his journal. There were four volumes of these, bound in boards with this introduction. —I, Lorenzo Wapshot, being

21 years of age and thinking that it will be my amusement to keep a sort of journal of my time and situation and the various events that may take place as I proceed along through life have concluded to make a minutes on this book daily of all circumstances that may transpire respecting not only my own concerns but of those throughout the town of St. Botolphs as far as I can conveniently ascertain. —It was in the second volume of the journal that he reported the events leading up to his father's famous return.

This day (Lorenzo wrote) we received news of the ship Topaze, my father Captn. She has been overdue three mos. Brackett esq. from the brig Luna tells us now that her rigging was much damaged by a tempist and that she was at Samoa 2 mos. for repairs, and can now be expected any day. Mother and Aunts Ruth and Patience hearing there was a heavy surf at Hales Point I harnessed the chaise and drove thence.

This day we were waited upon by David Marshman, 1st mate of the brig Luna who asked to speak privately with Mother and was shown into the back parlor for this purpose. He was served no tea and upon leaving Mother was rejoined by her sisters and much whispering ensued. None of the ladies took supper and I ate alone in the kitchen with the Chinaman. In the evening I walked to Cody's store and weighed myself. I weigh 165 lbs.

This day pleasant and warm; winds southerly. During the day the following vessels arrived viz: The Resiliance from Gibraltar. Captn Tobias Moffet. The Golden Doge from New Orleans. Captn Robert Folger. The Venus from Quito. Captn Edg. Small. The Unicorn from Antwerp. Captn Josh Kelley. Bathed in river. This afternoon the thirsty earth was refreshed with a most charming shower.

This day at about noon there was a cry of fire and lo the top of Mr. Dexter's house was discovered to be ignited. Water however was immediately applied in such copious quantities that its progress was directly stopped. A trifling damage was done to the roof. Walked this evening to Cody's store and weighed myself. I weigh 165 lbs. While I was at Cody's Newell Henry drew me aside with further news of the Topaze. He had the damnable effrontery to tell me my father's delay was occaisioned by no damage to his rigging but by his addiction to immoral practices viz drinking intemperately and indulging in lewdness with the natives whereupon I kicked him in the arse and walked home.

Was waited upon this morning at the counting house by Prince esq. president of the Birch Rod Club an organization of young men from hereabouts for the promotion of manly conduct and high moral character. Was brought before the club in the evening on the complaint of Henry esq. for kicking him in the arse. 1st mate Marshman of the brig Luna testified as to the veracity of Henry's allegation and H. Prince, serving as prosecutor for the defense made a most elegant and moving condemnation of gossip of all kinds whether or not they be a kernel of truth in it and the jury found for me and fined the plaintiff 3 doz fine apples. Upon returning home found Mother and sisters drinking rum punch.

This day clear at dawn. Captn Webb's little boy was trod upon by a horse and died before candlelight. Went to Cody's store and got weighed. I weigh 165 lbs. Walked with ladies in the pasture. Mother and sisters drinking rum punch.

This day was engaged in the gardain wheeling maneur. Mother and sisters drinking rum punch. It is Marshman's tale of Samoa that has undone them but they should not judge the absent unkindly nor forget that the flesh lusteth contrary to the spirit. I have spent considerable of my leisure time in this past year in the improvement of my mind but I find that much of it has been spent extremely foolish and that walking in the pasture at dusk with virtuous, amiable and genteel young ladies I experience none but swineish passions. I commenced to read Russell's Modern Europe sometime last summer. I have read the first two vols which I find very interesting and I shall improve the first opportunity to complete the work. By a retrospective view of the past may I find wisdom to govern and improve the future more profitably. To accomplish this and improve my character may the Almighty Ruler of the Universe grant His assistance and guide and direct me in all good things.

This day a wild animal caravan arrived at the River House and I went there in the evening to see the curiosities. At half-past six the gates to the tent were open, previous to which many had gathered and stood crouded together with their gallants like a vast flock of sheep when gathered before the shearer. It was absolutely disgusting to see delicate females and those too of the first respectability as well as many comely, strait and tall lads crouded and jammed and pushing and shoving in keeping their stations near the entrance of the tent and endeavoring to obtain as near a position as possible. The gate was at length opened and then it was a rush. The utmost exertions of several gate-keepers were hardly competent to regulate and prune the flood of ingression and the tent soon became filled to stuffing. Luckily I obtained a situation where by looking between several heads I could see the curiosities which included 1 lion, 3 monkies, 1 leopard and a learned bear this dumb beast having been taught to dance to music and add a sum of figures.

This day at 8 AM Sam Trowbridge rode over from Saul's Hill with the news that the Topaze was sighted. There was much livliness and stirring both at home and in the town amongst her other owners. Rode down-river with Judge Thomas in his chaise and was carried out to the Topaze by John Pendleton. Found father in fine spirits and has brought me as a present one rich sword called a kriss. Drank maderia in the cabin with father and Judge Thomas. The cargo is jute. The ship was walked up and made fast and the gangplank put down to where mother and sisters were waiting to greet father. They carried umbrellas. As father approached the ladies Aunt Ruth raised her umbrella high in the air and brought it down most savagely upon the back of his head. Aunt Hope beat him angrily on the port side and Mother charged him from the bow. When the ladies had done Father was taken directly by chaise to Dr. Howland's surgery where three stitches was taken in his ear and where he spent the night with me for company and where we drank wine and ate nuts and passed the time cheerfully in spite of his pain.

The early volumes of Lorenzo's journals were the best—accounts of the liveliness in the river and summer evenings when the St. Botolphs horse guards could be heard drilling on the green—and this was in a way surprising since he succeeded in improving his mind, served two terms in the state legislature and founded the St. Botolphs Philosophical Society, but learning did nothing for his prose and he would never write as well again as he had written about the wild-animal caravan. He lived to be eighty, never married and left his savings to his niece Honora, the only daughter of his younger brother Thaddeus.

Thaddeus went out to the Pacific on what may have been a voyage of expiation. He and his wife Alice remained there for eighteen years as missionaries, distributing copies of the New Testament, supervising the construction of coral block churches, healing the sick and burying the dead. Physically neither Thaddeus nor Alice was what is usually called to mind by the dedicated missionary. They beamed out of the family photographs—a handsome good-humored couple. They were dedicated, and in his letters Thaddeus reported approaching an island in an outrigger one evening where naked and beautiful women waited on him with ropes of flowers. "What a challenge to my piety," he wrote.

Honora was born on Oahu and sent to St. Botolphs, where she was raised by her Uncle Lorenzo. She had no children. Ebenezer had no children but Aaron begat Hamlet and Leander. Hamlet had no legal issue and Leander married Sarah Coverly and begat Moses and Coverly, whom we have seen watching the parade.

3

Mr. Pincher's horse galloped along Hill Street for about a hundred yards—maybe two—and then, her wind gone, she fell into a heavy-footed trot. Fatty Titus followed the float in his car, planning to rescue the charter members of the Woman's Club, but when he reached them the picture was so tranquil—it looked like a hayride—that he backed his car around and returned to the village to see the rest of the parade. The danger had passed for everyone but Mr. Pincher's mare. God knows what strains she had put on her heart and her lungs—even on her will to live. Her name was Lady, she chewed tobacco and she was worth more to Mr. Pincher than Mrs. Wapshot and all her friends. He loved her sweet nature and admired her perseverance, and the indignity of having a firecracker exploded under her rump made him sore with anger. What was the world coming to? His heart seemed to go out to the old mare and his tender sentiments to spread over her broad back like a blanket.

"Lady's going home," he called over his shoulder to Mrs. Wapshot. "She wants to get home and I'm going to let her."

"Couldn't you let us off?" Mrs. Wapshot asked.

"I ain't going to stop her now," Mr. Pincher said. "She's had a lot more to put up with than the rest of you. She wants to get home now and I ain't going to stop her."

Mrs. Wapshot and her friends resigned themselves to the news of their captivity. After all, none of them had been hurt. The water pitcher was broken and the lectern had been upset, but the lectern was whole. Lady's stable was on Hewitt Street, they knew, which meant going over the hill and through the back country to River Street; but it was a fine day and a good opportunity to enjoy the salt air and the summer scenery, and anyhow they didn't have any choice.

The old mare had begun the pull up Wapshot Hill and from here, above the trees, they had an excellent view of the village in the valley. To the northeast lay the brick walls of the table-silver factory, the railroad bridge and the morose, Victorian spire of the depot. Toward the center of town was a less sentimental spire—the Unitarian Church, founded in 1780. Its clock struck the half hour as they traveled. The bell had been cast in Antwerp and had a sweet, clear note. A second later the bell at Christ

Church (1870) struck the half hour with a gloomy note that sounded like a frying pan. This bell came from Altoona. A little below the crown of the hill the wagon rolled past old Mrs. Drinkwine's charming white house with her picket fence buried in red roses. The whiteness of the house, the feathery elms, the punctual church bells—even the faint smell of the sea—encouraged in these travelers a tendency to overlook the versatility of life as if it was only common sense to forget that Mrs. Drinkwine had once been a wardrobe mistress for Lee and J. J. Shubert and knew more about the seamy side of life than Louis-Ferdinand Céline.

But it was difficult, from the summit of Wapshot Hill, not to spread over the village the rich, dark varnish of decorum and quaintness—to do this or to lament the decadence of a once boisterous port; to point out that the Great Pissmire was now Alder Vale and that the Mariner's Jug was now the Grace Louise Tearoom. There was beauty below them, inarguable and unique—many fine things built for the contentment of hardy men—and there was decadence—more ships in bottles than on the water—but why grieve over this? Looking back at the village we might put ourselves into the shoes of a native son (with a wife and family in Cleveland) coming home for some purpose—a legacy or a set of Hawthorne or a football sweater—and swinging through the streets in good weather what would it matter that the blacksmith shop was now an art school? Our friend from Cleveland might observe, passing through the square at dusk, that this decline or change in spirit had not altered his own humanity and that whatever he was—a man come for a legacy or a drunken sailor looking for a whore—it did not matter whether or not his way was lighted by the twinkling candles in tearooms; it did not change what he was.

But our friend from Cleveland was only a visitor—he would go away, and Mr. Pincher and his passengers would not. Now, past Mrs. Drinkwine's and over the crown of the hill, the west of the village spread out below them—farmland and woods and in the distance Parson's Pond, where Parthenia Brown had drowned herself and where the icehouse, useless now, stood with its ramp sloping down into the blue water. They could see, from this high land, that there were no walls or barriers around the village and yet, as the wagon started slowly down the west side of Wapshot Hill and they approached Reba Heaslip's house, they might wonder how Reba could have carried on her life in a place that was not walled. Whenever Reba was introduced to a stranger she exclaimed: "I was BORN in the inner sanctum of the Masonic Temple." What she meant, of course, was that what was now the Masonic Temple had been her father's house, but would her jolting and exclamatory style have gotten her very far in a place like Chicago? She was a passionate antivivisectionist and was dedicated to the alteration or suppression of the celebration of Christmas—a holiday that seemed to her to inculcate and perpetuate ruinous improvidence, false standards and economic depravity. On Christmas Eve she joined her enthusiasms and went among the carol singers, passing out antivivisectionist tracts. She had been arrested twice by what she called the "fascist police." She had a white house like Mrs. Drinkwine's and a sign was nailed to her door. THIS IS THE HOUSE OF A VERY OLD LADY WHO HAS GIVEN THE LAST TEN YEARS OF HER LIFE TO THE ANTIVIVISECTIONIST CAUSE. MANY OF THE MEN OF HER FAMILY DIED FOR THEIR COUNTRY. THERE IS NOTHING OF VALUE OR INTEREST HERE. SALUTE YOUR FLAG! ROBBERS AND VANDALS PASS BY! The sign was weathered and had hung there for ten years and the ladies hardly noticed it.

On Reba's front lawn there was a skiff planted with petunias.

Going down the west side of Wapshot Hill with the full weight of the wagon forward on the shafts the mare picked her way slowly. Beyond Reba's there was a patch of woodland, charmingly dappled with sunlight, and this grove had on them all, even on Mr. Pincher, a happy effect as if it were some reminder of paradise—some happy authentication of the beauty of the summer countryside—for it was the kind of scene that most of them had hanging on their parlor walls and yet this was no photograph or painting through which they traveled with the spotty lights flowing over them. It was all real and they were flesh and blood.

Beyond the woods they came to Peter Covell's place.

Peter was a farmer. He had a small cash crop—sweet corn, gladioli, butter and potatoes—and in the past he had made some money building stone walls. A powerful man of perhaps seventy with rusty tools, a collapsed barn, chickens in his kitchen, cats in his parlor, lusty and sometimes drunk and always clean-spoken, he had pulled stones out of the earth with a mare that was older than Lady and had set them together into walls that would outlive the village, whatever its destiny. Dam the river and flood it for a reservoir (this could happen) and in the summer droughts people would drive or fly—this being in the future—to see the pattern of Covell's walls as they appeared above the receding water; or let the scrub take hold, maple saplings and horse brier, and fishermen and hunters, climbing the walls, would say that this must have been pasture once upon a time. His daughter Alice had never married, she loved the old man so, and even now on Sunday afternoons they climbed the hill hand in hand, carrying a spyglass to watch the ships in the bay. Alice raised collies. A sign hung on the house: COLLIES FOR SALE. Who wanted collies? She would have done better raising children or selling eggs.

All the unsold collies barked at the wagon as it went by.

Beyond Covells' there was Brown's River—a little stream or brook with a wooden bridge that set up peals of false thunder as they crossed it. On the other side of the river was the Pluzinskis' farm—a small brown house with glass ornaments on the lightning rods and two rose trees in the front yard. The Pluzinskis were hard-working foreigners who kept to themselves although their oldest son had won a scholarship at the Academy. Their farm, rectilinear and self-contained, was the opposite of Peter Covell's place as if, although they could not speak English, they had come much more naturally to the valley land than the old Yankee.

Beyond Pluzinskis' the road turned to the right and they could see the handsome Greek portico of Theophilus Gates' house. Theophilus was president of the Pocamasset Bank and Trust

Company and as an advocate of probity and thrift he could be seen splitting wood in front of his house each morning before he went to work. His house was not shabby, but it needed paint, and this, like his wood splitting, was meant to put honest shabbiness above improvident show. There was a FOR SALE sign on his lawn. Theophilus had inherited from his father the public utilities of Travertine and St. Botolphs and had sold them at a great profit. On the day these negotiations were completed he came home and put the FOR SALE sign on his grass. The house, of course, was not for sale. The sign was only meant to set in motion a rumor that he had sold the utilities at a loss and to help preserve his reputation as a poor, gloomy, God-fearing and overworked man. One more thing. When Theophilus invited guests for the evening they would be expected, after supper, to go into the garden and play hide-and-go-seek.

As they passed Gates' the ladies could see in the distance the slate roof of Honora Wapshot's house on Boat Street. Honora would not appear to them. Honora had once been introduced to the President of the United States and wringing his hand she had said: "I come from St. Botolphs. I guess you must know where *that* is. They say that St. Botolphs is like a pumpkin pie. No upper crust. . . ."

They saw Mrs. Mortimer Jones chasing up her garden path with a butterfly net. She wore a bulky house dress and a big straw hat.

Beyond the Joneses' was the Brewsters' and another sign: HOMEMADE PIE AND CAKES. Mr. Brewster was an invalid and Mrs. Brewster supported her husband and had sent her two sons through college with the money she made as a baker. Her sons had done well but now one of them lived in San Francisco and the other in Detroit and they never came home. They wrote her saying that they planned to come home for Christmas or Easter—that the first trip they made would be the trip to St. Botolphs—but they went to Yosemite National Park, they went to Mexico City, they even went to Paris, but they never, never came home.

At the junction of Hill and River streets the wagon turned

right, passing George Humbolt's, who lived with his mother and who was known as Uncle Peepee Marshmallow. Uncle Peepee came from a line of hardy sailors but he was not as virile as his grandfathers. Could he, through yearning and imagination, weather himself as he would have been weathered by a passage through the Straits of Magellan? Now and then, on summer evenings, poor Uncle Peepee wandered in his bare skin among the river gardens. His neighbors spoke to him with nothing more than impatience. "Go home, Uncle Peepee, and get some clothes on," they said. He was seldom arrested and would never be sent away for to send him away would reflect on the uniqueness of the place. What could the rest of the world do for him that could not be done in St. Botolphs?

Beyond Uncle Peepee's the Wapshot house could be seen in the distance and River Street itself, always a romantic picture, seemed more so on this late holiday morning. The air smelled of brine—the east wind was rising—and would presently give to the place a purpose and a luster and a sadness too, for while the ladies admired the houses and the elms they knew that their sons would go away. Why did the young want to go away? Why did the young want to go away?

Mr. Pincher stopped long enough for Mrs. Wapshot to climb down from the wagon. "I shan't thank you for the ride," she said, "but I will thank Lady. It was her idea." This was Mrs. Wapshot's style, and smiling good-by she stepped gracefully up the walk to her door.

4

Rosalie Young took the road to the shore that morning, unknown to the Wapshots as you are unknown to me, early, early, long before the parade had begun to form in St. Botolphs, way to the south. Her date stopped for her in his old convertible at the rooming house in the city where she lived. Mrs. Shannon, the landlady, watched them drive away through the glass panels of her front door. Youth was a bitter mystery to Mrs. Shannon but today the mystery was deepened by Rosalie's white coat and the care she had taken in painting her face. If they were going swimming, the landlady thought, she wouldn't have worn her new white coat, and if they weren't going swimming why did she carry a towel—one of Mrs. Shannon's towels? They might have been going to a wedding or an office picnic, a ball game or a visit to relations. It made Mrs. Shannon sad to know that she couldn't be sure.

But it was always difficult for a stranger to guess Rosalie's destination, she approached each journey with such great expectations. Sometimes in the autumn her date would tell his parents that he was going hunting and would then take Rosalie—who was under no kind of surveillance once she left the rooming house—out for a night in a tourist cabin on the turnpike, and when he picked her up on those Saturday afternoons she usually wore a chrysanthemum and an oak leaf pinned to her lapel and carried a small suitcase with an Amherst or Harvard label stuck to it as if all the pleasures of a football week end—the game, the tea dance, the faculty reception and the prom—were what she was expecting. She was never disappointed nor was she ever disabused. There was never a point, when she hung up her coat in the tourist cabin while he tried to burn off the damp with a fire, where the difference between this furtive evening and the goal-post snake dance would depress her, nor did she ever seem to reach a point where these differences challenged or altered her expectations. Most of her expectations were collegiate and now, as they found their way out of the city, she began to sing. Popular music passed directly from the radio and the bandstand into some retentive space in her memory, leaving a spoor of cheerful if repetitious and sentimental lyrics.

Going out of the city they passed those congested beaches that lie within its limits and that spread, with a few industrial interruptions, for miles to the south. Now, in the middle of the morning, the life of the beaches was in full swing and the peculiar smell of cooking grease and popcorn butter was stronger than any emanations of the Atlantic Ocean that seems there, held in the islands of a sinking coast, to be a virile and a sad presence. Thousands of half-naked bathers obscured the beach or hesitated knee deep in the ocean as if this water, like the Ganges, were purifying and holy so that these displaced and naked crowds, strung for miles along the coast, gave to this holiday and carnival surface the undercurrents of a pilgrimage in which, as much as any of the thousands they passed, Rosalie and her date were involved.

"You hungry?" he said. "You want something to eat now? Ma gave us enough for three meals. I've got some whisky in the glove case."

The thought of the picnic hamper reminded her of his plain, white-haired mother, who would have sent along something of herself in the basket—watchful, never disapproving, but saddened by the pleasures of her only son. He had his way. His neat, bleak and ugly bedroom was the axis of their house and the rapport between this man and his parents was so intense and tacit that it seemed secretive to Rosalie. Every room was dominated by souvenirs of his growth: guns, golf clubs, trophies from schools and camps and on the piano some music he had practiced ten years ago. The cool house and his contrite parents were strange to Rosalie and she thought that his white shirt that morning smelled of the yellow varnished floors where he took up his secretive life with Ma and Pa. Her date had always had a dog. He had, in his lifetime, run through four dogs, and Rosalie knew their names, their habits, their markings and their tragic ends. On the one time that she had met his parents the conversation had turned to his dogs and she had come to feel that they thought of his relationship to her—not maliciously or harmfully, but because these were the only terms they could find—as something like the exchange between him and a dog. I feel absolutely like a dog, she said.

They drove through a few holiday village squares where newspapers were stacked outside the one open drugstore and where
parades were forming. Now they were in the country, a few miles
inland, but there was not much change in feeling, for the road
was fenced with stores, restaurants, gift shops, greenhouses and
tourist cabins. The beach to which he was taking her was unpopular because the road was rough and the beach was stony, but
he was disappointed that day when he found two other cars in
the clearing where they parked, and they unloaded the hamper
and followed a crooked path to the sea—the open sea here.
Pink scrub roses grew along the path and she felt the salt air
form on her lips and tasted it with her tongue. There was a
narrow, gravelly beach at a break in the cliffs and then below
them they saw a couple like themselves and a family with children
and then beyond them the green sea. Turning away self-con-
sciously from the privacy he so sorely wanted then and that
the cliffs all around them made available he carried the picnic
hamper, the whisky bottle and the tennis ball down onto the
beach and settled himself in full view of the other bathers as if
this momentary gesture toward simple, public pleasure was made
for the sake of whatever his mother had been able to wrap up
of herself in the sandwiches. Rosalie went behind a stone and
changed from her clothes into a bathing suit. He was waiting
for her at the edge of the water and when she had made sure
that all her hair was under her bathing cap she took his hand
and they walked in.

The water was cruelly cold there, it always was, and when it
got up to her knees she dropped his hand and dived. She had
been taught to swim a crawl but she had never unlearned a
choppy, hurried stroke and with her face half buried in the green
she headed out to sea for ten feet, turned, surface-dived, shouted
with pain at the cold and then raced toward the beach. The
beach was sunny and the cold water and the heat of the sun
set her up. She dried herself roughly with a towel, snatched
off her cap and then stood in the sun, waiting for its heat to

reach her bones. She dried her hands and lighted a cigarette and he came out of the sea then, dried only his hands and dropped down beside her.

Her hair was yellow and she was fair—long limbed and full breasted with a skittish look that even in the robes of a choir girl, which she had worn, made her look high-tailed and un-dressed. He took her hand and raised it and brushed her arm, covered with the light hair of an early down, with his lips. "I'd adore to pick blueberries," she said loudly and for the benefit of the others on the beach. "I'd adore to pick blueberries but let's take your hat and we'll put the blueberries in that."

They climbed the stones above the beach, hand in hand, but the search for a privacy that would satisfy her was lengthy and they went from place to place until finally he stopped her and she agreed, timidly, that there was probably nothing better. He took her bathing suit off her shoulders and when she was naked she lay down cheerfully, gladly in the sunny dirt to take the only marriage of her body to its memories that she knew. Tender-ness and good nature lingered between them after they were done and she leaned on his shoulder while she stepped back into her bathing suit and they returned hand in hand to the beach. They went swimming again and unwrapped the sand-wiches that his worried mother had made them the night before.

There were deviled eggs and chicken joints, sandwiches, cakes, cookies, and when they had eaten what they could they put the rest away in the hamper and he jogged down the beach and pitched the tennis ball to her from there. The light ball wavered in the wind but she caught it and threw it back to him with a wing that, like her swimming stroke, was short of what was needed, and he caught the ball with a flourish and threw it back to her. Now the catching and the throwing, the catching and the throwing took on a pleasant monotony and through it she felt the afternoon passing. The tide was going out, leaving on the beach seriations of coarser gravel and strands of kelp whose flower shapes burst with a shot when she crushed them between

her fingers. The family group had begun to gather their possessions and call to their children. The other couple lay side by
side, talking and laughing. She lay down again and he sat beside
her and lighted a cigarette, asking, now, now, but she said no
and he walked off toward the water. She looked up and saw
him swimming in the waves. Then he was drying himself beside
her and offering her a cup of whisky but she said no, no, not
yet, and he drank it himself and looked out to sea.

Now the pleasure steamers, fat, white, crowded and unseaworthy, that had set out that morning were returning. (Among these
was the *Topaze*.) The swell of the sea had quieted a little. Her
date drank off his whisky and wrung the paper cup in his hand.
The couple on their left were getting up to go and when they
had gone he asked again now, now, and she said no, led on
by some vague vision of continence that had appeared to her.
She was weary of trying to separate the power of loneliness from
the power of love and she was lonely. She was lonely and the
sun drawing off the beach and the coming night made her feel
tender and afraid. She looked at him now, holding in at least
one chamber of her mind this vision of continence. He was staring out to sea. Lechery sat like worry on his thin face. He saw
the leonine reefs in the sea like clavicles and women's knees.
Even the clouds in heaven wouldn't dissuade him. The pleasure
boats looked to him like voyaging whorehouses and he thought
that the ocean had a riggish smell. He would marry some woman
with big breasts, she thought—the daughter of a paperhanger—
and go on the road selling disinfectants. Yes, yes, she said, yes
now.

Then they drank some more whisky and ate again and now
the homing pleasure boats had disappeared and the beach and
all but the highest cliffs lay in the dark. He went up to the car
and got a blanket, but now the search for privacy was brief;
now it was dark. The stars came out and when they were done
she washed in the sea and put her white coat on and together,
barefoot, they went up and down the beach, carefully gathering

the sandwich papers, bottles and egg shells that they and the others had left, for these were neat, good children of the middle class.

He hung the wet bathing suits on the door of the car to dry, patted her gently on the knee—the tenderest gesture of them all—and started the car. Once they had got onto the main road the traffic was heavy and many of the cars they passed had, like his, bathing suits hung from the door handles. He drove fast, and she thought cleverly, although the car was old. Its lights were weak and with the lights of an approaching car filling the pupils of his eyes he held to the road precariously, like a blind man running. But he was proud of the car—he had put in a new cylinder head and supercharger—proud of his prowess in negotiating the dilapidated and purblind vehicle over the curving roads of Travertine and St. Botolphs, and when they had gotten free of the traffic and were on a back road that was not, to his knowledge, patrolled, he took it as fast as it would go. The speed made Rosalie feel relaxed until she heard him swear and felt the car careen and bump into a field.

5

The heart of the Wapshot house had been built before the War of Independence, but many additions had been made since then, giving the house the height and breadth of that recurrent dream in which you open a closet door and find that in your absence a corridor and a staircase have bloomed there. The staircase rises and turns into a hall in which there are many doors among the book shelves, any one of which will lead you from one commodious room to another so that you can wander uninterruptedly and searching for nothing through a place that, even while you dream, seems not to be a house at all but a random construction put forward to answer some need of the sleeping mind. The house had been neglected in Leander's youth, but he had restored it during his prosperous years at the table-silver company. It was old enough and large enough and had seen enough dark acts to support a ghost but the only room that was haunted was the old water closet at the back of the upstairs hall. Here a primitive engine, made of vitreous china and mahogany, stood by itself. Now and then—sometimes as often as once a day—this contraption would perform its functions independently. There would be the clatter of machinery and the piercing whinny of old valves. Then the roar of waters arriving and the suck of waters departing could be heard in every room of the house. So much for ghosts.

The house is easy enough to describe but how to write a summer's day in an old garden? Smell the grass, we say. Smell the trees! A flag is draped from the attic windows over the front of the house, leaving the hall in darkness. It is dusk and the family has gathered. Sarah has told them about her journey with Mr. Pincher. Leander has brought the *Topaze* in to port. Moses has raced his sailboat at the Pocamasset club and is spreading his mainsail on the grass to dry. Coverly has watched the table-silver-company ball game from the barn cupola. Leander is drinking bourbon and the parrot hangs in a cage by the kitchen door. A cloud passes over the low sun, darkening the valley, and they feel a deep and momentary uneasiness as if they apprehended how darkness can fall over the continents of the mind. The wind freshens and then they are all cheered as if this reminded them of their recuperative powers. Malcolm Peavey is bringing his catboat up the river and it is so still that they can hear the sound she makes as she comes about. A carp is cooking in the kitchen, and, as everyone knows, a carp has to be boiled in claret with pickled oysters, anchovies, thyme, marjoram, basil and white onions. All of this can be smelled. But as we see the Wapshots, spread out in their rose garden above the river, listening to the parrot and feeling the balm of those evening winds that, in New England, smell so of maidenly things—of orris root and toilet soap and rented rooms, wet by an open window in a thun-

der shower; of chamber pots and sorrel soup and roses and
gingham and lawn; of choir robes and copies of the New Testament bound in limp morocco and pastures that are for sale,
blooming now with rue and fern—as we see the flowers, staked
by Leander with broken hockey sticks and mop and broom handles, as we see that the scarecrow in the cornfield wears the
red coat of the defunct St. Botolphs Horse Guards and that
the blue water of the river below them seems mingled with our
history, it would be wrong to say as an architectural photographer
once did, after photographing the side door, "It's just like a
scene from J. P. Marquand." They are not like this—these are
country people, and in the center of the gathering sits Aunt
Adelaide Forbes, the widow of a schoolteacher. Hear what Aunt
Adelaide has to say.

"Yesterday afternoon," says Aunt Adelaide, "about three
o'clock, three or three thirty—when there was enough shade
in the garden so's I wouldn't get sunstroke, I went out to pull
some carrots for my supper. Well, I was pulling carrots and
suddenly I pulled this very unusual carrot." She spread the fingers of her right hand over her breast—her powers of description
seemed overtaken, but then they rallied. "Well, I've been pulling
carrots all my life, but I never seen a carrot like this. It was
just growing in an awdinary row of carrots. There wasn't no
rocks or anything to account for it. Well, this carrot looked like—
I don't know how to say it—this carrot was the spit and image
of Mr. Forbes' parts." Blood rushed to her face but modesty
would not halt nor even delay her progress. Sarah Wapshot
smiled seraphically at the twilight. "Well, I took the other carrots
into the kitchen for my supper," Aunt Adelaide said, "and I
wrapped this unusual carrot up in a piece of paper and took it
right over to Reba Heaslip. She's such an old maid I thought
she'd be interested. She was in the kitchen so I give her this
carrot. That's what it looks like, Reba, I said. That's just what
it looks like."

Then Lulu called them in to supper where the smell of claret,
fish and spices in the dining room would make your head swim.

Leander said grace and served them and when they had all tasted
the carp they said that it hadn't a pondy taste. Leander had
caught the carp with a rig of his own invention, baited with
stale doughnuts. They talked about other carp that had been
taken from the fresh-water inlet to the river. There were six in
all—six or seven. Adelaide would remember one that the others
couldn't recall. Leander had caught three and Mr. Dexter had
caught two and a mill hand who lived on the other side of the
river—a Pole—had caught one. The fish had come from China
to St. Botolphs to be used in ornamental garden pools. In the
'90's they had been dumped into the stream to take their chances
and their chances had been good enough. Leander was saying
that he knew there were more carp when they all heard the
crash that, considering the dilapidation of the car, sounded ex-
traordinarily rich as if some miscreant had put an ax through
the lid of a jewel box. Leander and his sons got up from the
table and went out the side door.

It was a vast summer night. There was an unusual softness
to the dark air and the bland starlight and an unusual density
to the darkness so that even on his own land Leander had to
move cautiously to keep from stumbling over a stone or stepping
into a brier patch. The car had gone off the road at the bend
and run into an elm in the old field. Its red tail lamp and one
of its headlights were still burning and in this light the grass
and the leaves on the elm shone a bright green. Steam, as they
approached the car, was escaping from the radiator and hissing,
but as they crossed the field this hissing lessened and when they
reached the car it had stopped, although the smell of the vapors
was still in the air.

"He's dead," Leander said. "He's dead. What a Christly mess.
Stay here, Moses. I'll go up to the house and call the police.
You come with me, Coverly. I want you to drive Adelaide home.
They'll be enough trouble without her. He's dead," he muttered,
and Coverly followed him up the field and across the road to
the house where all the windows were being lighted, one by
one.

Moses seemed stunned. There was nothing for him to do and then a sound of crackling—he thought Leander or someone had returned and stepped on some brush, crossing a field—made him spin around but the field and the road were empty and he turned back to the car and saw a fire under the vents of the hood. At the same time the clammy smell of dirty steam and rubber was joined by the smell of heated metal and burning paint and while the hood contained the fire its paint began to blister. Then he seized the dead man's shoulders and tried to pull him out of the car while the fire crackled with the merriment of a hearth fire in a damp house at the end of the day and began to throw a golden light on the trees. The fear of an explosion that might send Moses to join the dead man made his movements hasty and constrained and while he wanted to get away from the fire he could not leave the man there on his pyre and he pulled and pulled until the body, released, sent them both backward into the field. There was sand there at the edge of the path and now he scooped this up with his hands and threw it onto the fire. The sand checked the fire and now he loaded it onto the hood and then knocked the hood open with a stick and threw sand onto the cylinder head until the fire was out and his fear of an explosion was ended and he was left alone in the field, he thought, with the wrecked car and the dead man. He sat down, exhausted, and saw that all of the windows of the farm across the road were lighted and then heard, north of the four corners, a siren and knew that Leander had got the police. He would sit there and catch his breath and his strength, he thought, until they came, when he heard the girl saying from somewhere in the darkness: I'm hurt, Charlie, I've hurt myself. Where are you? I'm hurt, Charlie. For a moment Moses thought: I'll leave her too; but when she spoke again he pushed himself to his feet and went around the car, looking for her. Charlie, she said, I've hurt myself, and then he found her and thinking that Moses was the dead man she said: Charlie, oh Charlie, where are we? and began to cry and he knelt beside her where she lay on the ground. By then the sound of the siren had passed the four corners and was bearing down the road and then he heard, from the darkness, Leander's voice and the voices of the police and saw their flashlights playing over the field—idly, inquisitively—heard their sighs as their idle, inquisitive lights touched the dead man and heard one of them tell another to go to the house and get a blanket. Then they began, idly, to discuss the fire, and Moses called to them and they brought their inquisitive lights over to where he knelt beside the girl. Now they played their lights on the girl, who kept up a bitter light sobbing and who, with her fair hair, seemed very young. "Don't move her, don't touch her," a policeman said importantly. "She may have sustained some internal injuries." Then one of them told another to get a stretcher and they put her on the stretcher—she was still sobbing—and carried her past the wrecked car and the dead man who was now covered with a blanket toward the many lights of the house.

Remember that crash on 7B—one of them said, but the question was put nervously and the others didn't answer. The strangeness of the night, the probing lights, the distant sound of fireworks and the dead man they had left in the field had unsettled them all and had unmanned at least one of them and now they followed closely the one course open to them: to bring the girl into the lighted house. Mrs. Wapshot stood in her door, her face composed in a sorrowful smile—an involuntary choice of expression with which she always confronted the unknown. She assumed that the girl was dead; more than that she assumed that she was the only child of a devoted couple, that she was engaged to marry a splendid man and that she had been standing at the threshold of a rich and useful life. But most of all she thought that the girl had been a child, for whenever Mrs. Wapshot saw a drunkard lying on the street or a whore tapping her windowpane the deep sadness she always felt in her breast lay in the recollection that these unfortunates had once been fragrant children. She was unsettled, but she restored herself with a kind of imperiousness as she spoke to the policemen when they carried the stretcher through the open door. "Take her to the spare room," she said, and when they hesitated, since they had never been in the house before and had no idea of where the spare room might be, she spoke as if they were stupid and had compounded the tragedy. "Take her up to the spare room," she commanded, for to Mrs. Wapshot all the world knew, or ought to know, the floor plan of West Farm. The "up" helped them and with this they started for the stairs.

The doctor was telephoned and he came over and the girl was put in the spare-room bed. Small stones and sand had cut the skin of her arms and shoulders and when the doctor came there was some indecision about whether he should first pronounce the man in the field dead or look at the girl but he decided on the girl and they all waited in the downstairs hall. "Get her something hot, get her something hot," they heard him tell Mrs. Wapshot, and she came down and made some tea in the kitchen. "Does that hurt?" they heard him ask the girl. "Does that hurt, does that hurt you at all?" and to all of this she answered no. "Now, what is your name?" he asked her, and she said, "Rosalie Young," and she gave an address in the city. "It's a rooming house," she said. "My folks live in Philadelphia." "Do you want me to notify your parents?" the doctor said, and she said warmly, "No, please don't, there isn't any reason why they should know." Then she began to cry again and Sarah Wapshot gave her the tea and the front door opened quietly and in came Emmet Cavis, the village undertaker.

Emmet Cavis had come to St. Botolphs as a traveling salesman for the gold-bead factory. He had impressed the village with his urbanity and his sharp clothes for those were the days when it was the responsibility of a drummer to represent for the people of isolated places the turbulence and color of urban life. He had made a few trips and had then returned with a mortician's diploma and had opened up an undertaking parlor and furniture store. Whether or not it had entered into his calculations, this transformation from a jewelry salesman to an undertaker had worked in his favor, for everything that he was associated with as a salesman—jewelry, promiscuity, travel and easy money—set him apart from the rest of the population and seemed, to the farm women at least, to be suitable attributes for the Angel of Death.

In his dealings with bewildered families he had, in the exchange of furniture and property for his services, been guilty now and then of sharp and dishonest practice; but it is a custom of that country to regard craft and dishonesty with respect. His cunning made him seem formidable and intelligent and like any good Yankee he had never trimmed the bereaved without remarking on The Uncertainty of All Earthly Things. He had retained and improved upon all his gifts as a commercial traveler and was the life of the village square. He could gossip brilliantly, tell a story in dialect and comfort a poor woman whose only child had been drowned in the surf. He put up, unwillingly, with the habits of mind his occupation had formed and when he spoke with Leander he judged him to be good for another fifteen years, but he suspected that his insurance policies might have elapsed and that the funeral would be modest if the two boys didn't interfere, as was sometimes the case, and insist on a cremation. What would the Day of Judgment be with nothing but ashes to show? He shook hands all around—neither hearty enough to be offensive nor diffident enough to seem sly—and then left the house with two policemen.

He told them what to do. Beyond opening the doors of the hearse he didn't raise a finger himself. "He goes right in there, boys, right on that platform. Just give him a push. Just give him a push there." He slammed the doors and tried the handle. He had the biggest car in St. Botolphs, as if first among the powers of death was richness, and he climbed into the driver's seat and drove slowly away.

6

By morning the news of the accident was known to almost everyone in St. Botolphs. The young man's death filled them with sadness; and they asked what Honora Wapshot would think of the stranger at the farm. Now it was only natural that they should think of Honora, for this childless matriarch had done much more for the family than give Leander the *Topaze*. She had, as they said, the wherewithal, and Moses and Coverly were, on a contingent basis, her heirs. It is not my fault that New England is full of eccentric old women and we will merely give Honora her due.

She was born, as we know, in Polynesia, and raised by her Uncle Lorenzo in St. Botolphs. She attended Miss Wilbur's Academy. "Oh, I was an awful tomboy," she often said of her youth, covering a smile with her hand and thinking, probably, of upset privies, tin cans tied to dog tails and other small-town pranks. She may have missed the tender love of her parents, who died in Polynesia, or been oppressed by her elderly uncle or been forced by something such as loneliness into the ways of a maverick but these were her ways. You could say of Honora that she had never subjected herself to the discipline of continuousness; but we are not dealing here with great cities and civilizations but with the society of an old port whose population diminished year by year.

After her graduation from Miss Wilbur's, Honora moved with Lorenzo into the city, where he served in the state legislature and where she occupied herself in social-service work that seemed to be mostly of a medical nature. She claimed that these were her proudest years and as an old lady she often said that she wished she had never given up social work, although it was hard to imagine why she should long, with such snarling and bitterness, for the slums. She liked, at times, to reminisce about her experiences as a samaritan. These tales could take your appetite away and make your body hair bristle, but this may have been no more than that attraction to morbidity that overtakes many good women late in life. We hear them on buses and trains, in kitchens and restaurants, talking in such sad and musical voices about gangrene that they only seem to express their dismay at discovering that the body, in spite of all its ringing claims to the contrary, is mortal. Cousin Honora did not feel that she should use a medical vocabulary and so she had worked out a compromise. What she did was to pronounce the first syllables of the word in question and mumble the rest. Thus hysterectomy became hystermumblemumble, suppuration became suppur-mumblemumble and testicles became testimumblemumbles.

When Lorenzo died he left Honora with a much larger trust than she might have expected. The Wapshot family had never—never in the darkest night with the owls chanting—discussed this sum. A month or two after Lorenzo's death Honora married a Mr. de Sastago who claimed to be a marquis and to have a castle in Spain. She sailed for Europe as a bride but she returned in less than eight months. Of this part of her life she only said: "I was once married to a foreigner and was greatly disappointed in my expectations. . . ." She took her maiden name again and settled down in Lorenzo's old house on Boat Street. The best way to understand her is to watch her during the course of a day.

Honora's bedroom is pleasant. Its walls are painted a light blue. The high, slender posts of her bed support a bare wooden frame that is meant to hold a canopy. The family has urged her to have this removed because it has fallen several times and might crash down in the middle of the night and brain the old lady while she dreams. She has not heeded these warnings and sleeps peacefully in this Damoclean antique. This is not to say that her furniture is as unreliable as the furniture at West Farm but there are three or four chairs around her house which, if you should be a stranger and sit in them, will collapse and dump you onto the floor. Most of her furniture belonged to Lorenzo and much of it was bought during his travels in Italy for he felt that this New World where he lived had sprung from the minds of Renaissance men. The dust that lies on everything is the world's dust, but the smell of salt marshes, straw floor matting and wood smoke is the breath of St. Botolphs.

Honora is waked this morning by the whistling of the 7:18 as it comes into the station and, half asleep, she mistakes this sound for the trumpeting of an angel. She is very religious and has joined with enthusiasm and parted with bitterness from nearly every religious organization in Travertine and St. Botolphs. Hearing the train she sees in her mind an angel in snowy robes with a slender trumpet. She has been called, she thinks cheerfully. She has been summoned to some unusual task. She always expected as much. She rises up on her pillows to hear the message and the train hoots again. The image of a locomotive replaces the angel, but she is not very disappointed. She gets out of bed, dresses and sniffs the air, which seems to smell of lamb chops. She goes down to breakfast with a good appetite. She walks with a stick.

A fire is burning in her dining room this July morning and she warms her hands at this to get the chill of age out of her bones. Maggie, her cook, brings a covered dish to the table and Honora, expecting lamb chops, is disappointed to discover a perch. This makes her very irritable, for she is subject to severe attacks of irritability, night sweats and other forms of nervousness. She does not have to admit these infirmities for if she feels out of sorts she can throw a dish at her cook. She bangs the metal cover against the platter now, like a cymbal, and when Maggie comes into the room she exclaims, "Perch. Whatever made you think I wanted perch for breakfast? Perch. Take it away. Take it away and cook me some bacon and eggs if it's not too much trouble." Maggie removes the fish and sighs, but not with any real despair. She is used to this treatment. People often ask why Maggie remains with Honora. Maggie is not dependent on Honora—she could get a better job tomorrow—and she does not love her. What she seems to recognize in the old lady is some naked human force, quite apart from dependence and love.

Maggie cooks some bacon and eggs and brings them to the table. She announces then that there has been an accident near West Farm. A man was killed and a young woman was taken into the house. "Poor soul," Honora says of the dead, but she says nothing else. Maggie hears the mailman's step on the walk and the letters fall through the brass slot and spill onto the floor. She picks up the mail—there are a dozen letters—and puts them on the table beside Honora's plate. Honora hardly glances at her mail. There may be letters here from old friends, checks from the Appleton Trust Company, bills, pleas and invitations. No one will ever know. Honora glances at the pile of envelopes, picks them up and throws them into the fire. Now we wonder why she burns her mail without reading it, but as she goes away from the fireplace back to her chair the light of a very clear emotion seems to cross her face and perhaps this is explanation enough. Admiring that which is most easily understood we may long for the image of some gentle old woman, kind to her servant and opening her letters with a silver knife, but how much more poetry there is to Honora, casting off the claims of life the instant they are made. When she has stowed away her breakfast she gets up and calls over her shoulder to Maggie, "I'll be in the garden if anyone wants me."

Mark, her gardener, is already at work. He comes to work at seven. "Good morning, Mark," Honora says gaily, but Mark is deaf and dumb. Before she employed Mark, Honora ran through every gardener in the village. The last one before Mark was an Italian who behaved badly. He threw down his rake and shouted, "She'sa no good, working for you, Missa Honora. She'sa no good. She'sa planta this, she'sa pullupa that, she'sa changes her mind every five minutes, she'sa no good." When he finished he went out of the garden leaving Honora in tears. Maggie ran out of the kitchen and took the old lady in her arms, saying, "You mustn't pay any attention to him, you mustn't pay any attention to him, Miss Wapshot. Everybody knows how wonderful you are. Everybody knows what a wonderful woman you are." Mark, being deaf, is protected from her interference and when she tells him to move all the rose bushes she might as well be talking to a stone.

It is hard for Honora to get down on her knees, but she does this and works in her garden until the middle of the morning. Then she goes into the house, quietly washes her hands, gets a hat, gloves and a bag and goes out through her garden to the four corners, where she catches a bus to Travertine. Whether this fairly stealthy departure is calculated or not no one will ever know. If Honora asks people for tea and is not home when they, wearing their best clothes, arrive, she has not consciously done something that will make them feel ill at ease, but she has acted characteristically. At any rate a few minutes after she leaves her garden a trust officer of the Appleton Bank rings her front doorbell. During the years in which she has lived on the income from Lorenzo's trust, Honora has never signed a form approving the bank's management. Now the trust officer has been told not to leave St. Botolphs until he has her signature. He rings the doorbell for some time before Maggie throws open a window and tells him that Miss Wapshot is in the garden. Talking with Mark is hopeless, of course, and when he rings the doorbell again Maggie shouts at him, "If she ain't in the garden I don't know where she's at but she might be at the farm where the other Wapshots live. That's over on Route 40. A big house beside the river." The trust officer starts for Route 40 just as Honora boards the bus for Travertine.

Honora doesn't put a dime into the fare box like the rest of the passengers. As she says, she can't be bothered. She sends the transportation company a check for twenty dollars each Christmas. They've written her, telephoned her and sent representatives to her house, but they've gotten nowhere. The bus is decrepit and the seats and several of the windows are held together with friction tape. Jarring and rattling, it gives, for a vehicle, an unusual impression of frailty. It is one of those lines that seem to carry the scrim of the world—sweet-natured but browbeaten women shoppers, hunchbacks and drunks. Honora looks out the window and at the river and the houses—those poignant landscapes against which she has played out most of her life and where she is known as the Wonderful Honora, the Splendid Honora, the Grand Honora Wapshot. When the bus stops at the corner in Travertine she goes up the street to Mr. Hiram's fish market. Mr. Hiram is in back, opening a crate of salt fish. Honora goes around and behind the counter to where there is a small tank of sea water for lobsters. She puts down her bag and stick, rolls up one sleeve and plunges her hand into the tank, coming up with a good four-pound lobster just as Mr. Hiram comes in from the back. "Put that down, Miss Honora," he shouts. "They ain't pegged, they ain't pegged yet."

"Well, they don't seem to be doing me any harm," says Honora. "Just get me a paper bag."

"George Wolf just brought them in," says Mr. Hiram, scurrying around for a paper bag, "and if one of those four pounders tooka hold of you you could lose a finger."

He holds the paper bag open and Honora drops the lobster into this, turns and plunges her hand into the tank again. Mr. Hiram sighs, but Honora comes up quickly with another lobster and gets it into the bag. When she has paid Mr. Hiram she carries her lobsters out to the street and walks to the corner where the bus is waiting to pick up passengers for St. Botolphs. She hands the bag of lobsters to the bus driver. "Here," she says. "I'll be back in a few minutes."

She starts for the dry-goods store but, as she walks by the five-and-ten-cent store, the smell of frankfurters draws her in. She sits at the counter. "Your frankfurters smell so deliciously," she tells the clerk, "that I can't resist having one. Our Cousin Justina used to play the piano in here, y'know. Oh, if she knew I remembered, she'd die. . . ." She eats two frankfurters and a dish of ice cream. "That was delicious," she tells the counter girl, and gathering up her things she starts down the street again toward the bus stop when she notices the sign above the Neptune movie theater: ROSE OF THE WEST. What harm can there be, she thinks, in an old lady going to a movie, but when she buys her ticket and steps into the dark, bad-smelling theater she suffers all the abrasive sensations of someone forced into moral uncleanliness. She does not have the courage of her vices. It is wrong, she knows, to go into a dark place when the world outside shines with light. It is wrong and she is a miserable sinner. She buys a box of popcorn and takes an aisle seat in the last row—a noncommittal position that seems to lighten her burden of guilt. She munches her popcorn and watches the movie suspiciously.

In the meantime Maggie is keeping her lunch warm on the back of the stove and her lobsters, battling for life in the paper bag, have made the trip to St. Botolphs and are now on their way back to Travertine. Mr. Burstyn, the trust officer, has driven to West Farm. Sarah has been courteous and helpful. "I haven't seen Honora myself," she says, "but she's expected. She's interested in some furniture in the barn. She may be there." He walks down the driveway to the barn. Mr. Burstyn is a city boy and the size of the barn and its powerful smells make him homesick. A large yellow spider on the barn floor comes straight toward him and he makes a wide circle around the insect. There is a staircase up to the loft. Two of the lifts are broken and a third is about to break and when he gets up into the loft there is no one there although it would be hard to make sure, for the loft is lighted by a single window hung thickly with spiderwebs and drifted with hayseed.

Honora sits through the movie twice. When she leaves the theater she feels weary and sad like any sinner. The lobby of the theater slopes like a kind of tunnel down toward the sidewalk. There is a small stretch here of some slippery composition stone and on it a spot of water or moisture from the iceman's load or a child's pop bottle. Someone may even have spat. Honora slips on this and crashes down onto the stone. Her purse flies in one direction and her stick in another and her three-cornered hat comes down over her nose. The girl, the woman, the hag, in fact, in the ticket window sees all of this and her heart seems to stop beating for she sees here, in the fallen old woman, the ruthlessness of time. She fumbles around for the key to the cash register and locks up the money. Then she opens the door to her little tower, sanctuary or keep and hurries to where Honora lies. She kneels beside her. "Oh, Miss Wapshot," she says. "Dear Miss Wapshot."

Honora raises herself by the arms and gets to her knees. Then slowly she swings her head around to this samaritan. "Leave me alone," she says. "Please leave me alone." The voice is not harsh or imperious. It sounds small, plaintive, the voice of a child with some inner trouble; a plea for dignity. Now more and more people come to her side. Honora is still on her hands and knees. "Please leave me alone," she tells the gathering. "Please mind your own business. Please go away and leave me alone." They recognize that what she is expressing is the privateness of pain and they move back. "Please leave me alone," she says, "please mind your own business." She straightens her hat and, using her stick for support, gets to her feet. Someone hands her the purse. Her dress is torn and dirty but she walks straight through the gathering to the corner where the bus to St. Botolphs is waiting. The driver who took her to Travertine earlier in the day has gone home to supper and has been replaced by a young man. "What," Honora asks him, "have you done with my lobsters?"

The bus driver tells her that the lobsters have been delivered and he has the good sense not to ask for her fare. So they travel up the River Road to St. Botolphs and Honora gets off at the four corners and enters her garden by the back gate.

Mark has done a good job. The paths and the flower beds look neat in the twilight—for it is nearly dark. The day has pleased her and she liked the movie. By half-closing her eyes she can still see the colored plains and the Indians riding down from the butte. Her kitchen windows are lighted and open on this summer night and as she approaches them she sees Maggie sitting at the kitchen table with Maggie's younger sister. She hears Maggie's voice. "Perch," says Maggie. "Perch, she says, rattling the dish cover and breathing smoke and fire. Whatever in the world made you think I wanted perch for breakfast? For weeks she's been telling me how she'd like a bit of perch and I bought a couple from the little Townsend boy yesterday with my own money and I cooked it for her nicely and all the thanks I get is this. Perch, she says. Whatever made you think I wanted perch for breakfast!"

Maggie is not bitter. Far from it; she and her sister are laughing

uproariously at the memory of Honora who stands now outside
the lighted windows of her own house in the dusk. "Well then,"
says Maggie, "I hear Mr. Macgrath coming up the walk and putting the mail into the slot and so I go down the hall to get
her letters and I give them to her and you know what she does?"
Maggie rocks back and forth in her chair with laughter. "She
takes these letters—there must be twelve of them altogether—
and throws them into the fire. Oh Lord, she's better than a
three-ring circus."

Honora walks past the window on the soft grass but they have
not heard her; they are laughing too loudly. Halfway down the
house she stops and leans heavily, with both hands, on her cane,
engrossed in an emotion so violent and so nameless that she
wonders if this feeling of loneliness and bewilderment is not
the mysteriousness of life. Poignance seems to drench her until
her knees are weak and she yearns so earnestly for understanding
that she raises her head and says half a prayer. Then she gathers
her forces, enters the front door and calls cheerfully down the
hall, "It's me, Maggie." Upstairs in her bedroom she drinks a
water glass full of port and while she is changing her shoes
the telephone rings. It is poor Mr. Burstyn, who has taken a
room at the Viaduct House, which is no place for a respectable
man to stay. "Well if you want to see me, come and see me,"
Honora says. "I'm not very hard to find. Excepting to visit Travertine I haven't been out of St. Botolphs in nearly seven years.
You can go and tell those men at the bank that if they want
someone to talk with me they'd better get someone with more
gumption than it takes to find an old lady." Then she hangs
up the receiver and goes down to supper with a good appetite.

7

The morning light and the bruit of the family going around
the upstairs hallway woke the girl. She felt at first the strangeness

of the place, although there were not many places with which she was familiar any more. The air smelled of sausage and even the morning light—golden with all its blue shadows—seemed foreign in a way that pained her and she remembered waking up on her first night at camp to find that she had wet the bed. Then she remembered the accident—all that—but not in detail; it loomed up in her mind like a boulder, too big to be moved and too adamant to be broken and have its contents revealed. All that stood in her mind like a dark stone. The sheets—linen and damp—brought her back to the pain of strangeness and she wondered why a person should feel, in the world where she was meant to live, so miserable and abraded. She got up out of bed to discover that her whole body was lame and sore. In the closet she found her coat and some cigarettes in the pocket. The taste of smoke diminished the painful sense of strangeness by a little and she carried a clamshell for an ash tray to the side of her bed and lay down again. She shivered, she trembled, she tried unsuccessfully to cry.

Now the house, or the part of it where she lay, was quiet. She heard a man calling good-by. On the wall she noticed that stuck behind the picture of a little Dutch girl were some palm fronds from Palm Sunday and she hoped that this was not the house of a priest. Then, in the downstairs hall, she heard the telephone ring and someone shouted, "Hello, Mabel. I may not be coming over today. No, she ain't paid me yet. She don't have any money. They get all their money from Honora. She don't have any money. No, I can't borrow no more money on my insurance. I told you, I told you, I did ass them, I assed them. Well, I need shoes myself the way she expects me to go upstairs and downstairs fifty times a day. They got somebody here now. Did you hear about the accident? There was an accident here last night. A car went off the road and a man was killed. Terrible. Well, he had a girl with him and they brought her in here and she's here now. I'll tell you later. I SAID I'LL TELL YOU LATER. They got her here now and that makes more work for me. How's Charlie? What are you going to have for

supper? Don't have the meat loaf. You don't have enough of
it. I said, don't have the meat loaf. Open a can of salmon and
make Charlie a nice salad. There isn't enough meat loaf. I just
told you. Open a can of salmon and get some of those nice
rolls from the bakery. Make him a pie for dessert. They got
nice pie apples now. Is he still constipated? They got pie apples,
they have so got pie apples, I saw them day before yesterday,
they got pie apples at Tituses'. You go down to Tituses' and
get some pie apples and make him an apple pie. Do what I
tell you. I'll tell you about the accident when I see you. I don't
know how long she's going to stay. I don't know. I got to make
the beds now. Good-by . . ."

After this the house was quiet again and then she heard someone climbing the stairs and the pleasant noise of dishes on a
tray. She put out her cigarette. "Good morning," Mrs. Wapshot
said. "Good morning, Rosalie. I'm going to call you Rosalie.
We don't stand on ceremony here."

"Good morning."

"The first thing I want you to do is to let me telephone your
parents. They'll be worried. But what am I talking about? That's
not the first thing I want you to do. The first thing I want you
to do is to eat a nice breakfast. Let me fix your pillows."

"Oh, I'm awfully afraid that I can't eat anything," the girl
said. "It's awfully nice of you but I just couldn't."

"Well, you don't have to eat everything on the tray," Mrs.
Wapshot said kindly, "but you've got to eat something. Why
don't you try and eat the eggs? That's all you have to eat; but
you must eat the eggs."

Then the girl began to cry. She laid her head sidewise on
the pillow and stared into the corner of the room where she
seemed to see a range of high mountains her look was so faraway
and heartbreaking. The tears rolled down her cheeks. "Oh, I'm
sorry," Mrs. Wapshot said. "I'm very sorry. I suppose you were
engaged to him. I suppose . . ."

"It isn't that," the girl sobbed. "It's just about the eggs. I
can't *bear* eggs. When I lived at home they made me eat eggs

for breakfast and if I didn't eat my eggs for breakfast well then I had to eat them for dinner. I mean everything I was supposed to eat and couldn't eat was always juss piled up on my dinner plate and the eggs were disgusting."

"Well, is there anything you would like for breakfast?" Mrs. Wapshot asked.

"I'd love some peanut butter. If I could have a peanut-butter sandwich and a glass of milk . . ."

"Well, I think that can be arranged," Mrs. Wapshot said, and carrying the tray and smiling she went out of the room and down the stairs.

She felt no resentment at this miscarriage of her preparations and was happy to have the girl in her house, as if she was, at bottom, a lonely woman, grateful for any company. She had wanted a daughter, longed for one; a little girl sitting at her knees, learning to sew or making sugar cookies in the kitchen on a snowy night. While she made Rosalie's sandwich it seemed to her that she possessed a vision of life that she would enjoy introducing to the stranger. They could pick blueberries together, take long walks beside the river and sit together in the pew on Sunday. When she took the sandwich upstairs again Rosalie said that she wanted to get up. Mrs. Wapshot protested but Rosalie's pleading made sense. "I'd just feel so much better if I could get up and walk around and sit in the sun; just feel the sun."

Rosalie dressed after breakfast and joined Mrs. Wapshot in the garden where the old deck chairs were. "The sun feels so good," she said, pushing up the sleeves of her dress and shaking back her hair.

"Now you must let me call your parents," Sarah said.

"I just don't want to call them today," the girl said. "Maybe tomorrow. You see, it always bothers them when I'm in trouble. I just don't like to bother them when I'm in trouble. And they'll want me to come home and everything. You see Daddy's a priest—rector really, I mean communion seven days a week and all that."

"We're low church here," Mrs. Wapshot said, "but some people I could name would like to see a change."

"And he's absolutely the most nervous man I ever knew,"
Rosalie said, "Daddy is. He's always scratching his stomach. It's
a nervous ailment. Most men's shirts wear out at the collar, I
guess, but Daddy's shirts wear out where he scratches himself."

"Oh, I think you ought to telephone them," Mrs. Wapshot
said.

"It's just because I'm in trouble. They always think of me as
making trouble. I went to this camp—Annamatapoiset—and I
had this sweater with an A on it for being such a marvelous
camper and when Daddy saw it he said I guess that A stands
for Always in Trouble. I just don't want to bother them."

"It doesn't seem right."

"Please, *please.*" She bit her lip; she would cry and Mrs. Wapshot swiftly changed the subject. "Smell the peonies," she said.
"I love the smell of peonies and now they're almost gone."

"That sun feels so good."

"Do you have a position in the city?" Mrs. Wapshot asked.

"Well, I was going to this secretarial school," Rosalie said.

"You planned to be a secretary?"

"Well, I didn't want to be a secretary. I wanted to be a painter
or a psychologist but first I went to Allendale School and I
couldn't bear the academic adviser so I never really made up
my mind. I mean he was always touching me and fiddling with
my collar and I couldn't bear to talk with him."

"So then you went to secretarial school?"

"Well, first I went to Europe, I went to Europe last summer
with some other girls."

"Did you like it?"

"You mean Europe?"

"Yes."

"Oh I thought it was divine. I mean there were some things
I was disappointed in, like Stratford. I mean it was just another
small town. And I couldn't bear London but I adored the Nether-
lands with all those divine little people. It was terribly quaint."

"Shouldn't you telephone this secretarial school you go to and tell them where you are?"

"Oh no," Rosalie said. "I flunked out last month. I blew up on exams. I knew all the material and everything but I just didn't know the words. The only words I know are words like divine and of course they don't use those words on exams and so I never understood the questions. I wish I knew more words."

"I see," Mrs. Wapshot said.

Rosalie might have gone on to tell her the rest of it and it would have gone something like this: I mean it just seems that all I ever heard about was sex when I was growing up. I mean everyone told me it was just marvelous and the end of all my problems and loneliness and everything and so naturally I looked forward to it and then when I was at Allendale I went to this dance with this nice-looking boy and we did it and it didn't stop me from feeling lonely because I've always been a very lonely person so we kept on doing it and doing it because I kept thinking it was going to keep me from being lonely and then I got pregnant, which was dreadful, of course, with Daddy being the priest and so virtuous and prominent, and they nearly died when they found out and they sent me to this place where I had this adorable little baby although they told everyone I was having an operation on my nose and afterwards they sent me to Europe with this old lady. . . .

Then Coverly came down the lawn from the house. "Cousin Honora called," he said, "and she's coming for tea or after supper, maybe."

"Won't you join us?" Mrs. Wapshot asked. "Coverly, this is Rosalie Young."

"How do you do," he said.

"Hello." He had that spooky bass voice meant to announce that he had entered into the kingdom of manhood, but Rosalie knew that he was still outside the gates and sure enough, while he stood there smiling at her he raised his right hand to his mouth and began thoughtfully to chew on a callus that had formed at the base of his thumb.

"Moses?"

"He's at Travertine."

"Moses has been sailing every day of his vacation," Mrs. Wap-shot said to Rosalie. "It's just as though I didn't have an older son."

"He wants to win a cup," Coverly said. They stayed in the garden until Lulu called them in to lunch.

After lunch Rosalie went upstairs and lying down in the still house she fell asleep. When she woke the shadows on the grass were long, and downstairs she could hear men's voices. She went down and found them all in the garden, once more, all of them. "It's our out-of-door sitting room," Mrs. Wapshot said. "This is Mr. Wapshot and Moses. Rosalie Young."

"Good evening, young lady," Leander said, charmed by her fairness, but not at all foxy. He spoke to her with a triumphant and bright disinterestedness as if she had been the daughter of an old friend and drinking companion. It was Moses who was surly—who hardly looked at her, although he was polite enough. It made Mrs. Wapshot unhappy to see any impediment in the relationships of the young. They ate cold carp in the homely dining room, half lighted by the summer twilight, half by what seemed to be an inverted bowl of stained glass, pieced together mostly out of gloomy colors. "These napkins are more holy than righteous," Mrs. Wapshot said, and most of her conver-sation at the table was made up of just such chestnuts, saws and hoary puns. She was one of those women who seemed to have learned to speak by rote. "May I please be excused," Moses mumbled as soon as he had cleared his plate, and he was out of the dining room and had one foot in the night before his mother spoke.

"Don't you want any dessert, Moses?"

"No, thank you."

"Where are you going?"

"Over to Pendletons'."

"I want you home early. Honora is coming."

"Yes."

"I wish Honora would come," Mrs. Wapshot said.

Honora will not come—she is hooking a rug—but they do not know and so rather than dwell with the Chekhovian delays of this family watching the night come in we might climb the stairs and pry into things of more pertinence. There is Leander's bureau drawer, where we find a withered rose—once yellow—and a wreath of yellow hair, the butt end of a Roman candle that was fired at the turn of the century, a boiled shirt on which an explicit picture of a naked woman is drawn in red ink, a necklace made of champagne corks and a loaded revolver. Or we might look at Coverly's book shelf—*War and Peace, The Complete Poetry of Robert Frost, Madame Bovary, La Tulipe Noire.* Or still better we might go to the Pocamasset Trust Company in the village where Honora's will lies in a safe deposit box.

8

Honora's will was no secret. "Lorenzo left me a little something," she had told the family, "and I have to consider his wishes as well as my own. Lorenzo was very devoted to the family and the older I grow the more important family seems to me. It seems to me that most of the people I trust and admire come from good New England stock." There was more of the same; and then she said that since Moses and Coverly were the last of the Wapshots she would divide her fortune between them, contingent upon their having male heirs. "Oh, the money will do so much good," Mrs. Wapshot had exclaimed, while institutes for the blind and the lame, homes for unwed mothers and orphan asylums danced in her head. The news of their inheritance did not elate the boys—it did not seem at first to penetrate or alter their feeling toward life, and Honora's decision only seemed to Leander to be a matter of course. What else would she have done with the money? But, considering the naturalness of her

choice, it came as a surprise to everyone that it should lead
them into something as unnatural as anxiety.

On the winter after Honora had made her will Moses came
down with a severe case of mumps. "Is he all right?" Honora
kept asking. "Will he be all right?" Moses recovered but that
summer a little gasoline stove in the galley of their sailboat exploded, burning Coverly in the groin. They were on tenterhooks
again. However, these forthright assaults on the virility of his
sons did not trouble Leander as much as those threats to the
continuation of the family that lay beyond his understanding.
Such a thing happened when Coverly was eleven or twelve and
went with his mother to see a performance of *A Midsummer Night's
Dream*. He was transported. When he got back to the farm he
would be Oberon. Girdling himself with a loose arrangement
of neckties, he tried flying from the back stairs into the parlor,
where his father was adding up the monthly accounts. He
couldn't fly, of course, and landed in a pile on the floor—his
neckties undone—and while Leander did not speak to him angrily
he felt, standing above his naked son in the presence of something mysterious and unrestful—Icarus! Icarus!—as if the boy
had fallen some great distance from his father's heart.

Leander would never take his sons aside and speak to them
about the facts of life, even although the continuation of Honora's numerous charities depended upon their virility. If they
looked out of the window for a minute they could see the drift
of things. It was his feeling that love, death and fornication ex-
tracted from the rich green soup of life were no better than
half-truths, and his course of instruction was general. He would
like them to grasp that the unobserved ceremoniousness of his
life was a gesture or sacrament toward the excellence and the
continuousness of things. He went skating on Christmas Day—
drunk or sober, ill or well—feeling that it was his responsibility
to the village to appear on Parson's Pond. "There goes old Leander Wapshot," people said—he could hear them—a splendid
figure of continuous and innocent sport that he hoped his sons
would carry on. The cold bath that he took each morning was

ceremonious—it was sometimes nothing else since he almost never used soap and got out of the tub smelling powerfully of the sea salts in the old sponges that he used. The coat he wore at dinner, the grace he said at table, the fishing trip he took each spring, the bourbon he drank at dark and the flower in his buttonhole were all forms that he hoped his sons might understand and perhaps copy. He had taught them to fell a tree, pluck and dress a chicken, sow, cultivate and harvest, catch a fish, save money, countersink a nail, make cider with a hand press, clean a gun, sail a boat, etc.

He was not surprised to find his ways crossed and contested by his wife, who had her own arcane rites such as arranging flowers and cleaning closets. He did not always see eye to eye with Sarah but this seemed to him most natural, and life itself appeared to regulate their differences. He was impulsive and difficult to follow—there was no telling when he would decide that it was time for the boys to swim the river or carve the roast. He went trout fishing each spring at a camp in the wilderness near the Canadian border and decided one spring that the time had come for Moses to accompany him. For once Sarah was angry and stubborn. She didn't want Moses to go north with his father and on the evening before they were to leave she said that Moses was sick. Her manner was seraphic.

"That poor boy is too ill to go anywhere."

"We're going fishing tomorrow morning," Leander said.

"Leander, if you take this poor boy out of a sickbed and up to the north woods I'll never forgive you."

"There won't be anything to forgive."

"Leander, come here."

They continued their discussion or quarrel behind the closed doors of Sarah's bedroom but the boys—and Lulu—could hear their angry and bitter voices. Leander got Moses out of bed before dawn on the next day. He had already packed the bait and fishing tackle and they started for the Langely ponds in the starlight while Sarah was still asleep.

It was May when they left—the valley of the West River was

all in bloom—and they had had a brace or more of those days when the earth smells like a farmer's britches—all timothy, manure and sweet grass. They were north of Concord when the sun came up and they stopped in some town in New Hampshire for lunch. They were far north of the lush river valley by then. The trees were bare and the inn where they stopped still seemed to be in the throes of a cold winter. The place smelled of kerosene and the waitress had a runny nose.

They were in the mountains then, the stony rivers full of black water—melted snow—and the sheen of reflected blue from the sky didn't much soften the impression of cold. Coming up into a pass Moses raised his head cheerfully to the voluptuous line of the mountains, the illusory blue, thunderous and deep, but the loud noise of wind in the bare trees reminded him of the gentle valley they had left that morning—shadbush and lilac and already some arbutus underfoot. They had then got to the approaches of French Canada—those farms and towns that seem, from the winter's cold and tedium, utterly unprotected: St. Evariste, St. Methode, the bleak country of the Holy Ghost, exposed to the lash of winter. Now the north wind was bitter, the clouds were a cheerless white and here and there on the ground he saw patches of old snow. They reached the village of Langely late in the day where the old launch—the *Cygnet*—that would take them uplake and into the wilderness was tied to a wharf and which Moses now loaded with their duffel bags and fishing tackle.

There was nothing at Langely but a post office and a store. It was late; it would be dark soon. The post-office windows were lighted but the shores of the lake were uninhabited and dark. Moses looked at the old launch, tied up at the wharf, her long bow and her helm shaped like a steering wheel. He recognized in the length of her mahogany bow, with its brass funnel and brass-bound bulkhead, that she was one of those boats built years ago, for the leisurely comings and goings of another generation of summer people. Four wicker chairs stood side by side on her deep stern deck. Weathered and raveled and threadbare, they had carried—how long ago?—women in summer dresses and men in flannels out to see the sun go down. Now her paint was dirty and her varnish was dim and she bemoaned her dereliction by rubbing the wharf in the northerly wind.

His father came down the path with the groceries and an old man followed him. It was the old man who took off the lines and pushed the boat into deep water with a hook. He must have been eighty. His teeth were gone and his mouth had sunk, accentuating the little thrust of his chin. He blinked his eyes behind a pair of dirty glasses and poked his tongue out between his teeth and when he got her into forward and full speed ahead he settled himself very stiffly. It was a seven-mile voyage to the camp. They carried their things up to a ramshackle place with a chimney made of soup cans and they lighted a fire and a lamp. Squirrels had gotten into the mattress. Mice and rats and porcupines had come and gone. Below them Moses heard the old man start the motor of his *Cygnet* and head back for the post office. The icy light of the afterglow, the noise of the launch as it faded and the smells of the stove all were so unlike their beginnings that morning in St. Botolphs that the world seemed to fall into two pieces or halves.

Here on this half were the deep lake, the old man with his superannuated *Cygnet* and the dirty camp. Here were salt and catsup and patched blankets and canned spaghetti and dirty socks. Here was a pile of rusted tin cans around the steps; here were *Saturday Evening Post* covers fixed with roofing nails to the bare walls beside the Fisherman's Prayer, the Fisherman's Lexicon, the Lament of the Fisherman's Widow, the Fisherman's Crying Towel and all the other inane and semicomic trash that has been published about fishing. Here was the smell of earthworms and gut, kerosene and burned pancakes, the smell of unaired blankets, trapped smoke, wet shoes, lye and strangeness. On the table near where he stood someone had stuck a candle into a root and beside this was a detective story, its first chapters eaten by mice.

On the other half was the farm at St. Botolphs, the gentle

valley and the impuissant river and the rooms that smelled now
of lilac and hyacinth and the colored engraving of San Marco
and all the furniture with claw feet. There were the Canton bowls
full of forget-me-nots, the damp linen sheets, the silver on the
sideboard and the loud ticking of the clock in the hall. The
difference seemed more strenuous than if he had crossed the
border from one mountain country into another, more strenuous
he guessed because he had not realized how deep his commit-
ment to the gentle parochialism of the valley was—the east wind
and the shawls from India—and had never seen how securely
conquered that country was by his good mother and her kind—
the iron women in their summer dresses. He stood, for the first
time in his life, in a place where their absence was conspicuous
and he smiled, thinking of how they would have attacked the
camp; how they would have burned the furniture, buried the
tin cans, holystoned the floors, cleaned the lamp chimneys and
arranged in a glass slipper (or some other charming antique)
nosegays of violets and Solomon's-seal. Under their administration lawns would reach from the camp to the lake, herbs and
salad greens would flourish at the back door and there would
be curtains and rugs, chemical toilets and clocks that chimed.

His father poured himself some whisky and when the stove
was hot he took some hamburgers and cooked them on the lid,
turning them with a rusty spoon as if he was following some
ritual in which he disregarded his wife's excellent concepts of
hygiene and order. When supper was finished the loons on the
lake had begun to cry and these cries seemed to bring into the
cabin, overheated now from the stove, a fine sense of their remoteness. Moses walked down toward the lake, pissed in the
woods and washed his hands and face in water that was so cold
his skin was still stinging when he undressed and climbed in
between two dirty blankets. His father blew out the lamp and
got into bed himself and they fell asleep.

The fishing was not at Langely, it was in the ponds deeper
in the woods, and they left for Folger's Pond at six the next
morning. The wind was still northerly and the sky was overcast.

They crossed the lake in a dinghy with a two-cylinder motor, heading for Kenton's swamp. Halfway across the lake the old dinghy sprang a leak. Moses sat in the stern, bailing with a bait can. At Lovell's Point his father throttled down the motor and turned the leaky boat into a great swamp. It was an ugly and a treacherous place but the landscape seemed to Moses enthralling. Rank on rank of dead trees lined the shore—tall, catatonic and ashen, they looked like the statuary of some human disaster. When the water got shallow Leander tipped the motor into the boat and Moses took the oars. The noise of setting them into the locks startled a flight of geese. "A little to port," his father said, "a little more to port . . ." Looking over his shoulder, Moses saw where the swamp narrowed to a stream and heard the roar of some falls. Then he saw the shapes of stones through the water, his oars struck and the bow grazed the shore.

He pulled the boat up and made it fast to a tree while his father examined a scraping of boat's paint on a stone near where they landed. It seemed to be last year's paint. Then Moses saw how anxious his father was to be the first man into the woods and while he unloaded the gear Leander looked around the trail for footprints. He found some but when he scraped them with a knife he saw that they were lined with mold and had been made by hunters. Then he started briskly up the trail. Everything was dead; dead leaves, dead branches, dead ferns, dead grass, all the obscenity of the woods death, stinking and moldy, was laid thickly on the trail. A little white light escaped from the clouds and passed fleetly over the woods, long enough for Moses to see his shadow, and then this was gone.

The trail went uphill. He got hot. He sweated. He watched his father's head and shoulders with feelings of admiration and love. It was the middle of the morning when they saw the clearing ahead of them through the trees. They pushed up the last slope and there was the pond and they were the first to have seen it since the hunters in the fall. The place was ugly but it had the exalting ugliness of the swamp. Leander looked into the bushes and found what he wanted—an old duck-shooting battery. He told Moses to get some wood for a fire and when the fire was lighted he took a can of tar out of his pack, rigged a crane of green wood over the fire and heated the tar. Then he swabbed the boat's seams with hot tar which hardened quickly in the cold. They floated the battery and rowed out onto the water against the north wind. In spite of the tar the battery leaked but they baited their hooks and began to troll.

Five minutes later Leander's rod bent, and with a grunt he set his hook and with Moses keeping the boat in motion he played a big trout that rose, a hundred feet to their stern, and then sounded and fought, taking his last sanctuary in the dim shade of the battery. Then Moses caught a fish and within an hour or so they had a dozen trout between them. Then it began to snow. For three hours they trolled in the snow squall without a strike, eating their dry sandwiches at noon. This was an ordeal and Moses had the sense to see that it was part of their trip. In the middle of the afternoon the squall blew off and then Leander had a strike. Then the fish began to bite again and before the sky began to darken they each had their limit. They pulled the battery up onto the banks—stupefied and brute tired— and stumbled down the trail to the lake, reaching this not much before dark. The wind had backed around to the northeast and from beyond the mouth of the swamp they could hear the roar of water but they crossed safely, with Moses bailing, and made the boat fast by her bow and stern. Moses lighted a fire while his father gutted four trout and fried them on the stove lid and when they had finished supper they mumbled their good nights, put out the lamp and went to bed.

That was a good trip and they returned to St. Botolphs with enough fish for all their friends and relations. On the next year it was time for Coverly to go. Coverly did have a runny nose, as it happened, but Sarah didn't mention this. However, late on the evening before they left, she came into his room carrying a cookbook and put it into his pack. "Your father doesn't know how to cook," she said, "and I don't know what you'll eat for four days so I'll give you this." He thanked her, kissed her good night and left with his father before dawn. The trip was the same—the stop for lunch and whisky, and the long voyage up the lake in the *Cygnet*. At the camp Leander threw some hamburgers onto the stove lid and when they had finished supper they went to bed. Coverly asked if he could read.

"What's your book, son?"

"It's a cookbook," Coverly said, looking at the cover. "Three hundred ways of preparing fish."

"Oh Goddamn it to hell, Coverly," Leander roared. "Goddamn it to hell." He took the book out of his son's hands, opened the door and threw it out into the night. Then he blew out the lamp, feeling once more—Icarus, Icarus—as if the boy had fallen away from his heart.

Coverly knew that he had offended his father but guilt would have been too exact a word for the pain and uneasiness he felt and this pain may have been aggravated by his knowledge of the conditions of Honora's will. The sense was not only that he had failed himself and his father by bringing a cookbook to a fishing camp; he had profaned the mysterious rites of virility and had failed whole generations of future Wapshots as well as the beneficiaries of Honora's largess—the Home for Aged Sailors and the Hutchens Institute for the Blind. He was miserable, and he would be made miserable again by the feeling that his human responsibilities had been abnormally enlarged by Honora's will. This was some time later, a year, perhaps, and anyhow later in the year and the matter was a simple one, simpler than fishing—the village fair which he attended late in August with his father as he always did. (Moses had planned to go, but he grounded the *Tern* on a sandbar and didn't get home until ten.) Coverly had an early supper in the kitchen. He wore his best white ducks and a clean shirt and had his allowance in his pocket. Leander gave him a toot on the whistle when the *Topaze* rounded the bend and swung the boat over to the dock, putting her into half-speed and then neutral but just touching the dock long enough for Coverly to jump aboard.

There was only a handful of passengers. Coverly went up to

the cabin and Leander let him take the wheel. The tide was going out and they moved against it slowly. It had been a hot day and now there were cumulus clouds or thunderheads standing out to sea in a light of such clearness and brilliance that they seemed unrelated to the river and the little village. Coverly brought the boat up to the wharf neatly and helped Bentley, the deck hand, make her fast, and knocked together the old deck chairs, upholstered with carpet scraps, and lashed a tarpaulin over the pile. They stopped in Grimes' bakery, where Leander ate a plate of baked beans. "Baked beans, the musical fruit," the old waitress said. "The more you eat, the more you toot." The mild crudeness of the joke had kept it fresh for her. Walking up Water Street toward the fairgrounds Leander let several loud farts. It was a summer evening so splendid that the power it had over their senses was like the power of memory and they could have kicked up their heels with joy when they saw ahead of them the matchboard fence and within it and above it the lights of the fair, burning gallantly against some storm clouds in which lightning could be seen to play.

Coverly was excited to see so many lights burning after dark and by the apparatus for the tightrope artist—a high pole secured by guy wires with a summit of fringed platforms and pedestals, all of it standing in the glare of two up-angled searchlights in whose powdery beams moth millers could be seen to swim like scraps of gum paper. There a girl with powdery skin and straw hair and a navel (Leander thought) deep enough to put your thumb into, and with rhinestones burning blue and red at her ears and breasts, walked and rode a bicycle over the tightwire, pushing her hair back now and then and hurrying a little it seemed, for the thunder was quickening and the gusty wind smelled clearly of rain and now and then people who were anxious or old or wearing their best clothes were leaving the bleachers and looking for shelter although not a drop of rain had fallen. When the high-wire act was over Leander took Coverly down to the head of the midway, where the argument for the cootch show had begun.

Burlymaque, burlymaque, see them strip the way you like, see them do the dance of the ages. If you're old you'll go home to your wife feeling younger and stronger and if you're young you'll feel happy and full of high spirits as youth should feel, said a man whose sharp face and sharp voice seemed wholeheartedly dedicated to chicanery and lewdness and who spoke to the crowd from a little red pulpit although they stayed at a safe distance from him as if he were the devil himself or at least the devil's advocate, a serpent. Lashed to poles at his back and billowing in the rain wind like idle sails were four large paintings of women in harem dress, so darkened by time and weather that the lights played on them to no purpose and they might have been advertising cough syrup and cure-alls. In the center was a gate in which some lights spelled GAY PAREE—the gate scuffed and battered from its long summer travels up and down New England. Burlymaque, burlymaque, hootchie cootch, hootchie cootch, said the devil, striking the top of his little red pulpit with a roll of unsold tickets. I'm going to ask the little ladies out here just once more, just one more time, to give you some idea, a little idea of what you'll see when you get inside.

Reluctantly, talking among themselves, shyly, shyly, as children called on to recite "Hiawatha" or "The Village Blacksmith," a pair of girls, dressed in skirts of some coarse, transparent cloth like the cloth hung at cottage windows, side by side for company, one adventuresome and one not so, their breasts hung lightly in cloth so that you could see the beginning of the curve, climbed up onto a ramshackle platform, the boards of which gave under their weight, and looked boldly and cheerfully into the crowd, one of them touching the back of her hair to keep it from blowing in the rain wind and holding with her other hand the opening in her skirt. They stood there until the pimp released them with the words that the show was about to begin, about to begin, last chance, your last chance to see these beauties dance, and Coverly followed his father up to the stand and then into a little tent where perhaps thirty men were standing apathetically around a little stage not so unlike the stage where he had seen his beloved Judy hit Punch over the head when he was younger. The roof of the tent was so shot with holes that the lights of the carnival shone through it like the stars of a galaxy—an illusion that charmed Coverly until he remembered what they were there for. Whatever it was, the crowd seemed sullen. Leander greeted a friend and left Coverly alone and listening to the pimp outside. "Burlymaque, hootchie cootch—I'm going to ask these little ladies out here just one more time before the show begins. . . ."

They waited and waited while the girls climbed up onto the platform and down again—up and down and the evening and the fair passed outside. A little rain began to fall and the walls of the tent to luff but the water did not cool the tent and sent up only in Coverly's mind memories of some mushroom-smelling forest where he wished he was. Then the girls retired, one of them to crank a phonograph and the other to dance. She was young—a child to Leander—not pretty but so fully in possession of the bloom of youth that it couldn't have mattered. Her hair was brown and as straight as a cow hand's except at the side where she had made two curls. She swore when she pricked her finger with a pin that held her skirt together and went on dancing with a drop of blood on her thumb. When she dropped her skirt she was naked.

Then, in this moth-eaten tent, filled with the fragrance of trampled grass, the rites of Dionysus were proceeding. A splintered tent post served for the symbol on the plate—that holy of holies—but this salute to the deep well of erotic power was step by step as old as man. The lowing of cattle and the voices of children came through the thin canvas walls that hid them. Coverly was rapt. Then a girl picked the cap off a farm hand in the front row and did something very dirty. Coverly walked out of the tent.

The fair was persevering in spite of the rain, which had left a pleasant, bitter smell in the air. The merry-go-round and the Ferris wheel were still turning. At his back Coverly could hear the scratchy music of the cootch show where his father was. To get out of the rain he wandered into the agricultural exhibit.

There was no one there but an old man and nothing that he wanted to see. Squashes, tomatoes, corn and lima beans were arranged on paper plates with prizes and labels. The irony of admiring squashes, under the circumstances, was not wasted on him. "Second prize. Olga Pluzinski," he read, staring miserably at a jar of tomato pickles. "Golden Bantam Corn. Raised by Peter Covell. Second prize, Jerusalem Artichokes . . ." He could still pick out, past the noise of the merry-go-round and the rain, the music where the girl was dancing. When the music stopped he went back and waited for his father. If Leander had seen Coverly leave the tent he didn't say so, but they walked to the village where the car was parked in silence. Coverly remembered his feelings at Langely. He had not only jeopardized his own rights—generations of unborn Wapshots were in jeopardy as well as the aged and the blind. He had even endangered that fitting and proper old age to which his parents were entitled and might have imperiled their way of life at West Farm. Everyone was asleep when they got home and they drank some milk, mumbled their good nights and went to bed.

But Coverly's troubles were not over. He dreamed about the girl. It was a humid day when he woke with a salt fog drifting upriver and catching, like bits of carded wool, in the firs. There was nothing about the morning into which he could escape. The rags of fog seemed to turn his mind and his body back onto themselves and their troubles. He groped among the piles of clothing on the floor to find his worsted bathing trunks. They were wet and smelled of a dead sea—the damp wool felt like a corruption on his skin and, thinking piously of saints and others who practiced mortification, Coverly drew them up over his groin and went down the back stairs. But even the kitchen that morning—the one room in the house that could be counted on to generate light and sense in the overcast—seemed like an abandoned hulk, dirty and cold, and Coverly went out the back door and down through the garden to the river. The tide was low and the mudbanks were exposed and reeking, but not so stinking, it seemed to Coverly, as the damp worsted wrapped around

his loins so that, with every movement he made, and warmed
now by his own miserable flesh, new odors of decayed sea water
were discharged. He went out to the tip of the diving board
and stood there on a scrap of potato sacking, warming the skin
of his chest with the skin of his arms and looking up and down
the cold, fog-hung valley where a little mortifying drizzle had
begun to form and drop like the condensation of moisture in
some subterranean prison. He dived and swam, shivering, out
to the middle of the river and then ran back up through the
wet garden, wondering if the joy of life was in him.

The boys took their mother to church at eleven and Coverly
got vehemently to his knees but he was not halfway through
his first prayer when the perfume of the woman in the pew ahead
of him undid all his work of mortification and showed him that
the literal body of Christ Church was no mighty fortress, for
although the verger had shut the oak doors and the only windows
open were not big enough for a child to enter by, the devil,
so far as Coverly was concerned, came and went, sat on his
shoulder, urged him to peer down the front of Mrs. Harper's
dress, to admire the ankles of the lady in front and to wonder
if there was any truth in the rumors about the rector and the
boy soprano. His mother nudged him with her elbow when it
was time for communion but he looked at her palely and shook
his head. The sermon was grueling and through it all Coverly's
mind turned over tirelessly the words of an obscene double limer-
ick about a bishop.

Late in the day, when the family were drinking tea, Coverly
went out to the back of the house. He smelled a clearing wind
and heard it stir in the trees and saw the overcast rise, the misera-
bleness of that day carried off and a band of yellow light spill
out of the west. Then he knew what he had to do and he made
his preparations; he washed his armpits and emptied his bank.
He had enough money to pay for her favors. He would join
the blessed company of men, so lightly screened by canvas from
the lowing of cattle and the voices of children. He walked, he
ran, he walked again, he took a short cut over the Waylands'

pasture to the dirt road to the fairgrounds, wondering why the simplicity of life had not appeared to him sooner.

It was dark by the time he reached the dirt road and in spite of the clearing wind it seemed to be a starless night. He did not stop or hesitate until he saw at the gates to the fairgrounds that all the lights were out. The fair was over, of course, and the carnival had gone. The gates hung open and why not, for after the cakes and squashes, the kewpie dolls and the exhibitions of needlework had been removed what was there to guard? With so many dark lanes and tree-shaded places not even the most harassed lovers would seek the shelter of the fairgrounds which, tenanted in these times no more than three or four days each year and nearly as old as Leander, breathed out into the night air the smell of rotted wood. But Coverly went on, into the space where the smell of trampled grass lingered in the air, down the ruts of the midway to where, or where as best he could see in the dark, she had gone through her rites. Oh, what can you do with a boy like that?

As for Moses, it was only a matter of chance that he was not already a father.

9

Henry Parker brought Rosalie's clothes out from the city in his produce truck and she stayed on at the farm, although she talked about going on to Chicago to visit a girl she had known in Allendale. But her plans to go, whenever she had made them, seemed to render the old square house and the valley in such a fine, golden light and to arouse such tenderness in her for everything she saw that she stayed on. Sometimes, walking on a beach and when there is no house near, we smell late in the day, on the east wind, lemons, wood smoke, roses and dust; the fragrance of some large house that we must have visited as children, our memories are so dim and pleasant—some place where we wanted to remain and couldn't—and the farm had come to seem like this for Rosalie.

She liked the old house best when it rained. When she woke in the morning and heard the noise of rain on the many roofs and skylights it was always with a great sense of comfort. She planned to read on the rainy days—to catch up on my reading, she said. All the books she chose were ambitious, but she never got through the first chapter. Sarah tried gently to direct her. *Middlemarch* is a very nice book or have you tried *Death Comes for the Archbishop?* After breakfast Rosalie would settle herself in the back parlor with some book and in the end she would take the old comic sections out of the woodbox and read these. She sometimes went into the village, where she was pleased to find that there was no question about her identity. You must be the young lady who's staying with the Wapshots, everyone said. She tried to be helpful around the house, sweeping the living room and wandering around with a dust cloth, but she was at that time of life when the ornaments and movables of middle age seemed like thorns and stones in her path and she was always knocking things over. She secretly did not understand why Mrs. Wapshot should bring so many flowers into the house and put them into vases and pitchers that kept tipping over. Her laughter was loud and sweet and almost everyone was glad to hear her voice; even her most distant footstep. She was good-natured about everything including the water pump, which broke down several times. When this happened Coverly drew water from a well near the woodshed for Rosalie and Mrs. Wapshot to wash with but the men took their baths in the brook.

Honora had never come to judge her. This was a family joke. "You can't go to Chicago until you've seen Cousin Honora," Leander said. The drill and stir of rain on the roofs assured her that her idle life at the farm was natural—that she was charged with nothing more than letting time slip through her hands. When she thought of her friend she tried to rationalize his death as we will, stumbling onto such conclusions as that it was time for him to go; he was meant to die young; and other persuasive and consoling sentimentalities. She dreamed of him once. She woke from a sound sleep, feeling that he was in trouble. It was late and the house was dark. She could hear the brook and in the woods an owl—a small and gentle chant. He is in trouble, she thought then, lighting a cigarette, and she seemed to see him, his back to her, naked in that he was defenseless, and lost, she could see, by the way he held his head and shoulders— lost or blinded, and wandering in some maze or labyrinth in great pain. She could not help him—she saw that—although she could feel the pain of his helplessness in the way he moved his hands like a swimmer. She supposed that he was being punished although she didn't know what sins he had committed. Then she went back to bed and to sleep but the dream was over as if he had wandered out of her ken or as if his wandering had ended.

Leander took her off for a day on the *Topaze*. It was lovely seaside weather and she stood on the forward deck while Leander watched her from the wheelhouse. A stranger approached her as they started across the bay and Leander was happy to see that she paid him very little attention and when he persisted she gave him a chilly smile and climbed up to the wheelhouse. "This is absolutely the funniest old boat I've ever seen," she said.

Now Leander did not like to have people speak critically of the *Topaze*. Her light words made him angry. His respect for the old boat might be a weakness but he thought that people who did not appreciate the *Topaze* were lightheaded. "I'm starving," Rosalie said. "All this *salt* air. I could eat an ox and it isn't ten o'clock." Leander's feelings were still smarting from her first words. "At the lake at this camp where I went to," she said, "there was a kind of boat that took people around, but it wasn't as much fun as this. I mean I didn't know the captain." She sensed the mistake she had made in speaking lightly of the *Topaze* and now she tried to make amends. "And the other boat wasn't as seaworthy," she said. "I suppose she's awfully seaworthy. I mean I suppose she was built in the days when people knew how to build seaworthy boats."

"She's thirty-two years old this spring," Leander said proudly. "Honora doesn't spend more than two or three hundred dollars on her a season and she's brought her passengers through thick and thin without harming a hair on their heads."

They went ashore together at Nangasakit and Leander watched her eat four hot dogs and wash them down with tonic. She didn't want to ride on the roller-coaster and he guessed that her ideas of pleasure were more sophisticated. He wondered if she drank cocktails in lounges. In speaking of her home she had spoken of both wealth and meanness and Leander guessed that her life had been made up of both. "Mother gives an enormous garden party, every summer," she had said, "with an orchestra sort of hidden in the bushes and millions of delicious cakes," and an hour later she had said, speaking of her own ineptitude as a housekeeper, "Daddy cleans the bathrooms at home. He gets into these old clothes and gets down on his hands and knees and scrubs the floors and tubs and everything. . . ." The hired orchestra and the housecleaning priest were equally strange to Leander and interested him, mostly in that her background seemed to stand between Rosalie and her enjoyment of Nangasakit. He would have liked to ride on the roller-coaster himself and he was disappointed when she refused. But they walked on the wrecked sea wall above the white sand and the green water and he was happy in her company. He thought—like Sarah—how much he would have liked a daughter, and the images of her career formed swiftly in his mind. She would marry, of course. He even saw himself throwing rice at her as she ran down the steps of Christ Church. But somehow her marriage went wrong. Her husband was killed in the war perhaps or turned out to be a drunk or a crook. In any case she came back to take care of Leander in his old age—to bring him his bourbon and cook his meals and listen to his stories on stormy nights. At three o'clock they went back to the boat.

Everyone liked Rosalie but Moses, who stayed out of her way

and was surly with her when they met. Mrs. Wapshot kept urging him to take her sailing and he always refused. It may have been that he associated her with that first night in the pasture and the fire or that—and this was more likely—that she seemed to him to be his mother's creation, to have stepped out of Sarah's brow. He spent most of his time at the Pocamasset boat club, where he raced the *Tern,* and he sometimes went fishing in the brook that flowed from Parson's Pond down behind the barn into the West River.

He planned to do this one morning and was up before dawn, although his chances of catching any fish that late in the summer were slim. It was dark when he made himself some coffee and pulled on his waders in the kitchen, his head full of pleasant recollections of other, similar, early mornings; the camp at Langely and skiing—the suffocating heat in ski lodges and the bad food and the running. Drinking coffee in the dark kitchen (the windows had begun to show some light) reminded him of all these things. He got some gear out of the hall closet, hitched his boots to his belt and trudged up the fields, planning to walk to Parson's Pond and then fish the stream down with wet flies, which were the only flies he had been able to find.

He cut into the woods a little below Parson's Pond. Other fishermen had made a path. It was humid in the woods and the smell of vegetation was heady and his heart seemed to rise when he heard the noise of water—like the garbled voices of prophets—and saw the first pool. His bladder was full, but he would save that for good luck if he needed it. He was so anxious to get a fly into the water that he had to reproach himself for haste. He had to put on leader and tie some respectable knots. While he did this he saw a trout traveling upstream—no more than the flicker of an eyelid—and somehow determined like a dog at evening with a newspaper in its mouth.

There were rags of mist over the water that early in the morning and what was that smell, he wondered, as strong as tanbark and much finer? He let himself into the brook, making sure of his footing, and made a fair cast. At least he was pleased himself and if he had been a trout he would have struck, his gastric juices flowing freely until he felt the hook in his jaw. He gathered in his line and made another cast, wading so deep in the pool that his crotch got wet, a blessing, he thought, hoping that the cold water would discourage his mind from ever leaving such simple pleasures, for with his maturity Moses had found in himself a taste for the grain and hair of life. He snagged a fly and then tying another waded on through some swift, shallow water into another pool, the prettiest of them all, but one where he had never caught a fish. The granite around the pool was square, like quarry stone, the water was black and slow-moving, overhung here and there with fir and wild apple, and although Moses knew that it was a pool where he wasted his time he could not convince himself that it was not inhabited by trout—whole families of shrewd two-pounders with undershot jaws. From this dark pool he waded through white water again to a place with meadowy banks where Turk's-cap lilies and wild roses grew and where it was easy to cast. While he was fishing this pool the sun came up and out—a flood of golden light that spread all through the woods and sank into the water so that every blue stone and white pebble showed—flooded the water with light until it was as golden as bourbon whisky—and the instant this happened he got a strike. His footing was bad. He nearly fell down, swearing loudly, but his rod was bent and then the trout surfaced with a crash and made for the logs at the mouth of the pool, but Moses kept him away from these, the fish zooming this way and that and the thrill of its life shooting up into Moses' arms and shoulders. Then, as the fish tired and he got out his landing net, he thought: What a life; what a grand life! He admired the rosy spots on the fish, broke its back and wrapped it in fern, ready now for a big day, a day in which he would catch his limit or over. But he fished that pool for an hour without getting another strike and then waded on to the next and the next, about as reflective as a race-track tout, but not insensitive to the stillness of the woods around him, the loud, prophetic noise of water and then, by looking down to the pool below him, to the fact that he was not alone. Rosalie was there.

She had come to bathe; she was really washing herself, rubbing soap between her toes and sitting naked in the warm sun on a stone. He snapped his reel so that she would not hear him take in the line and waded carefully, not to make any noise, to the banks of the pool where she could not see him but where he could see her through the leaves. He watched his gleaming Susanna, shamefaced, his dream of simple pleasure replaced by some sadness, some heaviness that seemed to make his mouth taste of blood and his teeth ache. She did not go in for washing much more than her feet. The water was too cold or the sun was too warm. She stood, picked a leaf off her buttocks and went into the green woods; vanished. Her clothes would be there. His head was confused and the smell of the dead trout in his pocket seemed like something from his past. He unwrapped the fish and washed it in the running water, but it looked like a toy. After a decent interval he went back to the farm, where his mother was waiting to ask him to bring water from the well, and after lunch he asked Rosalie to go sailing. "I'd adore to," she said.

They went down to Travertine in the old car and she knew more about sailing than he had expected. While he pumped the boat dry she put the battens into his sail and kept out of the way. There was a fresh southwest wind blowing and he took the racecourse, running for the first buoy with the wind at his stern, his centerboard up. And then the wind backed around to the east and the day darkened as swiftly as breath obscures a piece of glass. He took a wide tack for the second buoy but the water was rough and suddenly everything was sullen, angry and dangerous, and he could feel the pull of the old sea—the ebb tide—on his hull. Waves began to break over the bow and every one of them soaked Rosalie.

She hoped that he would head back for the boat club and she knew that he wouldn't. She had begun to shake with the cold and she wished she had never come. She had wanted his attention, his friendship, but as the hull rose clumsily and made an ominous thump and another sea broke over her shoulders she had some discouraging thoughts about her past and her hopes. Without a loving family, without many friends, dependent mostly upon men for her knowledge and guidance, she had found them all set on some mysterious pilgrimage that often put her life into danger. She had known a man who liked to climb mountains and as the *Tern* heeled over and shipped another sea she remembered her mountain-climbing lover, the crusts of fatigue in her mouth, the soreness of her feet, the dry sandwiches and the misty blue view from the summits that only raised in her mind the question of what she was doing there. She had tramped after bird watchers and waited home for fishermen and hunters and here she was on the *Tern*, half frozen and half drowned.

They rounded the second buoy and started back for the boat club and as they approached the mooring Rosalie went up to the bow. What happened was not her fault although Moses might have blamed her if he hadn't seen it. As she pulled the skiff toward her the light painter broke. The skiff rested thoughtfully, it seemed, in the chop for a second or two and then eased its bow around to the open sea and headed in that direction, nodding and dancing in the rough. Moses kicked off his sneakers and dived in, striking out for the skiff, and swam after it for some distance until he realized that the skiff was traveling more rapidly on the ebb tide and the wind than he could swim. Then he turned his head and saw the full scope of his mistake. When the painter broke the mooring had been lost and now, with her sails down and Rosalie calling to him, the *Tern* was heading out to the open sea.

It was foggy then. He could barely see the beach and the lights of the Pocamasset club and he struck out for these, but not hurriedly, for the ebb tide was strong and there were limits to his strength. He saw someone come out onto the porch of the boat club and he waved and shouted but he couldn't be heard or seen and after floating for a minute to rest he began the long haul to shore. When he felt sand under his feet it was a sweet sensation. The old committee boat was tied up to the wharf and he threw off the lines and headed her out into the fog, trying to guess the course the *Tern* would take. Then he let the motor idle and began to shout: "Rosalie, Rosalie, Rosalie, Rosalie. . . ."

She answered him in a little while and he saw the outlines of the *Tern* and told her what line to throw him, and lifted her, in his arms, off the bow. She was laughing and he had been so anxious that her cheerfulness seemed to him like a kind of goodness that he had not suspected her to have. Then they picked up the skiff and headed for shore and when the *Tern* was moored they went into the old clubhouse that looked as if it had been put together by old ladies and mice and had, in fact, been floated down the river from St. Botolphs. Moses built a fire and they dried themselves here and would have remained if old Mr. Sturgis hadn't come into the billiard room to practice shots.

Honora finished her hooked rug that afternoon—a field of red roses—and this and the gloomy sea-turn decided her to go to West Farm at last and be introduced to the stranger. She cut across the fields in the rain from Boat Street to River Street and let herself in the side door calling, "Hello. Hello. Is anyone home?" There was no answer. The house was empty. She was not nosy, but she climbed the stairs to the spare room to see if the girl might be there. The hastily made bed, the clothes scattered on chairs, and the full ash tray made her feel unfriendly and suspicious and she opened the closet door. She was in the closet when she heard Moses and Rosalie coming up the stairs, Moses saying, "What harm can there be in something that would make us both feel so good?" Honora closed the closet door as they came into the room.

What else Honora heard—and she heard plenty—does not concern us here. This is not a clinical account. We will only consider the dilemma of an old lady—born in Polynesia, educated at Miss Wilbur's, a philanthropist and samaritan—led by no more than her search for the truth into a narrow closet on a rainy afternoon.

10

No one saw Honora leave the house that day and if they had they wouldn't have been able to tell whether or not she was crying with the rain streaming over her face as she stamped across Waylands' pasture to Boat Street. The violence of her emotion may have stemmed from her memories of Mr. de Sastago, whose titles and castles turned out to be air. Her life had been virtuous, her dedication to innocence had been unswerving and she had been rewarded with a vision of life that seemed as unsubstantial as a paper match in a fairly windy place. She did not understand. She did not, as you might expect, take out her bewilderment on Maggie. She changed into dry clothes, drank her port and after supper she read the Bible.

At ten o'clock Honora said her prayers, turned out the light and got into bed. As soon as she turned out the light she felt wakeful and alert. It was the dark that made her wakeful. She was afraid of it. She looked boldly into the dark to assure herself that there was nothing to be afraid of but there seemed, in the dark, to be a stir, an increase of movement as if figures or spirits were arriving and gathering. She cleared her throat. She tried shutting her eyes, but this only heightened the illusion that the dark was populated. She opened her eyes again, determined to look squarely at the fantasy since she could not escape it.

The figures, although she couldn't see them clearly, were not numerous. There seemed to be twelve or fourteen—enough to circle her bed. They seemed to dance. Their movements were ugly and obscene and by looking narrowly into the dark she was able to recognize their forms. There were pumpkin heads cut with a dog-tooth smile; there were the buckram masks of cats and pirates that are sold to children at Halloween; there were skeletons, masked executioners, the top-heavy headdresses of witch doctors that she had seen photographed in the *National Geographic* magazine; there was everything that had ever seemed to her strange and unnatural. I am Honora Wapshot! she said aloud. I am a Wapshot. We have always been a hardy family.

She got out of bed, turned on a light and lighted the fire in her hearth, holding out her arms to the warmth. The light and the fire seemed to scatter the grotesques. I am a Wapshot, she said again. I am Honora Wapshot. She sat by the fire until midnight and then she went to bed and fell asleep.

Early in the morning she dressed and after breakfast hurried through her garden to catch the bus to Travertine. The rain was over but the day was sullen; the tail of the storm. There were only a few other passengers. One of these, a woman, left her seat in the rear when they had been traveling for a few minutes and sat down beside Honora. "I'm Mrs. Kissel," she said. "You don't remember me, but I recognized you. You're Honora Wapshot. I have a very embarrassing thing to tell you but I noticed when you got on the bus—" Mrs. Kissel lowered her voice to a whisper—"that your dress is undone all down the front. It's very embarrassing but I always think it's best to tell people."

"Thank you," Honora said. She clutched her coat over her dress.

"I always think it's best to tell people," Mrs. Kissel went on. "Whenever people tell me I'm always grateful. I don't care who they are. It reminds me of something that happened to me. Some years ago Mr. Kissel and I went up to Maine for his vacation. Mr. Kissel comes from Maine. He graduated from Bowdoin College. We went up in the sleeping cars. The train arrived at the station early in the morning and I had the most awful time getting my clothes on in that berth. I'd never been in a sleeping car before. Well, when we got off the train there were quite a few people there on the platform. The stationmaster was there, waiting for the mail, I guess, or something like that. Well, he came right over to me. I'd never seen him before in my life and I couldn't imagine what he wanted. Well, he came right over to me and he said 'Madam,' he said in a low voice, 'Madam, your corset is undone.' " Mrs. Kissel lifted her head and laughed for an instant like a young, young woman. "Oh, I'd never seen him before," she said, "and I never saw him again, but he came right over to me and told me that and I didn't resent it. Oh, I didn't resent it at all. I thanked him and went into the ladies' room and fixed it and then we took a carriage to the hotel. Those were the days when they had carriages."

Honora turned and stared at Mrs. Kissel, seized with jealousy, her neighbor seemed so simple and good and to have so few problems on her mind. They were at Travertine then and when the bus stopped Honora got off and marched up the street to the sign painter's.

11

Early the next morning Leander walked down the fish-smelling path to the wharf where the *Topaze* lay. A dozen passengers were waiting to buy their tickets and go aboard. Then he noticed that a sign had been hung on his wheelhouse. Then he thought at once of Honora and wondered what she had up her sleeve. The sign was painted on wood and must have cost five dollars. NO TRESPASSING, it said. THIS YACHT FOR SALE. FOR FURTHER IN-FORMATION SEE HONORA WAPSHOT 27 BOAT STREET. For a second his heart sank; his spirit seemed to wither. Then he was angry. The sign was hung, not nailed, to the wheelhouse, and he seized it and was about to throw it into the river when he realized that it was a good piece of wood and could be used for something else. "There won't be any voyage today," he told his passengers. Then he put the sign under his arm and strode through the group to the square. Of course most of the tradespeople in the village knew about the sign and most of them watched Leander. He saw no one and it was a struggle for him to keep from talking loudly to himself. He was, as we know, in his sixties; a little stooped, a little inclined to duckfoot, but a very handsome old man with thick hair and a boyish mien. The sign was heavy and made his arm lame and he had to change it from side to side before he got to Boat Street. His spirits by this time were fulminating. There wasn't much common sense left in him. He pounded on Honora's door with the edge of the sign.

Honora was sewing. She took her time getting to the door. First she reached for her stick and went around the parlor gathering up all the photographs of Moses and Coverly. She dumped these onto the floor behind the sofa. The reason she did this was that, although she liked having photographs of the boys around, she never wanted any of the family to catch her in such an open demonstration of affection. Then she straightened her clothes and started for the door. Leander was pounding on it. "If you mar the paint on my door," she called to him, "you'll pay for it." As soon as she opened the door he stormed into the hall and roared, "What in Christ's name is the meaning of this?"

"You don't have to be profane," she said. She put her hands over her ears. "I won't listen to profanity."

"What do you want from me, Honora?"

"I can't hear a word you say," she said. "I won't listen to swearing."

"I'm not swearing," he shouted. "I've stopped swearing."

"She's mine," Honora said, taking her hands down from her ears. "I can do anything I want with her."

"You can't sell her."

"I can too," Honora said. "The D'Agostino boys want to buy her for a fishing boat."

"I mean she's my usefulness, Honora." There was nothing pleading in his voice. He was still shouting. "You gave her to me. I'm used to her. She's my boat."

"I only loaned her to you."

"Goddamn it, Honora, the members of a family can't backbite one another like this."

"I won't listen to swearing," Honora said. Up went her hands again.

"What do you want?"

"I want you to stop swearing."

"Why did you do this? Why did you do this behind my back? Why didn't you tell me what was on your mind?"

"She belongs to me, I can do anything I want with her."

"We've always shared things, Honora. That rug belongs to me. That rug's mine." He meant the long rug in the hall.

"Your dear mother gave that rug to me," Honora said.

"She loaned it to you."

"She meant me to have it."

"That's my rug."

"It's nothing of the kind."

"Two can play at this game as well as one." Leander put down the sign and picked up an end of the rug.

"You put down that rug, Leander Wapshot," Honora shouted. "It's my rug."

"You put down that rug this instant. Do you hear me?"

"It's mine. It's my rug." He pulled the folds of the rug, which was long and so dirty that the dust from its warp made him sneeze, toward the door. Then Honora went to the other end of the rug, seized it and called for Maggie. When Maggie came out of the kitchen she grabbed Honora's end—they were all sneezing—and they all began to pull. It was a very unpleasant scene, but if we accept the quaintness of St. Botolphs we must also accept the fact that it was a country of spite fences and internecine quarrels and that the Pinchot twins lived until their death in a house divided by a chalk line. Leander lost, of course. How could a man win such a contest? Leaving Honora and Maggie in possession of the rug he stormed out of the house, his feelings in such a turmoil that he did not know where to go, and walking south on Boat Street until he came to a field he sat down in the sweet grass and chewed the succulent ends of a few stalks to take the bitterness out of his mouth.

During his lifetime Leander had seen, in the village, the num-

ber of sanctuaries for men reduced to one. The Horse Guards
had disbanded; the Atlantic Club was shut; even the boat club
had been floated down to Travertine. The only place left was
the Niagara Hose Company, and he walked back to the village
and climbed the stairs beside the fire engine to the meeting
room. The smell of many jolly beefsteak suppers was in the
air, but there was no one in the room but old Perley Sturgis
and Perley was asleep. On the walls were many photographs
of Wapshots: Leander as a young man; Leander and Hamlet;
Benjamin, Ebenezer, Lorenzo and Thaddeus. The photographs
of himself as a young man made him unhappy and he went
and sat in one of the Morris chairs near the window.

His anger at Honora had changed to a pervasive sense of
uneasiness. She had something up her sleeve and he wished
he knew what it was. He wondered what she could do and then
he realized that she could do anything she pleased. The *Topaze*
and the farm were hers. She paid the school bills and the interest
on the mortgage. She had even filled the cellar with coal. She
had offered to do all this in the kindest imaginable way. I have
the wherewithal, Leander, she had said. Why shouldn't I help
my only family? It was his fault—he couldn't blame her—that
he had never expected consequences for this largess. He knew
that she was meddlesome but he had overlooked this fact, borne
along on his conviction of the abundance of life—carp in the
inlet, trout in the streams, grouse in the orchard and money
in Honora's purse—the feeling that the world was contrived to
cheer and delight him. A ragged image of his wife and his sons
appeared to him then—thinly dressed and standing in a snowstorm—which was, after all, not so outrageous since couldn't
Honora, if she wanted, let them all experience hunger? This
image of his family roused in him passionate feelings. He would
defend and shelter them. He would defend them with sticks and
stones; with his naked fists. But this did not change the facts
of possession. Everything belonged to Honora. Even the rocking
horse in the attic. He should have led his life differently.

But out of the window he could see the blue sky above the

trees of the square and he was easily charmed with the appearance of the world. How could anything go wrong in such a paradise? "Wake up, Perley, wake up and we'll play some backgammon," he shouted. Perley woke up and they played backgammon
for matchsticks until noon. They had some lunch in the bakery
and played backgammon some more. In the middle of the afternoon it suddenly occurred to Leander that all he needed was
money. Poor Leander! We cannot endow him with wisdom and
powers of invention that he does not have and give him a prime-
ministerial breadth of mind. This is what he did.

He crossed the square to the Cartwright Block and climbed
the stairs. He said good afternoon to Mrs. Marston in the tele-
phone-company office—a pleasant white-haired widow surrounded by many potted plants that seemed to bloom and flourish in the fertile climate of her disposition. Leander spoke to
her about the rain and then went down the hall to the doctor's
office where a WALK IN sign hung from the doorknob like a bib.
In the waiting room there was a little girl with a bandaged hand,
leaning her head against her mother's breast, and old Billy
Tompkins with an empty pill bottle. The furniture seemed to
have been brought in from some porch, and the wicker chair
in which Leander sat squeaked as loudly as if he had sat down
on a nest of mice. The pack, hedges and jumpers of a fox hunt
appeared on the wallpaper and in these repeated images Leander
saw a reflection on the vitality of the village—a proneness to
dwell on strange and different ways of life. The door to the
inner office opened and a dark-skinned young woman who was
pregnant came out. Then the child with the bandaged hand was
led in by her mother. She was not in the office long. Then Billy
Tompkins went in with his empty pill bottle. He came out with
a prescription and Leander went in.

"What can I do for you, Captain Wapshot?" the doctor asked.

"I was playing backgammon with Perley Sturgis at the firehouse," Leander said, "and I had an idea. I wondered if you
could give me a job."

"Oh, I'm afraid not," the doctor said pleasantly enough. "I
don't even have a nurse."

"That wasn't the kind of work I had in mind," Leander said. "Can anyone hear us?"

"I don't believe so," the doctor said.

"Take me for an experiment," Leander said. "Please take me. I've decided that's what I want to do. I'll sign anything. I won't tell anyone. Operate on me. Do anything you want. Just give me a little money."

"You don't know what you're talking about, Captain Wapshot."

"Take me," Leander said. "I'm a very interesting specimen. Pure Yankee stock. Think of the blood in my veins. State senators. Scholars. Sea captains. Heroes. Schoolmasters. You can make medical history. You can make a name for yourself. You'll be famous. I'll give you the family history. I'll give you a regular pedigree. I don't care what you do with me. Just give me a little money."

"Please get out of here, Captain Wapshot."

"It would help humanity some, wouldn't it?" Leander asked. "It would help humanity. Nobody has to know. I won't tell anybody. I promise I won't tell anybody. I'll promise on the Bible. You can have a laboratory nobody knows about. I won't tell anyone. I'll go there whenever you say. I'll go there nights if you want me. I'll tell Mrs. Wapshot I'm traveling."

"Please get out of here, Captain Wapshot."

Leander picked up his hat and left. In the square a woman, from the other side of the river, was calling in Italian to her son. "Speak English," Leander told her. "Speak English. This is the United States." He drove back to the farm in the old Buick.

He was tired, and happy to see the lights of the farm. He was hungry and thirsty and his appetite seemed to embrace the landscape and the house. Lulu had burned something. There was a smell of burned food in the hall. Sarah was in the back parlor.

"Did you see the sign?" she asked.

"Yes," Leander said. "Was she here today?"

"Yes. She was here this afternoon."

"She hung it on the wheelhouse," Leander said. "I guess she hung it there herself."

"What are you talking about?"

"The sign."

"But it's on the gatepost."

"What do you mean?"

"The sign's on the gatepost. She put it there this afternoon."

"She wants to sell the farm?"

"Oh, no."

"What is it, what is it then? What in hell is it?"

"Leander. Please."

"I can't talk with anyone."

"You don't have to talk like that."

"Well, what is it? Tell me, Sarah, what is it?"

"She thinks that we ought to take in tourists. She's spoken to the Pattersons and they make enough money taking in tourists to go to Daytona every year."

"I don't want to go to Daytona."

"We have three extra bedrooms," Sarah said. "She thinks we ought to let them."

"That old woman has not got a scrap of the sense of the fitness of things left in her head," Leander shouted. "She'll sell my boat to foreigners and fill my house with strangers. She has no sense of fitness."

"She only wants . . ."

"She only wants to drive me out of my head. I can't make head nor tail of what she's doing. I don't want to go to Daytona. What makes her think I want to go to Daytona?"

"Leander. Please. Shhh . . ." In the dusk she saw the head-lights of a car come up the drive. She went down the hall to the side door and onto the stoop.

"Can you put us up?" a man called cheerfully.

"Well, I believe so," Sarah said. Leander followed her down the hall but when he heard the stranger, veiled by the dark, close the door of his car, he stepped back from the door.

"What do you charge?" the man asked.

"Whatever's customary," Sarah said. "Perhaps you'd like to look at the rooms?" A man and a woman came up the stairs.

"All we want are comfortable beds and a bathroom," the man said.

"Well, the bed has a nice hair mattress," Sarah said thoughtfully, "but there's some rust in the hot-water tank and we've had an awful time with the water pump this month, but I'd like you to see the rooms."

She opened the screen door and stepped into the hall to be followed by the strangers and Leander, standing there and trapped, opened the hall closet and crashed into the dark with its collection of old coats and athletic equipment. He heard the strangers enter his house and follow Sarah up the stairs. Just then the old water closet sounded the opening notes of a performance of unusual vehemence. As this noise abated Leander heard the stranger ask, "Then you don't have a room with a private bath?"

"Oh no," Sarah said, "I'm sorry," and there was sorrow in her voice. "You see this is one of the oldest houses in St. Botolphs and our bathroom is the oldest in the county."

"Well, what we were looking for was a place with a private bathroom," the stranger said, "and . . . "

"We always like to have a private bathroom," his wife said gently. "Even when we travel on trains we like to have one of those compartments."

"*De gustibus non est disputandum,*" Sarah said sweetly, but her sweetness was forced.

"Thank you for showing us the rooms."

"You're quite welcome."

The screen door slammed and when the car had gone down the drive Leander came out of the closet. He strode down the drive to where a sign, TOURIST HOME, was hung on his gatepost. It was about the size and quality of the sign on the *Topaze* and raising it in the air with all his might he brought it down on the stones, splitting the sign in two and jarring his own bones.

Later that night he walked over to Boat Street.

Honora's house was dark but Leander stood squarely in front of it and called her name. He gave her a chance to put on a wrapper and then shouted her name again.

"What is it, Leander?" she asked. He couldn't see her, but her voice was clear enough and he knew she had come to the window. "What do you want?"

"Oh you're so high and mighty these days, Honora. Don't forget that I know who you are. I can remember you feeding swill to the pigs and coming back from Waylands' with the milk pails. I have something to tell you, Honora. I have something important to tell you. It was a long time ago. It was right after you came back from Spain. I was standing in front of Moodys' with Mitch Emerson. When you walked through the square Mitch said something about you. I couldn't repeat what he said. Well, I took him out behind the lumberyard, Honora, and I walloped him until he cried. He weighed fifty pounds more than me and all the Emersons were hardy, but I made him cry. I never told you that."

"Thank you, Leander."

"And other things, too. I've always been dutiful towards you. I would have gone to Spain and killed Sastago if you'd asked me. There's not a hair on my body that has not turned white in your service. So why do you devil me?"

"Moses has to go," Honora said.

"What?"

"Moses has to go out in the world and prove himself. Oh, it's hard for me to say this, Leander, but I think it's right. He hasn't raised a finger all summer except to indulge himself and all the men of our family went out into the world when they were young; all the Wapshots. I've thought it over and I think he'll want to go but I'm afraid he'll be homesick. Oh, I was so homesick in Spain, Leander. I'll never forget it."

"Moses is a good boy," Leander said. "He'll do well anywhere." He straightened up, thinking proudly of his son. "What did you have in mind?"

"I thought he might go to someplace like New York or Washington, someplace strange and distant."

"That's a bully idea, Honora. Is that what all the trouble's been about?"

"What trouble?"

"Are you going to sell the *Topaze?*"

"The D'Agostino boys have changed their minds."

"I'll talk it over with Sarah."

"It won't be easy for any of us," Honora said, and then she sighed. Leander heard the tremulous sound, shaken and breaking like smoke and seeming to arise from such a deep base of the old lady's spirit that age had not changed its tenderness or its purity, and it affected him like the sigh of a child.

"Good night, Honora dear," he said.

"Feel that lovely breeze."

"Yes. Good night."

"Good night, Leander."

12

Moses' career at college had been unexceptional and—but for a few friendships—there was nothing about it that he would miss; not the skimmed milk on his porridge or Dunster House upended like a sow above the threadbare waters of the Charles. He wanted to see the world. For Leander the world meant a place where Moses could display his strong, gentle and intelligent nature; his brightness. When he thought of his son's departure it was always with feelings of pride and anticipation. How well Moses would do! Honora had tradition at her back, for all the men of the family had taken a growing-up cruise—Leander's father included—rounding the Horn before they shaved, some of them, and on the homeward voyage lewdly straddling the beauties of Samoa, who must have begun to show some signs

of wear and tear. Sarah's habitual reliance on sad conclusions—
life is only a casting off and we only live from day to day—
helped her to bear the pain of having her first born plucked
from his home. But where did all of this leave poor Coverly?

The relationship between the two brothers had been stormy
until a year or so ago. They had fought bare fisted and with
sticks, stones and iceballs. They had reviled one another and
had thought of the world as a place where the other would be
exposed as an evil-tempered fraud. Then all this bad feeling
had turned to tenderness and a brotherhood had bloomed that
had all the symptoms of love—the pleasure of nearness and the
pain of separation. They even took long walks together on the
beach at Travertine, airing their most intimate and improbable
plans. The knowledge that his brother was leaving gave Coverly
his first taste of love's dark side; it was gall. He didn't see how
he could live without Moses. Honora made the arrangements.
Moses would go to Washington and work for a Mr. Boynton
who was in some way indebted to her. If Moses had any regrets
or hints of regrets they were lost in the confusion of his feelings
and overridden by his passionate wish to get out of St. Botolphs
and try his strength in the world.

Sarah gathered those things that she thought Moses might
need when he took up his life in a strange place—his confirmation
certificate, a souvenir spoon he had bought at Plymouth Rock,
a drawing of a battleship he had made when he was six, his
football sweater, prayer book, muffler and two report cards—
but, hearing him shout loudly up the stairs to Coverly, she
sensed, in the notes of his voice, that he would leave these things
behind him and she put them away again. The closeness of Moses' departure drew Sarah and Leander together and refreshed
those charming self-deceptions that are the backbone of many
long-lived marriages. Leander felt that Sarah was frail and on
the evenings before Moses left he brought her a shawl to shield
her from the night air. Sarah felt that Leander had a beautiful
baritone voice and now with Moses going away she wished he
would take up his music again. Sarah was not frail—she had

the strength of ten—and Leander could not carry the simplest tune. "You have to remember about the night air," Leander told her when he brought her the shawl, and, looking up at him admiringly, Sarah would say, "It's a shame the boys have never heard you sing."

There was a farewell party. The men drank bourbon and the ladies had ginger ale and ice cream. "I came over by Waylands' pasture," Aunt Adelaide Forbes said, "and that pasture's just covered with cowflops. I have never seen so many cowflops in my whole life. There's just cowflops everywhere. You can't hardly take a step without ending up in a cowflop." Everyone was there and Reba Heaslip came up to Rosalie and said, "I was *born* in the inner sanctum of the Masonic Temple." They all talked about their travels. Mr. and Mrs. Gates had been to New York and had paid eighteen dollars a day for a room where you couldn't swing a cat around in. Aunt Adelaide had been taken to Buffalo when she was a child. Honora had been to Washington. Mildred Harper, the church organist, played the piano, and they sang from the old hymnal and song books—"Silver Threads Among the Gold," "Beulah Land" and "In the Gloaming." While they were singing Sarah saw Uncle Peepee Marshmallow's face in the window but when she went out onto the stoop to ask him in he had fled. Moses, going into the kitchen for a drink, found Lulu crying. "I ain't crying because you're going away, Moses," she said. "I'm crying because I had this bad dream last night. I dreamed I give you this gold watch and you broke it on some stones. Ain't that silly of me? Of course I don't have the money to buy you a gold watch and even if I did you aren't the kind of boy that'd break it, but just the same I dreamed this dream where I give you this gold watch and you broke it on some stones."

Moses left the next night on the 9:18, but there was no one to see him off but his parents. Rosalie was in her room, crying. "I won't go to the station," Honora had said in the same tone of voice she used at family funerals when she said that she would not go to the grave. No one knew where Coverly was but Sarah suspected that he was taking a walk on the beach at Travertine. Standing on the platform they could hear in the distance the noise of the train coming up the east bank of the river, a sound that made Sarah shiver, for she was at an age when trains seemed to her plainly to be the engines of separation and death. Leander put a hand on Moses' shoulder and gave him a silver dollar.

Moses' feelings were strenuous but not sad and he did not remember the skimming fleet at the ten-minute signal before a race or the ruined orchards where he hunted grouse or Parson's Pond and the cannon on the green and the water of the river shining between the hardware store and the five-and-ten-cent store where Cousin Justina once played the piano. We are all inured, by now, to those poetic catalogues where the orchid and the overshoe appear cheek by jowl; where the filthy smell of old plumage mingles with the smell of the sea. We have all parted from simple places by train or boat at season's end with generations of yellow leaves spilling on the north wind as we spill our seed and the dogs and the children in the back of the car, but it is not a fact that at the moment of separation a tumult of brilliant and precise images—as though we drowned—streams through our heads. We have indeed come back to lighted houses, smelling on the north wind burning applewood, and seen a Polish countess greasing her face in a ski lodge and heard the cry of the horned owl in rut and smelled a dead whale on the south wind that carries also the sweet note of the bell from Antwerp and the dishpan summons of the bell from Altoona but we do not remember all this and more as we board the train.

Sarah began to cry when Moses kissed her. Leander put an arm around her shoulder but she would have none of it and so they stood apart when Moses said good-by. As soon as the train started, Coverly, who had boarded it in Travertine, came out of the toilet where he was hidden and joined his brother and past the table-silver factory they went, past old Mr. Larkin's barn with this legend painted on it: BE KIND TO ANIMALS, past the Remsens' fields and the Watermans' dump, past the ice pond and the hair-tonic works, past Mrs. Trimble's the laundress, past

Mr. Brown's who ate a slice of mince pie and drank a glass of milk when the 9:18 rattled his windows, past the Howards' and the Townsends' and the grade crossing and the cemetery and the house of the old man who filed saws and whose windows were the last of the village.

13

It never rains but it pours. After saying good-by to Moses, Leander and Sarah came home to find this letter from Coverly on the hall table.

"Dear Mother and Father, I have gone away with Moses. I know that I should have told you and that not telling you was like lying but this is only the second lie I have ever told and I will never tell another. The other lie I told was about the screwdriver with the black handle. I stole it from Tinicum's hardware store. I love Moses so much that I couldn't be in St. Botolphs if he wasn't there. But we are not going to be together because we thought that if we separated we would have a better chance of proving our self-reliance to Cousin Honora. I am going to New York and work for Cousin Mildred's husband in his carpet factory and as soon as I have a place to live in I will write and tell you my address. I have twenty-five dollars.

"I love you both and would not want to hurt your feelings and I know there is no place finer in the world than St. Botolphs and our house and when I have made my mark I am coming back. I wouldn't be happy anywhere else. But now I am old enough to go out in the world and make my fortune. I can tell this because I have so many ideas about life where I never had any ideas before. I have taken the framed copy of Kiplings IF with me and I will think about this and about all the great men I have read about and I will go to Church.

"Your loving son, Coverly."

And two days later Rosalie's parents telephoned to say that

they would pick up Rosalie in an hour. They were driving to Oysterville. Soon after this a long black car that would have opened Emmet Cavis' eyes came up the driveway at West Farm and Rosalie ran down the path to greet her parents. "Where did you get that green dress?" Sarah heard Mrs. Young ask her daughter. It was the first or at least the second thing she said. Then they got out of the car and Rosalie, blushing and as confused and embarrassed as a child, introduced them to Sarah. As soon as Mrs. Young had shaken Sarah's hand she turned to Rosalie and asked, "Guess what I found yesterday? I found your scarab bracelet. I found it in my top bureau drawer. Yesterday morning before we had planned to go to Oysterville I decided to clean out my top bureau drawer. I just took the whole thing and dumped it out onto my bed—just dumped it out onto my bed and lo and behold there was your scarab bracelet."

"I'll go up and finish packing," said Rosalie, blushing and blushing, and she went in, leaving Sarah with her parents. The rector was a pursy man in clericals and sure enough, while they stood there, he began to scratch his stomach. Sarah disliked quick and unkind judgments and yet there seemed to be some striking stiffness and dryness in the man and something so pompous, monotonous and crusty in the notes of his voice that she felt irritable. Mrs. Young was a short woman, a little plump, and decked out with furs, gloves and a hat sewn with pearls— one of those middle-aged women of means, it seems, whose empty-headedness smacks of tragedy. "The funny thing about the scarab bracelet," she said, "was that I thought Rosalie lost it in Europe. She went abroad last year, you know. Eight countries. Well, I thought she lost her bracelet in Europe and I was so surprised to find it in my bureau drawer."

"Won't you come in?" Sarah asked.

"No thank you, no thank you. It's a quaint old house, I can see that. I love quaint old things. And some day when I'm old and James has retired I'm going to buy a quaint, run-down old house like this and do it all over myself. I love quaint old run-down places."

The priest cleared his throat and felt for his wallet. "We have a little pecuniary matter to settle," he said, "before Rosalie comes down. I've talked it over with Mrs. Young. We thought that twenty dollars might help repay you for . . ." Then Sarah began to cry, to cry for them all—Coverly, Rosalie and Moses and the stupid priest—and she felt such a sharp pain in her breast that it seemed as if she was weaning her children. "Oh, you must excuse me for crying," she sobbed. "I'm terribly sorry. You must excuse me."

"Well, here's thirty dollars then," the priest said, handing her the bills.

"Oh, I don't know what's come over me," Sarah sobbed. "Oh dear. Oh dear." She threw the money into the garden. "I've never been so insulted in my life," she sobbed, and went into the house.

Upstairs in the spare room Rosalie, like Mrs. Wapshot, was crying. Her bags were packed but Sarah found her lying face down on the bed and she sat beside her and put a hand tenderly on her back. "You poor child," she said. "I'm afraid they're not very nice."

Then Rosalie raised her head and spoke, to Sarah's astonishment, in anger. "Oh, I don't think you should talk like that about people's parents," she said. "I mean they are my parents, after all, and I don't think it's very nice of you to say that you don't like them. I mean I don't think that's very fair. After all they've done everything for me like sending me to Allendale and Europe and everybody says he's going to be a bishop and . . ." She turned then and looked at Sarah tearfully and kissed her good-by on the cheek. Her mother was calling her name up the stairs. "Good-by, Mrs. Wapshot," she said, "and please say good-by to Lulu and Mr. Wapshot for me. I've had a perfectly divine time. . . ." Then to her mother she called, "I'm coming, I'm coming, I'm coming, I'm coming," and she banged with her suitcases down the stairs.

Part Two

14

Writer's epistolary style (Leander wrote) formed in tradition of Lord Timothy Dexter, who put all punctuation marks, prepositions, adverbs, articles, etc., at end of communication and urged reader to distribute same as he saw fit. West Farm. Autumn day. 3 P.M. Nice sailing breeze from NW quarter. Golden light. Glittering riffle on water. Hornets on ceiling. An old house. Roofs of St. Botolphs in distance. Old river-bottom burg today. Family prominent there once. Name memorialized in many things in vicinity: lakes, roads, hills even. Wapshot Avenue now back street in honkytonk beach resort further south. Smell of hot dogs, popcorn, also salt air and grinding music from old merry-go-round calliope. Matchwood cottages for rent by day, week or season. Such a street named after forebear who rode spar in Java sea for three days, kicking at sharks with bare feet.

There's nothing but the blood of shipmasters and schoolteachers in writers' veins. All grand men! A true pork and beaner and something of a curiosity these days. Memories important or unimportant as the case may be but try in retrospect to make sense of what is done. Many skeletons in family closet. Dark secrets, mostly carnal. Cruelty, illicit love, candor, but no dirty linen. Decisions of taste involved. Voided bladder so many times; brushed teeth so many times; visited Chardon Street fancy house so many times. Who cares? Much modern fiction distasteful to writer because of above.

There may have been literature of New England port—factory town also—period of '70's and upwards, but if so I have never found same. Shipyards prospering in writer's early youth. Oak chips three feet deep in yards at foot of River Street. Lumber moved by oxen. Noise of adzes, hammers, heard all summer. Heartening sounds. Noise of seams being calked heard in late August. Soon will come the winter cold. Launching in September. Ships once crewed with flower of native youth, crewed then with lascars, Kanakas and worse. Bad times in offing. Grandfather on deathbed cried: "Shipping is dead!" Prosperous master. Writer raised among souvenirs of saltwater riches. Velvet cushions on deep window seats; now bare. Long garden in rear of house once upon a time. Geometric flower pots. Paths at right angles. Low box hedge. Four inches high. Father's fancy poultry. Fantails. Homers. Tumblers. No dung-heap stuff. Man to care for garden and birds in times gone by. Local character. Good man. Been to sea. Wonderful stories. Flying fish. Porpoises. Pearls. Sharks. Samoan girls. Beached six months in Samoa. Paradise. Never put his pants on once in six months. Let the pigeons out each afternoon. Each type separately. Tumblers interested writer most.

Sad times sometimes; sometimes gay. Thunderstorms. Christmas. Sounds of fish horn with which writer was called home to supper. Sailed with father on small schooner. Zoe. Moored at river in foot of garden on summer months. High sided; small, counter stern. Short overhang bow. Good cabin with transom and small galley. Thirty-foot water line. Moderate sail plan. Mainsail, foresail, two jibs set on jib-stay. One good-sized. She was dry in rough weather. She moved very well off the wind, quartering it or before it wing and wing, but "on the wind" or "up the wind" as they say today, she moved like real estate. Did not hold at all close going to windward and sagged off badly. Schooner crewed by Daniel Knight. Retired sailor. Old then. About five feet eight. 170 lbs. Broad-beamed and lively. Remembered square-riggers, Calcutta, Bombay, China, Java. Went out to Zoe in tender. First ceremony on getting aboard was meeting in cabin of father and crew. Libation of Barkham's rum and molasses. I was not in at slicing of mainbrace; but I can smell it now. More savory world then, than today. Smell of ship's-bread bakery. Green coffee beans roasted once a week. Perfumery of roasted coffee floated miles downriver. Lamp smoke. Smell of cistern water. Lye from privy. Wood fires.

Family consisted of self and brother, ten years my senior. Differences in ages seemed abysmal in early life. Later diminished. Brother named Hamlet after Prince of Denmark. Offshoot of father's devotion to Shakespeare. Unlike gloomy Prince, however. Very frisky. Played baseball for hose company; also lacrosse. Won many foot races. Much loved by mother. Later the darling of Chardon Street hookers. Familiar figure at the Narragansett House bar. Good fighter both with gloves in gymnasium and bare fisted in street when necessary.

In warm months writer slept in attic, surrounded by boyish museum of minerals and curiosities. Also facsimile of Chinese junk carved in ivory. Two feet long. Three balls of ivory within one another. Large as an apple. Brain corals. Sea shells as big as melons. Others like peas. Held to the human ear there was a sound like surf breaking on shore. Some shells with spikes. Two tame crows among cherished possessions. Taken from nest on Hale's island in April. Swordfish spur and eye socket. Powerful odor from same. Attic illuminated by skylight, approached by several steps. Fine view of river to the sea.

Sturgeon in river then. About three feet long. All covered with knobs. Leap straight up in air and fall back in water. Viewed from horse car running then between St. Botolphs and Travertine. One bobtailed car. You got in at the back end. Dingey Graves was driver. Been to sea. One voyage to Calcutta. Gave me free rides always and sometimes let me drive the horse. Hold the reins and see the sturgeon leap. Boyish happiness. Dingey was lovelorn. Harriet Atkinson was the object of his passon. She was of the first families but Dingey's financial and scholastic rating was a blank, They loved but never wedded. In such a place many dark lanes for lovers' meeting. Wooded river banks and groves. Love child raised by old-maid sister. Harriet exiled to Dedham. Dingey led life of quiet desperation, driving horse car.

Dingey was nephew of Jim Graves, prop of old River House

on waterfront. Honest gambler. Big chested. 5′11″. 200 lbs. Dark hair. River House bar very popular. Good liquor or so I was told. Ten cents per drink. Hard stuff. You got the bottle. Customers poured their own. Some lager. Cool lager. Some stock ale. Also native product. Barkham's rum. Made here for many years. No cocktails; mixed drinks served. Uncle Jim Graves never walked. Rode in hacks or barouches. Pair of horses. Never singles. Always one or more companions with him. Quiet. Much dignity. Wore good-sized diamond stud in necktie on boiled stiff shirt front. Also large ruby ring with stone inside hand. Always had big roll but never vulgar display. Clothes of excellent quality in style of those days. Prince Albert coat and some double-breasted vests with cutaway. Hair a bit long according to today's fashions. Mustache. Not walrus. Silk hat. Cards. Faro. Stud poker. Wheel. Sweatboard. No dice used as craps. Went with Uncle Jim and Dingey when of age to fancy house on Chardon Street, next door to sulphur, brimstone, deep-water Baptist Church. Whore with up-country accent. Lowell girl. Big thighs. Breath smelled of violets. Could hear the singing in the church. Uncle Jim ordered champagne by the basket. Well liked everywhere. Big shot. Big wagers. Big drinks. Never lost his head or legs. Never noisy. Died broke. Third-floor room of River House. Spare room. Cold. Went to see him. Forsaken by all. Like Timon. All fair-weather friends scattered. Not bitter. Gentleman to the end. Skin of ice in water pitcher. Shy flakes of snow falling.

On last summer of youth spent in valley J. G. Blaine, Presidential candidate, came to dinner. Sunday. Cousin Juliana visiting. Poor relation. Carried ivory ruler in apron pocket and gave writer cut on wrist when whistled on Sunday, went up stairs two at a time, said "awful" for "good." "Awful nice pudding." Crack! Porgies schooling in river then. Mackerel sharks—fourteen, fifteen feet long—chased porgies up to town dock in middle of afternoon. Big excitement. Ran up river bank to village. Water foaming white. Mysteries of the deep. Grand thunderstorm came down from the hills. Fierce rain. Stood under apple tree. Grand sunset after. Sharks went downriver with tide. Beautiful hour.

Skies all fiery. Stagecoach horns and train whistles. (Trains running then regularly.) Church bells ringing. Everybody and his grandmother out to see departure of sharks. Walked home in twilight. Wished for gold watch and chain on evening star. Venus? House ablaze with light. Carriages. Remembered Mr. Blaine for dinner. Late. Afraid of Juliana's ruler.

Front hall lamp lighted first time in two years. Moth millers all around lamp. Hall carpet seldom walked on. Felt coarse under bare feet. Barefooted most of summer. Five or six lamps burning in parlor. Grand illumination for those times. Splendid company. Mr. Blaine. Heavy man. Mother in garnet dress, later made into curtains. Something wrong. Juliana in best black dress, gold beads, lace cap, etc., squatted on floor. Big cigar in left hand. Speaking gibberish. Writer got upstairs without being seen. Troubled in spirit. Attic bedroom smelled of trunks, also swordfish spur. Would send you into the street on rainy weather. Made water in pot. No bathrooms at all. Washed in rain water collected in large tubs at back of house. Much troubled by spectacle of Juliana. Later voices on driveway. Men talking; lighting carriage lamps. Dogs barking for miles upriver.

In morning asked Bedelia. Hired girl. Never ask parents. Children seen, not heard. Very solemn, Bedelia. "Miss Juliana's a famous seer. She talks with the dead through the spirit of an Indian. Last night she talked with Mr. Blaine's mother and the little Hardwich boy who was drowned in the river." Never understood pious old lady talking with the dead. Can't think clearly about it now. Watched all day for Juliana. Didn't appear for noon meal. Tired out from talking with the dead. Showed up for supper. Same uniform. Black dress. Gray hair in little curls. Lace cap. Said grace in loud voice. "Dear Lord we thank Thee for these Thy blessings." Ate with good appetite. Always smelled like pantry, Juliana did. Cinnamony smell. Savory, sage and other spices. Not unpleasant. Watched for signs of seer, but saw only strict old lady. Dewlaps. Poor relation.

One more Indian. Joe Thrum. Lived on hoopskirts of town. Painted face orange. Smelly hut. Wore silk shirt. Big brass rings

in ears. Dirty. Ate rats or so writer believed. Last of savages.
Hate Indians, even in Wild West show. Great-great-grandfather
killed by same at Fort Duquesne. Poor Yankee! How far from
home. Strange water. Strange trees. Led into clearing at edge
of water stark naked at 4 P.M. Commenced fire-torture. 8 P.M.,
still living. Cried most piteously. Hate Indians, Chinamen, most
foreigners. Keep coal in bathtub. Eat garlic. Trail smell of polish
earth, Italian earth, Russian earth, strange earth everywhere.
Change everything. Ruin everything.

This was the first chapter of Leander's autobiography or confession, a project that kept him occupied after the *Topaze* was
put up the year his sons went away.

15

You come, as Moses did, at nine in the evening to Washington,
a strange city. You wait your turn to leave the coach, carrying
a suitcase, and walk up the platform to the waiting room. Here
you put down your suitcase and crane your neck, wondering
what the architect had up his sleeve. There are gods above you
in a dim light and, unless there are some private arrangements,
the floor where you stand has been trod by presidents and kings.
You follow the crowds and the sounds of a fountain out of this
twilight into the night. You put down your suitcase again and
gape. On your left is the Capitol building, flooded with light.
You have seen this so often on medallions and post cards that
it seemed incised on your memory only now there is a difference.
This is the real thing.

You have eighteen dollars and thirty-seven cents in your
pocket. You have not pinned the money to your underwear as
your father suggested but you keep feeling for your wallet to
make sure that it hasn't been lifted by a pickpocket. You want
a place to stay and, feeling that there will not be one around

the Capitol, you start off in the opposite direction. You feel springy and young—your shoes are comfortable and the good, woolen socks you wear were knitted by your dear mother. Your underwear is clean in case you should be hit by a taxicab and have to be undressed by strangers.

You walk and walk and walk, changing your suitcase from hand to hand. You pass lighted store fronts, monuments, theaters and saloons. You hear dance music and the thunder of tenpins from an upstairs bowling alley and wonder how long it will be before you begin to play a role against this new scene. You will have a job, perhaps in that marble building on your left. You will have a desk, a secretary, a telephone extension, duties, worries, triumphs and promotions. In the meantime you will be a lover. You will meet a girl by that monument on the corner, buy her some dinner in that restaurant across the street and be taken home by her to that apartment in the distance. You will have friends and enjoy them as these two men, swinging down the street in shirt sleeves, are enjoying one another. You may belong to a bowling club that bowls in the alley whose thunder you hear. You will have money to spend and you may buy that raincoat in the store window on your right. You may—who knows?—buy a red convertible like that red convertible that is rounding the corner. You may be a passenger in that airplane, traveling southeast above the trees, and you may even be a father like that thin-haired man, waiting for the traffic light to change, holding a little girl by one hand and a quart of strawberry ice cream in the other. It is only a question of days before the part begins, you think, although it must in fact have begun as soon as you entered the scene with your suitcase.

You walk and walk and come at last to a neighborhood where the atmosphere is countrified and domesticated and where signs hang here and there, advertising board and rooms. You climb some stairs and a gray-haired widow answers the door and asks your business, your name and your former address. She has a vacancy, but she can't climb the stairs because of a weak heart or some other infirmity and so you climb them alone to the third floor back where there is a pleasant-enough room with a window looking into some back yards. Then you sign a register and hang your best suit in the closet; the suit that you will wear for your interview in the morning.

Or you wake—like Coverly—a country boy in the biggest city in the world. It's the hour when Leander usually begins his ablutions and the place is a three-dollar furnished room, as small or smaller than the closets of your home. You notice that the walls are painted a baneful green which can't have been chosen because of its effect on a man's spirit—this is always discouraging—and so must be chosen because it is cheap. The walls seem to be sweating but when you touch the moisture it is as hard as glue. You get out of bed and look out of your window onto a broad street where trucks are passing, bringing produce up from the markets and railroad yards—a cheerful sight but one that you, coming from a small town in New England, regard with some skepticism, even with compassion, for although you have come here to make your fortune you think of the city as a last resort of those people who lack the fortitude and character necessary to endure the monotony of places like St. Botolphs. It is a city, you have been told, where the value of permanence has never been grasped and this, even early in the morning, seems to be a pitiful state of affairs.

In the hallway you find a wash basin where you shave your beard and while you are shaving a stout man joins you and watches critically. "You gotta stretch your skin, sonny," the stranger says. "Look. Let me show you." He takes a fold of his skin and pulls it tight. "Like that," he says. "You gotta stretch it, you gotta stretch your skin." You thank him for his advice and stretch your lower lip, which is all you have left to shave. "That's the way to do it," the stranger says. "That's the way. If you stretch your skin you'll have a nice, clean shave. Last you all day." He takes over the wash basin when you are finished and you go back to your room and dress. Then you climb down the stairs to a street full of shocks and wonders, for in spite of its Philosophical Society your home town was a very small place and you have never seen a high building or a dachshund; you have never seen a man in suede shoes or a woman blow her nose into a piece of Kleenex; you have never seen a parking meter or felt the ground under your feet shaken by a subway, but what you first notice is the fineness of the sky. You have come to feel—you may have been told—that the beauties of heaven centered above your home, and now you are surprised to find, stretched from edge to edge of the dissolute metropolis, a banner or field of the finest blue.

It is early. The air smells of cheap pastry, and the noise of trucking—the clatter of tail gates—is loud and cheerful. You go into a bakery for some breakfast. The waitress smiles at you openly and you think: Perhaps. Maybe. Later. Then you go out onto the street once more and gawk. The noise of traffic has gotten louder and you wonder how people can live in this maelstrom: how can they stand it? A man duckfoots past you wearing a coat that seems to be made out of machine waste and you think how unacceptable such a coat would be in St. Botolphs. People would laugh. In the window of a tenement you see an old man in an undershirt eating something from a paper bag. He seems to be by-passed so pitilessly by life that you feel sad. Then, in crossing the street, you are nearly killed by a truck. Safe on the curb again you wonder about the pace of life in this big city. How do they keep it up? Everywhere you look you see signs of demolition and creation. The mind of the city seems divided about its purpose and its tastes. They are not only destroying good buildings; they are tearing up good streets; and the noise is so loud that if you should shout for help no one would hear you.

You walk. You smell cooking from a Spanish restaurant, new bread, beer slops, roasting coffee beans and the exhaust fumes of a bus. Gaping at a high building you walk straight into a fire hydrant and nearly knock yourself out. You look around, hoping that no one saw your mistake. No one seems to have cared. At the next crossing a young woman, waiting for the light to change, is singing a song about love. Her song can hardly be heard above the noise of traffic, but she doesn't care. You have never seen a woman singing in the street before and she carries herself so well and seems so happy that you beam at her. The light changes and you miss your chance to cross the street because you are stopped in your tracks by a host of young women who are coming in the opposite direction. They must be going to work but they don't look anything like the table-silver girls in St. Botolphs. Not a single one of them is under the charge of modesty that burdens the beauties in your New England home. Roses bloom in their cheeks, their hair falls in soft curls, pearls and diamonds sparkle at their wrists and throats and one of them—your head swims—has put a cloth rose into the rich darkness that divides her breasts. You cross the street and nearly get killed again.

You remember then that you must telephone Cousin Mildred who is going to get you a job in the carpet works but when you go into a drugstore you find that all the telephones have dials and you have never used one of these. You think of asking a stranger for help but this request would seem to expose—in a horrible way—your inexperience, your unfitness to live in the city, as if your beginnings in a small place were shameful. You overcome these fears and the stranger you approach is kind and helpful. On the strength of this small kindness the sun seems to shine and you are thrilled by a vision of the brotherhood of man. You call Cousin Mildred but a maid says that she is sleeping. The maid's voice makes you wonder about the circumstances of your cousin's life. You notice your rumpled flannel pants and step into a tailor shop to have them pressed. You wait in a humid little fitting room walled with mirrors, and, pantless, the figure you see is inescapably intimate and discouraging. Suppose the city should be bombed at this moment? The tailor hands in your trousers, warm and cozy with steam, and you go out again.

Now you are on a main avenue and you head, instinctively, for the north. You have never seen such crowds and such haste before. They are all late. They are all bent with purpose and the interior discourse that goes on behind their brows seems much more vehement than anything in St. Botolphs. It is so vehement that here and there it erupts into speech. Then ahead of you you see a girl carrying a hat box—a girl so fair, so lovely, so full of grace and yet frowning so deeply as if she doubted her beauty and her usefulness that you want to run after her and give her some money or at least some reassurance. The girl is lost in the crowd. Now you are passing, in the store windows, those generations of plaster ladies who have evolved a seasonal cycle of their own and who have posed at their elegant linen closets and art galleries, their weddings and walks, their cruises and cocktail parties long before you came to town and will be at them long after you are dust.

You follow the crowd north and the thousands of faces seem like a text and a cheerful one. You have never seen such expensiveness and elegance and you think that even Mrs. Theophilus Gates would look seedy in a place like this. At the park you leave the avenue and wander into the zoo. It is like a paradise; greenery and water and innocence in jeopardy, the voices of children and the roaring of lions and in the underpasses obscenities written on the walls. Leaving the park you are surprised at the display of apartment houses and you wonder who can live in them all and you may even mistake the air-conditioning machinery for makeshift iceboxes where people keep a little milk and a quarter of a pound of butter fresh. You wonder if you will ever enter such a building—have tea or supper or some other human intercourse there. A concrete nymph with large breasts and holding a concrete lintel on her head causes you some consternation. You blush. You pass a woman who is sitting on a rock, holding a volume of the Beethoven sonatas in her lap. Your right foot hurts. There is probably a hole in your sock.

North of the park you come into a neighborhood that seems blighted—not persecuted, but only unpopular, as if it suffered acne or bad breath, and it has a bad complexion—colorless and seamed and missing a feature here and there. You eat a sandwich in one of those dark taverns that smells like a *pissoir* and where the sleepy waitress wears championship tennis sneakers. You climb the stairs of that great eyesore, the Cathedral of St. John The Divine, and say your prayers, although the raw walls of the unfinished basilica remind you of a lonely railroad station. You step from the cathedral into a stick-ball game and in the distance someone practices a sliding trombone. You see a woman with a rubber stocking waiting for a bus and in the window of a tenement a girl with yellow bangs.

Now the people are mostly colored and the air rings with jazz. Even the pills and elixirs in the cut-rate drugstore jump to boogie-woogie and on the street someone has written in chalk: JESUS THE CHRIST. HE IS RISEN. An old woman on a camp stool sings from a braille hymnal and when you put a dime into her hands she says, God bless you, God bless you. A door flies open and a woman rushes into the street with a letter in her hand. She stuffs it into a mailbox and her manner is so hurried and passionate that you wonder what son or lover, what money-winning contest or friend she has informed. Across the street you see a handsome Negress in a coat made out of cloth of gold. "Baloney John and Pig-fat's both dead," a man says, "and me married five years and still don't have a stick of furniture. Five years." "Why you always comparing me to other girls?" a girl asks softly. "Why you always telling me this one and that one is better than me? Sometimes it seems you just take me out to make me miserable, comparing me to this one and that one. Why you always comparing me to other girls?"

Now it is getting dark and you are tired. There is a hole for sure in your sock and a blister on your heel. You decide to go home by subway. You go down some stairs and board a train, trusting that you will end up somewhere near where you began, but you won't ask directions. The fear of being made ridiculous— a greenhorn—is overpowering. And so, a prisoner of your pride, you watch the place names sweep by: Nevins Street, Franklin Avenue, New Lots Avenue.

16

Writer enterprising although perhaps immodest to say so (Leander wrote). Bought sick calf in spring for two dollars. Nursed. Fatted. Sold in autumn for ten. Sent money to Boston for two-volume encyclopedia. Walked to post office to get same. Barefoot through autumn night. Heart beating. Remember every step of way on bare feet. Sand, thistles. Coarse and silky grass. Oyster shells and soft dirt. Unwrapped books outside of town on river path. Read in fading light. Dusk. Aalborg. Seat of a bishopric. Aardwolf. Aaron. Never forget. Never will forget. Joy of learning. Resolved to read whole encyclopedia. Memorize same. Memorable hour. Fires going out in west. Fires lighted on moon. Loved valley, trees and water. River smelled of damp church. Turn your hair gray. Grand night. Sad homecoming.

Father's star descending. Handsome man. Straight. Black haired. People said was spoiled and idle but never believed same. Loved same. Made four voyages to East Indies. Proud. Cousins found work for him in gold-bead factory but he refused. Why not? He was a proud man, not meant to make gold beads. Many family conferences. Dark country of visiting relations. Whispering in the parlor. No money, no supper, no wood for fires. Father sad.

And a grand and glorious autumn that was too. Leaves coming down like old cloth; old sails; old flags. Solid curtain of green in summer. Then north wind takes it away, piece by piece. See roofs and steeples, buried since June in leaves. Everywhere gold. Midas-like. Poor father! Mind coarsened with sorrow. Trees covered with gold bank notes. Gold everywhere. Gold knee deep on the ground. Dust in his pockets. Bits of thread. Nothing more. Uncle Moses came to the rescue. Mother's brother. Big, fat man. Uncouth. Ran wholesale business in Boston. Sold novelties to four-corner stores. Threads and needles. Buttons. Ginghams. A booming voice like a preacher. Shiny trousers. Threadbare. Walked the four miles from Travertine to St. Botolphs to save eight-cent horsecar fare. Famous walker. Once walked from Boston to Salem to foreclose on a creditor. Slept in livery stable. Walked home. Offered father house in Boston. Work. "The cities is where the money is, Aaron!" Father hated Moses. Had no choice. Moses always spoke of losses. Sad. Lost four thousand dollars one year. Lost six thousand dollars next year. Lived in big square house in Dorchester with For Sale sign on same. Wife made underwear of flour sacks. Two sons; both dead.

Good-by to St. Botolphs then. Let the tame crows go. Loaded few possessions onto wagon including Hallet & Davis rosewood piano. No room for swordfish spur, shells or corals. House for sale but no customers. Too big. Old-fashioned. No bathrooms. Furniture packed in Tingleys' wagon night before departure. Horses stabled in barn. Slept last time in attic. Waked by sound of rain 4 A.M. Sweet music. Left homestead by dawn's early light. Forever? Who knows? Brother and writer to ride on tail gate of wagon. Mother and father to travel by cars. Little wind before dawn. Boxed compass. Not enough to fill your sails. Stirring leaves. Good-by. Reached house on Pinckney Street after dark. Run-down place. Stair lifts rotted. Windows broken. Moses there. Shiny pants. Preacher's voice. "The house is not in good repair, Aaron, but surely you're not afraid of a little hard work." Slept first night on floor.

Went to visit Moses in Dorchester following Sunday. Walked all the way. Horsecars running but mother thought if he could walk to Salem and back we could walk to Dorchester. Burden of poor relations to set good example. Late winter morning. Overcast. Wind from north, northeast. Cold. Out in farming country barking dogs followed us. Strange figures we cut. Dressed for church, marching up dirt roads. Reached Uncle Moses' at two. Big house but Uncle Moses and Aunt Rebecca lived in kitchen. Sons, both dead. Moses carrying wood from shed to cellar. "Help me, boys, and I'll pay you," he says. Hamlet, father and me carried wood all afternoon. Got bark all over our best clothes. Mother was in the kitchen sewing. Night falls. Cold winds. Moses leads us over to the well. "Now we'll have a drink of Adam's ale, boys. There's nothing more refreshing." This was our payment. A drink of cold water. Started home at dark. Miles to go. Nothing to eat since breakfast. Sat down on the way to rest. "He's a Christly skin, Sarah," father says. "Aaron," mother says. "He buys and sells on the exchange like a prince," father says, "and he pays me and my sons with a cup of water for carrying his Christly firewood all afternoon." "Aaron," mother says. "He's known everywhere in the trade as a skin," father says. "He counts to make ten thousand and when he only makes five he claims to have lost five. All the goods he sells are shoddy and damaged in the loom. When his sons were sick he was too stingy to buy the medicine and when they died he buried them in pine-wood coffins and marked their graves with a slate." Mother and Hamlet walked on. Father put an arm around shoulders; held me tight. Mixed feelings, all deep, all good. Love and consolation.

Father. How to describe? Stern faced, sad hearted. Much loved, never befriended. Aroused pity, tenderness, solicitude, admiration among associates. Never stalwart friendship. Child of bold seafaring men. First tasted love in Samoa. Honest as the day was long. Perhaps unhappily married. Standards different in those times. Fatalistic. Never quarreled. Only Irish. Perhaps fastidious principles. Hatred for Moses deepened. Worked hard but complained of sharp practice. Mother's sisters often at house. Whispering. Father complained of numerous visitors. "My latchstring's always out for my relations," Mother said. Father often played checkers with writer. Shrewd checker player. Faraway looks.

Writer entered Latin school. Stood at head of class of forty. (Report card attached.) Country boy in high-water britches. Delivered newspapers in winter before dawn. Moon still in sky. Played on Common. Lacrosse. Snowball fights. Skating. Some baseball. Vague rules. No river embankment then. Copley Square

was a dump. Full of hoopskirt wires. River at low tide smelled
of sea gas. Trust writer was cheerful. Happy. Excepting father
no unhappy memories. Hard now to reconstruct. Epizootic epidemic. (1873.) All horses in city killed. Few oxen imported but
little sound of wheels, hoofs. Only street callers. Coalie-oilee
man. Knife sharpener. Played checkers late with father. Heard
bells ring. Church bells but no church. Loud. From all corners
of the compass. Praise, Laud and Honor. Among bells sounds
of people running. Went with father to roof. Excitement fast
growing. Bells louder on roof. Glory be to God on the highest.
Clamor. Saw great fire at waterfront; Great Boston Fire.

Ran downstairs, down Pinckney Street with father. Boston's
burning! Joined hose company on Charles Street. Ran at father's
side all the way to waterfront. First more smoke than flame.
Hellish smell of burning chattels. Shoes, wallpaper, clothes, plumage. Joined bucket brigade. Eyes sore from smoke. Coughing.
Father made writer rest back of safety cordon, but rejoined brigade later. Worked most of night. Walked home at dawn. Dead
tired. Smoky city. You could see from Washington and Winter
streets through to the harbor. Old South Church was scorched.
Way through to Fort Hill were smoking ruins. Dawn-light reddish
in smoke. Bad smell. Tents on Common for refugees. Strange
sight. Babies crying. Fires for cooking. Clink of water buckets
like ghostly cowbells. Scenes of upheaval, suffering and humor.
Down Charles Street the scavengers. Worse than Indians. Armies
of thieves. Sewing machines, dishes, celluloid collars, two dozen
left shoes, ladies' hats. Barbarians all. Hit the feathers at sunrise.

Moses burned out. Heavily insured. Cleared ten thousand.
Expected to clear twenty. Claimed to have lost ten. Crocodile
tears. Well-known skin. Opened up new business six weeks later
in new building. Continued sharp practice. Father complaining.
Aunts and cousins in and out of house like dog's hind leg. Whispering. Father not home for supper. Not home after. Never ask
questions. No sign of father for three days. Church on Sunday.
Took walk. Grand and glorious spring day after New England
rains. Cheerful. Passed brick house near junction of Pinckney

and Cedar. Heard woman's voice calling, "Boy, boy, oh you!"
Looked up to window. Saw naked woman. Big brindle bush of
hair like beard. Plain face. Man enters picture. Strikes woman.
Draws curtains. Went on walking to river. Resolved never to
walk by house looking for woman again. Resolved to keep mind
clean, body healthy. Ran a mile on riverbank. Had clean thoughts.
Admired sky. Water. God's creation. Walked straight back to
junction of Pinckney and Cedar streets. All resolves broken.
Shame faced. Looked in window and saw woman again. Dressed
now in voluminous house dress. Picking leaves off geranium
plants in window. Later found name was Mrs. Trexler. Member
of church in good standing. Poor soul.

Walked home at dusk. No father. Uncle Jared playing flute.
Mother at rosewood piano. Sterling silver flute. *Faite en France.*
Acis and Galatea. Writer heard music from room. Later Jared's
farewells. Was called then to kitchen where mother and brother
were having confab. Smelled trouble. Mother, saintly old woman.
God bless her! Never one to admit unhappiness or pain. Cried
at music, sunsets. Never human things. Remember her at West
River, wiping away tears while she watched sunsets, colored
clouds. Dry eyed at all funerals. Asked me to sit down. "Your
father has abandoned us," she said. "He left me a note. I burned
it in the fire. Moses knows. He says we can stay on here if we
persevere. Your school days are over. You will go to work. Hamlet is going to California. We will never talk about your father
again."

Writer first tasted sorrow then. Bewilderment. The first of
many hard knocks. Noticed kitchen. Dartmouth pump. Stain on
ceiling like South America. Mother's sewing bag made from scrap
of old silk dress worn at St. Botolphs in happy summertime.
Printing on stove: Pride of the Union. Saw everything. Gray in
mother's hair. Cracks in floor. Smoke on lamp chimney. A poor
Yankee trait. Writer remembers turning point in life as cracked
dishes, soot on glass, coal stove and pump.

Writer looked for work next morning. Plans afoot for Hamlet's
trip. Joined a company. Cousin Minerva put up the cash, sailed

in June. Hamlet, mother's favorite. Planned to begin sending money home in seven months. Save us all. Big farewell party for Hamlet. Moses, head cheese. All the rest too. Jared, Minerva, Eben, Rebecca, Juliana, many more. Jared did sleight of hand. Pulled brooch out of Minerva's topknot. Made watch disappear. Took same out of vase made of lava from Mount Vesuvius. Mead to drink. Homemade. Delicious. Mother played piano. Hamlet sang. Sympathetic tenor voice.

> "Youth and pleasure go together,
> Soon will come the winter cold."

Not a dry eye in the house. A dark night. Many lamps. Parting is such sweet sorrow. Not sweet for me.

Father gone. Hamlet sailing away. Writer left alone with dear old mother. God bless her! Stern company though. Writer led clean life. Cold bath every morning. Stone Hills boat club. Single-oared shells. Gymnasium twice a week. Missed father, brother. Father most. Lonely places. Bedroom hallway. Staircase turning. Looked for father in crowds. Straight back. Black coat. Walking home from work. Always looked for father in crowds. Looked in stations both north and south. Looked on waterfront. Watched disembarkations of all kinds. Passenger ships. Fishing boats. Ghosts rattle chains. Live in castle. Gauzy things with kindly voices mostly. Partial to blue light. Vanish at cock's crow. God give me such a ghost I cried.

Asked mother once for news of father but received no reply. Spoke later of old times. Asked me if I remembered St. Botolphs. Reminisced. Plums on Hales Island. Picked a bushel basket every year. Recalled famous church picnic with twenty-one varieties of pie. Sails. All good things. House still empty. Falling down. Old mother's eyes brightened. First time she ever seemed gay. Laughing, talking about old river-bottom place, Godforsaken. Took advantage of high spirits and asked once more for father. "Is he living or dead?"

"Remember one night last autumn when we had steak and tomatoes for supper?" she said. "The Boston police notified me while you were at work the day before that your father had been found dead in a Charles Street lodging. I made all the arrangements with no help from anyone. Early in the morning I took the body in the cars to St. Botolphs. Mr. Frisbee said the words. No one else was there at the grave. Then I came home on the cars and cooked a good supper for you so you wouldn't think that anything was wrong."

Blow to feelings not improved by receipt of enclosed letter from Hamlet: "Hello old scout. We reached this happy land after traveling 7 months and 9 days. I stood the trip well although the hardships of the voyage exceeded my anticipations. Out of a company of thirty, seven of our brother argonauts were taken by the grim reaper. My own skin is hale and hearty and we're a whip-cracking, bushy-bearded, sun-burned brother-hood, bound to make our million or go to H——.

"We made the passage from the Isthmus to San Francisco in the company of many women and children, going to be re-united with their loved ones. There is nothing in the world like the arrival of a ship in San Francisco to pluck at your heart-strings. I wish you could get out here and see the sights. I pity you in that musty old burg, compared to which San Francisco is an honest to G——d beehive. However the necessities of life were costly—board was four dollars a day and we lingered in San Francisco only a week and then came north where provisions still set me back two dollars a day. When you see Cousin Minerva don't spare the hard facts.

"Among us is an Irishman whose name is Clancy and is from Dedham. He is come out here to find a dowery for his daughter so that she can marry into the 'edicated' classes. There are also 3 carpenters, 2 shoemakers, a blacksmith and many other trades represented including the genteel art of music for one of the company has brought his violin with him and entertains us at night with symphonius strains. We had no sooner settled here than Howie Cockaigne and me got to work with our pick-axes in the bed of the river and when we had been digging for less than an hour two Mexicans came along and offered to buy the digging for an ounce of flour-gold and so we took the offer and had our first gold in less time than it takes to tell and you see that with gold selling at $5.60 an ounce and if our luck holds out we will be making forty or fifty dollars per day. Now under Captain Marsons leadership we are making a race in the river and turning its course so that we will be able to take the gold out of the dry bed.

"Don't expect many letters from me Old Scout because this happy land is still wild and as I am writing you now the ground is my chair and the night is my roof. But oh its a grand feeling to be out here and even with the professor playing symphonius strains on his violin and bringing back to me the sweet remembrance of all by-gone days there isn't a king or a merchant prince in the whole world that I envy for I always knew I was born to be a child of destiny and that I was never meant to be subservient to the wealth, fame, power, etc. of others or to wring my living from detestable, low, degrading, mean and ordinary kinds of business."

17

To create or build some kind of bridge between Leander's world and that world where he sought his fortune seemed to Coverly a piece of work that would take strength and perseverance. The difference between the sweet-smelling farmhouse and the room where he lived was abysmal. They seemed to have come from the hands of different creators and to deny one another. Coverly thought about this one rainy night on his way to Cousin Mildred's, wearing a rented tuxedo. "Come for dinner," she had asked him, "and then we'll go to the opera. That ought to be fun for you. It's Monday night so you'll have to dress. Everyone dresses on Mondays." Cousin Mildred's apartment was in one of those large buildings that Coverly, on his first day, had wondered if he would ever penetrate. Looking up at the building Coverly realized that by all the standards of St. Botolphs it would be condemned as expensive, pretentious, noisy and unsafe. It could not be compared to a nice farm. He took an elevator to the eighteenth floor. He had never approached such an altitude and he entertained himself with some imaginary return to St. Botolphs where he regaled Pete Meacham with a description of this city of towers. He felt worldly and saturnine like a character in a movie. A pretty maid let him in and took him into a parlor for which he was completely unprepared. The walls were half-paneled like the dining-room walls at West Farm. Most of the furniture he recognized since most of it had been stored in the hayloft when he was a boy. There, over the mantelpiece, hung old Benjamin himself, in his peignoir or Renaissance costume, staring out into the room with that harsh and naked look of dishonesty that had made him so unpopular with the family. Most of the lamps had come from the barn or the attic and Grandmother Wapshot's old moth-eaten sampler ("Unto Us a Son Is Given") was hanging on the wall. Coverly was studying old Benjamin's stare when Cousin Mildred blew in—a tall, gaunt woman in a red evening dress that seemed cut to display her bony shoulders. "Coverly!" she exclaimed. "My dear. How nice of you to come. You look just like a Wapshot. Harry will be thrilled. He adores Wapshots. Sit down. We'll have something to drink. Where are you staying? Who was the woman who answered the telephone? Tell me all about Honora. Oh, you do look like a Wapshot. I would have been able to pick you out in a crowd. Isn't it nice to be able to recognize people? There's another Wapshot in New York. Justina. They say she used to play the piano in the five-and-ten-cent store but she's very rich now. We've had Benjamin cleaned. Don't you think he looks better? Did you notice? Of course, he still looks like a crook. Have a cocktail."

The butler passed Coverly a cocktail on a tray. He had never drunk a martini cocktail before and to conceal his inexperience he raised the glass to his lips and drained it. He didn't cough and sputter but his eyes swam with tears, the gin felt like fire and some oscillation or defense mechanism in his larynx began to palpitate in such a way that he found himself unable to speak. He settled down to a paroxysm of swallowing. "Of course, this isn't my idea of a decent room at all," Cousin Mildred went on. "It's all Harry's idea. I'd much rather have called in a decorator and gotten something comfortable but Harry's mad for New England. He's an adorable man and a wizard in the carpet business, but he doesn't come from anyplace really. I mean he doesn't have anything nice to remember and so he borrows other people's memories. He's really more of a Wapshot than you or I."

"Does he know about Benjamin's ear?" Coverly asked hoarsely. It was still hard for him to speak.

"My dear, he knows the family history backwards and forwards," Cousin Mildred said. "He went to England and had the name traced back to Vaincre-Chaud and he got the crest. I'm sure he knows more about Lorenzo than Honora ever did. He bought all these things from your mother and I must say he paid for them generously and I'm not absolutely sure that your mother—I don't mean to say that your mother was untruthful, but you know that old traveling desk that always used to be full of mice? Well, your mother wrote and said that it belonged to Benjamin Franklin and I don't ever remember having heard that before."

This hint or slur at his mother's veracity made Coverly feel sad and homesick and annoyed with his cousin's rattling conversational style and the pretensions of simplicity and homeliness in her parlor and he might have said something about this, but the butler refilled his glass again and when he took another gulp of gin the oscillations in his larynx began all over again and he couldn't speak. Then Mr. Brewer came in—he was much shorter than his wife—a jolly pink-faced man with a quietness that might have been developed to complement the noise she made. "So you're a Wapshot," he said to Coverly when they shook hands. "Well, as Mildred may have told you, I'm very much interested in the family. Most of these things come from

the homestead in St. Botolphs. That cradle rocked four generations of the Wapshot family. It was made by the village undertaker. That tulip-wood table was made from a tree that stood
on the lawn at West Farm. Lafayette rode under this tree in
1815. The portrait over the mantelpiece is of Benjamin Wapshot.
This chair belonged to Lorenzo Wapshot. He used it during
his two terms in the state legislature." With this Mr. Brewer
sat down in Lorenzo's chair and at the feel of this relic beneath
him a smile of such sensual gratification spread over his face
that he might have been squeezed between two pretty women
on a sofa. "Coverly has the nose," Cousin Mildred said. "I've
told him that I could have picked him out in a crowd. I mean
I would have known that he was a Wapshot. It will be so nice
having him work for you. I mean it will be so nice having a
Wapshot in the firm."

It was quite some time before Mr. Brewer replied to this but
he smiled broadly at Coverly all during the pause and so it was
not an anxious silence and during it Coverly decided that he
liked Mr. Brewer tremendously. "Of course, you'll have to start
at the bottom," Mr. Brewer said.

"Oh, yes sir," Coverly exclaimed; his father's son. "I'll do
anything sir. I'm willing to do anything."

"Well, I wouldn't expect you to do anything," Mr. Brewer
said, tempering Coverly's earnestness, "but I think we might
work out some kind of apprenticeship, so to speak—some arrangement whereby you could decide if you liked the carpet
business and the carpet business could decide if it liked you. I
think we can work out something. You'll have to go through
personnel research. We do this with everyone. Grafley and
Harmer do this for us and I'll make you an appointment for
tomorrow. If they're done with you on Monday you can report
to my office then and go to work."

Coverly was not familiar with a correct dinner service, but
by watching Cousin Mildred he saw how to serve himself from
the dishes that the waitress passed and he only got into trouble
when he was about to drop his dessert into his finger bowl,

but the waitress, by smiling and signaling, got him to move his finger bowl and everything went off all right. When dinner was finished they went down on the elevator and were driven through the rain to the opera.

It is perhaps in the size of things that we are most often disappointed and it may be because the mind itself is such a huge and labyrinthine chamber that the Pantheon and the Acropolis turn out to be smaller than we had expected. At any rate, Coverly, who expected to be overwhelmed by the opera house, found it splendid but cozy. Their seats were in the orchestra, well forward. Coverly had no libretto and he could not understand what was going on. Now and then the plot would seem to be revealed to him but he was always mistaken and in the end more confused than ever. He fell asleep twice. When the opera ended he said good night and thank you to Cousin Mildred and her husband in the lobby, feeling that it would be to his disadvantage to have them drive him back to the slum where he lived.

Early the next morning Coverly reported to Grafley and Harmer, where he was given a common intelligence-quotient test. There were simple arithmetical problems, blocks to count and vocabulary tests, and he completed this without any difficulty although it took him the better part of the morning. He was told to come back at two. He ate a sandwich and wandered around the streets. The window of a shoe-repair place on the East Side was filled with plants and reminded him of Mrs. Pluzinski's kitchen window. When he returned to Grafley and Harmer he was shown a dozen or so cards with drawings or blots on them—a few of them colored—and asked by a stranger what the pictures reminded him of. This seemed easy, for since he had lived all his life between the river and the sea the drawings reminded him of fish bones, kelp, conch shells and other simples of the flood. The doctor's face was inexpressive and he couldn't tell if he had been successful. The doctor's reserve seemed so impenetrable that it irritated Coverly that two strangers should be closeted in an office to cultivate such an atmosphere of inhumanity. When he left he was told to report in the morning for two more examinations and an interview.

In the morning he found himself in stranger waters. Another gentleman—Coverly guessed they were all doctors—showed him a series of pictures or drawings. If they were like anything they were like the illustrations in a magazine although they were drawn crudely and with no verve or imagination. They presented a problem to Coverly, for when he glanced at the first few they seemed to remind him only of very morbid and unsavory things. He wondered at first if this was a furtive strain of morbidity in himself and if he would damage his chances at a job in the carpet works by speaking frankly. He wondered for only a second. Honesty was the best policy. All the pictures dealt with noisome frustrations and when he was finished he felt irritable and unhappy. In the afternoon he was asked to complete a series of sentences. They all presented a problem or sought an attitude and since Coverly was worried about money—he had nearly run through his twenty-five dollars—he completed most of the sentences with references to money. He would be interviewed by a psychologist on the next afternoon.

The thought of this interview made him a little nervous. A psychologist seemed as strange and formidable to him as a witch doctor. He felt that some baneful secret in his life might be exposed, but the worst he had ever done was masturbate and looking back over his life and knowing no one of his age who had not joined in on the sport he decided that this did not have the status of a secret. He decided to be as honest with the psychologist as possible. This decision comforted him a little and seemed to abate his nervousness. His appointment was for three o'clock and he was kept waiting in an outer room where many orchids bloomed in pots. He wondered if he was being observed through a peephole. Then the doctor opened a double or soundproof door and invited Coverly in. The doctor was a young man with nothing like the inexpressive manners of the others. He meant to be friendly, although this was a difficult feeling to achieve since Coverly had never seen him before and would never see him again and was only closeted with him because he wanted to work in the carpet factory. It was no climate for friendship. Coverly was given a very comfortable chair to sit in, but he cracked his knuckles nervously. "Now, suppose you tell me a little about yourself," the doctor said. He was very gentle and had a pad and a pencil for taking notes.

"Well, my name is Coverly Wapshot," Coverly said, "and I come from St. Botolphs. I guess you must know where that is. All the Wapshots live there. My great-grandfather was Benjamin Wapshot. My grandfather was Aaron. My mother's family are Coverlys and . . ."

"Well I'm not as interested in your genealogy," the doctor said, "as I am in your emotional make-up." It was an interruption, but it was a very courteous and friendly one. "Do you know what is meant by anxiety? Do you have any feelings of anxiety? Is there anything in your family, in your background that would incline you to anxiety?"

"Yes sir," Coverly said. "My father's very anxious about fire. He's awfully afraid of burning to death."

"How do you know this?"

"Well, he's got this rig up in his room," Coverly said. "He's got this suit of clothes—underwear and everything—hanging up beside his bed so in case of fire he can get dressed and out of the house in a minute. And he's got buckets full of sand and water in all the hallways and the number of the fire department is painted on the wall by the telephone and on rainy days when he isn't working—sometimes he doesn't work on rainy days— he spends most of the day going around the house sniffing. He thinks he smells smoke and sometimes it seems to me that he spends nearly a whole day going from room to room sniffing."

"Does your mother share this anxiety?" the doctor asked.

"No sir," Coverly said. "My mother loves fires. But she's anxious about something else. She's afraid of crowds. I mean she's afraid of being trapped. Sometimes on the Christmas holidays I'd go into the city with her and when she got into a crowd in

one of those big stores she'd nearly have a fit. She'd get pale
and gasp for breath. She'd pant. It was terrible. Well, then she'd
grab hold of my hand and drag me out of there and go up
some side street where there wasn't anybody and sometimes it
would be five or ten minutes before she got her breath back.
In any place where my mother felt she was confined she'd get
very uneasy. In the movies, for instance—if anybody in the movies was sent to jail or locked up in some small place why my
mother would grab her hat and her purse and run out of that
theater before you could say Jack Robinson. I used to have to
sprint to keep up with her."

"Would you say that your parents were happy together?"

"Well, I really never thought of it that way," Coverly said.
"They're married and they're my parents and I guess they take
the lean with the fat like everybody else but there's one thing
she used to tell me that left an impression on me."

"What was that?"

"Well, whenever I had a good time with Father—whenever
he took me out on the boat or something—she always seemed
to be waiting for me when we got home with this story. Well,
it was about, it was about how I came to be, I suppose you'd
say. My father was working for the table-silver company at the
time and they went into the city for some kind of banquet. Well,
my mother had some cocktails and it was snowing and they had
to spend the night in a hotel and one thing led to another but
it seems that after this my father didn't want me to be born."

"Did your mother tell you this?"

"Oh, yes. She told me lots of times. She told me I shouldn't
trust him because he wanted to kill me. She said he had this
abortionist come out to the house and that if it hadn't been
for her courage I'd be dead. She told me that story lots of times."

"Do you think this had any effect on your fundamental attitude
toward your father?"

"Well, sir, I never thought about it but I guess maybe it did.
I sometimes had a feeling that he might hurt me. I never used

to like to wake up and hear him walking around the house late at night. But this was foolish because I knew he wouldn't hurt me. He never punished me."

"Did she punish you?"

"Well, not very often, but once she just laid my back open. I guess perhaps it was my fault. We went down to Travertine swimming—I was with Pete Meacham—and I decided to climb up on the roof of the bathhouse where we could see the women getting undressed. It was a dirty thing to do but we hadn't even hardly got started when the caretaker caught us. Well my mother took me home and she told me to get undressed and she took my great-grandfather's buggy whip—that was Benjamin—and she just laid my back open. There was blood all over the wall. My back was such a mess she got scared, but of course she didn't dare call a doctor because it would be embarrassing, but the worst thing was I couldn't go swimming for the rest of that summer. If I went swimming people would see these big sores on my back. I wasn't able to go swimming all that summer."

"Do you think this had any effect on your fundamental attitude toward women?"

"Well, sir, where I come from, I think it's hard to take much pride in being a man. I mean the women are very powerful. They are kind and they mean very well, but sometimes they get very oppressive. Sometimes you feel as if it wasn't right to be a man. Now there's this story they tell about Howie Pritchard. On his wedding night he's supposed to have put his foot into the chamber pot and pissed down his leg so his wife wouldn't hear the noise. I don't think he should have done that. If you're a man I think you ought to be proud and happy about it."

"Have you ever had any sexual experiences?"

"Twice," Coverly said. "The first time was with Mrs. Maddern. I don't suppose I should name her but everybody in the village knew about her and she was a widow."

"Your other experience?"

"That was with Mrs. Maddern too."

"Have you ever had any homosexual experiences?"

"Well, I guess I know what you mean," Coverly said. "I did plenty of that when I was young but I swore off it a long time ago. But it seems to me that there's an awful lot of it around. There's more around anyhow than I expected. There's one in this place where I'm living now. He's always asking me to come in and look at his pictures. I wish he'd leave me alone. You see, sir, if there's one thing in the world that I wouldn't want to be it's a fruit."

"Now would you like to tell me about your dreams?"

"I dream about all kinds of things," Coverly said. "I dream about sailing and traveling and fishing but I guess mostly what you're interested in is bad dreams, isn't it?"

"What do you mean by bad dreams?"

"Well, I dream I do it with this woman," Coverly said. "I never saw this woman in real life. She's one of those beautiful women you see on calendars in barbershops. And sometimes," Coverly said, blushing and hanging his head, "I dream that I do it with men. Once I dreamed I did it with a horse."

"Do you dream in color?" the doctor asked.

"I've never noticed," Coverly said.

"Well, I think our time is about up," the doctor said.

"Well, you see, sir," Coverly said, "I don't want you to think that I've had an unhappy childhood. I guess what I've told you doesn't give you a true picture but I've heard a little about psychology and I guessed what you wanted to know about were things like that. I've really had an awfully good time. We live on a farm and have a boat and plenty of hunting and fishing and just about the best food in the world. I've had a happy time."

"Well, thank you, Mr. Wapshot," the doctor said, "and goodby."

On Monday morning Coverly got up early and had his pants pressed as soon as the tailor shop opened. Then he walked to his cousin's office in midtown. A receptionist asked if he had an appointment and when he said that he hadn't she said that she couldn't arrange one until Thursday. "But I'm Mr. Brewer's cousin," Coverly said. "I'm Coverly Wapshot." The secretary only smiled and told him to come back on Thursday morning. Coverly was not worried. He knew that his cousin was occupied with many details and surrounded by executives and secretaries and that the problems of this distant Wapshot might have slipped his mind. His only problem was one of money. He didn't have much left. He had a hamburger and a glass of milk for supper and gave the landlady the rent that night when he came in. On Tuesday he ate a box of raisins for breakfast, having heard somewhere that raisins were healthful and filling. For supper he had a bun and a glass of milk. On Wednesday morning he bought a paper, which left him with sixty cents. In the help-wanted advertisements there were some openings for stock clerks and he went to an employment agency and then crossed town to a department store and was told to return at the end of the week. He bought a quart of milk and marking the container off in three sections drank one section for breakfast, one for lunch and one for dinner.

The hunger pains of a young man are excruciating and when Coverly went to bed on Wednesday night he was doubled up with pain. On Thursday morning he had nothing to eat at all and spent the last of his money having his pants pressed. He walked to his cousin's office and told the girl he had an appointment. She was cheerful and polite and asked him to sit down and wait. He waited for an hour. He was so hungry by this time that it was nearly impossible for him to sit up straight. Then the receptionist told him that no one in Mr. Brewer's office knew about his appointment but that if he would return late in the afternoon she might be able to help him. He dozed on a park bench until four and returned to the office and while the receptionist's manner remained cheerful her refusal this time was final. Mr. Brewer was out of town. From there Coverly went to Cousin Mildred's apartment house but the doorman stopped him and telephoned upstairs and was told that Mrs. Brewer couldn't see anyone; she was just leaving to keep an engagement. Coverly went outside the building and waited and in a few minutes Cousin

Mildred came out and Coverly went up to her. "Oh yes, yes," she said, when he told her what had happened. "Yes, of course. I thought Harry's office must have told you. It's something about your emotional picture. They think you're unemployable. I'm so sorry but there's nothing I can do about it, is there? Of course your grandfather was second crop." She unfastened her purse and took out a bill and handed it to Coverly and got into a taxi and drove away. Coverly wandered over to the park.

It was dark then and he was tired, lost and despairing—no one in the city knew his name—and where was his home—the shawls from India and the crows winging their way up the river valley like businessmen with brief cases, off to catch a bus? This was on the Mall, the lights of the city burning through the trees and dimly lighting the air with the colors of reflected fire, and he saw the statues ranged along the broad walk like the tombs of kings—Columbus, Sir Walter Scott, Burns, Halleck and Morse—and he took from these dark shapes a faint comfort and hope. It was not their minds or their works he adored but the kindliness and warmth they must have possessed when they lived and so lonely and so bitter was he then that he would take those brasses and stones for company. Sir Walter Scott would be his friend, his Moses and Leander.

Then he got some supper—this friend of Sir Walter Scott— and in the morning went to work as a stock clerk for Warburton's Department Store.

18

Moses' work in Washington was highly secret—so secret that it can't be discussed here. He was put to work the day after he arrived—a reflection perhaps of Mr. Boynton's indebtedness to Honora or a recognition of Moses' suitability, for with his plain and handsome face and his descendance from a man who had been offered a decoration by General Washington, he fitted into the scene well enough. He was not smooth—the Wapshots never were—and compared to Mr. Boynton he sometimes felt like a man who eats his peas off a knife. His boss was a man who seemed to have been conceived in the atmosphere of career diplomacy. His clothes, his manners, his speech and habits of thought all seemed so prescribed, so intricately connected to one another that they suggested a system of conduct. It was not, Moses guessed, a system evolved at any of the eastern colleges and may have been formed in some foreign-service school. Its rules were never shown to Moses, so he could not abide by them, but he knew that rules must underlie this sartorial and intellectual diffidence.

Moses was happy at the boardinghouse that he had picked by chance, and found it tenanted mostly by people of his own age: the sons and daughters of mayors and other politicians; the progeny of respectable ward heelers who were in Washington, like himself, as the result of some indebtedness. He did not spend much time at the boardinghouse for he found that much of his social, athletic and spiritual life was ordained by the agency where he worked. This included playing volleyball, taking communion and going to parties at the X Embassy and the Z Legation. He was up to all of this although he was not allowed to drink more than three cocktails at any party and was careful not to make eyes at any woman who was in government service or on the diplomatic list, for security regulations had clapped a lid on the natural concupiscence of a city with a large floating population. On the autumn week ends he sometimes drove with Mr. Boynton to Clark County, where they went riding and sometimes stayed for dinner with Mr. Boynton's friends. Moses could stay on a horse, but this was not his favorite sport. It was a chance to see the countryside and the disappointing southern autumn with its fireflies and brumes, all of which stirred in him a longing for the brilliance of autumn at West Farm. Mr. Boynton's friends were hospitable people who lived in splendid houses and who, without exception, had made or inherited their money from some distant source such as mouthwash, airplane engines or beer; but it was not in Moses to sit on some broad terrace and observe that the bills for this charming picture had been footed by some dead brewer; and as for brewing he had never drunk such good bourbon in his life. It was true that, having come from a small place where a man's knowledge of his neighbors was intimate and thorough, Moses sometimes experienced the blues of uprootedness. His knowledge of his companions was no better than the knowledge travelers have of one another and he knew, by then, enough of the city to know that, waiting for a bus in the morning, the swarthy man with a beard and a turban might be an Indian prince in good standing or he might be a rooming-house eccentric. This theatrical atmosphere of impermanence—this latitude for imposture—impressed him one evening at an embassy concert. He was alone and had gone, at the intermission, out onto the steps of the building to get some air. As he pushed open the doors he noticed three old women on the steps. One was so fat, one so thin and haggard and one had such a foolish countenance that they looked like a representation of human folly. Their evening clothes reminded him of the raggle-taggle elegance of children on Halloween. They had shawls and fans and mantillas and brilliants and their shoes seemed to be killing them. When Moses opened the door they slipped into the embassy—the fat one, the thin one and the fool—so wary, so frightened and in such attitudes of wrongdoing that Moses watched. As soon as they got inside the building they fanned out and each of them seized a concert program that had been left on a chair or fallen to the floor. By this time a guard saw them and as soon as they were discovered they headed for the door and fled, but they were not disappointed, Moses noticed. The purpose of their expedition had been to get a program and they limped happily down the driveway in their finery. You wouldn't see anything like that in St. Botolphs.

The man who had the room next to Moses in the boarding-house was the son of a politician from somewhere in the West. He was competent and personable and an ideal of thrift and continence. He did not smoke or drink and saved every penny of his salary toward the purchase of half a saddle horse that was stabled in Virginia. He had been in Washington for two years and he invited Moses into his room one night and showed him a chart or graph on which he had recorded his social progress. He had been to dinner in Georgetown eighteen times. His hosts were all listed and graded according to their importance in the government. He had been to the Pan-American Union four times: to the X Embassy three times: to the B Embassy one time (a garden party) and to the White House one time (a press reception). You wouldn't find anything like that in St. Botolphs.

The intense and general concern with loyalty at the time when Moses arrived in Washington had made it possible for men and women to be discharged and disgraced on the evidence of a breath of scandal. Old-timers like to talk about the past when even the girls in the Library of Congress—even the archivists— could be booked for a clandestine week end at Virginia Beach, but these days were gone or at least in suspense for government servants. Public drunkenness was unforgivable and promiscuity was death. Private industry went its own way and a friend of Moses' who was in the meat-packing industry once made him this proposition: "I've got four dirty girls coming up from the shirt factory in Baltimore Saturday and I'm going to take them out to my cabin in Maryland. How about it? Just you and me and the four of them. They're pigs but they're not bad looking." Moses said no thanks—he would have said so anyhow—but he envied the meat packer his liberty. This new morality was often on his mind and by thinking about it long enough he was able to make some dim but legitimate connection between lechery and espionage, but this understanding did nothing to lessen this particular loneliness. He even wrote to Rosalie, asking her to visit him for a week end, but she never answered. The government was full of comely women but they all avoided the dark.

Feeling lonely one night and having nothing better to do he went out for a walk. He headed for the center of town and went into the lobby of the Mayflower to buy a package of cigarettes and to look around at a place that, for all its intended elegance, only reminded him of the vastness of his native land. Moses loved the lobby of the Mayflower. A convention was meeting and red-necked and self-respecting men from country towns were gathering in the lobby. Listening to them talk made him feel closer to St. Botolphs. Then he left the Mayflower and walked deeper into the city, and hearing music and being on a fool's errand he stepped into a place called the Marine Room and looked around. There were a band and dance floor and a girl singing. Sitting alone at a table was a blonde woman who seemed pretty at that distance and who looked as if she didn't work for the government. Moses took the table beside her and ordered a whisky. She did not see him at first because she was looking at herself in a mirror on the wall. She was turning her head, first one way and then another, raising her chin and taking the tips of her fingers and pushing her face into the firm lines that it must have had five or six years ago. When she had finished examining herself Moses asked if he could join her and buy her a drink. She was friendly—a little flurried, but pleased. "Well, it would be very nice to have your company," she said, "but the only reason I'm here is because Chucky Ewing, the band leader, is my husband and when I don't have anything better to do I just come down here and kill time." Moses joined her and bought her a drink and after a few farewell looks at herself in the mirror she began to talk about her past. "I used to vocalize with the band myself," she said, "but most of my training is operatic. I've sung in night clubs all over the world. Paris. London. New York . . ." She spoke, not with a lisp, but with an articulation that seemed childish. Her hair was pretty and her skin was white but this was mostly powder. Moses guessed that it would have been five or six years since she could be called beautiful but since she seemed determined to cling to what she had been he was ready to string along. "Of course, I'm really not a professional entertainer," she went on. "I went to finishing school and my family nearly died when I started entertaining.

They're very stuffy. Old family and all that sort of thing. Cliff dwellers." Then the band broke and her husband joined them and was introduced to Moses and sat down.

"What's the score, honey?" he asked his wife.

"There's a table in the corner drinking champagne," she said, "and the six gentlemen by the bandstand are drinking rye and water. They've each had four. There's two tables of Scotch and five tables of bourbon and some beer drinkers over on the other side of the bandstand." She counted the tables off on her fingers, still speaking in a very dainty voice. "Don't worry," she told her husband. "You'll gross three hundred."

"Where's the convention?" he said. "There's a convention."

"I know," she said. "Sheets and pillowcases. Don't worry."

"You got any hot garbage?" he asked a waiter who had come over to their table.

"Yes, sir, yes sir," the waiter said. "I've got some delicious hot garbage. I can give you coffee grounds with a little sausage grease or how about some nice lemon rinds and sawdust?"

"That sounds good," the band leader said. "Make it lemon rinds and sawdust." He had seemed anxious and unhappy when he came to the table but this leg-pulling with the waiter cheered him up. "You got any dishwater?" he asked.

"We got all kinds of dishwater," the waiter said. "We got greasy dishwater and we got dishwater with stuff floating around in it and we got moth balls and wet newspapers."

"Well, give me a little wet newspaper with my sawdust," the band leader said, "and a glass of greasy dishwater." Then he turned to his wife. "You going home?"

"I believe that I will," she said daintily.

"Okay, okay," he said. "If the convention shows I'll be late. Nice to have met you." He nodded to Moses and went back to the bandstand, where the other players had begun to stray in from the alley.

"Can I take you home?" Moses asked.

"Well, I don't know," she said. "We just have a little apartment in the neighborhood and I usually walk but I don't think there'd be any harm in you walking me home."

"Go?"

She got a coat from the hat-check girl and talked with the hat-check girl about a four-year-old child who was lost in the woods of Wisconsin. The child's name was Pamela and she had been gone four days. Extensive search parties had been organized and the two women speculated with deep anxiety on whether or not little Pamela had died of exposure and starvation. When this conversation ended, Beatrice—which was her name—started down the hall, but the hat-check girl called her back and gave her a paper bag. "It's two lipsticks and some bobby pins," she said. Beatrice explained that the hat-check girl kept an eye on the ladies' room and gave Beatrice whatever was left there. She seemed ashamed of the arrangement, but she recuperated in a second and took Moses' arm.

Their place was near the Marine Room—a second-story bedroom dominated by a large cardboard wardrobe that seemed on the verge or in the process of collapse. She struggled to open one of its warped doors and exposed a magpie wardrobe—maybe a hundred dresses of all kinds. She went into the bathroom and returned, wearing a kind of mandarin coat with a dragon embroidered up the back out of threads that felt thorny to Moses' hands. She yielded easily but when it was over she sobbed a little in the dark and asked, "Oh dear, what have we done?" Her voice was as dainty as ever. "Nobody ever likes me except in this way," she said, "but I think it's because I was brought up so strictly. I was brought up by this governess. Her name was Clancy. Oh, she was so strict. I was never allowed to play with other children. . . ." Moses dressed, kissed her good night and got out of the building without being seen.

19

Back at the farm Leander had banked the foundations of the old house with seaweed and had hired Mr. Pluzinski to clear the garden. His sons wrote him once or twice a month and he wrote them both weekly. He longed to see them and often thought, when he was drinking bourbon, of traveling to New York and Washington, but in the light of morning he couldn't find it in himself to ever leave St. Botolphs again. After all, he had seen the world. He was alone a lot of the time, for Lulu was spending three days a week with her daughter in the village and Mrs. Wapshot was working three days a week as a clerk in the Anna Marie Louise Gift Shoppe in Travertine. It was made clear to everyone, by Sarah's mien, that she was not doing this because the Wapshots needed money. She was doing it because she loved to, and this was the truth. All the energies that she possessed—and that she had used so well in improving the village—seemed to have centered at last in an interest in gift shops. She wanted to open a gift shop in the front parlor of the farmhouse. She even dreamed of this project, but it was something Leander wouldn't discuss.

It was hard to say why the subject of gift shops should excite, on one hand, Sarah's will to live, and on the other, Leander's bitterest scorn. As Mrs. Wapshot stood by a table loaded with colored-glass vases and gave a churchly smile to her friends and neighbors when they came in to spend a little money and pass the time, her equilibrium seemed wonderfully secure. This love of gift shops—this taste for ornamentation—may have been developed by the colorless surface of that shinbone coast or it may have been a most natural longing for sensual trivia. When she exclaimed—about a hand-carved salad fork or a hand-painted glass—"Isn't it lovely?" she was perfectly sincere. The gossip and the company of the customers let her be as gregarious as she had ever been in the Woman's Club; and people had always sought her out. The pleasure of selling things and putting silver and bills into the old tin box that was used for this purpose pleased her immensely, for she had sold nothing before in her life but the furniture in the barn to Cousin Mildred. She liked talking with the salesmen and Anna Marie Louise asked her advice about buying glass swans, ash trays and cigarette boxes. With some money of her own she bought two dozen bud vases that Anna Marie Louise had not wanted to buy. When the bud vases came she unpacked the barrel herself, tearing her dress on a nail and getting excelsior all over the place. Then she washed the vases and, arranging a paper rose in one, put it into the window. (She had had a lifelong aversion to paper flowers, but what could you do after the frosts?) Ten minutes after the vase had been put in the window it was sold and in three days they were all gone. She was very excited, but she could not talk it over with Leander and could only tell Lulu in the kitchen.

To have his wife work at all raised for Leander the fine point of sexual prerogatives and having made one great mistake in going into debt to Honora he didn't want to make another. When Sarah announced that she wanted to work for Anna Marie Louise he thought the matter over carefully and decided against it. "I don't want you to work, Sarah," he said. "You don't have anything to say about it," Sarah said. That was that. The question went beyond sexual prerogatives into tradition, for much of what Sarah sold was ornamented with ships at sea and was meant to stir romantic memories of the great days of St. Botolphs as a port. Now in his lifetime Leander had seen, raised on the ruins of that coast and port, a second coast and port of gift and antique shops, restaurants, tearooms and bars where people drank their gin by candlelight, surrounded sometimes by plows, fish nets, binnacle lights and other relics of an arduous and orderly way of life of which they knew nothing. Leander thought that an old dory planted with petunias was a pretty sight but when he stepped into a newly opened saloon in Travertine and found that the bar itself was made of a bifurcated dory he felt as if he had seen a ghost.

He spent much time in his pleasant room on the southwest corner of the house, with its view of the river and the roofs of the village, writing his journal. He meant to be honest and it seemed, in recording his past, that he was able to strike a level of candor that he had only known in his most lucky friendships. Young and old, he had always been quick to get out of his clothes, and now he was reminded of the mixed pleasures of nakedness.

Writer went to work day after confab about poor father (he wrote). Rose before dawn as usual. Got morning papers for delivery and looked at help-wanted ads. Vacancy at J. B. Whittier. Big shoe manufacturer. Finished newspaper route. Washed face. Put water on hair. Inked hole in sock. Ran all the way to Whittier's office. They were on the second story of frame building. Center of town. First person there. Only little light in sky. Spring dawn. Two other boys joined me, looking for same job. Birds singing in trees of Common. Glorious hour. Clerk—Grimes—opened door at eight o'clock. Let in applicants. Took me to Whittier's office. Half-past eight. Beard the lion. Heavy man, seated at desk with his back to door. He did not turn. Spoke over shoulder. "Can you write a letter? Go home and write a letter. Bring it in tomorrow morning. Same time." End of interview. Waited in outer office and watched two applicants go in and out with same results. Watched other applicants go home. Asked clerk—slender-faced—for sheet of paper and use of pen. Obliged. Headed paper J. B. Whittier. Wrote imaginary creditor. Asked to see boss again. Clerk helpful. Bearded lion for second time. "I've written my letter, sir." Reached for letter but did not turn. Read letter. Passed brown envelope over shoulder. Addressed to broker. Brewster, Bassett & Co. "Deliver this and wait for the receipted bill." Ran all the way to broker's. Caught breath while waiting for receipted bill. Ran all the way back. Gave bill to Whittier. "Sit down there in the corner," he says. Sat there for two hours without being noticed. More despotism in business in those days. Merchants often erratic. Tyrannical. No unions.

Finally spoke at end of two hours. "I want you in there." Points to outer office. "Clean out the spittoons and then ask Grimes what to do. He'll keep you busy."

Pleasant memories, all, even spittoons. Beginning business life. Full of self-confidence. Resolved to succeed. Kept journal of maxims. Always run. Never walk. Never walked in Whittier's presence. Always smile. Never frown. Avoid unclean thoughts. Buy mother gray silk dress. Turn of century approaching. Progress everywhere. New World. Dirigible in Music Hall. Phonograph in Horticultural Hall. First arc light on Summer Street. Had to change carbon stick every day. Early demonstration of telephone at Concord and Lexington Festival. Cold. Big crowds. No food. Rode to Boston on rooftop of train coach. Whittier bonafide merchant prince. Factory in Lynn. Office in Boston. Shoe prices from 67 cents a pair to $1.20. All sold to jobbers from West. South. Business in excess of a million a year. Worked from 7 to 6. Smiling. Running. Learning.

Grimes head clerk. Best friend in office. Slender man. Silky hair. Monkey-fingered, horny minded, sad. At times tiresome. Spoke often of wife. Conjugal bliss. Color in eyes deepened. Licked lips. Knew about Turkish customs. French customs. Armenian customs, etc. Sometimes tiresome as already said above. Writer captivated by thought of wife. Golden headed. Slut perhaps? Went home with Grimes for supper to meet same. Excited. Grimes unlocked door. Woman spoke from parlor. Heavy voice. Excitement gone. Big broad-shouldered woman. Red cheeks. Heavy boots caked with mud. "There's pork chops and greens for supper," she says. "I want to be at the hall at eight." Grimes puts on apron. Cooks supper. Runs between table and stove. Runs between stove and table. Wife stows away big meal; big eater. Not much to say. Puts on heavy coat and tramps off to meeting in muddy boots. A feminist. Grimes washes dishes. Monkey-fingered man. Sad.

Found self, although not yet of legal age, powerfully attracted to opposite sex. Picked up hooker on riverbank. Big hat. Dirty linen. Girlish airs, but not young. What matter. Writer on fool's errand. Red hair. Green eyes. Talked. "What a pretty sky," says she. "My how nice the river smells," says she. Very ladylike. River smells of mudbanks. Bad breath of the sea. Low tide. French kissed. Groin to groin. Put hand in front of dress. Little boys in bushes giggled. Tomfools. Walked in dusk, hip to hip. "I have a little room on Belmont Street," she says. No thanks. Took her to railroad embankment. Cinders. Cornflowers. Stars. Big weeds like tropical vegetation. Samoa. S——d her there. Grand and glorious feeling. Forget for an hour all small things. Venalities. Money worries. Ambitions. Felt refreshed, generous toward sainted old mother. Hooker named Beatrice. Met often afterwards. Later went to New York. Rattled her glass rings on Twenty-third Street windows. Winter nights. Tried to find her later. Disappeared. Above may be in bad taste. If so, writer apologizes. Man born to trouble as the sparks fly upward.

Smells. Heat. Cold. All things like that most clearly remembered. Air in office fetid in wintertime. Coal stoves. Walking home to supper through cold. Joyous. Air in streets straight from snow-capped mountains. Washington. Jefferson. Lafayette. Franconia. Etc. Like mountain city in winter. Inhale smell of dead leaves on Common. Inhale north wind. Sweeter than any rose. Never get enough of sun and moon. Always said to shut door. Got week's vacation in July. Grimes informed writer purpose was to give another boy—relation of Whittier's—chance at job. No good. Went to St. Botolphs with mother. Stayed with cousins. House still empty. Porch falling down. Garden overgrown. Few roses. Swam in river. Sailed. Caught three-pound trout in Parson's Pond. Much pleasure walking on lonely beaches. Happy hours. Waves roar, rattle like New York, New Haven & Hartford. Underfoot dead skates. Sea grass shaped like bull whips, flowers, petticoats. Shells, stones, sea tack. All simple things. In the golden light memories of paradise perhaps; youth, surely, innocence. On beaches the joy and gall of perpetual youth. Even today. Smell east wind. Hear Neptune's horn. Always raring to go. Pack sandwiches. Bathing suit. Catch ramshackle bus to beach. Irresistible. In blood perhaps. Father read Shakespeare to waves. Mouthful of pebbles. Demosthenes?

Planned life carefully. Gym. Sailing in summer. Read Plutarch. Never missed a day at the office. Not once. Raise in salary. Increase of responsibility. Other signs of success. A winter night. Clerks going home. Cleaning pens. Banking fires. Whittier called me in to sanctum sanctorum. Coarse-faced man. Strong. Suffered from flatulence. Kept whisky keg in corner of office. Drank from bunghole with straw. Kept me waiting half hour. Footsteps of last clerk—Grimes—heard going downstairs. "You like the business, Leander?" he says. "Yes sir." "Don't be so damned eager," he says. "You look like a house nigger." Clears throat. Uses spittoon. Slumps suddenly in chair. Sad? Sickness? Bad news? Bankruptcy? Failure? Worse? "I have no son," he says. "I'm sorry, Mr. Whittier." "I have no son," he says again. Raises big face. Tears all over cheeks. Tears running from eyes. "Work hard," he says. "Trust me. I'll treat you like a son. Now good night my boy." Pats me. Sends me home.

Mingled feelings of ambition and tenderness. My heart in the business. Whittier and Wapshot. Wapshot & Co. In love with the shoe business. Do anything for the boss. Visions of saving him from burning building, wrecked ship. Angry heirs at reading of will. Success ordained. Hurried through supper. Read Plutarch in cold room. Kept on gloves. Hat. Breath smoked. Got to office half hour early, next day. Ran. Smiled. Wrote letters. Shared lunch pail with Grimes. "How are you getting along with J. B.?" he asks. "All right," I said. "Has he asked you in yet and told you that he doesn't have a son?" Grimes said. "No," I said. "Well, he will," Grimes said. "He'll ask you in to his office late some day and tell you to work hard and trust him and he'll treat you like a son. He does it to everybody. Even Old Man Thomas. He's seventy-three years old. That's old for a son."

Writer tried to conceal hurt feelings. Grimes knew. Tried to turn experience to use. Continued to play role of eager son. Insincere but rules of business. Conceal natural independence. Seem dutiful. Obedient. As a result received many father-to-son talks. Advice typical of merchants at time. "Never extend credit to man with long hair. Never trust cigarette smokers; men with low-cut shoes." Business a religion. Full of shrewdness. Superstition too. In daydreams began to think of marrying Whittier's daughter. Only child. Harriet. Tried to discourage above ideas but received encouragement from old man himself. Asked to Whittiers' for dinner.

Bought black suit. When dressed on historic night went into kitchen to say good-by to mother. Hamlet not heard from. Anxious over favorite son. "Be sure and wipe your mouth with a napkin," she said. "I guess you know enough to get to your two feet when any ladies or older people come into the room. We come from a mannerly family. We weren't always poor. Be sure and use your napkin."

Walked to Whittiers' house in south end. Manservant opened door and took coat. House still standing. Now a slum. Good-sized house but not palatial as appeared then. Hothouse flowers. Wallpaper. Clock struck. Counted chimes. Fourteen. Mrs. Whittier met me at door of parlor, drawing room. Slender, gracious woman. Two necklaces. Four bracelets. Three rings. Greeted boss, then daughter. One necklace. Two bracelets. Two rings. Big girl. Horse-faced. Hopes dashed. No room for love, marriage. Human needs not so simple. Also had forgotten to empty bladder. Miserable. Spoil everything. Counted pictures on walls. Fourteen. All beautiful. Still lifes. Storms at sea. Italian or Egyptian woman at well. French priests playing dominoes. Foreign landscapes. Wallpaper even on ceiling.

Ate big dinner. Elegant surroundings but manners not so good as West Farm. Whittier broke wind twice. Both times loud. After repast Mrs. Whittier sang. Put on spectacles. Stood bright lamps on table. Sang of love. Shrill voice. Spectacles. Bright lamps made hostess seem old, pinched. After concert, writer said good night. Walked home. Found mother still in kitchen. Sewing by lamplight. Old now. Longing for Hamlet. "Did you have a nice time? Did you remember to use your napkin? Does your own home look ugly and dark? When I was a girl, I was younger than you, I went to visit my Brewster cousins in Newburyport.

They had carriage horses, servants, a big house. When I came back to St. Botolphs my home looked ugly and dark. It made me thoughtful."

Father-to-son talk four weeks later, at dark as customary. Clerks leaving. Fires dying. "Sit down, Leander, sit down," he said. "I told you that if you trusted me and worked hard I'd treat you like a son, didn't I? I never told that to anybody else. You know that, don't you? You believe me, don't you? Now I'm going to show you what I mean. Business practice is changing. I'm going to send a salesman on the road. I want you to be that salesman. I want you to go to New York for me, representing me. I want you to call on my customers, just as if you were my son. Take orders. Behave like a gentleman. When you go to New York I want you to realize what you're doing. I want you to realize that J. B. Whittier is more than a business. I want you to think of the firm as if it was your mother; our mother. I want you to think of it as if this dear old lady needed money and you were going to New York to make some money for her. I want you to comport yourself and dress yourself and talk as if you were representing this dear old lady. When you order your meals and stay in a hotel I want you to spend your money as if you realized it all belonged to this little old lady." Liberal display of the waterworks. We understood one another.

Sing of the night boats. All that writer knows. Fall River, Bangor, Portland, Cape May, Baltimore, Lake Erie, Lake Huron, Saint Louis, Memphis, New Orleans. Floating palaces. Corn-husk mattresses. Music over water. One-night card games, one-night friendships, one-night girls. All gone with dawn's early light. First passage calm. Ocean like glass. Many lights glittering on water. Sparse lights on shore line. People watching palace drift by from porches, lawns, bridges, cupolas. Set their clocks by her. Shared cabin with stranger. Put watch, cash and checks in sock, put sock on foot. Slept on corn-husk mattress yearning for night-boat nymphs. Going to big city to make fortune for little old lady. J. B. Whittier & Co.

Checked in at Hoffman House as ordered. First customer gave

order for eight hundred dollars. Second customer slightly higher. Sold five thousand dollars in three days. Wired for confirmation on last orders. Slept every night with watch, cash, etc., in sock. Returned on train, tired but happy. Went straight to office. J. B. waiting. Fell on writer's neck. Return of prodigal. Conquering hero. Took favorite son to Parker House for dinner. Whisky, wine, fish, flesh and fowl. Later to Chardon Street fancy house. Second visit. First time with Jim Graves. Died in St. Botolphs as stated above. Baptists still singing. "Lead, Kindly Light." Appeared to be favorite hymn.

White-haired boy. Advice sought on manufacturing, merchandising, etc. Subject of marriage finally broached. Same place, same time of day as other confidential talks. "You planning to marry my boy," he says, "or are you going to remain a bachelor all your life?" "I plan to marry and raise a family, sir," I said. "Shut the door and sit down," he said. "Have you got a young lady?" he asks. "No sir," I said. "Well, I've got the young lady for you," he said. "She lives with her parents in Cambridge. She's a Sunday-school teacher. She's no more than eighteen years old. Have a drink of whisky." He walked to the keg in the corner. Took turns at the straw. Sat down again. "Man born of woman," he said, "hath but a short span and he is full of misery." Waterworks beginning. Liberal display of tears. "I wronged this young lady, Leander. I forced her. But she'll make you a good wife." Loud sobbing. "She's not flighty or loose. I was the first one. You marry her and I'll give you a thousand dollars. You don't marry her and I'll see that you get no work in Boston or anyplace else where my name is known. Tell me on Monday. Go home and think it over." Got to his feet. Heavy man. Spring on swivel chair boomed. "Good night, my boy," he said. Down the curved stairs slowly. Night air smelled of mountains, but not for me. Colorless, hateful, northern city. All black but for gaslights; mustard-colored blankets on livery-stable hacks. Dirty snow underfoot. Gruel of snow; horse manure. Five years wasted in business. Father dead. Hamlet never coming home. Sole support of sainted old mother. What to do? Ate supper with mother. Went upstairs to cold room. Put on Mackinaw. Looked through book of resolutions. Avoid unclean thoughts. Run, never walk. Smile. Never frown. Go to gymnasium twice a week. Buy your mother a gray silk dress. No help here. Thought of Albany. Find work there. Lodgings. Begin life again. Decided on Albany. Pack on Sunday. Leave on Monday. Never see Whittier again. Went downstairs. Mother by stove in kitchen. Sewing. Mentioned Albany. "I hope you don't have any plans for going there," she said. "You've been a good boy, Leander, but you take after your father. It was always his feeling that if he could go someplace where he wasn't known he would become rich and happy. It was a great weakness. He was a weak man. If you want to go away at least wait until I die. Wait until Hamlet comes home. Remember that I'm old. I mind the cold. Boston is my only home."

Went to church on Sunday. God would be conscious of my trial. Got to my knees. Prayed for once with a full heart. Feast of Saint Mark. Lesson from Saint John. Looked around church wondering what symbol would reveal choice. Gordian knots, sheep and lions' heads, doves, swastikas, crosses, thorns and wheels. Watchful all through service. Nothing. Ask a stone. "I prayed for you," mother said. Took arm. "Albany is full of Irishmen and other foreigners. You won't go there." Jared came later. Played Acis and Galatea. Hated music. Was Acis hungry? Was Galatea sole support of aged mother? Mortals had worse trouble.

Woke before dawn on Monday. Two, three A.M. Irresolute and sleepless. Sat at window to try and reach decision. City sleeping. Few lights. Innocent-looking prospect. Remembered West Farm. Good old summertime! Remembered father. Life made unbearable by lack of coin. Moral of whole career appeared to be: Make Money. Hell hath no fire that burns like need. Poverty is the root of all evil. Who is the thief? A poor man. Who is the drunkard? A poor man too. Who makes his daughter spread her legs to strangers on Chardon Street? The poor man. Who leaves his son fatherless? The poor man.

Such reasoning quieted moral qualms somewhat although decision went against deepest instincts. Romantic perhaps. Dreamed often of fair wife, waiting in rose bower at end of day. White cottage. Lovebirds in flowering trees. Nellie Melba's *embonpoint*. All this lost. Saw no other course, however. Gentle light appearing in sky. Dusk. Sound of early-bird horsecar coming up Joy Street. Went first thing in morning to Whittier. "I'm game, sir," says I. Told me his plans. Go to visit girl that evening. Marry her in week or two. When time comes for accouchement take her to address in Nahant. Leave baby there. Infanticide? After birth of baby one thousand dollars would be deposited in National Trust Co., New York City, to writer's account.

Put on best black suit after supper and walked to address given in Cambridge. Spring night. Temperature in the sixties. South wind sounding in still-bare trees like kettle drums. Many stars. Gentle light. Unlike winter constellations. House on hoopskirts of Cambridge. Half-starved dogs barked at writer's footsteps. No sidewalks. Bare planks on mud. Small house among trees. Knocked woefully on door. Tall man opened. White hair. Sideburns. Drawn face. Sick perhaps? Sallow wife at back, holding lamp. Wick lying in yellow coal oil. How-do-you-dos ended, followed old couple into parlor, saw future wife.

Pretty child. Hair like raven's wing. Snow-white complexion. Slender wrists. Felt pity, sympathy too. Rolled by old wind-breaking goat in bushes after Sunday-school picnic. Boss was unpopular, even among Chardon Street beauties. Babes in the wood; she and me. "Father was reading from the Bible," says her mother. "Luke," says the old man. "Chapter seven; verse thirty-one." Reads the Bible for an hour. Closed with prayers. Everybody on their knees. Said good-by then. "Good-by, Mr. Wapshot" were the only words spoken by future spouse. Walked home, wondering. Was she stupid? Could she cook?

Took Clarissa to church following Sunday. In company with her parents. On way there made proposal of marriage. "I would like to marry you, Mr. Wapshot," she said. Some happiness then. Picture was not hopeless. Thought ahead to time after baby's birth. Stormy weather coming but why not peace and quiet after? Church was deep-water Baptist. Sunny day. Fell asleep during sermon. Late that evening told mother of plans. Sainted old lady did not bat an eyelash. Never told her facts in case. Laconism, like blindness, seems to develop other faculties. Powers of divination. Married following Sunday in Church of Ascension. Father Masterson tied bond. Fine old character. Mother only witness. God bless dear old lady. Went from church to North Station. Took cars to Franconia.

Tedious journey in local. Stopped at every back yard. So it seemed. Backside of every barn on way painted with advertisements. Elixirs. Liver pills. Old circus posters. Dried codfish. Tea. Coffee. Back of barn in St. Botolphs painted: Boston Store. Rock bottom prices.

Young black-haired wife, dressed in best. Made all own clothes. Great sweetness; grace. Remember slenderness of wrists, ankles. Fleeting joy, sadness on face. Much openness. Real meaning of beauty all flows from lovely woman. Poetry. Music. Makes everything touched upon seem like revelation. Writer's hand. Ugly train coach. "I once rode to Swamscott in the cars," she said. Musical voice made journey seem like poem. Swans. Music of harps. Fountains. Swamscott not much and trains to same like trains everywhere. Fragrant, supple child, carrying seed of troll. Deep feeling of pity. Also lead in pencil.

Arrival in Franconia. Took hack to boardinghouse. Eight dollars per week. American plan. North country. Cold nights even in midsummer. Pick-up supper in gloomy dining room. No matter. Love blind to cold pudding, sallow-faced landlady, stains on ceiling. Bridal chamber big farmhouse bedroom. Cumbrous bedstead painted with purple grapes. Iron wood stove blazing. Undressed in light, heat of fire.

No fishing in vicinity. Walked with bride in hills. Beautiful scenery. Milky-blue hills in distance. Old lakes. Old mountains. Poignant country, north of mill towns. Then booming. Later ruined. (Unable to meet competition from south and west.) So-called marginal farming. Sam Scat. Stony fields. Most hill towns abandoned even then. Foundation holes, ruined buildings in deep woods. Homesteads, schoolhouses, churches even. Woods in vicinity still wild. Deer, bears, some lynx. Young wife picked nosegay of posies from gardens planted by farmers' wives. Departed then. English roses. Sweet William. Lemon lilies. Phlox and primrose. Brought some back to bridal chamber. Put in water pitcher. Real love of flowers. Haying weather perfect. Writer worked in fields with farmer, sons. Thunderstorm at end of day. Dark clouds mounting. Cock's crow. Deep sound of stone hills falling. Get hay into barn before rain. Forked lightning. Heavy wagon reaches safety just as first drops fall. Encircling sound. Long after nightfall, departure of rain, embrace of wife returns to writer all good things. Magic of haying weather. Heat of sun. Chill of storm.

Vacation ends all too soon. Bid good-by to hills, fields, cow pastures, Elysian fields with real sorrow. Pinckney Street, Whittier, Grimes, etc. Sainted old mother was tender with wife, never so tender with anyone but Hamlet. Never spoke of trouble but seemed to sense babe-in-woods situation. Nothing of convenience in marriage, however. Made in heaven; so it seemed. Sweet child woke with writer in early morning. Darned socks, made marriage bed sweet, cleaned lamp chimneys, waxed rosewood piano. Thought often of future. Dispose of troll-child and raise own family. Live in rose-covered cottage after demise of sainted old mother. In church writer often thanked God for sweetness of spouse. Prayed with full heart. Never had occasion to thank same for anything else. Wife sang sometimes in evening, accompanied by sainted old mother on Hallet & Davis rosewood piano. Voice modest in range but true pitch and oh so clear. Sweet, good, loving, kindly spirit.

Little troll very lively. Abdomen swollen, but no disfigurement. Easily fatigued during dog days. Accouchement expected in October. Sent message to office one afternoon. Left office at three. Found bags packed, both wife's and writer's. Took late train to Nahant. Hired livery to Rutherford farm. Reached there nine o'clock or later. Dark house. Smelled salt in wind. Heard harsh, regular noise of waves. Used both bell pull and knocker. Door opened by sallow-faced woman in nightdress, wrapper. Hair in rags. "I don't know your names," says she. "I don't want to know them. The sooner you get out of here the better." Lighted lamp. Unpacked bags. Went to bed. Wife slept poorly. Often spoke in sleep. Unclear words. Listened all night to troubled speaking; also moiling of sea. Seemed from sound of waves to be flat, stony beach. Distinguished rattling, knocking sound of stones. Milkpail, cattle sounds before dawn. Woke early. Washed in cold water. "You'll take your meals in kitchen," said sallow-faced landlady. "So far as you're able you'll do your own work. I'm not going to be picking up after you."

Husband of same introduced self at breakfast. 5'6". 125 pounds. Runty. Poor specimen. Appeared to be henpecked. Former livery-stable proprietor or so claimed. Tales of prosperity. Once possessed biggest wardrobe in Nahant. Sixty-four horses. Seven grooms on payroll. All lost in epidemic. Documents of splendor displayed. Receipted feed bill for one thousand dollars. Also tailor bill, butcher bill, grocery bill, etc. All gone. Walked with Clarissa on beach. Dear wife gathered colored stones, shells in skirt. Day slow to pass. Situation seemed like Gordian knot and to cut same dreamed of future. Painted rosy picture of country cottage, children gathered around knees, pleasant life. Net result of such wool-gathering was to make wife weep.

Labor pains began at seven. Wet bed. Broke waters or some such term. Writer unfamiliar, even today, with obstetrical lingo. "Our Father who art in heaven," said Clarissa. Prayed continuously. Pain arduous. First experience with such things. Held wife in arms when seizures commenced. Sallow-faced landlady waited in next room. Sound of rocking chair. "Put blanket over her mouth," she said. "They'll hear her up at the Dexter place." Most violent seizure at eleven. Suddenly saw blood, baby's head. Landlady rushed in. Drove me away. Called henpecked husband to bring water, rags, etc. Much coming and going. Sallow-faced landlady emerged at 2 A.M. "You have a little daughter," says she. Magical transformation! Butter wouldn't melt in mouth.

Went in to see baby. Sleeping in soapbox. Clarissa also sleeping. Kissed brow. Sat in chair until morning. Went for walk on beach. Clouds shaped like curved ribbing of scallop shell. Light pouring off sea into same. Form of sky still vivid in memory. Returned to room on tiptoe. Opened door. Clarissa in bed, smiling. Masses of dark hair. Baby at breast, swollen with milk. Writer cried for first time since leaving West River. "Don't cry," Clarissa says. "I'm happy."

Heavy step of sallow-faced landlady. Transformation still in order. "God bless you, you dear, sweet little girl," she says to the baby. High, squeaky voice. "Look at her dear little fingers," says she. "Look at her dear little toes. I'll take her now." "Let her suck for a little while," says Clarissa. "Let her finish her dinner," says I. "Well, you ain't going to take the baby with you," says she, "and since you ain't going to take the baby with you and since she ain't going to be your baby there's no point in your suckling her." "Let her suck for a little while longer," says Clarissa. "I'm not one to judge others," says she, "and I don't put my nose in their business but if you hadn't done wrong you wouldn't be coming out here to have your baby in this God-forsaken place and when a baby drinks milk from a mother who's done wrong all the wickedness and sinfulness and lustfulness goes right into the baby through its mother's milk," says she. "You've got a wicked tongue," I said, "and we'd appreciate it if you'd leave us alone now." "Let her suck for a little while longer," Clarissa said. "I'm only doing what I'm paid to do," she said, "and what's more she's God's little creature and it ain't fair to have her imbibing all the weaknesses of another the first thing in her life." "Leave us alone," I said. "She's right, Leander," Clarissa said and she took the child off her pretty breast and gave it to the intruder. Then she turned her face away and cried.

She cried all the day long, she cried all night. She cried the bed full of tears. In the morning I helped her dress. She was too weak to dress herself, too weak even to lift her dark hair, and I lifted it for her and held it while she put it up with pins.

There was a nine-o'clock train to Boston and I sent a message for a livery to pick us up in time to get it. Then I packed the valises and carried them out to the side of the road. Then I heard the landlady screaming "You, you, where is she?" Oh, she looked then like a harpy. "She's run away. Go up to the Dexters', go up the Dexter path. I'll go down by the shell road. We've got to head her off." Off she goes in her muddy boots. Off goes former livery-stable proprietor with his manure fork. Pursued quarry over horizon. Heard baby crying in garden. Whimper, really. She had flown; but she had not gone far.

Pear tree in garden pruned to look like fountain, sunshade perhaps. Graceful tent of leaves. Under this she sat. Bodice unbuttoned. Camisole unlaced. Child at breast. Fretful crying. Did not speak; she and me. Eyes only. No explanations, names even. Child sucking, but crying also. A little rain began to fall; but not on us. Pear tree served as adequate shelter. Baby fell asleep. How long we sat there I don't know. Half hour perhaps. Watched oyster-shell road darken in rain. Still no drops touched us. "I have more tears than milk," she said. "I have more tears than milk. I've cried my breasts dry." Carried sleeping baby, sheltered by head, shoulders from rain, back to soapbox in kitchen near stove. Took livery to station.

Have no wish to dwell on sordid matters, sorrows, etc. Bestiality of grief. Times in life when we can count only on brute will to live. Forget. Forget. (By this Leander meant to say that Clarissa was drowned in the Charles River that night.) Took cars to St. Botolphs next morning with old mother and poor Clarissa.

Overcast day. Not cold. Variable winds. South, southwest. Hearse at station. Few rubbernecks watching. Father Frisbee said the words. Old man then; old friend. Purple face. Skirts blowing in wind. Showed old-fashioned congress boots. Thick stockings. Family lot on hill above river. Water, hills, fields restore first taste of sense. Never marry again. Roof of old house visible in distance. Abode of rats, squirrels, porcupines. Haunted house for children. Wind slacked off in middle of prayer. Distant, electrical smell of rain. Sound amongst leaves; stubble. Hath but a short span, says Father Frisbee. Full of misery is he. Rain more eloquent, heartening and merciful. Oldest sound to reach porches of man's ear.

20

The fat man who had given Coverly pointers on how to shave had begun to come into Coverly's room at night after supper and give him advice on how to get ahead in the world. He was a widower who had a house somewhere to the north where he went for week ends and who pinched pennies by living in the rooming house so that he would have a comfortable retirement. He had a job with Civil Service and it was his feeling that Coverly should get on the Civil Service lists. He brought him those newspapers that list Civil Service openings and kept pointing out opportunities for high-school graduates or opportunities for specialists who had been trained by the Civil Service schools in the city. There was a demand that year for Tapers and he pointed this out to Coverly as his best bet. The government would pay half of Coverly's tuition at the MacIlhenney Institute. It was a four-month course and if he passed his exams he would be taken into government service at seventy-five dollars a week. Advised and encouraged by his friend, Coverly enrolled in some night classes on Taping. This involved the translation of physics experiments into the symbols—or tape—that could be fed into a computation machine.

Coverly's schedule went like this. He punched Warburton's time clock at half-past eight and went down a back staircase into the basement. The air was spectacularly bad: the reek and the closeness of a department store backstage. The other stock boys were of varying ages—one of them was in his sixties—and they were all amused by Coverly's catarrhal accent and his references to life in St. Botolphs. They unpacked the merchandise as it came in and kept it flowing up the freight elevators to the departments overhead. When there were sales they worked sometimes as late as midnight, unloading racks of fur-trimmed coats or cartons of bed sheets. On three nights a week, when Coverly had finished work at Warburton's, he signed the monitor's book at the MacIlhenney Institute. This was in the fourth floor of an office building that seemed to contain a good many other schools—institutes of portrait photography, journalism and music. The only elevator that ran in the evening was a freight elevator, operated by an old man in overalls who could, by pursing his lips, give a fairly good imitation of a French horn. He performed the *William Tell* Overture while he took his passengers up and down and he liked to be complimented. There were twenty-four students in Coverly's class and the instructor was a young man who seemed to have put in a hard day himself by the time he got to them. The first lecture was an orientation talk on cybernetics or automation, and if Coverly, with his mildly rueful disposition, had been inclined to find any irony in his future relationship to a thinking machine, he was swiftly disabused. Then they got to work memorizing the code.

This was like learning a language and a rudimentary one. Everything was done by rote. They were expected to memorize fifty symbols a week. They were quizzed for fifteen minutes at the opening of each class and were given speed tests at the end of the two-hour period. After a month of this the symbols—like the study of any language—had begun to dominate Coverly's thinking, and walking on the street he had gotten into the habit of regrouping numbers on license plates, prices in store windows and numerals on clocks so that they could be fed into a machine. When the class ended he sometimes drank a cup of coffee with a friend who was going to school five nights a week. His name was Mittler and his second enrollment was at Dale Carnegie's and Coverly was very much impressed with how likeable Mittler had learned to make himself. Moses came over one Sunday to visit Coverly and they spent the day banging around the streets and drinking beer but when it came time for Moses to go back the separation was so painful for both of them that Moses never returned. Coverly planned to go to St. Botolphs for Christmas but he had a chance to work overtime on Christmas Eve and he took it, for he was in the city, after all, to make his fortune.

All things of the sea belong to Venus; pearls and shells and alchemists' gold and kelp and the riggish smell of neap tides, the inshore water green, and purple further out and the joy of distances and the roar of falling masonry, all these are hers, but she doesn't come out of the sea for all of us. She came for Coverly through the swinging door of a sandwich shop in the Forties where he had gone to get something to eat after classes at the MacIlhenney Institute. She was a thin, dark-haired girl named Betsey MacCaffery—raised in the badlands of northern Georgia—an orphan, her eyes red that night from crying. Coverly was the only customer in the shop. She brought him a glass of milk and a sandwich in an envelope and then went to the far end of the counter and began to wash glasses. Now and then she took a deep, tremulous breath—a sound that made her seem to Coverly, as she bent over the sink, tender and naked. When he had eaten half his sandwich he spoke to her:

"Why are you crying?"

"Oh Jesus," she said. "I know I shouldn't be here crying in front of strangers, but the boss just came in and found me smoking a cigarette and he gave me hell. There wasn't anybody in the store. It's always slow this late on rainy nights, but he can't blame me for that, can he? I don't have anything to do with the rain and I just can't stand out there in the rain asking people to come in. Well, it was slow and there hadn't been anybody in for nearly twenty—twenty-five or thirty minutes—and so I went out back and lighted a cigarette and then he came right in, sniffing like a pig, and gave me hell. He said these awful things about me."

"You shouldn't pay any attention to what he says."

"You English?"

"No," Coverly said. "I come from a place called St. Botolphs. It's a small town, north of here."

"The reason I asked was you don't talk like the others. I come from a small town myself. I'm just a small-town girl. I guess maybe that's the trouble with me. I don't have this thick skin you need to get along with in the city. I had so much trouble this week. I just took this apartment with my girl friend. I have or perhaps I should say I had this girl friend, Helen Bent. I thought she was my true-blue friend; true-blue. She certainly led me to believe she was my best friend. Well, since we were such good friends it seemed sensible for us to take an apartment together. We were inseparable. That's what people used to say about us. You can't ask Betsey unless you ask Helen, they used to say. Those two are inseparable. Well, we took this apartment together, my girl friend and I. That was about a month ago; a month or six weeks. Well, just as soon as we got moved in and settled and about to enjoy ourselves I discover that the whole thing is just a scheme. The only reason she wants to share this apartment with me is so she can meet men there. Formerly she was living with her family out in Queens. Well, I don't have any objections to having a boy friend now and then but it was only a one-room apartment and she was having them in every night and naturally it was very embarrassing for me. There were men going in and out of there so much that it didn't seem like home to me. Why, sometimes when it was time for me to go home to my own apartment where I was paying rent and had all my own furniture I'd just feel so heavyhearted about busting in on her with one of her friends that I'd go and sit in a late movie. Well, I finally spoke to her. Helen, I said, this place doesn't seem like home to me. There's no sense in my paying rent, I said, if I have to take up residence in a movie house. Well, she certainly showed her true colors. Oh, the spiteful things she said. When I come home the next day she's gone, television set and all. I was glad to see the last of her, of course, but I'm stuck with this apartment with nobody to share the rent and in a job like this I don't have any occasion to make girl friends."

She asked Coverly if he wanted anything more. It was nearly time to close and Coverly asked if he could walk her home.

"You sure come from a small town, all right," she said. "Anybody could tell you come from a small town, asking if you can walk me home, but it so happens I just live five blocks from here and I do walk home and I don't guess it would do me any harm, providing you don't get fresh. I've had too much of freshness. You've got to promise that you won't be fresh."

"I promise," Coverly said.

She talked on and on while she made the preparations for closing the store and when these were finished she put on a hat and coat and stepped with Coverly out into the rain. He was delighted with her company. What a citizen of New York, he thought—walking a counter girl home in the rain. As they approached her house she reminded him of his promise not to be fresh and he didn't ask to come up, but he asked her to have dinner with him some night. "Well, I'd adore to," she said. "Sunday's my only night off but if Sunday's all right with you I'd adore to have dinner with you on Sunday night. There's this nice Italian restaurant right around the corner we can go to—I've never been there, but this former girl friend of mine told me it was very good—excellent cooking, and if you could pick me up at around seven . . ." Coverly watched her walk through the lighted hall to the inner door, a thin girl and not a very graceful one, feeling, as surely as the swan recognizes its mate, that he was in love.

21

Northeaster (Leander wrote). Wind backed from SW. 3rd equinoctial disturbance of season. All in love is not larky and fractious.—In the attic the broken harp-string music of water drop-

ping into pails and pans had begun and, feeling chilled and
exposed to the somber view of the river in the rain, he put
away his papers and went down the stairs. Sarah was in Travertine. Lulu was away. He went into the back parlor, where he
was completely absorbed in building and lighting a fire—in
watching how it caught, in sniffing the perfume of clean wood
and feeling the heat as it reached his hands and then went
through his clothes. When he was warm he went to the window
to see the dark day. He was surprised to see a car turn in the
gates and come up the drive. It was one of the old sedans from
the taxi stand at the station.

The car stopped at the side door and he saw a woman lean
forward and talk to the driver. He did not recognize the passenger—she was plain and gray-haired—and he guessed that she
was one of Sarah's friends. He watched her from the window.
She opened the door of the car and walked up, through the
thin curtain of rain that fell from the broken gutters, to the
door. Leander was glad for any company and he went down
the hall and opened the door before she rang.

He saw a very plain woman, her coat darkened at the shoulders
with rain. Her face was long, her hat was trimmed gaily with
hard white feathers, like the feathers that are used to balance
badminton birds, and her coat was worn. Leander had seen,
he thought, hundreds of her kind. They were the imprimatur
of New England. Dutiful, pious and hardy, they seemed to have
patterned their spirits after the weeds that grow in high pastures.
They were the women, Leander thought, after whom the dirty
boats of the mackerel fleet were named: Alice, Esther, Agnes,
Maybelle and Ruth. That there should be feathers in her hat,
that an ugly pin made of seashells should be pinned to her flat
breast, that there should be anything feminine, any ornament
on such a discouraging figure, seemed to Leander touching.

"Come in," Leander said. "I expect you're looking for Mrs.
Wapshot?"

"I think you're the gentleman I'm looking for," she said with
a look so troubled and shy that Leander glanced down at his

clothes. "I'm Miss Helen Rutherford. Are you Mr. Wapshot?"

"Yes, I'm Leander Wapshot. Come in, come in out of the rain. Come into the parlor. I have a little fire." She followed Leander along the hall and he opened the door to the back parlor. "Sit down," he said. "Sit in the red chair. Sit by the fire. Give your clothes a chance to dry out."

"You have quite a big house here, Mr. Wapshot," she said.

"It's too big," Leander said. "Do you know how many doors there are in this house? There are one hundred and twenty-two doors in this house. Now what was it that you wanted to see me about?"

She made a sniffling sound as if she had a cold or might even have been crying and began to unbuckle a heavy brief case that she carried.

"Your name was given to me by an acquaintance. I'm an accredited representative of the Institute for Self-Improvement. We still have a few subscriptions open for eligible men and women. Dr. Bartholomew, the director of the institute, has divided human knowledge into seven branches. Science, the arts— both the cultural arts and the arts of physical well-being—religion . . ."

"Who gave you my name?" Leander asked.

"Dr. Bartholomew thinks it's more a question of inclination than background," the stranger said. "Many people who've been fortunate enough to have a college education are still ineligible by Dr. Bartholomew's standards." She spoke without emphasis or feeling, almost with dread, as if she had come about something else, and she kept her eyes on the floor. "Educators all over the world and some of the crowned heads of Europe have endorsed Dr. Bartholomew's methods and Dr. Bartholomew's essay on 'The Science of Religion' is in the Royal Library in Holland. I have a picture of Dr. Bartholomew here and . . ."

"Who gave you my name?" Leander asked again.

"Daddy," she said. "Daddy gave me your name." She began to wring her hands. "He died last summer. Oh, he was good to me, he was like a real daddy, there wasn't anything in the world that he wouldn't do for me. He was my best beau. On Sundays we used to take walks together. He was awfully intelligent but they cheated him. They did him out of everything. He wasn't afraid, though, he wasn't afraid of anything. Once we went to a show in Boston. That was on my birthday. He bought these expensive seats. They were supposed to be in the orchestra but when we came to sit in them they put us in the balcony. We paid for orchestra seats—he told me—and we're going down and sit in that orchestra. So he took my hand and we went downstairs and he told the usher—he was one of those stuck-up fellows—we paid for orchestra seats and we're going to sit in that orchestra. I miss him so much it's all I can think about. He never let me go anywhere without him. And then he died last summer."

"Where is your home?" Leander asked.

"Nahant."

"Nahant?"

"Yes. Daddy told me everything."

"What do you mean?" Leander said.

"Daddy told me everything. He told me how you came there after dark, like thieves, he said, and about how Mr. Whittier paid for everything and how Mother kept me from drinking her wicked milk."

"Who are you?" Leander said.

"I'm your daughter."

"Oh no," Leander said. "You're lying. You're a crazy woman. Get out of here."

"I'm your daughter."

"Oh no," Leander said. "You've thought this all up, you and those people in Nahant. You've made it all up. Now get out of my house. Leave me alone."

"You walked on the beach," she said. "Daddy remembered everything so's you'd believe me and give me money. He even remembered the suit you had. He said you had a plaid suit. He said you walked on the beach and picked up stones."

"Get out of my house," Leander said.

"I won't go away from here until you give me money. You never once asked was I living or dead. You never gave me a thought. Now I want some money. After Daddy died I sold the house and I had a little money and then I had to take this work. It's hard for me. It's too hard for me. I'm not strong. I'm out in all weathers. I want some money."

"I don't have anything to give you."

"That's what Daddy said. He said you'd try to get out of helping me. Daddy told me that's what you'd say, but he made me promise to come and see you." Then she stood and picked up her brief case. "God will be your judge," she said at the door, "but I know my rights and I can bring you into court and blacken your name." Then she went down the hall and when she got to the door Leander called after her, "Wait, wait, wait, please," and went down the hall. "I can give you something," he said. "I have a few things left. I have a jade watch fob and a golden chain and I can show you your mother's grave. It's in the village."

"I would spit on it," she said. "I would spit on it." Then she went out of the house to where the taxi was waiting and drove away.

22

A week or ten days after his dinner with Betsey, Coverly moved into her apartment. This took a lot of persuasion on Coverly's part but her resistance pleased him and seemed to express the seriousness with which she took herself. His case was based—indirectly—on the fact that she needed someone to look out for her, on the fact that she did not have, as she had said herself, the thickness of skin the city demanded. Coverly's feelings about her helplessness were poetic and absorbing and when he thought of her in her absence it was with a mixture of pity and bellicoseness. She was alone and he would defend her. There was this and there was the fact that their relationship unfolded with great validity and this informal marriage or union, played out in a strange and great city, made Coverly very happy. She was the beloved; he was the lover—there was never any question about this and this suited Coverly's disposition and gave to his courtship and their life together the liveliness of a pursuit. Her search for friends had been arduous and disappointing and it was these disappointments and exasperations that Coverly was able to redress. There was no pretentiousness in her—no memories of either hunt balls or razorback hogs—and she was ready and willing to cook his supper and warm his bones at night. She had been raised by her grandmother, who had wanted her to be a schoolteacher, and she had disliked the South so much that she had taken any job to get out of it. He recognized her defenselessness, but he recognized, at a much deeper level, her human excellence, the touching qualities of a wanderer, for she was that and said so and while she would play all the parts of love she would not tell him that she was in love. On the week ends they took walks, subway and ferryboat rides, and talked over their plans and their tastes, and late in the winter Coverly asked her to marry him. Betsey's reaction was scattered, tearful and sweet, and Coverly wrote his plans in a letter to St. Botolphs. He wanted to marry as soon as he had passed his Civil Service examinations and had been assigned to one of the rocket-launching stations where Tapers were employed. He enclosed a photograph of Betsey, but he would not bring his bride to St. Botolphs until he was given a vacation. He took these precautions because it had occurred to him that Betsey's southern accent and sometimes fractious manner might not go down with Honora and that the sensible thing to do would be to marry and produce a son before Honora saw his wife. Leander may have sensed this— his letters to Coverly were all congratulatory and affectionate— and it may have been at the back of his mind that with Coverly married they might soon all be on Easy Street. It would be way at the back of his mind. Sarah was heartbroken to know that Coverly would not be married at Christ Church.

Coverly passed his exams with flying colors in April and was surprised when the MacIlhenney Institute had a graduation ceremony. This was held in the fifth floor of the building in an academy of piano teaching where two classrooms had been thrown together to make an auditorium. All of Coverly's classmates appeared with their families or their wives, and Betsey wore a new hat. A lady, a stranger to them all, played "Pomp and Circumstance" on the piano and as their names were called they went up to the front of the room and got their diplomas from Mr. MacIlhenney. Then they went down to the fourth floor where they found Mrs. MacIlhenney standing by a rented tea urn and a plate of Danish pastry. Coverly and Betsey were married the next morning at the Church of the Transfiguration. Mittler was the only witness and they spent a three-day honeymoon on an island cottage that Mittler owned and loaned them. Sarah wrote Coverly a long letter about what she would send him from the farm when he was settled—the Canton china and the painted chairs—and Leander wrote a letter in which he said, among other things, that to make a son was as easy as blowing a feather off your knee. Honora sent them a check for two hundred dollars, but no message.

Coverly passed his Civil Service examination and was qualified as a Taper. He knew, by then, the location of most of the rocket-launching bases in the country and as soon as he was settled he would send for Betsey and they would begin their marriage. Although Coverly's status was civilian his assignment was cut at an army base and he was given transportation by the air force. His orders were cut in code. A week after his marriage he boarded an old C-54 with bucket seats and found himself, next day, in an airfield outside San Francisco. His feeling then was that he would be sent to Oregon or flown back to one of the desert stations. He telephoned Betsey and she cried when she heard his voice but he assured her that in a week or ten days they would be together again in a house of their own. He was very uxorious and lay down each night in his army bunk with Betsey's specter, slept with her shade in his arms and woke each morning with powerful longings for his sandwich-shop Venus and wife. There was some delay about the second stage of his journey and he was kept at the air-force base in San Francisco for nearly a week.

We all, man and boy, know what a transient barracks looks like and there would be no point in enumerating this barrenness. The fact that Coverly was a civilian did not give him any freedom and whether he went to the officers' club or the movies he had to report his whereabouts to the orderly room. He could see the hills of San Francisco across the bay and, thinking that this city—or some firing grounds in the vicinity—would be his destination, he wrote hopefully to Betsey about her coming West. "It was cold in the barracks last night and I sure wish you'd been in bed with me to warm it up." And so forth and so on. He lived among a dozen or so men who seemed to have been withdrawn from permanent installations in the Pacific because they were unfit. The most articulate of these was a Mexican who had not been able to stomach army food because there were no peppers in it. He told his story to anyone who would listen. As soon as he started eating army food he lost weight. He knew what the trouble was. He needed peppers. He had eaten peppers all his life. Even his mother's milk had been peppery. He pleaded with army cooks and doctors to get him some peppers but they wouldn't take his pleas seriously. He wrote to his Momma and she sent him some pepper seeds in an envelope and he planted them around an anti-aircraft gun emplacement where the soil was rich and where there was plenty of sun. He watered them and tended them and they had just begun to sprout when the commanding officer ordered them to be plowed under. It was unmilitary to raise vegetables on a gun emplacement. This order broke the Mexican's spirit. He lost weight; he became so emaciated that he had to be sent to the infirmary; and now he was being discharged from the army as a mental incompetent. He would have been happy to serve his flag, he said, if he could have peppers in his food. His plaint seemed reasonable enough but it got tiresome night after night and Coverly usually stayed out of the barracks until the lights were off.

He ate his meals at the officers' club, lost or won a dollar at the gambling machines, drank a glass of ginger ale at the bar and went to the movies. He saw Westerns, gangster careers, tales of happy and unhappy love both in brilliant colors and in black and white. He was sitting in the movies one evening when the public-address system called: "Attention, attention everybody. Will the following men report to Building Thirty-two with their gear. Private Joseph Di Gacinto. Private Henry Wollaston. Lieutenant Marvin Smythe. Mister Coverly Wapshot . . ." The audience hooted and whistled and called, "You'll be sorreee," as they went out into the dark. Coverly got his valise and went over to Building Thirty-two and was driven with the rest of the men to the airfield. They all had some theory about their destination. They were going to Oregon, Alaska or Japan. It had never occurred to Coverly that he might be leaving the country and he was worried. He pinned his hopes on Oregon but decided that if his destination was Alaska Betsey could follow him there. As soon as they boarded the plane the doors were shut and they taxied down the runway and took off. It was an old transport with a conservative speed, Coverly guessed, and if their destination was Oregon they would reach there before dawn. The plane was hot and stuffy and he fell asleep, and waking at dawn and looking from the port he saw that they were high over the Pacific. They flew westward all day, shooting crap and reading the Bible, which was all they had to read, and at dusk they picked up the lights of Diamond Head and landed on Oahu.

Coverly was assigned a bunk in another transient barracks and told to report to the airfield in the morning. No one would tell him if his travels were over, but he guessed, from the looks of the orderly-room clerks, that he had some way to go. He got rid of his valise and hitched a ride on a weapons carrier into Honolulu. It was a hot, stale-smelling night with thunder in the mountains. Memories of Thaddeus and Alice, of Honora and old Benjamin came to him and he walked in the footsteps of many Wapshots, but this was not much of a consolation. Half a world lay between him and Betsey, and all his plans of happiness, children, and the honor of the family name seemed cruelly suspended or destroyed. He saw a sign on a wall that said: AIRMAIL AN ORCHID LEI TO YOUR SWEETHEART FOR AS LITTLE AS THREE DOLLARS. This would be a way of expressing his tender feelings for Betsey and he asked an MP near the old palace where he could get a lei. He followed the MP's directions and rang the bell of a house where a fat woman in evening clothes let him in. "I want a lei," Coverly said sadly.

"Well, you come to the right place, honey," she said. "You come right in. You come right in and have a drink and I'll fix you up in a few minutes." She took his arm and led him into a little parlor where some other men were drinking beer.

"Oh, I'm sorry," Coverly said suddenly. "There's some mistake. You see, I'm married."

"Well, that don't make no difference," the fat lady said. "More'n half the girls I got working for me's married and I been happily married for nineteen years myself."

"There's been a mistake," Coverly said.

"Well, make up your mind," the fat woman said. "You come in here telling me you want to get laid and I'm doing the best I can for you."

"Oh, I'm sorry," Coverly said, and he was gone.

In the morning he boarded another plane and flew all day. A little before dark they circled for a landing and out of the ports Coverly could see, in the stormy light, a long, scimitar-shaped atoll with surf breaking on one coast, a huddle of buildings and a rocket-launching platform. The airstrip was small and the pilot took three passes before he made a landing. Coverly swung down from the door and crossed the strip to an office where a clerk translated his orders. He was on Island 93—an installation that was half military and half civilian. His tour of duty would be nine months with a two-week vacation at a rest camp in either Manila or Brisbane; take your pick.

23

Moses was promoted and he bought a car and rented an apartment. He worked hard at his office and still had a lot of nightwork assigned to him by Mr. Boynton. He saw Beatrice about once a week. This was a pleasant and irresponsible arrangement for he discovered very soon that Beatrice's marriage had gone on the rocks long before he had stepped into the Marine Room. Chucky was going around with the girl who sang in the band and Beatrice liked to talk about his perfidy and ingratitude. She had given him the money to organize the band. She had supported him. She had even bought his clothes. Beatrice meant to speak bitterly, but it wasn't in her. The dainty way in which she shaped her words seemed to exclude from them any of the deeper notes of human trouble. She had trouble—plenty of it—but she couldn't get it into her voice. She was thinking of traveling and spoke of beginning a new life in Mexico, Italy or France. She said she had plenty of money although if this was so Moses wondered why she put up with a broken-down cardboard wardrobe and wore such dilapidated furs. Going unexpectedly to her apartment one night, Moses was not let in until he had cooled his heels in the hallway for some time. From the noises inside he figured that she was entertaining another caller and when he was finally let in he wondered if his rival was hidden in the bathroom or stuffed into the wardrobe. But he was not in any way concerned with the life she led and he stayed long enough to smoke a cigarette and then went out to a movie.

It was the kind of relationship that was useful and peaceable enough until Moses began to lose interest and then Beatrice got ardent and demanding. She couldn't reach him at his office but she called his apartment, sometimes nightly, and when he went to see her she would cry and tell him about her artificial and socially ambitious mother and the sternness of Clancy. She moved from her apartment to a hotel and he helped carry her bags. She moved from this hotel to another and he helped her again. One early evening when he had just come in from supper she telephoned to say that she had gotten a singing engagement in Cleveland and would Moses put her on the train? He said that he would. She said she was home and gave him another address and he took a taxi.

The address was a delicatessen. He thought that perhaps her mother, in somewhat reduced circumstances, might have taken an apartment above the store, but there was no apartment entrance and he looked into the delicatessen. There in the back, dressed in a hat and coat and surrounded by suitcases, sat Beatrice. She was crying and her eyes were red. "Oh, thank you for coming, Moses dear," she said, as daintily as ever. "I'll be ready to go in just a minute. I want to catch my breath."

The room where she sat was the kitchen of the delicatessen. There were two other people there. Beatrice didn't explain or introduce them but Moses recognized one as Beatrice's mother. The resemblance was marked, although she was a very stout woman with a florid and handsome face. She wore an apron over her dress and her shoes were broken. The other woman was thin and old. This was Clancy. Here were the origins of Beatrice's splendid and unhappy memories. Her governess was a delicatessen cook.

The two women were making sandwiches. Now and then they spoke to Beatrice, but she didn't reply. They didn't seem troubled by her tear-stained face or her silence and the atmosphere in the kitchen was of a spent and ancient misunderstanding. The contrast between the stories Beatrice had told him of her unhappy childhood—her elegant and callous mother—and the clear lights of the delicatessen made her dilemma as keen and touching as the troubles of a child.

It was a fine delicatessen. The acid smell of pickles in brine came from some barrels near the door. Fresh sawdust had been scattered on the floor by Clancy—a little of it still clung to her apron—and from the door to the rear of the place, from the floor to the ceiling, were stacked cans of vegetables and fruit, shrimps, stone crabs, lobster meat, soups and chickens. There were baked turkeys and fowl in the glass cases, hams, turban-shaped rolls in the bread bins, sliced cucumbers in vinegar, creamed cheese, rollmops, smoked salmon, whitefish and stur-geon, and from this abundance of acid and appetizing smells poor Beatrice had invented an unhappy childhood with a hard-hearted mother and a stern governess.

A little sob came from Beatrice. She took a paper napkin from a container on the table and blew her nose into it. "If you could get a taxi and take my suitcases out, Moses dear," she said. "I'm too weak." He knew what her suitcases contained—that magpie wardrobe—and when he lifted them they felt like stone. He carried the bags out to the curb and got a cab and Clancy followed with a large paper bag full of sandwiches. "She'll eat them on the train," Clancy said to Moses. Beatrice said nothing to either her mother or the cook and in the taxi she sobbed some more and kept blowing her nose into the paper napkin.

Moses carried her bags through the station and put them on the Cleveland train and then Beatrice kissed him good-by daintily and began to cry in earnest. "Oh dear Moses, I've done some-thing awful, and I have to tell you. You know how they always investigate people, I mean they ask everybody you know about you, and a man came to see me one afternoon and I told him this long story about how you took advantage of me and promised to marry me and took all my money but I had to tell them some-thing because they would have thought I was immoral if I didn't and I'm sorry and I hope nothing bad happens to you." Then the conductor shouted all aboard and the train pulled out for Cleveland.

24

And now we come to the wreck of the *Topaze*.

This happened on May 30—her first voyage of the year. For two weeks Leander and the hired hand—Bentley—had been getting her into shape. The lilac was in bloom and in St. Botolphs there were hedges of lilac—there were whole groves and forests of it blooming the length of River Street and growing wild around the cellar holes on the other side of the hill. Going to the wharf in the early mornings Leander saw that the children walking to school all carried branches of lilac. He wondered if they gave it to their teachers, who must have lilac trees themselves, or used it to decorate the classrooms. All that week he saw children carrying lilac branches to school. Early on the morning of the thirtieth he cut some lilac himself and took it to the cemetery and then he went down to the *Topaze*.

Bentley had worked as a hired hand for Leander before. He was a young man who had been to sea and who had a bad name. He was known by everyone to be the illegitimate son of Theophilus Gates by a woman who called herself Mrs. Bentley and who lived in a two-family house near the table-silver factory. He was one of those neat, taciturn and competent seamen who tear the world to pieces about once a month. Landladies in many cities had admired him for his cleanliness, sobriety and industry until he would come home some rainy night with three bottles of whisky in a paper bag and drink them, one after the other. Then he would break the windows, piss on the floor and erupt in such a volcano of bitterness and obscenity that the police were usually called and he would start all over again in some other city or furnished room.

Another passenger or crew member that day was Lester Spinet, a blind man who had learned to play the accordion at the Hutchens Institute. It was Honora's idea that he should work on the *Topaze,* and she planned to pay him a salary herself. Leander was naturally pleased to have music on his boat and displeased at himself that he disliked the sound of the blind man's cane and the way he looked. Spinet was a heavy man with a massive head and face canted upward, as if some traces of light still reached his eyes. Spinet and Bentley were waiting for Leander that morning when he got to the wharf and they took on some passengers including an old lady with some lilac branches wrapped in a newspaper. The sky and the river were blue and it was everything, or almost everything, that a holiday should be, although it was a little close or humid and mixed with the smell of lilacs that came down from the river banks was a sour smell like the smell of wet paper. It might storm.

At Travertine he took on more passengers. Dick Hammersmith and his brother were on the wharf in bathing trunks, diving for coins, but there wasn't much business. As he headed for the channel he saw that the beach in front of the Mansion House was crowded and heard the shrieks of a child who was being ducked by her father. "Daddy isn't going to hurt you, Daddy only wants you to see how nice the water feels," the man said while the child's cries grew higher and more desperate. He passed through the channel between Hale and Gull rocks into the lovely bay, green inshore, blue in the deeper water and as purple as wine at forty fathoms. The sun shone and the air was warm and fragrant. From the wheelhouse he could see the passengers settling themselves on the forward deck with the charm and innocence of all holiday crowds. They would be dispersed, he knew, once he headed up into the wind, and he took a wide tack after the channel so that he would have their company for as long as possible. There were families with children and families without but very few old people had bought tickets that day. Bucks were photographing their girls and fathers were photographing their wives and children and although Leander had never taken a picture in his life he felt kindly toward these cameramen or anyone else who made a record of such a lighthearted thing as the crossing to Nangasakit. There was among the passengers, he guessed, a man with a wig or toupee, and turning the boat up into the wind he watched the stranger grab for his hairpiece and secure it to his head with a cap. At the same time many women grabbed for their skirts and hats, but the damage was done. The fresh breeze scattered them all. They gathered up their papers and their comic books and carrying deck chairs went over to the leeward side or back to the stern and Leander was alone.

The fact of his aloneness reminded Leander of Helen Rutherford, whom he had seen the night before. He had worked late on the boat and had gone into Grimes' bakery to get his supper. While he was eating he looked up and saw her standing at the window, reading the menu that was posted there. He got up from the table and went out to speak with her—he didn't know what he would say—but as soon as she recognized him she backed away from him in fear, saying, "Get away from me, get away from me."

In the spring dusk the square was deserted. They were alone. "I only want to . . ." Leander began.

"You want to hurt me, you want to hurt me."

"No."

"Yes, you do. You want to harm me. Daddy said you would. Daddy said for me to be careful."

"Please listen to me."

"Don't you move. Don't you come near me or I'll call the police officer."

Then she turned and walked up the Cartwright Block as if the soft air of evening were full of flints and missiles—a queer, frightened limp—and when she had turned up a side street Leander went back to the bakery to pay for his supper.

"Who's the nut?" the waitress asked. "She's been around here telling everybody she's got this secret that will set the river on fire. Oh, I hate nuts."

When Bentley came up to the wheelhouse, Leander saw that he had been drinking. Considering his own habits he had a long nose for the smell of rotted fruit that clung to the lips of someone else. Bentley still preserved the preternatural neatness of a man who is often tempted and deeply familiar with sloth. His curly hair shone with grease, his pale face was clean shaven with razor nicks on his neck and he had washed and scrubbed his denims until they were threadbare and smelled nicely of soap, but mixed with the smell of soap was the smell of whisky and Leander wondered if he would have to make the return voyage alone.

He could see the white walls of Nangasakit then and hear the music of the merry-go-round. On the wharf there was an old man with a card in his hat advertising the four-, five- and six-course shore dinners at the Nangasakit House. Leander stepped out of the wheelhouse and shouted his own refrain. "Return voyage at three thirty. Return voyage at three thirty. Please give yourself plenty of time to get back to the boat. Return voyage at three thirty. Please give yourself plenty of time to get back to the boat. . . ." The last to leave the boat was Spinet, who tapped his way down the wharf with a stick. Leander went to his cabin, ate a sandwich and fell sound asleep.

When he woke it was a little before three. The air was quite dark and he saw that it would storm. He poured some water into a basin and splashed his face. Going out onto the deck he saw a fog bank a mile or so out to sea. He wanted a hand on the return voyage and he put on his cap and walked up to Ray's Café, where Bentley usually did his drinking. Bentley was in no shape at all. He was not even in the bar but was sitting in a small back room with a bottle and a glass. "I guess you muss think I'm drunk," he began, but Leander only sat down wearily, wondering where he could get a deck hand in fifteen minutes. "You think I'm no good, but I got this girl out in Fort Sill, Oklahoma," Bentley said. "She thinks I'm good. I call her parrot. She's got this big nose. I'm going back to Fort Sill, Oklahoma, and love my parrot. She's got this two thousand dollars in the bank she wants to give me. You don't believe me, do you? You think I'm no good. You think I'm drunk, but I got this girl out in Fort Sill, Oklahoma. She loves me. She wants to give me this two thousand dollars. I call her parrot. She's got this big nose. . . ." It was not his fault, Leander knew, that he was a bastard, and it might not even be his fault that he was a cheerless bastard, but Leander needed a deck hand and he went out to the bar and asked Marylyn if her kid brother would want to pick up a dollar for the return voyage. She said sure, sure the kid was crazy to make a nickel, and she telephoned her mother and her mother opened the kitchen door and shouted for the boy but he couldn't be found and Leander walked back to his ship.

He watched his passengers come aboard with interest and some tenderness. They carried trophies—things they had won—thin blankets that would not keep the autumn cold from your bones; glass dishes for peanuts and jelly; and animals made out of oilcloth and paper, some of them with diamond eyes. There was a pretty girl with a rose in her hair and a man and his wife and three children, all of them wearing shirts made of the same flowered cloth. Helen Rutherford was the last to come aboard, but he was in the wheelhouse and didn't see her. She wore the same pot-shaped hat, ornamented with shuttlecock feathers, had the same seashell pinned to her breast and carried the old brief case.

Helen Rutherford had been trying to sell Dr. Bartholomew's wisdom in the cottages of Nangasakit for a week. On the morning of this, her last day, she had wandered into a neighborhood that seemed more substantial than anything else in the little resort. The houses were small—no bigger than bungalows—and yet all of them declaring by their mansards and spool railings and their porch latticework arched like the vents to a donjon that these were not summerhouses; these were places where men and women centered their lives and where children were conceived and reared. The sight might have cheered her if it hadn't been for the dogs. The place was full of dogs; and it had begun to seem to Helen that her life was a martyrdom to dogs. As soon as her footsteps were heard the dogs began to bark, filling her with timidity and self-pity. From morning until night dogs sniffed at her heels, snapped at her ankles, bit the skirts of her best gray coat and tried to run off with her brief case. As soon as she entered a strange neighborhood dogs that had been sunning themselves peacefully in clothesyards or sleeping by stoves, dogs who had been chewing bones or daydreaming or sporting with one another, would give up their peaceful occupations and sound the alarm. She had dreamed many times that she was torn to pieces by dogs. It seemed to her that she was a pilgrim and the soles of her shoes were so thin that she was virtually barefoot. She was surrounded, day after day, by strange houses and people and hostile beasts, and like a pilgrim she was now and then given a cup of tea and a piece of stale cake. Her lot was worse than a pilgrim's for God alone knew in which direction her Rome, her Vatican, would appear.

The first dog to come at her that day was a collie who snarled at her heels, a sound that frightened her more than a loud, straightforward bark. The collie was joined by a small dog who seemed friendly, but you could never tell. It was a friendly-seeming dog who had torn her coat. A black dog joined these two and then a police dog, woofing and belling like a hound from hell. She walked half a block, trailed by four dogs, and then all but the collie went back to their occupations. The collie was still a little behind, snarling at her heels. She hoped, she prayed, that someone would open a door and call him home. She turned to speak to him. "Go home, doggie," she said. "Go home, good doggie, go home, nice doggie." Then he sprang at her coat sleeve and she struck at him with her brief case. Her heart was beating so that she thought she would die. The collie sank his teeth into the old leather of the brief case and began a tug of war. "Leave that poor lady alone, you nasty cur," Helen heard someone say. A stranger appeared at her right with a kettle of water and let the dog have it. The dog went howling up the street. "Now you come into the house for a few minutes," the stranger said. "You come in and tell me what you're selling and rest your feet."

Helen thanked the stranger and followed her into one of the

little houses. Her savior was a short woman with eyes of a fine, pale blue and a very red face. She introduced herself as Mrs. Brown and in order to receive Helen she took off an apron and hung it over the back of a chair. She was a little woman with an extravagantly curved figure. Her breasts and buttocks stretched the cloth of her house dress. "Now tell me what it is that you're selling," she said, "and I'll see if I want any."

"I'm an accredited representative for Dr. Bartholomew's Institute for Self-Improvement," Helen said. "There are still a few subscriptions open for eligible men and women. Dr. Bartholomew feels that a college education is not a requirement. He feels . . ."

"Well, that's good," Mrs. Brown said, "because I'm not what you would call an educated woman. I graduated from the Nangasakit High School, which is one of the best high schools in the world—known all over the world—but the amount of education I got through learning is nothing to the amount of education that runs in my blood. I'm directly descended from Madame de Staël and many other well-educated and distinguished men and women. I suppose you don't believe me, I suppose you think I'm crazy, but if you'll notice that picture on the wall— it's a picture post card of Madame de Staël—and then notice my own profile you'll see the resemblance, no doubt."

"There are many four-colored portraits of famous historical men and women," Helen said.

"I'll stand right up beside the portrait so's you'll be sure to see the resemblance," Mrs. Brown said, and she went across the room and stood beside the card. "I guess you must have seen the resemblance by now. You see the resemblance, don't you? You must see it. Everybody else does. A man came here yesterday selling hot-water heaters and told me I looked enough like Madame de Staël to be her twin. Said we looked like identical twins." She smoothed her house dress and then went back and sat on the edge of her chair. "It's being directly descended from Madame de Staël and other distinguished men and women," she said, "that accounts for the education in my blood. I have very expensive tastes. If I go into a store to buy a pocketbook and there's a pocketbook for one dollar and a pocketbook for three dollars my eye goes straight to the one that costs three dollars. I've preferred expensive things all my life. Oh, I had great expectations! My great-grandfather was an ice merchant. He made a fortune selling ice to the niggers in Honduras. He wasn't a man to put much stock in banks and he took all his money to California and put it into gold bullion and coming back his ship sank in a storm off Cape Hatteras, gold and all. Of course it's still there—two and a half million dollars of it— and it's all mine, but do you think the banks around here would loan me the money to have it raised? Not on your life. There's over two and one half million dollars of my very own lying there in the sea and there's not a man or woman in this part of the country with enough gumption or sense of honor to loan me the money to raise my own inheritance. Last week I went up to St. Botolphs to see this rich old Honora Wapshot and she . . ."

"Is she related to Leander Wapshot?"

"She's the very same blood. Do you know him?"

"He's my father," Helen said.

"Well, for land's sakes, if Leander Wapshot's your father what are you doing going from door to door, trying to sell books?"

"He's disowned me." Helen began to cry.

"Oh, he has, has he? Well, that's easier said than done. It's crossed my mind to disown my own children, but I don't know how to go about it. You know what my daughter—my very own daughter—did on Thanksgiving Day? We all sat down to the table and then she picked up this turkey, this twelve-pound turkey, and she threw it onto the floor and she jumped up and down on it and she kicked it from here to there and then she took the dish with the cranberry sauce in it and she threw it all over the ceiling—cranberry sauce all over the ceiling—and then she began to cry. Well, I thought of disowning her then and there but it's easier said than done and if I can't disown my own daughter how's it Leander Wapshot can disown his?

Well," she said, getting to her feet and tying on her apron again, "I've got to get back to my housework now and I can't spend any more time talking but my advice to you is to go to that old Leander Wapshot and tell him to buy you a decent pair of shoes. Why, when I saw you walking down the street with the dogs behind you and the holes in your shoes I didn't feel it would be Christian not to come to your help but now that I know you're a Wapshot it seems that your own flesh and blood could come to your aid. Good-by."

Leander blew the warning whistle for his last voyage. From the wheelhouse he could see the rain falling onto the roller-coaster. He saw Charlie Matterson and his twin brother throw a tarpaulin over the last section of cars to come down. The merry-go-round was still turning. He saw the passengers in one of the boats of the Red Mill look up in surprise, as they were debouched from the mouth of a plaster-of-Paris ogre, to find it raining. He saw a young man gaily cover his girl's head with a newspaper. He saw people in the cottages up on the bluff lighting their kerosene lamps. He thought how sad it was that on this, their first trip away from home in so many years, it should rain. There were no stoves or fireplaces in the cottages. There was no escape from the damp and the doleful sounds of the rain for the matchboard walls of the cottages, salt soaked and tight, would resound when you touched them like the skin of a drum and you would hardly have settled down to a two-handed game of whist before the roof began to leak. There would be a leak in the kitchen and another over the card table and another over the bed. The vacationers could wait for the mail-man, but who would write to them?—and they couldn't write letters themselves for all their envelopes would be stuck together. Only the lovers, their bedposts jingling loudly and merrily, would be spared this gloom. On the beach Leander saw the last parties surrender, calling to one another to remember the blanket, re-member the bottle opener, remember the thermos and the picnic basket, until there was no one left but an old man who liked to swim in the rain and a young man who liked to walk in the rain and whose head was full of Swinburne and whose nickname was Bananas. Leander saw the Japanese, who sold fans and back scratchers, take in his silk and paper lanterns. He saw people standing in restaurant doorways and waitresses at windows. A waiter took in the naked tables of the Pergola Cantonese Restaurant and he saw a hand part some window curtains in the Nangasakit House, but he couldn't see the face that looked out. He saw how the waves, that had been riding in briskly, subsided in the rain so that they barely lapped the shore. The sea was still. Then the old man, who was standing waist deep in the water, suddenly turned and struggled up the beach, feeling the inward pull of the storm sea. He saw the gladness with which Bananas was watching these signs of danger. Then the sea, with a roar of stone, drew out beyond the line of sand to the stony beginnings of the harbor bottom, forming a wave that, when it broke (the first of a barrage that would sound all night), shook the beach and scooted up after the heels of the old man. He took off the lines and blew the whistle. Spinet started to play "Jingle Bells" as the *Topaze* went out to sea.

There was a channel at Nangasakit—a granite breakwater bearded with sea grass and a bell buoy rocking in the southwest sea, white foam spilling over the float as it tipped. The bell, Leander knew, could on this wind be heard inland. It could be heard by the card players rearranging pots and pans under their leaky roof, by the old ladies in the Nangasakit House and even by the lovers above the merry jingling of their bedposts. It was the only bell Leander had ever heard in his dreams. He loved all bells: dinner bells, table bells, doorbells, the bell from Antwerp and the bell from Altoona had all heartened and consoled him but this was the only bell that chimed on the dark side of his mind. Now the charming music fell astern, fainter and fainter, lost in the creaking of the old hull and the noise of seas breaking against her bow. Out in the bay it was rough.

She took the waves head on, like an old rocking horse. Waves broke over the glass of the wheelhouse so that Leander had to keep one hand on the windshield wiper to see. The water pouring down the decks began to come in at the cabin. It was dirty weather. Leander thought of the passengers—the girl with the rose in her hair and the man with three children, all wearing shirts cut of the same cloth as his wife's summer dress. And what about the passengers themselves, sitting in the cabin? Were they frightened? They were, nine times out of ten, their fear clothed lightly in idle speculation. They fished for their key rings and their small change, gave their privates a hitch and, if they had some talisman, a silver dollar or a St. Christopher medal, they rubbed it with their fingers. St. Christopher, be with us now! They readjusted their garters if they wore them, tightened the knots in their shoelaces and their neckties and wondered why their sense of reality should seem suspended. They thought of pleasant things: wheat fields and winter twilights, when five minutes after the lemony yellow light in the west was gone the snow began to fall, or hiding jelly beans under the sofa cushions on Easter Eve. The young man looked at the girl with the rose in her hair, remembering how generously she had spread her legs for him and now how fair and gentle she seemed.

In the middle of the bay Leander turned the boat toward Travertine. It was the worst of the trip, and he was worried. The following sea punished her stern. Her screw shook the hull at the crest of every wave and in the hollow she slipped to port. He set his bow on Gull Rock, which he could see clearly then, the gull droppings on top and the sea grass fanning out as the waves mounted and swallowed the granite pile. Beyond the channel he would be all right with nothing ahead of him but the run up the calm river to home. He put his mind on this. He could hear the deck chairs smashing against the stern rail and she had taken in so much water that she heeled. Then the rudder chain broke with the noise of a shot and he felt the power of the helm vanish into thin air beneath his hands.

There was a jury rudder in the stern. He thought quickly enough. He put her into half speed and stepped into the cabin.

Helen saw him, and she began to shriek. "He's a devil, he's a devil from hell that one there. He'll drown us. He's afraid of me. For eighteen weeks, nineteen on Monday, I've been out in all weathers. He's afraid of me. I have information in my possession that could put him into the electric chair. He'll drown us." It was not fear that stopped him, but a stunning memory of her mother's loveliness—the farm near Franconia and haying on a thundery day. He went back into the wheelhouse and a second later the *Topaze* rammed Gull Rock. Her bow caved in like an egg shell. Leander reached for the whistle cord and blew the distress signal.

They heard his whistle in what had been the parlor and was now the bar of the Mansion House and wondered what Leander was up to. He had always been prodigal with his whistle, tooting it for children's birthday parties and wedding anniversaries or at the sight of an old friend. It was one of the waiters in the kitchen—a stranger to the place—who recognized the distress signal and ran out onto the porch and gave the alarm. They heard him at the boat club and someone started up the old launch. As soon as Leander saw the boat leave the wharf he went back to the cabin, where most of the passengers were putting on life jackets, and told them the news. They sat quietly until the boat came alongside. He helped them aboard, including Spinet, including Helen, who was sobbing, and the boat chugged off.

He unscrewed the compass box from its stand and got his binoculars and a bottle of bourbon out of his locker. Then he went up to the bow to see the damage. The hole was a big one and the following sea was worrying her on the rocks. As he watched she began to ease off the rocks and he could feel the bow settle. He walked back toward the stern. He felt very tired—almost sleepy. His animal spirits seemed collapsed and his breathing, the beating of his heart, felt retarded. His eyes felt heavy. In the distance he saw a dory coming out to get him rowed by a young man—a stranger—and through this feeling of torpor or weariness he felt as if he watched the approach of someone of uncommon beauty—an angel, or a ghost of himself when he had been young and full of mettle. Tough luck, old-timer, the stranger said, and the illusion of ghosts and angels vanished.

Leander got into the dory. He watched the *Topaze* ease off the rocks and start up the channel herself with the sea pounding at her stern; and derelict and forsaken she seemed, like those inextinguishable legends of underwater civilizations and buried gold, to pierce the darkest side of his mind with an image of man's inestimable loneliness. She was heading through the channel, but she wouldn't make it. As each wave pushed her forward, she lost some buoyancy. Water was breaking over her bow. And then, with more grace than she had usually sailed, her stern upended—there was a loud clatter of deck chairs knocked helter-skelter along the sides of her cabin—and down went the *Topaze* to the bottom of the sea.

25

Leander wrote to both his sons. He did not know that Coverly was in the Pacific and it took three weeks for his letter to be forwarded to Island 93. Moses didn't get his father's letter at all. He was fired as a security risk ten days after Beatrice left for Cleveland. It was at a time when these dismissals were summary and unexplained and if there was some court of appeal Moses did not, at that time, have the patience or the common sense to seek it out. An hour after he had received his discharge he was driving north with all his possessions in the back of his car. The anonymity of his discharge gave it oracular proportions, as if some tree or stone or voice from a cave had put the finger on him, and the pain of being condemned or expelled by a veiled force may have accounted for his rage. He was far from the green pastures of common sense. He was angry at what had been done to him and angry at himself for having failed to come to reasonable terms with the world and he was deeply anxious about his parents, for if the news should get back to Honora that he had been discharged for reasons of security he knew they would suffer.

What he did was to go fishing. It may have been that he wanted to recapture the pleasures of his trips to Langely with Leander. Fishing was the only occupation he could think of that might refresh his common sense. He drove straight from Washington to a trout pond in the Poconos that he had visited before and where he was able to rent a cabin or shack that was as dilapidated as the camp at Langely. He ate some supper, drank a pint of whisky and went for a swim in the cold lake. All this made him feel better and he went to bed early, planning to get up before dawn and fish in the Lakanana River.

He was up at five and drove north to the river, as anxious to be the first fisherman out as Leander had been anxious to be the first man in the woods. The sky was just beginning to fill with light. He was disappointed and perplexed then when a car ahead of him turned off and parked on the road shoulder that led to the stream. Then the driver of the car ahead hurried out of his car and looked over his shoulder at Moses in such agony and panic that Moses wondered—so soon after dawn— if he had crossed the path of a murderer. Then the stranger unbuckled his belt, dropped his trousers and relieved himself in full view of the morning. Moses gathered up his tackle and smiled at the stranger, happy to see that he was not another trout fisherman. The stranger smiled at Moses for his own reasons; and he took the path to the water and didn't see another fisherman that day.

Lakanana Pond emptied into the river and the water, regulated by a dam, was deep and turbulent and in many places over a man's head. The sharp fall of the land and the granite bed of the stream made it a place where there was nowhere a respite from the loud noise of water. Moses caught one trout in the morning and two more late in the day. Here and there a bridle path from the Lakanana Inn ran parallel to the stream and a few riders hacked by but it was not until late in the day that any of them stopped to ask Moses what he had caught.

The sun by then was below the trees and the early dark seemed to deepen the resonance of the stream. It was time for Moses to go and he was taking in his line and putting away his flies when he heard the hoofs and the creaking leather of some riders. A middle-aged couple stopped to ask about his luck while he was pulling off his boots. It was the urbanity of the couple that struck Moses—they looked so terribly out of place. They were both of them heavy and gray-headed—the woman dumpy and the man choleric, short-winded and obese. It had been a warm day but they were dressed correctly in dark riding clothes—bowlers, sticks, tattersalls and so forth. All of this must have been very uncomfortable. "Well, good luck," the woman said in the cheerful, cracked voice of middle age, and turned her horse away from the stream. Out of the corner of his eye Moses saw the horse rear but by the time he turned his head so much dust had been raised by the scuffle of hoofs that he didn't see how she fell. He ran up the bank and got the fractious horse by the bridle as her husband began to roar: "Help, help. She's dead, she's dead, she's been killed." The horse reared again while Moses' hand was on the bridle. He let go and the hack galloped off. "I'll go for help, I'll go for help," the husband roared. "There's a farm back there." He cantered off to the north and the dust settled, leaving Moses with what seemed to be a dead stranger.

She was on her knees, face downward in the dirt, the tails of her coat parted over the broad, worn seat of her britches and her boots toed in like a child's, so stripped of her humanity, so defeated—Moses remembered the earnest notes of her voice—in her attempt to enjoy the early summer day, that he felt a flash of repugnance. Then he went to her and more out of consideration for his own feelings than anything else—more out of his desire to return to her the form of a woman than to save her life—he straightened out her legs and she rolled with a thump onto her back. He rolled up his coat and put it under her head. A cut in her forehead, over the eye, was bleeding and Moses got some water and washed the cut, pleased to be occupied. She was breathing, he noticed, but this exhausted his medical knowledge. He knelt beside her wondering in what form and when help would come. He lighted a cigarette and looked at the stranger's face—pasty and round and worn it seemed with such anxieties as cooking, catching trains and buying useful presents at Christmas. It was a face that seemed to state its history plainly—she was one of two sisters, she had no children, she could be inflexible about neatness and she probably collected glass animals or English coffee cups in a small way. Then he heard hoofs and leather and her bereaved husband bore down in a cloud of dust. "There's nobody at the farm. I've wasted so much time. She ought to be in an oxygen tent. She probably needs a blood transfusion. We've got to get an ambulance." Then he knelt down beside her and put his head on her breast, crying, "Oh my darling, my love, my sweet, don't leave me, don't leave me."

Then Moses ran up the path to his car and, driving it a little way through the woods, he got it onto the loose dirt of the bridle path where the man still knelt by his wife. Then, opening the door, they managed together to lift her into the car. He started back for the road, the wheels of the car spinning in the loose dirt, but he was able to keep it moving and was cheered when they got onto the black-top road. There were choking and grunting sounds of grief from the back seat. "She's dying, she's dying," the stranger sobbed. "If she lives I'll repay you. Money is no consideration. Please hurry."

"You know you both seem pretty old for horseback riding," Moses said.

He knew there was a hospital in the next village and he made good time until he got stuck, on the narrow road, behind a slow-moving truck loaded with live chickens. Moses blew his horn but this only made the truck driver more predatory and how could Moses communicate to him that the thread of a woman's life might depend on his consideration? He passed the truck at the crown of a hill but this only excited the driver's malevolence and, roaring downhill, his chicken crates swaying wildly from side to side, he tried, unsuccessfully, to repass Moses. They had come down at last into the leafy streets of the village and the road to the hospital. Many people were walking at the side of the road and then Moses saw signs nailed to the trees advertising a hospital lawn party. They were out of luck. The hospital was surrounded by the booths, lights and music of a country fair.

A policeman stopped them when they tried to approach the hospital and waved them toward a parking lot. "We want to get to the hospital," Moses shouted. The policeman leaned toward them. He was deaf. "We have a woman here who is dying," the stranger cried loudly. "This is a matter of life and death." Moses got past the policeman and through the fair, approaching a brick building, darkened by many shade trees. The place was shaped like a Victorian mansion and may have been one, modified now by fire escapes and a brick smokestack. Moses got out of the car and ran through an emergency entrance into a room that was empty. He went from there into a hall where he met a gray-haired nurse carrying a tray. "I have an emergency in my car," he said. There was no kindliness in her face. She gave him that appalling look of bitterness that we exchange when we are too tired, or too exacerbated by our own ill luck, to care whether our neighbors live or die. "What is the nature of the emergency?" she asked airily. Another nurse appeared. She was no younger but she was not so tired. "She was thrown by a horse, she's unconscious," Moses said. "Horses!" the old nurse exclaimed. "Dr. Howard has just come in," the second nurse said. "I'll get him now."

A few minutes later a doctor came down the hall with the second nurse and they wheeled a table out of the emergency room down a ramp to the car and Moses and the doctor lifted the unconscious woman onto this. They accomplished this in a summer twilight, surrounded by the voices of hawkers and the sounds of music that came from the fair beyond the trees. "Oh, can't somebody stop this?" the stranger asked, meaning the music. "I'm Charles Cutter. I'll pay any amount of money. Send them home. Send them home. I'll pay for it. Tell them to stop the music at least. She needs quiet."

"We couldn't do that," the doctor said quietly, and with a marked upcountry accent. "That's how we raise the money to keep the hospital running." In the hospital they began to cut off the woman's clothes and Moses went into the hallway, followed by her husband. "You'll stay, you'll stay a little while with me, won't you?" he asked Moses. "She's all I have and if she dies, if she dies I don't know what I'll do." Moses said that he would stay and wandered down the hall to an empty waiting room. A large, bronze plaque on the door said that the waiting room was the gift of Sarah P. Watkins and her sons and daughters, but it was difficult to see what the Watkins family had given. There were three pieces of imitation-leather furniture, a table and a collection of old magazines. Moses waited here until Mr. Cutter returned. "She's alive," he sobbed, "she's alive. Thank God. Her leg and her arm are broken and she has a concussion. I've called my secretary and asked them to send a specialist on from New York. They don't know whether she'll live or not. They won't know for twenty-four hours. Oh, she's such a lovely person. She's so kind and lovely."

"Your wife will be all right," Moses said.

"She isn't my wife," Mr. Cutter sobbed. "She's so kind and lovely. My wife isn't anything like that. We've had such hard times, both of us. We've never asked for very much. We haven't even been together very much. It couldn't be retribution, could it? It couldn't be retribution. We've never harmed anyone. We've taken these little trips each year. It's the only time we ever have together. It couldn't be retribution." He dried his tears and cleaned his spectacles and went back down the hall.

A young nurse came to the door, looking out at the carnival and the summer evening, and a doctor joined her.

"B2 thinks he's dying," the nurse said. "He wants a priest."

"I called Father Bevier," the doctor said. "He's out." He put a hand on the nurse's slender back and let it fall along her buttocks.

"Oh, I could use a little of that," the nurse said cheerfully.

"So could I," the doctor said.

He continued to stroke her buttocks and desire seemed to make the nurse plaintive and in a human way much finer and the doctor, who had looked very tired, seemed refreshed. Then, from the dark interior of the place, there was a wordless roar, a spitting grunt, extorted either by extreme physical misery or the collapse of reasonable hope. The doctor and the nurse separated and disappeared in the dark at the end of the hall. The grunt rose to a scream, a shriek, and to escape it Moses walked out of the building and crossed the grass to the edge of the lawn. He was on high land and his view took in the mountains, blackened then by an afterglow—a brilliant yellow that is seen in lower country only on the coldest nights of February.

In the trees on his left the fair or carnival had hit its gentle, countrified stride. An orchestra on a platform was playing "Smiles" and on the second chorus one of the players put down his instrument and sang a verse through a megaphone. Strings of lights—white and faded reds and yellows—were hung from booth to booth to light, with the faint candle power of these arrangements, the dark of the maples. The noise of voices was not loud and the men talking up hamburgers and fortune's wheel called with no real insistence. He walked over to a booth and bought a paper cup of coffee from a pretty country girl. When she had given him his change she moved the sugar bowl an inch this way and that, looked at the doughnut jar with a deep sigh and pulled at her apron. "You're a stranger?" she asked. He said that he was. The girl moved down the counter to wait on some other people who were complaining about the chilly mountain dusk.

In the next booth a young man was pitching baseballs at a pyramid of wooden milk bottles. His aim and his speed were superb. He stared at the milk bottles, drawing back a little and narrowing his eyes like a rifleman, and then winged a ball at them with the energy of sheer malevolence. Down they came, again and again, and a small crowd of girls and bucks gathered to watch the performance but when it was ended and the pitcher turned toward them they said so long, so long, Charlie, so long, and drifted away, arm in arm. He seemed to be friendless.

Beyond the baseball pitcher there was a booth selling flowers that had been picked in the village gardens and there were wheels and a bingo game and the wooden stand where the musicians continued without a break their selection of dance music. Moses was surprised to find them so old. The pianist was old, the saxophone player was bent and gray and the drummer must have weighed three hundred pounds, and they seemed attached to their instruments by the rites, conveniences and habits of a long marriage.

When they had finished their last set a man announced some local talent and Moses saw a child, at the edge of the platform, waiting to go on. She seemed to be a child but when the band played her fanfare she lifted up her hands, shuffled into the light and began a laborious tap dance, counting time painfully and throwing out to the audience, now and then, a leering smile. The taps on her silver shoes made a metallic clang and shook the lumber of the platform and she seemed to have left her youth in the shadows. Powdered, rouged, absorbed in the mechanics of her dance and the enjoinder to seem flirtatious, her freshness was gone and all the bitterness and disappointments of a lascivious middle age seemed to sit on her thin shoulders. At the end she bowed to the little applause, smiled her tart smile once more and ran into the shadows where her mother was waiting with a coat to put over her shoulders and a few words of encouragement and when she stepped back into the shadows Moses saw that she was no more than twelve or thirteen.

He threw his paper cup into a can, and finishing his circuit of the carnival saw, walking through the deep grass smell and the summer gloom, a group, a family perhaps, in which there was a woman wearing a yellow skirt. The color of the skirt set up in him a yearning, a pang that put his teeth on edge, and he remembered that he had once loved a girl who had a skirt of the same color although he could not remember her name.

"I want a specialist, a brain specialist," Moses heard his friend shouting when he returned to the hospital. "Charter a plane if it's necessary. Money is no consideration. If he wants a consultant, tell him to bring a consultant. Yes. Yes." He was using a telephone in an office across the hall from the waiting room that had been given by the Watkins family and where it had grown dark without anyone's bothering to turn on a lamp. Only a few lights seemed to burn in the hospital at all. The bereaved and elderly lover sat among covered typewriters and adding machines and when he had finished his conversation he looked up to Moses and either because the light caught his spectacles or because his mood had changed, he seemed very officious. "I want you to consider yourself on my payroll as of this morning," he said to Moses. "If you have other engagements to fulfill you can cancel them, confident that I will more than make this worth your while. The hospital has given me a room for the night and I want you to go back to the inn and get my toilet articles. I've made out a list," he said, passing such a list to Moses. "Estimate your mileage and keep track of the time and I will see that you are amply reimbursed." Then he picked up the telephone and asked for long distance and Moses stepped out into the dark hall.

He had nothing better to do and he was glad to drive back to the inn, not so much from a commendable sense of charity and helpfulness as from his desire to draw into a sensible perspective the events of the last few hours. Back at the inn he gave the manager—like a true Wapshot—the most meager account of what had happened. "She was in an accident," he said. He went upstairs to the room that had been occupied by poor Mr. Cutter and his paramour. All the things on the list were easy to find—everything but a bottle of rye but after looking in the medicine cabinet and behind the books in the shelves he looked under the bed and found a well-stocked bar. He had a drink

of Scotch himself in a toothbrush glass. Back at the hospital
Mr. Cutter was still on the telephone. He put his hand over
the mouthpiece. "Now you get some sleep, my boy," he said
mingling paternalism and officiousness. "If you don't have a
place, go back to the inn and ask them to give you a room.
Report back here at nine o'clock. Remember that money is no
consideration. You're on my payroll." Moses went back to the
bridle path to get his fishing tackle, which he found unharmed
except for a fall of dew, and spent the night in his rented shack.

26

The next day at dusk, Mr. Cutter's paramour regained consciousness, and in the morning Moses arranged to have his car driven
to New York and flew to the city with Mr. Cutter and the patient
in a chartered ambulance plane. He was not quite sure where
he stood on Mr. Cutter's payroll, but he had nothing better to
do. He went to Coverly's address as soon as he got to New
York, not knowing that his brother was on Island 93. Betsey
was there and he took her out to dinner. She was not the girl
he would have married, but he found her likable enough. A
day or so later he had an interview with Mr. Cutter and a few
days later he was enrolled in the Fiduciary Trust Company Bond
School at a better salary than he had received in Washington
and with a more brilliant future. The letter Leander wrote to
him in Washington lay on the hall floor of his apartment and
it went like this:

"Slight mishap to Topaze on 30th. All hands removed with
dry feet. Sank in channel and was removed as navigational hazard
by Coast Guard on Tues. Beached and patched at Mansion
House. She's at your mooring now (Tern's) and has been at
same since mishap. Afloat but not seaworthy. Beecher estimates
cost of repairs at $400. Till empty here and Honora very unco-

operative. Can you help? Please try my son and see what you can do. These are d—d difficult days for your old father.

"Topaze gone, how will I fare? Geezer as old as me begins to cherish his time on this earth but with Topaze gone days pass without purpose, meaning, color, form, appetite, glory, squalor, regret, desire, pleasure or pain. Dusk. Dawn. All the same. Feel hopeful sometimes in early morning but soon discouraged. Sole excitement is to listen to horse races on radio. If I had a stake could quickly recoup price to repair Topaze. Lack even small sum for respectable bet.

"Was generous giver myself. On several occasions gave large sums to needy strangers. One-hundred-dollar bill to cab starter at Parker House. Fifty dollars to old lady selling lavender at Park Street Church. Eighty dollars to stranger in restaurant who claimed son needed operation. Other donations forgotten. Cast bread upon waters, so to speak. No refund as of today. Tasteless to remind you but never spared the horses with family. Extra suit of sail for Tern. Three hundred dollars for dahlia bulbs. English shoes, mushrooms, hothouse posies, boat club dues and groaning board consumed much of windward anchor.

"Try to help old father if within means. If not, feel out acquaintances. There is one easy spender in every group of men. Sometimes gambler. Topaze good investment. Has shown substantial profit for every season, but one. Grand business expected in Nangasakit this year. Good chance of returning loan by August. Regret handkerchief tone of letter. Laugh and the world laughs with you. Weep and you weep alone."

The mooring that Leander mentioned was a mushroom anchor and chain in the river at the foot of the garden, and the old launch could be seen from there. Mrs. Wapshot stared at the *Topaze* one afternoon when she was picking sage. She felt a stirring in her mind and her body that might mean that she was going to have a vision. Now in fact so many of Mrs. Wapshot's imaginings had come true that she was entitled to call them visions. Years and years ago, when she was walking by Christ

Church, some force of otherness seemed to stop her by the vacant lot that adjoined the church and she had a vision of a parish house—red brick with small-paned casement windows and a neat lawn. She had begun her agitation for a parish house that afternoon and a year and a half later her vision—brick for brick—was a reality. She had dreamed up horse troughs, good works and pleasant journeys to have them materialize oftener than not. Now, coming back from the garden with a bouquet of sage, she looked down the path to the river where the *Topaze* lay at her mooring.

It was a gray afternoon along the coast, but not an unexciting one—there might be a storm, and the prospect seemed to please her, as if she held on her tongue, like a peppercorn, the flavor of the old port and the stormy dusk. The air was salty and she could hear the sea breaking at Travertine. The *Topaze* was dark, of course, dark and she seemed unsalvageable in that light— one of those hulks that we see moored by coal yards in city rivers, kept afloat through some misguided tenderness or hope, wearing sometimes a For Sale sign and sometimes the last habitation of some crazy old hermit whose lair is pasted up with pearly-skinned and spread-legged beauties and whose teeth are pulled. The first thing that crossed her mind when she saw the dark and empty ship was that she would not sail again. She would not cross the bay again. Then Mrs. Wapshot had her vision. She saw the ship berthed at the garden wharf, her hull shining with fresh paint and her cabin full of light. She saw, by turning her head, a dozen or more cars parked in the cornfield. She even saw that some of them had out-of-state license plates. She saw a sign nailed to the elm by the path: VISIT THE S. S. TOPAZE, THE ONLY FLOATING GIFT SHOPPE IN NEW ENGLAND. In her mind she took the path down the garden and crossed the wharf to board the ship. Her cabin was all new paint (the life preservers were gone), and lamps burned on many small tables, illuminating a cargo of ash trays, cigarette lighters, playing-card cases, wire arrangements for holding flowers, vases, embroidery, hand-painted drinking glasses and cigarette boxes that played "Tales from the Vienna Woods" when you opened them. Her vision was in detail and splendidly lighted and warm as well, for she saw a Franklin stove at one end of the cabin with a fire in the grate and the perfume of wood smoke mingled with the smell of sachets, Japanese linen and here and there the smell of tallow from a lighted candle. The S. S. *Topaze,* she thought again, The Only Floating Gift Shoppe in New England, and then she let the stormy dusk reclaim the dark ship and went very happily into the house.

27

Leander did not understand why Theophilus Gates would not lend him enough money to have the bow of the *Topaze* repaired while he would loan Sarah all the money she wanted to turn the old launch into a floating gift shop. That is what happened. The day after her vision Sarah went to the bank and the day after that the carpenters came and began to repair the wharf. The salesmen began to arrive—three and four a day—and Sarah began to stock the *Topaze,* spending money, as she said herself, like an inebriated sailor. Her happiness or rapture was genuine although it was hard to see why she should find such joy in a gross of china dogs with flowers painted on their backs, their paws shaped in such a way that they could hold cigarettes. There may have been some vengefulness in her enthusiasm—some deep means of expressing her feelings about the independence and the sainthood of her sex. She had never been so happy. She had signs painted: VISIT THE S. S. TOPAZE, THE ONLY FLOATING GIFT SHOPPE IN NEW ENGLAND, and posted at all the roads leading into the village. She planned to open the *Topaze* with a gala tea and a sale of Italian pottery. Hundreds of invitations were printed and mailed.

Leander made a nuisance of himself. He broke wind in the

parlor and urinated against an apple tree in full view of the boats on the river and the salesmen of Italian pottery. He claimed to be aging swiftly and pointed out how loudly his bones creaked when he stooped to pick a thread off a carpet. Tears streamed capriciously from his eyes whenever he heard a horse race on the radio. He still shaved and bathed each morning, but he smelled more like Neptune than ever and clumps of hair grew out of his ears and nostrils before he could remember to clip them. His neckties were stained with food and cigarette ash, and yet, when the night winds woke him and he lay in bed and traced their course around the dark compass, he still remembered what it was to feel young and strong. Deluded by this thread of cold air he would rise in his bed thinking passionately of boats, trains and deep-breasted women, or of some image—a wet pavement plastered with yellow elm leaves—that seemed to represent requital and strength. I will climb the mountain, he thought. I will kill the tiger! I will crush the serpent with my heel! But the fresh winds died with the morning dusk. There was a pain in his kidney. He could not get back to sleep and he would limp and cough through another day. His sons did not write him.

On the day before the *Topaze* opened as a gift shop, Leander paid a call on Honora. They sat in her parlor.

"Would you like some whisky?" Honora asked.

"Yes, please," Leander said.

"There isn't any," Honora said. "Have a cookie."

Leander glanced down at the plate of cookies and saw they were covered with ants. "I'm afraid ants have gotten into your cookies, Honora," he said.

"That's ridiculous," Honora said. "I know you have ants at the farm, but I've never had ants in this house." She picked up a cookie and ate it, ants and all.

"Are you going to Sarah's tea?" Leander asked.

"I don't have time to spend in gift shops," Honora said. "I'm taking piano lessons."

"I thought you were taking painting lessons," Leander said.

"Painting!" Honora said scornfully. "Why, I gave up my painting in the spring. The Hammers were in some financial difficulty so I bought this piano from them and now Mrs. Hammer comes and gives me a lesson twice a week. It's very easy."

"Perhaps it runs in the family," Leander said. "Remember Justina?"

"Justina who?" Honora asked.

"Justina Molesworth," Leander said.

"Why, of course I remember Justina," Honora said. "Why shouldn't I?"

"I meant that she played the piano in the five and ten," Leander said.

"Well, I have no intention of playing the piano in the five and ten," Honora said. "Feel that refreshing breeze," she said.

"Yes," Leander said. (There was no breeze at all.)

"Sit in the other chair," she said.

"I'm quite comfortable here, thank you," Leander said.

"Sit in the other chair," Honora said. "I've just had it reupholstered. Although," she said as Leander obediently changed from one chair to the other, "you won't be able to see out of the window from there and perhaps you were better off where you were."

Leander smiled, remembering that to talk with her, even when she was a young woman, had made him feel bludgeoned. He wondered what her reasons were. Lorenzo had written somewhere in his journal that if you met the devil you should cut him in two and go between the pieces. It would describe Honora's manner although he wondered if it wasn't the fear of death that had determined her crabwise progress through life. It could have been that by side-stepping those things that, through their force—love, incontinence and peace of mind—throw into our faces the facts of our mortality she might have uncovered the mystery of a spirited old age.

"Will you do me a favor, Honora?" he asked.

"I won't go to Sarah's tea if that's what you want," she said. "I've told you I have a music lesson."

"It isn't that," Leander said. "It's something else. When I die I want Prospero's speech said over my grave."

"What speech is that?" Honora asked.

"Our revels now are ended," Leander said, rising from his chair. "These our actors, as I foretold you, were all spirits and are melted into air, into thin air." He declaimed, and his declamatory style was modeled partly on the Shakespeareans of his youth, partly on the bombast and singsong of prize-ring announcements and partly on the style of the vanished horsecar and trolley-car conductors who had made an incantation of the place names along their routes. His voice soared and he illustrated the poetry with some very literal gestures. ". . . and, like the baseless fabric of this vision, the cloud-capped towers, the gorgeous palaces, the solemn temples, the great globe itself, yea, all which it inherit, shall dissolve, and, like this insubstantial pageant faded, leave not a rack behind." He dropped his hands. His voice fell. "We are such stuff as dreams are made on, and our little life is rounded with a sleep." Then he said good-by and went.

Early the next morning Leander saw that there would be no sanctuary or peace for him in the farm that day. The stir of a large ladies' party—magnified by the sale of Italian pottery— was inescapable. He decided to visit his friend Grimes, who was living in an old people's home in West Chillum. It was a trip he had planned to make for years. He walked into St. Botolphs after breakfast and caught the bus to West Chillum there. It was on the other side of Chillum that the bus driver told him they had reached the Twilight Home and Leander got off. The place from the road looked to him like one of the New England academies. There was a granite wall, set with sharp pieces of stone to keep vagrants from resting. The drive was shaded with elms, and the buildings it served were made of red brick along architectural lines that, whatever had been intended when they were built, now seemed very gloomy. Along the driveway Leander saw old men hoeing the gutters. He entered the central building and went to an office, where a woman asked what he wanted.

"I want to see Mr. Grimes."

"Visitors aren't allowed on weekdays," the woman said.

"I've just come all the way from St. Botolphs," Leander said.

"He's in the north dormitory," she said. "Don't tell anyone I said you could go in. Go up those stairs."

Leander walked down the hall and up some broad wooden stairs. The dormitory was a large room with a double row of iron beds down each side of a center aisle. Old men were lying on fewer than half the beds. Leander recognized his old friend and went over to the bed where he was lying.

"Grimes," he said.

"Who is it?" The old man opened his eyes.

"Leander. Leander Wapshot."

"Oh Leander," Grimes cried and the tears streamed down his cheeks. "Leander, old sport. You're the first friend to come and see me since Christmas." He embraced Leander. "You don't know what it's like for me to see a friendly face. You don't know what it's like."

"Well, I thought I'd pay you a little call," Leander said. "I meant to come a long time ago. Somebody told me you had a pool table out here so I thought I'd come out and play you a little pool."

"We have a pool table," Grimes said. "Come on, come on, I'll show you the pool table." He seized Leander's arm and led him out of the dormitory. "We've got all kinds of recreation," he said excitedly. "At Christmas they sent us a lot of gramophone records. We have gardens. We get plenty of fresh air and exercise. We work in the gardens. Don't you want to see the gardens?"

"Anything you say, Grimes," Leander said unwillingly. He did not want to see the gardens or much more of the Twilight Home. If he could sit quietly for an hour somewhere and talk with Grimes he would feel repaid for the trip.

"We grow all our own vegetables," Grimes said. "We have fresh vegetables right out of the garden. I'll show you the garden first. Then we'll play a little pool. The pool table isn't in very good shape. I'll show you the gardens. Come on. Come on."

They left the central buildings by a back door and crossed to the gardens. They looked to Leander like the rigid and depressing produce gardens of a reformatory. "See," Grimes said. "Peas. Carrots. Beets. Spinach. We'll have corn soon. We sell corn. We may grow some of the corn you eat at your table, Leander." He had led Leander into a field of corn that was just beginning to silk. "We have to be quiet now," he said in a whisper. They went through the corn to the edge of the garden and climbed a stone wall marked with a No Trespassing sign and went into some scrub woods. They came in a minute to a clearing where there was a shallow trench dug in the clay.

"See it?" Grimes whispered. "See it? Not everybody knows about it. That's potter's field. That's where they bury us. These two men got sick last month. Charlie Dobbs and Henry Fosse. They both died one night. I had an idea what they were doing then but I wanted to make sure. I came out here that morning and I hid in the woods. Sure enough, about ten o'clock this fat fellow comes along with a wheelbarrow. He's got Charlie Dobbs and Henry Fosse in it. Stark naked. Dumped on top of one another. Upside down. They didn't like each other, Leander. They never even spoke to one another. But he buried them together. Oh, I couldn't look. I couldn't watch it. I've never felt right after that. If I die in the night they'll dump me naked into a hole side by side with somebody I never knew. Go back and tell them, Leander. Tell them at the newspapers. You were always a good talker. Go back and tell them. . . ."

"Yes, yes," Leander said. He was backing through the woods, away from the clearing and his hysterical friend. They climbed the stone wall and walked through the corn patch. Grimes gripped Leander's arm. "Go back and tell them, tell them at the newspapers. Save me, Leander. Save me. . . ."

"Yes, I will, Grimes, yes, I will."

Side by side the old men returned through the garden and Leander said good-by to Grimes in front of the central building. Then he went down the driveway, obliged to struggle to give the impression that he was not hurried. He was relieved when he got outside the gates. It was a long time before the bus came along and when one did appear he shouted, "Hello there. Stop, stop, stop for me."

He could not help Grimes; he could not, he realized when the bus approached St. Botolphs and he saw a sign, VISIT THE S.S. TOPAZE, THE ONLY FLOATING GIFT SHOPPE IN NEW ENGLAND, help himself. He hoped that the tea party would be over but when he approached the farm he found many cars parked on the lawn and the sides of the driveway. He swung wide around the house and went in at the back door and up the stairs to his room. It was late then and from his window he could see the *Topaze*—the twinkling of candles—and hear the voices of ladies drinking tea. The sight made him feel that he was being made ridiculous; that a public spectacle was being made of his mistakes and his misfortunes. He remembered his father then with tenderness and fear as if he had dreaded, all along, some end like Aaron's. He guessed the ladies would talk about him and he only had to listen at the window to hear. "He drove her onto Gull Rock in broad daylight," Mrs. Gates said as she went down the path to the wharf. "Theophilus thinks he was drunk."

What a tender thing, then, is a man. How, for all his crotch-hitching and swagger, a whisper can turn his soul into a cinder. The taste of alum in the rind of a grape, the smell of the sea, the heat of the spring sun, berries bitter and sweet, a grain of sand in his teeth—all of that which he meant by life seemed taken away from him. Where were the serene twilights of his old age? He would have liked to pluck out his eyes. Watching the candlelight on his ship—he had brought her home through gales and tempests—he felt ghostly and emasculated. Then he went to his bureau drawer and took from under the dried rose and the wreath of hair his loaded pistol. He went to the window.

The fires of the day were burning out like a conflagration in some industrial city and above the barn cupola he saw the evening star, as sweet and round as a human tear. He fired his pistol out of the window and then fell down on the floor.

He had underestimated the noise of teacups and ladies' voices and no one on the *Topaze* heard the shot—only Lulu, who was in the kitchen, getting some hot water. She climbed the back stairs and hurried down the hall to his room and screamed when she opened the door. When he heard her voice Leander got to his knees. "Oh, Lulu, Lulu, you weren't the one I wanted to hurt. I didn't mean you. I didn't mean to frighten you."

"Are you all right, Leander? Are you hurt?"

"I'm foolish," Leander said.

"Oh, poor Leander," Lulu said, helping him to his feet. "Poor soul. I told her she shouldn't have done it. I told her in the kitchen many times that it would hurt your feelings, but she wouldn't listen."

"I only want to be esteemed," Leander said.

"Poor soul," Lulu said. "You poor soul."

"You won't tell anyone what you saw," Leander said.

"No."

"You promise me."

"I promise."

"Swear that you won't tell anyone what you saw."

"I swear."

"Swear on the Bible. Let me find the Bible. Where's my Bible? Where's my old Bible?" Then he searched the room wildly, lifting up and putting down books and papers and throwing open drawers and looking into book shelves and chests, but he couldn't find the Bible. There was a little American flag stuck into the mirror above his bureau and he took this and held it out to Lulu. "Swear on the flag, Lulu, swear on the American flag that you won't tell anyone what you saw."

"I swear."

"I only want to be esteemed."

28

Although the administration of Island 93 was half military and half civilian, the military, having charge of transportation, communication and provisions, often dominated the civilian administrators. So Coverly was called to the military communications office one early evening and handed a copy of a cable that had been sent by Lulu Breckenridge. YOUR FATHER IS DYING. "Sorry, fellow," the officer said. "You can go to communications but I don't think they'll do anything for you. You're signed up for nine months." Coverly dropped the cable into the wastebasket and walked out of the office.

It was after supper and the latrines were being fired and the smoke rose up through the coconut palms. In another twenty minutes the movies would begin. When Coverly had gone a little way beyond the building he began to cry. He sat down by the road. The light was changing and the light goes quickly in the islands and it was that hour when the primitive domesticity of a colony of men without women begins to assert itself: the washing, letter-writing and the handicrafts with which men preserve some reason and dignity. No one noticed Coverly because there was nothing unusual in a man sitting by the side of the road and no one could see he was crying. He wanted to see Leander and cried to think that all their plans had taken him to the flimflam of a tropical island a little while before the movies began while his father was dying in St. Botolphs. He would never see Leander again. Then he decided to try to go home and dried his tears and walked to the transportations office. There was a young officer there who seemed, in spite of Coverly's civilian clothes, disappointed not to have him salute. "I want some emergency transportation," Coverly said.

"What's the nature of the emergency?" Coverly noticed that the officer had a tic in his right cheek.

"My father is dying."

"Have you any proof of this?"

"There's a cable at communications."

"What do you do?" the officer asked.

"I'm one of the Tapers," Coverly said.

"Well, you might get excused from work for a week. I'm sure you can't get any emergency transportation. The major's at the club but I know he won't help you. Why don't you go and see the chaplain?"

"I'll go and see the chaplain," Coverly said.

It was dark then and the movies had begun and all the stars hung in the soft dark. The chapel was about a quarter of a mile from the offices and when he got there he could see a blue gasoline lamp above the door and behind the lamp a large sign that said WELCOME. The building was a considerable tribute to human ingenuity. Bamboo had been lashed into a scaffolding and this was covered with palm matting—all of it holding to the conventional lines of a country church. There was even a steeple made of palm matting and there was an air of conspicuous unpopularity about the place. The doorway was plastered with WELCOME signs and so was the interior and on a table near the door were free stationery, moldy magazines and an invitation for rest, recreation and prayer.

The chaplain, a first lieutenant named Lindstrom, was there, writing a letter. He wore steel-rimmed GI spectacles on a weak and homely face, and he was a man who belonged to the small places of the earth—to little towns with their innocence, their bigotry and their devilish gossip—and he seemed to have brought, intact to the atoll, the smell of drying linen on a March morning and the self-righteous and bitter piety with which he would thank God, at Sunday dinner, for a can of salmon and a bottle of lemonade. He invited Coverly to sit down and offered him some stationery and Coverly said he needed help.

"I don't remember your face," Lindstrom said, "so I guess

you're not a member of my congregation. I never forget a face. I don't see why the men don't come here and worship. I think I have one of the nicest chapels in the West Pacific and last Sunday I only had five men at the service. I'm trying to see if I can't get one of the photographers to come down from headquarters and take a picture of the place. I think there ought to be a photograph of this chapel in *Life* magazine. I have to share it with Father O'Leary, but he didn't give me much help when there was work involved. He didn't seem to care where his men worshiped. He's over to the officers' mess, playing poker right now. It's none of my business how he spends his time but I don't think a minister of the gospel ought to play cards. I've never held a playing card in my hand. Of course it's none of my business, but I don't approve of the methods he uses to get his congregation together, either. He had twenty-eight men here last Sunday. I counted them. But you know how he did it? There was a whisky ration last Saturday and he went down and pulled the men out of line and made them come to confession. No confession, no whisky. Anybody could fill up a church if they did things like that. I put out the stationery and the magazines and I painted the Welcome signs myself and whenever my wife sends me cookies—my wife bakes oatmeal cookies; she could make a fortune if she wanted to open a bakery—now when my wife sends me cookies I put them in a dish out here but that's as far as I'll go."

"I want some emergency transportation," Coverly said. "I want to go home. My father's dying."

"Oh, I'm sorry, my boy," Lindstrom said. "I'm very sorry. I can't get you emergency transportation. I don't know why they send people to me. I don't know why they do this. You can go and see the major. A man got some emergency transportation last month. At least that's what I heard. You go to the major and I'll pray for you."

The major was playing poker and drinking whisky at the officers' club and he left the card table gruffly, but he was an amiable or sentimental drinker, and when Coverly said that his father was dying he put an arm around his shoulder, walked him over to the transportation office and got a clerk out of the movies to cut his orders.

He left before dawn in an old DC-4, covered with oil and with a picture of a bathing beauty painted on its fuselage. He slept on the floor. They got to Oahu in the disorder of a hot summer dusk with more lightning playing in the mountains. He left for San Francisco in a transport at eleven the next night. There was a crap game and the uninsulated plane was very cold and Coverly sat in a bucket seat, wrapped in a blanket. The drone of the motors reminded him of the *Topaze* and he fell asleep. When he woke the sky was a rosy color and the flight clerk was passing out oranges and saying that he could smell the land wind. A solid cloud ceiling broke as they neared the coast and they could see the burned summer hills of San Francisco. A few hours after clearing military customs Coverly hitched a ride on a bomber to Washington and went from there to St. Botolphs on the train. He took a taxi from the station out to the farm in the middle of the morning and saw, for the first time, the signs on the main road on the elm tree, VISIT THE S.S. TOPAZE, THE ONLY FLOATING GIFT SHOPPE IN NEW ENGLAND. He got out of the cab and looking around he saw his father, searching for four-leaf clovers in the meadow by the river, and he ran to him. "Oh, I knew you'd come, Coverly," Leander called. "I knew that you or Moses would come," and he embraced his son and laid his head on his shoulder.

Part Three

29

At the turn of the century there were more castles in the United States than there were in all of Merrie England when Gude King Arthur ruled that land. The search for a wife took Moses to one of the last of these establishments to be maintained—the bulk of them had been turned into museums, bought by religious orders or demolished. This was a place called Clear Haven, the demesne of Justina Wapshot Molesworth Scaddon, an ancient cousin from St. Botolphs who had married a five-and-ten-cent-store millionaire. Moses had met her at a cotillion or dance that he had gone to with a classmate from Bond School and through her had met her ward, Melissa. Melissa seemed to Moses, the instant he saw her, to be, by his lights, a most desirable and beautiful woman. He courted her and when they became lovers he asked her to marry him. So far as he knew, this sudden decision had nothing to do with the conditions of Honora's will. Melissa agreed to marry him if he would live at Clear Haven. He had no objections. The place—whatever it was—would shelter them for the summer and he felt sure that he could prevail on her to move into the city in the fall. So one rainy afternoon he took a train to Clear Haven, planning to love Melissa Scaddon and to marry her.

The conservative sumptuary tastes that Moses had formed in St. Botolphs had turned out to coincide with the sumptuary tastes of New York banking, and under his dun-colored raincoat Moses wore the odd, drab clothes of that old port. It was nearly dark when he set out, and the journey through the northern slums, and the rainfall catching and returning like a net the smoke and filth of the city, made him somber and restive. The train that he took ran up the banks of the river and, sitting on the land side of the car, he watched a landscape that in the multitude of its anomalies would have prepared him for Clear Haven if he had needed any preparation, for nothing was any more what it had aimed to be or what it would be in the end and the house that had meant to express familial pride was now a funeral parlor, the house that had meant to express worldly pride was a rooming house, Ursuline nuns lived in the castle that was meant to express the pride of avarice, but through this erosion of purpose Moses thought he saw everywhere the impress of human sweetness and ingenuity. The train was a local and the old rolling stock creaked from station to station, although at some distance from the city the stops were infrequent and he saw now and then from the window those huddled families who wait on the platform for a train or a passenger and who are made by the pallid lights, the rain and their attitudes to seem to be drawn together by some sad and urgent business. Only two passengers remained in the car when they reached Clear Haven and he was the only one to leave the train.

The rain was dense then, the night was dark and he went into a waiting room that held his attention for a minute for there was a large photograph on the wall, framed in oak, of his destination. Flags flew from the many towers of Clear Haven, the buttresses were thick with ivy and considering what he went there for it seemed far from ridiculous. Justina seemed to have had a hand in the waiting room for there was a rug on the floor. The matchboard walls were stained the color of mahogany and the pipes that must heat the place in winter rose gracefully, two by two, to disappear like serpents into holes in the ceiling. The benches around the walls were divided at regular intervals with graceful loops of bent wood that would serve the travelers as arm rests and keep the warm hams of strangers from touching one another. Stepping out of the waiting room he found a single cab at the curb. "I'll take you up to the gates," the driver said. "I can't take you up to the house but I'll leave you at the gates."

The gates, Moses saw when he got out of the taxi, were made of iron and were secured with a chain and padlock. There was a smaller gate on the left and he went in there and walked through the heavy rain to the lights of what he guessed was a gatehouse or cottage. A middle-aged man came to the door—he was eating—and seemed delighted when Moses gave his name. "I'ma Giacomo," he said. "I'ma Giacomo. You comea with me." Moses followed him into an old garage, rank with the particular damp of cold concrete that goes so swiftly to the bone. There, in the glare, stood an old Rolls-Royce with a crescent-windowed tonneau like the privy at West Farm. Moses got into the front while Giacomo began to work the fuel pump and it took him some time to get the car started. "She'sa nearly dead," Giacomo said. "She'sa no good for night driving." Then they backed like a warship out into the rain. There were no windshield wipers or Giacomo did not use them and they traveled without headlights up a winding drive. Then suddenly Moses saw the lights of Clear Haven. There seemed to be hundreds of them—they were so numerous that they lighted the road and lifted his spirits. Moses thanked Giacomo and carried his suitcase through the rain to the shelter of a big porch that was carved and ribbed like the porch of a cathedral. The only bell he saw to ring was a contraption of wrought-iron leaves and roses, so fanciful and old that he was afraid it might come down on his head if he used it, and he pounded on the door with his fist. A maid let him in and he stepped into a kind of rotunda and at the same time Melissa appeared in another door. He put down his bag, let the rain run out of the brim of his hat and gathered his beloved up in his arms.

His clothes were wet and a little rancid as well. "I suppose you could change," Melissa said, "but there isn't much time. . . ." He recognized in her look of mingled anxiety and pleasure the suspense of someone who introduces one part of life into another, feeling insecurely that they may clash and involve a choice or a parting. He felt her suspense as she took his arm and led him across a floor where their footsteps rang on the black-and-white marble. It was unlike Moses, but to tell the truth he looked neither to the left where he heard the sounds of a fountain nor to the right where he smelled the sweet earth of a conservatory, feeling, like Cousin Honora, that to pretend to have been born and bred in whatever environment one found oneself was a mark of character.

He was in a sense right in resisting his curiosity, for Clear Haven had been put together for the purpose of impressing strangers. No one had ever counted the rooms—no one, that is, but a vulgar and ambitious cousin who had spent one rainy afternoon this way, feeling that splendor could be conveyed in numbers. She had come up with the sum of ninety-two but no one knew whether or not she had counted the maid's rooms, the bathrooms and the odd, unused rooms, some of them without windows, that had been created by the numerous additions to the place, for the house had grown, reflecting the stubborn and eccentric turns of Justina's mind. When she had bought the great hall from the Villa Peschere in Milan she had cabled the architect, telling him to attach it to the small library. She would not have bought the hall if she had known that she would be offered the drawing room from the Château de la Muette a week later, and she wrote the architect asking him to attach this to the little dining room and advising him that she had bought four marble fountains representing the four seasons. Then the architect wrote saying that the fountains had arrived and that since there was no room for them in the house would she approve his plans for a winter garden to be attached to the hall from Milan? She cabled back her approval and bought that afternoon a small chapel that could be attached to the painted room that Mr. Scaddon had given her on her birthday. People often said that she bought more rooms than she knew how to use; but she used them all. She was not one of those collectors who let their prizes rot in warehouses. On the same trip she had picked up a marble floor and some columns in Vincenzo but the most impressive addition to Clear Haven that she was able to find on that or any of her later trips were the stones and timbers of the great

Windsor Hall. It was to this expatriated hall now that Melissa took Moses.

Justina sat by the fire, drinking sherry. She was, by Leander's reckoning, about seventy-five then, but her hair and her eyebrows were ink black and her face, framed in spit curls, was heavily rouged. Her eyes were glassy and shrewd. Her hair was raised off her forehead in a high construction, plainly old-fashioned and reminding Moses of the false front on the Cartwright Block in St. Botolphs. It was the same period. But she reminded him mostly of what she had been—a foxy old dancing mistress.

She greeted Moses with marked disinterest but this was not surprising in a woman whose distrust of men was even more outspoken than Cousin Honora's. Her dress was rich and simple and her imperious and hoarse voice ranged over a complete octave of requited social ambitions. "The Count D'Alba, General Burgoyne and Mrs. Enderby," she said, introducing Moses to the others in the room. The count was a tall, dark-skinned man with cavernous and hairy nostrils. The general was an old man in a wheel chair. Mrs. Enderby wore a pince-nez, the lozenge-shaped lenses of which hung so limply from the bridge of her nose that they gave her a very dropsical look. Her fingers were stained with ink. Melissa and Moses went to some chairs by the fire but these were so outrageously proportioned that Moses had to boost himself up and found, when he was seated, that his legs did not reach the floor. A maid passed him a glass of sherry and a dish in which there were a few old peanuts. The sherry was not fit to drink and when he tasted it Melissa smiled at him and he remembered her accounts of Justina's parsimony and wished he had brought some whisky in his suitcase. Then a maid stood in a distant doorway and rang some chimes and they went down a hall into a room that was lighted with candles.

The dinner was a cup of soup, a boiled potato, a scrap of fish and some kind of custard, and the conversation, that was meant to move at Justina's dictates, suffered from the fact that she seemed either tired, absent-minded or annoyed by Moses' arrival. When the general spoke to her about the illness of a friend she expressed her fixed idea about the perfidiousness of men. It was her opinion that the husband of her friend was responsible for the illness. Unmarried women—she said—were much healthier than wives. When the meal was finished they returned to the hall. Moses was still hungry and he hoped that there was some breakdown in the kitchen arrangements and that if he did live at Clear Haven he would not be expected to get along on such meager fare. Justina played backgammon with the general and the count sat down at the piano and started a medley of that lachrymose music that is played for cocktails and that is so limpid in its amorousness, so supine and wistful in its statement of passion that it will offend the ears of a man in love. Suddenly all the lights went out.

"The main fuse is gone again," Justina said, rolling her dice in the firelight.

"Can I fix it?" Moses asked, anxious to make a good impression.

"I don't know," Justina said. "There are plenty of fuses."

Melissa lighted a candle and Moses followed her down a hall. They could hear a babble of voices from the kitchen where the servants were striking matches and looking for candles. She opened a door into a further corridor and started down a steep flight of worn, wooden stairs into a cellar that smelled of earth. They found the fuse box and Moses changed the old fuse for a new one, although he noticed that the wiring was in some cases bare or carelessly patched with friction tape. Melissa blew out her candle and they returned to the hall, where the count had resumed his forlorn music and where the general hitched his wheel chair up to Moses and led him to a glass case near the fireplace where there were some moldy academic robes that the late Mr. Scaddon had worn when he was given an honorary degree from Princeton.

It pleased Moses to think that the palace and the hall stood four square on the five-and-ten-cent stores of his youth with their appetizing and depraved odors. His most vivid memories were of the girls—the girl with acne at the cosmetic counter,

the full-busted girl selling hardware, the indolent girl in the
candy department, the demure beauty selling oilcloth and the
straw-haired town whore on probation among the wind-up toys—
and if there was no visible connection between these memories
and the hall at Clear Haven the practical connection was inarguable. Moses noticed that when the general spoke of J. P. Scaddon
he avoided the phrase "five-and-ten-cent store" and spoke only
of merchandising. "He was a great merchant," the general said,
"an exceptional man, a distinguished man—even his enemies
would admit that. For the forty years that he was president of
the firm his days were scheduled from eight in the morning
until sometimes after midnight. When I say that he was distinguished I mean that he was distinguished by his energies, his
powers of judgment, his courage and imagination. He possessed
all these things to an unusual degree. He was never involved
in any shady deals and the merchandising world as we see it
today owes something to his imagination, his intelligence and
his fine sense of honor. He had, of course, a payroll that employed over a million people. When he opened stores in Vene-
zuela and Belgium and India his intention was not to make himself or his stockholders any richer, but to raise the standard of
living generally. . . ."

Moses listened to what the general said but the thought that
he would lay Melissa had given to that day such stubborn light
and joy that it was an effort to keep his ardor from turning to
impatience while he listened to this praise of the late millionaire.
She was beautiful and it was that degree of beauty that fills even
the grocery boy and the garage mechanic with solemn thoughts.
The strong, dark-golden color of her hair, her shoulder bones
and *gorge* and the eyes that appeared black at that distance had
over Moses such a power that, as he watched her, desire seemed
to darken and gild her figure like the cumulative coats of varnish
on an old painting, and he would have been gratified if some
slight hurt had befallen her, for that deep sense of involvement
we experience when we see a lovely woman—or even a woman
with nothing left to her but the loveliness of intent—trip on

the iron steps of a train carriage or on a curbing of the street—
or when, on a rainy day, we see the paper bag in which she is
carrying her groceries home split and rain down around her
feet and into the puddles on the sidewalk oranges, bunches of
celery, loaves of bread, cold cuts wrapped in cellophane—that
deep sense of involvement that can be explained by injury and
loss was present with Moses with no explanation. He had half
risen from his chair when the old lady snapped:

"Bedtime!"

He had underestimated the power of desire to draw his features
and he was caught. From under her dyed eyebrows Justina looked
at him hatefully. "I'm going to ask you to take the general to
his room," she said. "Your room is just down the hall so there
won't be any inconvenience. Melissa's room is on the other side
of the house"—she said this triumphantly and made a gesture
to emphasize the distance—"and it's not convenient for her to
take the general up. . . ."

The stamp of desire on his face had betrayed him once and
he did not want to be betrayed by disappointment or anger
and he smiled broadly—he positively beamed—but he wondered
how, in the labyrinth of rooms, he would ever find his way to
her bed. He could not go around knocking on all the doors
nor could he open them on screaming maids or the figure of
Mrs. Enderby taking off her beads. He might stir up a hornet's
nest of servants—even the Count D'Alba—and precipitate a scandal that would end with his expulsion from Clear Haven. Melissa
was smiling so sweetly that he thought she must have a plan
and she kissed him decorously and whispered, "Over the roof."
Then she spoke for the benefit of the others. "I'll see you in
the morning, Moses. Pleasant dreams."

He pushed the general's chair into the elevator and pressed
the button for the third floor. The elevator rose slowly and the
cables gave off a very mournful sound, but filled again with stubborn joy Moses was insensitive to the premonitory power of
such lifts and elevators—the elevators in loft buildings, castles,
hospitals and warehouses—that, infirm and dolorous to hear,

seem to touch on our concepts of damnation. "Thank you, Mr. Wapshot," the old man said when Moses had wheeled his chair to the door. "I'll be all right now. We're very glad to have you with us. Melissa has been very unhappy, very unhappy and unsettled. Good night." Back in his own room Moses shucked his clothes, brushed his teeth and stepped out onto the balcony of his room, where the rain still fell, making in the grass and the leaves a mealy sound. He smiled broadly with a great love of the world and everything in it and then, in his skin, started the climb over the roofs.

This seemed to be the greatest of the improbabilities at Clear Haven but considering what it was that he sought, to be a naked man scrambling over the leads presented nothing that was actually very irregular or perplexing. The rain on his skin and hair felt fresh and soft and the chaos of wet roofs fitted easily into the picture of love; and it was the roofs of Clear Haven, to be seen only by the birds or a stray airplane, where the architect had left bare the complexity of his task—in a sense his defeat— for here all the random majesty of the place appeared spatchcocked, rectified and jumbled; here, hidden in the rain, were the architect's secrets and most of his failures. Peaked roofs, flat roofs, pyramidal roofs, roofs inset with stained-glass skylights and chimneys and bizarre systems of drainage stretched for a quarter of a mile or more, shining here and there in the light from a distant dormer window like the roofs of a city.

As far as he could see in the rainy dark the only way to get to the other side of the house lay past this distant row of dormers and he had started for them when a length of wire, stretched knee-high across a part of the roof, tripped him up. It was an old radio aerial, he guessed charitably, since he was not hurt, and started off again. A few minutes later he passed a rain-soaked towel and a bottle of sun-tan lotion and still further along there was an empty bottle of vermouth, making the roof seem like a beach on which someone, unknown he felt sure to Justina, had stretched out his bones in the sun. As he approached the ledge to the first lighted dormer he saw straight into a small room, decked with religious pictures, where an old servant was ironing. The lights in the next window were pink, and glancing in briefly he was surprised to see the Count D'Alba standing in front of a full-length mirror without any clothes on. The next window was Mrs. Enderby's and she sat at a desk, dressed as she had been at dinner, writing in a book. He had gone out of the range of her desk light when his right foot, seeking a hold, moved off into nothing but the rainy dark and only by swinging and throwing his weight onto the slates did he keep from falling. What he had missed was an airshaft that cut straight through the three stories of the hall and that would have been the end of him. He peered down at this, waiting for the chemistry of his alarmed body to quiet and listening then to see if Mrs. Enderby or the others had heard the noise he made when he threw himself down. Everything was quiet and he made the rest of his climb more slowly, swinging down at last onto the balcony of Melissa's room where he stood outside her window, watching her brush her hair. She sat at a table by a mirror and her nightgown was transparent so that even in the dim light of the room he could see the fullness of her breasts, parting a little as she leaned toward the mirror.

"You're drenched, my darling, you're drenched," she said. Her look was opaque and wanton; she raised her mouth to be kissed and he unknotted the ribbons of her gown so that it fell to her waist and she drew his head down from her lips to salute her breasts. Then, naked and unshy, she crossed the floor and went into the bathroom to finish her toilet and Moses listened to the noises of running water and the sounds of opening and closing drawers, knowing that it was sensible for a lover to be able to estimate these particular delays. She came back, walking he thought in glory and turning out the lights that she passed on her way, and at dawn, stroking her soft buttocks and listening to the singing of the crows, she told him that he would have to go and he climbed in his skin back over the chaos of roofs.

It was daybreak then and Moses, unable to sleep, dressed and went out. Coming down the stairs, he saw in the strong light of morning that everything sumptuous was dirty and worn. The velvet padding on the banister was patched, there were cigar ashes on the stair carpet and the needlepoint bench at the turning was missing a leg. Coming down into the rotunda Moses saw a large gray rat. They exchanged a look and then the rat—too fat or arrogant to run—moved into the library. Crystals were missing from the chandelier, bits of marble from the floor were gone and the hall seemed like an old hotel where expensiveness and elegance had been abandoned by its company to old men, old women and the near poor. The air was stale and the chests that stood at regular intervals along the wall were ringed white from glasses. Most of the chests were missing a claw or a piece of hardware. Continuing along the hall Moses realized that he had never seen so many chests and he wondered what they contained. He wondered if the Scaddons had bought them by mail, ordered them from some dealer or succumbed to a greed for these massive, ornate and, so far as he knew, useless things. He wondered again what they contained but he did not open one and let himself out a glass door onto a broad lawn.

The women that Moses loved seemed to be in the morning sky, gorged with lights, in the river, the mountains and the trees, and with lust in his trousers and peace in his heart he walked happily over the grass. Below the house there was an old-fashioned Roman plunge with a marble curb and water spouting out of lions' mouths and, having nothing better to do, Moses took a swim. A day that had begun brilliantly darkened suddenly and it began to rain, and Moses went back to the house to get some breakfast and talk with Justina.

Moses had written to Leander about Justina and Leander had replied without a salutation and with this title: "The Rise of a Mercenary B——ch." Under the heading he had written: "Justina; daughter of Amos and Elizabeth Molesworth. Only child. Father was sporting gent. Goodlooker but unable or unwilling to meet domestic obligations. Deserted wife & child. Was never heard from. Elizabeth supported self and daughter as dress-maker. Worked day & night. Ruined eyesight. Mouth always full of pins. Little Justina was changeling from onset or so it appeared to me. Marked tastes for queenly things. Scraps of velvet. Peacock feathers, etc. Only childhood game ever indulged in was to play queen in topshelf finery. Out of place in such a town as St. Botolphs. Subject to much ridicule. Was taken on as apprentice dancing mistress by Gracie Tolland. Held sway in Eastern Star Hall above drugstore; feed store also. Place smelled of floor oil. Later played piano for movies in old Masonic Temple and J. P. Scaddon five & dime store. Waltz me around again Willie. Piano always badly out of tune.

"J. P. Scaddon then competing with Woolworth and Kresge. Millionaire but not above visiting backwoods stores. Beheld Justina tickling the ivories. Love at first sight! Transported same to New York. Amy Atkinson served as duenna. Later married Justina. Newspaper accounts omitted any mention of St. Botolphs, dressmaking mother, dancing mistress. Appeared to have sprung full-grown into high society. Justina well equipped to scrap for social position in New York bear pit. Became benefactress of Dog & Cat Hospital. Often photographed in newspaper, surrounded by grateful bow-wows. Was once asked to contribute small sum of money to local Sailor's Home. Refused. Anxious to keep severance of ties with home-place in good condition. No children. Hobnobbed with dukes and earls. Entertained royalty. Opened big house on Fifth Avenue. Also country place. Clear Haven. All dreams come true."

Later in the morning Moses found Justina in the winter garden—a kind of dome-shaped greenhouse attached to one of the extremities of the castle. Many of the window lights were broken and Giacomo had repaired these by stuffing bed pillows into the frames. There seemed to have been flower beds around the walls in the past and in the center of the room were a fountain and a pool. When Moses entered the room and asked to speak with her, Justina sat down in an iron chair.

"I want to marry Melissa."

Justina touched that façade of black hair that was like the Cartwright Block and sighed.

"Then why don't you? Melissa is twenty-eight years old. She can do what she wants."

"We would like your approval."

"Melissa has no money and no expectations," the old woman said. "She owns nothing of value but her beads. The resale value of pearls is very disappointing and they're almost impossible to insure."

"That wouldn't matter."

"You know very little about her."

"I only know that I want to marry her."

"I think there are some things about her past that you should know. Her parents were killed when she was seven. Mr. Scaddon and I were delighted to adopt her—she has such a sweet nature—but we've had our troubles. She married Ray Badger. You knew that?"

"She told me."

"He became an alcoholic through no fault, I think, of Melissa's. He had some very base ideas about marriage. I hope you don't entertain any such opinions."

"I'm not sure what you mean."

"Mr. Scaddon and I slept in separate rooms whenever this was possible. We always slept in separate beds."

"I see."

"Even in Italy and France."

"It will be some time before we can hope to travel," Moses said, hoping to change the subject.

"I don't think Melissa will ever be able to travel," Justina said. "She's not left Clear Haven since her divorce."

"Melissa's told me this herself."

"It seemed a confining life for a young woman," Justina said. "Last year I bought her a ticket to go around the world. She was agreeable, but when all her luggage had been brought aboard and we were drinking some wine in her cabin she decided that she couldn't go. Her distress was extreme. I brought her back to Clear Haven that afternoon." She smiled at Moses. "Her hats went around the world."

"I see," Moses said. "Melissa's told me this and I would like to live here until our marriage."

"That can be arranged. Is your father still alive?"

"Yes."

"He must be very old. My memories of St. Botolphs are not pleasant. I left there when I was seventeen. When I married Mr. Scaddon I must have received a hundred letters from people in the village, asking for financial help. This did nothing to improve my recollections. I did try to be helpful. For several years I took some child—an artist or a pianist—and gave them an education, but none of them worked out." She unclasped her hands and gestured sadly as if she had dropped the students from a great height. "I had to let them all go. You lived up the river, didn't you? I remember the house. I suppose you have some heirlooms."

"Yes." Moses was unprepared for this and he answered hesitantly.

"Could you give me some idea of what they are?"

"Cradles, highboys, lowboys, things like that. Cut glass."

"I wouldn't be interested in cut glass," Justina said. "However, I've never collected Early American furniture and I've always wanted to. Dishes?"

"My brother Coverly would know more about this than I," Moses said.

"Ah yes," Justina said. "Well, it does not matter to me whether you and Melissa marry. I think Mrs. Enderby is in her office now and you can ask her to set a date. She will send out the invitations. And be careful of that loose stone in the floor. You might trip and hurt yourself." Moses found Mrs. Enderby and after he listened to some frowsty memories of her youth on the Riviera she told him that he could be married in three weeks. He looked for Melissa but the maids told him she had not come down and when he started to climb the stairs to her part of the house he heard Justina's voice at his back. "Come down, Mr. Wapshot."

Melissa didn't come down until lunch and this meal, although it was not filling, was served with two kinds of wine and dragged on until three. After lunch they walked back and forth on the terrace below the towers like two figures on a dinner plate and looking for some privacy in the gardens they ran into Mrs. Enderby. At half-past five, when it was time for Moses to go and he took Melissa in his arms, a window in one of the towers flew open and Justina called down, "Melissa, Melissa, tell Mr. Wapshot that if he doesn't hurry he'll miss his train."

After work on Monday Moses packed his clothing in two suitcases and a paper box, putting in among his shirts a bottle of bourbon, a box of crackers and a three-pound piece of Stilton cheese. Again he was the only passenger to leave the train at Clear Haven but Giacomo was there to meet him with the old Rolls and drive him up the hill. Melissa met him at the door and that evening followed the pattern of his first night there except that the fuses didn't blow. Moses wheeled the general to the elevator at ten and started once more over the roofs, this time on such a clear, starlit night that he could see the airshaft that had nearly killed him. Again in the morning at dawn he climbed back to his own quarters and what could be pleasanter than to see that heavily wooded and hilly countryside at dawn from the high roofs of Clear Haven. He went to the city on the train, returned in the evening to Clear Haven, yawned purposefully during dinner and pushed the old general to the elevator at half-past nine.

30

While Moses was eating these golden apples, Coverly and Betsey had settled in a rocket-launching station called Remsen Park.

Coverly had only spent one day at the farm. Leander had urged him to return to his wife—and had gone to work himself at the table-silver factory a few days later. Coverly had joined Betsey in New York and, after a delay of only a few days, was transferred to this new station. This time they traveled together. Remsen Park was a community of four thousand identical houses, bounded on the west by an old army camp. The place could not be criticized as a town or city. Expedience, convenience and haste had produced it when the rocket program was accelerated; but the houses were dry in the rain and warm in the winter; they had well-equipped kitchens and fireplaces for domestic bliss and the healthy need for national self-preservation could more than excuse the fact that they were all alike. At the heart of the community there was a large shopping center with anything you might want—all of it housed in glass-walled buildings. This was Betsey's joy. She and Coverly rented a house, furnished even to the pictures on the wall, and set up housekeeping with the blue china and the painted chairs that Sarah sent them from St. Botolphs.

They had been in Remsen Park for only a little while when Betsey decided that she was pregnant. She felt sick in the morning and stayed in bed late. When she got up, Coverly had gone to work. He had left coffee for her in the kitchen and had washed his own dishes. She ate a late breakfast, sitting at the kitchen window so that she could see the houses of Remsen Park stretching away to the horizon like the pattern on a cloth. The woman in the house next door came out to empty her garbage. She was an Italian, the wife of an Italian scientist. Betsey called good morning to her and asked her to come in and have a cup of coffee but the Italian woman only gave her a sullen smile and returned to her own kitchen. Remsen Park was not a very friendly place.

Betsey hoped that she would not be disappointed in her pregnancy. Her mind seemed to strike an attitude of prayer, as involuntary as the impulse with which she swore when she slammed her finger in a window. Dear God, she thought briefly, make me a mother. She wanted children. She wanted five or six. She smiled suddenly, as if her wish had filled the kitchen with the love, disorder and vitality of a family. She was braiding the hair of her daughter, Sandra, a beautiful girl. The other four or five were in the room. They were happy and dirty and one of them, a little boy with Coverly's long neck, was holding in his hands the halves of a broken dish, but Betsey had not scolded him, Betsey had not even frowned when he broke the dish, for the secret of his clear, resilient personality was that his growth had never been impeded by niggardly considerations. Betsey felt that she had a latent talent for raising children. She would put the development of personality above everything. The phantom children that played around her knees had never received from their parents anything but love and trust.

When the housework was done it was time for Betsey to take the iron out and have the cord repaired. She walked out of Circle K and down 325th Street to the shopping center and went into the super market, not because she needed anything but because the atmosphere of the place pleased her. It was vast and brightly lighted and music came down from the high blue walls. She bought a giant jar of peanut butter to the strains of "The Blue Danube" and then a pecan pie. The cashier seemed to be a pleasant young man. "I'm a stranger here," Betsey said. "We've just moved from New York. My husband's been out in the Pacific. We have one of those houses in Circle K and I just wondered if you could give me some advice. My ironing cord is frayed, it just gave out the day before yesterday when I was doing my husband's shirts, and I just wondered if you happened to know of an electrical-appliance or repair store in the vicinity that might fix it for me so that I could have it tomorrow because tomorrow's the day when I do my big shopping and I thought I could come in here and buy my groceries and then pick up the iron on my way home."

"Well, there's a store four, no, five doors down the street," the young man said, "and I guess they can fix it for you. They fixed my radio for me once and they're not highway robbers

like some of the people's come in here." Betsey thanked him
kindly and went out into the street and wandered along to the
electrical store. "Good morning," Betsey said cheerfully, putting
her iron on the counter. "I'm a stranger here and when my
ironing cord went yesterday while I was doing my husband's
shirts I said to myself that I just didn't know where to take it
and have it repaired but this morning I stopped in at the Grand
Food Mart and that cashier, the nice one with the pretty, wavy
hair and those dark eyes, told me that he recommended your
store and so I came right over here. Now what I'd like to do
is to come downtown and do my shopping tomorrow afternoon
and pick up my iron on my way home because I have to get
some shirts ironed for my husband by tomorrow night and I
wondered if you could have it ready for me by then. It's a good
iron and I gave a lot of money for it in New York where we've
been living although my husband was out in the Pacific. My
husband's a Taper. Of course I don't understand why the cord
on such an expensive iron should wear out in such a short time
and I wondered if you could put on an extra-special cord for
me because I get a great deal of use out of my iron. I do all
my husband's shirts, you know, and he's high up in the Taping
Department and has to wear a clean shirt every day and then I
do my own personal things as well." The man promised to give
Betsey a durable cord and then she wandered back to Circle K.

But her steps slowed as she approached the house. Her family
of phantom children was scattered and she could not call them
back again. Her period was only seven days late and her pregnancy might not be a fact. She ate a peanut-butter sandwich
and a wedge of pecan pie. She missed New York and thought
again that Remsen Park was an unfriendly place. Late in the
day the doorbell rang and a vacuum-cleaner salesman stood in
the door. "Well now, come right in," Betsey said cheerfully.
"You come right in. I don't have a vacuum cleaner now and I
don't have the money to buy one at the moment. We only just
moved from New York but I'm going to buy one as soon as I
have the money and perhaps if you've got some new attachments

I might buy one of those because I'm determined to buy a new vacuum cleaner sooner or later and I'll need the attachments anyhow. I'm pregnant now and a young mother can't do all the housework without the proper equipment; all that stooping and bending. Would you like a cup of coffee? I imagine you must get tired and footsore going around with that heavy bag all day long. My husband's in the Taping Department and they work him hard but it's a different kind of tiredness, it's just in the brain, but I know what it is to have tired feet."

The salesman opened his sample case in the kitchen before he drank his coffee and sold Betsey two attachments and a gallon of floor wax. Then, because he was tired, and this was his last call, he sat down. "I was living alone in New York all the time my husband was in the Pacific," Betsey said, "and we just moved out here and of course I was happy to make the move but I don't find it a very friendly place. I mean I don't think it's friendly like New York. In New York I had lots of friends. Of course I was mistaken, once. I was mistaken in my friends. You know what I mean? There were these people named Hansen who lived right down the hall from me. I thought they were my real friends. I thought at last I'd found some lifelong friends. I used to see them every day and every night and she wouldn't buy a dress without asking me about it and I loaned them money and they were always telling me how much they loved me, but I was deceived. Sad was the day of reckoning!" The light in the kitchen was dim and Betsey's face was drawn with feeling. "They were hypocrites," she said. "They were liars and hypocrites."

The salesman packed his things and went away. Coverly came home at six. "Hello, sugar," he said. "Why sit in the dark?"

"Well, I think I'm pregnant," Betsey said. "I guess I'm pregnant. I'm seven days late and this morning I felt sort of funny, dizzy and sick." She sat on Coverly's lap and put her head against his. "I think it's going to be a boy. That's what it feels like to me. Of course there's no point in counting your chickens before your eggs are hatched but if we do have a baby one of the things I want to buy is a nice chair because I'm going to breast feed this baby and I'd like to have a nice chair to sit in when I nurse him."

"You can buy a chair," Coverly said.

"Well, I saw a nice chair in the furniture center a couple of days ago," Betsey said, "and after supper why don't we walk around the corner and look at it? I haven't been out of the house all day and a little walk would be good for you, wouldn't it? Wouldn't it be good for you to stretch your legs?"

After supper they took their walk. A fresh wind was blowing out of the north—straight from St. Botolphs—and it made Betsey feel vigorous and gay. She took Coverly's arm and at the corner, under the fluorescent street lamp, he bent down and gave her a French kiss. Once they got to the shopping center Betsey wasn't able to concentrate on her chair. Every suit, dress, fur coat and piece of furniture in the store windows had to be judged, its price and way of life guessed at and some judgment passed as to whether or not it should enter Betsey's vision of happiness. Yes, she said to a plant stand, yes, yes to a grand piano, no to a breakfront, yes to a dining-room table and six chairs, as thoughtfully as Saint Peter sifting out the hearts of men. At ten o'clock they walked home. Coverly undressed her tenderly and they took a bath together and went to bed for she was his potchke, his fleutchke, his notchke, his motchke, his everything that the speech of St. Botolphs left unexpressed. She was his little, little squirrel.

31

During the three weeks before their marriage, Moses and Melissa deceived Justina so successfully that it pleased the old lady to watch them say good night to one another at the elevator and she spoke several times at dinner of Melissa's part of the house as that part of the house that Moses had never seen. Moses' training as a mountain climber kept him from tiring in his nightly trip over the roofs but one evening, when they had wine with dinner and he was hurried, he tripped over the wire once more and sprawled, full-length, on the slates, cutting his chest. Then, with his skin smarting, a deep physical chagrin took hold of him and he discovered in himself a keen dislike of Clear Haven and all its antics and a determination to prove that the country of love was not bizarre; and he consoled himself with thinking that in a few days he would be able to put a ring on Melissa's finger and enter her room at the door. She had, for some reason, made him promise not to urge her to leave Clear Haven, but he felt that she would change her mind by autumn.

On the eve of his wedding Moses walked up from the station, carrying a rented cutaway in a suitcase. On the drive he met Giacomo, who was putting light bulbs into the fixtures along the drive. "She'sa two hundred feefty light bulbs!" Giacomo exclaimed. "She'sa likea Saint's Day." It was dusk when the lights gave Clear Haven the cheerful look of a country fair. When Moses took the general up the old man wanted to give him a drink and some advice, but he excused himself and started over the roofs. He was covering the stretch from the chapel to the clock tower when he heard Justina's voice, quite close to him. She was at D'Alba's window. "I can't see anything, Niki," she said, "without my glasses."

"Shhh," D'Alba said, "he'll hear you."

"I wish I could find my glasses."

"Shhhh."

"Oh, I can't believe it, Niki," Justina said. "I can't believe that they'd disappoint me."

"There he goes, there he goes," D'Alba said as Moses, who had been crouching in the dark, made for the shelter of the clock tower.

"Where?"

"There, there."

"Get Mrs. Enderby," Justina said. "Get Mrs. Enderby and have her call Giacomo and tell him to bring his crow gun."

"You'll kill him, Justina."

"Any man who does such a thing deserves to be shot."

What Moses felt while he listened to their talk was extreme irritation and impatience, for having started on his quest he did not have the reserve to brook interruptions, or at least interruptions from Justina and the count. He was safe in the shelter of the tower and while he stood there he heard Mrs. Enderby and then Giacomo join the others.

"She'sa nobody there," Giacomo said.

"Well, fire anyway," Justina said. "If there's someone there you'll frighten them. If there isn't you won't do any harm."

"She'sa no good, Missa Scaddon," Giacomo said.

"You fire, Giacomo," Justina said. "You either fire or hand me that gun."

"Wait until I get something to cover my ears," Mrs. Enderby said. "Wait until . . ."

Then there was the ear-clapping blast of Giacomo's crow gun and Moses heard the shot strike on the roof around him and in the distance the ring of breaking glass.

"Oh why do I feel so sad?" Justina asked plaintively. "Why do I feel so sad?" D'Alba shut the window and when his lights were turned on and his pink curtains drawn, Moses continued his climb. Melissa ran to him weeping when he swung down onto the balcony of her room. "Oh my darling, I thought they'd shot you," she cried. "Oh my sweetheart, I thought you were dead."

Coverly could not get away from Remsen Park, but Leander and Sarah came to the wedding. They must have left St. Botolphs at dawn. Emmet Cavis drove them in his funeral car. Moses was delighted to see them and proud, for they played out their parts with the wonderful simplicity and grace of country people. As for the invitations to the wedding—Justina had dusted off her old address book, and poor Mrs. Enderby, wearing a hat and a scrap of veiling, had addressed the four hundred envelopes and come to the dinner table for a week with ink-stained fingers and an ink-spotted blouse, her eyes red from checking Justina's addresses against a copy of the *Social Register* that could have been printed no later than 1918. Giacomo mailed the cards with his blessing ("She'sa lovely, Missa Scaddon") and the cards were delivered to brownstones in the East Fifties that had been transformed from homesteads into showrooms for Italian neckties, art galleries, antique dealers, walk-up apartments and offices of such organizations as the English-Speaking Union and the Svenskamerikanska Förbundet. Further uptown and further east the invitations were received by the tail-coated doormen of eighteen- and twenty-story apartment buildings where the names of Justina's friends and peers struck a spark in no one's memory. Up Fifth Avenue invitations were delivered to more apartment houses as well as to institutes of costume design, slapdash rooming houses, finishing schools and to the offices of the American Irish Historical Society and the Sino-American Amity, Inc. They were exposed to the sootfall among other uncollected mail (old bills from Tiffany and copies of *The New Yorker*) in houses with boarded-up front doors. They lay on the battered tables of progressive kindergartens where children could be heard laughing and weeping and they fell into the anonymous passageways of houses that, built with an open hand, had been remodeled with a tight one and where people cooked their dinners in the morning room and the library. An invitation was received at the Jewish Museum, at the downtown branch of Columbia University, at the French and the Jugoslavian consulates, at the Soviet Delegation to the United Nations, at several fraternity houses, actors' clubs, bridge clubs, milliners and dressmakers. Further afield invitations were received by the Mother Superiors of the Ursuline Order, the Poor Clares and the Sisters of Mercy. They were received by the overseers of Jesuit schools and retreats, Franciscan Fathers, Cowley Fathers, Paulists and Misericordia Sisters. They were delivered to mansions remodeled into country clubs, boarding schools, retreats for the insane, alcohol cures, health farms, wildlife sanctuaries, wallpaper factories, drafting rooms and places where the aged and the infirm waited sniffily for the

angel of death in front of their television sets. When the bells
of Saint Michael's rang that afternoon there were no more than
twenty-five people in the body of the church and two of these
were rooming-house proprietors who had come out of curiosity.
When the time came Moses said the words loudly and with a
full heart. After the ceremony most of the guests returned to
Clear Haven and danced to the music of a phonograph. Sarah
and Leander performed a stately waltz and said good-by. The
maids filled the old champagne bottles with cheap sauterne and
when the summer dusk had fallen and all the chandeliers were
lighted the main fuse blew once more. Giacomo repaired it and
Moses went upstairs and entered Melissa's room by the door.

32

The rocket-launching sites at Remsen Park were fifteen miles
to the south and this presented a morale problem for there were
hundreds or thousands of technicians like Coverly who knew
nothing about the beginnings or the ends of their works. The
administration met this problem by having public rocket launchings on Saturday afternoons. Transportation was furnished so
that whole families could pack their sandwiches and beer and
sit in bleachers to hear the noise of doom crack and see a fire
that seemed to lick at the vitals of the earth. These firings were
not so different from any other kind of picnic, although there
were no softball games or band concerts; but there was beer
to drink and children strayed and were lost and the jokes the
crowd made while they waited for an explosion that was calculated to pierce the earth's atmosphere were very human. Betsey
loved all of this, but it hardly modified her feeling that Remsen
Park was unfriendly. Friends were important to her and she said
so. "I just come from a small town in Georgia," she said, "and
it was a very friendly place and I just believe in stepping up

and making friends. After all, we only pass this way once." As often as she made the remark about passage, it had not lost its strength. She was born; she would die.

Her overtures to Mrs. Frascati continued to be met with sullen smiles and she invited the woman in the next house—Mrs. Galen—in for a cup of coffee, but Mrs. Galen had several college degrees and an air of elegance and privilege that made Betsey uneasy. She felt that she was being scrutinized and scrutinized uncharitably and saw there was no room for friendship here. She was persistent and finally she hit on it. "I met the liveliest, nicest, friendliest woman today, honey," she told Coverly when she kissed him at the door. "Her name's Josephine Tellerman and she lives on M Circle. Her husband's in the drafting room and she says she's lived on nearly every rocket-launching reservation in the United States and she's just full of fun and her husband's nice too and she comes from a nice family and she asked us why didn't we come over some night and have a drink."

Betsey loved her neighbor. This simple act of friendship brought her all the delights and hazards of love. Coverly knew how dim and senseless Circle K had seemed to her until the moment when she met Josephine Tellerman. Now he was prepared to hear about Mrs. Tellerman for weeks and months. He was glad. Betsey and Mrs. Tellerman would do their shopping together. Betsey and Mrs. Tellerman would be on the telephone every morning. "My friend Josephine Tellerman tells me that you have some very nice lamb chops," she would tell them at the butcher. "My friend Josephine Tellerman recommended you to me," she would tell them at the laundry. Even the vacuum-cleaner salesman, ringing her doorbell at the end of a hard day, would find her changed. She would be friendly enough, but she would not open the door. "Oh, hello," she would say. "I'd like to talk with you but I'm very sorry I don't have the time this afternoon. I'm expecting a telephone call from my friend Josephine Tellerman."

The Wapshots went over to the Tellermans' for a drink one night and Coverly found them friendly enough. The Tellermans' house was furnished exactly like the Wapshots', including the Picasso over the mantelpiece. In the living room the women talked about curtains, and Coverly and Max Tellerman talked about cars in the kitchen while Max made the drinks. "I've been looking at cars," Max said, "but I decided I wouldn't buy one this year. I have to cut down. And I don't really need a car. You see I'm sending my kid brother through college. My folks have split up and I feel pretty responsible for this kid. I'm all he's got. I worked my way through college—Jesus, I did every-thing—and I don't want him to go through that rat race. I want him to take it easy for four years. I want him to have everything he needs. I want him to feel that he's as good as the next fellow for a few years. . . ." They went back into the living room, where the women were still talking about curtains. Max showed Coverly some photographs of his brother and went on talking about him and at half-past ten they said good night and walked home.

Betsey was no gardener but she bought some canvas chairs for the back yard and some wooden lattice to conceal the garbage pail. They could sit there on summer nights. She was pleased with what she had done and one summer night the Tellermans came over to christen—as Betsey said—the back yard with rum. It was a warm night and most of their neighbors were in their yards. Josie and Betsey were talking about bedbugs, cockroaches and mice. Coverly was speaking affectionately of West Farm and the fishing there. He wasn't drinking himself and he disliked the smell of rum that came from the others, who were drinking a lot. "Drink, drink," Josie said. "It's that kind of a night."

It was that kind of a night. The air was hot and fragrant and from the kitchen, where he mixed the drinks, Coverly looked out of the window into the Frascatis' back yard. There he saw the young Frascati girl in a white bathing suit that accentuated every line of her body but the crease in her buttocks. Her brother was spraying her gently with a garden hose. There was no horse-play, there were no outcries, there was no sound at all while the young man dutifully sprayed his beautiful sister. When Coverly had mixed the drinks he carried them out. Josie had begun to talk about her mother. "Oh, I wish you people could have met my mother," she said. "I wish you kids could have met my mother." When Betsey asked Coverly to fill the glasses once more he said they were out of rum. "Run down to the shopping center and get a bottle, honey," Josie said. "It's that kind of a night. We only live once."

"We only pass this way once," Betsey said.

"I'll get some," Coverly said.

"Let me, let me," Max said. "Betsey and I'll go." He pulled Betsey out of her chair and they walked together toward the shopping center. Betsey felt wonderful. It's that kind of a night, was all she could think to say, but the fragrant gloom and the crowded houses where the lights were beginning to go out and the noise of sprinklers and the snatches of music all made her feel that the pain of traveling and moving and strangeness and wandering was ended and that it had taught her the value of permanence and friendship and love.

Everything delighted her then—the moon in the sky and the neon lights of the shopping center—and when Max came out of the liquor store she thought what a distinguished, what an athletic and handsome man he was. Walking home he gave Betsey a long, sad look, put his arms around her and kissed her. It was a stolen kiss, Betsey thought, and it was that kind of a night, it was the kind of a night where you could steal a kiss. When they got back to Circle K, Coverly and Josie were in the living room. Josie was still talking about her mother. "Never an unkind word, never a harsh look," she was saying. "She used to be quite a pianist. Oh, there was always a big gang at our house. On Sunday nights we all used to gather around the piano and sing hymns, you know, and have a wonderful time." Betsey and Max went to the kitchen to make drinks. "She was unhappy in her marriage," Josie was saying. "He was a real sonofabitch, there's no two ways about it, but she was philosophical, that was the secret of her success; she was philosophical about him and just from hearing her talk you'd think she was the happiest married woman in the world but he was . . ."

"Coverly," Betsey screamed. "Coverly, help."

Coverly ran down the hall. Max was standing by the stove. He had torn Betsey's dress. Coverly swung at him, got him on the side of the jaw and set him down on the floor. Betsey screamed and ran into the living room. Coverly stood over Max, cracking his knuckles. There were tears in his eyes. "Hit me again if you want to, kick me if you want to," Max said. "I couldn't punch a hole in a paper bag. That was a lousy thing for me to do, you know, but I just can't help myself sometimes and I'm glad it's over and I swear to God I'll never do it again, but Jesus Christ Coverly sometimes I get so lonely I don't know where to turn and if it wasn't for this kid brother of mine that I'm sending through college I think I'd cut my throat, so help me God, I've thought of it often enough. You wouldn't think, just looking at me, that I was suicidal, would you, but so help me God I am an awful lot of the time.

"Josie's all right. She's a darned good sport," Max said, still speaking from the floor, "and she'll stay with me through thick and thin and I know that, but she's very insecure, you know, oh she's very insecure and I think it's because she's lived in so many different places. She gets melancholy, you know, and then she takes it out on me. She says I take advantage of her. She says I don't bring in the money for the food. I don't bring in the money for the car. She needs new dresses and she needs new hats and I don't know what she doesn't need new and then she gets real sore and goes off on a buying spree and sometimes it's six months or a year before I can pay the bills. I still owe bills all over the whole United States. Sometimes I don't think I can stand it any more. Sometimes I think I'm going to pack my bag and take to the road. That's what I think, I think I'm entitled to a little fun, a little happiness, you know, and so I take a pass here and a pass there but I'm sorry about Betsey because you and Betsey have been real good friends to us but sometimes I don't think I can go on unless I have a little fun.

I just don't think I have the strength to go on. I just don't think I can stand it any more."

In the living room Josie had taken Betsey into her arms. "There, there, honey," Josie was saying, "there, there, there. It's all over. Nothing happened. I'll fix your dress. I'll get you a new dress. He just had too much to drink, that's all. He's got the wandering hands. He's got the wandering hands and he just had too much to drink. Those hands of his, he's always putting them someplace where they don't belong. Honey, this isn't the first time. Even when he's asleep those hands of his are feeling around all the time until they get hold of something. Even when he's asleep, honey. There, there, don't you worry about it any more. Think of me, think of what I have to put up with. Thank God you've got a nice, clean husband like Coverly. Think of poor me, think of poor Josie trying to be cheerful all the time and going around picking up after him. Oh, I'm so tired of it. I'm so tired of trying to make his mistakes good. And if we get a couple of dollars ahead he sends it to his kid brother in Cornell. He's in love with this kid brother, he loves him more than he loves me or you or anybody. He spoils him. It makes my blood boil. He's living up there like a regular prince in a dormitory with his own bathroom and fancy clothes while I'm mending and sewing and scrubbing to save the price of a cleaning woman so that he can send this college boy an allowance or a new sports jacket or a tennis racket or something. Last year he was worried because the kid didn't have an extra-special heavy overcoat and I said to him, I said, Max, I said, now look here. You're worrying yourself sick because he doesn't have a winter coat, but what about me? Did it ever occur to you that I didn't have a good winter coat? Did it ever cross your mind that your loving wife is just as entitled to a coat as your kid brother? Did you ever look at it that way? And you know what he said? He said it was cooler up where this college is than it was in Montana where we was living. It didn't make any impression on him at all. Oh, it's terrible to be married to a man who's got something on his mind like that all the time.

Sometimes it just makes my blood boil, seeing how he spoils him. But we have to take the lean with the fat, don't we? Into every real friendship a little rain must fall. Let's pretend it was that, honey, shall we, let's pretend it was just a little rain. Let's go and get the men and drink a friendship cup and let bygones be bygones. Let's pretend it was just a little rain."

In the kitchen they found Max still sitting on the floor and Coverly standing by the sink, cracking his knuckles, but Betsey went to Coverly and pleaded with him in a whisper to forget it. "We're all going to be friends again," Josie said loudly. "Come on, come on, it's all forgotten. We're all going into the living room and drink a friendship cup and anyone who won't drink out of the friendship cup is a rotten egg." Max followed her into the living room and Betsey led Coverly behind. Josie filled a large glass with rum and Coke. "Here's for auld lang syne," she said. "Let bygones be bygones. Here's to friendship." Betsey began to cry and they all drank from the glass. "Well, I guess we are friends again, aren't we," Betsey said, "and I'll tell you, I'll tell you just to prove it, I'll tell you something I had in the back of my mind and that's even more important to me after this. Saturday is my birthday and I want you and Max to come over for dinner and make it a real celebration with champagne and tuxedos—a regular party and I think it's all the more important now that we've had this little trouble."

"Oh, sweetheart, that's the nicest invitation anyone's ever given me," Josie said, and she got up and kissed Betsey and then Coverly and linked her arm in Max's. Max held his hand out to Coverly and Betsey kissed Josie again and they said good night—softly, softly for it was late then, it was after two o'clock and theirs were the only lights burning in the circle.

Josie didn't call Betsey in the morning and when Betsey tried to call her friend either the line was busy or no one answered, but Betsey was too absorbed in the preparations for the party to care much. She bought a new dress and some glasses and napkins and on the night before the party she and Coverly ate supper in the kitchen in order to keep the dining space clean. Coverly had to work on Saturday and he didn't get home until after five. Everything was ready for the party. Betsey had not put on her new dress yet and was still wearing her bathrobe with her hair in pins but she was excited and happy and when she kissed Coverly she told him to hurry and take his bath. The table was set with one of the cloths, the old candlesticks and the blue china from West Farm. There were dishes of nuts and other things to eat with cocktails on all the tables. Betsey had laid out Coverly's clothes and he took a shower and was dressing when the telephone rang. "Yes, dear," Coverly heard Betsey say. "Yes, Josie. Oh. Oh, then you mean you can't come. I see. Yes, I see. Well, what about tomorrow night? Why don't we put it off until tomorrow night? I see, oh I see. Well, why don't you come tonight for just a little while? We can bundle Max up in blankets and you could leave right after dinner if you wanted. I see. I see. Yes, I see. Well, good-by. Yes, good-by."

Betsey was sitting on the sofa when Coverly came back to the living room. Her hands were in her lap, her face was haggard and wet with tears. "They can't come," she said. "Max is sick and has a cold and they can't come." Then a loud sob broke from her but when Coverly sat down and put an arm around her she resisted him. "For two days I haven't done anything but work and think about my party," she cried. "I haven't done anything else for two days. I wanted to have a party. I just wanted to have a nice party. That's all I wanted."

Coverly kept telling her that it didn't matter and gave her a glass of sherry and then she decided to call the Frascatis. "All I want now is to have a little party," she said, "and I have all this food and maybe the Frascatis would like to come. They haven't been very neighborly but maybe that's because they're foreigners. I'm going to ask the Frascatis."

"Why don't we forget the whole thing?" Coverly said. "We can eat our supper or take in a movie or something. We can have a good time together."

"I'm going to ask the Frascatis," Betsey said, and she went

to the telephone. "This is Betsey Wapshot," she said cheerfully, "and I've meant to call you again and again but I've been a bad neighbor, I'm afraid. We've been so busy since we've moved in that I haven't had the time and I'm ashamed of myself for having been such a bad neighbor but I just wondered if you and your husband wouldn't like to come over tonight and have supper with us."

"Thank you but we already had supper," Mrs. Frascati said. She hung up.

Then Coverly heard Betsey calling the Galens. "This is Betsey Wapshot," she said, "and I'm sorry I haven't called you sooner because I've wanted to know you better but I wondered if you and your husband would like to come over tonight for supper."

"Oh, I'm terribly sorry," Mrs. Galen said, "but the Teller-mans—I think they're friends of yours—Max Tellerman's young brother has just come home from college and they're bringing him over to see us."

Betsey hung up. "Hypocrite," she sobbed. "Hypocrite. Oh she'd break her back, wouldn't she, to get in good with the Galens and she just wouldn't tell me, her best friend, she just wouldn't have the nerve to tell me the truth."

"There, there, sugar," Coverly said. "It isn't that important. It doesn't matter."

"It matters to me," Betsey cried. "It's a matter of life and death to me, that's what it is. I'm going over there and see, I'm going over there and see if that Mrs. Galen's telling me the truth. I'm just going over there and see if that Max Teller-man's sick in bed or if he isn't. I'm just going over there and see."

"Don't, Betsey," Coverly said. "Don't, honey."

"I'm just going over there and see, that's what I'm going to do. Oh I've heard enough about this brother of his but when it comes time to introduce him around their old friends aren't good enough. I'm going over and see." She stood—Coverly tried to stop her, but she went out the door. In her bathrobe and slippers she marched, bellicosely, up the street to the next circle.

The Tellermans' windows were lighted, but when she rang the bell no one answered and there was no sound. She went around to the back of the house where the curtains on the picture window hadn't been drawn and looked into their living room. It was empty but there were some cocktail glasses on the table and by the door was a yellow leather suitcase with a Cornell sticker on it. And as she stood there in the dark it seemed that the furies attacked Betsey; that through every incident—every moment of her life—ran the cutting thread, the wire of loneliness, and that when she thought she had been happy she had only deceived herself for under all her happiness lay the pain of loneliness and all her travels and friends were nothing and everything was nothing.

She walked home and later that night she had a miscarriage.

33

Betsey was in the hospital for two days and then she came home but she didn't seem to get better. She was unhappy as well as sick and Coverly felt that she was pushing some kind of stone that had nothing to do with their immediate life—or even with her miscarriage—but with some time in her past. He cooked her supper each night when he came home from the laboratory and talked or tried to talk with her. When she had been in bed for two weeks or longer he asked her if he could call the doctor. "Don't you dare call the doctor," Betsey said. "Don't you dare call the doctor. The only reason you want to call the doctor is to have him come and prove that there isn't anything wrong with me. You just want to embarrass me. It's just meanness." She began to cry but when he sat on the edge of the bed she turned away from him. "I'll cook the supper," he said. "Well, don't cook anything for me," Betsey said. "I'm too sick to eat."

When Coverly stepped into the dark kitchen he could see into the Frascatis' lighted kitchen where Mr. Frascati was drinking wine and patting his wife on the rump as she went between the stove and the table. He slapped the Venetian blinds shut and, finding some frozen food, cooked it after his fashion, which was not much. He put Betsey's supper on a tray and took it into her room. Fretfully she worked herself up to a sitting position in the pillows and let him put the tray on her lap but when he went back into the kitchen she called after him, "Aren't you going to eat with me? Don't you want to eat with me? Don't you even want to look at me?" He took his plate into the bedroom and ate off the dressing table, telling her the news of the laboratory. The long tape he had been working on would be done in three days. He had a new boss named Pancras. He brought Betsey a dish of ice cream and washed up and walked down to the shopping center to buy her some mystery stories at a drugstore. He slept on the sofa, covered with an overcoat and feeling sad and lewd.

Betsey remained in bed another week and seemed more and more unhappy. "There's a new doctor at the laboratory, Betsey," Coverly said one night. "His name is Blennar. I've seen him in the cafeteria. He's a nice-looking fellow. He's a sort of marriage counselor, and I thought . . ."

"I don't want to hear about him," Betsey said.

"But I want you to hear about him, Betsey. I want you to talk with Dr. Blennar. I think he might help us. We'll go together. Or you could go alone. If you could tell him your troubles . . ."

"Why should I tell him my troubles? I know what my troubles are. I hate this house. I hate this place, this Remsen Park."

"If you talked with Dr. Blennar . . ."

"Is he a psychiatrist?"

"Yes."

"You want to prove I'm crazy, don't you?"

"No, Betsey."

"Psychiatrists are for crazy people. There's nothing wrong with me." Then she got out of bed and went into the living room. "Oh, I'm sick of you, sick of your earnest damned ways, sick of the way you stretch your neck and crack your knuckles and sick of your old father with his dirty letters asking is there any news, is there any good news, is there any news. I'm sick of Wapshots and I don't give a damn who knows it." Then she went into the kitchen and came out with the blue dishes that Sarah had sent them from West Farm and began to break them on the floor. Coverly went out of the living room onto the back steps but Betsey followed him and broke the rest of the dishes out there.

On the day after they were married they had gone out to sea in a steamer of about the same vintage as the *Topaze* but a good deal bigger. It was a fine day at sea, mild and fair and with a haze suspended all around them so that, but for the wake rolled away at their stern, their sense of direction and their sense of time were obscured. They walked around the decks, hand in hand, finding in the faces of the other passengers great kindliness and humor. They went from the bow down to the shelter of the stern where they could feel the screw thumping underfoot and where many warm winds from the galley and the engine room blew around them and they could see the gulls, hitchhiking their way out to Portugal. They did not raise the island—it was too hazy—and warped in by the lonely clangor of sea bells they saw the place—steeples and cottages and two boys playing catch on a beach—rise up around them through the mist.

The cottage was far away—a place that belonged to Leander's time—a huddle of twelve or sixteen cottages, so awry and weather-faded that they might have seemed thrown up to accommodate the victims of some disaster had you not known that they had been built for those people who make a pilgrimage each summer to the sea. The house they went to was like West Farm, a human burrow or habitation that had yielded at every point to the crotchets and meanderings of a growing family. They put down their bags and undressed for a swim.

It was out of season, early or late, and the inn and the gift shop were under lock and key and they went down the path, hand in hand, as bare as the day they were born with no thought of covering themselves, down the path, dust and in some places ashes and then fine sand like the finest sugar and crusty—it would set your teeth on edge—down onto the coarser sand, wet from the high tide and the sea, ringing then with the music of slammed doors. There was a rock offshore and Betsey swam for this, Coverly following her through the rich, medicinal broths of the North Atlantic. She sat naked on the rock when he approached her, combing her hair with her fingers, and when he climbed up on the rock she dived back into the sea and he followed her to shore.

Then he could have roared with joy, kicked up his heels in a jig and sung a loud tune, but he walked instead along the edge of the sea picking up skimmers and firing them out to beyond the surf where they skittered sometimes and sometimes sank. And then a great sadness of contentment seemed to envelop him—a joy so fine that it gently warmed his skin and bones like the first fires of autumn—and going back to her then, still picking skimmers and firing them, slowly, for there was no rush, and kneeling beside her, he covered her mouth with his and her body with his and then—his body raked and exalted—he seemed to see a searing vision of some golden age that bloomed in his mind until he fell asleep.

The next night when Coverly came home, Betsey had gone. The only message she left him was their canceled savings-account bankbook. He wandered around the house in the dim light. There was nothing here that she had not touched or rearranged, marked with her person and her tastes, and in the dusty light he seemed to feel a premonition of death, he seemed to hear Betsey's voice. He put on a hat and took a walk. But Remsen Park was not much of a place to walk in. Most of its evening sounds were mechanized and the only woods was a little strip on the far side of the army camp and Coverly went there. When he thought of Betsey he thought of her against scenes of travel—trains and platforms and hotels and asking strangers for help with her bags—and he felt great love and pity. What he could not understand was the heaviness of his emotional investment in a situation that no longer existed. Making a circle around the woods and coming back through the army camp and seeing the houses of Remsen Park he felt a great homesickness for St. Botolphs— for a place whose streets were as excursive and crooked as the human mind, for water shining through trees, human sounds at evening, even Uncle Peepee pushing through the privet in his bare skin. It was a long walk, it was past midnight when he got back, and he threw himself naked onto their marriage bed that still held the fragrance of her skin and dreamed about West Farm.

Now the world is full of distractions—lovely women, music, French movies, bowling alleys and bars—but Coverly lacked the vitality or the imagination to distract himself. He went to work in the morning. He came home at dark, bringing a frozen dinner which he thawed and ate out of the pot. His reality seemed assailed or contested; his gifts for hopefulness seemed damaged or destroyed. There is a parochialism to some kinds of misery— a geographical remoteness like the life led by a grade-crossing tender—a point where life is lived or endured at the minimum of energy and perception and where most of the world appears to pass swiftly by like passengers on the gorgeous trains of the Santa Fe. Such a life has its compensations—solitaire and star-wishing—but it is a life stripped of friendship, association, love and even the practicable hope of escape. Coverly sank into this emotional hermitage and then there was a letter from Betsey.

"Sweetie," she wrote, "I'm on my way back to Bambridge to see Grandma. Don't try to follow me. I'm sorry I took all the money but as soon as I get work I'll pay it all back to you. You can get a divorce and marry somebody else who will have children. I guess I'm just a wanderer and now I'm wandering again." Coverly went to the telephone and called Bambridge. Her old grandmother answered. "I want to speak with Betsey," Coverly shouted. "I want to speak with Betsey." "She ain't here," the old lady said. "She don't live here any more. She done married Coverly Wapshot, and went to live with him somewheres

else." "I'm Coverly Wapshot," Coverly shouted. "Well, if you're
Coverly Wapshot what you bothering me for?" the old lady
asked. "If you're Coverly Wapshot why don't you speak to Betsey
yourself? And when you speak to her you tell her to get down
on her knees to say her prayers. You tell her it don't count
unless she gets down on her knees." Then she hung up.

34

And now we come to the unsavory or homosexual part of our
tale and any disinterested reader is encouraged to skip. It came
about like this. Coverly's immediate superior was a man named
Walcott but in charge of the whole Taping Department was a
young man named Pancras. He had a sepulchral voice, beautifully
white and even teeth and he drove a European racing car. He
never spoke to Coverly beyond a good morning or an encourag-
ing smile when he passed through the long Tapers' room. It
may be that we overestimate our powers of concealment and
that the brand of loneliness and unrequital is more conspicuous
than we know. In any case, Pancras suddenly approached Coverly
one evening and offered him a ride home. Coverly would have
been grateful for any company, and the low-slung racing car
had a considerable effect on his spirits. When they turned off
325th Street onto Circle K, Pancras said he was surprised not
to see Coverly's wife on the doorstep. Coverly said she was visiting in Georgia. Then you must come home and have supper
with me, Pancras said. He throttled the car, and off they roared.

Pancras' house was, of course, exactly like Coverly's, but it
was near the army post and stood on a larger piece of land. It
was elegantly furnished and a pleasant change for Coverly from
the disorder of his own housekeeping. Pancras made him a drink
and began to butter Coverly's parsnips. "I've wanted to talk

with you for a long time," he said. "Your work is excellent—brilliant in fact—and I've wanted to say so. We're sending someone to England in a few weeks—I'm going myself. We want to compare our tapings with the English. And we want someone who can get along, of course. We need someone personable, someone with some social experience. There's a good chance that you might make the trip if you're interested."

These words of esteem made Coverly happy, although Pancras showered on him so many open and lingering glances that he felt uneasy. His friend was not effeminate; far from it. His voice was the deepest bass, his body seemed to be covered with hair and his movements were very athletic, but Coverly somehow had the feeling that if he was touched on the bun he would swoon. He could see that it was ungrateful and dishonest to accept the man's charming house and his hospitality while he entertained suspicions about his private life; and to tell the truth he was thoroughly enjoying himself. Coverly could not contemplate the consummation of any such friendship but he could enjoy the atmosphere of praise and tenderness that Pancras created and in which he seemed to bask. The dinner was the best meal Coverly had eaten in months and after dinner Pancras suggested that they take a walk through the army garrison and into the woods. It was exactly what Coverly would have liked to do and so they walked out in the evening and made a circle through the woods, talking in friendly and serious voices about their work and their pleasure. Then Pancras drove Coverly home.

In the morning, before he had started work, Walcott warned Coverly about Pancras. He was queer. This news excited in Coverly bewilderment, sadness and some stubbornness. He felt as Cousin Honora felt about the cart horse. He did not want to be a cart horse, but he did not want to see them exposed to cruelty. He did not see Pancras for a day or two and then one evening, when he was about to eat his dinner from the pot, the racing car roared into K Circle and Pancras rang the bell. He took Coverly back to his own house for supper and they walked again in the woods. Coverly had never found anyone so interested in his recollections of St. Botolphs and he was happy to be able to talk about the past.

After another evening with Pancras it was apparent to Coverly what his friend's intentions were, although he did not know how to behave himself and saw no reason why he should not eat dinner with a homosexual. He claimed to himself to be innocent or naïve, but this pretense was the thinnest. The queer never really surprise us. We choose our neckties, comb our hair with water and lace our shoes in order to please the people we desire; and so do they. Coverly had enough experience in friendship to know that the exaggerated attentions he was receiving from Pancras were amorous. He meant to be seductive and when they took their walk after supper he seemed to emanate a stir of erotic busyness or distress. They had come to the last of the houses and had reached the army installation—barracks and a chapel and a walk lined with whitewashed stone and a man sitting on a step hammering out a bracelet from a piece of rocket scrap. It was the emotional no man's land of most army posts—tolerable enough in the push of war but now more isolated and lonely than ever. They walked through the barracks area into the woods and sat down on some stones.

"We're going to England in ten days," Pancras said.

"I'll miss you," Coverly said.

"You're coming," Pancras said. "I've arranged the whole thing."

Coverly turned to his companion and they exchanged a look of such sorrow that he thought he might never recover. It was a look that he had recoiled from here and there—the doctor in Travertine, a bartender in Washington, a priest on a night boat, a clerk in a shop—that exacerbating look of sexual sorrow between men; sorrow and the perverse wish to flee—to piss in the Lowestoft soup tureen, write a vile word on the back of the barn and run away to sea with a dirty, dirty sailor—to flee, not from the laws and customs of the world but from its force and vitality. "Only ten more days," his companion sighed, and suddenly Coverly felt a dim rumble of homosexual lust in his trousers. This lasted for less than a second. Then the lash of his conscience crashed down with such force that his scrotum seemed injured, at the prospect of joining this pale-eyed company, wandering in the dark like Uncle Peepee Marshmallow. A second later the lash came down again—this time for having scorned a human condition. It was Uncle Peepee's destiny to wander through the gardens and Coverly's vision of the world must be a place where this forlornness was admitted. Then the lash crashed down once more, this time at the hands of a lovely woman who scorned him bitterly for his friend and whose eyes told him that he was now shut away forever from a delight in girls—those creatures of morning. He had thought with desire of going to sea with a pederast and Venus turned her naked back on him and walked out of his life forever.

It was a withering loss. Their airs and confessions, their memories and their theories about the atomic bomb, their secret stores for Kleenex and hand lotion, the warmth of their breasts, their power of succumbing and forgiveness, that sweetness of love that had passed his understanding—was gone. Venus was his adversary. He had drawn a mustache on her gentle mouth and she would tell her minions to scorn him. She might allow him to talk to an old woman now and then, but that was all.

It was in the summer—the air was full of seed and pollen—and with that extraordinary magnification of grief—he might have been looking through a reading glass—Coverly saw the wealth of berries and seed pods in the ground around his feet and thought how richly all of nature was created to inseminate its kind—all but Coverly. He thought of his poor, kind parents at West Farm, dependent for their happiness, their security, their food upon a prowess that he didn't have. Then he thought of Moses and the wish to see his brother was passionate. "I can't go to England with you," he told Pancras. "I have to go and see my brother." Pancras was supplicatory and then downright angry and they came out of the woods in single file.

In the morning Coverly told Walcott that he didn't want to

go to England with Pancras and Walcott said this was all right
and smiled. Coverly looked back at him grimly. It was a knowl-
edgeable smile—he would know about Pancras—it was the smile
of a Philistine, a man content to have saved his own skin; it
was the kind of crude smile that held together and nourished
the whole unwholesome world of pretense, censure and cruelty—
and then, looking more closely, he saw that it was a most friendly
and pleasant smile, the smile at the most of a man who recognizes
another man to have known his own mind. Coverly asked for
two days' annual leave to go and visit Moses.

He left the laboratory at noon, packed a bag and took a bus
to the station. Some women were waiting on the platform for
the train but Coverly averted his eyes from them. It was not
his right to admire them any more. He was unworthy of their
loveliness. Once aboard the train he shut his eyes against anything in the landscape that might be pleasing, for a beautiful
woman would sicken him with his unworthiness and a comely
man would remind him of the sordidness of the life he was about
to begin. He could have traveled peaceably then only in some
hobgoblin company of warty men and quarrelsome women—
some strange place where the hazards of grace and beauty were
outlawed.

At Brushwick the seat beside him was occupied by a gray-
haired man who carried one of those green serge book bags
that used to be carried in Cambridge. The worn green cloth
reminded Coverly of the New England winter—a simple and
traditional way of life—going back to the farm for Christmas
and the snow-dark as it gathered over the skating pond and
the barking of dogs way off. With the book bag between them,
the stranger and Coverly began to talk. His companion was a
scholar. Japanese literature was his field. He was interested in
the *Samurai Sagas* and showed Coverly a translation of one. It
was about some homosexual samurai and when Coverly had absorbed this his traveling companion produced some prints of
the samurai in action. Then the valves of Coverly's heart felt
abraded and he seemed to listen at his organs, as we will at a

door, to see if there was any guilty arousal there. Then, blushing like Honora—coloring like any spinster who finds the whole sky-high creaking edifice of her chastity shaken—Coverly grabbed for his suitcase and fled to another car. Feeling sick, he went to the toilet, where someone had written on the wall in pencil a homosexual solicitation for anyone who would stand by the water cooler and whistle "Yankee Doodle." How could he refresh his sense of moral reality; how could he put different words in Pancras' mouth or pretend that the prints he had been shown were of geisha crossing a bridge in the snow? He stared out of the window at the landscape, seeking in it, with all his heart, some shred of usable and creative truth, but what he looked into were the dark plains of American sexual experience where the bison still roam. He wished that instead of going to the MacIlhenney Institute he had gone to some school of love.

He saw the entrance and the pediment of such a school and imagined the curriculum. There would have been classes on the moment of recognition; lectures on the mortal error of confusing worship with tenderness; there would have been symposiums on indiscriminate erotic impulses and man's complex and demoniac nature and there would have been descriptions of the powers of anxiety to light the world with morbid and lovely colors. Representations of Venus would be paraded before them and they would be marked on their reactions. Those pitiful men who counted upon women to assure them of their sexual nature would confess to their sins and miseries, and libertines who had abused women would also testify. Those nights when he had lain in bed, listening to trains and rains and feeling under his hip bread crumbs and the cold stains of love—those nights when his joy overshot his understanding—would be explained in detail and he would be taught to put an exact and practical interpretation on the figure of a lovely woman bringing in her flowers at dusk before the frost. He would learn to estimate sensibly all such tender and lovely figures—women sewing, their laps heaped with blue cloth—women singing in the early dark to their children the ballads of that lost cause. Charles Stuart—women walking out of the sea or sitting on rocks. There would be special courses for Coverly on the matriarchy and its subtle influence—he would have to do make-up work here—courses in the hazards of uxoriousness that, masquerading as love, expressed skepticism and bitterness. There would be scientific lectures on homosexuality and its fluctuating place in society and the truth or the falsity of its relationship to the will to die. That hairline where lovers cease to nourish and begin to devour one another; that fine point where tenderness corrodes self-esteem and the spirit seems to flake like rust would be put under a microscope and magnified until it was as large and recognizable as a steel girder. There would be graphs on love and graphs on melancholy and the black looks that we are entitled to give the hopelessly libidinous would be measured to a millimeter. It would be a hard course for Coverly, he knew, and he would be on probation most of the time, but he would graduate. An upright piano would play "Pomp and Circumstance" and he would march across a platform and be given a diploma and then he would go down the stairs and under the pediment in full possession of his powers of love and he would regard the earth with candor and with relish, world without end.

But there was no such school, and when he got into New York, late that night, it was raining and the streets around the station seemed to exhale an atmosphere of erotic misdemeanor. He got a hotel room and, looking for the truth, decided that what he was was a homosexual virgin in a cheap hotel. He would never see the resemblance he bore to Cousin Honora, but, as he cracked his knuckles and stretched his neck, his train of thought was like the old lady's. If he was a pederast he would be one openly. He would wear bracelets and pin a rose in his buttonhole. He would be an organizer of pederasts, a spokesman and prophet. He would force society, government and the law to admit their existence. They would have clubs—not hole-in-the-wall meeting places, but straightforward organizations like the English-Speaking Union. What bothered him most was his inability to discharge his responsibilities to his parents, and he sat down and wrote Leander a letter.

A morning train took Coverly out to Clear Haven and when he saw his brother he thought how solid this friendship was. They embraced—they swatted one another—they got into the old Rolls and in a second Coverly had dropped from the anguish of anxiety to a level of life that seemed healthy and simple and reminded him only of good things. Could it be wrong, he wondered, that he seemed, in spirit, to have returned to his father's house? Could it be wrong that he felt as if he were back at the farm, making some simple journey down to Travertine to race the *Tern?* They passed the gates and went up through the park while Moses explained that he was living at Clear Haven only until autumn; that it had been Melissa's home. Coverly was impressed with the towers and battlements, but not surprised since it was a part of his sense of the world that Moses would always have better luck than he. Melissa was still in bed, but she would be down soon. They would have a picnic at the pool. "This is the library," Moses said. "This is the ballroom, this is the state dining room, this is what they call the rotunda." Then Melissa came down the stairs.

She took Coverly's breath away; her golden skin and her dark-blond hair. "It's so nice to meet you," she said, and while her voice was pleasant enough it could never be compared to the power of her appearance. She seemed a triumphant beauty to Coverly—an army with banners—and he couldn't take his eyes off her until Moses pushed him toward a bathroom where they put on their bathing trunks. "I think we'd better wear hats," Melissa said. "The sun's terribly bright." Moses opened a coat closet, passed Melissa a hat and, rummaging around for one himself, brought down a green Tyrolean hat with a brush in the band. "Is this D'Alba's?" he asked. "Lord, no," Melissa said. "Pansies *never* wear hats." It was all that Coverly needed. He plunged into the coat closet and grabbed the first hat he saw—an old Panama that must have belonged to the late Mr. Scaddon. It was much too big for him—it drooped down over his ears—but with at least this one symbol of his male virility intact he walked behind Moses and Melissa down toward the pool.

Melissa didn't swim that day. She sat at the edge of the marble curb, spreading the cloth for lunch and pouring the drinks. There was nothing she did or said that did not charm and delight poor Coverly and incline him to foolishness. He dived. He swam the length of the pool four times. He tried to do a back dive and failed, splashing water all over Melissa. They drank martinis and talked about the farm, and Coverly, who was not used to liquor, got tipsy. Starting to talk about the Fourth of July parade he was sidetracked by a memory of Cousin Adelaide and ended up with describing the rocket launchings on Saturday afternoons. He didn't mention Betsey's departure and when Moses asked for her he spoke as if they were still living happily together. When lunch was finished he swam the length of the pool once more and then lay down in the shade of a boxwood tree and fell asleep.

He was tired and didn't know, for a moment, when he woke where he was, seeing the water gush out of the green lions' heads and the towers and battlements of Clear Haven at the head of the lawn. He splashed some water on his face. The picnic cloth was still spread on the curb. No one had removed the cocktail glasses or the plates and chicken bones. Moses and Melissa were gone and the shadow of a hemlock tree fell across the pool. Then he saw them coming down the garden path from the greenhouse where they had spent some pleasant time and there was such grace and gentleness between them that he thought his heart would break in two; for her beauty could arouse in him only sadness, only feelings of parting and forsakenness, and thinking of Pancras it seemed that Pancras had offered him much more than friendship—that he had offered him the subtle means by which we deface and diminish the loveliness of a woman. Oh, she was lovely, and he had betrayed her! He had sent spies into her kingdom on rainy nights and encouraged the usurper.

"I'm sorry we left you alone, Coverly," she said, "but you were sleeping, you were *snoring*. . . ." It was late, it was time for Coverly to dress and catch his train.

Any railroad station on Sunday afternoon seems to lie close to the heart of time. Even in midsummer the shadows seem autumnal and the people who are gathered there—the soldier, the sailor, the old lady with flowers wrapped in a paper—seem picked so arbitrarily from the community, seem so like those visited by illness or death, that we are reminded of those solemn plays in which it appears, toward the end of the first act, that all the characters are dead. "Do your soft shoe, Coverly," Moses asked. "Do your buck and wing," "I'm rusty, brother," Coverly said. "I can't do it any more." "Oh, try, Coverly," Moses said. "Oh, try . . ." Cloppety, cloppety, cloppety went Coverly up and down the platform, ending with a clumsy shuffle-off, a bow and a blush. "We're a very talented family," he told Melissa. Then the train came down the track and their feelings, like the scraps of paper on the platform, were thrown up pellmell in a hopeless turbulence. Coverly embraced them both—he seemed to be crying—and boarded the train.

When he got back to the empty house in Remsen Park there was a reply from Leander to the letter he had written his father from New York. "Cheer up," Leander wrote. "Writer not innocent, and never claimed to be so. Played the man to many a schoolboy bride. Woodshed lusts. Rainy Sundays. Theophilus Gates tried to light farts with candle ends. Later President of Pocamasset Bank and Trust Co. Had unfortunate experience in early manhood. Unpleasant to recall. Occurred after disappearance of father. Befriended stranger in gymnasium. Name of Parminter. Appeared to be good companion. Witty. Comely physique. Writer at loneliest time of life. Father gone. Hamlet away. Brought Parminter home for supper on several occasions. Old mother much taken by elegant manners. Fine clothes. I'm glad you have a gentleman for a friend, says she. Parminter brought her posies. Also sang. Good tenor voice. Gave me a pair of gold cuff links on birthday. Sentimental inscription. Tickled pink. Me.

"Vanity was my undoing. Very vain of my physique. Often

admired self in mirror, scantily clad. Posed as dying gladiator. Discobolus. Mercury in flight. Guilty of self-love, perhaps. Retribution might be what followed. Parminter claimed to be spare-time artist. Offered to pay writer hard cash for posing. Seemed like agreeable prospect. Happy at thought of having shapely limbs appreciated. Went on designated night to so-called studio. Climbed narrow staircase to bad-smelling room. Not large. Parminter there with several friends. Was asked to undress. Cheerfully complied. Was much admired. Parminter and friends commenced to undress. Appeared to be pederasts.

"Writer grabbed britches and made escape. Rainy night. Anger. Perturbation. Poor cod appeared to be seat of mixed feelings. Up and down. Felt as if same had been put through clothes wringer. Such feelings gave rise to question: Was writer pederast? Sex problems hard nut to crack in 19th-century gloom. Asked self: Was pederast? In shower after ball games. Swimming in buff with chums at Stone Hills. In locker room asked self: Was pederast?

"Had no wish to see Parminter after exposé. Not so easy to shake. Appeared at home on following evening. Unregenerate. Unashamed. Posies for old mother. Sloe-eyed looks for me. Unable to explain situation. Might as well tell mother moon was made of green cheese. Far from ignorant in regards to such things since St. Botolphs produced several such specimens but never seemed to cross mind that gentleman friend belonged in such category. Writer unwilling to meet situation with meanness. Agreed to eat supper with Parminter at Young's Hotel. Hoped to preserve climate of speckless reason. Gentle parting at crossroads. You go that way. I'll go this.

"Parminter in high-low spirits. Eyes like hound dog. Itchy teakettle. Drank much whisky. Ate little food. Writer made parting speech. Hoped to continue friendship, etc. Net result was like poking adder with sharp stick. Recrimination. Threats. Cajolery. Etc. Was asked to return gold cuff links. Accused of flirtatiousness. Also of being well-known pederast. Paid share of check and left dining room. Went to bed. Later heard name being called. Gravel on window. Parminter in back yard calling me. Thought then of slop pail. Sin of pride, perhaps. Hellfire in offing. Everything in due course. Opened door of commode. Removed lid of chamberpot. Ample supply of ammunition. Carried same to window and let figure in yard have both barrels. Finis.

"Man is not simple. Hobgoblin company of love always with us. Those who hang their barebums out of streetfront windows. Masturbate in YMCA showers. Knights, poets, wits in this love's flotsam. Drapers. Small tradesmen. Docile. Cleanly. Soft-voiced. Mild of wit. Flavorless. Yearn for the high-school boy who cuts the grass. Die for the embraces of the tree surgeon. Life has worse trouble. Sinking ships. Houses struck by lightning. Death of innocent children. War. Famine. Runaway horses. Cheer up my son. You think you have trouble. Crack your skull before you weep. All in love is not larky and fractious. Remember."

35

It would be, Moses thought, a sentimental summer, for they could hear fountains in their room and she made his bed a kind of Venice and who cared about the watery soups and custards that they mostly seemed to get for dinner? Melissa was loving and contented and how could Justina make any of this her province? A few days after the wedding Mrs. Enderby called Moses into her office and said that he would be billed three hundred dollars a month for room and board. He apprehended then that loving a woman who could not move from a particular place might create some problems, but this was only an apprehension and he agreed politely to pay the toll. A few nights later he returned from Bond School and found his wife, for the first time since he had known her, in tears. Justina's wedding present had arrived. Giacomo had removed their capacious and lumpy marriage bed and replaced it with twin beds—narrow and hard as slate. Melissa stood at the door to her balcony, weeping over this, and it appeared to Moses then that he might have overlooked the depth of the relationship between his golden-skinned wife and that truculent and well-preserved crone, her guardian. He dried her tears and thanked Justina for the beds at dinner. After dinner he and Giacomo put the twin beds back into the storeroom where they had been and returned the old bed. Watching Melissa undress that night (he could see past her shoulder in the moonlight the lawns and the gardens and the plunge) and resisting the thought that these ramparts were real for her, that she should think that the thorns on the roses that surrounded the walls were piercing, he asked if they could leave before autumn and she reminded him that he had promised not to ask this.

A few mornings later, going to his closet, Moses discovered that all his suits were gone but the soiled seersucker suit he had worn the day before. "Oh, I know what's happened, darling," Melissa said. "Justina's taken your clothes and given them to the church for a rummage sale." She got out of bed, wearing nothing, and went anxiously to her own closet. "That's what she's done. She's taken my yellow dress and my gray and my blue. I'll go down to the church and get them back."

"You mean she's taken my clothes for a rummage sale without asking?"

"Yes, darling. She's never understood that everything in Clear Haven isn't hers."

"How long has this been going on?"

"For years."

As it happened Melissa was able to buy their clothes back from the church for a few dollars and with this forgotten he was able to take up his sentimental life. Moses had long since forgotten the dislike of Clear Haven that had formed in his mind when he stumbled on the roof and it began to seem to him an excellent place for the first months of his marriage, for even the benches in the garden were supported by women with enormous marble breasts and in the hall his eye fell repeatedly on naked and comely men and women in the pursuit or the glow of love. They were on the needlepoint chairs, they reached for one another from the tops of the massive andirons, they supported the candles for the dinner table and the bowl of the glass from which Justina drank the water for her pills. He seemed to work even the lilies in the garden into his picture of love and when Melissa picked them and carried them in her arms like lumber, their truly mournful perfume falling this way and that, he kicked up his heels with joy. Night after night they drank some whisky in their room, some sherry in the hall, sat through the wretched dinner and then went together down to the plunge, and they were excusing themselves one evening after dinner when Justina said:

"We're going to play bridge."

"We're going swimming," Moses said.

"The pool lights are broken," Justina said. "You can't swim in the dark. I'll have Giacomo fix the lights tomorrow. Tonight we'll play bridge."

They played bridge until after eleven and, in the company of the old general, the count and Mrs. Enderby, it was a stifling evening. When Moses and Melissa excused themselves on the next night Justina was ready. "The pool lights aren't fixed yet," she said, "and I feel like some more bridge." Playing bridge that night and the night after, Moses felt restless, and it appeared to him to be significant that he was the only one who left Clear Haven; that since his wedding he had not seen a strange or a new face in the house and that, so far as he knew, not even Giacomo ever left the grounds. He complained to Melissa and she said that she would ask some people for drinks on Saturday and she asked Justina's permission on the next night at dinner. "Of course, of course," Justina said, "of course you want to have some young people in, but I can't let you entertain guests until I've had the rugs cleaned. I'm having estimates made and they ought to be cleaned in a week or two and you can have your little party." On Saturday morning Justina announced through Mrs. Enderby that she was tired and would spend the week end in her room, and Melissa, encouraged by Moses, telephoned three couples who lived in the neighborhood and asked them for drinks on Sunday. Late Sunday afternoon Moses laid a fire in the hall and brought the bottles out of their hiding place. Melissa made something to eat and they sat on the only comfortable sofa in the room and waited for their guests.

It was a rainy afternoon and the rain played on the complicated roofs of the old monument a pleasant air. Melissa turned on a lamp when she heard a car come up the drive and she went down the hall and through the rotunda. Moses heard her voice in the distance, greeting the Trenholmes, and he gave the fire a poke and stood as a couple, who were made by their youthfulness and their pleasant manners to seem innocuous, came into the room. Melissa passed the crackers and when the Howes and the Van Bibbers joined them the vapid music of their voices mingled pleasantly with the sounds of the rain. Then Moses heard from the doorway the hoarse, strong notes of Justina's voice.

"What is the meaning of this, Melissa?"

"Oh, Justina," Melissa said gallantly. "I think you know all these people."

"I may know them," Justina said, "but what are they doing here?"

"I've asked them for cocktails," Melissa said.

"Well, that's very inconvenient," Justina said. "This day of all days. I told Giacomo he could take up the rugs and clean them."

"We can go into the winter garden," Melissa said timidly.

"How many times have I told you, Melissa, that I don't want you to take guests into the winter garden?"

"I'll call Giacomo," Moses said to Justina. "Here, let me get you some whisky."

Moses gave Justina her whisky and she sat on the sofa and regarded the dumb-struck company with a charming smile. "If you insist on inviting people here, Melissa," she said, "I wish

you would ask my advice. If we're not careful the house will
be full of pickpockets and hoboes." The guests retreated toward
the door and Melissa walked them out to the rotunda. When
she returned to the hall she sat down in a chair, not beside
Moses, but opposite her guardian. Moses had never seen her
face so dark.

The rain had let up. Close to the horizon the heavy clouds
had split as if they had been lanced and a liquid brilliance gorged
through the cut, spread up the lawn and came through the glass
doors, lighting the hall and the old woman's face. The hundred
windows of the house would glitter for miles. Ursuline nuns,
bird watchers, motorists and fishermen would admire the illusion
of a house bathed in flame. Feeling the light on her face and
feeling that it became her, Justina smiled her most narcissistic
smile—that patrician gaze that made it seem as if all the world
were hung with mirrors. "I only do this because I love you so,
Melissa," she said, and she worked her fingers loaded with diamonds, emeralds and glass in the light that was fading.

Then the stillness of a trout pool seemed to settle over the
room. Justina seemed to make a lure of false promises and Melissa to watch her shadow as it fell through the water to the
sand, trying to find in her guardian's larcenous words some truth.
Justina's face gleamed with rouge and her eyebrows shone with
black dye and it seemed to Moses that somewhere in the *maquil-
lage* must be the image of an old woman. Her face would be
seamed, her clothes would be black, her voice would be cracked
and she would knit blankets and sweaters for her grandchildren,
take in her roses before the frost and speak mostly of friends
and relations who had departed this life.

"This house is a great burden," Justina said, "and I have no
one to help me bear it. I would love to give it all to you, Melissa,
but I know that if you should predecease Moses he would sell
it to the first bidder."

"I promise not to," Moses said cheerfully.

"Oh, I wish I could be sure," she sighed. Then she rose, still
beaming, and went to her ward. "But don't let there be any

hard feeling between us, sweet love, even if I have broken up your little party. I warned you about the rugs, but you've never had much sense. I've always been able to wrap you around my fingers."

"I won't have this, Justina," Moses said.

"Keep out of this, Moses."

"Melissa is my wife."

"You're not her first husband and you won't be her last and she's had a hundred lovers."

"You're wicked, Justina."

"I'm wicked, as you say, and I'm rude and I'm boorish and I discovered, after marrying Mr. Scaddon, that I could be all these things and worse and that there would still be plenty of people to lick my boots." Then she turned to him again her best smile and he saw for once how truly powerful this old dancing mistress had been in her heyday and how she was like an old Rhine princess, an exile from the abandoned duchies of upper Fifth Avenue and the dusty kingdoms of Riverside Drive. Then she bent and kissed Melissa and removed herself gracefully from the room.

Melissa's lips were drawn as if to check her tears. Moses went to her eagerly, thinking that he could take her out of the atmosphere of breakage that the old woman had left in the room, but when he put his hands on her shoulders she twisted out of his reach.

"Would you like another drink?"

"Yes."

He put some whisky and ice in her glass.

"Shall we go up?"

"All right."

She walked ahead of him; she didn't want him at her side. The encounter had damaged her grace and she sighed as she walked. She held her whisky glass in both hands before her like a grail. She seemed to emanate weariness and pain. It was her charming custom to undress where she could be seen but this evening she went instead to the bathroom and slammed the door. When she returned she was wearing a drab gray dress that Moses had never seen before. It was shapeless and very old; he could tell because there were moth holes in it. A row of steel buttons, pressed to look like ships in full sail, ran from the tight neck to the sagging hem, and the shape of her waist and her breasts was lost in the folds of gray cloth. She sat at the dressing table and removed her earrings, her bracelets and pearls, and began to brush the curl out of her hair.

Now Moses knew that women can take many forms; that it is in their power in the convulsions of love to take the shape of any beast or beauty on land or sea—fire, caves, the sweetness of haying weather—and to let break upon the mind, like light on water, its most brilliant imagery, and it did not dismay him that this gift for metamorphosis could be used to further all kinds of venal and petty schemes for self-aggrandizement. Moses had learned that it was wise to keep in mind the guises most often taken by the women he loved so that when a warm-hearted woman appeared suddenly, for some reason of her own, to have become a spinster he would be prepared and in not much danger of losing the hopefulness that sustained his patience, for while women could metamorphose themselves at will he found that they could not sustain these impersonations for long and that if he could endure, patiently, a disguise or distemper or false modesty, it would soon wear thin. Now he watched the changes that had come over his golden-skinned wife, trying to discover what it was that she represented.

She represented chastity—an infelicitous and implacable chastity. She represented an unhappy spinster. She glanced scornfully at where he had let his clothes drop to the floor, averting her eyes at the same time from where he stood in his skin. "I wish you would learn to pick up your things, Moses," she said in a singsong voice that he didn't recognize at all. It had in it the forced sweetness of a lonely and a patient woman, forced by a reduction of circumstances to take care of a dirty boy. When she had done what she could to take the softness out of her hair she stood and moved in little steps toward the door.

"I'm going down."

"If you'll wait a minute, darling."

"I think if I go *down* now I might be able to help. After all, the poor servants have a great deal to do." Her smile was pure hypocrisy. She drifted out of the room.

Moses' determination to see through this clumsy disguise put him into a position that verged on foolishness and while he dressed his lined face shone with false cheer. She would have exhausted the part by midnight, he thought, so his yearning would have to wait until then; but there it was, a sense of fullness and strength that seemed to increase in the lamplight. When he went down to the hall he noticed that the bottles he had foolishly left there had been appropriated by Justina and that he would never see them again. He had a glass of bad sherry and a peanut. Melissa was among the lemon trees, twisting off the dead leaves. Even as she did this she seemed to sigh. She was a poor relation now, a shadowy figure, not meant to play a large part in life but philosophically resigned to small things. When she had finished cleaning up the lemon trees she took an ash tray off the table and emptied it—conspicuously—into the fire. When the chimes rang she pushed the general's chair to the door, first tucking the blanket tenderly around his legs, and at the table she picked at her food and talked about the dog-and-cat hospital.

They played bridge until ten, when Melissa yawned daintily and said she was tired. Moses excused himself and was disheartened to see with what small steps she preceded him down the hall. At the stairs he put his arm around her waist—he had to feel for it in the folds of her drab dress—and kissed her cheek. She did not try to move out of his arm. Up in their room when he closed the door, shutting out the rest of the house, he watched to see what she would do. She went to a chair and picked up a circular sent from a dry-cleaning firm in the village and began to read this. Moses lifted the paper lightly out of her hands and kissed her. "All *right,*" she said.

He took off his clothes, jubilantly, thinking that in another minute she would be in his arms, but she went instead to her dressing table, tipped many pins out of a small gold box, separated a strand of hair with her fingers, coiled it, laid it flat against her skull and pinned it there. He hoped that she would make only a few curls and he looked at the clock, wondering if it would be ten or fifteen minutes. He liked her hair to be full and he watched with a feeling of foreboding as she took strand after strand, coiled it and laid it flat with a pin against her skull. This did not delay or alter his hopefulness or lessen his need, and trying to distract himself he opened a magazine and looked at some advertisements, but with the kingdom of love so soon to be his the pictures had no meaning. When the hair over her brow was all secured to her skull she started on the sides and he saw that he had a considerable wait ahead of him. He sat up, swung his feet onto the floor and lighted a cigarette. The sense of fullness and strength in his groin was at its apex, and cold baths, long walks in the rain, humorous cartoons and glasses of milk would not help him—she had begun to pin up the hair at the back of her neck—when the feeling of fullness changed subtly to a feeling of anguish that spread from his loins deep into his bowels. He put out his cigarette, drew on some pajama pants and wandered out onto the balcony. He heard her close the bathroom door. Then, with a sigh of real misery, he heard her start to run water for a bath.

It never took Melissa less than three quarters of an hour to bathe. Moses could often wait cheerfully for her, but his feelings that night were painful. He remained on the balcony, picking out by name the stars that he knew and smoking. When, three quarters of an hour later, he heard her pull the plug in the tub he returned to the room and stretched out, his yearning rising to new summits of purity and happiness, on the bed. From the bathroom he could hear the clink of bottles on glass and the opening and closing of drawers. Then she opened the bathroom door and came out—not naked but dressed in a full, heavy nightgown and busily running a piece of dental floss between her teeth. "Oh, Melissa," he said.

"I doubt that you love me," she said. It was the thin, dispassionate voice of the spinster and it reminded him of thin things: smoke and dust. "I sometimes think you don't love me at all," she said, "and of course you put too much emphasis on sex, oh much too much. The trouble is that you don't have enough to think about. I mean you're really not interested in business. J. P. used to be so tired when he came home from work that he could hardly eat his dinner. Most men are too tired to think about love every morning and every afternoon and every night. They're tired and anxious and they lead normal lives. You don't like your job and so you think about sex all the time. I don't suppose it's because you're really depraved. It's just because you're idle."

He heard the squeaking of chalk. His bower was replaced with the atmosphere of a schoolroom and his roses seemed to wither. In the glass he saw her pretty face—opaque and wanton—formed to express passion and sweetness, and thinking of her capabilities he wondered why she had put them down. That he presented difficulties—the flights and crash landings of a sentimental disposition—that he sometimes broke wind and picked his teeth with a kitchen match, that he was neither brilliant nor beautiful belonged in the picture—but he did not understand. He did not understand, picking back over her words, what right she had to make the love that kept his mind open, and that made even the leaking of a rain gutter seem musical, a creation of pure idleness.

"But I love you," he said hopefully.

"Some men bring work home from the office," she said. "Most men do. Most of the men that I know." Her voice seemed to dry as he listened to it, to lose its deeper notes as her feelings narrowed. "And most men in business," she went on thinly, "have to do a lot of traveling. They're away from their wives a lot of the time. They have other outlets than sex. Most healthy men do. They play squash."

"I play squash."

"You've never played squash since I've known you."

"I used to play."

"Of course," she said, "if it's absolutely necessary for you to make love to me I'll do it, but I think that you ought to understand that it's not as crucial as you make it."

"You've talked yourself out of a fuck," he said bleakly.

"Oh, you're so hateful and egotistical," she said, swinging her head around. "Your thinking is so crude and mean. You only want to hurt me."

"I wanted to love you," he said. "The thought of it has made me cheerful all day. When I ask you tenderly you go to your dressing table and stuff your head with pieces of metal. I felt loving," he said sadly. "Now I feel angry and violent."

"And I suppose all your bad feelings are directed towards me?" she asked. "I've told you before that I can't be all the things you want. I can't be wife, child and mother all at once. It's too much to ask."

"I don't want you to be my mother and my child," he said hoarsely. "I have a mother and I will have children. I won't lack those things. I want you to be my wife and you stuff your head with pins."

"I thought we had agreed before," she said, "that I can't give you everything you want. . . ."

"I have no stomach for talk," he said. He took off his pajamas and dressed and went out. He walked down the driveway and took the back road to the village of Scaddonville. It was four miles and when he got there and found the streets dark he turned back on a lane that went through the woods where the mildness of a summer night seemed at last to replace his vexation. Dogs in distant houses heard his footsteps and went on barking long after he had passed. The trees moved a little in the wind and the stars were so numerous and clear that the arbitrary lines that form the Pleiades and Cassiopeia in her chair seemed nearly visible. There seemed to be some indestructible good health in a dark path on a summer night—it was a place and a season where it was impossible to cherish bad feeling. In the distance he saw the dark towers of Clear Haven and he returned up the driveway and went to bed. Melissa was asleep when he left in the morning.

Melissa was not in their room when he returned in the evening and looking around him hopefully for some change in her mood he saw that their room had been given a thorough cleaning. This in itself might have been a good sign but he saw that she had taken the perfume bottles off her dressing table and thrown out all the flowers. He washed and put on a soft coat and went down. D'Alba was in the hall, sitting in the golden throne, reading a Mickey Mouse comic and smoking a big cigar. His taste in comics was genuine but Moses suspected that the rest of the picture was a pose—a nod toward J. P.'s tradition of near-illiterate merchant princes. D'Alba said that Melissa was in the laundry. This was a surprise. She had never gone near the laundry since Moses knew her. He went down that shabby hall that cut away from the rest of the house like a backstage alley and down the dirty wooden stairs into the basements. Melissa was in the laundry, stuffing sheets into a washing machine. Her golden hair was dark with steam. She didn't reply when Moses spoke to her and when he touched her she said, "Leave me alone."

She said that the bedding in the house had not been washed for months. The maids kept drawing from the linen closets and she had found the laundry chute full of sheets. Moses knew enough not to suggest that she send the sheets to a laundry. He could sense that cleanliness was not her purpose. She had successfully discredited her beauty. She must have found the dress she was wearing in a broom closet and her golden-skinned arms were red with hot water. Her hair was stringy and her mouth was set in an expression of extreme distaste. He loved her passionately and when he saw all of this his face fell.

Other than the dark brown photograph of her mother, sitting in a carved chair, holding a dozen roses head down, he did not know her family. The parents, the aunts, uncles, brothers and sisters to whom we can sometimes trace a change of character were unknown to him and if she was overtaken now by the shadow of some aunt it was an aunt he had never seen. Watching her stuff sheets into the washing machine he wished briefly, for once, that her status had not been that of an orphan. Her energies seemed penitential and he would let it go at that. He had not fallen in love with her because of her gift with arithmetic, because of her cleanliness, her reasonable mind or any other human excellence. It was because he perceived in her some extraordinary inner comeliness or grace that satisfied his needs. "Don't you have anything to do but sit there?" she asked sorely. He said yes, yes, and went up the stairs.

Justina met him in the hall with great cordiality. Her eyes were wide and her voice was an excited whisper when she asked if Melissa was in the laundry. "Perhaps we should have told you before you married," she said, "but you know that Melissa has been very, very—" the word she wanted was too crude and she settled for a modulation—"she has never been very tractable. Come," she said to Moses, "come and have a drink. D'Alba has some whisky, I think. We need something more than sherry tonight." The picture she evoked was cozy and although Moses felt the naked edge of her mischievousness he had nothing better to do than walk in the garden and stare at the roses. He went down the hall at her side. D'Alba produced a bottle of whisky from underneath the throne and they all had a drink. "Is she having a breakdown?" D'Alba asked. They were halfway through the soup when Melissa appeared, wearing her broom-closet dress. When she came to the table Moses stood but she did not look in his direction and she did not speak during the meal. After dinner Moses asked if she would like to take a walk but Melissa said that she had to hang out the sheets.

Justina met Moses at the door the next night with a long and an excited face and said that Melissa was ill. "Indisposed perhaps would be a better word," she said. She asked Moses to have a drink with her and D'Alba but he said that he would go up and see Melissa. "She's not in your room," Justina said. "She's moved to one of the other bedrooms. I don't know which one. She doesn't want to be disturbed." Moses looked first into their bedroom to make sure she was not there and then went down the hall, calling her name loudly, but there was no reply. He tried the door of the room next to theirs and looked into a room with a canopied bed but at some time in the past a large piece of the ceiling had fallen and fragments of plaster hung from this cavity. The curtains were drawn and the damps of the room were sepulchral—ghostly he would have said if he had not had such a great scorn for ghosts. The next door that he opened led into an unused bathroom—the tub was filled with newspapers tied into bundles—and the room was lighted luridly by a stained-glass window, and the next door that he opened led into a storeroom where brass bedsteads and rocking chairs, oak mantelpieces and sewing machines, mahogany chiffoniers with rueful lines and other pieces of respectable and by-passed furniture were stacked up to the ceiling, antedating, he guessed, Justina's first glimpse of Italy. The room smelled of bats. The next door opened into an attic where there was a water tank as big as the plunge and there was an aeolian harp attached to the next door that he opened and asthmatic and airy as the music was it made his flesh rough when it began to ring as it would have been roughened by the hissing of an adder. This door led to the tower stairs and he climbed them up and up to a large raftered room with lancet windows and no furniture and over the mantelpiece this motto in gold: LOOK AWAY FROM THE BODY INTO TRUTH AND LIGHT. He ran down the tower stairs and had opened the door of a nursery—Melissa's, he guessed— and another bedroom with a fallen ceiling before the foolish music of the aeolian harp had died away. Then with so much stale air in his nose and his lungs he opened a window and stuck his head out into the summer twilight where he could hear, way below him, the sounds of dinner. Then he opened a door into a room that was clean and light and where Melissa, when she saw him, buried her face in pillows and cried when he touched her, "Leave me alone, leave me alone."

Her invalidism, like her chasteness, seemed to be an imposture, and he reminded himself to be patient, but sitting at a window, watching the lawns darken, he felt very forlorn at having a wife

who had promised so much and who now refused to discuss
with him the weather, the banking business or the time of day.
He waited there until dark and then went down the stairs. He
had missed his dinner but a light was still burning in the kitchen,
where a plump old Irishwoman, who was mopping the drain-
boards, cooked him some supper and set it on a table by the
stove. "I guess you're having trouble with your sweetheart,"
she said kindly. "Well, I was married myself to poor Mr. Reilly
for fourteen years and there's nothing I don't know about the
ups and downs of love. He was a little man, Mr. Reilly was,"
she said, "and when we was living out in Toledo everybody
used to say he was runty. He never weighed over a hundred
and twenty-five pounds and look at me." She sat down in a
chair opposite Moses. "Of course I wasn't so heavy in those
days but towards the end I would have made three of him. He
was one of those men who always look like a little boy. I mean
the way he carried his head and all. Even now, just looking out
of the train window sometimes in a strange city I see one of
these little men and it reminds me of Mr. Reilly. He was a meno-
pause baby. His mother was past fifty when he was born. Why,
after we was married sometimes we'd go into a bar for a beer
and the barkeep wouldn't serve him, thinking he was a boy.
Of course as he got old his face got lined and towards the end
he looked like a dried-up little boy, but he was very loving.

"He never seemed to be able to get enough of it," she said.
"When I remember him that's the way I remember him—that
sad look on his face that meant he was loving. He always wanted
his piece and he was lovely—lovely things he'd say to me while
he caressed and unbuttoned me. He liked a piece in the morning.
Then he'd comb his hair on the left side, button up his britches
and go off to a good day's work in the foundry, so cheerful
and cocky. In Toledo he was coming home for his dinner in
the middle of the day and he liked a piece then and he couldn't
go to sleep without his piece. He couldn't sleep. If I woke him
up in the middle of the night to tell him I heard burglars downstairs there was no use my talking. The night Mabel Ransome's

house burned down and I stayed up watching the fire until two in the morning he never listened to what I said. When thunderstorms woke him at night or the north wind in winter he'd always wake up in a very loving mood.

"But I didn't always feel like loving," she said sadly. "Heartburn or gas would get me down and then I had to be very careful with him. I had to choose me words. Once I refused him without thinking. Once when he commenced to gentle me I spoke roughly to him. Forget about it for a little while Charlie, I says. Helen Sturmer tells me her husband don't do it but once a month. Why don't you try to be like him? Well, it was like the end of the world. You should have seed the way his face got dark. It was terrible to behold. The very blood in his veins got dark. I never seed him so crossed in my whole life. Well, he went out of the house then. Come suppertime he isn't home. I went to bed expecting him to come in but when I wakes up the bed is empty. Four nights I wait for him to come home but he don't show up. Finally I put this advertisement in the paper. This was when we was living in Albany. Please come home Charlie. That's all I say. It cost me two-fifty. Well, I put the advertisement in on Friday night and on Saturday morning I hear his key in the lock. Up the stairs he comes all smiles with this big bunch of roses and one idea in his mind. Well it's only ten o'clock in the morning and my housework isn't half done. The breakfast dishes are in the sink and the bed isn't made. It's very hard for a woman to be loving before her work is done but even with the dust all over the tables I knew my lot.

"Sometimes it was a hardship for me," she said. "It kept me from ever broadening my mind. There's lots of important things he kept me from seeing, like after the war when the parade went right by our windows with Marshal Foch and all. I looked forward to that parade but I never got to see it. He was on top of me when Lindbergh flewed the Atlantic and when that English king, whatever his name was, put down his crown for love and made a speech about it over the radio I never heard a word of it. But when I remember him now that's the way I remember him—that sad look on his face that meant he was loving. He never seemed to be able to get enough of it and now, God bless the poor man, he's lying in a cold, cold grave."

It was not until Saturday that Melissa came down, and, asking her to walk with him after dinner, Moses noticed how she hesitated at the door to the terrace as if she apprehended that the summer night might end her imposture. Then she joined him but she kept a meaningful distance between them. He suggested that they go down through the garden, hoping that the smell of roses and the sound of fountains would prevail, but she continued to keep a protective distance between them although when they left the garden she took a path through some pine woods that he had not seen before and that ended in a plot that turned out to be the animal cemetery. Here were a dozen headstones, overgrown with weeds, and Moses followed Melissa, reading the inscriptions:

> Here lie the bones and feathers of an amiable bird,
> A cold December twilight saw his fall.
> His voice, raised in sweet song, was never heard,
> Because the bird was very small.

> Here lie the bones of Sylvia Rabbit.
> She was sat on by Melissa Scaddon on June 17th
> And died of contusions.

> Here lie the bones of Theseus the Whippet.

> Here lie the bones of Prince the Collie,
> He will be missed by One and All.

> Here lie the bones of Hannibal.

> Here lie the bones of Napoleon.

> Here lie the bones of Lorna, the kitchen cat.

The lot exhaled the power of a family, Moses thought, and the glee they took in their own nonsense, and looking from the headstones to Melissa's face he saw hopefully that her expression seemed to be softened by the foolish graveyard, but he decided to take his time and followed her out of the lot down a path to the barns and greenhouses, when they both stopped to hear the loud, musical singing of some night bird. It sounded in the distance, on the early dark, with the brilliance of a knife, and Melissa was captivated. "You know J. P. wanted to have nightingales," she said. "He imported hundreds and hundreds of nightingales from England. He had a special nightingale keeper and a nightingale house. When we came back from England the first thing we did on the boat after breakfast was to go down into the hold and feed mealy worms to the nightingales. They all died. . . ."

Then looking past her, to the roof of the barn where the night bird seemed to be perched, Moses saw that it was not a bird at all; it was the plaintive song of a rusty ventilator as it turned on the night wind; and feeling that this discovery might change the sentimental mood that the twilight, the graveyard and the song promised he led her hurriedly into the old greenhouse and made a bed of his clothing on the floor. Much later that night, when they had returned to the house, and Moses, his bones feeling light and clean with love, was waiting for sleep, he had every reason to wonder if she had not transformed into something else.

This suspicion was renewed the next night when he stepped into their room and found her on the bed wearing a single stocking and reading a love story she had borrowed from one of the maids and when he kissed her and joined her where she lay her breath smelled, not unpleasantly, of candy. But on the next night, walking across the lawns from the station, Moses was reminded of those noisome details in her past that Justina liked to dwell on. She was on the terrace with Jacopo, one of the young gardeners. She was cutting Jacopo's hair. Even at a distance the sight made Moses uneasy and sad, for the insatiableness that he adored left the possibilities of inconstancy open and he conceived for Jacopo a hatred that was murderous. Lewd and comely and laughing while she snipped and combed his hair, he seemed to Moses to be one of those figures who stand outside the brightly lighted centers of our consciousness and defeat our love of candor and our confidence in the sweetness of life, but Melissa sent Jacopo away when Moses joined them and displayed her affection for Moses brilliantly in greeting him and he did not worry about the gardener or anything else until, a few nights later, walking down the hall, he heard laughter from their bedroom and found Melissa and a stranger drinking whisky on the balcony. This was Ray Badger.

Now the dubiousness of visiting a former wife did not, Moses supposed, concern him. His rival, if Badger was still a rival, had a hard-finish suit, a cast in one eye and patent-leather hair. He meant to be charming, when Moses joined them, but the memories he shared with Melissa—he had fed the nightingales—were confined to the past at Clear Haven and Moses was kept out of the conversation. Melissa had seldom mentioned Badger and if she had been unhappy with him it did not show that evening. She was delighted with his company and his recollections—delighted and sad, for when he had left them she spoke sentimentally to Moses about her former husband. "He's just like an eighteen-year-old boy," she said. "He's always done what other people wanted him to do and now, at thirty-five, he's just realized that he never expressed himself. I feel so *sorry* for him. . . ." Moses reserved judgment on Badger and found at dinner that Justina was his advocate. She did not speak to her guest and seemed to be in a deeply emotional state. She announced that she was selling all her paintings to the Metropolitan Museum. A curator was coming for lunch the next day to appraise them. "There is no one I can trust to keep my things together," she said. "I can't trust any of you."

Badger gave Moses a cigar after dinner and they went together out onto the terrace. "I suppose you wonder why I've come back," Badger said, "and I may as well explain myself. I'm in the toy business. I don't know whether you knew that or not, and I've just had an unusually lucky piece of business. I've got the patent on a penny bank—it's a plastic reproduction of an old iron bank—and Woolworth's given me an order for sixty thousand. I have a confirmation for the order in New York. I've invested twenty-five thousand of my own in the thing, but right now I've got a chance to pick up a patent on a toy gun and I'll sell my interest in the bank for fifteen thousand. I was wondering who to sell it to and I thought of you and Melissa—I read about your marriage in the paper—and I thought I'd come out here and give you the first chance. On the Woolworth order alone you'll double your investment and you can count on another sixty thousand from the stationery stores. If you could get over to the Waldorf late tomorrow afternoon for a drink I'll show you the patent and the design and the correspondence from Woolworth."

"I wouldn't be interested," Moses said.

"You mean you don't *want* to make any money? Oh, Melissa will be very disappointed."

"You haven't talked this over with Melissa."

"Well, not *really,* but I know that she'll be very disappointed."

"I haven't fifteen thousand dollars," Moses said.

"You mean to tell me that you don't have fifteen thousand dollars?"

"That's right," Moses said.

"Oh," Badger said. "What about the general? Do you know if he's worth anything?"

"I don't know," Moses said. He followed Badger back into the hall and saw him give the old man a cigar and push his wheel chair out onto the terrace. When Moses repeated the conversation to Melissa it did not change her sentimental feelings for Badger. "Of course he's not in the toy business," she said. "He's never really been in any business at all. He just tries to get along and I feel so sorry for him."

The fact that Justina was parting with her art treasures because she knew no one trustworthy made the next day both elegiac and exciting.

Mr. Dewitt, the curator, was due at one and it happened to

be Moses who let him into the rotunda. He was a slight man who wore a brown felt hat that was so many sizes too small for him that he looked like Boob McNutt. Moses wondered if he hadn't picked out the wrong hat at a cocktail party. His face was slender and deeply lined—he tipped his head a little as if his baggy eyes were nearsighted—and the length and triangularity of his nose were extraordinary. This thin and angular organ seemed elegant and lewd—a vice, a penance, a gift of the devil's— and reinforced a general impression of elegance and lewdness. He must have been fifty—the bags under his eyes couldn't have been formed in a shorter time—but he carried himself gracefully and spoke with a little impediment as if a hair had gotten onto his tongue. "Not pork, not pork!" he exclaimed, sniffing the stale air of the rotunda. "I'm simply pasted together." When Moses assured him that they would have chicken he put on some horn-rimmed glasses and, looking around the rotunda, noticed the big panel at the left of the stairs. "What a charming forgery," he cried. "Of course I think the Mexicans make the most charming forgeries, but this is delightful. It was made in Zurich. There was a factory there in the early nineteen hundreds that turned them out by the carload. The interesting thing is their lavish use of carmine. None of the originals are nearly as brilliant." Then some smell in the rotunda turned his mind back to the thought of lunch. "You're sure it isn't pork?" he asked again. "My tummy is a wreck." Moses reassured him and they went down the long hall to where Justina was waiting for them. She was triumphantly gracious and sounded all those rich notes of requited social ambition that made her voice seem to carry up into the hills and down to the shadow of the valleys.

Mr. Dewitt clasped his hands when he saw all the pictures in the hall but Moses wondered why his smile should be so fleeting. He carried his cocktail over to the big Titian.

"Astonishing, astonishing, perfectly astonishing," Mr. Dewitt said.

"We found that Titian in a ruined palace in Venice," Justina said. "A gentleman at the hotel—an Englishman, I recall—knew about it and showed us the way. It was like a detective story. The painting belonged to a very old countess and had been in her family for generations. I don't clearly recall what we paid her but if you will get the catalogue, Niki?"

D'Alba got the catalogue and leafed through it. "Sixty-five thousand," he said.

"We found the Gozzoli in another hovel. It was Mr. Scaddon's favorite painting. We found it through the assistance of another stranger. I believe we met him on a train. The painting was so dirty and so covered with cobwebs when we first saw it and hung in such a dark room that Mr. Scaddon decided against it but we later realized that we could not be too particular and in the morning we changed our minds."

The curator sat down and let D'Alba fill his glass and when he turned to Justina she was reminiscing about the dirty palace where she had found the Sano di Pietro.

"These are all copies and forgeries, Mrs. Scaddon."

"That's impossible."

"They're copies and forgeries."

"The only reason you're saying this is because you want me to give my pictures to your museum," Justina said. "That's it, isn't it? You want to have my pictures for nothing."

"They're worthless."

"We met a curator at the Baroness Grachi's," Justina said. "He saw our paintings in Naples where they were being crated for the steamer. He offered to vouch for their authenticity."

"They're worthless."

A maid came to the door and rang the chimes for lunch, and Justina stood, her self-possession suddenly refreshed. "We will be five for lunch, Lena," she told the maid. "Mr. Dewitt won't be staying. And will you telephone the garage and tell Giacomo that Mr. Dewitt will walk to the train?" She took D'Alba's arm and went down the hall.

"Mrs. Scaddon," the curator called after her, "Mrs. Scaddon."

"There isn't much you can do," Moses said.

"How far is it to the station?"

"A little over a mile."

"You don't have a car?"

"No."

"And there aren't any taxis?"

"Not on Sunday."

The curator looked out the window at the rain. "Oh this is outrageous, this is the most outrageous thing I've ever experienced. I only came as a favor. I have an ulcer and I have to eat regularly and it will be four o'clock before I get back into the city. You couldn't get me a glass of milk?"

"I'm afraid not," Moses said.

"What a mess, what a mess, and how in heaven's name could she have supposed that those paintings were authentic? How could she have fooled herself?" He gave up with a gesture and started down the hall to the rotunda, where he put on the little hat that made him look like Boob McNutt. "This may kill me," he said. "I'm supposed to eat regularly and avoid excitement and physical exertion. . . ." Off he went in the rain.

When Moses joined the others at lunch there was no talk at all and the silence was so oppressive that his hearty appetite showed some signs of flagging. Suddenly D'Alba dropped his spoon and said tearfully, "My lady, oh my lady!"

"Document," Justina snapped. Then she swung her head around to Badger and said fiercely, "Please try and eat with your mouth shut!"

"I'm sorry, Justina," Badger said. Maids cleared off the soup plates and brought in some chicken but at the sight of the dish Justina waved it away. "I can't eat a thing," she said. "Take the food back to the kitchen and put it into the icebox." Everyone bowed his head, sorry for Justina and bereft of a meal, for on Sunday afternoons the iceboxes were padlocked. She put her hands on the edge of the table, glaring heavily at Badger, and rose. "I suppose you want to get into town, Badger, and tell everyone about this."

"No, Justina."

"If I hear a word out of you about this, Badger," she said, "I'll tell everyone I know that you've been in *prison.*"

"Justina."

She started for the door, not bent but straighter than ever, with D'Alba in tow, and when she reached the door she threw out her arms and cried, "My pictures, my pictures, my lovely, lovely pictures." Then D'Alba could be heard opening and closing the elevator doors and there was the mournful singing of the cables in the shaft as she went up.

It was a gloomy afternoon and Moses spent it studying syndicalism in the little library. When it began to get dark he shut his books and wandered through the house. The kitchen was empty and clean but the iceboxes were still padlocked. He heard music from the hall and thought that D'Alba must be playing, for it was cocktail music—the languid music of specious sorrow and mock yearning, of barroom twilights and unfresh peanuts; of heartburn and gastritis and those paper napkins that clung like wet leaves to the foot of your cocktail glass—but when he stepped into the room he saw that it was Badger. Melissa sat beside him on the piano bench and Badger was singing dolefully:

"I've got those guest-room blues,
I'm feeling blue all the time,
I've got those guest-room blues,
Surrounded by things that aren't mine.
The bed is lumpy and has sprained my back,
And I hear the choo-choo whistling that will taka me back,
I've got those guest-room blues . . . "

When Moses approached the piano they both looked up. Melissa sighed deeply and Moses felt as if he had violated the atmosphere of a tryst. Badger gave Moses a jaded look and closed the piano. He seemed to be in an emotional turbulence that Moses was at some pains not to misunderstand. He got up from the piano bench and walked out onto the terrace, a figure of grief and unease, and Melissa turned her head and followed him with her eyes and all her attention.

Now Moses knew that if we grant men vestigial sexual rites—that if the ease of his stance when a hockey stick was first put into his hands, if the pleasure he took in the athletic equipment in the closet at West Farm or the sense, during a football scrimmage on a rainy day, of looking, during the last minutes of light and play, deep into the past of his kind, had any validity—there must be duplicate rites and ceremonies for the opposite sex. By this Moses did not mean the ability to metamorphose swiftly, but something else, linked perhaps to the power beautiful women have of evoking landscapes—a sense of rueful distance—as if their eyes had come to rest on a horizon that had never been seen by any man. There was some physical evidence for this—their voices softened and the pupils of their eyes dilated, and they seemed to be recollecting some distaff voyage over distaff waters to a walled island where they were committed by the nature of their minds and their organs to some secret rites that would refresh their charming and creative stores of sadness. Moses did not expect ever to know what was going on in Melissa's mind but as he saw her pupils dilate now and a deeply thoughtful cast fall over her beautiful face he knew that it would be hopeless to inquire. She was recalling the voyage or she had seen the horizon and the effect of this was to stir up in her vague and stormy longings, but that Badger seemed to fit somehow into her memories of the voyage was what made him anxious.

"Melissa?"

"Justina is so mean to him," Melissa said, "and she has no right to be. And you don't like him."

"I don't like him," Moses said, "that's true."

"Oh, I feel so sorry for him." She got up from the bench and started for the terrace after Badger. "Melissa," Moses said, but she was gone in the dark.

It was about ten o'clock when Moses went upstairs. The door to their room was locked. He called his wife's name and she didn't reply and then he was enraged. Then some part of him that was as unsusceptible to compromise as his sexual pride was inflamed and this rage seemed to settle in his gut like stone. He pounded on the door and tried to break the lock with his shoulders and was resting from these exertions when the cold air, coming through the space between the door and the sill, reminded him that Badger was sleeping in the room where he had slept when he first made his trip over the roofs.

He ran down the back stairs and across the rotunda and took the old elevator to the bedrooms on the other side of the house. Badger's door was shut but when he knocked no one answered. When he opened the door and stepped in the first thing he heard was the loud noise of rain from the balcony. There was no sign of Badger in the room. Moses went out onto the balcony and swung up onto the roof and sure enough, about a hundred yards away from him and moving very cautiously, bent at the waist and sweeping the air around his feet with his hands like a swimmer (he must have been tripped up by the old radio wire), was Badger. Moses called his name. Badger began to run.

He seemed to know the way; he steered clear of the airshaft anyhow. He ran toward the pyramidal roof that the chapel made and then turned right and ran along the pitched slate roof of the hall. Moses came around the other side but Badger retreated and got back onto the straightaway and began running toward D'Alba's lighted dormer. Halfway across the flat roof Moses outstripped him and clapped a hand on his shoulder.

"It isn't what you think," Badger said. Then Moses hit him and down Badger went on his bum and he must have sat on a nail because he let out such a hoarse, loud roar of pain that the count stuck his head out of a window.

"Who's there, who's there?"

"It's Badger and me," Moses said.

"If Justina hears about this she'll be wild," the count said. "She doesn't like people to walk on the roofs. It makes leaks. And what in the world are you doing?"

"I'm on my way to bed," Moses said.

"Oh, I wish you'd give a civil answer to a sensible question once in a while," the count said. "I'm terribly, terribly tired of your sense of humor and so is Justina. It's a terrible comedown for her to have people like you in the house after having spent her life in the highest society including royalty, and she told me herself . . ." The voice got fainter as Moses continued along the ledge to above Melissa's balcony, his feelings blasted with anger. Then he sat on the roof with his feet in the rain gutter for half an hour, composing an obscene indictment of her intractableness and seeming to release this into the night until the stony rage in his gut diminished. Then, realizing that if he was to find any usable truth in the situation, he would have to find it in himself, he swung down onto the balcony, undressed and got into bed where Melissa was asleep.

But Moses had wronged Badger. There had not been a lecherous thought in his head when he started over the roofs. He had been very drunk. But there was some magnanimity in the man—a trace of the raw material of human excellence—or at least enough scope in his emotions to set the scene for a conflict, and when he woke early the next morning he reproached himself for his drunkenness and his crazy schemes. He could see the world out of his window then all blue and gold and round as a bull's eye but all the sapphire-colored lights in heaven merely chilled Badger's spirit and excited in him a desire to retire into some dark, badly ventilated place. The world, in the partial lights of early morning, appeared to him as hypocritical and offensive as the smile of a door-to-door salesman. Nothing was true, thought Badger; nothing was what it appeared to be, and the enormity of this deception—the subtlety with which the color of the sky deepened as he dressed—angered him. He got down through the rotunda without meeting anyone—not even a rat— and telephoned Giacomo, although it was not six o'clock, and Giacomo drove him to the station.

The early train was a local and all the passengers were night-shift workmen, returning home. Looking into their tired and dirty faces Badger felt a longing for what he thought to be their humble ways. If he had been brought up simply his life would have had more meaning and value, the better parts of his disposition would have been given a chance to develop and he would not have wasted his gifts. Shaken with drink and self-reproach, he felt it plain that morning that he had wasted them beyond any chance of their renewal, and images of his earlier life—a high-spirited and handsome boy, bringing in the terrace furniture before a thunderstorm—rose up to reinforce his self-condemnation. Then at the nadir of his depression light seemed to strike into Badger's mind, for it was the force of his imagination rebelling against utter despair, to raise white things in his head—cities or archways at least of marble—signs of prosperity, triumph and splendor.

Then whole palladia seemed to mushroom beneath Badger's patent-leather hair, the cities and villas of a younger world, and he made the trip into the city in a hopeful mood. But sitting over his first cup of coffee in the hole-in-the-wall where he lived Badger saw that his marble white civilizations were helpless before invaders. These snowy, high-arched constructions of principle, morality and faith—these palaces and memorials—were overrun with hordes of war-whooping, half-naked men, dressed in the stinking skins of beasts. In they rode at the north gate and as Badger sat huddled over his cup, he saw one by one his temples and palaces go. Out the south gate rode the barbarians, leaving poor Badger without even the consolation of a ruin; leaving him with a nothingness and with his essence, which was never much better than the perfume of a wood violet gone.

"*Mamma e Papa Confettiere arrivan' domani sera,*" Giacomo said. He was screwing light bulbs once more into the long string of fixtures that were hung in the trees of the driveway. Melissa met Moses sweetly at the door as she had done on his first night there and told him that some old friends of Justina's were arriving on the next night. Mrs. Enderby was in the office, telephoning invitations, and D'Alba was running around the hall in an apron, giving orders to a dozen maids that Moses had never seen before.

The place was upside down. Doors were thrown open onto bat-smelling parlors and Giacomo took the bed pillows out of the broken windows in the winter garden where palm trees and rose bushes were being unloaded from trucks. There was no place to sit down and they had sandwiches and drinks in the hall where the Scaddonville Symphony Orchestra (eight ladies) undressed the harp of its cracked mackintosh and tuned their instruments. Then the glee of the old upside-down palace on the eve of a party reminded Moses of West Farm, as if this house, like the other, lay deep in their consciousness—even in the dreams of the fly-by-night maids, who exhumed and burnished the old rooms as if they were improving their wisdom. Bats were found in the big basement kitchens and two of the maids came screaming up the stairs with dish towels over their heads but this small incident discouraged no one and only seemed to heighten the antic atmosphere, for who, these days, was rich enough to have bats in their kitchen? The big chests in the cellar were filled with beef and wine and flowers and all the fountains played in the gardens and water poured out of the green-mouthed lions in the plunge and a thousand lights or more burned in the house and the driveway was beaded with lights like a country fair and lights burned here and there in the garden, forlorn and unshaded like the lights in rooming-house hallways and with all the doors and windows open at ten or eleven and the night air suddenly cold and a thin moon in the sky over the broadest lawns Moses was reminded of some wartime place, some poignance of furlough and leave-takings, headlines and good-by dances in beery ports like Norfolk and San Francisco where the dark ships waited in the roads for the lovers in their beds and none of it might ever happen again.

And who were Mamma and Papa Confettiere? They were the Belamontes, Luigi and Paula, the last of the *haut monde* of the *prezzo unico botteghe*. She was the daughter of a Calabrian farmer and Luigi was spawned in the back of a Roman barbershop that smelled of violets and old hair, but at the age of eighteen he had saved enough money to stock a *prezzo unico* store. He was the Woolworth, he was the Kress, he was the J. P. Scaddon of Italy and had made himself into a millionaire with villas in the south and castles in the north by the time that he was thirty. He had retired in his fifties and for the last twenty years had motored around Italy with his wife in a Daimler, throwing hard candies out of the windows of their car to the children in the street.

They left Rome after Easter. The date was announced in the newspapers and over the radio so that a crowd would have gathered outside the gates of their house for the first free candy of the season. They drove north toward Civitavecchia, scattering candy to the left and the right—a hundred pounds here, three hundred pounds there—circumventing Civitavecchia and all the larger cities on their route for they had once nearly been torn limb from limb by a crowd of twenty thousand children in Milan and had also caused serious riots in Turin and Leghorn. Piedmont and Lombardy saw them and southward they traveled through Portomaggiore, Lugo, Imola, Cervia, Cesena, Rimini and Pesaro, tossing out handfuls of lemon drops, peppermints, licorice sticks, anise and horehound drops, sugar plums and cherry suckers along streets that, as they climbed Monte Sant'Angelo and came down into Manfredonia, had begun to be covered with fallen leaves. Ostia was shut when they passed there and shut were the hotels of Lido di Roma, where they scattered the last of their store to the children of fishermen and caretakers, turning northward and home again under the fine skies of a Roman winter.

Moses took a suitcase to work in the morning and rented a suit of tails at lunch. He walked up from the station to the hall in a late summer dusk when the air already smelled of autumn. Then he could see Clear Haven in the early dark with every one of its windows lighted for Mamma and Papa Confettiere. It was a cheerful sight and, letting himself in at the terrace doors, he was cheered to see how the place had been restored, how shining and quiet it was. A maid who came down the hall with some silver on a tray walked stealthily and, other than the sound of a fountain in the winter garden and the hum of water rising in some pipes within the walls, the house was still.

Melissa had dressed and they drank a glass of wine. Moses was standing in the shower when all the lights went out. Then every voice in what had been a hushed place was raised in alarm and dismay and someone who was stuck in the old elevator cage began to pound on the walls. Melissa brought a lighted candle into the bathroom and Moses was pulling on some trousers when the lights went on again. Giacomo was around. They drank another glass of wine on the balcony, watching the cars arrive. Jacopo was directing them to park on the lawns. God knows where Mrs. Enderby had found the guests, but she had found enough for once and the noise of talk, even from the third floor, sounded like the October sea at Travertine.

There must have been a hundred people in the hall when Moses and Melissa went down. D'Alba was at one end and Mrs. Enderby at the other, steering servants toward people with empty glasses, and Justina stood by the fireplace beside an elderly Italian couple, swarthy, egg-shaped, merry and knowing, Moses discovered when he shook hands with them, not a word of English. The dinner was splendid, with three wines and cigars and brandy on the terrace afterward, and then the Scaddonville Symphony Orchestra began to play "A Kiss in the Dark," and they all went in to dance.

Badger was there, although he had not been invited. He walked up from the station after dinner and hung around the edges of the dance floor, a little drunk. He could not have said why he had come. Then Justina saw him and the corrosive glance she gave him and the fact that she was not wearing any jewelry reminded Badger of his purpose. That evening had for him the savor of a man who finds his destiny and adores it. This was his finest hour. He went upstairs and started once more over those roofs (he could hear the music in the distance) that he had crossed often enough for love himself, but that he crossed now with a much deeper sense of purpose. He headed for Justina's balcony at the north end of the house and entered that big chamber with its vaulted ceiling and massive bed. (Justina never slept in this; she slept on a little cot behind a screen.) The decision against her jewelry must have been made suddenly for it was all heaped on the cracked and peeling surface of her dressing table. He found a paper bag in her closet—she collected paper and string—and filled this with her valuables. Then, trusting in Divine Providence, he left boldly by the door, went down the stairs, crossed the lawns with the music growing fainter and fainter and caught the 11:17 into the city.

When Badger boarded the train he had no idea of how he would dispose of the jewelry. He may have thought of prying some of the stones out of their settings and selling them. The train was a local—the last—taking back to the city people who had been visiting friends and relations. They all seemed tired; some of them were drunk; and, sweating and sleeping fitfully in the overheated coach, they seemed, to Badger, to share a great commonality of intimacy and weariness. Most of the men had taken off their hats but their hair was matted with the pressure of hat brims. The women wore their finery but they wore it awry and their curls had begun to come undone. Many of them slept with their heads on the shoulders of their men, and the smells—and the looseness of most of the faces he saw—made Badger feel as if the coach was some enormous bed or cradle in which they all lay together in a state of unusual innocence. They shared the discomforts of the coach, they shared a destination and for all their shabbiness and fatigue they seemed to Badger to share some beauty of mind and purpose, and looking at the dyed red head of the woman in front of him he attributed to her the ability to find, a shade below the level of consciousness, an imagery of beauty and grandeur like those great, ruined palladia that rose in Badger's head.

He loved them all—Badger loved them all—and what he had done he had done for them, for they failed only in their inability to help one another and by stealing Justina's jewelry he had done something to diminish this failure. The red-headed woman in the seat in front moved him with love, with amorousness and with pity, and she touched her curls so often and with such simple vanity that he guessed her hair had just been dyed and this in turn touched him as Badger would have been touched to see a sweet child picking the petals off a daisy. Suddenly the red-headed woman straightened up and asked in a thick voice, "Wassa time, wassa time?" The people in front of her to whom the question was addressed did not stir and Badger leaned forward and said that it was a little before midnight. "Thank you, thank you," she said with great warmth. "You're a genemun after my own heart." She gestured toward the others. "Won't even tell me what time is because they think I'm drunk. Had a liddle accident." She pointed to some broken glass and a puddle on the floor where she seemed to have dropped a pint bottle. "Jess because I had a liddle accident and spilled my good whisky none of these sonofbitches will tell me time. You're a genemun, you're a genemun and if I didn't have a little accident and spill my whisky give you a drink." Then the motion of Badger's cradle overtook her and she fell asleep.

Mrs. Enderby had given the alarm twenty minutes after the theft and two plain-clothes men and an agent from the insurance company were waiting for Badger when he got off the train in Grand Central. Wearing tails, and carrying a paper bag that seemed to be full of hardware, he was not hard to spot. They followed him, thinking that he might lead them to a ring. He walked jubilantly up Park Avenue to Saint Bartholomew's and tried the doors, which were locked. Then he crossed Park Avenue, crossed Madison and walked up Fifth to Saint Patrick's, where the doors were still open and where many charwomen were mopping the floors. He went way forward to the central altar, knelt and said his Lamb of God. Then—the rail was down and he was too enthralled to think of being conspicuous—he walked across the deep chancel and emptied his paper bag on the altar. The plain-clothes men picked him up as he left the cathedral.

It was not one o'clock when the police department called Clear Haven to tell Justina that they had her jewelry. She checked the police list against a typewritten list that had been pasted to the top of her jewel box. "One diamond bracelet, two diamond and onyx bracelets, one diamond and emerald bracelet," etc. She tried the policeman's patience when she asked him to count the pearls in her necklace, but he did. Then Papa Confettiere called for music and wine. "Dancinga, singinga," he shouted, and gave the ladies' orchestra a hundred-dollar bill. They struck up a waltz and then the fuses blew for the second time that night.

Moses knew that Giacomo was around—he had seen him in the halls—but he went to the cellar door anyhow. A peculiar smell surrounded him but he didn't reflect on it and he didn't notice the fact that as he went down the back hallway sweat began to pour off his body. He opened the cellar door onto a pit of fire and a blast of hot air that burned all the hair off his face and nearly overcame him. Then he staggered down the hall to the kitchens where the maids were cleaning up the last of the dishes and asked the major-domo if anyone was upstairs. He counted off the help and said that no one was and then Moses told them to get out; that the house was on fire. (How Mrs. Wapshot would have been disappointed with this direct statement of fact; how cleverly she would have led the guests and servants out onto the lawn to see the new moon.)

Then Moses called the fire department from the kitchen telephone, noticing, as he picked up the receiver, that much flesh had been burned off his right hand by the cellar doorknob. His lips were swollen with adrenaline and he felt peculiarly at ease. Then he ran down to the hall where the guests were still waltzing and told Justina that her house was burning. She was perfectly composed and when Moses stopped the music she asked the guests to go out on the lawn. They could hear the bull horn in the village beginning to sound. There were many doors onto the terrace and as the guests crowded out of the hall, away from the lights of the party, they stepped into the pink glow of fire, for flames had blown straight up the clock tower and while there were still no signs of fire in the hall the tower was blazing like a torch. Then the fire trucks could be heard coming down the road toward the drive and Justina started down the hall to greet them at her front door as she had greeted J. C. Penney, Herbert Hoover and the Prince of Wales, but as she started down the hall a rafter somewhere in the tower burned loose from its shorings, crashed through the ceiling of the rotunda and then all the lights in the house flickered and went out.

Melissa called to her guardian in the dark and the old woman joined them—now she seemed bent—and walked between them out to the terrace where D'Alba and Mrs. Enderby took her arms. Then Moses ran around to the front of the house to move the cars of the guests. They seemed to be all that was worth saving. "For the last six nights I been trying to discharge my conjugal responsibilities," one of the firemen said, "and every time I get started that damned bull horn . . ." Moses bumped a dozen cars down over the grass to safety and then went through the crowd, looking for his wife. She was in the garden with most of the other guests and he sat beside her at the pool and put his burned hand into the water. The fire must have been visible for miles then, for crowds of men, women and children were climbing over the garden walls and pouring in at all the gates. Then the Venetian room took fire and, saturated with the salts of the Adriatic, it bloomed like paper, and the iron works of the old clock, bells and gears had begun to crash down through the remains of the tower. A brisk wind carried the flames deep into the northwest and then slowly the garden and the whole valley began to fill up with a bitter smoke. The place burned until dawn and looked, in the morning light with only its chimneys standing, like the hull of some riverboat.

Later the next afternoon Justina, Mrs. Enderby and the count flew to Athens and Moses and Melissa went happily into New York.

But Betsey returned, long before this. Coming home one night Coverly found his house lighted and shining and his Venus with a ribbon in her hair. (She had been staying with a girl friend in Atlanta and had been disappointed.) Much later that night, lying in bed, they heard the sounds of rain and then Coverly put on some underpants and went out the back door and walked through the Frascatis' yard and the Galens' to the Harrows', where Mr. Harrow had planted some rose bushes in a little crescent-shaped plot. It was late and all the houses were dark. In the Harrows' garden Coverly picked a rose and then walked back through the Galens' and the Frascatis' to his own house and laid the rose between Betsey's legs—where she was forked—for she was his potchke once more, his fleutchke, his notchke, his little, little squirrel.

Part Four

36

In the early summer both Betsey and Melissa had sons and Honora was as good as or better than her word. A trust officer from the Appleton Bank brought the good news to Coverly and Moses and they agreed to continue Honora's contributions to the Sailor's Home and the Institute for the Blind. The old lady wanted nothing more to do with the money. Coverly came on from Remsen Park to New York and planned with Moses to visit St. Botolphs for a week end. The first thing they would do with Honora's money was to buy Leander a boat and Coverly wrote his father that they were coming.

Leander gave up his job at the table-silver company with the announcement that he was going back to sea. He woke early on Saturday morning and decided to go fishing. Struggling, before dawn, to get into his rubber boots reminded him of how rickety his limbs—or what he called his furniture—had gotten. He twisted a knee and the pain shot and multiplied and traversed his whole frame. He got the trout rod, crossed the fields and started fishing in the pool where Moses had seen Rosalie. He was absorbed in his own dexterity and in the proposition of trying to deceive a fish with a bird's feather and a bit of hair. The foliage was dense and pungent and in the oaks were whole carping parliaments of crows. Many of the big trees in the woods had fallen or been cut during his lifetime but nothing had changed the loveliness of the water. Standing in a deep pool, the sun falling through the trees to light the stones on the bottom, it seemed to Leander like an Avernus, divided by the thinnest film of light from that creation where the sun warmed his hands, where the crows carped and argued about taxes and where the wind could be heard; and when he saw a trout it seemed like a shade—a spirit of the dead—and he thought of all his dead fishing companions whom he seemed cheerfully to commemorate by wading this stream. Casting, gathering in his line, snagging flies and talking to himself, he was busy and happy and he thought about his sons; about how they had gone out in the world and proved themselves and found wives and would now be rich and modest and concerned with the welfare of the blind and retired seamen and would have many sons to carry on their name.

That night Leander dreamed that he was in strange country. He saw no fire and smelled no brimstone but he thought that he was walking alone through hell. The landscape was like the piles of broken and eroded stone near the sea but in all the miles he walked he saw no trace of water. The wind was dry and warm and the sky lacked that brilliance that you see above water, even at a great distance. He never heard the noise of surf or saw a lighthouse although the coasts of that country might not have been lighted. The thousands or millions of people that he passed were, with the exception of an old man who wore some shoes, barefoot and naked. Flint cut their feet and made them bleed. The wind and the rain and the cold and all the other torments they had been exposed to had not lessened the susceptibility of their flesh. They were either ashamed or lewd. Along the path he saw a young woman but when he smiled at her she covered herself with her hands, her face dark with misery. At the next turn in the path he saw an old woman stretched out on the shale. Her hair was dyed and her body was obese and a man as old as she was sucking her breasts. He saw people astride one another in full view of the world but the young, in their beauty and virility, seemed more continent than their elders and he saw the young, in many places, gently side by side as if carnality was, in this strange country, a passion of old age. At another turn in the path a man as old as Leander, in the extremities of eroticism, approached him, his body covered with brindle hair. "This is the beginning of all wisdom," he said to Leander, exposing his inflamed parts. "This is the beginning of everything." He disappeared along the shale path with the index finger up his bum and Leander woke to the sweet sounds of a southerly wind and a gentle summer morning. Separated from his dream, he was sickened at its ugliness and grateful for the lights and sounds of day.

Sarah said that morning that she was too tired to go to church. Leander surprised everyone by preparing to go himself. It was a sight, he said, that would make the angels up in heaven start flapping their wings. He went to early communion, happily, not convinced of the worth of his prayers, but pleased with the fact that on his knees in Christ Church he was, more than in any other place in the world, face to face with the bare facts of his humanity. "We praise thee, we bless thee, we worship thee, we glorify thee," he said loudly, wondering all the time who was that baritone across the aisle and who was that pretty woman on his right who smelled of apple blossoms. His bowels stirred and his cod itched and when the door at his back creaked open he wondered who was coming in late. Theophilus Gates? Perley Sturgis? Even as the service rose to the climax of bread and wine he noticed that the acolytes' plush cushion was nailed to the floor of the chancel and that the altar cloth was embroidered with tulips but he also noticed, kneeling at the rail, that on the ecclesiastical and malodorous carpet were a few pine or fir needles that must have lain there all the months since Advent, and these cheered him as if this handful of sere needles had been shaken from the Tree of Life and reminded him of its fragrance and vitality.

On Monday morning at about eleven the wind came out of the east and Leander hurriedly got together his binoculars and bathing trunks and made himself a sandwich and took the Travertine bus to the beach. He undressed behind a dune and was disappointed to find Mrs. Sturgis and Mrs. Gates preparing to have a picnic on the stretch of beach where he wanted to swim and sun himself. He was also disappointed that he should have such black looks for the old ladies who were discussing canned goods and the ingratitude of daughters-in-law while the surf spoke in loud voices of wrecks and voyages and the likeness of things; for the dead fish was striped like a cat and the sky was striped like the fish and the conch was whorled like an ear and the beach was ribbed like a dog's mouth and the movables in the surf splintered and crashed like the walls of Jericho. He waded out to his knees and wetted his wrists and forehead to prepare his circulation for the shock of cold water and thus avoid a heart attack. At a distance he seemed to be crossing himself. Then he began to swim—a sidestroke with his face half in the water, throwing his right arm up like the spar of a windmill— and he was never seen again.

37

So, coming back to give him a boat, his sons heard the words said for those who are drowned at sea. Moses and Coverly drove down from New York without their wives and arrived in the village late on the day of the service. Sarah did not cry until she saw her sons, and held out her arms to be kissed, but the manners and the language of the village helped to sustain her. "It was a very long association," she said. They sat in the parlor and drank some whisky and Honora joined them, kissed the boys and had a drink herself. "I think you make a great mistake to have the service at the church," she told Sarah. "All his friends are dead. There will be no one there but us. It would be better to have it here. And another thing. He wanted Prospero's speech said over his grave. I think you boys had better go to the church and speak with the rector. Ask him if we can't have the service in the little chapel and tell him about the speech."

The boys drove over to Christ Church and were let into an office where the rector was trying to work an adding machine. He seemed impatient at the little help Divine Providence gave him in practical matters. He refused Honora's requests gently and firmly. The chapel was being painted and could not be used and he could not approve introducing Shakespeare into a holy service. Honora was disappointed to hear about the chapel. This anxiety about the empty church was the form her grief seemed to take.

She looked old and bewildered that day, her face haggard and leonine. She got some shears and went into the fields to cut flowers for Leander—loosestrife, cornflowers, buttercups and daisies. She worried about the empty church all through lunch. Going up the church steps she took Coverly's arm—she clutched it as if she was tired or frail—and when the doors were opened and she saw a crowd she stopped short on the threshold and asked in a loud voice, "What are all these people doing here? Who are all these people?"

They were the butcher, the baker, the boy who sold him newspapers and the driver of the Travertine bus. Bentley and Spinet were there, the librarian, the fire chief, the fish warden, the waitress from Grimes' bakery, the ticket seller from the movie theater in Travertine, the man who ran the merry-go-round in Nangasakit, the postmaster, the milkman, the stationmaster and the old man who filed saws and the one who repaired clocks. All the pews were taken and people were standing at the back. Christ Church had not seen such a crowd since Easter.

Honora raised her voice once during the service when the rector began to read from St. John. "Oh no," she said loudly. "We've always had Corinthians." The rector changed his place and there seemed to be no discourtesy in this interruption for it was her way and in a sense the way of the family and this was the funeral of a Wapshot. The cemetery adjoined Christ Church and they walked behind Leander, two by two, up the hill to the family lot in that stupefaction of grief with which we follow our dead to their graves. When the prayers were finished and the rector had shut his book Honora gave Coverly a push. "Say the words, Coverly. Say what he wanted." Then Coverly went to the edge of his father's grave and although he was crying he spoke clearly. "Our revels now are ended," he said. "These our actors, as I foretold you, were all spirits and are melted into air, into thin air. We are such stuff as dreams are made on, and our little life is rounded with a sleep."

After the service the boys kissed their mother good-by and promised to return soon. It would be the first trip they made and Coverly did return, on the Fourth of July, with Betsey and his son, William, to see the parade. Sarah closed her floating gift shop long enough to appear on the Woman's Club float once more. Her hair was white and only two of the founding members remained, but her gestures, the sadness of her smile and the air of finding that the glass of water on her lectern tasted of rue were all the same. Many people would remember the Independence Day when some hoodlum had set off a fire-cracker under Mr. Pincher's mare.

Honora was not there and after the parade when Coverly tele-phoned to see if he could bring Betsey and the baby to Boat Street Honora put him off. He was disappointed, but he was not surprised. "Some other time, Coverly dear," she said. "I'm late now." A novice at observing her might have guessed that she was late for her piano lesson but as soon as she had mastered "The Jolly Miller" she had shut the lid on her piano and become a baseball fan. What she was late for was the starting pitch at Fenway Park. She had arranged with a cab driver in the village to drive her to and from the games once or twice a week when the Red Sox were in Boston.

She wears her three-cornered hat and her black clothes to the game and climbs up the ramp to her seat in the balcony with the ardor of a pilgrim. The climb is long and she stops at a turn to catch her breath. She clasps one hand, her fingers outspread, to her breast, where the noise of respiration is harsh. "Can I help you?" a stranger asks, thinking that she is sick. "Can I help you, lady?" but this gallant and absurd old woman does not seem to hear him. She takes her seat, arranges her program and her score card and taps a Catholic priest who is sitting near her on the shoulder with her stick. "Forgive me,

Father," she says, "if I seem remiss in my use of language, but I do get carried away. . . ." She sits in the clear light of harmlessness and as the game proceeds she cups her hands to her mouth and shouts, "Sacrifice, you booby, *sacrifice!*" She is the image of an old pilgrim walking by her lights all over the world as she was meant to do and who sees in her mind a noble and puissant nation, rising like a strong man after sleep.

Betsey loved the floating gift shop and spent most of the afternoon there with Sarah, admiring the fish-net floats, mounted to hold ivy, the hand-painted flatirons and coal scuttles, the luncheon sets from the Philippines and the salt and pepper shakers shaped like dogs and cats. Coverly walked alone through the empty rooms of the farm. There would be a thunderstorm. The light was getting dim and the telephone in the hall had begun to ring erratically, sensitive to every random charge of electricity. He saw the threadbare rugs, the bricks, neatly encased in scraps of carpeting, that would keep the doors from slamming now that the wind had begun to rise, and on a corner table an old pewter pitcher, filled with bayberry and bittersweet, all covered with dust. In the storm light the fine, square rooms stood for a way of life that seemed to be unusually desirable, although it could have been the expectancy of the storm that accounted for the intensity of Coverly's feeling. Memories of his childhood could be involved and he could remember those thunderstorms—Lulu and the dog hidden in the coat closet—that plunged the sky, the valley and the rooms of the house into darkness and how tenderly they felt for one another, carrying buckets and pitchers and lighted candles from room to room. Outside he could hear the tossing noise of the trees, and the teakwood table in the hall—that famous barometer—made a creaking sound. Then, before the rain began, the old place appeared to be, not a lost way of life or one to be imitated, but a vision of life as hearty and fleeting as laughter and something like the terms by which he lived.

But Leander got the last word. Opening Aaron's copy of Shakespeare, after it had begun to rain, Coverly found the place marked with a note in his father's hand. "Advice to my sons," it read. "Never put whisky into hot water bottle crossing borders of dry states or countries. Rubber will spoil taste. Never make love with pants on. Beer on whisky, very risky. Whisky on beer, never fear. Never eat apples, peaches, pears, etc. while drinking whisky except long French-style dinners, terminating with fruit. Other viands have mollifying effect. Never sleep in moonlight. Known by scientists to induce madness. Should bed stand beside window on clear night draw shades before retiring. Never hold cigar at right-angles to fingers. Hayseed. Hold cigar at diagonal. Remove band or not as you prefer. Never wear red necktie. Provide light snorts for ladies if entertaining. Effects of harder stuff on frail sex sometimes disastrous. Bathe in cold water every morning. Painful but exhilarating. Also reduces horniness. Have haircut once a week. Wear dark clothes after 6 P.M. Eat fresh fish for breakfast when available. Avoid kneeling in unheated stone churches. Ecclesiastical dampness causes prematurely gray hair. Fear tastes like a rusty knife and do not let her into your house. Courage tastes of blood. Stand up straight. Admire the world. Relish the love of a gentle woman. Trust in the Lord."

The Wapshot Scandal

To W. M.

All the characters in this work are fictional,
as is much of the science.

Part One

1

The snow began to fall into St. Botolphs at four-fifteen on Christmas Eve. Old Mr. Jowett, the stationmaster, carried his lantern out onto the platform and held it up into the air. The snowflakes shone like iron filings in the beam of his light, although there was really nothing there to touch. The fall of snow exhilarated and refreshed him and drew him—full-souled, it seemed—out of his carapace of worry and indigestion. The afternoon train was already an hour late, and the snow (whose whiteness seems to be a part of our dreams, since we take it with us everywhere) came down with such open-handed velocity, such swiftness, that it looked as if the village had severed itself from its context on the planet and were pressing its roof and steeples up into the air. The remains of a box kite hung from the telephone wires overhead—a reminder of the year's versatility. "Oh, who put the overalls in Mrs. Murphy's chowder?" Mr. Jowett sang loudly, although he knew that it was all wrong for the season, the day and the dignity of a station agent, the steward of the town's true and ancient boundary, its Gate of Hercules.

Going around the edge of the station he could see the lights of the Viaduct House, where at the very moment a lonely traveling salesman was bending down to kiss a picture of a pretty girl in a mail-order catalogue. The kiss tasted faintly of ink. Beyond the Viaduct House were the rectilinear lights of the village green, but the village itself was circular and did not conform in any way to the main road that wound seaward to Travertine, or to the railroad track, or even to the curve of the river, but to the pedestrian needs of its inhabitants, putting them within walking distance of the green. Thus it was the shape, really, of an ancient place, and seen from the air on a fairer day might have been in Etruria. Mr. Jowett could see into the windows, across from the Viaduct House and above the ship chandler's, of the Hastings apartment, where Mr. Hastings was decorating the Christmas tree. Mr. Hastings stood on a ladder, and his wife and children passed him ornaments and told him where to hang them. Then suddenly he bent and kissed his wife. It was the sum of his feeling for the holiday and for the storm, Mr. Jowett thought, and it made him very happy. He seemed to feel happiness in the stores and houses, happiness everywhere. Old Dog Tray trotted happily up the street, on his way home, and Mr. Jowett thought affectionately of the dogs of St. Botolphs. There were wise dogs, foolish dogs, bloodthirsty and thieving dogs, and as they raided clotheslines, upset garbage pails, bit the mailman and disturbed the sleep of the just, they seemed like diplomats and emissaries. They seemed, in their chaffing way, to keep the place together.

The last of the shoppers were going home, carrying a pair of mittens for the ash man, a brooch for Grandmother and a Teddy bear stuffed with sawdust for baby Abigail. Like Old Dog Tray, everybody was going home, and everybody had a home to go to. It was one place in a million, Mr. Jowett thought. Even with his pass, he had never wanted much to travel. The village, he knew, had, like any other, its brutes and its shrews, its thieves and its perverts, but like any other it meant to conceal these facts under a shine of decorum that was not hypocrisy but a guise or mode of hope. At that hour most of the inhabitants were decorating their Christmas trees. The druidical significance of bringing a green tree into the house at the solstice had certainly never crossed the minds of any of the natives, but they treated their chosen trees (at the time of which I'm writing) with more instinctive respect than is the case today. The trees were not, at the end of their usefulness, stuck into ashcans or fired into the ditch by the railroad tracks wearing a few strands of angel's hair. The men and boys burned them ceremoniously in the back yard, admiring the surge of flame and the smell of balsam smoke. People did not, as they presently would, say that the Tremaines' tree was skinny, that the Wapshots' tree had a bare place in the middle, that the Hastings' tree was stumpy and that the Guilfoyles must have suffered economic reverses, since they had only paid fifty cents for their tree. Fancy illuminations, competitiveness and disregard for the symbols involved would all come, but they would come later. The lights, at the time of which I am writing, were spare and rudimentary and the ornaments were commemorative like the table silver, and were handled respectfully, as if one were counting over the bones of the family. They were, naturally, in disrepair—the birds without tails, the bells without clappers and the angels sometimes without wings. It was a conservatively dressed population that performed this tree-trimming ceremony. All the men wore trousers and all the women wore skirts, excepting Mrs. Wilston, who was a widow, and Alby Hooper, who was an itinerant carpenter. They had been drinking bourbon for two days and wore nothing at all.

On the ice pond—Parson's Pond at the north end of town—two boys were struggling to keep clear enough ice for a hockey game in the morning. They skated back and forth, pushing coal shovels ahead of them. It was an impossible task. This was clear to both of them, and yet they continued to go back and forth, toward and away from the roar of the falls at the dam, with an unaccountable feeling of eagerness. When the snow got too deep for skating, they propped their shovels against a pine tree and sat down in its shelter to unlace their skates.

"You know, Terry, I miss you when you're away at school."

"They throw so much work at me in school that I don't have a chance to miss anyone."

"Smoke?"

"No, thanks."

The first boy took from his pocket a pouch full of sassafras root that had been ground in a clean pencil sharpener, poured some of this onto a square of coarse, yellow toilet paper, and rolled a loose cigarette that flared up like a torch, lighting his

thin face, with its momentary look of suavity, and dropping embers all over his trousers. Drawing on his cigarette, he could
taste its components—the raw gassy flavor of burning toilet paper
and the sweetness of sassafras. He shuddered as it touched his
lungs, and yet he was rewarded by his smoke with a sense of
wisdom and power. When their skates were unlaced and the
fire in the cigarette had died, they started back toward the village.
The first house they passed was the Ryders', distinguished in
St. Botolphs because, for as long as anyone could remember,
the parlor window shades had been drawn and the parlor door
locked. What did the Ryders have hidden in their parlor? There
was no one in the village who hadn't wondered. Was there a
dead body there, a perpetual-motion machine, a collection of
eighteenth-century furniture, a heathen altar, a laboratory for
hellish experiments on dogs and cats? People had made friends
of the Ryders in the hope of getting into their parlor, but no
one had ever succeeded. The Ryders themselves, a peculiar but
not really unfriendly family, were decorating their tree in the
dining room, which was where they lived. Next to the Ryders'
was the Tremaines' and, passing here, the boys could see a gleam
of something yellow—copper or brass—a clue to the richness
of color in that house. Traveling through Persia as a young man,
Dr. Tremaine had cured the shah of boils and had been rewarded
with rugs. The Tremaines had rugs on their tables, their piano,
their walls and their floors, and the brilliant dyes could be seen
through the lighted windows. Suddenly, for one of the boys—
the smoker—the bitterness of the storm and the warmth of color
in the Tremaines' house seemed to converge. It was like a discovery, and so exciting that he began to run. His friend jogged
along beside him to the corner, where they could hear the bells
of Christ Church.

The rector was about to bless the carolers who stood in his
living room. A rancid and exciting smell of the storm came from
their clothes. The room was neat and clean and warm, and had
been—before they entered in their snowy clothes—fragrant. Mr.
Applegate had cleaned the room himself, they knew, because

he was unmarried and did not employ a housekeeper. He did not enjoy having women in his sanctuary. He was a tall man with an astonishing and somehow elegant curvature of the spine, formed by an enlarged lower abdomen, which he carried in a stately and contented way, as if it contained money and securities. Now and then he patted his paunch—his pride, his friend, his solace, his margin for error. With his spectacles on he gave the impression of a portly and benign ecclesiastic, but when he removed his eyeglasses to clean them his gaze was penetrating and haggard and his breath smelled of gin.

His life was a lonely one, and the older he grew the more harried he was by doubts about the Holy Ghost and the Virgin Mary, and it was true that he drank. When he first took over the parish, the spinsters had embroidered his stoles and illuminated his prayer books, but when it appeared that he was not interested in their attentions, they urged the vestry and bishop to discharge him as a drunk. Drunkenness was not what infuriated them. His claim to be celibate, his unmarriedness, had offended their womanhood and they longed to see him disgraced, defrocked, scourged and harried down the Wilton Trace past the old pill factory to the village boundaries. On top of this, Mr. Applegate had recently begun to suffer from an hallucination. It seemed to him that as he passed the bread and wine he could hear the substance of his parishioners' prayers and petitions. Their lips did not move, so he knew this was an hallucination, a kind of madness, but as he moved from one kneeling form to another he seemed to hear them asking, "Lord God of Hosts, shall I sell the laying hens?" "Shall I take up my green dress?" "Shall I cut down the apple trees?" "Shall I buy a new icebox?" "Shall I send Emmett to Harvard?" " 'Drink this in remembrance that Christ's Blood was shed for thee, and be thankful,' " he said, hoping to scour his mind of this galling illusion, but he still seemed to hear them asking, "Shall I fry sausage for breakfast?" "Shall I take a liver pill?" "Shall I buy a Buick?" "Shall I give Helen the gold bracelet or wait until she's older?" "Shall I paint the stairs?" It was the feeling that all exalted human experience was an imposture, and that the chain of being was a chain of humble worries. If he had confessed to the vice of drinking and to his serious doubts about blessedness, he would end up licking postage stamps in some diocesan office, and he felt too old for this. "Almighty God," he said loudly, "bless these Thy servants in the task of celebrating the birth of Thine only Son, by Whom and with Whom in the unity of the Holy Ghost all honor and glory be to Thee, O Father Almighty world without end. Amen!" The blessing smelled distinctly of juniper. They sang an Amen and a verse of "Christus Natus Hodie."

Absorbed and disarmed by the business of singing, their faces seemed unusually open, like so many windows, and Mr. Applegate was pleased to look into them, they seemed at that moment so various. First was Harriet Brown, who had worked for the circus, singing romantic music for the living statues. She was married to a wastrel, and it was she who kept the family together these days, baking cakes and pies. Her life had been stern, and her pale face was sternly marked. Next to Harriet stood Gloria Pendleton, whose father ran the bicycle-repair shop. They were the only colored family in the village. The ten-cent necklace that Gloria wore seemed to be of inestimable value, and she dignified everything she touched. This was not a primitive or a barbaric beauty, it was the extraordinary beauty of race, and it seemed to accentuate the plumpness and the paleness of Lucille Skinner, who stood on her right. Lucille had studied music in New York for five years. Her education was estimated to have cost in the neighborhood of ten thousand dollars. She had been promised an operatic career, and wouldn't your head swim at the thought of San Carlo and La Scala, that uproarious applause that seems to be the essence of the world's best and warmest smile! Sapphires and chinchilla! But the field is crowded, as everyone knows, and dominated by unscrupulous people, and she had come home to make an honest living teaching the piano in her mother's front parlor. Her love of music—it was true of most of them, Mr. Applegate thought—had been a consuming and disenchanting passion. Next to Lucille stood Mrs. Coulter, the wife of the village plumber. She was Viennese, and she had been a seamstress before her marriage. She was a frail, dark-skinned woman with shadows like lampblack under her eyes. Beside her stood old Mr. Sturgis, who wore a celluloid collar and a brocade ascot, and who had sung in public whenever possible ever since he had been admitted to his college glee club, fifty years ago.

Behind Mr. Sturgis stood Miles Howland and Mary Perkins, who would be married in the spring but who had been lovers since last summer, although no one knew. He had first undone her clothes in the pine copse behind Parson's Pond during a thunderstorm, and after this they had thought mostly of how, where, when next—moving, on the other hand, through a world lit by the intelligent and trusting faces of their parents, whom they loved. They took a picnic lunch to Bascom's Island and didn't put their clothing on the whole day long. Lovely, it was lovely. Was this sinful? Would they burn in Hell, suffer agues and strokes? Would he be killed by a bolt of lightning during a baseball game? Later that same Christmas Eve, he would serve on the altar at Holy Communion, wearing fresh white and scarlet and raking the dark church, as he appeared to pray, for the shape of her face. In the light of all the vows he had taken, that was heinous, but how could it be, since if his flesh had not informed his spirit he would never have known this sense of strength and lightness of his bones, this fullness of heart, this absolute belief in the glad tidings of Christmas, the star and the kings? If he walked her home from church in the storm her kind parents might ask him to spend the night and she might come to him. In his mind he heard the creaking of the stairs, saw the color of her instep, and he thought, in his innocence, how wonderful was his nature that he could at the same moment praise his Saviour and see the shape of his lady's foot. Beside Mary stood Charlie Anderson, who had the gift of an unusually sweet tenor voice, and beside him were the Basset twins.

In the dark, mixed clothing they had put on for the storm, the carolers looked uncommonly forlorn, but the moment they began to sing they were transformed. The Negress looked like an angel, and dumpy Lucille lifted her head gracefully and seemed to cast off her misspent youth in the rainy streets around Carnegie Hall. This instantaneous transformation of the company was thrilling, and Mr. Applegate felt his faith renewed, felt that an infinity of unrealized possibilities lay ahead of them, a tremendous richness of peace, a renaissance without brigands, an ecstasy of light and color, a kingdom! Or was this gin! The carolers seemed absolved and purified as long as the music lasted, but when the final note was broken off they were just as suddenly themselves. Mr. Applegate thanked them, and they started for his front door. He drew old Mr. Sturgis aside and said tactfully, "I know you enjoy very good health, but don't you think this snowstorm might be a little too severe for you to go out in? It said on the radio that there hasn't been such a snowstorm in a hundred years."

"Oh, no, thank you," said Mr. Sturgis, who was deaf. "I had a bowl of crackers and milk before I came out."

The carol singers left the rectory for the village green.

The music could be heard in the feed store, where Barry Freeman was closing up. Barry had graduated from Andover Academy, and during Christmas vacation of his senior year he had worn his new tuxedo to the Eastern Star Dance. There was general laughter as soon as he appeared. He approached one girl and then another, and when they all refused to dance with him he tried to cut in, but he was laughed off the floor. He stood against the wall for nearly half an hour before he put on his coat and walked home through the snow. His appearance in a tuxedo had not been forgotten. "My oldest daughter," a woman might say, "was born two years after Barry Freeman wore his monkey suit to the Eastern Star Dance." It was a turning point in his life. It may have accounted for the fact that he had never married and would go home on Christmas Eve to an empty house.

The music could be heard in Bryant's General Store ("Rock Bottom Prices"), where old Lucy Markham was talking on the telephone. "Do you have Prince Albert in the can, Miss Mark-ham?" a child's voice asked.

"Yes, dear," Miss Markham said.

"Now, you stop hectoring Miss Markham," said Althea Swee-ney, the telephone operator. "You're not supposed to use the telephone for hectoring people on Christmas Eve."

"It's against the law," said the child, "to interfere in private telephone conversations. I'm just asking Miss Markham if she has Prince Albert in the can."

"Yes, dear," said Miss Markham.

"Then let him out," said the child, her voice breaking with laughter. Althea turned her attention to a more interesting con-versation—an eighty-five-cent call to New Jersey, made from Prescott's drugstore.

"It's Dolores, Mama," a strange voice said. "It's Dolores. I'm in a place called St. Botolphs. . . . No, I'm not drunk, Mama. I'm not drunk. I just wanted to wish you a Merry Christmas, Mama. . . . I just wanted to wish you a Merry Christmas. And a Merry Christmas to Uncle Pete and Aunt Mildred. A Merry Christmas to all of them . . ." She was crying.

" '. . . on the Feast of Stephen,' " sang the carolers, " 'when the snow lay round about . . .' " But the voice of Dolores, with its prophecy of gas stations and motels, freeways, and all-night supermarkets, had more to do with the world to come than the singing on the green.

The singers turned down Boat Street to the Williamses' house. They would not be offered any hospitality here, they knew—not because Mr. Williams was mean but because he felt that hospitality might reflect on the probity of the bank of which he was president. A conservative man, he kept in his study a portrait photograph of Woodrow Wilson framed in an old ma-hogany toilet seat. His daughter, home from Miss Winsor's, and his son, home from St. Mark's, stood with their father and mother in the doorway and called "Merry Christmas! Merry Christmas!" Next to the Williamses' was the Brattles', where they were asked in for a cup of cocoa. Jack Brattle had married the Davenport girl from Travertine. It had not been a happy marriage, and, having heard somewhere that parsley was an aphrodisiac, Jack had planted eight or ten rows of parsley in his garden. As soon as the parsley matured, rabbits began to raid it, and, going into his garden one night with a shotgun, Jack blew an irreparable hole in the stomach of a Portuguese fisherman named Manuel Fada, who had been his wife's lover for years. He stood trial on a manslaughter charge in the county court and was acquitted, but his wife ran off with a yard-goods salesman, and now Jack lived with his mother.

Next to the Brattles were the Dummers, where the carol singers were passed dandelion wine and sweet cookies. Mr. Dummer was a frail man who sometimes did needlework and who was the father of eight. His enormous children ranged behind him in the living room, like some excessive authentication of his vigor. Mrs. Dummer seemed pregnant again, although it wasn't easy to tell. In the hallway was a photograph of her as a pretty young woman, posed beside a cast-iron deer. Mr. Dummer had labeled the picture "Two Dears." The singers pointed this out to one another as they left the house for the storm.

Next to the Dummers were the Bretaignes, who ten years ago had been to Europe, where they had bought a crèche, which everyone admired. Their only daughter, Hazel, was there with her husband and children. During Hazel's marriage ceremony, when Mr. Applegate asked who gave the girl away, Mrs. Bretaigne got up from her pew and said, "I do. She's mine, she's not his. I took care of her when she was sick. I made her clothes. I helped her with her homework. He never did anything. She's mine, and I'm the one to give her away." This unconventional behavior did not seem to have affected Hazel's married happiness. Her husband looked prosperous and her children were pretty and well behaved.

At the foot of the street was old Honora Wapshot's house, where they knew they would get buttered rum, and in the storm the old house, with all its fires burning, all its chimneys smoking, seemed like a fine work of man, the kind of homestead some greeting-card artist or desperately lonely sailor sweating out a hangover in a furnished room might have drawn, brick by brick, room by room, on Christmas Eve. Maggie, the maid, let them in and passed the rum. Honora stood at the end of her parlor, an old lady in a black dress that was sprinkled liberally with either flour or talcum powder. Mr. Sturgis did the honors. "Say us the poem, Honora," he asked.

She backed up toward the piano, straightened her dress, and began:

> "Announced by all the trumpets of the sky,
>   Arrives the snow, and, driving o'er the fields,
>   Seems nowhere to alight; the whited air
>   Hides hills and woods, the river and the heaven,
>   And veils the farmhouse at the garden's end. . . ."

She got through to the end without making a mistake, and then they sang "Joy to the World." It was Mrs. Coulter's favorite, and it made her weep. The events in Bethlehem seemed to be not a revelation but an affirmation of what she had always known in her bones to be the surprising abundance of life. It was for this house, this company, this stormy night that He had lived and died. And how wonderful it was, she thought, that the world had been blessed with a savior! How wonderful it was that she should have such a capacity for joy! When the carol ended she dried her tears and said to Gloria Pendleton: "Isn't it wonderful?" Maggie filled their glasses again. Everyone protested, everyone drank a cup, and going back into the snow again they felt, like Mr. Jowett, that there was happiness everywhere, happiness all around them.

But there was at least one lonely figure on the scene, lonely and furtive. It was old Mr. Spofford, moving with the particular agility of a thief, down the path to the river. He carried a mysterious sack. He lived alone at the edge of town, supporting himself by repairing watches. His family was formerly well-to-do, and he had traveled and been to college. What could he be carrying to the river on Christmas Eve in an epochal snowstorm? It must be some secret, something he meant to destroy, but what documents might a lonely old man possess, and why should he choose this of all nights to hide his secret in the river?

The sack he carried was a pillowcase, and in it were nine live kittens. They made a lumpy burden, mewing loudly for milk, and their mistaken vitality distressed him. He had tried to give them away to the butcher, the fish man, the ash man and the druggist, but who wants a stray cat on Christmas Eve, and he couldn't take care of nine himself. It was not his fault that his old cat conceived—it was no one's fault, really—and yet the closer he got to the river, the heavier was his burden of guilt. It was the destruction of their vitality, their life, that pained him. Animals are not supposed to apprehend death, and yet the struggle in the pillowcase was vigorous and apprehensive; and he was cold.

He was an old man, and he hated the snow. Pushing on toward the river, he seemed to see in the storm the mortality of the planet. Spring would never come again. The valley of the West River would never again be a bowl of grass and violets. The lilacs would never bloom again. Watching the snow blow over the fields, he knew in his bones the death of civilizations—Paris buried in snow, the Grand Canal and the Thames frozen over, London abandoned, and in the caves of the escarpment at Innsbruck a few survivors huddled over a fire of chair and table legs. This cruel, this dolorous, this Russian winter, he thought; this death of hope. Cheer, valor, all good feelings had been extinguished in him by the cold. He tried to cast the hour into the future, to invent some gentle thaw, some clement southwest wind—blue and moving water in the river, tulips and hyacinths in bloom, the plump stars of a spring night hung about the tree of heaven—but he felt instead the chill of the glacier, the ice age, in his bones and in the painful beating of his heart.

The river was frozen, but there was some open water along the banks where the current turned. It would be easiest to drop a stone into the pillowcase, but this might hurt the kittens that he meant to murder. He knotted the top of the sack, and as he approached the water the noise in the pillowcase got louder and more plaintive. The banks were icy. The river was deep. The snow was blinding. When he put his sack into the water, it floated, and in trying to submerge it he lost his balance and fell into the water himself. "Help! Help! Help!" he cried. "Help! Help! Help! I'm drowning!" But no one heard him, and it would be weeks before he was missed.

Then the train whistle sounded—the afternoon train that had pushed its cowcatcher through the massive drifts, bringing home the last to come, bringing them back to the old houses on Boat Street, where nothing was changed and nothing was strange and nobody worried and nobody grieved, and where in an hour or two the souls of men would be sifted out, the good getting toboggans and sleds, skates and snowshoes, ponies and gold pieces, and the wicked receiving nothing but a lump of coal.

2

The Wapshot family settled in St. Botolphs in the seventeenth century. I knew them well, I made it my business to examine their affairs, indeed I spent the best years of my life, its very summit, on their chronicle. They were friendly enough. When you met them on the streets of St. Botolphs they behaved as if this chance meeting were something they had anticipated but if you told them anything—told them that the West River had flooded or that Pinkham's Folly had burned to the ground—they would convey, in a fleeting smile, the fact that you had made a mistake. One did not tell the Wapshots anything. Their resistance to receiving information seemed to be a family trait. They thought well of themselves; they esteemed themselves so healthy that it seemed impossible to them that they would not have known about the flood or the fire, even though they might have been in Europe. I went to school with the boys, raced with

Moses at the Travertine Boat Club and played football with them both. They used to cheer one another loudly as if shouting the family name across a playing field would give it some immortality. I spent a lot of pleasant time at their house on River Street and yet what I remember is that it was always in their power to make me feel alone, to make it painfully clear that I was an outsider.

Moses, when I knew him best, had the kind of good looks and presence that sweeps a young man triumphantly through secondary school and disappointingly enough not much farther. He had dark yellow hair and a sallow complexion. Everybody loved Moses, including the village dogs, and he comported himself with the purest, the most impulsive humility. Everybody did not love Coverly. He had a long neck and a disagreeable habit of cracking his knuckles. Sarah Wapshot, their mother, was a fair and slender woman who wore a pince-nez, mispronounced the word "interesting" and claimed to have read *Middlemarch* sixteen times. She used to leave her books in the garden and their set of George Eliot was foxed and buckled by the rain. Their father, Leander, was one of those Massachusetts Yankees who look forever like a boy although toward the end he looked like a boy who had seen the Gorgon. He had a high color, fine blue eyes and thick white hair. He said "marst" for "mast" and "had" for "hard" and spent the last years of his life running a launch between Travertine and the amusement park in Nangasakit. Leander drowned while swimming. Mrs. Wapshot died two years later and ascended into heaven, where she must have been kept very busy since she was a member of that first generation of American women to enjoy sexual equality. She had exhausted herself in good works. She had founded the Woman's Club, the Current Events Club, and was a director of the Animal Rescue League and the Lambert Home for Unwed Mothers. As a result of all these activities the house on River Street was always filled with dust, its cut flowers long dead, the clocks stopped. Sarah Wapshot was one of those women whose grasp of vital matters had forced them to consider the simple tasks of a house to be in some way perverted. Coverly married a girl named Betsey MacCaffery from the Georgia badlands; a counter girl in a Forty-second Street milk bar. At the time of which I'm writing he worked at the Talifer Missile Site. Moses had thrown up his job as a banking apprentice to work for Leopold and Company, a shady brokerage house. He married Melissa Scaddon. Both Moses and Coverly had sons.

Spread them out on some ungiven summer evening on the lawn between their house and the banks of the West River, in the fine hour before dinner. Mrs. Wapshot is giving Lulu, the cook, a lesson in landscape painting. They have set up their easel a little to the right of the group. Mrs. Wapshot is holding a paper frame up to the river view and saying: *"Cherchez la motif, Lulu. Cherchez la motif."* Leander is drinking bourbon and admiring the light. For a man who is, in all his ways, plainly provincial, Leander's life has possessed more latitude than one would have guessed. He once traveled as far west as Cleveland with a Shakespearean company and, a few years later, ascended one hundred and twenty-seven feet in a hot-air balloon at the county fair. He is proud of himself, proud of his sons; pride is some part of the calm and inquisitive gaze he gives to the river banks, thinking that all the rivers of the world are old but that the rivers of his own country seem oldest.

Coverly is burning tent moths out of the apple trees. Moses folds a sail. From the open windows of their house they can hear the Waldstein Sonata being played by their cousin Devereaux, who is practicing for his concert debut in the fall. Devereaux has a harried, dark face and is not quite twelve years old. "Light and shadow, light and shadow," says old Cousin Honora of the music. She would say the same for Chopin, Stravinsky or Thelonious Monk. She is a redoubtable old woman in her seventies, dressed all in white. (She will switch to black on Labor Day.) Her money has saved the family repeatedly from disgrace or worse and while her own home is on the other side of town she gives this landscape and its cast a proprietary look. The parrot, in his cage by the kitchen door, exclaims: "Julius Caesar,

I am thoroughly *disgusted.*" It is all he ever says.

How orderly, clean and sensible the world seems; above all how light, as if these were the beginnings of a world, a chain of mornings. It is late in the day, late in this history of this part of the world, but this lateness does nothing to eclipse their ardor. Presently there is a cloud of black smoke from the kitchen—the rolls are burning—but it doesn't really matter. They eat their supper in a cavernous dining room, play a little whist, kiss one another good night and go to sleep to dream.

3

The trouble began one afternoon when Coverly Wapshot swung down off the slow train, the only south-bound train that still stopped at the village of St. Botolphs. It was in the late winter, just before dark. The snow was gone but the grass was dead and the place seemed not to have rallied from the February storms. He shook hands with Mr. Jowett and asked about his family. He waved to the bartender in the Viaduct House, waved to Barry Freeman in the feed store and called hello to Miles Howland, who was coming out of the bank. The late sky was brilliant and turbulent but it shed none of its operatic lights and fires onto the darkness of the green. This awesome performance was contained within the air. Between the buildings he could see the West River with its, for him, enormous cargo of pleasant memory and he took away from this brightness the unlikely impression that the river's long history had been a purifying force, leaving the water fit to drink. He turned right at Boat Street. Mrs. Williams was sitting in her parlor, reading the paper. The only light at the Brattles' was in the kitchen. The Dummers' house was dark. Mrs. Bretaigne, who was saying good-by to a caller, welcomed him home. Then he turned up the walk to Cousin Honora's.

Maggie answered the door and he gave her a kiss. "They ain't nothing but dried beef," Maggie said. "You'll have to kill a chicken." He went down the long hall past the seven views of Rome into the library, where he found his old cousin with an open book on her lap. Here was home-sweet-home, the polished brass, the apple-wood fire. "Coverly dear," Honora said in an impulse of love and kissed him on the lips. "Honora," Coverly said, taking her in his arms. Then they separated and scrutinized one another cannily to see what changes had been made.

Her white hair was still full, her face leonine, but her new false teeth were not well fitted and they made her look like a cannibal. This hinted savagery reminded Coverly of the fact that his cousin had never been photographed. In all the family albums she appeared either with her back to the camera as she ran away or with her face concealed by her hands, her handbag, her hat or a newspaper. Any stranger looking at the albums would have thought she was wanted for murder. Honora thought Coverly looked underfed and she said so. "You're skinny," she said.

"Yes."

"I'll have Maggie bring you some port."

"I'd rather have a whisky."

"You don't drink whisky," Honora said.

"I didn't used to," Coverly said, "but I do now."

"Will wonders never cease?" Honora asked.

"If you're going to kill a chicken," Maggie said from the doorway, "you'd better kill it now or you won't get supper much before midnight."

"I'll kill the chicken now," Coverly said.

"You'll have to speak louder," Honora said. "She can't hear."

Coverly followed Maggie back through the house to the kitchen. "She's crazier than ever," Maggie said. "Now she claims she can't sleep. She claims she ain't slept for years. Well, so I come into the parlor one afternoon with her tea and there she is. Sound asleep. Snoring. So I say, 'Wake up, Miss Wapshot. Here's your tea.' She says, 'What do you mean, wake up? I wasn't asleep,' she says. 'I was just lost in deep meditation.' And now she's thinking of buying an automobile. Dear Jesus, it would be like setting a hungry lion loose in the streets. She'll be running over and killing innocent little children if she don't kill herself first."

The relationship between the old women stood foursquare on a brand of larcenous backbiting that appeared to contain so little in the way of truth that it could be passed off as comical. Maggie's hearing was perfect but for some years Honora had told everyone she was deaf. Honora was eccentric but Maggie told everyone in the village that she was mad. The physical and mental infirmities they invented for one another had a pristine quality that made it nearly impossible to believe there was any grimness in the contest.

Coverly found a hatchet in the back pantry and went down the wooden steps to the garden. Somewhere in the distance he could hear children's voices, distinctly accented with the catarrhal pronunciations of that part of the world. There was a gaggle of sound from the hen house beyond the hedge. He felt uncommonly happy in this sparsely populated place; felt some marked loosening of his discontents. It was the hour, he knew, when the pinochle players would be drifting across the green to the firehouse and when the yearnings of adolescence, exacerbated by the smallness of the village, would be approaching a climax. He could remember sitting himself on the back steps of the house on River Street, racked with a yearning for love, for friendship and renown, that had made him howl.

He went on through the hedge to the hen house. The laying hens had retired but four or five cockerels were feeding in their yard. He chased them into their house and after an undignified scuffle caught one by its yellow legs. The bird squawked for mercy and Coverly spoke to it soothingly, he hoped, as he lay its neck on the block and chopped off its head. He held the struggling body down and away from him to let the blood drain into the ground. Maggie brought him a bucket of scalding water and an old copy of the St. Botolphs *Enterprise* and he plucked and eviscerated the bird, losing his taste for chicken, step by step. He brought the carcass back to the kitchen and joined his old cousin in the library, where Maggie had set out whisky and water.

"Can we talk now?" Coverly asked.

"I guess so," Honora said. She put her elbows on her knees and leaned forward. "You want to talk about the house on River Street?"

"Yes."

"Well, nobody'll rent it and nobody'll buy it and it would break my heart to see it torn down."

"What is the matter?"

"The Whitehalls rented it in October. They moved in and moved right out again. Then the Haverstraws took it. They lasted a week. Mrs. Haverstraw told everybody in the stores that the house was haunted. But who," she asked, raising her face, "would there be to haunt the place? Our family has always been a very happy family. None of us have ever paid any attention to ghosts. But just the same it's all over town."

"What did Mrs. Haverstraw say?"

"Mrs. Haverstraw spread it around that it's the ghost of your father."

"Leander," Coverly said.

"But what would Leander want to come back and trouble people for?" Honora asked. "It wasn't that he didn't believe in ghosts. He just never had any use for them. I've heard him say many times that he thought ghosts kept low company. And you know how kind he was. He used to escort flies and moth millers out the door as if they were guests. What would he come back for except to eat a bowl of crackers and milk? Of course he had his faults."

"Were you with us," Coverly asked, "the time he smoked a cigarette in church?"

"You must have made that up," Honora said, fending for the past.

"No," Coverly said. "It was Christmas Eve and we went to Holy Communion. I remember that he seemed very devout. He was up and down, crossing himself and roaring out the responses. Then before the Benediction he took a cigarette out of his pocket and lighted it. I saw then that he was terribly drunk. I told him, 'You can't smoke in church, Daddy,' but we were in one of the front pews and a lot of people had seen him. What I wanted then was to be the son of Mr. Pluzinski the farmer. I don't know why, except that the Pluzinskis were all very serious. It seemed to me that if I could only be the son of Mr. Pluzinski I would be happy."

"You ought to be ashamed of yourself," Honora said. Then she sighed, changed her tone and added uneasily: "There was something else."

"What?"

"You remember how he used to give away nickels on the Fourth of July."

"Oh, yes." Coverly then saw the front of their house in many colors. A large flag hung from the second floor, its crimson stripes faded to the color of old blood. His father stood on the porch, after the parade and before the ball game, passing out new nickels to a line of children that reached up River Street. The trees were all leafed out and in his reverie the light was quite green.

"Well, as you may remember he kept the nickels in a cigar box. He had painted it black. When I was going through the house I found the box. There were still some nickels in it. Many of them were not real. I believe he made them himself."

"You mean . . ."

"Shhhh," said Honora.

"Supper's ready," said Maggie.

Honora seemed tired after supper so he kissed her good night in the hallway and walked to his own home on the other side of town. The place had been empty since fall. There was a key on the windowsill and the door swung open onto a strong smell of must. This was the place where he had been conceived and born, where he had awakened to the excellence of life, and there was some keen chagrin at finding the scene of so many dazzling memories smelling of decay; but this, he knew, was the instinctual foolishness that leads us to love permanence when there is none. He turned on the lights in the hall and the parlor and got some logs from the shed. He was absorbed in laying and lighting a fire but when the fire was set he began to feel, surrounded by so many uninhabited rooms, an unreasonable burden of apprehension, as if his presence there were an intrusion.

It was his and his brother's house, by contract, inheritance and memory. Its leaks and other infirmities were his responsibility. It was he who had broken the vase on the mantelpiece and burned a hole in the sofa. He did not believe in ghosts, shades, spirits or any other forms of unquietness on the part of the dead. He was a man of twenty-eight, happily married, the father of a son. He weighed one hundred and thirty-eight pounds, enjoyed perfect health and had eaten some chicken for dinner. These were the facts. He took a copy of *Tristram Shandy* down from the shelf and began to read. There was a loud noise in the kitchen that so startled him the sweat stood out on his hands. He raised his head long enough to embrace this noise in the realm of hard fact. It could be a shutter, a loose piece of firewood, an animal or one of those legendary tramps who were a part of local demonology and who were supposed to inhabit the empty farms, leaving traces of fire, empty snuff cans, a dry cow and a frightened spinster. But he was strong and young and even if he should encounter a tramp in the dark hallway he could take care of himself. Why should he feel so intensely uncomfortable? He went to the telephone intending to ask the operator the time of night but the telephone was dead.

He went on reading. There was noise from the dining room. He said something loud and vigorous to express his impatience and his apprehensions but the effect of this was to convince him overwhelmingly that he had been heard. Someone was listening. There was a cure for this foolishness. He went directly to the empty room and turned on the light. There was nothing there and yet the beating of his heart was accelerated and painful and sweat ran off his palms. Then the dining room door slowly closed of itself. This was only natural since the old house sagged badly and while half the doors closed themselves the other half wouldn't close at all. He went through the swinging door on into the pantry and the kitchen. Here again he saw nothing but felt again that there had been someone in the room when he turned on the light. There were two sets of facts—the empty room and the alarmed condition of his skin. He was determined to scotch this and he went out of the kitchen into the hallway and climbed the stairs.

All the bedroom doors stood open, and here, in the dark, he seemed to yield to the denseness of the lives that had been lived here for nearly two centuries. The burden of the past was palpable; the utterances and groans of conception, childbirth and death, the singing at the family reunion in 1893, the dust raised by a Fourth of July parade, the shock of lovers meeting by chance in the hallway, the roar of flames in the fire that gutted the west wing in 1900, the politeness at christenings, the joy of a young husband bringing his wife back after their marriage, the hardships of a cruel winter all took on some palpableness in the dark air. But why was the atmosphere in this darkness distinctly one of trouble and failure? Ebenezer had made a fortune. Lorenzo had introduced child-welfare legislation into the state laws. Alice had converted hundreds of Polynesians to Christianity. Why should none of these ghosts and shades seem contented with their work? Was it because they had been mortal, was it because for every last one of them the pain of death had been bitter?

He returned to the fire. Here was the physical world, fire-lit, stubborn and beloved, and yet his physical response was not to the parlor but to the darkness in the rooms around him. Why, sitting so close to the fire, did he feel a chill slide down his left shoulder and a moment later coarsen with cold the skin of his chest, as if a hand had been placed there? If there were ghosts, he believed with his father that they kept low company. They consorted with the poorhearted and the faint. He knew that we sometimes leave after us, in a room, a stir of love or rancor when we are gone. He believed that whatever we pay for our loves in money, venereal disease, scandal or ecstasy, we leave behind us, in the hotels, motels, guest rooms, meadows and fields where we discharge this much of ourselves, either the scent of goodness or the odor of evil, to influence those who come after us. Thus it was possible that this passionate and eccentric cast had left behind them some ambiance that made his presence seem like an intrusion. It was time to go to bed and he got some blankets out of a closet and made up a bed in the spare room, nearest the stairs.

He woke at three. There was enough radiance from the moon or the night sky itself to light the room. What had waked him, he knew immediately, was not a dream, a reverie or an apprehension; it was something that moved, something that he could see, something strange and unnatural. The terror began with his optic nerves and reverberated through his whole person but it was in the beam of his eye that the terror had begun. He was able to trace the disturbance back through his nervous system to his pupil. The eye counted on reality and what he had seen or thought he had seen was the ghost of his father. The chaos set into motion by this hallucination was horrendous and he shook with psychic and physical cold, he shook with terror, and sitting up in bed he roared: "Oh, Father, Father, Father, why have you come back?"

The loudness of his voice was some consolation. The ghost seemed to leave the room. He thought he could hear stair lifts give. Had he come back to look for a bowl of crackers and milk, to read some Shakespeare, come back because he felt like all the others that the pain of death was bitter? Had he come back to relive that moment when he had relinquished the supreme privileges of youth—when he had waked feeling less peckery than usual and realized that the doctor had no cure for autumn, no medicine for the north wind? The smell of his green years would still be in his nose—the reek of clover, the fragrance of women's breasts, so like the land-wind, smelling of grass and trees—but it was time for him to leave the field for someone

younger. Spavined, gray, he had wanted no less than any youth
to chase the nymphs. Over hill and dale. Now you see them;
now you don't. The world a paradise, a paradise! Father, Father,
why have you come back?

There was the noise of something falling in the next room.
The knowledge that this was a squirrel, as it was, would not
have brought Coverly to his senses. He was too far gone. He
grabbed his clothing, flew down the stairs and left the front
door standing open. He stopped on the sidewalk long enough
to draw on his underpants. Then he ran to the corner. Here
he put on his trousers and shirt but he ran the rest of the way
to Honora's barefoot. He scribbled a farewell note, left it on
her hall table and caught the milk train north, a little after dawn,
past the Markhams', past the Wilton Trace, past the Lowells',
who had changed the sign on their barn from BE KIND TO ANIMALS
to GOD ANSWERS PRAYERS, past the house where old Mr. Spofford
used to live and repair watches.

4

Going back to Talifer where he lived with Betsey, Coverly had
the choice of concluding that he was demented or that he had
seen his father's ghost. He chose the latter, of course, and yet
he could not say so to his wife; he could not explain to his
brother Moses why the house on River Street was empty. The
specter of his father seemed to sit beside him in the plane that
took him west. Oh, Father, Father, why have you come back!
What, he wondered, would Leander have made of Talifer?

The site for Missile Research and Development had a population of twenty thousand, divided, like any society, whatever its
aspirations, into first class, second class, third class and steerage.
The large aristocracy was composed of physicists and engineers.
Tradesmen made up the middle class, and there was a vast prole-

tariat of mechanics, ground crewmen and gantry hands. Most
of the aristocracy had been given underground shelters and while
this fact had never been publicized it was well known that in
the case of a cataclysm the proletariat would be left to scald.
This made for some hard feeling. The vitals of the place were
the twenty-nine gantries at the edge of the desert, the mosque-
shaped atomic reactor, the underground laboratories and han-
gars and the two-square-mile computation and administration
center. The concerns of the site were entirely extraterrestrial,
and while common sense would scotch any sentimental and transparent ironies about the vastness of scientific research under-
taken at Talifer and the capacity for irrational forlornness, loneliness and ecstasy among the scientists, it was a way of life that
presented some strenuous intellectual contrasts.

Security was always a problem. Talifer was never mentioned
in the newspapers. It had no public existence. This concern with
security seemed to inhibit life at every level. One Saturday afternoon Betsey was watching television. Coverly had taken Binxey
for a trip to the shopping center. Out of her window she saw
that Mr. Hansen, who lived across the street, was taking down
his storm windows and putting up his screens. He had a steplad-
der, which he planted carefully in his flowerbeds, then he raised
and unhooked his windows and carried them into the garage.
His wife and children seemed to be off. There were no other
signs of life around the place. When he had removed the windows
from the first floor he started on the upstairs bedrooms. His
ladder didn't reach these and he had to work by leaning out
of the open windows, unhooking the frames and drawing them
on their rectilinear bias into the house. The hardware for one
of the windows seemed warped or rusted. It would not come
loose. He straddled the windowsill and yanked at the frame.
He fell out of the window and landed with a thud onto a little
terrace that he had paved with cement block a few weeks earlier.
Betsey looked out of the window long enough to see that his
body was inert. Then she returned to her television set. Twenty
minutes later she heard a siren and an ambulance came down

the street and took the still inert form away on a stretcher. She
learned that evening that he had been instantly killed. Some
children had given the alarm. But why hadn't she? How could
she account for her unnatural behavior? The general concern
for security seemed to be at the bottom of her negligence. She
had not wanted to do anything that would call attention to herself, that would involve giving testimony or answering questions.
Presumably her concern for security had led her to overlook
the death of a neighbor.

Coverly would have had some difficulty explaining to Leander
that while he had been trained as a taper and subprogrammer,
he had been switched to public relations when he was transferred
from the Remsen to the Talifer site. This was a mistake, made
by one of the computations machines in personnel, but there
was no appeal. They lived in a mixed neighborhood. Betsey
wanted a shelter and Coverly had applied for a transfer to another
neighborhood but the government-operated real-estate office
was swamped with such applications and anyhow Coverly was
not unhappy where he was. Ginkgo trees had been planted along
the sidewalks where children roller-skated, and song birds had
nested in the trees. Sitting in his back yard before dinner he
could watch the sere and moving mountain twilight—that sour
and powerful glow—beyond the distant gantries. They had a
little garden and a grill for cooking meat. The house on their
right was owned by a man named Armstrong, who was in the
World Relations Department. Armstrong had developed a dry,
manly and monosyllabic prose style for ghosting the chronicles
of astronauts. The house on their left was owned by a gantry-
crew man named Murphy, who got drunk and beat up his wife
on Saturday nights. The Wapshots did not get along with the
Murphys. One morning when Coverly was at work the signal
board indicated that there was a telephone call for him. He left
the security area to take the call. It was Betsey. "She stole my
garbage pail," Betsey said.

"I don't understand, sugar," Coverly said.

"Mrs. Murphy," Betsey said. "The garbage man came this

morning, he always comes on Tuesdays, and when he took away the garbage she took that nice, new, tin, galvanized garbage pail of mine and carried it right up to the back of her house, leaving me with that cracked, plastic old thing they brought from Canaveral."

"Well, I can't do anything about it now," Coverly said. "I'll be home at half-past five."

Betsey was still excited when he returned. "You go right over there now and get it back," she said. "They'll fill it up with garbage and claim that it's theirs. You should have painted our name on it. You go right over there now and get it away from them. There he is, he's cutting the grass."

Coverly left the house and walked to the boundary of his lot. Pete Murphy had just started up his lawn mower. The distant mountains were blue. The time of day, the sameness of the houses, the popping noise of the one-cylinder engine and the two men in their white shirt sleeves gave to the scene some unwonted otherness, as if Coverly were not about to accuse his neighbor, or his neighbor's wife, of theft, but was about to remark that merchandising indices showed in their uptrend the inarguable power of direct-mail advertising. In short, their reality and their passions seemed challenged. The distant mountains had been formed by fire and water but the houses in the valley looked so insubstantial that they seemed, in the dusk, to smell of shirt cardboards. Coverly cracked his knuckles nervously and signaled to Pete with a jerk of his head. Pete pushed the lawn mower directly past him and muffled Coverly's words with noise of the motor. Coverly waited. Pete made a second circle of the lawn and then throttled down the motor and stopped in front of Coverly.

"My wife tells me you stole our garbage pail," Coverly said.

"So what?"

"Are you in the habit of helping yourself to other people's property?" Coverly was more perplexed than angry.

"Listen, chicken," Murphy said. "Where I grew up you either helped yourself or you ate dirt."

"But this doesn't happen to be where you grew up," said Coverly. It was the wrong tack. He seemed to be footnoting the dispute. Then, confident of his rightness, he spoke sternly and in a full voice, marred by some old-fashioned or provincial haughtiness.

"Would you be good enough to return our garbage pail?" he asked.

"Listen," Murphy said. "You're trespassing. You're on my land. Get off my land or you'll go home a cripple for life. I'll gouge out your eyes. I'll break your nose. I'll tear off your ears."

Coverly swung a right from the hip, and Murphy, a big man and a coward, it seemed, went down. Coverly stood there, a little bewildered. Then Murphy came forward on his hands and knees and sank his teeth into Coverly's shin. Coverly roared. Betsey and Mrs. Murphy came running out of their kitchens. Just then a missile left its pad and, in the dusk, shed a light as bright as the light of a midsummer's day over the valley and the site, throwing the shadows of the combatants, their houses and their ginkgo trees blackly onto the grass, while air waves demarked the earth-shaking roar so that it sounded like the humble click of track joints. The missile ascended, the light faded with it, and the two women took their husbands home.

Oh, Father, Father, why have you come back?

The computation and administration center where Coverly worked appeared from a distance to be a large, one-story building but this single story merely contained the elevator terminals and the security offices. The other offices and the hardware were underground. The one visible story was made of glass, tinted darkly to the color of oily water. The darkened glass did not diminish but it did alter the light of day. Beyond these dim glass walls one could see some flat pasture land and the buildings of an abandoned farm. There was a house, a barn, a clump of trees and a split-rail fence, and the abandoned buildings with the gantries beyond them had a nostalgic charm. They were signs of the past, and whatever the truth may have been, they appeared to be signs of a rich and a natural way of life. The

abandoned farm evoked a spate of vulgar and bucolic imagery—
open fires, pails of fresh milk and pretty girls swinging in apple
trees—but it was nonetheless persuasive. One turned away from
this then to the dark, oil-colored glass and moved into another
world, buried six stories beneath the cow pasture. It was a new
world in every way. Its newness was most apparent in an atmosphere of enthusiasm and usefulness that seems lost to most of
us today. To observe that the elevators sometimes broke down,
that one of the glass walls had cracked, and that the pretty recep-
tionists in the security office had a primitive and an immemorial
appeal was like burdening oneself with the observations of some
old man, pushed by time past the boundaries of all usefulness.
The crowds that went to and from the computation center had
a look of contentment and purpose that you won't find in the
New York or Paris subways, where we seem to regard one another
with the horror and dismay of a civilization of caricaturists. Leaving his office late one night Coverly had heard Dr. Cameron,
the site director, ending a dispute with one of his lieutenants.
The doctor was shouting, "You'll never get a Goddamned man
onto the Goddamned moon, and if you do, it won't do you
any Goddamned good."

Oh, Father, Father, why have you come back?

Betsey had hoped to be transferred to Canaveral and was disappointed in Talifer. They had been there two months then but
no one had come to call. She had made no friends. In the evening
she could hear the sounds of talk and laughter but she and
Coverly were never included in these gatherings. From her window Betsey could see Mrs. Armstrong working in her flower
garden and she interpreted this interest in flowers as the sign
of a kindly nature. One day, when Binxey was taking his nap,
Betsey went next door and rang the bell. Mrs. Armstrong answered the door. "I'm Betsey Wapshot," Betsey said, "and I'm
your next-door neighbor. My husband Coverly was trained as
a subprogrammer but they've got him on public relations right
now. I've seen you in your garden and I thought I'd pay you a
call." The woman kindly invited her in. She seemed not inhospi-

table but subdued. "What I wanted to ask you about," Betsey said, "was my neighbors. We've been here two months now but we just seem to have been too busy to make friends. We don't know anybody and so I thought I'd like to give a little cocktail party and see who's who. I want to know who to ask."

"Well, my dear, I'd wait a little while, if I were you," Mrs. Armstrong said. "For some reason this seems to be quite a conservative community. I think you'd better meet your neighbors before you invite them."

"Well, I come from a small town," Betsey said, "where everybody's neighbors, and I often say to myself that if I can't trust in the friendliness of strangers, well, then what in the world is there that I can trust in?"

"I see what you mean," said Mrs. Armstrong.

"I've lived in all kinds of places," Betsey said. "High society. Low society. My husband's family came over on the *Arbella*. That's the ship that came after the *Mayflower* but it had a higher class of people. It seems to me that people are all the same, under their skins. What I want you to do is to give me a list of twenty-five or thirty of the most interesting people in the neighborhood."

"But, my dear, I'm afraid I couldn't do that."

"Why not?"

"There isn't time."

"Well, it wouldn't take very long, would it?" Betsey asked. "I've got a pencil and paper right here. Now just tell me who lives in the house on the corner."

"The Seldons."

"Are they interesting?"

"Yes, they're quite interesting but they're not terribly friendly."

"What's his first name?"

"Herbert."

"Who lives in the house next to them?"

"The Trampsons."

"Are they interesting?"

"Yes, they're terribly interesting. He and Reginald Tappan discovered the Tappan Constant. He's been nominated for a Nobel Prize but he's not terribly friendly."

"And then on the other side of them?" Betsey asked.

"The Harnecks," Mrs. Armstrong said. "But I must warn you, my dear, that you'll be making a mistake if you ask them before you've been introduced."

"And that's where I think you're wrong," Betsey said. "You just wait and see. Who lives on the other side of them?"

In the end she went away with a list of twenty-five names. Mrs. Armstrong explained that she would be unable to come to the party herself because she was going to Denver. With the thought of a party to occupy her Betsey was happy and at peace with the world. She explained her plans to the proprietor of a liquor store in the shopping center. He told her what she would need and gave her the telephone number of a couple—a maid and barman—who would mix the drinks and prepare the food. At the stationery store she bought a box of invitations and happily spent an afternoon and an evening addressing these. On the day of the party the couple arrived at three. Betsey dressed herself and her little son, Coverly came home at five, when the first guests were expected, and the scene was set.

When no one had come by half-past five Coverly opened a beer and the barman made a whisky and ginger ale for Betsey. Cars went to and fro on the street but none of them stopped at the Wapshots'. She could hear the sounds of a tennis game from a court in the next block; laughter and talk. The bartender said kindly that the neighborhood was a strange one. He worked in Denver and he longed to get back to a place where people were more courteous and predictable. He halved limes, squeezed lemons, arranged a row of cocktail glasses on the table and filled these with ice. At six o'clock the maid took a paper-back novel out of her bag and sat down to read. At a little after six the back doorbell rang and Betsey hastened to answer it. It was the delivery man from the dry-cleaners. Coverly heard Betsey ask him in for a drink. "Oh, I'd love to, Mrs. Wapshot," the

man said, "but I have to go home now and cook my supper.
I'm living alone now, I guess I told you. My wife ran off with
one of the butchers in the food express. The lawyer told me
to put the kids in an orphanage, he said I'd get custody quicker
that way, so I'm all alone. I'm so alone that I talk with the flies.
There's a lot of flies where I live but I don't kill them. I just
talk with them. They're like friends. 'Hello, flies,' I say. 'We're
all alone, you and me. You're looking good, flies.' I suppose
you might think I was crazy for talking with the flies but that's
the way it is. I don't have anybody else to talk to."

Coverly heard the door close. Betsey drew some water in the
sink. When she came back into the room her face was pale.
"Well, let's have a party," Coverly said. "Let's you and I have
a party." He got her another drink and passed her a tray of
sandwiches but she seemed so stiff with pain that she could not
turn her head and when she drank her whisky she spilled some
on her chin. "The things you read about in these paper books,"
the maid said. "I don't know. I been married three times but
right here in this book they're doing something and I don't
know what it is. I mean I don't know what they're doing. . . ."
She glanced at the little boy and went on reading. Coverly asked
the couple if they wouldn't like a drink but they both politely
refused and said that they didn't drink on duty. Their presence
seemed to amplify a pain of embarrassment that was swiftly turning into shame; their eyes seemed to be the eyes of the world,
civil as they were, and Coverly finally asked them to go. They
were enormously relieved. They had the good taste not to say
that they were sorry; not to say anything but good-by. "We'll
leave everything out for the latecomers," Betsey called gallantly
after them as they went out the door.

It was her last gallantry. The pain in her breast threatened
to overwhelm her. Her spirit seemed about to break under the
organized cruelty of the world. She had offered her innocence,
her vision of friendly strangers, to the community and she had
been wickedly spurned. She had not asked them for money, for
help of any kind, she had not asked them for friendship, she

had only asked that they come to her house, drink her whisky and fill the empty rooms with the noise of talk for a little time and not one of them had the kindness to come. It was a world that seemed to her as hostile, incomprehensible and threatening as the gantry lines on the horizon, and when Coverly put an arm around her and said, "I'm sorry, sugar," she pushed him away from her and said harshly, "Leave me be, leave me be, you just leave me be."

In the end Coverly, by way of consolation, took Betsey to a coffee house in the commercial center. They bought their tickets and sat in canvas chairs with mugs of coffee to drink. A young woman with yellow hair drawn back over her ears was plucking a small harp and singing:

> "Oh Mother, dear Mother, oh Mother,
>   Why is the sky so dark?
>   Why does the air smell of roach powder?
>   Why is there no one in the park?"

> "It's nothing, my darling daughter,
>   This isn't the way the world ends,
>   The washing machine is on spinner,
>   And I'm waiting to entertain friends."

> "But Mother, dear Mother, please tell me,
>   Why does your Geiger counter tick?
>   And why are all those nice people
>   Jumping into the creek?"

> "It's nothing, it's nothing, my darling,
>   It's really nothing at all,
>   My Geiger counter simply records
>   An increase in radioactive fall."

> "But Mother, dear Mother, please tell me,
>   Before I go up to bed,
>   Why are my yellow curls falling,
>   Falling off of my head?
>   And why is the sky so red?
>   Why is the sky so red . . ."

There was something in Coverly's nature—something provincial no doubt—that made this sort of lamentation intolerable and he seized Betsey's hand and marched out of the coffee house, snorting like someone much older. It wasn't much of a night.

Oh, Father, Father, why have you come back?

5

Moses and Melissa Wapshot lived in Proxmire Manor, a place that was known up and down the suburban railroad line as the place where the lady got arrested. The incident had taken place five or six years before, but it had the endurance of a legend, and the lady had seemed briefly to be the genius of the pretty place. The facts are simple. With the exception of one unsolved robbery, the eight-man police force of Proxmire Manor had never found anything to do. Their only usefulness was to direct traffic at weddings and large cocktail parties. They listened day and night on the interstate police radio to the crimes and alarms in other communities—car thefts, mayhem, drunkenness and murder—but the blotter in Proxmire Manor was clean. The burden of this idleness on their self-esteem was heavy as, armed with pistols and bandoleers of ammunition, they spent their days writing parking tickets for the cars left at the railroad station. It was like a child's game, ticketing commuters for the most trifling infractions of the rules the police themselves invented, and they played it enthusiastically.

The lady—Mrs. Lemuel Jameson—had similar problems. Her children were away at school, her housework was done by a maid, and while she played cards and lunched with friends, she was often made ill-tempered by abrasive boredom. Coming home from an unsuccessful shopping trip in New York one afternoon, she found her car ticketed for being a little over a white line. She tore the ticket to pieces. Later that afternoon, a policeman found the pieces in the dirt and took them to the police station, where they were pasted together.

The police were excited, of course, at this open challenge to their authority. Mrs. Jameson was served with a summons. She called her friend Judge Flint—he was a member of the Club—and asked him to fix it. He said that he would, but later that afternoon he had an attack of acute appendicitis and was taken to the hospital. When Mrs. Jameson's name was called in traffic court and there was no response, the police were alert. A warrant for her arrest was issued, the first such warrant in years. In the morning two patrolmen, heavily armed and in fresh uniforms and in the company of an old police matron, drove to Mrs. Jameson's house with the warrant. A maid opened the door and said that Mrs. Jameson was sleeping. With at least a hint of force, they entered the beautiful drawing room and told the maid to wake Mrs. Jameson. When Mrs. Jameson heard that the police were downstairs she was indignant. She refused to move. The maid went downstairs, and in a minute or two Mrs. Jameson heard the heavy steps of the policemen. She was horrified. Would they dare enter her bedroom? The ranking officer spoke to her from the hall. "You get out of bed, lady, and come with us or we'll get you up." Mrs. Jameson began to scream. The police matron, reaching for her shoulder holster, entered the bedroom. Mrs. Jameson went on screaming. The matron told her to get up and dress or they would take her to the station house in her nightclothes. When Mrs. Jameson started for the bathroom, the matron followed her and she began to scream again. She was hysterical. She screamed at the policemen when she encountered them in the upstairs hallway, but she let herself be led out to the car and driven to the station house. Here she began to scream again. She finally paid the one-dollar fine and was sent home in a taxi.

Mrs. Jameson was determined to have the policemen fired, and the moment she walked into her house she began to organize her campaign. Counting over her neighbors for someone who would be eloquent and sympathetic, she thought of Peter Dolmetch, a free-lance television writer, who rented the Fulsoms' gatehouse. No one liked him, but Mrs. Jameson sometimes invited him to her cocktail parties, and he was indebted to her. She called and told him her story. "I can't believe it, darling," he said. She said that she was asking him, because of his natural eloquence, to defend her. "I'm against Fascism, darling," he said, "wherever it raises its ugly head." She then called the mayor and demanded a hearing. It was set for eight-thirty that night. Mr. Jameson happened to be away on business. She called a few friends, and by noon everyone in Proxmire Manor knew that she had been humiliated by a policewoman, who followed her into the bathroom and sat on the edge of the tub while she dressed, and that Mrs. Jameson had been taken to the station house at the point of a gun. Fifteen or twenty neighbors showed up for the hearing. The mayor and his councilmen numbered seven, and the two patrolmen and the matron were also there. When the meeting was called to order, Peter stood and asked, "Has Fascism come to Proxmire Manor? Is the ghost of Hitler stalking our tree-shaded streets? Must we, in the privacy of our homes, dread the tread of the Storm Troopers' boots on our sidewalks and the pounding of the mailed fist on the door?" On and on he went. He must have spent all day writing it. It was all aimed at Hitler, with only a few passing references to Mrs. Jameson. The audience began to cough, to yawn, and then to excuse themselves. When the protest was dismissed and the meeting adjourned, there was no one left but the principals, and Mrs. Jameson's case was lost, but it was not forgotten. The conductor on the train, passing the green hills, would say, "They arrested a lady there yesterday"; then, "They arrested a lady there last month"; and presently, "That's the place where the lady got arrested." That was Proxmire Manor.

The village stood on three leafy hills north of the city, and was handsome and comfortable, and seemed to have eliminated, through adroit social pressures, the thorny side of human nature. This knowledge was forced on Melissa one afternoon when a neighbor, Laura Hilliston, came in for a glass of sherry. "What I wanted to tell you," Laura said, "is that Gertrude Lockhart is a slut." Melissa heard the words down the length of the room as she was pouring sherry, and wondered if she had heard correctly, the remark seemed so callous. What kind of tidings were these to carry from house to house? She was never sure—how could one be, it was all so experimental?—of the exact nature and intent of the society in which she lived, but did it really embrace this kind of thing?

Laura Hilliston laughed. Her laughter was healthy and her teeth were white. She sat on the sofa, a heavy woman with her feet planted squarely on the rug. Her hair was brown. So were her large, soft eyes. Her face was fleshy, but with a fine ruddiness. She was long married and had three grown sons, but she had recently stepped out of the country of love—briskly and without a backward glance, as if she had spent too much time in its steaming jungles. She was through with all *that,* she had told her wretched husband. She had put on some perfume for the visit, and she wore a thick necklace of false gold that threw a brassy light up onto her features. Her shoes had high heels, and her dress was tight, but these lures were meant to establish her social position and not to catch the eyes of a man.

"I just thought you ought to know," Laura said. "It isn't mere gossip. She has been intimate with just about everybody. I mean the milkman, and that old man who reads the gas meter. That nice fresh-faced boy who used to deliver the laundry lost his job because of her. The truck used to be parked there for hours at a time. Then she began to buy her groceries from Narobi's, and one of the delivery boys had quite a lot of trouble. Her husband's a nice-looking man, and they say he puts up with it for the sake of the children. He adores the children. But what I really wanted to say is that we're getting her out. They have a twenty-eight-thousand-dollar mortgage with a repair clause, and Charlie Peterson at the bank has just told them that they'll have to put a new roof on the house. Of course, they can't afford this, and so Bumps Trigger is going to give them what they paid for the place, and they'll have to go somewhere else. I just thought you might like to know."

"Thank you," Melissa said. "Will you have some more sherry?"

"Oh, no, thank you. I must get along. We're going to the Wishings'. Aren't you?"

"Yes, we are," Melissa said.

Laura put on a short mink jacket and stepped out of the house with that grace, that circumspection, that gentle and unmistakable poise of a lady who has said farewell to love.

Then the back doorbell rang. The cook was out with the baby, and so Melissa went to the back door and let in one of Mr. Narobi's grocery boys. She wondered if he was the one Mrs. Lockhart had tried to seduce. He was a slender young man with brown hair and blue eyes that shed their light evenly, as the eyes of the young will, and were so unlike the eyes of the old—those haggard lanterns that shed no light at all. She would have liked to ask him about Mrs. Lockhart, but this, of course, was not possible. She gave him a quarter tip, and he thanked her politely, and she went upstairs to bathe and dress for the Wishings' dance.

The Wishings' dance was an annual affair. As Mrs. Wishing kept explaining, they gave it each year before the rugs were put down. There was a three-piece orchestra, a fine dinner, with glazed salmon, *boeuf en daube,* a dark flowery claret and a bar for drinks. By quarter after ten, Melissa felt bored and would have asked Moses to take her home, but he was in another room. Lovely and high-spirited, she was seldom bored. Watching the dancers, she thought of poor Mrs. Lockhart, who was being forced out of this society. On the other hand, she knew how easy, how mistaken it was to assume that the exceptions—the drunkard and the lewd—penetrate, through their excesses, the carapace of immortal society. Did Mrs. Lockhart know more about mankind than she, Melissa? Who did have the power of penetration? Was it the priest who saw how their hands trembled when they reached for the chalice, the doctor who had seen them stripped of their clothing, or the psychiatrist who had seen them stripped of their obdurate pride, and who was now dancing with a fat woman in a red dress? And what was penetration worth? What did it matter that the drunken and unhappy woman in the corner dreamed frequently that she was being chased through a grove of trees by a score of naked lyric poets? Melissa was bored, and she thought her dancing neighbors were bored, too. Loneliness was one thing, and she knew herself how sweet it could make lights and company seem, but boredom was something else, and why, in this most prosperous and equitable world, should everyone seem so bored and disappointed?

Melissa went to the bathroom. The Wishings' house was large and she lost her way. She stepped by mistake into a dark bedroom. The moment she entered the room another woman, who must have been waiting, embraced her, groaning with ardor. Then realizing her mistake she said: "I'm terribly sorry," and went out the door. Melissa saw only that she had dark hair and full skirts. She stood in the dark room for a moment, trying, with no success at all, to fit this encounter somewhere into the distant noise of dance music. It could only mean that two of her neighbors, two housewives, had fallen in love and had planned a rendezvous in the middle of the Wishings' dance. But who could it have been? None of her neighbors seemed possible. It must have been someone from out of town; someone from the wicked world beyond Proxmire Manor. She stepped into the lighted hallway and found her way to where she had been going in the first place and all she seemed able to do was to forget the encounter. It had not happened.

She asked Bumps Trigger to get her a drink, and he brought her back a glass of dark bourbon. She felt a profound nostalgia, a longing for some emotional island or peninsula that she had not even discerned in her dreams. She seemed to know something about its character—it was not a paradise—but its elevating possibilities of emotional richness and freedom stirred her. It was the stupendous feeling that one could do much better than this; that the reality was not Mrs. Wishing's dance; that the world was not divided into rigid parliaments of good and evil but was ruled by the absolute authority and range of her desire.

She began to dance, then, and danced until three, when the band stopped playing. Her feelings had changed from boredom to a ruthless greed for pleasure. She did not ever want the party to stop, and stayed until dawn, when she yielded to Moses' attentions. Moses was a very attentive husband. He was attentive in boathouses and leaky canoes, on beaches and mossy banks, in motels, hotels, guest rooms, sofas, and day beds. The house rang nightly with his happy cries of abandon but within this lather of love there were rigid canons of decency and some forms of sexual commerce seemed to him shocking and distasteful. In the light of day (excepting Saturdays, Sundays and holidays) his standards of decency were exacting. He would smash any man in the nose who told a dirty story in mixed company and once spanked his little son for saying damn. He was the sort of paterfamilias who inspires sympathy for the libertine. Nightly he romanced Melissa, nightly he climbed confidently into bed, while the poor libertine enjoys no such security. He—love's wanderer—must write letters, spend his income on flowers and jewelry, squire women to restaurants and theaters and listen to interminable reminiscences—How Mean My Sister Was to Me and The Night the Cat Died. He must apply his intelligence and his manual dexterity to the nearly labyrinthine complications of women's clothing. He must anticipate problems of geography, caprices of taste, jealous husbands, suspicious cooks, all for a few hours', sometimes a few moments', stolen sweetness. He is denied the pleasures of friendship, he is a suspicious character to the police, and it is sometimes difficult for him to find employment, while the world smiles gently on that hairy brute, his married neighbor. This volcanic area that Moses shared with Melissa was immense, but it was the only one. They agreed on almost nothing else. They drank different brands of whisky, read different books and papers. Outside the dark circle of love they seemed almost like strangers, and glimpsing Melissa down a long dinner table he had once wondered who was that pretty woman with light hair. That this boisterousness, this attentiveness, was not entirely spontaneous was revealed to Melissa one morning when she opened a drawer in the hall table and found a series of clipped memos dated for a month or six weeks and titled: "Drink Score." The entries ran: "12 noon 3 martinis. 3:20 1 pickmeup. 5:36 to 6:40 3 bourbons on train. 4 bourbons before dinner. 1 pint moselle. 2 whiskies after." The entries didn't vary much from day to day. She put them back into the drawer. It was something else to be forgotten.

6

Incredible as it may seem, Honora Wapshot had never paid an income tax. Judge Beasely, who was nominally in charge of her affairs, assumed that she was cognizant of the tax laws and had never questioned her on the subject. Her oversight, her criminal negligence, might have been explained by her age. She may have felt herself too old to begin something new such as paying taxes or she may have felt that she would die before she was apprehended. Now and then the thought of her dereliction would waveringly cross her mind and she would suffer a fleeting pang of guilt, but, as she saw it, one of the privileges of age was a high degree of irresponsibility. In any case, she had never paid a tax and thus, one evening, a man named Norman Johnson got off the same train that had brought Coverly to St. Botolphs the night he saw his father's ghost.

Mr. Jowett guessed from his clothing that he was a salesman and directed him to the Viaduct House. Mabel Moulton, who had been running the hotel since her father's stroke, led him up the stairs to a room on the second floor back. "It isn't much," she explained, "but it's all we have." She left him alone to amplify her observation. The single window looked out across the river to the table-silver factory. In the corner there was a pitcher and a basin for washing. He saw a chamber pot under the bed. These primitive arrangements disturbed him. Imagine using a chamber pot at a time when men freely explored space! But did astronauts use chamber pots? Motormen's helpers? What *did* they use? He dropped this subject to sniff the air of the room but the Viaduct House was a very old hotel and forgiveness was all you could bring to its odors. He hung both the suit he wore and the one in his bag in the closet. The collection of tin coat-racks there chimed the half-hour when he touched them. This ghostly music startled him and then the stillness of the place rushed in. There were footsteps in the room overhead. A man's? A woman's? The heels were hard but the step was heavy and he guessed they belonged to a man. But what was he doing? First the stranger walked from the window to the closet. Then he walked from the closet to the bed. Then he walked from the bed to the washstand and then from the washstand back to the window. His step was brisk, quick and urgent, but his comings and goings were senseless. Was he packing, was he dressing, was he shaving or was he, as Johnson knew from his own experience, simply moving aimlessly around an empty place, wondering what it was that he had forgotten?

Johnson, wearing a shirt and underpants, sat on the edge of the bed. (His underpants were printed with poker hands and dice.) He opened a bottle of sherry and drank a glass. In the heterogeneous and resurgent stream of faces that surrounds us there are those that seem to be the coins of a particular realm, that seem to have a sameness of feature and value. One would have seen Johnson before; one would see him again. He had the kind of long face to which the word "maturity" could not in any sense be applied. Time had been a series of unsuspected losses and rude blows, but in half-lights and cross-lights this emotional scar tissue was unseen and the face seemed earnest, simple and inscrutable. Some of us go around the world three times, divorce, remarry, divorce again, part with our children, make and waste a fortune, and coming back to our beginnings we find the same faces at the same windows, buy our cigarettes and newspapers from the same old man, say good morning to the same elevator operator, good night to the same desk clerk, to all those who seem, as Johnson did, driven into life by misfortune like the nails into a floor.

He was a traveler, familiar with the miseries of loneliness, with the violence of its sexuality, with its half-conscious imagery of highways and thruways like the projections of a bewildered spirit; with that forlorn and venereal limbo that must have flowed over the world before the invention of Venus, unknown to good and evil, ruled by pain. His father had died when he was a boy and he had been raised by his mother and her sister, a schoolteacher and a seamstress. He had been a good boy, industrious and hard-working, and while the rest of the kids were running up and down the street after a football he had sold arch supporters, magazine subscriptions, hot-water heaters, Christmas cards and newspapers. He stored his dimes and nickels in empty prune-juice jars and deposited them in his savings account once a week. He paid his own tuition for two years at the university and then he was drafted into the infantry. He could have gotten a deferred job at the ore-loading docks in Superior and made a fortune during the war but he didn't learn this until it was too late.

He landed in Normandy on the fourth day of the invasion. His burly first sergeant shot himself in the foot as soon as they landed and his bloodthirsty company commander cracked up after three hours of combat. The modest and decent men like himself were the truly brave. He was wounded on his third day in combat and flown back to a hospital in England. When he returned to his company he was transferred to headquarters and he stayed there until his discharge. That was four years out of his life, four years cut out of the career of a young man. When he got back to Superior his aunt was dead and his mother was dying. When he buried her he was left with three thousand dollars in medical bills, a fourteen-hundred-dollar bill from the undertaker and a seven-thousand-dollar mortgage on a house nobody wanted to buy. He was twenty-seven years old. He poured himself another glass of sherry. "I never had an electric train," he said aloud. "I never had a dog."

He got a job in the Veterans Administration in Duluth and learned another lesson. Most men were born in debt, lived in debt and died in debt. Conscientiousness and industry were no match for the burdens of indebtedness. What he needed was an inspiration, a gamble, and standing on a little hill outside Superior one night he had an inspiration. In the distance he could see the lights of Duluth. Below him were the flat roofs of a cannery. The evening wind from Duluth blew in his direction and on this wind he heard the barking of dogs. His thinking took these lines: Two thousand people lived on the hill. Everyone on the hill had a dog. Every dog ate at least a can of food a day. People loved their dogs and were ready to pay good money to feed them but who knew what went into a can of dog food? What did dogs like? Table scraps, garbage and horse buns. Stray dogs always had the finest coats and enjoyed the best health. All he needed was a selling point. Ye Olde English Dog Food! England meant roast beef to most people. Put a label like that on a can and dog owners would pay as high as twenty-five cents. The noise from the cannery fitted in with all of this and he went happily to bed.

He experimented with dogs in the neighborhood and settled on a formula that was ninety per cent floor sweepings from the breakfast-food factory, ten per cent horse buns from the riding stable and enough water to make the mixture moist. He had a label designed and printed with a heraldic shield and "Ye Olde English Dog Food" in a florid script. The cannery agreed to process a lot of a thousand and he rented a truck and took a load to the cannery in ashcans. When the cans were labeled and crated and stored in his garage he felt that he possessed something valuable and beautiful. He bought a new suit and began going around to the markets of Duluth with a sample can of Olde English.

The story was the same everywhere. The grocers bought from

the jobbers and when he approached the jobbers they explained that they couldn't handle his food. The dog food they sold was pushed by the Chicago meat-packers on a price tie-in basis with the rest of their products and he couldn't compete with Chicago. He tried peddling his dog food on the hill but you can't sell dog food door to door and he learned a bitter lesson. The independent doesn't have a chance. Duluth was full of hungry dogs and he had a thousand cans of feed stored in his garage but as an independent he was helpless to bring them profitably together. Remembering this, he had another glass of sherry.

It was dark by then. The light had gone from the window and he dressed to go down for supper. He was the only customer in the dining room, where Mabel Moulton brought him a bowl of greasy soup in which a burnt match was swimming. The burnt match, like the chamber pot, made his hatred of St. Botolphs implacable. "Oh, I'm awful sorry," Mabel said, when he showed her the match. "I'm awful sorry. You see, my father had a stroke last month and we're awful shorthanded. Things aren't the way we'd like to have them. The pilot light on the gas range isn't working and the cook has to keep lighting the range with matches and I expect that's how a match got into your soup. Well, I'll take away your soup and bring you the pot roast and I'll make sure there's no matches in that. Notice that I'm taking off your plate with my *left* hand. I sprained my left hand last winter and it's never been right since but I keep doing things with it to see if I can't get it back into condition that way. The doctor tells me that if I keep using it, it'll get better. Of course it's easier for me to use my right hand all the time but every now and then . . ." She saw that he was unfriendly and moved on. She had waited on a thousand lonely men and most of them liked to hear about her aches, pains and sprains while she admired the pictures of their wives, children, houses and dogs. It was a light bridge of communication but it was better than nothing and it passed the time.

Johnson ate his pot roast and his pie and went into the bar. It was crudely lighted by illuminated beer signs and smelled like a soil excavation. The only customers were two farmers. He went to the end of the bar farthest from them and drank another glass of sherry. Then he bowled a game on the miniature bowling machine and went out the side door onto the street. The town was dark; turned back on itself, totally unfamiliar with the needs of travelers, wanderers, the great flowing world. Every store was shut. He glanced at the Unitarian church across the green. It was a white frame building with columns, a bell tower and a spire that vanished into the starlight. It seemed incredible to him that his people, his inventive kind, the first to exploit glass store fronts, bright lights and continuous music, should ever have been so backward as to construct a kind of temple that belonged to the ancient world. He went around the edges of the green and turned up Boat Street as far as Honora's. Lights burned here and there in the old house but he saw no one. He went back to the bar and watched a fight on television.

The favorite was an aging club fighter named Mercer. The challenger was a man named Santiago who could have been Italian or Puerto Rican. He was fleshy, muscular and stupid. Mercer had it all his way for the first two rounds. He was a fair, slight man, his face lined, so Johnson thought, with common domestic worries. He would have kissed his wife good-by in some kitchen an hour ago and he was fighting to keep up the payments on the washing machine. Agile, intelligent and tough, he seemed unbeatable until early in the third round when Santiago opened a cut over his right eye. Blood streamed down Mercer's face and chest and he slipped on the bloody canvas. Santiago reopened the cut in the fifth and Mercer was blinded again and staggered helplessly around the ring. The fight was stopped in the sixth. Mercer's spirit would be crushed, his wife and children would be heartbroken and his washing machine would be taken away. Johnson went upstairs, got into a suit of pajamas printed with scenes of a steeplechase and read a paper-back novel.

His novel was about a young woman with millions of dollars

and houses in Rome, Paris, New York and Honolulu. In the first chapter she made it with her husband in a ski hut. In the second chapter she made it with a butler in the pantry. In the third chapter her husband and the butler made it in the swimming pool. The heroine then made it with a chambermaid. Her husband discovered them and joined the fun. The cook then made it with the postman and the cook's twelve-year-old daughter made it with the groom. On it would go for six hundred pages. It would end, he knew, in religious institutions. The heroine, having practiced every known indecency, would end up in a cloistered order with a shaven head and a lead ring. The last you saw of her depraved husband would be his feet in the rude sandals of a monk as he pressed through a snowstorm carrying a vial of antibiotics to a sick whore in the mountains. It seemed like a poor fare for a lonely man and he felt from the hard mattress where he lay an accrual of loneliness from the thousands like himself who had lain there, hankering not to be alone. He turned off the light, slept and dreamed of swans, a lost suitcase, a snow-covered mountain. He saw his mother lifting the ornaments off the Christmas tree with trembling hands. He woke in the morning feeling natural, boisterous and even loving, but the stranger with a hidden face is always waiting by the lake, there is always a viper in the garden, a dark cloud in the west. The eggs that Mabel brought him for breakfast were swimming in grease. As soon as he stepped out of the Viaduct House a dog began to bark at him. The dog followed him across the green, snapping at his ankles. He ran up Boat Street and some children on their way to school laughed uproariously at his panic. When he got to Honora's his high spirits were spent.

Maggie answered the doorbell and led him into the library, where Honora was sitting by the window, picking over a large assortment of fireworks heaped in a washbasket. At the sound of a man's footsteps she took off her spectacles. She hoped to look younger. She could not see much without her glasses and when Johnson entered the library the indistinctness with which she saw his face made her think that he was a young man with keen appetites, enthusiasms, an open heart. She felt for his very blurred image an impulse of friendship or pity. "Good morning," she said. "Please sit down. I was just looking over my fireworks. I bought these last year, you know, and I thought I'd have a little party, you know, but it was very dry last July, it didn't rain for six weeks and the fire chief asked me not to shoot them off. I put them in the coat closet and I completely forgot about them until this morning. I love fireworks," she said. "I love to read the labels on the packages and imagine what they'll look like. I *love* the smell of gunpowder."

"I'd like to know something about your Uncle Lorenzo," Johnson said.

"Oh, yes," Honora said. "Is this about the commemorative plaque?"

"No," Johnson said. He opened his briefcase.

"Well, a man came last year," Honora said, "and urged me to have a commemorative plaque made for Lorenzo. At first I thought he represented some committee but then I discovered that he was just a salesman. You're not a salesman?"

"No," Johnson said. "I'm from the government."

"Well, Lorenzo served in the state legislature, you know," Honora said. "He introduced the child-labor laws. You see, my parents were missionaries. You wouldn't know it to look at me, would you, but I was born in Polynesia. My parents sent me back here to school but they died before I could return. Lorenzo raised me. He was never an awfully friendly man." She seemed deeply reflective. "But you might have described him as both my father and mother," she said with a sigh of obvious discontent.

"This was his house?"

"Oh, yes."

"Your uncle left you his estate?"

"Yes, he had no other family."

"I have some correspondence here from the Appleton Bank and Trust Company. They estimate the value of your uncle's estate at the time of his death to have been about a million dollars. They claim to have paid you an annual income ranging from seventy thousand to a hundred thousand dollars."

"I don't know," Honora said. "I give most of my money away."

"Have you any proof of this?"

"I don't keep records," Honora said.

"Have you ever paid an income tax, Miss Wapshot?"

"Oh, no," Honora said. "Lorenzo made me promise that I wouldn't give any of his money to the government."

"You are in grave trouble, Miss Wapshot." Then he felt tall and strong, felt the supreme importance of those who bring black tidings. "This will lead to a criminal indictment."

"Oh, dear," Honora said.

She had been caught and she knew it; caught like any clumsy thief waving a water pistol at a bank teller. If her knowledge of the tax laws was not much more than a dream, she knew them to be the laws of her country and her time. What she did then was to go to the fireplace and light the pile of shavings, paper and wood that the gardener had laid on the irons. The reason she did this was that fire was for her a sovereign pain-killer. When she was discontented with herself, troubled, bewildered or bored, to light a fire seemed to incinerate her discontents and transform her burdens into smoke. She approached the light and heat of a fire like an aboriginal. The shavings and paper exploded into flame, filling the library with a dry, gaseous heat. Honora stoked the blaze with dry apple wood; felt that once the fire was hot enough she would have burned away her fears of the poor farm and the jail. A log exploded and an ember landed in the basket of fireworks. A Roman candle was the first to go. "Mercy," Honora said. Purblind without her spectacles, she reached for a vase of flowers to extinguish the Roman candle but her aim was off and she got Johnson square in the face with a pint or so of bitter flower water and a dozen hyacinths. By this time the Roman candle had begun to ejaculate its lumps of colored fire and these ignited something called The Golden Vesuvius. A rocket took off in the direction of the piano and then the lot went up.

7

The two stories about Honora Wapshot that were most frequently told in the family concerned her alarm clock and her
penmanship. These were not told so much as they were performed, each member of the family taking a part, singing an
aria so to speak, while everyone joined in on the Grand Finale
like some primitive anticipation of the conventions of nineteenth-
century Italian opera. The alarm clock incident belonged to the
remote past when Lorenzo had been alive. Lorenzo was determined to appear pious and liked to arrive at Christ Church for
morning worship at precisely quarter to eleven. Honora, who
may have been genuinely pious but who detested appearances,
could never find her gloves or her hat and was always tardy.
One Sunday morning Lorenzo, in a rage, led his niece by the
hand into the drugstore and bought her an alarm clock. So they
went to church. Mr. Briam, Mr. Applegate's predecessor, had
started on an interminable sermon about the chains of St. Paul
when the alarm clock went off. Since most of the congregation
was asleep they were startled and confused. Honora shook the
clock and then proceeded to unwrap it but by the time she got
through to the box in which it sat the ringing had stopped.
Mr. Briam then picked up the chains of St. Paul and the alarm
clock, on repeat, began to ring again. This time Honora pretended that it wasn't her clock. Sweating freely, she sat beside
this impious engine while Mr. Briam went on about the significance of chains until the mechanism had unwound. It was an
historic Sunday. The tales about her penmanship centered on
a morning when she had written to the local coal dealer protest-
ing his prices and then had written to Mr. Potter to share with
him his sorrow over the sudden loss of his sainted wife. She
got the letters in the wrong envelopes but since Mr. Potter could

read nothing of her letter but the signature he was touched by her thoughtfulness and since Mr. Sumner, the coal dealer, was unable to read the letter of condolence he received he mailed it back to Honora. She had been taught Spencerian penmanship but something redoubtable or coarse in her nature was left unexpressed by this style and the conflict between her passions and the tools given to her left her penmanship illegible.

At about this time Coverly received a letter from his old cousin.

Someone more persevering might have broken the letter down word by word and diagnosed its content but Coverly was not this gifted or patient. He was able to decipher a few facts. A holly tree that grew behind her house had been attacked by rust. She wanted Coverly to return to St. Botolphs and have it sprayed. This was followed by an indecipherable paragraph on the Appleton Bank and Trust Company in Boston. Honora had set up trusts for Coverly and his brother and he supposed she was writing of these. The income enabled Coverly to live much more comfortably than he would have been able to on his government salary and he hoped nothing was wrong here. This was followed by a clear sentence stating that Dr. Lemuel Cameron, director of the Talifer site, had once received a scholarship endowed by Lorenzo Wapshot. She closed with her customary observations on the rainfall, the prevailing winds and the tides.

Coverly guessed that her reference to the holly tree meant something very different but he didn't have the emotional leisure to discover what was at the back of the old woman's mind. If there was trouble with the Appleton Bank and Trust Company—and his quarterly check was late—there was nothing much he could do. The remark about Dr. Cameron might or might not have been true since Honora often exaggerated Lorenzo's bounty and had, like any other old woman, a struggle to remember names. The letter arrived at a bad time in his affairs and he forwarded it on to his brother.

Betsey had not rallied from the failure of her cocktail party. She hated Talifer and squarely blamed Coverly for making her live there. She avenged herself by sleeping alone and by not speaking to her husband. She complained loudly to herself about the noise, the neighborhood, the kitchen, the weather and the news in the papers. She swore at the mashed potatoes, cursed the pot roast, she damned the pots and pans to hell and spoke obscenely to the frozen apple tarts, but she did not speak to Coverly. Every surface of life—table, dishes and the body of her husband—seemed to be abrasive facets of a stone that lay in her path. Nothing was right. The sofa hurt her back. She could not sleep in her bed. The lamps were too dim to read by, the knives were too dull to cut butter, the television programs bored her although she watched them faithfully. The greatest of Coverly's hardships was the breakdown in their sexual relationship. It was the crux, the readiest source of vitality in their marriage, and without this her companionship became painful.

Coverly tried to throw a ring of light around her figure and saw or thought he saw that she might be heartlessly overburdened by a past of which he knew nothing. We are all, he thought, ransomed to our beginnings, and the sum in her case might have been exorbitant. This might account for that dark side of her nature that seemed more mysterious to him than the dark face of the moon. Were there instruments of love and patience that could explore this darkness, discover the wellsprings of her misery and by charting it all draw it all into the area of reasonableness; or was this the nature of her kind of woman to stand forever half in a darkness that was unknown to herself? She looked nothing like a moon goddess, sitting in front of the television set, but of all the things in the world her spirit with its irreconcilable faces seemed most like the moon to him.

One Saturday morning when he was shaving he heard Betsey's voice—strident and raised in anger—and he went downstairs in his pajamas to see what was the matter. Betsey was upbraiding a new cleaning woman. "I just don't know what the world's coming to," Betsey said. "I just don't *know*. I suppose you expect me to pay you good money for just sitting around, for just sitting around smoking my cigarettes and watching my television." Betsey turned to Coverly. "She can hardly speak English," Betsey said, "and she doesn't even know how to work a vacuum cleaner. She doesn't even know how to do that. And you. Look at you. Here it is nine o'clock and you're still in your pajamas and I suppose you're going to spend the day just sitting around the house. It just makes me sick *and* tired. Well, you take her upstairs and you show her how to work the vacuum cleaner. Now you march, both of you. You get upstairs and do something useful for a change."

The cleaning woman had dark hair and olive skin. Her eyes were wet with tears. Coverly got the vacuum cleaner and carried it up the stairs, admiring the stranger's ample rump. There was between them the instantaneous rapport of unhappy children. Coverly plugged in the cord and turned on the motor but when he smiled at the stranger things took a different turn. "Now we put it in here," Betsey heard him say. "That's right. That's the way. We have to get it into the corners, way into the corners. Slowly, slowly, slowly. Back and forth, back and forth. Not too fast . . . " Downstairs Betsey thought angrily that Coverly had at last found something useful to do on Saturday mornings and that at least one room would be clean. She went into the bathroom where she had a vision—not so much of the emancipation of her sex as the enslavement of the male.

Routine progress—a feminine President and a distaff Senate— did not appear in Betsey's reverie. Indeed, in her vision the work of the world was still largely done by men, although this had been enlarged to include housework and shopping. She smiled at the thought of a man bent over an ironing board; a man dusting a table; a man basting a roast. In her vision all the public statuary commemorating great men would be overthrown and dragged off to the dump. Generals on horseback, priests in robes, solons in tailcoats, aviators, explorers, inventors, poets and philosophers would be replaced by attractive representations of the female. Women would be granted complete sexual independence and would make love to strangers as casually as they bought a pocketbook, and coming home in the evening they would brazenly describe to their depressed husbands (sprinkling Adolph's meat tenderizer on the London broil) the high points of their erotic adventures. She would not go so far as to imagine any legislation that would actually restrict the rights of men; but she saw them as so browbeaten, colorless and depressed that they would have lost the chance to be taken seriously.

Now the love song of Coverly Wapshot was slapstick and vainglorious and at the time of which I'm writing he had developed an unfortunate habit of talking like a Chinese fortune cookie. "Time cures all things," he would say or, "The poor man goes before the thief." In addition to his habit of cracking his knuckles he had acquired an even more irritating habit of nervously clearing his throat. At regular intervals he would emit from his larynx a reflective, apologetic, complaining and irresolute noise. "Grrgrum," he would say to himself as he washed the dishes. "Arhum, arrhum, grrumph," he would say as if these noises subtly expressed his discontents. He was the sort of man who at the PR conventions he sometimes attended always dropped his name tag (Hello! I'm Coverly Wapshot!) into the wastebasket along with the white carnation that was usually given to delegates. He seemed to feel that he lived in a small town where everyone would know who he was. Nothing, of course, could be further from the truth. Betsey was one of those women who, like the heroines in old legends, could turn herself from a hag into a beauty and back into a hag again so swiftly that Coverly was kept jumping.

Coverly, like some despot, was given to the capricious rearrangement of the facts in his history. He would decide cheerfully and hopefully that what had happened had not happened although he never went so far as to claim that what had not happened had happened. That what had happened had not happened was a refrain in his love song as common as those lyrical stanzas celebrating erotic bliss. Now Betsey was a complaining woman or, as Coverly would put it, Betsey was not a complaining woman. She had been unhappy at Remsen and had wanted to be transferred to Canaveral, where she saw herself sitting on a white beach, counting the wild waves and making eyes at a life-guard. If Betsey had been painted she would have been painted against the landscapes of northern Georgia where she had spent her mysterious childhood. There would be razorback hogs, a dying chinaberry tree, a frame house that needed paint and as far as the eye could see acres of swept red dirt that would turn slick and wash off in the lightest rains. There was not enough topsoil in that part of the state to fill a bait can. Coverly had seen this landscape fleetingly from the train window and of her past he only knew that she had a sister named Caroline. "I was so disappointed in that girl Caroline," Betsey said. "She was my only, only sister and I just wanted to enjoy a real sisterhood with her but I was disappointed. When I was working in the five-and-dime I gave her all my salary for her trousseau but when she got married she just went away from Bambridge and she never once wrote me or told me her whereabouts in any way, shape or form." Then Caroline began to write Betsey and there was a *bouleversement* in Betsey's feeling for her sister. Coverly was pleased with this since, with the exception of the television set, Betsey's loneliness in Talifer was unrelieved and it did not seem to be in his power to make the place more sociable. In the end Caroline, who was divorced, was invited to visit.

What had not happened or what might possibly have happened and been overlooked by Coverly's way of thinking began with Caroline's visit. She arrived on a Thursday. All the windows were lighted when Coverly came home from work and when he stepped into the house he could hear their voices from the living room. Betsey seemed happy for the first time in months and met him with a kiss. Caroline looked up at him and smiled, the color and cast of her eyes concealed by a large pair of spectacles that reflected the room. She was not a heavy woman but she sat like a heavy woman, her legs wide apart and her arms hung gracelessly between them. She was wearing a traveling costume—blue pumps that pinched her feet and a tight blue skirt that was rucked and seamed like a skin. Her smile was sweet and slow and she got to her feet and gave Coverly a wet kiss.

"Why, he looks just like Harvey," she said. "Harvey was this boy in Bambridge and you look just like him. He was a nice-looking boy. His family had a nice house on Spartacus Street."

"They didn't live on Spartacus Street," Betsey said. "They used to live on Thompson Avenue."

"They lived on Spartacus Street until his father got the Buick agency," Caroline said. "Then they moved to Thompson Avenue."

"I thought they always lived on Thompson Avenue," Betsey said.

"It was that other boy that used to live on Thompson Avenue," Caroline said. "The one that had curly hair and crooked teeth."

There was a bottle of bourbon on the coffee table and they each had a drink. When Betsey went into the kitchen to heat up the supper Caroline remained with Coverly. It was at this point that Coverly would decide that what had happened had not happened. Caroline spoke to him in a whisper. "I just been dying to meet the man Betsey married," Caroline said. "Nobody in Bambridge ever thought Betsey'd get married, she's so *queer.*"

There was a moment before Coverly decided, as he would, that what had been said had not been said when he was confronted with the venom in this remark. He could only conclude that "queer" in Georgia meant charming, original and fair.

"I don't understand," he said.

"Why, she's just queer, that's all," Caroline whispered. "Everybody in Bambridge knew Betsey was queer. I don't think it was her fault. I just think it was because Step-pappy was so mean to her. He used to whip her, he used to take off his belt and whip her with no provocation whatever. I just think he whipped the common sense right out of her."

"I didn't know any of this," Coverly said; or didn't say.

"Well, Betsey was never one to tell anybody anything," Caroline whispered. "That was one of the queer things about her."

"Dinner's served," Betsey said in her sweetest and most trusting manner. This much, in retrospect, would appear to be true.

The talk about Bambridge went on through dinner and it was

a conversation that, led by Caroline, seemed strangely morbid. "Bessie Pluckette has another mongoloid idiot," Caroline exclaimed, not cheerfully but with definite enthusiasm. "Unfortunately it's just as healthy as it can be and poor Bessie can just expect to spend the rest of her life taking care of it. Poor thing. Of course she could put it into the state institution but she just doesn't have the heart to have her little son starved to death and that's what they do in the state institution, they starve them to death. Alma Pierson had a mongoloid too but mercifully that one died. And remember that Brasie girl, Betsey, the one with the shriveled right arm?" She turned to Coverly and explained. "She has this shriveled right arm, no longer than your elbow and right at the end of it there's this teeny-weeny hand. Well, she learned how to play the piano. Isn't that wonderful? I mean she could only play chords of course with this teeny-weeny hand but she could play the rest of the music with her left hand. Her left hand was normal. She took piano lessons and everything, that is, she took piano lessons until her father fell down the elevator shaft at the cotton mill and broke both legs." Was this morbidity, Coverly wondered, or were these the facts of life in Georgia?

Caroline stayed three days and was (if one forgot her remarks before dinner) a tolerable guest excepting that her knowledge of tragic, human experience was inexhaustible and that she left lipstick stains on everything. She had a broad mouth and she painted it heavily and there were purple lipstick stains on the cups and glasses, the towels and napkins; the ashtrays were full of stained cigarette ends and in the toilet there was always a piece of Kleenex stained purple. This seemed to Coverly not carelessness but much more—some atavistic way of impressing herself upon this household in which she would spend so short a time. The purple stains seemed to mark her as a lonely woman. When Coverly went to the site on the day she left Caroline was asleep and she had gone by the time he got home. She had left a smear of purple lipstick on his son's forehead; there seemed to be purple lipstick everywhere he looked, as if she had marked her departure this way. Betsey was watching television and eating from a box of candy that Caroline had given her as a present. She did not look up when he came in and brushed away the place on her cheek where he kissed her. "Leave me be," she said, "leave me be. . . ."

After Caroline's departure Betsey's discontents only seemed to increase. Then there was a night that, according to Coverly's habit of eliminating facts, especially did not happen. He was kept late at the site and didn't get home until half-past seven. Betsey sat in the kitchen, weeping. "What's the matter, sugar-luve," he asked, or didn't ask.

"Well, I made myself a nice cup of tea," Betsey sobbed, "and a piece of hot Danish and I was just sitting down to enjoy myself when the telephone rang and there was this woman selling magazine subscriptions and she talked and by the time she was done talking my tea and my Danish were all cold."

"That's all right, sugar," Coverly said. "You can heat it up again."

"It isn't all right," Betsey said. "It just isn't all right. Nothing's all right. I hate Talifer. I hate it here. I hate you. I hate wet toilet seats. The only reason I live here is because there's no place else in the world for me to go. I'm too lazy to get a job and I'm too plain to find another man."

"Would you like to take a trip, sugar, would you like a change?"

"I been all over this country, it's the same everywheres."

"Oh, come back, sugar, come back," he said, speaking in great love and tiredness. "I feel as if I were walking up a street calling after you, asking you to come back and you never turn your head. I know what the street looks like, I've seen it so often. It's nighttime. There's a place on the corner where you can buy cigarettes and papers. Stationery. I can see you walking up this street and I'm behind you, calling you to come back, to come back, but you never turn your head." Betsey went on sobbing, and thinking that his words had moved her Coverly put an arm around her shoulders but she wrenched herself convulsively out of his embrace and screamed: "Leave me be." The scream, like the piercing and hideous noise of brakes, seemed to be apart from the fitness of things.

"But, sugar."

"You beat me," she screamed. "You took off your belt and you beat me and you beat me and you beat me."

"I never beat you, sugar. I never hit anybody but Mr. Murphy the night he stole our garbage pail."

"You beat me and beat me and beat me," she screamed.

"When was this, sugar, when did I do this?"

"Tuesday, Wednesday, Thursday, Friday, I can't remember every time." She fled to her room and shut the door. He was stunned (or would have been stunned if any of this had happened) and it was a minute or two before he realized (or would have realized) that Binxey was crying in terror. He seized the little boy as an object of reason, love, animal warmth. He crushed him in his arms and took him into the kitchen. This was no time, it seemed, for reflection or decision. He cooked some hamburgers and after supper told the boy an asinine story of space travel as he did each night. These stories were no worse than the stories of talking rabbits he had been told as a boy but the talking rabbits had the charm of innocence. He turned off the light, kissed the boy good night and stopped at the bedroom door to ask Betsey if she wanted some dinner. "Let me alone," she said. He drank a beer, read an old copy of *Life*, went to the window and looked at the lights on the street.

Here was (or would have been had he admitted the facts) the forlornness, the pain of an unexampled dilemma. The thief and the murderer all have their brotherhood and their prophets but he had none. Psychiatry, psychiatry, the word came to his mind as we put one foot in front of the other, but if he went to a doctor he would jeopardize his security clearance and his job. Any association with mental instability made a man unemployable in Talifer. The only way he could cling to his conviction that the devastating blows of life fell in some usable sequence was to claim that these special blows had not fallen; and so making this claim he made a bed on the sofa and went to sleep.

This curious process of claiming that what had happened had

not happened and what was happening was not happening went on in the morning when Coverly went to get a shirt and found that Betsey had cut the buttons off all of his shirts. This was inadmissible. He fastened a shirt with his tie, tucked it into his trousers and went to work but in the middle of the morning he went to the men's room and wrote Betsey a note:

"Darling Betsey," he wrote, "I am going away. I am desperate and I am not interested in desperation, especially quiet desperation. I have no address but I don't suppose that makes much difference because in all the years we've been together you've never sent me a postcard and I don't suppose you're going to start writing me piles of letters now. I have thought of taking Binxey with me but of course this would be against the law. I love him more than I have ever loved anyone in the world and please be kind to him. You might want to know why I am going away and why I am desperate although I somehow cannot imagine you asking yourself any questions about my disappearance. I don't know any of your family excepting Caroline and I sometimes wish I knew them better because I sometimes think you've got me mixed up with someone who caused you pain long ago. I know that I have a very difficult personality my family always said that Coverly was very odd and perhaps I am much more to be blamed than I will ever know. I do not like to cherish resentments, I do not like to be bitter or resentful and yet I often am. In the mornings of our life together when the alarm wakes me the first thing I want to do is to take you in my arms but if I do I know you will fling yourself away from me and so that is the way the days begin and usually the way they end. I won't bother about saying anything else. As I said in the beginning I am not interested in desperation, particularly quiet desperation and so I am going away."

Coverly mailed the letter, bought some shirts, cleared some annual leave and left for Denver that night, where he checked into a fourth-string hotel. There were cigarette butts on the bathroom floor and a pier glass arranged at the foot of the bed for questionable reasons. He had some drinks and went to a movie. When he came in at about midnight the elevator man asked if he wanted a girl, a boy, some dirty pictures or filthy comics. He said no thanks and went to bed. He went to a museum in the morning, to another movie and was having a drink at dusk in a bar when he felt his spirit genuflect, bend, stoop and kneel before what happened to be the image of those worn Indian moccasins, ornamented with beads, that Betsey wore around the house. He had another drink and went to another movie. When he came in the elevator operator asked again if he wanted a girl, a boy, a dirty massage, filthy pictures or obscene comics. He wanted Betsey.

The secrets of a marriage are most scrupulously guarded. Coverly might speak freely of his infidelities; it was his passion for fidelity that he would hide. It didn't matter that she had accused him wrongly and cut the buttons off his shirts. It wouldn't matter if she burned holes in his underpants and served him arsenate of lead. If she locked the door against him he would climb in at the window. If she locked the bedroom door he would break the lock. If she met him with a tirade, a shower of bitter tears, an ax or a meat cleaver it didn't matter. She was his millstone, his ball and chain, his angel, his fate, and she held in her hands the raw material of his most illustrious dreams. He called her then and said he was coming home. "That's all right," Betsey said. "That's all right."

He had some trouble making connections for the return trip and it was not until ten that he got back the next night. Betsey was in bed, filing her nails. "Hi, sugar," he said and sat on the bed, making a groaning sound. "Well, all right," Betsey said, but she flung her nail file onto the table, preserving this much of her sovereignty. She went into the bathroom, closing the door, and Coverly heard the various sounds of running water, diverse and cheerful as the fountains in Tivoli. But she did not return. What had happened? Had she hurt herself? Had she climbed out the window? He threw open the bathroom door and found her sitting naked on the edge of the tub, reading an old copy of *Newsweek*. "What's the matter, sugar?" he asked.

"Nothing," Betsey said. "I was just reading."

"But that's an old copy," Coverly said. "That's about a year old."

"Well, it's very interesting," Betsey said. "I find it very interesting."

"But you're not interested in current events," Coverly said. "I mean you don't even know the name of the vice president, do you?"

"That's none of your business," said Betsey.

"But do you know the name of the vice president?"

"That's just none of your business," Betsey said.

"Oh, sugar," groaned Coverly, his feeling swamped with love, and he raised her up in his arms. Then the verdure of venery, that thickest of foliage, filled the room. Sounds of running water. Flights of wild canaries. Lightly, lightly, assisting one another at every turn they began their effortless ascent up the rockwall, the chimney, the flume, the long traverse, up and up and up until over the last ridge one had a view of the whole, wide world and Coverly was the happiest man in it. But according to him none of this had happened. How could it have?

8

Judge Beasely's offices were on the second floor of the Cartwright Block. Enid Moulton, Mabel's sister, let Honora into the farther room where the judge sat examining or pretending to examine papers. Honora guessed that he had been asleep and she looked at him gloomily. Time, that she had seen turn so many things and men into their opposites, had forced him into the image of a hawk. She did not mean that he seemed predatory—only that the thinness of his face made what had always been a sharp nose hooked like a beak and that his thin gray hair lay on his scalp like moulting feathers. He humped his shoulders like a roosted bird. His voice was cracked but then it always had been. The skin of his nose had peeled here and there, showing a violet-colored underskin. He had been a lady-killer—she remembered that—and at eighty he still seemed proud of his prowess. Above his desk was a large, varnished painting of some antlered deer, leaving a gloomy wood to drink at a pond. The frame of the picture was festooned with Christmas tinsel. Honora gave this a glance. "I see you're all ready for Christmas," she said meanly.

"Hmmm," he said, uncomprehending.

Honora told him her problem, trying to estimate its magnitude by the degrees of consternation on his thin face. His memory, his reason, seemed not impaired but retarded. When she was done he made a temple of his fingers. "County court won't convene for another five weeks," he said, "so they can't indict you until then. Have they put a lien on your accounts?"

"I don't believe so," Honora said.

"Well, my advice, Honora, is that you go directly to the bank, withdraw a substantial sum of money and leave the country. Extradition proceedings are complicated and prolonged and the tax authorities are not altogether pitiless. They will invite you to return, of course, but I don't think a lady as venerable as you will be subjected to any unpleasantness."

"I am too old to travel," Honora said.

"You are too old to go to the poor farm," he said. The light in his eye seemed as uncomprehending as a bird and he seemed, like a drake, to have to turn his head from side to side to bring her into his vision. She said nothing more, neither thank you nor good-by, and left the office. She stopped at the hardware store and bought a length of clothesline. When she got back to her own house she climbed directly to the attic.

Honora admired all sorts of freshness: rain and the cold morning light, all winds, all sounds of running water in which she thought she heard the chain of being, high seas but especially the rain. Liking all of this she felt, stepping into the airless attic holding a length of clothesline with which she meant to hang herself, an alien. The air was so close it would make your head swim; spicy as an oven. Flies and hornets at the single window made the only sounds of life. Calcutta trunks, hatboxes, a helm inlaid with mother-of-pearl (hers), a torn mainsail and a pair of oars stood by the window. She looped the clothesline she carried over a rafter on which was printed: PEREZ WAPSHOT'S GRAND MENAGERIE AND ANIMAL CIRCUS. Red curtains hung from the rafter marking the stage where they had performed on wet days, rain gentling that small, small world. Rodney Townsend had waked her as the sleeping beauty with a kiss. It was her favorite part. She went to the window to see the twilight, wondering why the last light of day demanded from her similes and resolutions. Why, all the days of her life, had she compared its colors to apples, to the sere pages of old books, to lighted tents, to sapphires and ashes? Why had she always stood up to the evening light as if it could instruct her in decency and courage?

The day was gray, it had been gray since morning. It would be gray at sea, gray at the ferry slip where the crowds waited, gray in the cities, gray at the isthmus, gray at the prison and the poor farm. It was a harsh and an ugly light, stretched like some upholstery webbing beneath the damask of the year. Responsive to all lights, the dark left her feeling vague and sad. The rewards of virtue, she knew, are puerile, odorless and mean, but they are none the less rewards and she could not seem to find enough virtue in her conduct to reflect upon. She had meant to bring Mrs. Potter chicken broth when Mrs. Potter was dying. She had meant to attend her funeral when she died. She had meant to spread the fireplace ashes on the lawn. She had meant to return Mrs. Bretaigne's copy of *The Bitter Tea of General Yen.* She had counted every stud, nail, pew, light and organ pipe in Christ Church while Mr. Applegate, year after year, had unfolded the word of God. Patroness, Benefactor, Virgin and Saint!

She had been proud of her ankles, proud of her hair, proud of her hands, proud of her power over men and women although she knew enough about love to know that this impulse has no reflection. Pridefully she had given toys to the poor on Christmas.

Pridefully she had smiled at this image of her magnanimity. Pridefully she had invented a whispering chorus of admiration. Glorious Honora, Generous Honora, Peerless Honora Wapshot. One brought energy to life, there was nothing to equal its velocity, its discernment, but could the spirit of an old woman take wing on the rain wind? She had no boisterousness left. Her usefulness was over. She tied a noose in the clothesline and dragged a trunk to beneath the rafter. This would be a trap for her gallows. The trunk lid was ajar and she saw that the papers inside had been rifled. They were family papers, private things. Who would have done this? Maggie. She was into everything: Honora's desk, Honora's pockets. She pieced together the torn letters in the fireplace. Why? Was it like the magic that an empty house works on a child? The King and Queen are dead. She roots through Daddy's stud box, puts on Mummy's beads, stirs up the humble contents of every drawer. Honora put on her glasses and looked at the disordered paper. "The President and the Board of Trustees of the Hutchens Institute for the Blind request . . ." Beneath this was a letter in faded ink: "Dear Honora, I shall be in Boston for perching cloathing for summer and fawl but will return thursday. I thinch its plaine enof now that Lorenzo wold like to have bought my land when he was theare. I am ankshus to sell. I know thears no prospect of getting a faire prise from him, jidging from the past. Dishonesty is his polesy but if you spoke with him it might affect a saile. . . ." Below this she read: "He who reads me when I am ashes is my son in wishes."

It was in Leander's hand, some pages of that execrable journal or autobiography that had occupied the last months of his life.

Cousin Honora Wapshot is a skin-flint [he had written]. Headcheese of every local charity. Dispenser of skinny chickens and pullet's eggs to the poor. Prays loudly in church for those who travail and are heavy-laden but will not loan one hundred bucks to only, only cousin for safe investment and guaranteed income in local water-powered tack factory. No work in St. Botolphs. No coin. Village dying or dead. Writer at age nineteen forced by Honora's parsimony to take job as night desk clerk in Travertine Mansion House ten miles down river.

Travertine Mansion House ranked with wonders of the ages. Compared in free literature to monuments in Karnak, Acropolis in Greece, Pantheon in Rome. Large, frame, brine-soaked firetrap with two-story piazzas, palatial public rooms, 80 bedrooms, 8 baths. Wash-basins and chamber-pots still widely in use. Accounted for poignant smell in hallways. Public rooms and some suites lighted by gas but many chambers still dependent on kerosene lamps for illumination. Palm trees in lobby. Music played for all meals, excepting breakfast. American plan. Twelve dollars a day and upwards. Writer worked at desk from 6 P.M. until last gun was fired, usually around midnight. Salary was seventeen dollars including board wages. Wore swallow-tail coat and flower in buttonhole. Speaking tubes but no telephones. Limited bell system connected to drycell batteries. Fine view of beach from piazza. Tennis courts and croquet lawn at side of hotel. Some saddle horses brought up from livery stable. Some boating. Principle evening recreation was attendance at lectures. Glories of Rome. Glories of Venice. Glories of Athens. Also some philosophical and religious subjects.

Among guests was Shakespearean actress. Lottie Beauchamp. Pronounced Beecham. Played supporting roles with Farquarson Grant Stratford and Avon Shakespearean Co. Traveled with own bed-linen, silver, jams and jellies. Mlle. Beauchamp as she was then known to writer appeared at desk late in evening with sad tale. Had lost pearl necklace on beach. Remembered where she had left it but was reluctant to venture on dark shore alone. Writer accompanied star-boarder on search. Mild night. Moon, stars, etc. Gentle swell. Found necklace on stone in sheltered cove. Admired scenery, warmth of night air, moon riding in west. Mlle. Beauchamp breathing heavily. Pleasant hour ensued. Writer dozed off. Woke to find famous Thespian jumping up and down in moonlight, holding breasts to keep from jouncing. Moon madness? What are you doing? Well, you don't want me to have a child do you? says she. Jumped up and down. Never experienced such behavior before or since. Seemed to work.

Lottie Beauchamp was 5'6". 117 lbs. Age unknown. Paine's Celery Compound Complexion. Light brown hair. Would be called blonde nowadays. Excellent shape but excessive topside structure by modern standards. Golden voice. Could raise your hackles, also bring tears to every eye. Noticeable English accent but not foreign sounding or in any other way unpleasant. Fastidious nature. Traveled with own bed-linen as noted above. Hot house flowers in bedroom. Spoke however of humble beginnings. Daughter of a Leeds mill worker. Mother was drunkard. Familiar with cold, hunger, poverty, destitution, etc., in childhood. A dungheap rose. Enjoyed ample stock of artistic temperament. Very volatile. Complained liberally to management about lack of hot water and lumpiness of bed but was always gracious to servants. Sometimes repented of life as actress. All mummery and sham. Needed tenderness. Writer happy to accommodate. No question of wrongdoing or so it seemed.

End of September business at Mansion House slow as cold molasses. Some northerly winds. Also fine weather. Bright sun. Warm air. Breeze up and down the mast. Wouldn't blow a butterfly off your mainsail. Walked often on beach with Thespian before commencing tour of duty. Delightful company. Lingered in various coves, nooks, also aboard catboat. Property of hotel. Tern. Fifteen foot. Marconi rig. Wide waisted. Sailed like a butter-tub. Small cabin with no amenities. So the days passed.

Maiden ladies composed majority of clientele at season's end. Some dear old ladies; some lemons. Front-porch committee commanded by Dr. Helen Archibald. Famous dietician. Also hygienist. Led daily course in calisthenics in music saloon For Women Only. Never privileged to see same but expect consisted of knee bends performed to old music box tunes. Big music box. Called Regina. Music produced by flat metal disks, two feet in diameter. Wide selection. Opera. Marches. Songs of love.

Front-porch committee bored with counting whitecaps. Got wind of romance. Famous dietician evinced sudden interest in sea-shells. Shells of no particular interest on Travertine beach.

Sand dollars. Starfish. Usual produce of cold northern waters. Few colored stones gleaming like jewels when wet. Colorless when dry. Purpose of famous dietician's seaside excursions was to spy. Shadowed Lottie and me like moral gumshoe. Pretending to look for shells. Upsoaring of self. Tramped the beach for hours. Got sand in shoes. Ruined several costumes. Vigilance was rewarded. Writer, rising from recumbent position in sheltered cove, saw famous dietician scurrying back to Mansion House in full possession of damaging facts. All interest in seashells forgotten. Was unable to pursue same, being clad only in birthday suit. Lottie very calm. Planned campaign. She would return to Mansion House alone. Gallant. Unafraid to beard front-porch committee. Writer would travel cross-country and approach hostelry from opposite direction. Did so. Walked through scrub pine woods to village of Travertine and then down dirt road to shore via so-called Great Western. Changed clothes and took up position behind desk at 6 P.M. with fresh flower in buttonhole. String trio tuning instruments in Grand Dining Salon. Handyman lighting gas chandeliers. (No daylight saving time. September dusk fell swiftly.) All h——l broke loose.

Front-porch committee led by self-designated Grand Marshal and Chief Bottle Washer Dr. Helen Archibald approached hotel manager and issued ultimatum. Unable to hear terms from desk but surmised they dealt with Lottie. Committee then entered dining salon in full panoply, sat down and put on pince-nezs and other assorted storm windows, pretending to study menus. (Menus printed for every meal.) Other guests entered and were seated. Music of string trio did nothing to relieve tension. Soup is being served when Lottie comes downstairs in salmon or coral-colored dress. Beautiful! She is waylaid by hotel proprietor who urges her sotto voce to dine in her suite at the expense of the management. No soap. On sweeps Lottie into the lion's den. Considerable noise of dropped soup spoons. Also storm windows. Then silence. Grand Marshal for the opposition deals the first and only blow. "I will not eat off the same dishes as that whore," says she. Then up spake the desk clerk in the swallow-tail coat. "Apologize to Miss Beauchamp, Dr. Archibald." "You're fired," says the manager. "When was this?" says I. "The day before yesterday," says he and the forces of Venus retired in confusion. Lottie took a trip to Travertine and went up to Boston on freight train with load of cranberries. I walked to St. Botolphs, carrying my straw suitcase and, finding Cousin Honora's dark, spent the night at the Viaduct House. Only concern was indignation at having been fired. Was never fired before or since during fifty-five years in business.

Went up to Boston on noon cars. Joined Lottie as per arrangement in Brown's Hotel. Very tough joint. Lottie preparing to open two weeks season with Farquarson and Freedom. Urged writer to take job with company as bitplayer, walk-on, crowd recruiter and bouncer. Theater more free and easy than today. Great attraction of times was Count Johannes. Audience came armed with over-ripe produce. Missiles began to fly before first act ended. Actors served as moving targets for remainder of performance. Sometimes produced bushel baskets and nets to catch vegetables. No reflection on theatrical greats intended. Julia Marlowe as Parthenia in Ingomar. Glorious! E. H. Sothern in Romeo and Juliet. Basset D'Arcy's Lear. Howard Athenaeum then open. Also Boston Museum, Old Boston Theatre and Hollis Street Theatre.

Accepted position with Farquarson and Freedom. Played Marcellus in opening production of Hamlet with Farquarson as Hamlet and Lottie as Ophelia. Played numerous soldiers, sailors, gentlemen, guards and sundry watch-men during two-week season. Opened National Tour in Congress Opera House, Providence, R.I.

Tour included Worcester, Springfield, Albany, Rochester, Buffalo, Syracuse, Jamestown, Ashtabula, Cleveland, Columbus and Zanesville. Suspected Lottie of concupiscence in Jamestown. Found naked stranger in clothes closet in Ashtabula. Caught redhanded in Cleveland. Sold gold cuff-links and returned to Boston via steam-cars on March 18th. No hard feelings. Laugh and the world laughs with you. Weep and you weep alone.

9

When Moses had Honora's letter he was much more alarmed than his brother. He had mortgaged his trust on the strength of Honora's age and he wrote directly to Boston. The Appleton Bank and Trust Company did not reply and when he telephoned Boston they told him that the trust officer was skiing in Peru. On Sunday night Moses took a plane to Detroit, starting on a wild-goose chase across the country to see if he could raise fifty thousand dollars on the strength, largely, of his charm. Fifty thousand dollars would barely cover his obligations.

On Monday night, alone in the house with the cook and her son, Melissa had a sentimental dream. The landscape was romantic. It was evening, and since there was no trace anywhere of mechanical things—automobile tracks and the noise of planes— it seemed to her to be evening in another century. The sun had set, but a polished afterglow lighted up the sky. There was a winding stream with alders, and on the farther banks the ruins of a castle. She spread a white cloth on the grass and set this with long-necked wine bottles and a loaf of new bread, whose fragrance and warmth were a part of the dream. Upstream a man was swimming naked in a pool. He spoke to her in French, and it was part of the dream's lightness that it all transpired in another country, another time. She saw the man pull himself up onto the banks and dry himself with a cloth while she went on setting out the things for supper.

She was waked from this dream by the barking of a dog. It was 3 A.M. She heard the wind. It was changing its quarter and beginning to blow from the northwest. She was about to fall asleep when she heard the front door come open. Sweat started at her armpits and her young heart strained its muscles, although she knew it was only the wind that had opened the door. Not long ago, a thief had broken into a house in the neighborhood. In the garden, behind a lilac bush, a pile of cigarette ends had been found, where he must have waited patiently for hours for the lights of the house to be turned out. He had made an opening in a window with a glass cutter, rifled a wall safe of cash and jewelry, and left by the front door. In reporting the theft, the police had described his movements in detail: He had waited in the garden. He had entered by a back window. He had gone through the kitchen and pantry into the dining room. But who was he? Had he been tall or short, heavy or slender? Had his heart throbbed with terror in the dark rooms, or had he experienced the thief's supreme sense of triumph over a pretentious and gullible society? He had left traces of himself—cigarette ends, footprints, broken glass and a rifled safe—but he had never been found, and so he remained disembodied and faceless.

It was the wind, she told herself; no thief would have left the door standing open. Now she could feel the cold air spreading through the house, rising up the stairs and moving the curtains in the hall. She got out of bed and put on a wrapper. She turned on the hall light and started down the stairs, asking herself what it was she was afraid of in the dark rooms below. She was afraid of the dark, like a primitive or a child, but why? What was there about darkness that threatened her? She was afraid of the dark as she was afraid of the unknown, and what was the unknown but the force of evil, and why should she be afraid of this? She turned on the lights one after another. The rooms were empty, and the wind was enjoying the liberty of the place, scattering the mail on the hall table and peering under the edge of the rug. The wind was cold, and she shivered as she closed and locked the front door, but now she was unafraid and very much herself. In the morning she had a cold.

The doctor came several times during that week, and when she got no better he ordered her to go to the hospital. In the middle of the morning, she went upstairs to pack. She had been to the hospital in recent years only once, to have her son, and then the drives of pregnancy had carried her unthinkingly through her preparations. This time she carried no life within her; she carried, instead, an infection. And, alone in her bedroom, choosing a nightgown and a hairbrush, she felt as if she had been singled out to make some mysterious voyage. She was not a sentimental woman, and she had no sad thoughts about parting from the pleasant room she shared with her husband. She felt weary but not sick, although there was a cutting pain in her chest. A stranger watching her would have thought she was insane. Why did she empty the carnations into the wastebasket and rinse out the vase? Why did she count her stockings, lock her jewelry box and hide the key, glance at her bank balance, dust off the mantelpiece and stand in the middle of the room, looking as if she were listening to distant music? The foolish impulse to dust the mantelpiece was irresistible, but she had no idea why she did it, and anyhow it was time to go.

The hospital was new, and conscientious efforts had been made to make it a cheerful place, but her loveliness—you might say her elegance—was put at a disadvantage by the undisguisable atmosphere of regimentation, and she looked terribly out of place. A wheelchair was brought for her, but she refused to use it. She would have looked crestfallen and ridiculous, she knew, with her coat bunched up around her middle and her purse in her lap. A nurse took her upstairs and led her into a pleasant room, where she was told to undress and get into bed. While she was undressing, someone brought her lunch on a tray. It was a small matter, but she found it disconcerting to be given a chop and some canned fruit while she was half-naked and before the clocks had struck noon. She ate her lunch dutifully and the doctor came at two and told her she could count on being in the hospital ten days or two weeks. He would call Moses. She fell asleep, and woke at five with a fever.

The imagery of her fever was similar to the imagery of love. Her reveries were spacious, and she seemed to be promised the revelation of some truth that lay at the center of the labyrinthine and palatial structures where she wandered. The fever, as it got higher, eased the pain in her breast and made her indifferent to the heavy beating of her heart. The fever dreams seemed like a healthy employment of her imagination to distract her from the struggle that went on in her breast. She was standing at the head of a broad staircase with red walls. Many people were climbing the stairs. They had the attitudes of pilgrims. The climb was grueling and lengthy, and when she reached the summit she found herself in a grove of lemon trees and lay down on the grass to rest. When she woke from this dream, her nightgown and the bed linen were soaked with sweat. She rang for a nurse, who changed them.

She felt much better when this was done, and felt that the fever had been a crisis and that, passing safely through it, she had triumphed over her illness. At nine the nurse gave her some medicine and said good night. Some time later she felt the lassitude of fever returning. She rang, but no one came, and she could not resist the confusion in her mind as her temperature rose. The labored beating of her heart sounded like a drum. She confused it with a drum in her mind, and saw a circle of barbaric dancers. The dance was long, rising to a climax, and at the moment of the climax, when she thought her heart would burst, she woke, shaking with a fresh chill and wet with sweat. A nurse finally came and changed her clothing and her linen again. She was relieved to be dry and warm. The two attacks of fever had weakened her but left her with a feeling of childish contentment. She felt wakeful, got out of bed and by supporting herself on the furniture made her way to the window to see the night.

While she watched, clouds covered the moon. It must have been late because most of the windows were dark. Then a window in the wall at her left was lighted, and she saw a nurse introduce a young woman and her husband into a room identical to the one where she sat in the dark. The young woman was pregnant but not having labor pains. She undressed in the bathroom and got into bed, while her husband was unpacking her bag. The window, like all the others, was hung with a Venetian blind, but no one had bothered to close it. When the unpacking was

done, he unfastened the front of her nightgown, knelt beside
the bed and laid his head on her breasts. He remained this way
for several minutes without moving. Then he got up—he must
have heard the nurse approach—and covered his wife. The nurse
came in and snapped the blinds shut.

Melissa heard a night bird calling, and wondered what bird
it was, what it looked like, what it was up to, what its prey was.
There was a deep octave of thunder, magnificent and homely,
as if someone in heaven had moved a chest of drawers. Then
there was some lightning, distant and discolored, and a moment
later a shower of rain dressed the earth. The sound of the rain
seemed to Melissa, with the cutting pain in her breast, like the
repeated attentions of a lover. It fell on the flat roofs of the
hospital, the lawns and the leaves in the wood. The pain in
her chest seemed to spread and sharpen in proportion to her
stubborn love of the night, and she felt for the first time in
her life an unwillingness to leave any of this; a fear as senseless
and powerful as her fear of the dark when she went down to
shut the door; a horror of death.

10

Now that was the year when the squirrels were such a pest and
everybody worried about cancer and homosexuality. The squirrels upset garbage pails, bit delivery men and entered houses.
Cancer was a commonplace but men and women, at its mercy,
were told that their pain was some trifling complication while
behind their backs their brothers and their sisters, their husbands
and wives, would whisper: "All we can hope is that they will
go quickly." This cruel and absolute hypocrisy was bound to
backfire and in the end no one could tell or count upon being
told if that pain in the middle was the knock of death or some
trifling case of gas. Most maladies have their mythologies, their

populations, their scenery and their grim jokes. The Black Plague had masques, street songs and dances. Tuberculosis in its heyday was like a civilization where a caste of comely, brilliant and doomed men and women fell in love, waltzed and invented privileges for their disease; but here was the grappling hand of death disinfected by a social conspiracy of all its reality. "Why, you'll be up and around in no time at all," says the nurse to the dying man. "You want to dance at your daughter's wedding, don't you? Don't you want to see your daughter married? Well, then, we can't expect to get better if we're not more cheerful, can we?" She cleans his arm with alcohol and prepares the syringe. "Your wife tells me you're a great mountain-climber but if you want to get better and climb the mountains again you'll have to be more cheerful. You do want to climb the mountains again, don't you?" The contents of the syringe flow into his veins. "I've never climbed a mountain myself," the nurse says, "but I expect it must be very exciting when you get to the top. I don't think I'd like the climbing part of it very much but the view from the summit must be lovely. They tell me that in the Alps roses grow in the snow banks and if you want to see all these things again you'll have to be more careful." Now he is drowsy and she raises her voice. "Oh, you'll be up and around in no time at all," she exclaims and softly, softly she closes the door to his room and says to his family, gathered in the corridor: "I've put him to sleep again and all we can do is hope and pray that he will never wake up." Melissa was one of those unfortunate people who was to suffer from this attitude.

Moses returned from his wild-goose chase as soon as he learned of Melissa's illness, having borrowed enough money to at least give an impression of solvency. The fact that Melissa was convalescent when he returned might have seemed to account for the fact that he did not describe to her his financial embarrassments but this was not so. He would not have been able to describe them to her under any circumstances; no more could Coverly state that he had seen the ghost of his father. Had Moses lived in Parthenia he would have felt free to put a

FOR SALE sign in his living room window and another in the windshield of his convertible but to do this in Proxmire Manor would have been subversive. He expressed his worries not in irritability but in a manner that was very broad and jocular. Melissa then had this forced jocularity to cope with as well as the absurd conviction that she had cancer. She could not convince herself that she was cured nor could she trust what the doctor told her. She telephoned the hospital and asked to speak with her nurse. She asked the nurse if they could meet for a drink. "Why not?" the nurse asked. "Sure. Why not?" She went off duty at four and Melissa planned to meet her at the traffic light by the hospital at four-fifteen.

They went to a bar near there, a roadside place. The nurse ordered a double martini. "I'm tired," she said. "I'm worn out. My sister, she's married, she called me last night and said would I take care of the baby while she and her husband go to a cocktail party. So I said sure, I'd take care of the baby if it was just for cocktails, an hour or two. So I went there at six and you know when they came home? Midnight! The baby didn't shut her eyes once. She bawled all the time. Kind sister, that's me."

"I wanted to ask you about my x-rays," Melissa said. "You saw them."

"What are you afraid of," the nurse asked, "cancer?"

"Yes."

"That's what they're all afraid of."

"I don't have cancer?"

"Not to my knowledge." She raised her face and watched the wind carry some leaves past the window. "Leaves," she said, "leaves, leaves, look at them. I've got a little apartment with a back yard and it's me that rakes the leaves. I spend all my spare time raking leaves. Just as soon as I get one bunch cleaned up down comes another. As soon as you get rid of the leaves it begins to snow."

"Would you like another drink?" Melissa asked.

"No, thanks. You know, I wondered what you wanted to see me about but I didn't think it was cancer. You know what I thought you wanted?"

"What?"

"Heroin."

"I don't understand."

"I thought maybe you wanted me to smuggle some heroin out to you. You'd be surprised at the number of people who think I can get them drugs. Top-ranking people, some of them. Oh, I could name names. Shall we go?"

She stood, late one afternoon, at her window watching the ring of golden light that crowned the eastern hills at that season and time of day. It rested on the Babcocks' lawn, the Filmores' ranch house, the stone walls of the church, the Thompsons' chimney—lambent, and as yellow and clear as strained honey, and a ring because, as she watched, she saw at the base of the hills a clear demarcation between the yellow light and the rising dark, and watched the band of light lift past the Babcocks' lawn, the Filmores' ranch house, the stone walls of the church and the Thompsons' chimney, up into thin air. The street was empty, or nearly so. Everyone in Proxmire Manor had two cars and no one walked with the exception of old Mr. Cosden, who belonged to the generation that took constitutionals. Up the street he came, his blue eyes fixed on the last piece of yellow light that touched the church steeple, as if exclaiming to himself, "How wonderful, how wonderful it is!" He passed, and then a much stranger figure took her attention—a tall man with unusually long arms. He was a stray, she decided; he must live in the slums of Parthenia. In his right hand he carried an umbrella and a pair of rubbers. He was terribly stooped and to see where he was going had to crane his neck forward and upward like an adder. He had not bent his back over a whetstone or a workbench or under the weight of a brick hod or at any other honest task. It was the stoop of weak-mindedness, abnegation and bewilderment. He had never had any occasion to straighten his back in self-esteem. Stooped with shyness as a child, stooped with loneliness as a youth, stooped now under an invisible burden of social disregard, he walked now with his long arms reaching nearly to his knees. His wide, thin mouth was set in a silly half-grin, meaningless and sad, but the best face he had been able to hit on. As he approached the house, the beating of her heart seemed to correspond to his footsteps, the cutting pain returned to her breast, and she felt the return of her fear of darkness, evil and death. Carrying his umbrella and rubbers, although there was not a cloud in the sky, he duck-footed out of sight.

A few days later, Melissa was driving back from the village of Parthenia. The street was lighted erratically by the few stores that hung on at the edge of town—general stores smelling of stale bread and bitter oranges, where those in the neighborhood who were too lazy, too tired and too infirm to go to the palatial shopping centers bought their coffee rings, beer and hamburgers. The darkness of the street was sparsely, irregularly, checkered with light, and she saw the tall man crossing one of these apertures, throwing a long, crooked shadow ahead of him on the paving. He held a heavy bag of groceries in each arm. He was no more stooped than before—the curvature of his spine seemed set—but the bags must be heavy, and she pitied him. She drove on, evoking defensively the worlds of difference that lay between them and the chance that he would have misunderstood her kindness had she offered to give him a ride. But when she had completed her defense it seemed so shallow, idle and selfish that she turned the car around in her own driveway and drove back toward Parthenia. Her best instinct was to help him— to make some peace between his figure and her irrational fear of death—and why should she deny herself this? He would have passed the lighted stores by this time, she decided, and she drove slowly up the dark street, looking for his stooped figure. When she saw him she turned the car around and stopped. "Can I help you?" she asked. "Can I give you a ride? You seem to have so much to carry." He turned and looked at the beautiful stranger without quite relaxing his half-grin, and she wondered if he wasn't a deaf-mute as well as weak-minded. Then a look of distrust touched the grin. There was no question about what he was feeling. She was from that world that had gulled him, pelted him with snowballs and rifled his lunchbox. His mother had told him to beware of strangers and here was a beautiful stranger, perhaps the most dangerous of all. "No!" he said. "No, no!" She drove on, wondering what was at the bottom of her impulse; wondering, in the end, why she should scrutinize a simple attempt at kindness.

On Thursday the maid was off, and Melissa took care of the baby. He slept after lunch, and she woke him at four, lifting him out of his crib and letting the blankets fall. They were alone. The house was quiet. She carried him into the kitchen, put him in his highchair and opened a can of figs. Sleepy and docile and pale, he followed her with his eyes, and smiled sweetly when their eyes met. His shirt was stained and wet, and she wore a wrapper. She sat by him at the table, with her face only a few inches from his, and they spooned the figs out of the can. He shuddered now and then with what seemed to be pleasure. The quiet house, the still kitchen, the pale and docile boy in his stained shirt, her round white arms on the table, the comfortable slovenliness of eating from a can were all part of an intimacy so intense and yet so tranquil that it seemed to her as if she and the baby were the same flesh and blood, subjects of the same heart, all mingled and at ease. What a comfort, she thought, is one's skin. . . . But it was time then to change the boy, time to dress herself, time to take up cheerfully the other side of her life. Carrying the child through the living room she saw, out of the window, the stooped figure with his rubbers and umbrella.

A wind was blowing and he moved indifferently through a diagonal fall of yellow leaves, craning his neck like an adder, his back bent under its impossible burden. She held the baby's head against her breast, foolishly, instinctively, as if to protect his eyes from some communicable evil. She turned away from the window, and shortly afterward there was a loud pounding on the back door. How had he found where she lived, and what did he want? He might have recognized her car in the driveway; he might have asked who she was, the village was that small. He had not come to thank her for attempted kindness. She felt sure of that. He had come—in his foolishness—to accuse her of something. Was he dangerous? Was there any danger left in Proxmire Manor? She put the boy down and went toward the back door, summoning her self-respect. When she opened it, there was Mr. Narobi's good-looking grocery boy. He made it all seem laughable—came in beaming and with a kind of radiance that seemed to liberate her from this absurd chain of anxieties.

"You're new?" she asked.

"Yes."

"I don't know your name."

"Emile. It's a funny name. My father was French."

"Did he come from France?"

"Oh, no, Quebec. French Canadian."

"What does he do?"

"When people used to ask me that, I used to say, 'He plays the harp!' He's dead. He died when I was little. My mother works at the florist's—Barnum's—on Green Street. Maybe you know her?"

"I don't think I do. Would you like a beer?"

"Sure. Why not? It's my last stop."

She asked if he wanted something to eat, and got him some crackers and cheese. "I'm always hungry," he said.

She brought the baby into the kitchen and they all three sat at the table while he ate and drank. Stuffing his mouth with cheese, he seemed to be a child. His gaze was clear and disarming. She couldn't meet it without a stir in her blood. And was this sluttishness? Was she worse than Mrs. Lockhart? Would she be dragged figuratively out of Proxmire Manor at the tail of a cart? She didn't care.

"Nobody ever gave me a beer before," he said. "They give me Cokes, sometimes. I guess they don't think I'm old enough. But I drink. Martinis, whisky, everything."

"How old are you?"

"Nineteen. Now I have to go."

"Please don't go," she said.

He stood at the table, covering her with his wide gaze, and

she wondered what would happen if she reached out to him. Would he run out of the kitchen? Would he shout, "Unhand me!"? He seemed ripe; he seemed ready for the picking; and yet there was something else in the corner of his eyes—reserve, wariness. He perhaps had a vision of something better, and if he had, she would encourage him with all her heart. Go and love the drum majorette, the girl next door.

"Oh, I'd like to stay," he said. "It's nice here. But it's Thursday, and I have to take my mother shopping. Thank you very much."

He went to the house three or four times a week. Melissa was usually alone in the late afternoons and he timed his visits. Sometimes she seemed to be waiting for him. No one had ever been so attentive. She seemed interested in all the facts of his life—that his father had been a surveyor, that he drove a second-hand Buick, that he had done well at school. She usually gave him a beer and sat with him in the kitchen. Her company excited him. It made him feel that he might do well. Some of her worldliness, some of her finesse, would rub off on him and get him out of the grocery business. Suddenly, one afternoon, she said quite shyly, "You know, you're divine."

He wondered if she hadn't lost her marbles. He had heard that women sometimes did. Had he been wasting his time? He didn't want to fool around with a woman who had lost her marbles. He knew he wasn't divine. If he was, someone would have said so before and if he had been divine and had been convinced of this, he would have concealed it—not through modesty but through an instinct of self-preservation. "Sometimes I think I'm good-looking," he said earnestly to try and modify her praise. He finished his beer. "Now I have to get back to the store."

11

Melissa went shopping in New York a few days later. She stood on the platform with her neighbor, Gertrude Bender, waiting for the midmorning train. As the train came around the curve the station agent pushed out on a wagon one of those yellow wooden boxes that are used for transporting coffins. This simple fact of life came as a blow to Melissa's high spirits. "It must be Gertrude Lockhart," her friend whispered. "They're sending her back to Indiana."

"I didn't know she was dead," Melissa said.

"She hung herself in the garage," her friend said, still whispering, and they boarded the train.

Now it was not true that nothing happened in Proxmire Manor; the truth was that eventfulness in the community took such eccentric curves that it was difficult to comprehend. It was not a force of discreetness that kept Melissa from knowing Gertrude Lockhart's story; it was that the story was more easily forgotten than understood. She had been considering her widespread reputation for licentiousness, a singularly winsome woman; light-boned, quick, a little nervous. Her skin was very white. This was not a point of beauty, a stirring pallor. She just happened to have a white skin. Her hair was ash-blond but it had lost its shine. Her eyes were bright, small, dark and set close together. Her ears were too big, a fact that made her seem basically unserious. At the fourth- or fifth-string boarding school she had attended she had been known as Dirty Gertie. She was married, happily enough, to Pete Lockhart and had three small children. Her downfall began not with immortal longings but with an uncommonly severe winter when the main soil line from their house to the septic tank froze. The toilets backed up into the bathtubs and sinks. Nothing drained. Her husband went off to work. Her children caught the school bus. At half-past eight she found herself alone in a house that had, in a sense, ceased to function. The place was not luxurious but it appeared to be civilized; it appeared to promise something better than relieving herself in a bucket. At nine o'clock she took a drink of whisky and began to call the plumbers of Parthenia. There were seven and they were all busy. She kept repeating that her case was an emergency. One firm offered, as a favor, to stir up for her a retired plumber and presently an old man in an old car came to the house. He looked sadly at the mess in the bathtubs and the sinks and told her that he was a plumber, not a ditchdigger, and that she would have to find someone to dig a trench before he could repair the drain. She had another drink, put on some lipstick and drove into Parthenia.

She went first to the state employment office where eighteen or twenty men were sitting around looking for work but none of them was willing to dig a ditch and she saw as one of the facts of her life, her time, that standards of self-esteem had advanced to a point where no one was able to dig a hole. She went to the liquor store to get some whisky and told the clerk her problems. He said he thought he could get someone to help. He made a telephone call. "I've got you somebody," he said. "He's not as bad as he sounds. Give him two dollars an hour and all the whisky he can drink. His father-in-law fired him out of the house a couple of weeks ago and he's on the bum, but he's a nice guy." She went home and had another drink. Sometime later the doorbell rang. She had expected an old man with the shakes but what she saw was a man in his thirties. He wore tight jeans and a dark pullover and stood on her steps with his hands thrust into his back pockets, his chest pushed forward in a curious way as if this were a gesture of pride, friendship or courtship. His skin was dark, rucked deeply around the mouth like the seams on a boot, and his eyes were brown. His smile was bare amorousness. It was his only smile, but she didn't know this. He would smile amorously at his shovel, amorously into his whisky glass, amorously into the hole he had dug, and when it was time to go home he would smile amorously at the ignition switch on his car. She offered him some whisky but he said he would wait. She showed him where the tools were and he began to dig.

He worked for two hours and uncovered and cleared the frozen drain. She was able to clear out the bathtubs and sinks. When he returned the tools she asked him in for his whisky. She was quite drunk herself by then. He poured himself a water glass of whisky and drank it off. "What I really need," he said, "is a shower. I'm living in a furnished room. You have to take turns at the bathtub." She said he could take a shower, knowing full well what was afoot. He drank off another glass of whisky and she led him upstairs and opened the bathroom door. "I'll just get out of these things," he said, pulling off his sweater and dropping his jeans.

They were still in bed when the children came home. She opened the door and called sweetly down the stairs: "Mummy's resting. There are cookies on top of the icebox. Be sure and take your vitamin pills before you go out to play." When the children went out she gave him ten dollars, kissed him good-by and slipped him out the back door. She never saw him again.

The old plumber fixed the drain and on the weekend Pete filled in the trench. The weather remained bitter. One morning, a week or ten days later, she was wakened by her husband's huffing and puffing. "There isn't time, darling," she said. She slipped on a wrapper, went downstairs and tried to open a package of bacon. The package promised to seal in the bacon's smoky flavor but she couldn't get the package open. She broke a fingernail. The transparent wrapper that imprisoned the bacon seemed like some immutable transparency in her life, some invisible barrier of frustrations that stood between herself and what she deserved. Pete joined her while she was struggling with the bacon and continued his attack. He was very nearly successful—he had her backed up against the gas range—when they heard the thunder of their children's footsteps in the hall. Pete went off to the train with mixed and turbulent feelings. She got the children some breakfast and watched them eat it with the extraordinary density of a family gathered at a kitchen table on a dark winter morning. When the children had gone off to get the school bus she turned up the thermostat. There was a dull explosion from the furnace room. A cloud of rank smoke came out of the cellar door. She poured herself a glass of whisky to steady her nerves and opened the door. The room was full of smoke but there was no fire. Then she telephoned the oil-burner repairman they employed. "Oh, Charlie isn't here," his wife said brightly. "He's up in Utica with his bowling team. They're in the semi-finals. He won't be back for ten days." She called every oil-burner man in the telephone directory but none of them was free. "But someone must come and help me," she exclaimed to one of the women who answered the phone. "It's zero outside and there's no heat at all. Everything will freeze." "Well, I'm sorry but I won't have a man free until Thursday," the stranger said. "But why don't you buy yourself an electric heater? You can keep the temperature up with those things." She had some more whisky, put on some lipstick and drove to the hardware store in Parthenia where she bought a large electric heater. She plugged it into an outlet in the kitchen and pulled the switch. All the lights in the house went out and she poured herself some more whisky and began to cry.

She cried for her discomforts but she cried more bitterly for their ephemeralness, for the mysterious harm a transparent bacon wrapper and an oil burner could do to the finest part of her spirit; cried for a world that seemed to be without laws and prophets. She went on crying and drinking. Some repairmen came and patched things up but when the children came home from school she was lying unconscious on the sofa. They took their vitamin pills and went out to play. The next week the washing machine broke down and flooded the kitchen. The first repairman she called had gone to Miami for his vacation. The second would not be able to come for a week. The third had gone to a funeral. She mopped up the kitchen floor but it was two weeks before a repairman came. In the meantime the gas

range went and she had to do all the cooking on an electric
plate. She could not educate herself in the maintenance and
repair of household machinery and felt in herself that tragic
obsolescence she had sensed in the unemployed of Parthenia
who needed work and money but who could not dig a hole. It
was this feeling of obsolescence that pushed her into drunkenness and promiscuity and she was both.

One afternoon when she was very drunk she threw her arms
around the milkman. He pushed her away roughly. "Jesus, lady,"
he said, "what kind of a man do you think I am?" In a blackmail-
ing humor he stuffed the icebox with eggs, milk, orange juice,
cottage cheese, vegetable salad and eggnog. She took a bottle
of whisky up to her bedroom. At four o'clock the oil burner
went out of order. She was back on the telephone again. No
one could come for three or four days. It was very cold outside
and she watched the winter night approach the house with the
horror of an aboriginal. She could feel the cold overtake the
rooms. When it got dark she went into the garage and took
her life.

They held a little funeral for her in the undertaking parlor
in Parthenia. The room where her monumental coffin stood was
softly lighted and furnished like a cocktail lounge and the music
from the electric organ was virtually what you would have heard
in a hotel bar in someplace like Cleveland. She had, it turned
out, no friends in Proxmire Manor. The only company her husband was able to muster was a handful of near strangers they
had met on various cruise ships. They had taken a two-week
Caribbean cruise each winter and the ceremony was attended
by the Robinsons from the S.S. *Homeric,* the Howards from S.S.
United States, the Gravelys from the *Gripsholm* and the Leonards
from the *Bergensfjord.* A clergyman said a few trenchant words.
(The oil-burner repairmen, electricians, mechanics and plumbers
who were guilty of her death did not attend.) During the clergyman's remarks Mrs. Robinson (S.S. *Homeric)* began to cry with
a violence and an anguish that had nothing to do with that time
or place. She groaned loudly, she rocked in her chair, she sobbed

convulsively. Mrs. Howard and Mrs. Leonard and then the men began to sob and wail. They did not cry over the loss of her person; they scarcely knew her. They cried at the realization of how bitterly disappointing her life had been. Melissa knew none of this, of course, traveling that morning on the same train that carried Mrs. Lockhart's remains on the first leg of their trip back to Indiana.

Gertrude Bender, with whom Melissa sat, had silver-gilt hair skinned back in a chignon with such preciseness and skill that Melissa wondered how it had been accomplished. She had matching silver-gilt furs, and rattled six gold bracelets. She was a pretty, shallow woman who wielded the inarguable powers of great wealth and whose voice was shrill. She talked about her daughter Betty. "She's worried about her schoolwork but I tell her, 'Betty,' I tell her, 'don't you worry about your schoolwork. Do you think what I learned in school got me where I am today? Develop a good figure and learn the forks. That's all that matters.' "

In the seat in front of Melissa there was an old lady whose head was bowed under the weight of a hat covered with cloth roses. A family occupied the facing seats across the aisle—a mother and three children. They were poor. Their clothing was cheap and threadbare, and the woman's face was worn. One of her children was sick and lay across her lap, sucking his thumb. He was two or three years old, but it was hard to guess his age, he was so pale and thin. There were sores on his forehead and sores on his thin legs. The lines around his mouth were as deep as those on the face of a man. He seemed sick and miserable, but stubborn and obdurate at the same time, as if he held in his fist a promise to something bewildering and festive that he would not relinquish in spite of his sickness and the strangeness of the train. He sucked his thumb noisily and would not move from his position in the midst of life. His mother bent over him as she must have done when she nursed him, and sang him a lullaby as they passed Parthenia, Gatesbridge, Tuxon Valley and Tokinsville.

Gertrude said, "I don't understand people who lose their looks when they don't have to. I mean what's the point of going through life looking like an old laundry bag? Now take Molly Singleton. She goes up to the Club on Saturday nights wearing those thick eyeglasses and an ugly dress and wonders why she doesn't have a good time. There's no point in going to parties if you're going to depress everyone. I'm no girl and I know it, but I still have all the partners I want and I like to give the boys a thrill. I like to see them perk up. It's amazing what you can do. Why, one of the grocery boys wrote me a love letter. I wouldn't tell Charlie—I wouldn't tell anyone, because the poor kid might lose his job—but what's the sense of living if you don't generate a little excitement once in a while?"

Melissa was jealous. That the rush of feeling she suffered was plainly ridiculous didn't diminish its power. She seemed, unknowingly, to have convinced herself of the fact that Emile worshiped her, and the possibility that he worshiped them all, that she might be at the bottom of his list of attractions, was a shock. It was all absurd, and it was all true. She seemed to have rearranged all of her values around his image; to have come unthinkingly to depend upon his admiration. The fact that she cared at all about his philandering was painfully humiliating, but it remained painful.

She left New York in the middle of the afternoon and called Narobi's when she got back. She ordered a loaf of bread, garlic salt, endives—nothing she needed. He was there fifteen or twenty minutes later.

"Emile?" she asked.

"Yes."

"Did you ever write a letter to Mrs. Bender?"

"Mrs. who?"

"Mrs. Bender."

"I haven't written a letter since last Christmas. My uncle sent me ten dollars and I wrote a letter and thanked him."

"Emile, you must know who Mrs. Bender is."

"No, I don't. She probably buys her groceries somewhere else."

"Are you telling the truth, Emile?"

"Sure."

"Oh, I'm making such a damn fool of myself," she said, and began to cry.

"Don't be sad," he said. "Please don't! I like you very much, I think you're fascinating, but I wouldn't want to make you sad."

"Emile, I'm going to Nantucket on Saturday, to close up the house there. Would you like to come with me?"

"Oh, gee, Mrs. Wapshot," he said. "I couldn't do that. I mean I don't know." He knocked over a chair on his way out.

Melissa had never seen Mrs. Cranmer. She could not imagine what the woman looked like. She then got into the car and drove to the florist shop on Green Street. There was a bell attached to the door and, inside, the smell of flowers. Mrs. Cranmer came out of the back, taking a pencil from her bleached hair and smiling like a child.

Emile's mother was one of those widows who keep themselves in a continuous state of readiness for some call, some invitation, some meeting that will never take place because the lover is dead. You find them answering the telephone in the back-street cab stands of little towns, their hair freshly bleached, their nails painted, their high-arched shoes ready for dancing with someone who cannot come. They sell nightgowns, flowers, stationery and candy, and the lowest in their ranks sell movie tickets. They are always in a state of readiness, they have all known the love of a good man, and it is in his memory that they struggle through the snow and the mud in high heels. Mrs. Cranmer's face was painted brightly, her dress was silk, and there were bows on her high-heeled pumps. She was a small, plump woman, with her waist cinctured in sternly, like a cushion with a noose around it. She looked like a figure that had stepped from a comic book, although there was nothing comic about her.

Melissa ordered some roses, and Mrs. Cranmer passed the order on to someone in the back and said, "They'll be ready in a minute." The doorbell rang and another customer came in—a thick-featured man with a white plastic button in his right

ear that was connected by an electrical cord to his vest. He spoke
heavily. "I want something for a deceased," he said. Mrs. Cranmer was diplomatic, and through a series of delicate indirections
tried to discover his relationship to the corpse. Would he like
a blanket of flowers, at perhaps forty dollars, or something a
little less expensive? He gave his information readily, but only
in reply to direct questions. The corpse was his sister. Her children were scattered. "I guess I'm the closest she has left," he
said confusedly, and Melissa, waiting for her roses, felt a premonition of death. She must die—she must be the subject of some
such discussion in a flowershop, and close her eyes forever on
a world that distracted her with its beauty. The image, hackneyed
and poignant, that came to her was of life as a diversion, a festival
from which she was summoned by the secret police of extinction,
when the dancing and the music were at their best. I do not
want to leave, she thought. I do not ever want to leave. Mrs.
Cranmer gave her the roses, and she went home.

12

The Moonlite Drive-In was divided into three magnificent parts.
There was the golf links, the roller rink and the vast amphitheater
itself, where thousands of darkened cars were arranged in the
form of an ancient arena, spread out beneath the tree of night.
Above the deep thunder from the rink and the noise from the
screen, you could hear—high in the air and so like the sea that
a blind man would be deceived—the noise of traffic on the great
Northern Expressway that flows southward from Montreal to
the Shenandoah, engorging in its clover leaves and brilliantly
engineered gradings the green playing fields, rose gardens,
barns, farms, meadows, trout streams, forests, homesteads and
churches of a golden past. The population of this highway gathered for their meals in a string of identical restaurants, where

the murals, the urinals, the menus and the machines for vending sacred medals were uniform. It was some touching part of the autumn night and the hazards of the road that so many of these travelers pleaded for the special protection of gentle St. Christopher and the blessings of the Holy Virgin.

An exit (Exit 307) curved away from the Northern Expressway down toward the Moonlite, and here was everything a man might need: the means for swift travel, food, exercise, skill (the golf links), and in the dark cars of the amphitheater a place to perform the rites of spring—or, in this case, the rites of autumn. It was an autumn night, and the air was full of pollen and decay. Emile sat on the back seat with Louise Mecker. Charlie Putney, his best friend, was in the front seat with Doris Pierce. They were all drinking whisky out of paper cups, and they were all in various stages of undress. On the screen a woman exclaimed, "I want to put on innocence, like a bright, new dress. I want to feel clean again!" Then she slammed a door.

Emile was proud of his skin, but the mention of cleanliness aroused his doubts and misgivings. He blushed. These parties were a commonplace of his generation, and if he hadn't participated in them he would have gotten himself a reputation as a prude and faggot. Four boys in his high school class had been arrested for selling pornography and heroin. They had approached him, but the thought of using narcotics and obscene pictures disgusted him. His sitting undressed in the back seat of a car might be accounted for by the fact that the music he danced to and the movies he watched dealt less and less with the heart and more and more with overt sexuality, as if the rose gardens and playing fields buried under the Expressway were enjoying a revenge. What is the grade-crossing tender standing in the autumn sun thinking of? Why has the postmaster such a dreamy look? Why does the judge presiding at General Sessions seem so restless? Why does the cab driver frown and sigh? What is the shoeshine boy thinking of as he stares out into the rain? What darkens the mind and torments the flesh of the truck driver on the Expressway? What are the thoughts of the old gardener dusting his roses, the garage mechanic on his back under the Chevrolet, the idle lawyer, the sailor waiting for the fog to lift, the drunkard, the soldier? The times were venereal, and Emile was a child of the times.

Louise Mecker was a tomato, but her looseness seemed only to be one aspect of a cheerful disposition. She did what she was expected to do to get along, and this was part of it. And yet in her readiness she sometimes seemed to debase and ridicule the seat of desire, toward which he still preserved some vague and tender feelings. When the lilac under his bedroom window bloomed in the spring and he could smell its fragrance as he lay in bed, some feeling, as strong as ambition but without a name, moved him. Oh, I want—I want to do so well, he thought, sitting naked at the Moonlite. But what did he want to do? Be a jet pilot? Discover a waterfall in Africa? Manage a supermarket? Whatever it was, he wanted something that would correspond to his sense that life was imposing; something that would confirm his feeling that, as he stood at the window of Narobi's grocery store watching the men and women on the sidewalk and the stream of clouds in the sky, the procession he saw was a majestic one.

He thought of Melissa, who by giving him a beer had penetrated into his considerations. In the last six or eight months he had been bewildered by the sudden interest men and women took in his company. They seemed to want something from him and to want it ardently, and although he was not an innocent or a fool, he was genuinely uncertain about what it was they wanted. His own desires were violent. While he was shaving in the morning, a seizure of sexual need doubled him up with pain and made him groan. "Cut yourself, dear?" his mother asked. Now he thought of Melissa. He thought of her—oddly enough— as a tragic figure, frail, lonely and misunderstood. Her husband, whoever he was, would be obtuse, stupid and clumsy. Weren't all men his age? She was a fair prisoner in a tower.

Halfway through the feature, they got dressed and, with the cutout open and the radio blaring "Take It Easy, Greasy," roared out of the Moonlite onto the Expressway, jeopardizing their lives and the lives in every car they passed (men, women and children in arms), but gentle St. Christopher or the mercies of the Holy Virgin spared them, and they got Emile safely home. He climbed the stairs, kissed his mother good night—she was studying an article in *Reader's Digest* about the pancreas—and went to bed. Lying in bed, he decided, quite innocently, that he was tired of tomatoes, movies and paper cups, and that he would go to Nantucket.

13

Melissa had bought the plane tickets and made all the arrangements, and she asked Emile not to speak to her on the plane. He wore new shoes and a new pair of pants, and walked with a bounce in order to feel the thickness of the new soles and to feel the nice play of muscle as it worked up his legs and back into his shoulders. He had never been on a plane before, and he was disappointed to find that it was not so sleek as the planes in magazine advertisements and that the fuselage was dented and stained with smoke. He got a window seat and watched the activity on the field, feeling that as soon as the plane was airborne he would begin a new life of motion, comfort and freedom. Hadn't he always dreamed of going here and there and making friends in different places and being easily accepted as a man of strength and intelligence and not a grocery boy without a future or a destiny, and had he ever doubted that his dreams would come true? Melissa was the last one to get on, and was wearing a fur coat, and the dark skins made her appear to him like a visitor from another continent where everything was beautiful, orderly and luxurious. She didn't look in his direction. A drunken sailor took the seat beside Emile and fell asleep. Emile was disappointed. Watching the planes that passed over Parthenia and Proxmire Manor, he had assumed that the people who traveled in them were of a high order. In a little while they were off the ground.

It was charming. At the distance of a few hundred feet, all the confused and mistaken works of man seemed orderly. He smiled down broadly at the earth and its population. The sensation he had looked forward to, of being airborne, was not what he had anticipated, and it seemed to him that the engines of the plane were struggling to resist gravity and hold them in their place among the thin clouds. The sea they were crossing was dark and colorless, and as they lost sight of land he felt in himself a corresponding sense of loss, as if at this point some sustaining bond with his green past had been cut. The island, when he saw it below them on the sea, with a cuff of foam on its northeast edge, looked so small and flat that he wondered why anyone should want to go there. When he left the plane she was waiting for him by the steps and they walked through the airport and got a cab. She told the driver, "First I want to go into the village and get some groceries, and then I want to go to Madamquid."

"What do you want to go to Madamquid for?" the driver asked. "There's nobody out there now."

"I have a cottage out there," she said.

They drove across a bleak landscape but one so closely associated with her youth and her happiness that the bleakness escaped her. In the village, they stopped at the grocery store where she had always traded, and she asked Emile to wait outside. When she had bought the groceries, a boy wearing the white apron and bent in exactly the same attitude as Emile was when she first saw him carried them out to the taxi. She gave him a tip and looked up and down the street for Emile. He was standing in front of the drugstore with some other young men his age.

Her courage left her then. The society of the bored and the disappointed, from which she had hoped to escape, seemed battlemented, implacable and splendid—a creation useful to concert halls, hospitals, bridges and courthouses, and one that she was not fit to enter. She had wanted to bring into her life the freshness of a journey and had achieved nothing but a galling sense of moral shabbiness. "You want me to get your boyfriend?" the cab driver asked.

"He's not my boyfriend," Melissa said. "He's just come out to help me move some things."

Emile saw her then, and crossed the street, and they started for Madamquid. She felt so desperate that she took his hand, not expecting him to support her, but he turned to her with wonderful largess, a smile so strong and tender that she felt the blood pour back into her heart. They were heading out to the point where there was nothing to see but the cream-colored dunes, with their scalp locks of knife grass, and the dark autumn ocean. He was perplexed by this. One of the several divisions in his world was that group of people who went away for the summer—who closed their houses in June and bought no more groceries until September—and never having enjoyed any such migratory privileges himself, he had imagined the places where they went as having golden sands and purple seas, the houses palatial and pink-walled, with patios and swimming pools, like the houses he saw in the movies. There was nothing like that here, and he couldn't believe that even in the long, hot days of summer this place would look less of a wilderness. Were there fleets of sailboats, deck chairs and beach umbrellas? There was no trace of summery furniture now. She pointed out the house to him and he saw a big, shingled building on a bluff. He could see that it was big—it was big all right—but if you were going to build a summer house why not build something neat and compact, something that would be nice to look at? But maybe he was wrong, maybe there was something to be learned here; she seemed so pleased at the sight of the old place that he was willing to suspend judgment. She paid off the cab driver and tried to open the front door, but the lock had rusted in the salt air and he had to help. He finally got the door open, and she went in and he carried in the bags and then, of course, the groceries.

She knew well enough that the place was homely—it was meant to be—but the lemony smell of the matchboard walls seemed to her like the fragrance of the lives that had been spent there in the sunny months. Her sister's old violin music, her brother's German textbooks, the water color of a thistle her aunt had painted seemed like the essence of their lives. And while she had quarreled with her brother and her sister and they no longer communicated with each other, all her memories now were kind and gentle. "I've always been happy here," she said. "I've always been terribly happy here. That's why I wanted to come back. It's cold now, of course, but we can light some fires." She noticed then, on the wall at her left, the pencil markings where each Fourth of July her uncle had stood them up against the matchboard and recorded their growth. Afraid that he might see this incriminating evidence of her age, she said, "Let's put the groceries in the icebox."

"That's a funny word, icebox," he said. "I never heard it before. It's a funny thing to call a frigidaire. But you speak differently, you know—people like you. You say lots of different things. Now, you say divine—you say lots of things are divine—but, you know, my mother, she wouldn't ever use that word, excepting when she was speaking of God."

Frightened by the chart in the hallway, she wondered if there was anything else incriminating in the house, and remembered the gallery of family photographs in the upstairs hall. Here were pictures of her in school uniforms, in catboats, and many pictures of her playing on the beach with her son. While he put the groceries away, she went upstairs and hid the pictures in a closet. Then they walked down the bluff to the beach.

It was surprisingly warm for that time of year. The wind was southerly; in the night it would probably change around to the southwest, bringing rain. All along the beach, the waves from Portugal rolled in. There was the noise of a detonation, the roar of furling water, and then the glistening discharge fanned out on the sand, faded and sank. Ahead of her, at the high-water mark, she saw a sealed bottle with a note inside and ran to pick it up. What did she expect? The secret of the Spada treasure, or a proposal of marriage from a French sailor? She handed Emile the bottle and he broke it open on a stone. The note was written in pencil. "To whomever in the whole wide world may read this I am a 18 yr old college boy, sitting on the beach at Madamquid on Sept. 8. . . ." His sense of the act of setting his name and address adrift on the tide was rhapsodic, but the bottle must have returned to where he stood a little while after he had walked away. Emile asked if he could go swimming, and then bent down to unlace his new shoes. One of the laces knotted and his face got red. She dropped to her knees and undid it herself. He got out of his clothes hurriedly in order to display his youth and his brawn, but he asked her earnestly if she minded if he took off his underpants. He stood with his back to her while he did this, and then walked off into the sea. It was colder than he had expected. His shoulders and his buttocks tightened and his head shook. Naked and shivering, he seemed pitiful, vain and fair—a common young man trying to find some pleasure and adventure in his life. He dove into a wave and then came lunging back to where she stood. His teeth were chattering. She threw her coat over him and they went back to the house.

She had been right about the wind. After midnight or later, it came out of the southwest, spouting rain, and as she had done ever since she was a child, she got out of bed and crossed the room to close the windows. He woke and heard the sound of her bare feet on the wooden floor. He couldn't see her in the dark, but as she came back toward the bed her step sounded heavy and old.

It rained in the morning. They walked on the beach, and Melissa cooked a chicken. Looking for a bottle of wine, she found a long-necked green bottle of Moselle, like the bottle she had set out in her dream of the picnic and the ruined castle. Emile ate most of the chicken. At four they took a cab to the airport, and flew back to New York. In the train out to Proxmire Manor he sat several seats ahead of her, reading the paper.

Moses met her at the station and was pleased to have her back. The baby was awake; and Melissa sat in a chair in their bedroom singing, "Sleep, my little one, sleep. Thy father guards the sheep. . . ." She sang until both the baby and Moses were asleep.

14

In the meantime things at the Wapshots' in Talifer were very gloomy. There were no checks from Boston and no explanation and Betsey was complaining. One Sunday afternoon after Coverly had cooked some lunch and washed the dishes Betsey returned to her television set. Their little son had been crying since before lunch. Coverly asked the boy why he cried but he only went on crying. Would he like to take a walk, would he like a lollipop, could Coverly build him a house of blocks? "Oh, leave him alone," Betsey said and turned up the volume. "He can watch TV with me." The boy, still sobbing, went to his mother and Coverly put on a jacket and went out. He took a bus to the computer center and walked across the fields to the farmland. It was late in the season, purple asters bloomed along the path and the air was so heavy with pollen that it gave him a not unpleasant irritation in his nostrils; the whole world smelled like some worn and brilliant carpet. The maples and beeches had turned and the moving lights of that afternoon among the trees made the path ahead of him seem like a chain of corridors and chambers, yellow and gold consistories and vaticans, but in spite of this show of light he seemed still to hear the music from the television, to see the lines at Betsey's mouth and to hear the crying of his little son. He had failed. He had failed at everything. Poor Coverly will never amount to anything. He had heard it said often enough by his aunts from behind the parlor door. He will marry a bony woman and beget a morbid child. He will never succeed at anything. He will never pay his debts. He stooped to tighten a shoelace and at that exact moment a hunting arrow whistled over his head and sank into the trunk of a tree on his right.

"Hey," Coverly shouted, "hey. You damned near killed me." There was no reply. The archer was concealed by a screen of yellow leaves and why should he confess to his nearly murderous mistake? "Where are you," Coverly shouted, "where the hell are you?" He ran into the brush beside the path and in the distance saw an archer, all dressed in red, climbing a stone wall. He looked exactly like the devil. "You, you," Coverly called after him but the distance was too great for him to catch the brute. There was no reply, no echo. He startled a pair of crows who flew off toward the gantries. That the arrow would have killed him had he not stopped to tighten his shoelace exploded in his consciousness, accelerated the beating of his heart and made his tongue swell. But he was alive, he had missed death at this chance turning as he had missed it at a thousand others and suddenly the color, fragrance and shape of the day seemed to stir themselves and surround him with great force and clarity.

He saw nothing unearthly, heard no voices, came at the experience through a single fact—the deathly arrow—and yet it seemed the most volcanic, the most like a turning point, in his life. He felt a sense of himself, his uniqueness, a raptness that he had never felt before. The syllables of his name, the coloring of his hair and eyes, the power in his thighs seemed intensified into something like ecstasy. The voices of his detractors behind the parlor door—and he had listened to them earnestly all the years of his life—now seemed transparently covetous and harmful, the voices of people loving enough but whose happiness would best be served if he did not make any discoveries of himself. His place in the autumn afternoon and the world seemed indisputable, and with such a feeling of resilience, how could anything harm him? The sense was not that he was inviolate but headstrong and that had the arrow struck him he would have fallen with the brilliance of that day in his eyes. He was

not the victim of an emotional and a genetic tragedy; he had
the supreme privileges of a changeling and he would make something illustrious of his life. He examined the arrow and tried
to pull it out of the tree but the shaft broke. The feathers were
crimson and he thought that if he gave the broken arrow to
his son the boy might stop crying, and when the boy saw the
crimson feathers he did.

Coverly's resolve to do something illustrious settled on a plan
to diagnose the vocabulary of John Keats, a project that in turn
depended upon a friend named Griza. Most of the employees
lunched in the subterranean cafeteria but Coverly usually took
the elevator up and ate a sandwich in the sunlight. This choice
was odd enough to serve as the basis for a friendship. One of
the technicians in the computer room also ate a sandwich in
the sun, and this and the fact that they both came from Massachusetts made them fast friends. In the spring they threw a baseball;
in the autumn they spiraled a football back and forth with a
conspicuous sense of simpler things than the gantry line on the
horizon. Griza was the son of a Polish immigrant but he had
been raised in Lowell and his wife was the granddaughter of a
Yankee farmer. He was one of the technicians who serviced the
big computer and might have been recognized as one. There
were no mandates for dress in the computation center and no
established hierarchies but over the months the outlines of a
society and a list of sumptuary laws had begun to emerge, expressing, it seemed, an inner love of caste. The physicists wore
cashmere pullovers. The senior programmers wore tweeds and
colored shirts. Coverly's rank wore business suits and the technicians seemed to have settled on a uniform that included white
shirts and dark ties. They were separated from the rest of the
center by the privilege of manipulating the console and by the
greater privilege of technical knowledge and limited responsibility. If a program failed repeatedly, they could be sure it was
not their fault, and this gave them all the briskness and levity
that you sometimes see in the deck hands on a ferry boat. Griza
had never been to sea but he walked as if he walked on a moving

deck and looked somehow as if he slept in a bunk, kept watches and did his own laundry. He was a slight man with less than a stomach—that whole area seemed limber and concave; he used a fixative on his hair and combed it in a careful cross-hatch at the nape of his neck, a style that had been popular with street boys ten years earlier. Thus he seemed to have one foot in the immediate past. Coverly expected him, sooner or later, to confess to some eccentric ambition. Was he building a raft in his cellar for a trip down the Mississippi? Was he perfecting a machine for compressing empty beer cans? A simplified contraceptive? A chemical solvent for autumn leaves? A project like this seemed necessary to settle the lines of his character, but Coverly was mistaken. Griza hoped to work at the site until the retirement age, when he planned to invest his savings in a parking lot in Florida or California.

From his position at the computer Griza seemed to know a great deal about the politics at the site. He did not seem to have the disposition of a gossip and yet Coverly came away from their lunch hours each day with a wealth of information. The receptionist at the security center was pregnant. Cameron, the director of the site, wouldn't last six weeks. The top brass were bitterly divided in their opinions. They quarreled over whether or not coherent radio signals had been received from Tau Ceti and Epsilon Eridani, they disputed the existence of other civilizations in the solar system, they challenged the intelligence of dolphins. Griza passed along his news indifferently but there was always plenty of it. Coverly cultivated Griza with the hope that Griza might help him. He wanted Griza to put the vocabulary of Keats through the computer. Griza seemed undecided but he did invite Coverly to come home with him for supper one night.

When they finished work they took a bus to the end of the line and began to walk. It was a part of the site that Coverly had never seen. "We're in the emergency housing section," Griza explained. It was a trailer camp although most of the trailers stood on cement block foundations. Some of them were massive and had two levels. There were street lights, gardens, picket fences and inevitably a pair of painted wagon wheels, a talisman of the rural and mythical past. Coverly wondered if they had come from the farm near the computation center. Griza stopped at the door of one of the more modest trailers, opened the door and let Coverly in.

There was one long and pleasant room that seemed to serve a number of purposes. Griza's mother was standing at the stove. His wife was putting a fresh diaper on their daughter. Old Mrs. Griza was a heavy, gray-haired woman who wore a Christmas tree ornament on her dress. Christmas was far away and this ornament had the appeal of those farmhouses you pass, coming down from the ski trails in the north where the colored Christmas lights burn way past Epiphany and are sometimes not dismantled until the snow melts, as if Christmas had been unself-consciously enlarged to embrace the winter. Her face was broad and kindly. Young Mrs. Griza wore a torn man's shirt and a pair of tartan slacks that she had outgrown. Her face was large, her long hair pretty and disheveled, her eyes were beautiful when they were open wide, which they seldom were that evening. The cast of her eyes and her mouth was downward, suggesting sullenness, and it was this sullenness, so swiftly contradicted by the light and authority of her smile, that made her face compelling. Gentling and dressing the baby she seemed nearly imperious. Griza opened two cans of beer and he and Coverly sat down at the end of the room farthest from the stove.

"We're a little crowded in here now," the old lady said. "Oh, I wish you could have seen the house we had in Lowell! Twelve rooms. Oh, it was a lovely house; but we had rats. Oh, those rats. Once I went down cellar to get a stick of wood for the stove and this big man rat jumped at me, jumped right at me! Well, he missed me, thank God, went right over my shoulder but ever after that I was afraid of them. I mean when I saw how fearless they was. We used to have a nice centerpiece in the dining room. Fruit, you know, or wax flowers, but I come down one morning and there was this nice centerpiece all chewed up. Rats. It broke my heart. I mean it made me feel I didn't have anything I could call my own. Mice too. We had mice. They used to get into the pantry. One year I made a big batch of jelly and the mice chewed right through the wax tops and spoiled the jelly. But the mice was nothing compared to the termites. I always noticed the living-room floor was kind of springy and one morning when I was pushing the vacuum cleaner a whole section of the floor give way and sagged into the cellar. Termites. Termites and carpenter ants. It was a combination. The termites ate the underpinnings of the house and the carpenter ants ate the porch. But the worst was bedbugs. When my cousin Harry died he left me this big bed. I didn't think anything about it. I felt funny in the night, you know, but I'd never seen a bedbug in my life and I couldn't imagine what it was. Well, one night I turned on the light good and quick and there they were. There they were! Well, by this time they'd spread all over the house. Bedbugs everywhere. We had to have everything sprayed and, oh, my, the smell was dreadful. Fleas too. We had fleas. We had this old dog named Spotty. Well, he had fleas and the fleas got off him into the rugs and it was a damp house, the fleas bred in the rugs and you know there was one rug there when you stepped onto it there would be a cloud of fleas, thick as smoke, fleas all over you. Well, supper's ready."

They ate frozen meat, frozen fried potatoes and frozen peas. Blindfolded one could not have identified the peas, and the only flavor the potatoes had was the flavor of soap. It was the monotonous fare of the besieged, it would be served everywhere on the site that night, but where were the walls, the battering rams, where was the enemy that could be accounted for this tasteless porridge? Coverly was happy there and they talked about New England during the meal. While the women washed the dishes Coverly and Griza spoke about running the Keats vocabulary through the computer. Griza's invitation to dinner seemed to have been a gesture of trust or assent and he agreed to run the vocabulary through the hardware if Coverly would make the preparations. They drank a glass of whisky and ginger ale and Coverly went home.

On the next night Coverly arranged his life along these lines. He left the computation center at five, cooked supper, bathed and put his son to bed. Then he returned to the computation center with his soft leather copy of Keats and began to translate this, on an electrical typewriter, into binary digits. "I stood tip-toe upon a little hill," he began, "the air was cooling, and so very still. . . ." It took him three weeks to get through it all including *King Stephen.* It was half-past eleven one night when he typed: "To feel forever its soft fall and swell,/Awake for ever in a sweet unrest,/Still, still to hear her tender-taken breath,/ And so live ever—or else swoon to death."

15

Griza said that if everything went on schedule he would run the tape through late on a Saturday afternoon. He telephoned Coverly on Friday night and told him to come in at four. The tape was stored in Coverly's office and at four he brought it up to the room where the console stood. He was very excited. He and Griza seemed to be alone in the center. Somewhere an unanswered telephone was ringing. His instructions, converted into binary digits, asked the machine to count the words in the poetry, count the vocabulary and then list those words most frequently used in the order of their usage. Griza put the instructions and the tape into a pair of towers and pulled some switches on the console. He was in that environment where he felt most like himself and swaggered around like a deck hand. Coverly was sweating with excitement. To make some conversation he asked Griza about his mother and his wife but Griza, ennobled by the presence of the console, did not reply. The typewriter began loudly to clatter and Coverly turned. When the machine stopped Griza tore the paper off its rack and passed it to Coverly. The number of words in the poetry came to fifteen thousand three hundred and fifty-seven. The vocabulary was eight thousand five hundred and three and the words in the order of their frequency were: "Silence blendeth grief's awakened fall/The golden realms of death take all/Love's bitterness exceeds its grace/That bestial scar on the angelic face/Marks heaven with gall."

"My God," Coverly said. "It rhymes. It's poetry."

Griza was going around turning off the lights. He didn't reply.

"But it's poetry, Griza," Coverly said. "Isn't that wonderful? I mean there's poetry within the poetry."

Griza's indifference was implacable. "Yuh, yuh," he said. "We better get out of here. I don't want to get caught."

"But you see, don't you," Coverly said, "that within the poetry of Keats there is some other poetry." It was possible to imagine that some numerical harmony underlay the composition of the universe, but that this harmony embraced poetry was a bewildering possibility and Coverly then felt himself to be a citizen of the world that was emerging; a part of it. Life was filled with newness; there was newness everywhere! "I guess I'd better tell somebody," Coverly said. "It's a discovery, you know."

"Keep cool," Griza said. "You tell somebody, they'll know I was using the console on off hours and I'll get my arse reamed." He had turned off all the lights and they moved into the corridor. Then at the end of the corridor a door opened and Dr. Lemuel Cameron, director of the site, came toward them.

Cameron was a short man. He walked with a stoop. His ruthlessness and his brilliance were legendary and Griza and Coverly were frightened. Cameron's hair was a lusterless black, cut so long that a curl hung over his forehead. His skin was dark and sallow with a fine flush of red at the cheek. His eyes were mournful but it was their brows, their awnings, their hairy settings, that made his appearance seem distinguished and formidable. His brows were an inch thick, brindled with gray and tufted like the pelt of a beast. They looked like structural beams, raised into a position that would support the weight of his knowledge and his authority. We know that heavy eyebrows support nothing, not even thin air, nor are they rooted in the intellect or the heart, but it was his brows that intimidated the two men.

"What's your name?" he asked. The question was directed at Coverly.

"Wapshot," he said.

If Cameron had been a recipient of Lorenzo's bounty, he showed no signs of it.

"What are you doing here?" he asked.

"We've just made a word-count of the vocabulary of John Keats," Coverly said in his most earnest manner.

"Ah, yes," Cameron said. "I'm interested in poetry myself although it's not commonly known." Then, raising his face and giving them a smile that was either gassy or insincere, he recited with practiced expression:

> "How many worlds around their suns
>   Have woven night and day,
>   For countless thinking things like men,
>   Now deep in stone or clay!
>   Their story caught in light now comes
>   To us, unskilled to know
>   The comedy, the tragedy, the glint of friend or foe.
>   In that faint and cryptic message
>   From afar and long ago."

Coverly said nothing and Cameron looked at him narrowly.

"I've seen you before?" he asked.

"Yes, sir."

"Where?"

"On the mountain."

"Come to my office on Monday," he said. "What time is it?"

"Quarter to seven," Coverly said.

"Have I eaten?" he asked.

"I don't know, sir," said Coverly.

"I wonder," he said, "I wonder." He went up on the elevator alone.

16

Coverly reported to Cameron's office on Monday morning. He clearly recalled his first encounter with the old genius. This had been in the mountains, three hundred miles north of Talifer, where Coverly had gone skiing one weekend with some other men from the office. They reached the place late in the afternoon and would have time for only one run before dark. They were waiting for the chair lift when they were asked to step aside. It was Cameron.

He was with two generals and a colonel. They were all much bigger and younger than he. There was an appreciable stir at his arrival but he was, after all, a legendary skier. His contribution to the theory of thermal heat had been worked out from his observation of the molecular action on the base of his skis. He wore fine ski clothes and had a scarlet headband above his famous eyebrows. His eyes were brilliant that afternoon and he moved toward the lift with the preciseness and grace (Coverly thought) of someone who enjoys unchallenged authority. He went up the mountain, followed by his retinue and then by Coverly and his friends. There was a hut or refuge at the summit where they stopped to smoke. There was no fire in the refuge. It was very cold. When Coverly had adjusted his bindings he found that he and Cameron were alone. The others had gone down. The presence of Cameron made Coverly uneasy. Without speaking, without making a sound, he seemed to project around him something as palpable as an electromagnetic field. It was late, it would be dark very soon, but all the mountain peaks, all of them buried in snow, still stood in the canted light of day like the gulfs and trenches of an ancient sea bed. What moved Coverly in the scene was its vitality. Here was a display of the inestimable energies of the planet; here in the last light was a sense of its immense history. Coverly knew enough not to speak of this to the doctor. It was Cameron who spoke. His voice was harsh and youthful. "Isn't it remarkable," he said, "to think that only two years ago it was generally thought that the heterosphere was divided into two regions."

"Yes," Coverly said.

"First of course we have the homosphere," the doctor explained. He spoke with the forced courtesy of some professors. "Within the homosphere the primary components of air are uniformly mixed in their standard proportions by weight of 76 percent nitrogen, 23 percent oxygen and one percent argon, apart from water vapor." Coverly turned to see him. His face was drawn by the intense cold. His breath smoked. His habit of explanation seemed impervious to the majesty of their circumstances. Coverly felt that he barely saw the light and the mountains. "We have within the homosphere," he went on, "the troposphere, the stratosphere and the mesosphere with, beyond the mesopause, oxygen and nitric acid, ionized by Lyman Beta components and above this oxygen and some nitric oxide, ionized by short ultraviolet ray. The electronic density above the mesopause is 100,000 a cubic centimeter. Above this it rises to 200,000 and then to a million. Then the gross density of atoms becomes so low that the electron density diminishes. . . ."

"I think we'd better go down," Coverly said. "It's getting dark. Would you like to go first?"

Cameron refused and called good luck to Coverly as Coverly poled off. He made the first turn and the second but the third turn was already dark and he took a spill. He was not hurt but, getting to his feet, he happened to look overhead and saw Dr. Cameron descending sedately in the chair lift.

Coverly met his friends below the chair-lift station and went on to an inn where they had a drink in the bar. Cameron and his retinue came in a few minutes later and took a table in a corner. It was no trouble to hear what Cameron was saying. It seemed that he could not control the penetrativeness of his voice. He was talking about running the trail and talking about it in detail; the hairpin turns, the long stretch of washboard, the icy schusses and the drifted snow. Here was a man responsible in a sense for the security of the nation, who could not be counted upon to tell the truth about his skiing. He was notorious for his insistence upon demonstrable truths and yet in this matter was a consummate liar. Coverly was fascinated. Had he brought another and a finer sense of truth to the face of the mountain? Had he judged from the chair lift that the trail was too steep and swift for his strength? Had he guessed that if he admitted to judicious timidity he might have impaired the respectfulness of his team? Had his disregard for the common truth involved some larger sense of truth? Coverly didn't know whether or not he had been seen from the chair lift.

A secretary led Coverly into Cameron's office that morning. "Your interest in poetry," the old man began at once, "is my principal reason for asking you here, for what could be more poetic than those hundred thousand million suns that make up the glittering jewelry of our galaxy? This vastness of power is utterly beyond our comprehension. It seems certain that we are receiving light from more than a hundred billion billion suns. It is conservatively estimated that one star in a thousand carries a planet hospitable to some form of life. Even if this estimate should prove a million times too big there would still be a hundred billion such planets in the known universe. Would you like to work for me?" the doctor asked.

"I don't think you understand, Dr. Cameron," Coverly said. "You see, my only training is in taping and preprogramming. When I was transferred from Remsen the machine made a slip-up and I ended in public relations; but I don't think you understand that—"

"Don't you tell me what I understand and what I don't understand," Cameron shouted. "If what you're trying to tell me is that your ignorance is limpid and abysmal, you're trying to tell me something I already know. You're a blockhead. I know it. That's why I want you. Blockheads are difficult to find these days. On your way out tell Miss Knowland to have you transferred to my staff. Write me a twenty-minute commencement address along the lines of what I've just said and plan to leave with me for Atlantic City next week. What time is it?"

"Quarter to ten," Coverly said.

"Hear that bird?" the doctor asked.

"Yes," Coverly said.

"What is he saying?" the doctor asked.

"I'm not sure," Coverly said.

"He's calling my name," said Cameron, a little angrily. "Can't you hear it? He's calling my name. Cameron, Cameron, Cameron."

"It does sound like that," said Coverly.

"Do you know the constellation Pernacia?"

"Yes," said Coverly.

"Did you ever notice that it contains my initials?"

"I'd never thought of it that way," Coverly said. "I see now, I see it now."

"How long can you hold your breath?" Cameron asked.

"I don't know," Coverly said.

"Well, try." Coverly took a deep breath and Cameron looked at his wristwatch. He held his breath for a minute and eight seconds. "Not bad," Cameron said. "Now get out of here."

17

We are born between two states of consciousness; we spend our lives between the darkness and the light, and to climb in the mountains of another country, phrase our thoughts in another language or admire the color of another sky draws us deeper into the mystery of our condition. Travel has lost the attributes of privilege and fashion. We are no longer dealing with midnight sailings on three-stacked liners, twelve-day crossings, Vuitton trunks and the glittering lobbies of Grand Hotels. The travelers who board the jet at Orly carry paper bags and sleeping babies, and might be going home from a hard day's work at the mill. We can have supper in Paris and, God willing, breakfast at home, and here is a whole new creation of self-knowledge, new images for love and death and the insubstantiality and the importance of our affairs. Most of us travel to improve on the knowledge we have of ourselves, but none of this was true for Cousin Honora. She went to Europe as a fugitive.

She had developed, over the years, a conviction that St. Botolphs was the fairest creation on the face of the earth. Oh, it was not magnificent, she well knew; it was nothing like the postcards of Karnak and Athens that her Uncle Lorenzo had sent her when she was a child. But she had no taste for magnificence. Where else in the world were there such stands of lilac, such lambent winds and brilliant skies, such fresh fish? She had lived out her life there, and each act was a variation on some other act, each sensation she experienced was linked to a similar sensation, reaching in a chain back through the years of her long life to when she had been a fair and intractable child, unlacing her skates, long after dark, at the edge of Parson's Pond, when all the other skaters had gone home and the barking of Peter Howland's collies sounded menacing and clear as the bitter cold gave to the dark sky the acoustics of a shell. The fragrant smoke from her fire mingled with the smoke from all the fires of her life. Some of the roses she pruned had been planted before she was born. Her dear uncle had lectured her on the ties that bound her world to Renaissance Europe, but she had always disbelieved him. What person who had seen the cataracts in the New Hampshire mountains could care about the waterworks of kings? What person who had smelled the rich brew of the North Atlantic could care about the dirty Bay of Naples? She did not want to leave her home and move on into an element where her sensations would seem rootless, where roses and the smell of smoke would only remind her of the horrible distances that stood between herself and her own garden.

She went alone to New York on a train, slept restlessly in a hotel bedroom, and one morning she boarded a ship for Europe. In her cabin she found that the old judge had sent her an orchid. She detested orchids, and she detested improvidence, and the gaudy flower was both. Her first impulse was to fire it out of the porthole, but the porthole wouldn't open, and on second thought it seemed to her that perhaps a flower was a necessary part of a traveler's costume, a sign of parting, a proof that one was leaving friends behind. There was loud laughter, and talk, and the noise of drinking. Only she, it seemed, was alone.

Removed from the scrutiny of the world, she could seem a little foolish—she spent some time trying to find a place to hide the canvas money belt in which she kept her cash and documents. Under the sofa? Behind the picture? In the empty flower vase or the medicine cabinet? A corner of the carpet was loose and she hid her money belt there. Then she stepped out into the corridor. She wore black clothes and a tricorne hat, and looked a little as George Washington might have looked had he lived to be so old.

The festivities in the crowded staterooms had moved out into the corridor, where men and women stood drinking and talking. She couldn't deny that it would have been pleasanter if a few friends had come down to put a social blessing on her departure. Without the orchid on her shoulder, how could these strangers guess that in her own home she was a celebrated woman, known to everyone and famous for her good works? Mightn't they, glancing at her as she passed, mistake her for one of those cussed old women who wander over the face of the earth trying to conceal or palliate that bitter loneliness that is the fitting reward for their contrary and selfish ways? She felt painfully disarmed and seemed to have only the fewest proofs of her identity. What she wanted then was some common room, where she could sit down and watch things.

She found a common room, but it was crowded and all the seats were taken. People were drinking and talking and crying, and in one corner a grown man stood saying goodbye to a little girl. His face was wet with tears. Honora had never seen or dreamed of such mortal turmoil. The go-ashore was being sounded, and while many of the farewells were cheerful and lighthearted, many of them were not. The sight of a man parting from his little daughter—it must be his little daughter, separated from him by some evil turn of events—upset Honora terribly. Suddenly the man got to his knees and took the child in his arms. He concealed his face in her thin shoulder, but his back could be seen shaking with sobs, while the public-address system kept repeating that the hour, the moment, had come. She felt the tears form in her own eyes, but the only way she could think of to cheer the little girl was to give her the orchid, and by now the corridors were too crowded for Honora to make her way back to her stateroom. She stepped over the high brass sill onto a deck.

The gangways were thronged with visitors leaving the ship. The stir was tremendous. Below her she could see a strip of dirty harbor water, and overhead there were gulls. People were calling to one another over this short distance, this still unaccomplished separation, and now all but one of the gangways were up, and the band began to play what seemed to her to be circus music. The loosening of gigantic hemp lines was followed by the stunning thunder of the whistle, so loud it must ruffle the angels in Heaven. Everyone was calling, everyone was waving—everyone but her. Of all the people standing on the deck, only she had no one to part with, only her going was lonely and meaningless. In simple pride, she took a handkerchief out of her pocketbook and began to wave it to the faces that were so swiftly losing their outline and their appeal. "Good-bye, good-bye, my dear, dear friend," she called to no one. "Thank you. . . . Thank you for everything. . . . Good-bye and thank you. . . . Thank you and good-bye."

At seven o'clock she put on her best clothes and went up to dinner. She shared a table with a Mr. and Mrs. Sheffield, from

Rochester, who were going abroad for the second time. They were traveling with orlon wardrobes. During dinner they told Honora about their earlier trip to Europe. They went first to Paris, where they had nice weather—nice drying weather, that is. Each night, they took turns washing their clothes in the bathtub and hanging them out to dry. Going down the Loire they ran into rain and were not able to do any wash for nearly a week, but once they reached the sea the weather was sunny and dry, and they washed everything. They flew to Munich on a sunny day and did their wash in the Regina Palast, but in the middle of the night there was a thunderstorm and all their clothing, hung out on a balcony, got soaked. They had to pack their wardrobes wet for the trip to Innsbruck, but they reached Innsbruck on a clear and starry night and hung everything out to dry again. There was another thunderstorm in Innsbruck, and they had to spend a day in their hotel room, waiting for their clothes to dry. Venice was a wonderful place for laundry. They had very little trouble in Italy, and during their Papal audience Mrs. Sheffield convinced herself that the Pope's vestments were made of orlon. They remembered Geneva for its rainy weather, and London was very disappointing. They had theater tickets, but nothing would dry, and they had to spend two days in their room. Edinburgh was even worse, but in Skye the clouds lifted and the sun shone, and they took a plane home from Prestwick with everything clean and dry. The sum of their experience was to warn Honora against planning to do much wash in Bavaria, Austria, Switzerland and the British Isles.

Toward the end of this account, Honora's face got very red, and suddenly she leaned across the table and said, "Why don't you stay home and do your wash? Why do you travel halfway around the world, making a spectacle of yourself in front of the waiters and chambermaids of Austria and France? I've never owned a stitch of orlon, or whatever you call it, but I expect I'll find laundries and dry cleaners in Europe just as at home, and I'm sure I'd never travel for the pleasure of hanging out a clothesline."

The Sheffields were shocked and embarrassed. Honora's voice carried, and passengers at the nearby tables had turned to stare at her. She tried to extricate herself by calling a waiter. "Check," she called. "Check. Will you please bring me my check?"

"There is no check, madam," the waiter said.

"Oh, yes," she said, "I forgot," and limped out of the room.

She was too angry at the Sheffields to be remorseful, but she was faced again with the fact that her short temper was one of her worst qualities. She wandered around the decks to cool off, admiring the yellowish shroud lights and thinking how like a second set of stars they were. She was standing on the stern deck, watching the wake, when a young man in a pin-striped suit joined her. They had a pleasant conversation about the stars, and then she went to bed and slept soundly.

In the morning, after a hearty breakfast, Honora arranged for a deck chair on the leeward side. She then settled herself with a novel *(Middlemarch)* and prepared to relax and enjoy the healthfulness of the sea air. Nine quiet days would conserve her strength and perhaps even lengthen her life. It was the first time that she had ever planned a rest. Sometimes after lunch on a hot day she would shut her eyes for five minutes but never for longer. In the mountain hotels where she went for a change of air she had always been an early riser, a marathon chair rocker and a tireless bridge player. Up until now there had always been things to do, there had always been demands on her time, but now her old heart was weary and she should rest. She pressed her head against the chair cushion and drew the blanket over her legs. She had seen thousands of travel advertisements in which people her age stretched out in deck chairs, watching the sea. She had always wondered what pleasant reveries passed through their minds. Now she waited for this enviable tranquillity to steal over her. She shut her eyes, but she shut them emphatically; she drummed her fingers on the wooden armrest and wriggled her feet. She counseled herself to wait, to wait, to wait for repose to overtake her. She waited perhaps ten minutes before she sat up impatiently and angrily. She had never learned to sit still, and, as with so much else in life, it seemed too late now for her to learn.

Her sense of life was a sense of motion and embroilments, and even if to move gave her a keen pain in the heart, she had no choice but to move. To be stretched out in a deck chair that early in the day made her feel idle, immoral, worthless and—what was most painful of all—like a ghost, neither living nor dead; like some bitterly unwilling bystander. To tramp around the decks might tire her, but to be stretched out under a blanket like a corpse was a hundred times worse. Life seemed like a chain of brilliant reflections on water, unrelated perhaps to the motion of the water itself but completely absorbing in their color and shine. Might she kill herself with her love of things? Were the forces of life and death identical? And would the thrill of rising on a fine day be the violence that ruptured the vessels of her heart? The need to move, to talk, to make friends and enemies, to involve herself was irresistible, and she struggled to get to her feet, but her lameness, her heaviness, the age of her body and the shape of the deck chair made this impossible. She was stuck. She grasped the armrests and struggled to raise herself, but she fell back helplessly. Again she struggled to get up. She fell back again. There was a sudden sharp pain in her heart, and her face was flushed. Then she thought that she would die in another few minutes—die on her first day at sea, be sewn into an American flag and dropped overboard, her soul descending into Hell.

But why should she go to Hell? She knew well enough. It was because she had been all her life a food thief. As a child, she had waited and watched until the kitchen was empty and had then opened the massive icebox doors, grabbed a drumstick off the cold chicken and dipped her fingers into the hard sauce. Left alone in the house, she had climbed to the top pantry shelf on an arrangement of chairs and stools and eaten all the lump sugar in the silver bowl. She had stolen candy from the highboy, where it was saved for Sunday. She had, when the cook's back was turned, ripped a piece of skin off the Thanksgiving turkey before grace was said. She had stolen cold roast potatoes, dough-nuts set out to cool, beef bones, lobster claws and wedges of pie. Her vice had not been cured by her maturity, and when, as a young woman, she invited the altar guild to tea, she ate half the sandwiches before they arrived. Even as an old woman leaning on a stick, she had gone down to the pantry in the middle of the night and stuffed herself with cheese and apples. Now the time had come to answer for her gluttony. She turned desper-ately to the man in the deck chair on her left. "I beg your par-don," she said, "but I wonder if . . ." He seemed to be asleep. The deck chair on her right was empty. She shut her eyes and called on the angels. A second later, the moment after her prayers had gone up, a young officer stopped to wish her good morning and to extend an invitation from the captain to join him on the bridge. He pulled her out of her chair.

On the bridge she shot the sun with a hand sextant and remi-nisced. "When I was nine years old, my Uncle Lorenzo bought me a twelve-foot sloop," she said, "and for the next three years there wasn't a fisherman at Travertine I couldn't outsail." The captain asked her for cocktails. At lunch the steward seated her with a twelve-year-old Italian boy who spoke no English. They got along by smiling at one another and making signs. In the afternoon she played cards until it was time to go down and get ready for the captain's cocktail party. She went to her state-room and took out of her suitcase a rusty curling iron that had served her faithfully for thirty-five years or more. She plugged this into an outlet in the bathroom. All the lights in the cabin went off, and she yanked out the plug.

A moment later, there were sounds of running in the corridors, and people called confusedly to one another in Italian and En-glish. She hid her curling iron in the bottom of her suitcase and drank a glass of port. She was an honest woman, but she was too stunned, at the moment, to confess to the captain that she had blown a fuse.

She seemed to have done much more. Opening the door to her stateroom, she found the corridor dark. A steward ran by, carrying a lamp. She closed the door again and looked out of her porthole. Slowly, slowly, the ship was losing way. The high white crest at the bow slacked off.

In the corridors and on the decks there were more calls and sounds of running. Honora sat miserably on the edge of her berth, having, through her own clumsiness, her own stupidity, halted this great ship in its passage across the sea. What would they do next? Take to the boats and row to some deserted island, rationing their biscuits and water? It was all her fault. The children would suffer. She would give them her water ration and share her biscuits, but she did not think she had the strength to confess. They might put her in the brig or drop her overboard.

The sea was calm. The ship drifted with the swell, and had begun to roll a little. The voices of men, women and children echoed off the corridors and over the water. "It's the generators," she heard someone say. "Both generators have blown." She began to cry.

She dried her tears and stood by the porthole, watching the sunset. She could hear the orchestra playing in the ballroom, and she wondered if people were dancing in the dark. Way below her, in the crew's quarters, someone had put out a fishing line. They must be fishing for cod. She wished she had a line herself, but she didn't dare ask for one, because they might then discover that she had stopped the ship.

A few minutes before dark, all the lights went on, there was a cheer from the deck, and the ship took up its course. Honora watched the white crest at the bow form and rise as they headed once more for Europe. She didn't dare go up to the dining room, and made a supper of Saltines and port wine. Later she took a turn around the decks, and the young man in the pin-striped suit asked if he could join her. She was happy to have his company and the support of his arm. He said that he was traveling to get away from things, and she guessed that he was a successful young businessman who wanted, quite naturally, to see the world before he settled down with a wife and children. She wished, fleetingly, that she had a daughter he could marry.

Then she could find him a nice position in St. Botolphs, and they could live in one of the new houses in the east end of the village and come and visit her, with their children, on Sundays. When she tired, she was quite lame. He helped her down to her cabin and said good night. He had excellent manners.

She looked for him in the dining room the next day, and she wondered if he was traveling in some other class, or belonged to the fast set that didn't come down for lunch but instead ate sandwiches in the bar. He joined her on deck at dusk that night, when she was waiting for the dinner chimes to ring.

"I don't see you in the dining room," she said.

"I spend most of my time in my cabin," he said.

"But you shouldn't be so unsociable," she said. "You ought to make friends—an attractive young man like you."

"I don't think you'd like me," he said, "if you knew the truth."

"Well, I don't know what you're talking about," she said. "If you're a member of the working class or something like that, it wouldn't make any difference to me. I went up to Jaffrey last summer for a rest, you know, and I met this very nice lady and befriended her, and she said the same thing to me. 'I don't think you'd like me,' she said, 'if you knew who I was.' So then I asked her who she was, and she said she was a cook. Well, she was a very nice woman, and I continued to play cards with her, and it didn't make any difference to me that she was a cook. I'm not stuck-up. Mr. Haworth, the ashman, is one of my best friends, and often comes into the house for a cup of tea."

"I'm a stowaway," the young man said.

She took a deep breath of sea air. The news was a blow. Oh, why should life appear to be a series of mysteries? She had imagined him to be prosperous and successful, and he was merely a lawless outcast. "Where do you sleep?" she asked. "Where do you eat?"

"I sleep in the heads," he said. "I haven't eaten for two days."

"But you must eat."

"I know," he said wistfully. "I know. You see, what I thought

I might do is to confide in someone—a passenger—and then, if they were friendly, they could order dinner in their stateroom and I could share it."

For a second she was wary. He seemed importunate. He had moved too swiftly. Then his stomach gave a loud rumble, and the thought of the hunger pangs he must be suffering annihilated her suspicions. "What's your name?" she asked.

"Gus."

"Well, I'm in Cabin 12 on B Deck," she said. "You come down there in a few minutes, and I'll see that you get some supper."

When she got to her cabin, she rang for the waiter and ordered a six-course meal. The young man arrived and hid in the bathroom. When the table was set with covered dishes, he came out of hiding, and it did her heart good to see him eat.

When he had finished his dinner, he took out a package of cigarettes and offered it to her as if she was not an old lady but a dear friend and companion. She wondered if, under the beneficial influence of the sea air, her appearance had grown more youthful. She accepted a cigarette and blew out four matches trying to get it lighted. When it was finally ignited, the smoke cut her throat like a rusty razor. She had a paroxysm of coughing, and scattered embers down the front of her dress. He did not seem to notice this loss of dignity—he was telling her the story of his life—and she held the cigarette elegantly between her fingers until the fire died. Smoking a cigarette definitely made her feel younger. He was married, he told her. He had two little children—Heidi and Peter—but his wife ran away with a sailor and took the children to Canada. He didn't know where they were. He worked as a file clerk for an insurance office and led a life that was so lonely and empty that he had boarded the ship one day during his lunch hour and stayed aboard when she sailed. What was there to lose? He would at least see a little of the world, even if he was sent home in the brig. "I miss the kiddies," he said. "That's the main thing. You know what I did last Christmas? I bought one of those little trees you get in the five-and-ten, and I decorated it, in this room where I live, and I bought presents for the kiddies, and then on Christmas Day I just pretended that they came to see me. Of course, it was all make-believe, but I opened the presents and everything, just as if they were there."

After dinner Honora taught him to play backgammon. He picked up the game very quickly, she thought, and was a remarkably intelligent young man. It seemed a great shame to her that he should waste his youth and his intelligence in loneliness, sorrow and boredom. He was not handsome; his face was too changeable, and his grin was a little foolish. But he was really just a boy, she thought, and with experience and kindness his face would change. They played backgammon until eleven, and, to tell the truth, she had not felt so happy, or at least at ease, since she had begun her travels. When they said good night, he lingered at the door, and seemed, with his inward and foolish—or was it sly?—grin, to be implying that she might let him sleep in the spare berth in her cabin. Enough was enough, and she closed the door in his face.

He did not appear the next day, and she wondered where in the great ship he was hidden, hungry and alone. The bouillon and sandwiches that were passed on the promenade deck only reminded her of the cruel inequalities of life, and she did not enjoy her lunch. She spent most of the afternoon in her cabin, in case he should need her help. Just before the dinner chimes rang, there was a soft knock at the door, and he came in. After dinner she got out the backgammon board, but he seemed restless, and she won every game. She pointed out that he needed a haircut, and when he said that he didn't have any money, she gave him five dollars. He said good night at ten, and she invited him to return the next evening for his dinner.

He didn't come. When the dinner chimes rang at seven, she called a waiter and ordered dinner so that it would be ready for him, but he didn't come. She was sure then that he had been caught and thrown into the brig, and she thought of going to the captain, as the young man's advocate, and explaining the loneliness and the emptiness of his life. She decided, however, not to act until morning, and she went to bed. In the morning, as she was admiring the ocean, she saw him on the main deck, laughing and talking with Mrs. Sheffield.

She was indignant. She was jealous, although she tried to rationalize this weakening of her position as a sensible fear that if he confided in Mrs. Sheffield, Mrs. Sheffield would betray him. He saw Honora, clearly enough—he waved to her—but he went on talking gaily with Mrs. Sheffield. Honora was angry. She even seemed to be in pain, stripped as she was of that sense of ease and comfort she had enjoyed while they played backgammon in her cabin, stripped of a sense of her unique usefulness, her indispensability. She went around the bow to the leeward side of the ship, to admire the waves from there. She noticed that, with her feelings unsettled, the massive, agate-colored seas, veined with white, seemed mightier. She heard footsteps on the deck and wondered was it he? Had he come at last, to apologize for talking with Mrs. Sheffield and to thank her for her generosity? She was sure of one thing: Mrs. Sheffield wouldn't take a stowaway into her cabin and give him supper. The footsteps passed, and so did some others, but the intenseness of her anticipation did not. Would he never come? Then someone stopped at her back and said, "Good morning, darling."

"Don't call me 'darling,' " she said, turning around.

"But you are 'darling' to me."

"You haven't got your hair cut."

"I lost your money on the horse races."

"Where were you last night?"

"A nice man in the bar treated me to sandwiches and drinks."

"What were you telling Mrs. Sheffield?"

"I wasn't telling her anything. She was telling me about her orlon wardrobe, but she's asked me to have drinks with them before lunch."

"Very well, then, they can give you lunch."

"But they don't know I'm a stowaway, darling. You're the only one who knows. I wouldn't trust anyone else."

"Well, if you want some lunch," she said, "I might be in my cabin at noon."

"You'd better make it half-past one or two. I don't know when I'll get away from the Sheffields," he said, and walked off.

At half-past twelve she went down to her cabin to wait for him—for, like many of the old, she traveled with her clocks fifteen or twenty minutes fast, and was a half-hour early for all her engagements, sitting empty-handed in waiting rooms and lobbies and corridors, feeling quite clearly that her time was running out. He blew in a little after two, and he refused at first to hide in the bathroom. "If you want me to go to the captain and tell him there's a stowaway aboard, I'll do it," she said. "If that's what you want, I'll do it. There's no point in having the news percolate up to him from the kitchens, and it will if the waiter sees you here." In the end, he hid in the bathroom and she ordered lunch. After lunch he stretched out on the sofa and fell asleep. She sat in a chair, watching him, tapping her foot on the carpet and drumming her nails on the arm of her chair. He snored. He muttered in his sleep.

She saw then that he was not young. His face was lined and sallow; there was gray in his hair. She saw that his youthfulness was a ruse, an imposture calculated to appeal to some old fool like herself, although she was doubtless not the only dupe. Asleep, he looked aged, sinful and cunning, and she felt that his story of the two children and the lonely Christmas had been a lie. There was no innocence in him beyond the naïveness with which he would count upon preying on the lonely. He seemed a fraud, a shabby fraud, and yet she could not inform on him; she could not even bring herself to wake him. He slept until four, woke, pierced all of her skepticism with one of his most youthful and engaging grins, said that he was late and went out. The next time she saw him, it was three in the morning and he was taking her money belt out from under the carpet.

He had hit something, made some noise that waked her. She was terrified—not by him but by the possibilities of evil in the world; by the fear that her sense of reality, her saneness, was no more inviolable than the doors and windows that sheltered her. She was too angry to be afraid of him.

She had turned on the light switch nearest to the bed. This lit a single bulb in the ceiling, a feeble and sorry light that made this scene of robbery and treachery in the darkest hour and the vastness of the ocean seem like a nausea fantasy. He turned on her his sliest grin, his look of a long-lost loving son. "I'm sorry I woke you up, darling," he said.

"You put that money back."

"Now, now, darling," he said.

"You put that money back this instant."

"Now, now, darling, don't get excited."

"That's my money," she said, "and you put it back where you found it." She pulled a wrapper over her shoulders and swung her feet onto the floor.

"Now, listen, darling," he said, "stay where you are. I don't want to hurt you."

"Oh, you don't, do you?" she said, and she picked up a brass lamp and struck him full on the skull.

His eyes rolled upward and his smile faded. He weaved to the left and the right and then fell in a heap, striking his head on the arm of a chair. She seized the money belt and then spoke to him. She shook him by the shoulders. She felt his pulse. He seemed to have none. "He's dead," she said to herself. She didn't know his last name, and since she didn't believe what he had told her about himself, she knew nothing about the man she had killed. His name wasn't on the passenger list, he had no legitimacy. Even the part he played in her life had been an imposture. If she shoved his body out the porthole into the sea, who would ever know? But this was the wrong thing to do. The right thing was to get the doctor, whatever the conse- quences, and she went into the bathroom and dressed hastily. Then she stepped into the deserted corridor. The purser's and doctor's offices were locked and dark. She climbed a flight of stairs to the main deck, but the ballroom and the bar and the lounges were all empty. An old man in his pajamas stepped out of the darkness and came toward her. "I can't sleep either, sister," he said. "Gin knits up the raveled sleeve of care. You know how old I am? I'm seven days younger than Herbert Hoover and one hundred and five days older than Winston Churchill. I don't like young people. They make too much noise. I have three grandchildren and I can stand them for ten minutes. Not a second more. My daughter married a prince. Last year I gave them fifteen thousand. This year he must have twenty-five. It's the way he asks me for the money that burns me up. 'It is very painful for me to ask you for twenty-five thousand,' he says. 'It is very painful and humiliating.' My little grandchildren can't speak English. They call me Nonno. . . . Take a load off your feet, sister. Sit down and talk with me and help to pass the time."

"I'm looking for the doctor," Honora said.

"I have an unfortunate habit of quoting Shakespeare," the old man said, "but I will spare you. I know a lot of Milton, too. Also Gray's 'Elegy,' and Arnold's 'The Scholar Gypsy.' How far away those streams and meadows seem! My conscience is uneasy. I've killed a man."

"You did?" Honora asked.

"Yes. I had a fuel-oil business in Albany. That's my home. I did a gross business of over two million a year. Fuel, oil and maintenance. One night a man called and said his burner was making a funny noise. I told him nothing could be done until morning. I could have got him a serviceman, or I could have gone there myself, but I was drinking with friends, and why should I go out on a cold night? Half an hour later, the house burned down, cause undetermined. . . . It was a man, his wife and three little children. Five coffins in all. I often think about them."

Honora remembered then that she had left her cabin door open and that the corpse could be seen by anyone who passed. "Sit down. Sit down, sister," the old man said, but she waved him away and limped back down the stairs. Her cabin door stood open, but the corpse was gone. What had happened? Had someone come and disposed of the body? Were they now searching the ship for her? She listened, but there was no sound of footsteps—nothing but the titanic, respiratory noise of the sea, and somewhere a door banging as the ship heeled a little. She closed and locked her door and poured herself some port. If they were going to come and get her, she wanted to be fully dressed, and anyhow she couldn't sleep.

She stayed in her cabin until noon, when her telephone rang and the purser asked if she would come to his office. He only wanted to know if she wouldn't like to have her bags shipped from Naples to Rome. Having prepared herself for an entirely different set of questions and answers, she seemed very absent-minded. But what had happened? Did she have some accomplice aboard who had pushed the stowaway's body out the porthole? Almost everyone smiled at her, but how much did they know? Had he picked himself up off the floor of her cabin, and was he now nursing his wounds somewhere? The enormousness of the ship and its thousands of doors discouraged her from trying to find him. She looked for him in the bar and the ballroom, and she investigated the broom closet at the end of her corridor. Passing an open cabin door, she thought she heard him laughing, but when she stopped, the laughter stopped, and someone shut the door. She examined the lifeboats—a traditional sanctuary, she knew, for stowaways—but all the lifeboat covers were fast. She would have felt less miserable if she had had some familiar work to do, such as raking and burning leaves, and she even thought of asking the stewardess if she couldn't sweep the corridor, but she perceived the impropriety of this.

She did not see the stowaway again until the day they were to dock in Naples. The sky and the sea were gray. The air was moist and dispiritingly humid. It was one of those timeless days, she thought, so unlike the stunning best of spring and autumn— one of those gloomy days of which the year, after all, is forged. He came swinging down the deck late in the afternoon with a woman on his arm. The woman was not young, and she had a bad complexion, but they were looking into one another's eyes like lovers and laughing. As he passed Honora, he spoke to her. "Excuse me," he said.

This final cheapness infuriated her. She went down to her cabin. Everything was packed—her book and her mending—and she had nothing to distract her. What she then did is hard to explain. She was not an absent-minded or a thoughtless woman, but she had been raised in gaslight and candlelight and had never made her peace with electrical appliances or other kinds of domestic machinery. They seemed to her mysterious and at times capricious, and because she came at them hastily and in total ignorance they often broke, backfired or exploded in her face. She could never imagine that she was to blame, and felt instead that an obscure veil hung between her and the world of machinery. This indifference to engines, along with her impetuousness and her anger at the stowaway, may have accounted for what she then did. She looked at herself in the mirror, found her appearance lacking, took her old curling iron out of the bottom of the suitcase, and plugged it in again.

They drifted into the Bay of Naples without a light showing. Powerless, helmless, they floated stern foremost on the ebb tide. Two tugs came out from the port to tow them in, and a portable generator on the dock was connected to the ship's lines so that there was light enough to disembark. Honora was one of the first to go ashore. The noise of Neapolitan voices sounded to her like a wilderness, and, stepping onto the Old World, she felt in her bones the thrill of that voyage her forefathers had made how many hundreds of years ago, coming forth upon another continent to found a new nation.

Part Two

18

The cast of characters in the Nuclear Revolution changed so swiftly that Dr. Cameron has long since been forgotten excepting for a few disorders he incited. A crucifix hung on the wall behind his desk. The figure of Christ was silver or leaden and it was the kind of thing tourists pick up in the back streets of Rome and carry to the Vatican for a Papal blessing. It had no value or beauty and its only usefulness was to state that the doctor was a convert, a sinful one perforce, since he was known to believe in neither the divine nor scientific ecology of nature, but the priest who had given him instruction had stressed the mercifulness of Our Lord and the old man believed passionately that there was some blessedness in the nature of things although his transgressions were repeated and spectacular. He believed, and said so publicly, that matrimony was not an adequate means of genetic selection. He had administered, for the Air Force, some experiments in the manipulation of chromosomal structures for the production of what we call courage. He believed in sperm banks and, for the immediate future, a clear command of the chemistry of personality. He loosely embraced his belief in blessedness, his science and his own unquiet nature by thinking of himself as a frontiersman, approaching a future in which he would be obsolete. He was a gourmet and knew the foolishness of stuffing himself with snails, beef filets, sauces and wines but he classed his interest in good food as a mark of obsolescence. He similarly classified as obsolete his own sexual drives—that nagging inquietude in his middle. His wife had been dead for twenty years and he had kept a series of mistresses and housekeepers, but the older and more powerful he grew, the more discretion was demanded of him and he had not been safely able to enjoy a relationship with anyone in the United States.

He was one of those blameless old men who had found that lasciviousness was his best means of clinging to life. In the act of love his heart sent up a percussive beating like a gallows drum in the street, but lewdness was his best sense of forgetfulness, his best way of grappling with the unhappy facts of time. With age his desires had grown more irresistible as his fear of death and corruption mounted. Once, lying in bed with Luciana, his mistress, a fly had come in at the window and buzzed around her white shoulders. The fly had, to his old man's mind, seemed like a singular reminder of corruption and he had got out of bed, bare as a jay bird, and raced and jumped around the room with a rolled-up copy of *La Corriere della Sera* trying, unsuccessfully, to kill the pest but when he got back to bed there was the fly, still buzzing around her breasts.

It was in the arms of his mistress that he felt the chill of death go off his bones; it was in the arms of his mistress that he felt himself invincible. She lived in Rome and he met her there about once a month. There was a legitimate side to these trips—the Vatican wanted a missile—and a side more clandestine than his erotic sport. It was in Rome that he met with those sheiks and maharajas who wanted a rocket of their own. The commands from one part of his body to another would begin with a ticklish sensation that in a day or two, depending upon how hard he drove himself, would become irresistible. Then he would take a jet to Italy and return a few days later in a most relaxed and magnanimous frame of mind. Thus he flew one afternoon from Talifer to New York and spent the night at the Plaza. His need for Luciana mounted hour by hour like some simple impulse of hunger and lying in his hotel bed he granted himself the privilege of putting her together—lips, breasts, arms and legs. Oh, the wind and the rain and to hold in one's arms a willing love! He was suffering, as he would put it, from a common inflammation.

In the morning it was foggy and leaving the hotel he listened for the sound of planes to discover if the airport was closed but it was impossible to hear anything above the clash of traffic. He took a taxi to Idlewild and waited in turn to pick up his ticket. Some mistake had been made and he was booked on a tourist flight. "I would like this changed to first class," he said.

"I'm sorry, sir," the girl said, "but there is no first-class space." She did not look at him and went on filing papers.

"I have made thirty-three flights on this line in the last year," the doctor said, "and I think I am entitled to a little preferential treatment."

"We do not give preferential treatment," the girl said. "It is against the law." She had obviously never seen him on television and was unimpressed by the bulk of his eyebrows.

"Now you listen to me, young lady . . ." His voice sawed, soared, made enemies for him everywhere within earshot. "I am Dr. Lemuel Cameron. I am traveling on government business and if I should report your attitude to your superiors—"

"I am very sorry, sir," she said, "but things are backed up because of the fog. The only available first-class space we have is for the evening flight next Thursday if you wish to wait."

Her imperviousness to his importance, her indifference or overt dislike flustered him and he remembered all the others who had looked at him with skepticism or even antagonism as if his whole brilliant career had been a fatuous self-delusion. It was especially her kind, the girls in uniform with overseas caps, their hair dyed, their skirts tight, who seemed as remote to him as a generation of leaves. Where did they go when the flight was over, the office shut? They seemed to bang down a shutter between himself and them, they seemed made of different ingredients than the men and women of his day, they seemed supremely indifferent to his appearance of wisdom and authority.

"I must explain," he said, speaking softly, "that I have a top priority and that I can demand a seat if necessary."

"Your flight is loading at gate eight," she said. "If you wish to wait until Thursday evening I can get you first-class space."

He went down a long corridor to where a shabby-looking huddle of men and women were waiting to board the plane. They were mostly Italians, mostly working class, waiters and maids going home for a month to see Mamma and show off their ready-made clothes. He liked to stretch his legs in first class, sip his first-class wine and admire the caves of heaven from a first-class port as they traveled swiftly toward Rome but the tourist flight was very different from what he was accustomed to and reminded him of the early days of aviation. When he found his seat he beckoned to the hostess, another impermeable young woman with a brilliant smile, a tight skirt and hair dyed silver and gold. "I've been promised first-class space if there's a cancellation," he said, partly to acquaint her with the facts, partly to make clear to this motley group around him that he was not one of them. "I'm very sorry, sir," she said with a smile that was dazzling in its insincerity, "but there is no first-class space on this flight." Then she kindly ushered into the seats beside him a sickly-looking Italian boy and his mother, who had a baby in her arms. He smiled at them fleetingly and asked if they were going to Rome. "Sí," the woman said wearily, "ma non speaka the English." As soon as they were seated she took a bottle of medicine out of a brown paper bag and offered it to her son. The boy didn't want the medicine. He put his hands over his mouth and turned toward Cameron. *"Si deve, si deve,"* the mother said. *"No, mamma, no, mamma,"* the boy pleaded but she forced him to drink. A little of the medicine spilled onto his clothing and it had a vile and sulphurous smell. The stewardess closed the cabin door and the pilot announced in Italian and then in English that the ceiling was zero and that they had not received their clearance but that it was expected that the fog, the *nebbia,* would lift.

Cameron's legs were cramped and to lift himself out of these unpleasant surroundings he thought about Luciana. He went over her points, her features, as if he were describing them to an acquaintance. He explained the fact that while she was Tuscan she was not heavy, not even in the buttocks, and that if it hadn't been for her walk, that marvelous Roman walk, she could have passed for a Parisienne. She was fine, he pointed out to his acquaintance. She had a fineness that you seldom find in Italian beauties; fine wrists, fine hands, slim, round arms. Oh, the wind and the rain and to hold in one's arms a willing love! That span of blood that leaps from the groin to the brain had made its passage and he was again committed to a painful inflammation. He recalled, in some detail, a piece of erotic slapstick that he had performed on his last visit. His inflammation mounted and mounting with it was a curb of self-disgust, a stubborn love of decency that kept abreast of his unruly flesh. That his body was a fool was well known to him; that it should demand instantaneous requital in a public airplane cabin with his nearest companions a sickly boy and his mother was a measure of its foolishness, but his conscience, clutching at its vision of decency, seemed even more foolish. Then the little boy on his left turned and vomited the medicine his mother had made him drink. The vomit had a bitter smell, bitter as flower water.

Cameron was shocked out of his venereal reverie by this ugly fact of life. The boy's sickness instantly cooled the lewdness of his thinking. He helped the stewardess wipe up the mess with paper towels and courteously accepted the apologies of the mother. He was himself again, judicious, commanding, enlightened. Then the pilot announced in two languages that they were taking the plane into a hangar to wait for their clearance. The ceiling was still zero but they expected a change in the wind and a clearing within the hour.

They drove into a hangar, where there was nothing to watch. A few of the passengers stretched their legs in the aisle. No one complained, except laughingly, and most of them spoke in Italian. Cameron closed his eyes and tried to rest but Luciana stepped trippingly into his reveries. He urged her to go, to leave him in peace, but she only laughed and undid her clothing. He opened his eyes to clear his head with a view of the world. The baby was crying. The stewardess brought the baby a bottle and the captain announced that the fog was general. In a few minutes they would be transported by bus to a New York hotel and would wait for their clearance there. They would be served a courtesy meal by the airline and the flight was scheduled for four that afternoon.

The doctor groaned. Why couldn't they be put up at the International Hotel? he asked the stewardess. She explained that all planes were grounded and the airport hotels were full. A bus drove into the hangar and they boarded it with perfect passivity and returned to the city, where they were received in what was very definitely a third-class hotel. It was nearly noon and Cameron went into the bar and ordered a drink and lunch. "Are you with flight seven?" the waitress asked. He said that he was. "Well, I'm very sorry," she said, "but passengers for flight seven have to eat in the dining room where they serve the *plat du jour.*"

"I will pay for my lunch," Cameron said. "And please bring me a drink."

"The courtesy of cocktails is not extended to tourist passengers," the waitress said.

"I will pay for my drink and I will pay for my lunch," Cameron said.

"That won't be necessary," the waitress said, "if you go into the other dining room."

"Does it look to you as if I couldn't pay for my lunch?" Cameron asked.

"I am just trying to explain to you," the waitress said, "that the airline is responsible for your meals."

"I understand," said Cameron. "Now please bring me what I have ordered."

After lunch he watched a television play in his hotel room and rang for a bottle of whisky at four. At six the airline called to say that the flight was scheduled for midnight and that they would board the bus in front of the hotel at eight o'clock. He ate some supper in a restaurant around the corner and joined the other passengers, whom he had begun to detest. They boarded the plane at half-past eleven and were airborne on schedule but the plane was old and noisy and flew so low that he could clearly see the lights of Nantucket when they passed the island. He had his whisky bottle with him and he sipped at this until he fell asleep to suffer an excruciating dream about Luciana. When he woke it was dawn and they were coming in for a landing but it was not Rome; it was Shannon, where they made an unscheduled stop for motor repairs. He cabled Luciana from Shannon but it was five before they took off again and they didn't reach Rome until a little after dawn the next day.

The airport bar and restaurant were shut. He telephoned Luciana. She was asleep, of course, and cross at being waked. She had not received his cable. She could not see him until evening. She would meet him at Quinterella's at eight. He pleaded with her to let him see her sooner—to let him come to her then. "Please, my darling, please," he groaned. She broke the connection. He took a cab into Rome and got a room at the Eden. It was still early in the morning and the people on the streets were dressed for work and hurrying, with that international sameness of people hurrying to work on a hot morning anywhere. He took a shower and lay down on his bed to rest, yearning for her and cursing her, but his anger did nothing to palliate his need and the crudeness of his thinking seemed like one of the realities of hell. Oh, the wind and the rain and to hold in one's arms a willing love!

There was the day to kill. He had never seen the Sistine Chapel or any of the other sights of the city and he thought he could do that. It might clear his head. He dressed and went out onto the street looking for one of those famous museums or churches about which one heard so much. Presently he came to a square where there were three churches that looked old. The doors of the first and the second were locked but the third was open and he stepped into a dark place that smelled heavily of spices. There were four women in a front pew and a priest in soiled lace was celebrating mass. He looked around him, anxious to appreciate the art treasures, but there seemed to be a roof leak above the chapel on his right and while he guessed that the painting there must be valuable and beautiful it was cracked and stained with water like the wall of any furnished room. The next chapel was decorated with naked men blowing on trumpets and the next was so dark that he could see nothing. There was a sign in English saying that if you put ten lire in the slot the lights would go on and he did this, revealing a large and bloody picture of a man in the death agonies of being crucified upside down. He did not ever like to be reminded of the susceptibilities of his flesh to pain and he quickly left the church for the smashing light and heat of the square. There was a café with an awning and he sat there and drank a *campari*. A young woman, crossing the street, reminded him of Luciana, but even if she was a tart it was Luciana and not her he wanted. Luciana was a tart but she was his tart and somewhere in the crudeness of his drives was a touching strain of romance. Luciana, he thought, was the kind of woman who could make the simple act of stepping into her pumps seem as if she had slammed a door on time.

Oh, the wind and the rain and to hold in one's arms a willing love! Why should life seem so pitilessly to harry him, why should the only reality seem to be obscene? He thought of the quantum theory, of Mittledorf's Constant, of the discovery of helium in the tetrasphere, but they had no bearing on his sorrow. Are we all unmercifully imbedded in time, insensate, purblind, vain, cold to the appeals of love and reason and stripped of our gifts for reflection and self-assessment? Had the time come for him, and was his only reminder of reasonableness, of the stalwart he had been, a smell of vomit? He had seen brilliant colleagues orbit off into impermeable foolishness and vanity, claiming discoveries they had not discovered, discarding useful men for sycophants, running for Congress, circulating petitions and uncovering international and imaginary networks of enemies. He was no less interested in cleanliness and decency than he had ever been, but he seemed less well equipped to honor these interests. His thinking had the disgusting crudeness of pornography. He seemed to see some image of himself, separate and distant like a figure in a movie, forlorn and unredeemable, going about some self-destructive business in the rainy back streets of a strange city. Where was his goodness, his excellence, his common sense?

I used to be a good man, he thought piteously. He shut his eyes in pain and in that movie that played interminably across the fine skin of his eyelids he saw himself stumbling over wet cobblestones under old-fashioned street lamps, falling, falling, falling from usefulness into foolishness, from high spirits into crudeness. Then he was tormented by that cretinous and sordid cylinder in the head or mind on which are inscribed old hymns and dance tunes, the musical junkyard, that territory where camp-fire songs, singing commercials, marches and fox trots gather and fester in their idiotic repetitiousness and appear at will, their puerile verses and their vulgar melodies in a state of perfect preservation. "Got those racetrack blues," sang this chamber of his mind. It was a tune he had heard forty years ago on a crank-up phonograph and yet he could not stop the singing:

> Got those racetrack blues,
> I'm feelin' blue all the time.
> Got those racetrack blues,
> With all my dough on the line.

He left the café and started back to the Eden but his mind went on caroling:

> But the track is muddy, and I don't mean maybe,
> And I'll never get the money to buy shoes for baby.

He climbed up the Via Sistina and the song went on:

> I've got those racetrack blues,
> I'm feelin' blue all the time. . . .

A young man was waiting for him in the lobby; one of those elegantly barbered youths who hang around the Pincio. He introduced himself as Luciana's brother and said she must pay her dressmaker for the costume she would wear that evening. He took an envelope from his pocket and presented Cameron with a note in Luciana's hand and a bill for a hundred thousand lire. Cameron returned it to the stranger and said he would pay the bill that evening. "Shesa no comea if you don'ta paya," the youth said. "Tell her to call me," Cameron said. He took the elevator up and the telephone was ringing when he entered his room. She was herself. He could imagine her twisting the telephone cord in her fingers. "You paya the bill," she said, "or I no see you. You givea him the money." For a second he thought of breaking the connection, breaking off the affair, but the noise of Roman traffic in the Roman streets reminded him of how far he was from home, that in fact he had no home, no friends, and that an ocean lay between him and his usefulness. He had come too far, he had come too far. Conduct and time were linear and serial; one was hurled through life with the bitch of remorse nipping at one's hocks. No power of reason or justice or virtue could bring him to his senses.

There was a soft knock on the door and her soft-eyed agent stepped into the room. Cameron made him wait but the noises outside his window spelled his doom. After an hour with her he would be his high-minded and magnanimous self again but in order to achieve this he must be swindled, humiliated and gulled. She had jockeyed him into a position of helplessness. "All right," he said, and they walked through the heat down to the Banco di Santo Spirito, where he cashed a draft for three hundred thousand lire and gave the boy his money. Then, and it was the only kind of disdain or self-expression left to him, he walked past the youth and out of the bank.

The day passed miserably. He took a shower at seven and went out to the Via Veneto for a *campari*. She was always late, he had never known a woman who wasn't, and it would probably be nine before she got to Quinterella's. She might, for once, play it safe; she might guess that his patience was not inexhaustible and that he had a mind of his own. But had he? If she asked him to drop to his knees and bark like a dog would he dare to refuse? He stayed at the café until eight and then started down the hill. His feelings were heavy—lustful and melancholy— and it dismayed him that in thinking of Luciana his mind could display such foulness. He started across the Piazza del Popolo. Somewhere a church bell rang. The discordant iron bells of

Rome had always surprised him, carrying on, with their contemporaries the fountains, a losing battle against the noise of traffic. Then from the hills there was a peal of thunder. The explosion seemed to ring back from the excitements of his youth, and what a strong, fine youth he had been. A second later the air of Rome was filled with a dense, gray rain. It seemed to fall with a wicked vehemence.

He was stuck by the fountain in the middle of the square. By the time there was a halt in the traffic he was as wet as if he had plunged into the fountain; but he ran across the square to the shelter of a church porch. The porch was crowded with Romans and he had to push to find a place among them. There was no delicacy or shyness in the way in which the crowd jostled one another but he held himself with as much probity as he could muster. When the rain let up, and it let up as suddenly as it had fallen, he stepped back into the *piazza* and looked down at his clothes. His shirt clung to his skin, his tie had lost its shape, there was no press left in his pants and when he pulled the folds of his jacket away from his shoulders he saw that his pocket had been picked.

This was a blow. It stopped him short. What he felt was too violent for indignation. It was the enormous sadness of having lost some lights or vitals—six inches of intestine, a gall bladder or a group of back teeth—the melancholy and enfeebling shock of surgery. His wallet could be replaced, there was plenty of money where that had come from, but for a moment the loss seemed stinging and irreplaceable and he felt guilty. Neither absent-mindedness nor drunkenness nor any other fault of his had helped the thief and yet he felt gulled and foolish, an old idiot who had come into a time of life when he would begin to mislay his possessions, lose his tickets and money and become a burden to the world. Somewhere a bell struck the half-hour and the crude iron note reminded him of Luciana, of the crudeness and fitness of the bounding act of love. The thought of her overtook his feeling of loss, he straightened up in spite of his wet clothing. Oh, the wind and the rain and to hold in one's arms a willing love! He stepped into a large pile of dog manure.

It took him nearly five minutes to scrape this off his shoe and like the boy's sickness on the plane it had a tonic effect on his feelings; it aroused some momentary misgivings. It was the sum of obstacles—the delayed flight, the sick child, the thunderstorm—that might in the end cure his ardor. But the restaurant was only a step away and in a few minutes he would be with his swan, his swan who would lead him off to a paradise all laced with green and gold. He strode up to the door of the restaurant, but it was locked. Why were the windows dark? Why did the place seem abandoned? Then on the door he saw a photograph of Enrico Quinterella framed in a boxwood wreath with a bow, who, that very afternoon somewhere in Rome, surrounded by his wife and children had received extreme unction and departed this life.

Death had shut up the place; put out the light. Signore Quinterella was dead. Then he felt an exalting surge of deliverance, a return to himself; his mind seemed to fill with the astringency of all decent things. Luciana was a slut, her bed a pit and he was free to live sensibly, free to judge right from wrong. Here was a sense of pureness without the force of repression and his gratitude to the contingencies that had liberated him was pious. He walked back to the Eden like a new man, slept deeply and felt in the depths of sleep that he had been granted some bounty. He took a New York plane in the morning and was back in Talifer that afternoon, convinced that there was some blessedness in the nature of things.

19

Coverly, without having been given a clue to his usefulness, packed and left for Atlantic City one evening with Cameron and his team. The ambiguity of his position was embarrassing. One of the team told Coverly that Cameron was to speak to a conference of scientists on a detonative force that was a million times the force of terrestrial lightning and that could be produced inexpensively. It was all that Coverly was able to grasp. Cameron sat apart from the others and read a paper-back which, Coverly saw, by craning his neck, was called *Cimarron: Rose of the South West.* It was the first time that Coverly had associated with men of this echelon and he was naturally inquisitive but he couldn't understand their point of view, indeed he couldn't understand their language. They talked about thermal runions, tolopters, strabometers, trenchions and podules. It was another language and one that seemed to him with the bleakest origins. You couldn't trace here the elisions and changes worked by a mountain range, a great river or the nearness of the sea. Coverly supposed that the palest of them could smite a mountain but they were the most unlikely people to imagine as being armed with the powers of doom-crack. They spoke of lightning in their synthetic language but with the voices of men—strained from time to time with nervousness, broken with coughing and laughter, shaded and colored a little with regional differences. One of them was an aggressive pederast and Coverly wondered if this sexual cynicism had anything to do with his attitude as a scientist. One of them wore a suit coat that bunched around his shoulders. One of them—Brunner—wore a necktie painted with a horseshoe. One of them had a nervous habit of pulling at his eyebrows and they were all heavy smokers. They were men born of women and subject to all the ravening caprices of the flesh. They could destroy a great city inexpensively, but had they made any progress in solving the clash between night and day, between the head and the groin? Were the persuasions of lust, anger and pain any less in their case? Were they spared toothaches, nagging erections and fatigue?

They checked into the Haddon Hall, where Coverly was given a room of his own. Brunner, who was friendly, suggested that Coverly might like to attend some of the open lectures and so he did. The first was by a Chinese on the legal problems of

interstellar space. The Chinese spoke in French and a simulta-
neous translation was broadcast through transistor radios. The
legal vocabulary was familiar but Coverly couldn't grasp its appli-
cation to the cosmos. He could not easily apply phrases like
National Sovereignty to the moon. The following lecture dealt
with experiments in sending a man into space in a sac filled
with fluid. The difficulty presented was that men immersed in
fluid suffered a grave and sometimes incurable loss of memory.
Coverly wanted to approach the scene with his best seriousness—
with a complete absence of humor—but how could he square
the image of a man in a sac with the small New England village
where he had been raised and where his character had been
formed? It seemed, in this stage of the Nuclear Revolution, that
the world around him was changing with incomprehensible velocity but if these changes were truly incomprehensible what
attitude could he take, what counsel could he give his son? Had
his basic apparatus for judging true and false become obsolete?
Leaving the lecture hall he ran into Brunner and asked him to
lunch. His motive was curiosity. Compared to Brunner's high-
minded scientific probity the rhythms of his own nature seemed
wayward and sentimental. Brunner's composure challenged his
own disciplines and his own usefulness and he wondered if his
pleasure in the unscientific landscape of the Atlantic City boardwalk was obsolete. On his right were the singing waves and on
his left a generous show of that mysterious culture that springs
up at the edges of the sea and that, with its overt concern with
mystery—seers, palmists, fortunetellers, gambling games and
tea-leaf diviners—seems like a product of the thunderous discourse between the ocean and the continent. Seers seemed to
thrive in the salty air. He wondered what Brunner made of the
scene. Did the smell of fried pork excite his memory or what
he called his playback? Would the sighing of the waves present
him with a romantic vision of the possibilities of adventure?
Coverly looked at his companion but Brunner stared out so flatly,
so impassively at the scene that Coverly didn't ask his question.
He guessed that Brunner saw what was to be seen—brine, a

boardwalk, some store fronts—and that if he went beyond the moment, which seemed unlikely, he would have seen the store fronts demolished and replaced by public playgrounds, ball fields and picnic groves. But who was wrong? The possibility that Coverly was wrong made him very uncomfortable. Brunner said that he had never eaten a lobster and so they went into an old matchboard lobster palace at a turn in the walk.

Coverly ordered a bourbon. Brunner sipped a beer and whistled loudly at the prices. He had a very large head and a heavy but not a dark beard. He must have shaved that morning, perhaps carelessly, but the outlines of his brown beard were, by noon, clearly defined. He was pale and his pallor seemed heightened by the largeness and the redness of his ears. The redness stopped abruptly at the point where his ears joined his head. The rest of him was all pallor; it was not a Levantine or a Mediterranean pallor—it was probably an inherited characteristic or the product of a bad diet—but it was, to give him credit, a virile pallor, thick-skinned and lit by those flaming ears. He had his charms, they all had, and it was Coverly's feeling that these were based on the possession of a vision of surmountable barriers, a sense of the future, a means for expressing his natural zeal for progress and change. He drank his beer as if he expected it to incapacitate him and here was another difference. With a single exception they were all temperate men. Coverly was not temperate but his intemperance was his best sense of the abundance of life.

"You live in Talifer?" Coverly asked. He knew that Brunner did.

"Yes. I have a little pad on the west side. I live alone. I was married but that was no go."

"I'm sorry," Coverly said.

"There's nothing to be sorry about. The marriage was no go. We couldn't optimize." He tackled his salad.

"You live alone?" Coverly asked.

"Yes." He spoke with his mouth full.

"How do you spend your evenings?" Coverly asked. "I mean, do you go to the theater?"

Brunner laughed kindly. "No, I don't go to the theater. Some of the team have outside interests but I can't say that I have."

"But if you don't have any outside interests what do you do in the evenings?"

"I study. I sleep. Sometimes I go to a restaurant on Route 27 where you can get all the chicken you can eat for two-fifty. I'm keen on chicken and when I get my appetite dialed up I can put away a very satisfactory payload."

"You go with friends?"

"Nope," he said with dignity. "I go alone."

"Do you have any children?" Coverly asked.

"Nope. That's one of the reasons my wife and I couldn't finalize. She wanted children. I didn't. I had a bad time when I was a kid and I didn't want to put anybody else through that."

"What do you mean?"

"Well, my mother died when I was about two and Dad and Grandma brought me up. Dad was a free-lance engineer but he couldn't hold a job for long. He was a terrible alcoholic. You see, I felt more than most people, I think I felt more than most people that I had to get away. Nobody understood me. I mean, my name didn't mean anything but the name of an old drunk. I had to make my name mean something. So when this lightning thing turned up I felt better, I began to feel better. Now my name means something, at least to some people it does."

Here then was the lightning, a pure force of energy, veined when one saw it in the clouds as all the world is veined—the leaf and the wave—and here was a lonely man, familiar with blisters and indigestion, whose humble motives in inventing a detonative force that could despoil the world were the same as the child actress, the eccentric inventor, the small-town politician. "I only wanted my name to mean something." He must have been forced more than most men to include in the mystery of death the incineration of the planet. Waked by a peal of thunder he must have wondered more than most if this wasn't the end, hastened in some way by his wish to possess a name.

The waitress brought their lobsters then and Coverly ended his interrogation.

When Coverly got back to the hotel there was a note for him in Cameron's hand. He was to meet Cameron outside a conference room on the third floor at five o'clock and drive him to the airport. He guessed from this that he had been attached to Cameron's staff as a chauffeur. He spent the afternoon in the hotel swimming pool and went up to the third floor at five. The door to the conference room was locked and sealed with wire and two secret servicemen in plain clothes waited in the corridor. When the meeting ended it was announced to them by telephone and they broke the seals and unlocked the door. The scene inside was disorderly and bizarre. The doors and windows of the room had been draped, as a security precaution, with blankets. Physicists and scientists were standing on chairs and tables, removing these. The air was cloudy with smoke. It was a moment before Coverly realized that no one was speaking. It was like the close of an especially gruesome funeral. Coverly said hello to Brunner but his lunch companion didn't reply. His face was green, his mouth set in a look of bitterness and revulsion. Could the tragedy and horror of what Cameron had told them account for this silence? Were these the faces of men who had just been told the facts of the millennium? Had they been told, Coverly wondered, that the planet was uninhabitable; and if they had, what was there to cling to in this hotel corridor with its memories of call girls, honeymoon couples and old people down for a long weekend to take the sea air? Coverly looked confusedly from these pale, these obviously terrified faces down to the dark cabbage roses that bloomed on the rug. Cameron, like the others, passed Coverly without speaking and Coverly followed him obediently out to the car. Cameron said nothing on the trip to the airport nor did he say good-bye. He boarded a small Beechcraft— he was going on to Washington—and when the plane had taken off Coverly noticed that he had forgotten his briefcase.

The responsibilities attached to this simple object were frightening. It must contain the gist of what he had said that afternoon and from the faces of his audience Coverly guessed that what he had said concerned the end of the world. He decided to return to the hotel at once and unload the briefcase on one of the team. He drove back to the city with the briefcase in his lap. He asked at the desk for Brunner and was told that Brunner had checked out. So had all the others. Looking around him at the shady or at least heterogeneous faces in the lobby he wondered if any of them were foreign agents. To behave inconspicuously seemed to be his best course of action and he went into the dining room and had some dinner. He kept the briefcase on his lap. Toward the end of his dinner there was a series of percussive explosions from outside the hotel and he thought that the end had come until the waitress explained that it was a display of fireworks put on for the entertainment of a convention of gift-shop proprietors.

With the briefcase secured under his armpit he stepped out of the hotel to see the fireworks. It seemed fitting to him that a meeting that had dealt with detonative powers should end with such a spendthrift, charming and utterly harmless display. Folding chairs had been set up on the boardwalk for the audience. The display was fired from a set of mortars on the beach. He heard the sound of a projectile dropped into a shell, followed its trajectory by a light trail of cinders as it mounted up past the evening star. There was a blast of white light—it took the sound a moment to reach them—and then there was a confusion of gold streamers, arced like stems, ending in silent balls of colored fire. All this was reflected in the windowpanes of the hotels, and the faces of the gift-shop proprietors, turned up to admire this ingenuous show, seemed excellent and simple. There was a scattering of applause, a touching show of politeness and enthusiasm, the sort of clapping one hears when the dance music ends. The black smoke could be seen clearly against the twilight, changing shapes as it drifted off to sea. Coverly sat down to enjoy himself, to hear the walls of the mortar shell ring again, to follow the trajectory of cinders, the arc of stars, the blooming colors, the sighs of hundreds and the decencies of applause. The show ended with a barrage, a gentle mockery of warfare, demonic drumming and all the thousands of hotel windows flashing white fire. The last explosion shook the boardwalk harmlessly, there was a shower of dancing-school applause and he started back for his hotel. When he entered his room he wondered if it hadn't been rifled. All the drawers were open and clothing was scattered over the chairs; but he had to measure this chaos against the fact that he was not a neat traveler. He slept with the briefcase in his arms.

In the morning Coverly, carrying the briefcase against his chest the way girls carry their schoolbooks, flew from Atlantic City to an international airport where he waited for a plane to the West. There was, on one hand, the railroad station in St. Botolphs, with its rich aura of arrivals and departures, its smells of coal gas, floor oil and toilets, and its dark waiting room, where some force of magnification seemed brought to bear on the lives of the passengers waiting for their train to arrive; and on the other hand, this loft or palace, its glass walls open to the overcast sky, where spaciousness, efficiency and the smell of artificial leather seemed not to magnify but to diminish the knowledge the passengers had of one another. Coverly's plane was due to leave at two, but at quarter to three they still waited at the gate. A few of the passengers were grumbling, and two or three of them had copies of an afternoon paper that reported a jet crash in Colorado with a death list of seventy-three. Was the jet that had crashed the one they were waiting for? Had they, standing in the dim sunlight, received some singular mercy? Had their lives been saved? Coverly went to the information desk to ask about his flight. The question was certainly legitimate, but the clerk reacted sullenly, as if the purchase of a plane ticket was a contract to walk humbly and in darkness. "There is some delay," he said, unwillingly. "There may be some motor trouble or the connecting flight from Europe may be delayed. You won't board until half-past three." Coverly thanked him for this favor and went up some stairs to a bar. On a gilt easel at the right of the door was a photograph of a pretty singer in evening clothes, a delegate of all those thousands who beam at us from the thresholds of bars and hotel dining rooms; but she didn't go on until nine and would probably be asleep or taking her wash out to the laundromat.

Inside, there was piped-in music and the bartender wore military livery. Coverly took a stool and ordered a beer. The man beside him was swaying comfortably on his stool. "Where you going?" he asked.

"Denver."

"Me, too," the stranger exclaimed, striking Coverly on the back. "I've been going to Denver for three days."

"That's right," the bartender said. "He missed eight flights now. Isn't it eight?"

"Eight," the stranger said. "It's because I love my wife. My wife's in Denver, and I love her so much I can't get on the plane."

"It's good for business," the barkeeper said.

In the gloom at the end of the bar two conspicuous homosexuals with dyed yellow hair were drinking rum. A family sat at a table eating lunch and conversing in advertising slogans. It seemed to be a family joke.

"My!" the mother exclaimed. "Taste those bite-sized chunks of white Idaho turkey meat, reinforced with riboflavin, for added zest."

"I like the crispy, crunchy potato chips," the boy said. "Toasted to a golden brown in health-giving infrared ovens and topped with imported salt."

"I like the spotless rest rooms," said the girl, "operated under the supervision of a trained nurse and hygienically sealed for our comfort, convenience and peace of mind."

"Winstons taste good," piped the baby in his highchair, "like a cigarette should. Winstons have *flavor.*"

The dark bar had the authority of a creation, but it was a creation evolved independently from the iconography of the universe. With the exception of the labels on the bottles there was nothing familiar in the place. Its light were cavernous, its walls were dark mirrors. There was not even a truncated piece of driftwood or a coaster shaped like a leaf to remind him of the world outside. That beauty of sameness that makes the star and the shell, the sea and the clouds all seem to have come from the same hand was lost. The music was interrupted for the announcement that Coverly's flight was boarding, and he paid for his beer and grabbed his briefcase. He stopped in the men's room, where someone had written something exceedingly human on the wall, and then followed the lighted numbers down the long corridor to his gate. There was still no plane in sight, but none of the passengers had been moved by the delay or the news of the crash to change their plans. They stood there passively as if the sullen clerk had in fact sold them humility with their tickets. Coverly's topcoat was too warm for that climate, but most of the other passengers had come from places that were colder or warmer than here. From a duct directly overhead, the continuous music poured gently into their ears. "It's going to be all right," an old lady beside Coverly whispered to an even older companion. "It isn't dangerous. It isn't any more dangerous than the trains. They carry millions of passengers every year. It's going to be all right." The fingers of the older, knobbed like driftwood, touched her cheeks, and in her eyes was the fear of death. Death was what the scene meant to her— the frisky mechanics in their white coveralls, the numbered runways, the noise of an incoming 707. A baby cried. A man ran a comb through his hair. The objects and sounds around Coverly seemed to group themselves into some immutable statement. These were the facts—this music, the fear of death endured by the old stranger, the flatness of the field, and way in the distance the roofs of some houses.

The plane came in, they boarded, and the stewardess seated Coverly between the old lady and a man whose breath smelled of whisky. The stewardess wore high-heeled shoes, a raincoat and dark glasses. Coverly saw under her raincoat the skirts of a red silk dress. As soon as she had closed the plane, she went

to the toilet and reappeared in the gray skirt and white silk blouse
of her profession. Her eyes, when she took off her glasses, were
haggard, and she peered out of them in pain. "Joe Burner,"
said the man on Coverly's right, and Coverly shook his hand
and introduced himself. "I'm pleased to meet you, Cove," the
stranger said. "I have a little present here I'd like to give you."
He took a small box from his pocket, and when Coverly opened
it he found a gilt tie clip. "I travel a lot," the stranger explained,
"and I give away these tie clips wherever I go. I have them
manufactured for me in Providence. That's the jewelry capital
of the United States. I give away two or three thousand clips a
year. It's a nice way of making friends. Everybody can use a
tie clip."

"Thank you very much," Coverly said.

"I knit socks for astronauts," said the old lady on Coverly's
left. "Oh, I know it's silly of me, but I love those boys, and I
can't bear to think of them having cold feet. I've sent ten pairs
of socks down to Canaveral in the last six weeks. They don't
thank me, it's true, but they've never returned them, and I like
to think that they use them."

"I'm taking a few days off, to see an old friend who's dying
of cancer," said Joe Burner. "I have at this date twenty-seven
friends who are dying of cancer. Some of them know it. Some
of them don't. But not a one of them has more than a year to
live."

They were wrapped then in a heard and unheard convulsion
of sound and pushed roughly back against their seats by the
force of gravity as the plane went down the strip and began
its strenuous push for altitude. A large panel fell out of the
ceiling and crashed into the aisle, and the glasses and bottles
in the pantry rattled noisily. When they had risen above the
scattered clouds, the passengers unbuckled their seat belts and
resumed their lives, their habits. "Good afternoon," said the
loudspeaker. "This is Captain MacPherson welcoming you to
Flight 73, nonstop to Denver. We have reports of a little turbulence in the mountains but we expect it to clear by scheduled
landing time. We are sorry about the delay, and wish to take

this occasion to thank you all for your patience in not doing nothing about it." The speaker clicked off.

Coverly could not see that anyone else was perplexed. Was he mistaken in assuming that navigational competence implied a rudimentary grasp of English? Joe Burner had begun to tell Coverly the story of his life. His style was nearly bardic. He began with the characters of his parents. He described his birthplace. Then he told Coverly about his two older brothers, his interest in sandlot baseball, his odd jobs, the schools he had attended, the wonderful buttermilk pancakes that his mother used to make and the friends that he had won and lost. He told Coverly his annual grosses, the size of his office staff, the nature of his three operations, the wonderfulness of his wife and the amount of money it had cost him to landscape his seven-room, two-bath house on Long Island. "I have something very unique," he said. "I have this lighthouse on my front lawn. Four, five years ago, this big estate on Sands Point was auctioned off for taxes, and Mother and I went down there to see if there was anything we could use. Well, they had this little lake with a lighthouse on it—just ornamental, of course—and when it came time to buy the lighthouse, the bidding was very slow. Well, I bid thirty-five dollars, just for the heck of it, and you know what? That lighthouse was mine. Well, I have this friend in the trucking business—you have to know the right people—and he went down there and got it off the lake. I don't know to this day how he did it. Well, I've got this other friend in the electric business, and he wired it up for me, and now I've got this lighthouse right on my front lawn. It makes the place look real nice. Of course, some of the neighbors complain—you find clinkers in every gang—so I don't turn it on every night, but when we have people in to play cards or watch the television, I turn it on, and it looks beautiful."

The sky by then was the dark blue of high altitudes, and the atmosphere in the plane was as genial as a saloon. The white blouse the hostess wore came loose whenever she bent over to serve a cocktail. She tucked it in each time she straightened up. The seat backs were as high as the walls of an old box pew, and the passengers had a limited degree of privacy and a limited view of one another. Then the bulkhead door opened, and Coverly saw the captain come down the aisle. His color was bad, and his eyes were as haggard as the eyes of the stewardess. Perhaps he was a friend of the pilot and crew who had crashed a few hours earlier in Colorado. Would he, would anyone else, have the fortitude to face this disaster calmly? Would the charred bones of seventy-three bodies mean any less to him than they did to the rest of the world? He nodded to the stewardess, who followed him aft to the pantry. They did not exchange a word, but she put some ice into a paper cup and poured whisky into it. He carried his drink forward and closed the door. The old lady was dozing, and Joe Burner, having finished with his autobiography, had begun to tell his stock of jokes. Without any warning, the plane dropped about two thousand feet.

The confusion was horrible. Most of the drinks hit the ceiling, men and women were thrown into the aisles, children were screaming. "Attention, attention," said the public-address system. "Hear this, everyone."

"Oh, my God," the stewardess said, and she went aft and strapped herself in. "Attention, attention," said the amplified voice, and Coverly wondered then if this might be the last voice that he heard. Once, when he was being prepared for a critical operation, he had looked out of his hospital window into the window of an apartment house across the street, where a fat woman was dusting a grand piano. He had already been given Sodium Pentothal and was swiftly losing consciousness, but he resisted the drug long enough to feel resentment at the fact that the last he might see of the beloved world was a fat woman dusting a grand piano.

"Attention, attention," the voice said. The plane had leveled off in the heart of a dark cloud. "This is not your captain. Your captain is tied up in the head. Please do not move, please do not move from your seats, or I will cut off your oxygen supply. We are traveling at five hundred miles an hour, at an altitude of forty-two thousand feet, and any disturbance you create will only add to your danger. I have logged nearly a million air miles and am disqualified as a pilot only because of my political opinions. This is a robbery. In a few minutes my accomplice will enter the cabin by the forward bulkhead, and you will give him your wallets, purses, jewelry and any other valuables that you have. Do not create any disturbance. You are helpless. I repeat: You are helpless."

"Talk to me, talk to me," the old lady asked. "Please just say something, anything."

Coverly turned and nodded to her, but his tongue was so swollen with fear that he could not make a sound. He worked it around desperately in his mouth to stir up some lubrication. The other passengers were still, and on they rocketed through the dark—sixty-five or seventy strangers, their noses pressed against the turmoil of death. What would be its mode? Fire? Should they, like the martyrs, inhale the flames to shorten the agony? Would they be truncated, beheaded, mutilated and scattered over three miles of farmland? Would they be ejaculated into the darkness and yet not lose consciousness during the dreadful fall to earth? Would they be drowned, and while drowning display their last talent for inhumanity in trampling one another at the flooding bulkheads? It was the darkness that gave him most pain. The shadow of a bridge or a building can fall across our spirit with all the weight of a piece of bad news, and it was the darkness that seemed to compromise his spirit. All he wanted then was to see some light, a patch of blue sky. A woman, sitting forward, began to sing "Nearer, My God, to Thee." It was a common church soprano, feminine, decent, raised once a week in the company of her neighbors. "E'en though it be a cross that raiseth me," she sang, "still all my song shall be, nearer, my God, to Thee. . . ."

A man across the aisle took up the hymn, joined quickly by several others, and when Coverly remembered the words, he sang:

> "Though like a wanderer,
> Weary and lone,

> Darkness comes over me,
> My rest a stone. . . ."

Joe Burner and the old lady were singing, and those who didn't know the words came in strong on the refrain. The bulkhead door opened, and there was the thief. He wore a felt hat and a black handkerchief tied over his face with holes cut for the eyes. It was, except for the felt hat, the ancient mask of the headsman. He wore black rubber gloves and carried a plastic wastebasket to collect their valuables. Coverly roared:

> "There let my way appear,
> Steps into heaven,
> All that Thou sendest me
> In mercy given. . . ."

They sang more in rebelliousness than in piety; they sang because it was something to do. And merely in having found something to do they had confounded the claim that they were helpless. They had found themselves, and this accounted for the extraordinary force and volume of their voices. Coverly stripped off his wristwatch and dropped his wallet into the basket. Then the thief, with his black-gloved hands, lifted the briefcase out of Coverly's lap. Coverly let out a groan of dismay and might have grabbed at the case had not Burner and the old lady turned on him faces so contorted with horror that he fell back into his seat. When the thief had robbed the last of them, he turned back to the bulkhead, staggering a little against the motion of the plane—a disadvantage that made his figure seem familiar and harmless. They sang:

> "Then with my waking thoughts,
> Bright with Thy praise,
> Out of my stormy griefs,
> Altars I'll raise. . . ."

"Thank you for your cooperation," said the public-address system. "We will make an unscheduled landing in West Franklin in about eleven minutes. Please fasten your seat belts and observe the no-smoking signal."

The clouds outside the ports began to lighten, to turn from gray to white, and then they sailed free into the blue sky of late afternoon. The old lady dried her tears and smiled. To lessen the pain of his confusion Coverly suddenly concluded that the briefcase had contained an electric toothbrush and a pair of silk pajamas. Joe Burner made the sign of the cross. The plane was losing altitude rapidly, and then below them they could see the roofs of a city that seemed like the handiwork of a marvelously humble people going about useful tasks and raising their children in goodness and charity. The moment when they ceased to be airborne passed with a thump and a roar of the reverse jets, and out of the ports they could see that international wilderness that hedges airstrips. Scrub grass and weeds, a vegetable slum, struggled in the sandy bottom soil that formed the banks of an oily creek. Someone shouted, "There they *go!*" Two passengers opened the bulkhead. There were confused voices, and when someone asked for information, the complexity of human relationships so swiftly re-established itself that those who knew what was going on pridefully refused to communicate with those who didn't and the first man into the forward cabin spoke to them with condescension. "If you'll quiet down for a minute," said he, "I'll tell you what we know. We've released the crew and the captain has made radio contact with the police. The thieves got away. That's all I can tell you now."

Then faintly, faintly, they heard the sirens approaching over the airstrip. The first to come was a fire crew, who put a ladder up against the door and got it open. Next to come were the police, who told them they were all under arrest. "You're going to be let off in lots of ten," one of the policemen said. "You're going to be questioned." He was gruff, but they were magnanimous. They were alive, and no incivility could disturb them. The police then began to count them off in lots. The ladder of the fire truck was the only way of getting down from the plane, and the older passengers mounted this querulously, their faces working with pain. Those who waited seemed immersed in the passivity of some military process; seemed to suffer that suspense of discernment and responsibility that overtakes any line of soldiers. Coverly was No. 7 in the last lot. A gust of dusty wind blew against his clothing as he went down the ladder. A policeman took him by the arm, a touch he bitterly and instantly resented, and it was all he could do to keep from flinging the man's arm off. He was put with his group into a closed police van with barred windows.

A policeman took him again by the arm when he left the van and again he had to struggle to control himself. What was this testiness of his flesh? he wondered. Why did he loathe this stranger's touch? Rising before him was the Central Police Headquarters—a yellow-brick building with a few halfhearted architectural flourishes and a few declarations of innocent love written in chalk on the walls. The wind blew dust and papers around his feet. Inside he found himself in the alarming and dreary atmosphere of wrongdoing. It was a passage into a world to which he had been granted merely a squint—that area of violence he glimpsed when he spread newspapers on the porch floor before he painted the screens. Roslyn man shoots wife and five children. . . . Murdered child found in furnace. . . . They had all been here, and had left in the air a palpable smell of their bewilderment and dismay, their claims of innocence. He was led to an elevator and taken up six flights. The policeman said nothing. He was breathing heavily. Asthma? Coverly wondered. Excitement? Haste?

"Do you have asthma?" he asked.

"You answer the questions," the policeman said.

He led Coverly down a corridor like the corridor in some depressing schoolhouse and put him in a room no bigger than a closet, where there was a wooden table, a chair, a glass of water and a questionnaire. The policeman shut the door, and Coverly sat down and looked at the questions.

Are you the head of a household? he was asked. Are you divorced? Widowed? Separated? How many television sets do you own? How many cars? Do you have a current passport? How often do you take a bath? Are you a college graduate? High school? Grammar school? Do you know the meaning of "marsupial"; "seditious"; "recondite"; "dialectical materialism"? Is your house heated by oil? Gas? Coal? How many rooms? If you were forced to debase the American flag or the Holy Bible, what would be your choice? Are you in favor of the federal income tax? Do you believe in the International Communist Conspiracy? Do you love your mother? Are you afraid of lightning? Are you for the continuation of atmospheric testing? Do you have a savings account? Checking account? What is your total indebtedness? Do you own a mortgage? If you are a man, would you classify your sexual organs as being size 1, 2, 3, or 4? What is your religious affiliation? Do you believe John Foster Dulles is in Heaven? Hell? Limbo? Do you often entertain? Are you often entertained? Do you consider yourself to be liked? Well liked? Popular? Are the following men living or dead: John Maynard Keynes. Norman Vincent Peale. Karl Marx. Oscar Wilde. Jack Dempsey. Do you say your prayers each night? . . .

Coverly attacked these questions—and there were thousands of them—with the intentness of a guilty sinner. He had given his watch to the thief, and had no idea of how long it took him to fill out the questionnaire. When he was done, he shouted, "Hullo. I'm finished. Let me out of here." He tried the door and found it open. The corridor was empty. It was night, and the window at the end of the hall showed a dark sky. He carried his questionnaire to the elevator and rang. As he stepped out of the elevator on the street floor, he saw a policeman sitting at a desk. "I lost something very valuable, very important," Coverly said.

"That's what they all say," the policeman said.

"What do I do now?" asked Coverly. "I've answered all the questions. What do I do now?"

"Go home," the policeman said. "I suppose you want some money?"

"I do," Coverly said.

"You're all getting a hundred from the insurance company," the policeman said. "You can put in a claim later if you've lost more." He counted out ten ten-dollar bills and looked at his watch. "The Chicago train comes through in about twenty minutes. There's a cab stand at the corner. I don't suppose you'll want to fly again for a while. None of the others did."

"Have they all finished?" Coverly asked.

"We're holding a few," the man said.

"Well, thank you," Coverly said, and walked out of the building into a dark street in the town of West Franklin, feeling in its dust, heat, distant noise and the anonymity of its colored lights the essence of his loneliness. There was a newsstand at the corner, and a cab parked there. He bought a paper. "Disqualified Pilot Robs Jet In Midair," he read. "A Great Plane Robbery took place at 4:16 this afternoon over the Rockies . . ." He got into the cab and said, "You know, I was in that plane robbery this afternoon."

"You're the sixth fare who's told me that," the driver said. "Where to?"

"The station," Coverly said.

20

It was late the next afternoon when Coverly finally made his way from Chicago back to Talifer. He went to Cameron's office at once but he was kept waiting nearly an hour. Now and then he could hear the old man's voice, through the closed door, raised in anger. "You'll never get a Goddamned man on the Goddamned moon," he was shouting. When Coverly was finally let in, Cameron was alone. "I've lost your briefcase," Coverly said.

"Oh, yes," the doctor said. He smiled his unfortunate smile.

Then it was a toothbrush and some pajamas, Coverly thought. It was nothing, after all!

"There was a robbery on the plane coming West," Coverly said.

"I don't understand," Cameron said. The light of his smile was undiminished.

"I have a newspaper here," Coverly said. He showed Cameron the paper he had bought in West Franklin. "They took everything. Our watches, wallets, your briefcase."

"Who took it?" Cameron asked. His smile seemed to brighten.

"The thieves, the robbers. I suppose you might call them pirates."

"Where did they take it?"

"I don't know, sir."

Cameron left his desk and went to the window, putting his back to Coverly. Was he laughing? Coverly thought so. He had duped the enemy. The briefcase had been empty! Then Coverly saw that he was not laughing at all. These were the painful convulsions of bewilderment and misery; but what did he cry for? His reputation, his absent-mindedness, his position; for the world itself that he could see outside his window, the ruined farm and the gantry line? Coverly had no means of consoling him and stood in a keen agony of his own, watching Cameron, who seemed then small and old, racked by these uncontrollable muscular spasms. "I'm sorry, sir," Coverly said. "Get the hell out of here," Cameron muttered and Coverly left.

It was closing time and the bus he took home was crowded. He tried to judge himself along traditional lines. Had he refused to yield up the briefcase he might have wrecked the plane and killed them all; but mightn't this have been for the best? What could he anticipate or what could he look back upon with any calm? When he went back to work in the morning what office would he report to? What had Cameron wanted of him in the first place? What sense could he make of the old man sobbing at his window? Would Betsey, when he got home, be watching

TV? Would his little son be in tears? Would there be any supper? Some vision of St. Botolphs in the light of a summer evening appeared to him. It was that hour when the housewives called their children in for supper with those small bells that used to be used for summoning servants to the table. Silver or not, they all had a silvery note and Coverly recalled this silvery ringing now from all the back stoops of Boat Street and River Street, calling children in from the banks of the river.

His own place was brightly lighted. Betsey ran into his arms when he entered the house. "I just been hoping and praying, sweetie, that you'd get home for supper," she said, "and now my prayers are answered, my prayers are answered. We've been asked out to dinner!" Coverly could not work this in with any-thing that had happened in the last twenty-four hours and he settled for a mode of emotional and intellectual improvisation. He was tired but it would have been cruel to frustrate Betsey's only invitation. He kissed his son, tossed him into the air a few times and made a strong drink. "This nice woman," Betsey said, "her name is Winifred Brinkley, well, she came to the house collecting money for the Heart Drive and I told her, I just told her that I thought this was the lonesomest place on the face of the earth. I just didn't care who knew it. She then told me she thought it was lonesome too and that wouldn't we like to come to a little dinner party at her house tonight. So then I told her you were in Atlantic City and I didn't know when you would return but I just prayed and prayed that you'd get back in time and here you are!"

Coverly took a bath and changed while Betsey transported a high school boy who was going to stay with Binxey. The Brinkleys lived in the neighborhood and they walked there, arm in arm. Now and then Coverly bent his long neck and gave Betsey a kiss. Mrs. Brinkley was a thin, sprightly woman, brilliantly made up and loaded down with beads. She kept saying "Crap." Mr. Brinkley had an uncommonly receding forehead, a lack or infirm-ity that was accentuated by the fact that his gray, curly hair was arranged in loops over this receding feature like the curtains in some parlor. He seemed gallantly to be combating an air of fatigue and inconsequence by wearing a gold collar pin, a gold tie clip, a large bloodstone ring and a pair of blue-enamel cuff links that flashed like semaphores when he poured the sherry. Sherry was what they drank but they drank it like water. There were two other guests—the Cranstons from the neighboring city of Waterford. "I just had to ask somebody from out of town," Mrs. Brinkley said, "so we wouldn't have to listen to all that crap about Talifer."

"One thing I know, one thing I've learned," Mr. Cranston said, "and that is that you've got to have balls. That's what matters in the end. Balls." He wore a crimson hunting shirt and had yellow curls and a face that seemed both cherubic and menacing. His gray-haired wife seemed much older and more intelligent than he and in spite of his talk it was easiest to imagine him, not in the bouncing act of love, but in some attitude of bewilderment and despair while his wife stroked his curls and said: "You'll find another job, honey. Don't worry. Something better is bound to come along." Mrs. Brinkley's youngest child had just returned from a tonsillitis operation at the government hospital and during sherry they all talked about their tonsils and adenoids. Betsey positively shone. Coverly had never had his tonsils or adenoids removed and he was a little out of things until he brought up appendicitis. This carried them to the dinner table, where they then talked about dentistry. The dinner was the usual, washed down with sparkling Burgundy. After dinner Mr. Cranston told a dirty story and then got up to leave. "I hate to rush," he said, "but you know it takes us an hour and a half to get back and I have to work in the morning."

"Well, it shouldn't take you an hour and a half," Mr. Brinkley said. "How do you go?"

"We take the Speedway," Mr. Cranston said.

"Well, if you get outside Talifer before you take the Speedway," Mr. Brinkley said, "you'll save about fifteen minutes. Maybe twenty. You go back to the shopping center and turn right at the second traffic light."

"Oh, I wouldn't do it that way," Mrs. Brinkley said. "I'd go straight out past the computation center and take the clover leaf just before you get to the restricted area."

"Oh, you would, would you," said Mr. Brinkley. "That way you'd run right into a lot of construction. Just do what I say. Go back to the shopping center and turn right at the second traffic light."

"If they go back to the shopping center," Mrs. Brinkley said, "they'll get stuck in all that traffic at Fermi Circle. If they don't want to go out by the computation center, they could head straight for the gantries and then turn right at the road block."

"My God, woman," Mr. Brinkley said, "will you shut your big damned mouth?"

"Aw, crap," said Mrs. Brinkley.

"Well, thanks a lot," said the Cranstons, heading for the door. "I guess we'll just take the Speedway the way we used to." They were gone.

"Now you got them all mixed up," Mr. Brinkley said. "I don't know what makes you think you can give directions. You can't even find your way around the house."

"If they'd gone the way I told them in the beginning," Mrs. Brinkley said fiercely, "they would have been perfectly all right. There isn't any construction out by the restricted area. You just made that up."

"I did not," Mr. Brinkley said. "I was out there Thursday. That whole place is torn up."

"You were in bed with a cold on Thursday," Mrs. Brinkley said. "I had to keep bringing you trays."

"Well, I guess we'd better go," Coverly said. "It was awfully nice and thank you very much."

"If you would just learn to shut your mouth," Mr. Brinkley shouted at his wife, "the whole world would be very grateful. You shouldn't be allowed to drive a car, let alone give people directions."

"Thank you," said Betsey shyly at the door.

"Who smashed up the car last year?" Mrs. Brinkley screamed. "Who was the one who smashed up the car? Please tell me that."

They walked home, stopping now and then to exchange a kiss, and that journey ended like any other.

21

Coverly had not seen Cameron again. He killed some days at his desk, revising his commencement address about the jewelry of heaven. He was ordered, one morning, to report to security. He guessed that he would be charged with the loss of the briefcase and wondered if he would be arrested. Coverly was one of those men who labor under a preternaturally large sense of guilt that, like some enormous bruise, concealed by his clothing, could be carried painlessly until it was touched; but once it was touched it would threaten to unnerve him with its pain. He was a model of provincial virtues—truthful, punctual, cleanly and courageous—but once he was accused of wrongdoing by some powerful arm of society his self-esteem collapsed in a heap. Yes, yes, he was a sinner. It was he who had butchered the ambassador, hocked the jewelry and sold the blueprints to the enemy. He approached the security offices feeling deeply guilty. There was a long corridor painted buttercup yellow and eight or ten men and women were ahead of him. It seemed like a doctor's or a dentist's anteroom, a consular anteroom, a courthouse corridor, an employment office; it seemed, this scene for waiting, to be an astonishingly large part of the world. One by one the other men and women were called by name and let in at a door at the end of the yellow corridor. None of them returned so there must have been another way out but their disappearance seemed to Coverly ominous. Finally his name was called and a pretty secretary, her face composed in a censorious scowl, ushered him into a large office that looked like an old-fashioned courtroom.

There was an elevated bench behind which sat a colonel and two men in civilian clothes. A recording clerk sat below the bench. On the left was an American flag in a standard. The flag was heavy silk with a gold fringe and would never have left its stand, not even for a fine parade in auspicious weather.

"Coverly Wapshot?" the colonel asked.

"Yes, sir."

"Could I please have your security card?"

"Yes, sir." Coverly passed over his security card.

"You know a Miss Honora Wapshot of Boag Street, St. Botolphs?"

"It's Boat Street, sir."

"You know this lady?"

"Yes, sir, I've known her all my life. She's my cousin."

"Why didn't you report to this office the fact of her criminal indictment?"

"Her what?" What could she have done? Arson? Been caught shoplifting at the five-and-dime? Bought a car and run it into a crowd? "I don't know anything about her criminal indictment," Coverly said. "She's been writing me about a holly tree that grows behind her house. It has some kind of rust and she wants it sprayed. That's all I know about her. Could you tell me what she was charged with?"

"No. I can tell you that your security clearance has been suspended."

"But, Colonel, I don't understand any of this. She's an old lady and I can't be held responsible for what she does. Is there any appeal, is there any way I can appeal this?"

"You can appeal through Cameron's office."

"But I can't go anywhere, sir, without a security clearance. I can't even go to the men's room."

The clerk filled out a slip that looked like a fishing license and passed it to Coverly. It was, he read, a limited security clearance with a ten-day expiration. He thanked the clerk and went out a side door as another suspect was let in.

Coverly went at once to Cameron's office, where the receptionist said that the old man was out of town and would be gone at least two weeks. Coverly then asked to see Brunner, the scientist who had lunched with him in Atlantic City, and the girl cleared him through to Brunner's office. Brunner wore the cashmere pullover of his caste and sat in front of a colored writing board covered with equations and a note saying: "Buy sneakers." There was a wax rose in a vase on his desk. Coverly told Brunner his problems and Brunner listened to him sympathetically. "You never see any classified material, do you?" he asked. "It's the kind of thing the old man likes to fight. Last year they fired a janitor in the computation center because it appears that his mother worked briefly as a prostitute during the Second World War." He excused himself and returned with another member of the team. Cameron was in Washington and was going from there to New Delhi. The two scientists suggested that Coverly go down to Washington and catch the old man there. "He seems to like you," Brunner said, "and if you spoke to him, he could at least extend your temporary clearance until he returns. He's up for a Congressional hearing at ten tomorrow morning. It's in Room 763." Brunner wrote the number down and passed it to Coverly. "If you get there early perhaps you could speak to him before he goes on. I don't think there'll be many spectators. This is the seventeenth time he's been grilled this year and there has been a certain loss of interest."

22

Whether or not Cameron would speak to Coverly after their last interview was highly questionable; but it appeared to be Coverly's only chance and he decided to take it, moved mostly by his indignation at the capriciousness of the security officers who could confuse his old cousin's eccentricities with national security. He flew to Washington that night and went to Room

763 in the morning. His temporary security clearance served and he had no trouble getting in. There were very few spectators. Cameron came in at another door at quarter after ten and went directly to the witness stand. He was carrying what appeared to be a violin case. The chairman began to question him at once and Coverly admired the quality of his composure and the density of his eyebrows.

"Dr. Cameron?"

"Yes, sir." His voice was much the best in the room; the most commanding, the most virile.

"Are you familiar with the name Bracciani?"

"I have answered this question before. My answer is on record."

"The records of previous hearings have nothing to do with us today. I have requested the records of earlier hearings but my colleagues have refused them. Are you familiar with the name Bracciani?"

"I see no reason why I should come to Washington repeatedly to answer the same questions," the doctor said.

"You are familiar with the name Bracciani?"

"Yes."

"In what connection?"

"Bracciani was my name. It was changed to Cameron by Judge Southerland in Cleveland, Ohio, in 1932."

"Bracciani was your father's name?"

"Yes."

"Your father was an immigrant?"

"All of this is known to you."

"I have already told you, Dr. Cameron, that my colleagues have withheld the records of earlier hearings."

"My father was an immigrant."

"Was there anything in his past that would have encouraged you to disown his name?"

"My father was an excellent man."

"If there was nothing embarrassing, disloyal or subversive in your father's past, why did you feel obliged to disown his name?"

"I changed my name," the doctor said, "for a variety of reasons. It was difficult to spell, it was difficult to pronounce, it was difficult to identify myself efficiently. I also changed my name because there are some parts of this country and some people who still suspect anything foreign. A foreign name is inefficient. I changed my name as in going from one country to another one changes one's currency."

A second senator was recognized; a younger man. "Isn't it true, Dr. Cameron," he asked, "that you are opposed to any investigation beyond our own solar system and that you have refused money, cooperation and technical assistance to anyone who has challenged your opinions?"

"I am not interested in interstellar travel," he said quietly, "if that's what you meant to ask me. The idea is absurd and my opinion is based on fundamental properties such as time, acceleration, power, mass and energy. However, I would like to make it clear that I do not assume our civilization to be the one intelligent civilization in the universe." That fleeting smile passed over his face, a jewel of forced and insincere patience, and he leaned forward a little in his chair. "I feel that life and intelligence will have developed at about the same speed as on earth wherever the proper surroundings and the needed time have been provided. Present data—and these are extremely limited—suggest that life may have developed on the planets of about six percent of all stars. I feel myself that the spectrum of light reflected from the dark areas of Mars shows characteristics that prove the presence of plant life. As I've said, I think the possibilities of interstellar travel absurd; but interstellar communication is something else again.

"The number of civilizations with whom we might possibly communicate depends upon six factors. One: The rate at which stars like our sun are being formed. Two: The fraction of such stars that have planets. Three: The fraction of such planets that can sustain life. Four: The fraction of livable planets upon which life has arisen. Five: The fraction of the latter that have produced beings with a technology adequate for interstellar communica-

tion. Six: The longevity of this high technology. About one in
three million stars has the probability of a civilization in orbit.
However, this could still mean millions of such civilizations within
our galaxy alone and, as you gentlemen all know, there are bil-
lions of galaxies." The hypocritical smile again passed over his
face. Gas? Coverly wondered. "It seems unlikely to me," he went
on, "that technologies would develop on a planet covered with
water. Some of my colleagues are enthusiastic about the intelligence of the dolphin but it seems to me that the dolphin is
not likely to develop an interest in interstellar space." He waited
for the hesitant and scattered laughter to abate. "The twenty-
one-centimeter band—that is, one thousand four hundred and
twenty megacycles—emitted by the colliding atoms of hydrogen
throughout space has produced some interesting signals, especially from Tau Ceti, but I am very skeptical about their coher-
ence. I do believe that scientists in every advanced civilization
will have discovered that the energy value of each unit or quantum of radiation, whether in the form of light or radio waves,
equals its frequency times a value known to us, and perhaps
to some of you, as Planck's Constant.

"Optical masers appear to be our most promising means of
interstellar communication." Now he was deep in his classroom
manner and nothing would stop him until he had inflicted on
them all the tedium, excitement and pain of a lecture period.
"The optical version of these masers can produce a beam of
light so intense and narrow that, if transmitted from the earth,
it would illuminate a small portion of the moon." Again there
was the fleeting, the sugary smile. "Extraneous wavelengths are
eliminated so that unlike most light beams this one is pure
enough to be modulated for voice transmission. A maser system
could be detected with our present technology if it were transmit-
ting from a solar system ten light years away. We must study
the spectra of light from nearby stars for emission lines of peculiar sharpness and strength. This would be unmistakable evidence
of maser transmissions from a planet orbiting that star. The
light signals would be elaborately coded. In the case of a system

one thousand light years away it would take two thousand years to ask a question and receive an answer. A superior civilization would load its signal beam with vast amounts of information. A highly advanced civilization, having triumphed over hunger, disease and war, would naturally turn its energies into the search for other worlds. However, a highly advanced civilization might take another direction." Here his voice so grated with censoriousness and reproach that it woke two senators who were dozing. "A highly advanced civilization might well destroy itself with luxury, alcoholism, sexual license, sloth, greed and corruption. I feel that our own civilization is seriously threatened by biological and mental degeneration.

"But to get back to your original question." He used the smile this time to indicate a change of scenery; they were in another part of the forest. "The earth-moon system extends its influence for a considerable distance into space. The earth's gravity, magnetism and reflected radiation have no appreciable influence. At the climax of the sunspot cycle the sun erupts, putting clouds of gas into space. Magnetic storms of great violence usually break out on earth a day or so later. But the nature of interplanetary space is absolutely unknown. We know nothing about the shape, composition and magnetic characteristics of the clouds from the sun. We don't even know whether they follow a spiraling or a direct path. Mapping the solar system is virtually impossible because of the uncertainty as to the precise distance between the planets and the sun."

"Dr. Cameron?" Another senator had been recognized.

"Yes."

"We have some sworn testimony here on the subject of what some of your colleagues have described as an ungovernable temper. Dr. Pewters testified that on August 14th, during a discussion of the feasibility of moon travel, you tore down the Venetian blinds in his office and stamped on them." Cameron smiled indulgently. "Hugh Tompkins, an enlisted man and a driver from the motor pool, claims that when he was delayed, through no fault of his own, in reaching your office, you slapped him several times in the face, ripped the buttons off his uniform and used obscene language. Miss Helen Eckert, a stewardess for Pan American Airlines, states that when your flight from Europe was forced to land in Chicago rather than in New York you created such a disturbance that you seriously threatened the safety of the flight. Dr. Winslow Turner states that during a symposium on interstellar travel you threw a heavy glass ashtray at him, cutting his face severely. There is a deposition here, from the doctor who stitched up the cut."

"I plead guilty to all these offenses," the doctor said charmingly.

"Dr. Cameron?" asked another senator.

"Yes."

"Critics of your administration at Talifer state that you have neither terminated, suspended nor reduced experiments that have so far cost the government six hundred million dollars and that appear to be fruitless. They state that a total of four hundred and seventeen million has been spent on abortive missiles and another fifty-six million on inoperative tracking experiments. They state that your administration has been characterized by mismanagement, waste and duplication."

"I don't, in this instance, know what you mean by fruitless, abortive and inoperative, Senator," Cameron said. "Talifer is an experimental station and our work cannot be reduced to linear mathematics. All my decisions, viewed in the full light of all factors, seem to me to have been proper at the time and I assume full responsibility for them all."

"Dr. Cameron?" The next senator to be recognized was a stout man and seemed oddly shy for a politician.

"Yes."

"My question is perhaps not germane, it involves my constituents, indeed it involves their well-being, their health, but as you know the microbes that breed in missile fuel have been traced to an outbreak of respiratory disease in the vicinity of Talifer."

"I beg your pardon, Senator, but there is absolutely no scientific proof tracing these microbes to the unfortunate outbreak of respiratory disease. No scientific proof at all. We do know that microbes breed in the fuel—a fungus of the genus Loremendrum that produces airborne spores and special mutants. These are no more significant than the microbes that breed in gasoline, kerosene and jet fuel. In volumes so large a concentration of contaminants can quickly become a troublesome amount of residue."

"Dr. Cameron?" One saw this time an old man, slim and with the extraordinary pallor of an uncommonly long life span. Indeed, he seemed more dead than alive. At a little distance his shaking hands appeared to be bone. He wore a piped vest and a well-cut suit and had the stance of a dandy, a dandy's air of self-esteem. His nose was enormous and purple and hooked to the bridge was a pince-nez from which depended a long, black ribbon. His voice was not feeble but he spoke with that helplessness before emotion of the very old and now and then dried, with a broad linen handkerchief, a trickle of saliva that ran down his chin.

"Yes," the doctor said.

"I was born in a small town, Dr. Cameron," the old man said. "I think the difference between this noisy and public world in which we now live and the world I remember is quite real, quite real." There was an embarrassing pause as he seemed to wait for his heart to pump enough blood for his brain to carry on. "Men of my age, I know, are inclined to think sentimentally of the past and yet even after discounting these deplorable sentiments I think I can find much in the past that is genuinely praiseworthy. However . . ." He seemed again to have forgotten what he planned to say; seemed again to be waiting for the blood to rise. "However, I have lived through five wars, all of them bloody, crushing, costly and unjust, and I think inescapable, but in spite of this evidence of man's inability to live peacefully with his kind I do hope that the world, with all its manifest imperfections, will be preserved." He dried his cheeks with his handkerchief. "I am told that you are famous, that you are great, that you are esteemed and honored everywhere and I respect your honors unequivocally but at the same time I find in your thinking some narrowness, some unwillingness, I should say, to acknowledge those simple ties that bind us to one another and to the gardens of the earth." He dried his tears again and his old shoulders shook with a sob. "We possess Promethean powers but don't we lack the awe, the humility, that primitive man brought to the sacred fire? Isn't this a time for uncommon awe, supreme humility? If I should have to make some final statement, and I shall very soon for I am nearing the end of my journey, it would be in the nature of a thanksgiving for stout-hearted friends, lovely women, blue skies, the bread and wine of life. Please don't destroy the earth, Dr. Cameron," he sobbed. "Oh, please, please don't destroy the earth."

Cameron courteously overlooked this outburst and the questioning went on.

"Is it true, Dr. Cameron, that you believe in the inevitability of hydrogen warfare?"

"Yes."

"Would you give us an estimate of the number of survivors?"

"I'm sorry, but I can't. It would be the roughest guesswork. I think there will be a substantial number of survivors."

"In the case of reverses, Dr. Cameron, would you be in favor of destroying the planet?"

"Yes," he said. "Yes, I would. If we cannot survive, then we are entitled to destroy the planet."

"Who would decide that we had reached the ultimate point of survival?"

"I do not know."

The old man, having dried his tears, was up on his feet again. "Dr. Cameron, Dr. Cameron," he asked, "don't you think that there might be some bond of warmth amongst the peoples of the earth that has been underestimated?"

"Some what?" Cameron was not discourteous, but he was dry.

"Some bond of human warmth," the old man said.

"Men and women," the doctor said, "are chemical entities,

easily assessable, easily altered by the artificial increase or elimination of chromosomal structures, much more predictable, much more malleable, than some plant life and in many cases much less interesting."

"Is it true, Dr. Cameron," the old man went on, "that your reading is confined to *Western Romances?*"

"I think I read as much as most men of my generation," the doctor replied. "I sometimes go to the movies. I watch television."

"But isn't it true, Dr. Cameron," the old man asked, "that the humanities have not been a part of your education?"

"You are talking to a musician," the doctor said.

"Did I understand you to say that you're a musician?"

"Yes, Senator. I am a violinist. You seem to have suggested that my lack of familiarity in the humanities would account for my cool-headedness about the demolition of the planet. This is not true. I love music and music is surely one of the most exalted of the arts."

"Did I understand you to say that you play the violin?"

"Yes, Senator, I play the violin."

He opened the violin case, took out an instrument, which he rosined and tuned, and played a Bach air. It was a simple piece of beginner's music and he played it no better than any child but when he finished there was a round of applause. He put the violin away.

"Thank you, Dr. Cameron, thank you." It was the old man who was once more on his feet. "Your music was charming and reminded me of a reverie I often enjoy when some man from another planet who has seen our earth says to his friends: 'Come, come, let us rush to the earth. It is shaped like an egg, covered with fertile seas and continents, warmed and lighted by the sun. It has churches of indescribable beauty raised to gods that have never been seen, cities whose distant roofs and smokestacks will make your heart leap, auditoriums in which people listen to music of the most serious import and thousands of museums where man's drive to celebrate life is recorded and preserved. Oh, let us rush to see this world! They have invented musical instruments to stir the finest aspirations. They have invented games to catch the hearts of the young. They have invented ceremonies to exalt the love of men and women. Oh, let us rush to see this world!" He sat down.

"Dr. Cameron?" It was the voice of a senator who had just come in. "You have a son?"

"I had a son," the doctor said. There was a splendid edge to his voice.

"You mean to say that your son is dead?"

"My son is in a hospital. He is an incurable invalid."

"What is the nature of his illness?"

"He is suffering from a glandular deficiency."

"What is the name of the hospital?"

"I don't recall."

"Is it the Pennsylvania State Hospital for the Insane?"

The doctor colored, he seemed touched. He was on the defensive for a moment. Then he rallied.

"I don't recall."

"In discussing your son's illness has the subject of your treatment of him ever arisen?"

"All the discussions of my son's illness," the doctor said forcefully, "have unfortunately been confined to psychiatrists. These discussions are not sympathetic to me because psychiatry is not a science. My son is suffering from a glandular deficiency and no idle investigation of his past life will alter this fact."

"Do you recall an incident when your son was four years old and you punished him with a cane?"

"I don't recall any specific incident. I probably punished the boy."

"You admit to punishing the boy?"

"Of course. My life is highly disciplined. I cannot tolerate a hint of disobedience or unreliability in my organization, my associates or myself. My life, my work, involving the security of the planet, would have been impossible if I had relaxed this point of view."

"Is it true that you beat him so cruelly with a cane that he had to be taken to the hospital and kept there for two weeks?"

"As I have said, my life is highly disciplined. If I should relax my disciplines I would expect to be punished. I treat those around me in the same way."

He replied with dignity but the damage had been done.

"Dr. Cameron," the senator asked.

"Yes, sir."

"Do you ever remember employing a housekeeper named Mildred Henning?"

"That's a difficult question." He put a hand to his eyes. "I may have employed this woman."

"Mrs. Henning, will you please come in."

An old, white-haired woman dressed in mourning came through the door and when the formalities of recognition had been established she was asked to testify. Her voice was cracked and faint. "I worked for him six years in California," she said, "and toward the end I just stayed on to try and protect the boy, Philip. He was always after him. Sometimes it seemed like he wanted to kill him."

"Mrs. Henning, will you please describe the incident you mentioned to us earlier."

"Yes. I have the dates here. I had to call the county health officer and so I have the dates. It was the nineteenth of May. He, the doctor, left some change, some silver, on his bureau and the boy helped himself to a twenty-five-cent piece. You couldn't blame him. He never had a penny for himself. When the doctor came home that night he counted his money, he was very methodical. When he seen that he was short some he asked the boy if he took it. Well, he was a good, honest boy and he owned right up to it. So then the doctor took him to his room, the boy had a room at the back of the house and there was a closet and he told him to go into the closet. Then he went into the bathroom and got him a glass of water and he gave him the water and then he locked the closet door. This was about quarter to seven. I didn't say anything because I wanted to help the boy and I knew if I opened my big mouth it would only make things worse for the boy. So I served the doctor his dinner with a straight face and then I listened and I waited but I didn't go near the closet where the poor boy was locked in the dark. So then I went to the closet in my bare feet and I whispered to him but he was crying so, he was so miserable that he couldn't do anything but sob and I told him not to worry, that I was going to lie down on the floor by the closet and stay all night and I did. I lay there until dawn and then I whispered good-bye to him and I went down and cooked the breakfast. Well, the doctor went to the site at eight and then I tried to unlock the door but it was a good strong lock and none of the keys in the house would open it and still the poor boy was crying so that he couldn't speak hardly and he had drunk his water and had nothing to eat and there was no way of getting any water or food in to him. So when my housework was done I got a chair and sat by the door and talked with him until half-past six when the doctor come home and I thought he'd let the boy out then but he didn't go near the back of the house and ate his supper just as if nothing was wrong. Well, then I waited, I waited until he started to get ready for bed and then I called the police. He told me to get out of the house, he told me I was fired and when the police come he tried to get them to throw me out but I got the policeman to open the closet and the poor little fellow—oh, he was so sick—come out but I had to go although it broke my heart to leave him alone and I never saw the doctor again until today."

"Do you recall this incident, Dr. Cameron?"

"Do you suppose, with my responsibilities, that I can afford to entertain such recollections?"

"You don't recall punishing the boy?"

"If I punished him I only meant to teach him right from wrong." His voice still had its edge, still soared, but he took no one with him.

"You don't recall locking your son in a closet for two days with nothing to eat or drink?"

"I gave him water."

"Then you do recall the incident?"

"I only wanted to teach him right from wrong."

"Do you visit your son?"

"From time to time." Something was carrying him on, some energy. He smiled.

"Do you remember the last time you visited him?"

"I can't recall."

"Would it have been ten years ago?"

"I can't recall."

"Would you recognize your son?"

"Of course."

"Daddy, Daddy."

The man who spoke from the open door seemed older than his father. His hair was white; his face was swollen. He was crying and he crossed the hearing room, knelt where his father sat, awkwardly for he was not a child, and put his head on the doctor's knee. "Daddy," he cried, "oh, Daddy. It's raining."

"Yes, dear." It was the most eloquent thing he had said. He no longer saw the hearing room or his persecutors. He seemed immersed in some human, some intensely human balance of love and misgiving as if the feelings were a storm with a circumference and an eye and he was in the stillness of the eye. "It's raining, Daddy," the man said. "Stay with me. Don't go out in the rain. Stay with me just once. They tell me you've hurt me but I don't believe them. I love you, Daddy. I'll always love you, Daddy. I write you all the time, Daddy, but you never answer my letters. Why don't you answer my letters, Daddy? Why don't you ever answer my letters?"

"I don't answer your letters because I'm ashamed of them," the doctor said hoarsely but not as if he spoke to someone childish or insane but to an equal, his son. "I send you everything you need. I sent you some nice stationery but you write me on wrapping paper, you write me on laundry lists, you even write me on toilet paper." His voice rose in anger and rang off the marble walls. "How in hell do you expect me to answer letters when you write them on toilet paper? I'm ashamed to receive them, I'm ashamed to see them. They remind me of everything in life I detest."

"Daddy, Daddy," the man cried.

"We'll go now, Philip. We have to go." There was an attendant with him. The attendant took his patient by the arm.

"No, I want to stay with Daddy. It's raining and I want to stay with Daddy."

"Come along, Philip."

"Daddy, Daddy," he cried, all the way to the door, and when it closed he could still be heard as Mrs. Henning must have heard his voice in the closet so many years ago.

"I move," the old man said, "that we propose, if that lies within our power, a suspension of Dr. Cameron's security clearance." The proposal seemed to be within their power. The motion was passed and the meeting was adjourned. Cameron remained in the witness chair and Coverly went out with the others.

23

Emile and Melissa planned to meet in Boston. Melissa told Moses that she had to go north to see her aunt. Her aunt was in Florida but Moses didn't question her explanation.

She and Emile flew in separate planes. He arrived an hour later than she, and went to her room, where they spent the afternoon. Later they went out for a walk. It was very cold, and, looking at the façades and campaniles of Copley Square, she was moved by the thought that Boston had once thought itself the sister city of Florence, that vale of flowers. The wind scored her face. He stopped to look at a ring in a jeweler's window. It was a man's ring, a star sapphire set in gold. The ring did not interest her but it seemed to hold him. She shook with the cold while he admired the stone. "I wonder how much it costs. I'm going in and ask."

"Don't, Emile," she said. "I'm frozen. And anyhow, those things are always terribly expensive."

"I'll just ask. It won't take a minute."

She waited for him in the shelter of the door. "Eight hundred dollars!" he exclaimed when he came out. "Think of that. Eight hundred dollars."

"I told you it would be expensive."

"Eight hundred dollars. But it was pretty, though, wasn't it? And I suppose if you needed money you could always sell it. I mean, they must fix the price on things like that, don't you think? It would be sort of like an investment. You know, if I had eight hundred dollars I might buy a ring like that. I just might. People when they saw the ring, they would always know that you were worth eight hundred dollars. Waiters. Like that. I mean they would respect you when you were wearing a ring like that."

It seemed to her that he was deliberately debasing their relationship and forcing her into the humiliating position of buying him the ring, but she was mistaken; the idea had never occurred to him.

"Do you want me to buy you the ring, Emile?"

"Oh, no, I wasn't thinking about that. It just caught my eye. You know how things catch your eye."

"I'll buy it for you."

"No, no, forget about it."

They had dinner in a restaurant and went to a movie. Walking back to the hotel he bought a newspaper, and he sat reading it in her room while she undressed and brushed her hair. "I'm hungry," he said suddenly. His tone was petulant. "At home I get a bowl of cornflakes or a sandwich, something before I go to bed." He stood up, put his hands on his stomach and shouted, "I'm hungry. I just don't get enough to eat in these restaurants. I'm still growing. I have to have three big meals a day and sometimes something in between!"

"Well, why don't you go down and get something to eat?"

"Well."

"Do you need money?"

"Sort of."

"Here," she said. "Here's some money. Go down and get some supper."

He went out, but he didn't return. At midnight she locked the door and went to sleep. In the morning she dressed, went to the jeweler's and bought the ring. "Oh, I remember you," the clerk said, "I saw you last night. I saw you standing outside the door when your son came in to ask the price." It was a blow, and she supposed she could be seen flinching. She thought that perhaps the winter dark and the pale light in the street had made her seem old. "You're a very generous mother," the clerk said when he took her check and passed her the box. She called Emile's room and when he came down she gave him the ring. His pleasure and gratitude were not, she thought, mercenary and crass but only a natural response to the ancient tokens of love, the immemorial power of stones and fine gold. It was a foggy afternoon, all the planes were grounded, and they went back on the train, sitting in different cars.

He sat by the window, watching the landscape. Somewhere south of Boston the train passed a suburban tract of houses. They were new, and although the architects and the gardeners had rung a few changes here and there, the effect was monotonous. What interested him was that rising in the center of the development was a large, ugly, loaf-shaped and colorless escarpment of granite. The roads must circumvent it expensively. Its sides were too steep to hold the foundations of a house. It seemed, in its uselessness, triumphantly obdurate and perverse. It was the only form on the landscape that had not succumbed to change. It could not be dynamited. It could not be quarried and carried away piecemeal. It was useless, and it was invincible. Some boys his age were climbing the steep face, and he guessed this was their last refuge.

It was late and it was getting cold, and he could remember the sense of the season and the hour when it was time to leave off playing and go home to study. Near where he lived there was a similar rock, and he had climbed it on winter afternoons, to smoke cigarettes and talk with his friends about the future.

He could remember grasping for handholds on the steep face, and how the rough stone pulled at his best school clothes, but what he remembered most clearly was how once his feet were on the ground, he had a sense of awakening to a whole new life, the arrival at a new state of consciousness, as clearly unlike his past as sleep is unlike waking. Standing at the foot of the cliff at that hour and season—about to go home and study but not yet on the path—he would stare at the yards and the trees and the lighted houses with a galvanic sense of discovery. How forceful and interesting the world had seemed in the early winter light! How new it all seemed! He must have been familiar with every window, roof, tree and landmark in the place, but he felt as if he were seeing it all for the first time.

How old he had grown since then.

They met ten days or two weeks later, in a New York hotel. She was there first and ordered some whisky and roast-beef sandwiches. When he came in, she poured herself a drink and made one for him, and he ate both the sandwiches she had ordered. She was wearing a bracelet, made of silver bells, that she had bought long ago in Casablanca. She had been given a Mediterranean cruise as a Christmas present by a rich elderly cousin, and in her travels she had never been able to escape a genuine and oppressive sense of gratitude to the old lady. When she saw Lisbon she thought, Oh, Cousin Martha, I wish you could see Lisbon! When she saw Rhodes she thought, Oh, Cousin Martha, I wish you could see Rhodes! Standing in the Casbah at dusk she thought, Oh, Cousin Martha, I wish you could see how purple the skies are above Africa! Remembering this she gave the silver bells a shake.

"Do you have to wear that bracelet?" he asked.

"Of course not," she said.

"I hate that kind of junky stuff," he said. "You've got lots of nice jewelry—those sapphires. I don't see why you want to wear junk. Those bells are driving me crazy. Every time you move they jingle. They get on my nerves."

"I'm sorry, darling," she said. She took off the bracelet. He seemed ashamed or confused by his harshness; he had never before been harsh or callous with her.

"Sometimes I wonder why it happened to me like this," he said. "I mean, I couldn't have had anything better, I know. You're beautiful and you're fascinating—you're the most fascinating woman I ever saw—but sometimes I wonder—wondered—why it should happen to me this way. I mean, some fellows, right away they get a pretty young girl, she lives next door, their folks are friendly, they go to the same schools, the same dances, they go dancing together, they fall in love and get married. But I guess that's not for poor people. No pretty girls live next door to me. There aren't any pretty girls on my street. Oh, I'm glad it happened to me the way it did, but I can't stop wondering what it would have been like some other way. I mean like in Nantucket that weekend. That was the big football weekend, and I was thinking, there we were, all alone in that gloomy old house—that was a real gloomy place, rainy and everything—while some fellows were driving in convertibles to the football game."

"I must seem terribly old."

"Oh, no. No, you don't. It isn't that. . . . Only once. That was in Nantucket, too. It was raining in the night. It began to rain and you got up to shut the window."

"And I seemed terribly old?"

"Just for a minute. . . . Not really. But you see, you're used to comfort, you're different. Two cars, plenty of clothes. I'm just a poor kid."

"Does it matter?"

"Oh, I know you think it doesn't, but it does. When you go into a restaurant you never look at the prices. Now, your husband, he can buy you all these things. He can buy you anything you want, he's loaded, but I'm just a poor kid. I guess I'm sort of a lone wolf. I guess most poor people are. I'll never live in a house like yours. I'll never get to join a country club. I'll never have a place at the beach. And I'm still hungry," he said, looking at the empty sandwich plate. "I'm still growing, you know. I have to have lunch. I don't want to seem ungrateful or anything but I'm hungry."

"You go down to the dining room, darling," she said, "and get some lunch. Here's five dollars." She kissed him and then as soon as he was gone she left the hotel herself.

24

She wandered around the streets—she had no place to go—wondering what had been the first in the chain of events that had brought her to where she was. The barking of a dog, the dream of a castle or her boredom at Mrs. Wishing's dance. She went home, and regard this lovely woman then, getting off the train in Proxmire Manor. See what she does. See what happens to her.

She wears a mink coat and no hat. Her car is a convertible. She drives up the hill to her house, whose whiteness seems to authenticate her purity. How could anyone who lives in such a decorous environment be sinful? How could anyone who has so much Hepplewhite—so much Hepplewhite in good condition—be shaken by unruly lusts? She embraces her only son with tears in her eyes. This love for the boy seems to be one more thing to be crowded into her soul. Alone in her bedroom she doubled over with need and groaned like a bitch in rut. He seemed—his phantom—to cross the room and while she knew the plainness of his mind his skin seemed to shine; he seemed to be some golden Adam. She wanted to forget him. She wanted absolution. She had taken a lover, but was this so revolutionary? She had perhaps been mistaken in her choice, but wasn't this, in the history of things, as common as rain? She thought briefly of confessing to Moses but she knew his pride well enough to know that he would fire her out of the house. She felt herself gored. She had hoped to be a natural woman, sensual but unromantic, able to take a lover cheerfully and to leave him cheerfully when the time came. What had been revealed to her was the force of guilt and lust within her own disposition. She had transgressed the canons of a decorous society and she seemed impaled on the decorum she despised. The pain was unbearable and she went downstairs and poured herself a drink. She would have been ashamed, that early in the day, to ask the cook for ice and she watered the whisky in the bathroom and drank it there.

The drink made her feel better. She quickly had another. She was not able to exorcise the image of Emile but she was able, slowly, and with the help of the whisky, to put the image in a different light. He came toward her with his arms out and drew her down but now he seemed evil, he seemed to intend to debase and destroy her. She had been innocent, she had been wronged! That was it. The comfort of attributing evil to him was enormous. He had preyed on her innocence! But now, remembering the trip to Nantucket when she had received from him only the most heartening and gentle lasciviousness, could she claim to be innocent, to have been wronged? The comfort of absolution vanished and she drank some more whisky. By the time Moses came home she was quite drunk.

Moses said nothing. He thought she must have received some bad news. She seemed drowsy, she dropped a lighted cigarette on the rug and going in to dinner she stumbled and nearly fell. When Moses went out to put the cars in the garage she went to the bar and drank some whisky from a bottle. As drunk as she was she could not sleep. Moses did not touch her but as he lay beside her she thought that a small scar in the hair on Emile's belly was more precious to her than the enormousness of all of Moses' love. When Moses went to sleep she went downstairs and poured herself more whisky. She drank until three o'clock but when she went to bed the image of Emile, her golden Adam, was still vivid. To distract herself she planned the renovation of her kitchen. She removed the old range, refrigerator, dishwasher and sink, chose a new linoleum, a new garbage disposal unit, a new color scheme, a new means of lighting. Was this some foolishness of hers or of her time that, caught in the throes of a hopeless love, the only peace of mind that she could find was in imagining new stoves and linoleum?

She went to the doctor for an examination the next afternoon. She stretched out on the examination table, wearing a slip. The room was uncomfortably warm. The doctor touched her, she thought, with a gentleness that was not clinical, although this might, she knew, be the summit of her confused feelings, distorted by lewd dreams, drunkenness and a nearly sleepless night. As he handled her breasts she thought she saw in his face the undisguisable sadness of desire. She turned her face away but now her breathing was deep and tortured and her accumulated frustrations, her sorrow for Moses and her lust for Emile threatened to overwhelm her. What could she do? Discuss the weather? Criticize the Zoning Board? Evoke what seemed to her then to be the fragile and dishonest chain of circumstances that kept them from ruin? He seemed to linger, lasciviously, over the examination and she felt the bonds of her common sense give one by one until her feelings were wild. She reached up and caressed the back of his neck and he made no move to discourage her. When she heard him fumbling with his clothing she closed her eyes. The moment was explosive and instantaneous. She nearly lost consciousness. While he was dressing the telephone rang. "Yes, yes," he said, "but as you know, Ethel, we don't expect her to live through the day." Melissa dressed and put on her furs. "When can I see you again?" the doctor asked. She didn't reply. Six or seven patients were waiting in the front room. One of them, an old man, was groaning in pain. She was in great pain herself, a keener pain, she thought, because his suffering was blameless. She stepped out into the street, into the afternoon. The parking meters ticked. Chopped meat and bacon were on sale. A fountain splashed in the public park. She smiled and waved to a friend who passed in a car. The consummate skill with which she could appear respectable was crushing and she detested impostors. Here was the light of late afternoon—the store fronts seemed lit with fire—and she seemed, by her misery, shut away from the light.

Was she sick? It was the charitable judgment, she knew, that the street and its people would pass on her and she rebelled against it bitterly for if she was sick so was Moses, so was Emile, so was the doctor, so was mankind. The world, the village, would forgive her her sins if she would go to Dr. Herzog, whom she had last seen dancing with a fat woman in a red dress, and unburden herself three times a week for a year or two of her memories and confusions. But wasn't it her detestation of bigotry and anesthesia that had gotten her into trouble, her loathing of mental, sexual and spiritual hygiene? She could not believe that her sorrows might be whitewashed as madness. This was her body, this was her soul, these were her needs.

Her little son came to meet her when she entered the house and she took him most tenderly in her arms. When he had gone back in the kitchen she poured herself a drink in the bathroom to blunt the pain. She then telephoned her minister and asked if she could see him at once. His wife, Mrs. Bascom, answered the telephone and kindly invited Melissa to come. Mrs. Bascom, smelling pleasantly of perfume and sherry, let her into the rectory. She would have spent the afternoon playing bridge. It would be sentimental of her, Melissa knew, to long for a life that centered on bridge parties, but the woman's simplicity and good cheer excited in Melissa a dreadful yearning. Mrs. Bascom's containment seemed as substantial as a well-built house, its windows shining with light, while Melissa felt herself to be cruelly exposed to every inclemency. Mrs. Bascom led her into a parlor where the rector was kneeling by an open fireplace, lighting some paper and kindling with a match. "Good afternoon," he said, "good afternoon, Mrs. Wapshot." For some reason he pronounced her name "Wapshirt." He was a portly man, his hair stained a discouraging gray like the last snows of winter and with a strong, plain face. "I thought we'd have a little fire," he said. "There's nothing like a fire, is there, to stimulate conversation? Sit down, do sit down. I have a confession to make." She flinched at the word. "Mrs. Bascom's bridge club, one of her *three* bridge clubs, met this afternoon and I decided to give myself a vacation and spent the whole afternoon watching television. Now I know a lot of people disapprove of television but during my, shall we say, dissipation this afternoon I saw some very interesting playlets and some splendid acting, some splendid performances. I wouldn't be at all surprised to discover that the standards of acting on television today are a great deal higher than those we find in the theater. I saw one very interesting playlet about a woman who was tempted—tempted, I say, there was nothing at all unsavory—by the monotony of her middle-class life to abandon her family in favor of a business enterprise. She had a most unpleasant mother-in-law. Not really unpleasant, I suppose, but a woman, you might say, whose character had been formed by a series of unfortunate circumstances. She was a possessive woman. She felt that the heroine neglected her husband. Well, the mother-in-law was wealthy and they had every reason to expect a substantial inheritance when she passed away. They took a picnic to a lake—oh, it was very well done—and during a storm the mother-in-law drowned. The next scene was in the lawyer's office where the will was read and where they discovered to their astonishment that they had been cut off with a single dollar. Well, the wife, rather than being disappointed, discovered new sources of strength in herself at this turn of events and was able to rededicate herself—to undergird her dedication, so to speak—to her family once more. It was all very revealing and it seems to me that if we looked at television oftener and saw the sorrows and the problems of others we might be less selfish, less egotistical, less likely to be overwhelmed by our own little problems."

Melissa had come to him for compassion but she felt then that she might better have asked for compassion from a barn door or a stone. For a moment his stupidity, his vulgarity, seemed inviolable. But if he had no compassion for her, wasn't it then her responsibility to extend some compassion to him, to try and understand, to try at least to tolerate the image of a stout and simple man applauding the asininities on television? What touched her, as he leaned toward the fire, was the antiquity of his devotions. No runner would ever come to his door with the news that the head of the vestry had been martyred by the local police and had she used the name of Jesus Christ, out of its liturgical context, she felt that he would have been terribly embarrassed. He was not to blame, he had not chosen this moment of history, he was not alone in having been overwhelmed at the task of giving the passion of Our Lord ardor and reality. He had failed, he seemed sitting by his fire to be a failure as she was and to deserve, like any other failure, compassion. She felt how passionately he would have liked to avoid her troubles; to discuss the church fair, the World Series, the covered-dish supper, the high price of stained glass, the perfidy of Communism, the comfortableness of electric blankets, anything but her trouble.

"I have sinned," Melissa said. "I have sinned and the memory is grievous, the burden is intolerable."

"How have you sinned?"

"I have committed fornication with a boy. He is not twenty-one."

"Has this happened often?"

"Many times."

"And with others?"

"With one other but I feel that I can't trust myself."

He shielded his eyes with his hands and she saw that he was shocked and disgusted. "In matters like this," he said, his eyes still shielded, "I work with Dr. Herzog. I can give you his telephone number or I'll be happy to call him myself and make an appointment."

"I will not go to Dr. Herzog," Melissa said, weeping. "I cannot."

She left the rectory and at home telephoned Narobi's. The cook had ordered the groceries and she asked for a case of quinine water, a bunch of water cress and a box of peppercorns. "Your cook had a case of quinine water delivered this morning," Mr. Narobi said. He was unpleasant. "Yes, I know," Melissa said. "We're having guests." Emile came a little while later.

"I'm sorry I left you in New York," Melissa said.

"That's all right." He laughed. "I was just hungry."

"I want to see you."

"Sure," he said. "Where?"

"I don't know."

"Well, there's this shack," he said. "Some of the fellows and me have this shack down by the cove. I'll check in at the store and meet you there in half an hour."

"All right."

"You go over the railroad bridge," he said, "down to the cove. There's a dirt road there by the dump. I'll get there early and make sure no one's around."

She hardly saw the place beyond the wall near where she lay. "You know," he said, "for lunch I had the Manhattan clam chowder and then a hot roast-beef sandwich with two vegetables and pie with ice cream and I'm still hungry."

25

Emile and Mrs. Cranmer lived on the second floor of a two-family frame house. The house was painted a dark green with white trim—the green turned black in the rain and was one of a species, gregarious in that one seldom finds them alone. They appear in the suburbs of Montreal, reappear across the border in Northern lumber and mill towns, flourish in Boston, Baltimore, Cleveland and Chicago and go underground briefly in the wheat states to appear again in the depressed neighborhoods of Sioux City, Wichita and Kansas City, forming an irregular and mighty chain of quasi-nomadic domiciles that reaches across the entire continent.

On her walk home in the evening from Barnum's Mrs. Cranmer passed the house that had been hers when Mr. Cranmer was alive. It was a large brick and stucco house. Twelve rooms! The dimensions and conveniences of the place returned to her like an incantation. The house had been sold by the bank to an

Italian family named Tomasi. In spite of her struggle to accept
the doctrines of equality that had been taught to her in school
she still felt some bitterness that people from another country,
people who had not yet learned the language and the customs
of the United States, could possess the house of someone who
was native born like herself. The economic facts were inescapable
and she knew them but this didn't cure her bitterness. The house
still seemed to be hers, still seemed in her custody, still reminded
her of the richness of her life with Mr. Cranmer. The Tomasis
spent most of their time in the kitchen and the front windows
were usually dark but this evening a fringed lamp in one of
the windows was lighted and beyond the lamp she could see,
hanging on the wall, the enlarged photographs of some foreigners, the men with mustaches and high collars and the women
in black. There was a powerful otherness for her in looking
into the lighted windows of a house where her life had been
centered. On she went in her comic-strip shoes.

The evening paper was in the mailbox. She usually looked
at this in the kitchen. The most sensational stories dealt with
the covert moral revolution that was being waged on men of
Emile's age. They robbed, they pillaged, they drank, they raped
and when they were locked up in jail they ripped out the plumb-
ing. She reasoned that their parents were to blame and she
sent up to heaven a completely sincere prayer of thanksgiving
over the fact that Emile was such a good boy. In her own youth
she had seen some wildness but the world had seemed more
commodious and forgiving. She had never been able to settle
on who was to blame. She feared that the world might have
changed too swiftly for her intelligence and her intuition. She
had no one to help her sift out the good from the evil. When
she had finished with the paper she usually went into her room
and unfastened those gallant bindings that signified that she
had known the love of a good man. She was never unready,
she was never slovenly. She put on clean slippers and a clean
cotton dress and then as a rule she cooked the supper. This

night she went directly into her bedroom, lay on her bed in the dark and cried.

Driving back from the shack Emile felt that he was discovering in himself a new vein of seriousness, a new aspect of maturity. The kitchen was lighted when he came in but his mother was not at the stove and then he heard her crying in her room. He knew at once why she cried but he was completely unprepared. His heart moved him at once into her dark room, where she looked more desolate, more than ever like a child, dumped by her misery onto the bed, utterly mystified and forsaken. He felt crushed with the force of her grief. "I just can't believe it," she sobbed. "Just can't believe it. I thought you were such a good boy, I thanked God night after night for your goodness and all the time right under my nose you were doing that. Mr. Narobi told me. He came to the store today."

"It isn't true, Mother. Whatever Mr. Narobi said isn't true."

She worked her face in the wet pillow like a child and he felt as if she were a child, his daughter, treated cruelly by some stranger.

"That's what I prayed you'd say, that's what I hoped you'd say but I can't believe anything any more. Mr. Narobi told me all about it and why should he tell me if it wasn't true? He couldn't make that all up."

"It isn't true, Mother."

"But why did he tell me all this then, why did he tell me all these lies? He said there's this woman you've been going off with. He said she's always calling the store when she doesn't need anything and that he knows what's going on."

"It isn't true."

"But why did he tell me these lies then? Perhaps he's jealous," she asked in a reckless hopefulness. "You know the year before last he asked me to marry him. Of course I'll never marry again, but he seemed cross when I said so." She sat up and dried her tears.

"Perhaps that's it."

"He came here one night when I was alone. He brought me a box of candy and asked me to marry him. When I said no he was angry, he said I'd be sorry. Do you think that's what he's trying to do? Make me sorry?"

"Yes, that must be it."

"Isn't that funny? To think that someone should want to do me harm. Isn't that funny? Don't people do the strangest things?"

She washed her face and began to cook supper and Emile went to his room, worried about the sapphire ring, hidden in a drawer. He would feel safer if it was in his pocket. He opened the drawer and was taking the ring out of the box when he turned and saw her standing in the doorway. "Give that to me," she said. "Give that to me, you devil. Whoever put the devil into you, who was it? Give me that ring. Is this how she paid you, you dirty, rotten snake? Don't think I'm going to cry over you. I cried my last true tears at your father's grave. I know what it was to be loved by a good man and nobody can take that away from me. You stay in your room until I tell you to come out."

Moses answered the door the next evening when Mrs. Cranmer rang. She was wearing a hat, gloves and so forth and he couldn't imagine what she wanted. She had no car and must have walked over from the bus stop. He thought at first that she had the wrong address. She might have been a cook or a seamstress, looking for work. To speak to him directly, as she did, seemed to drain her courage and self-esteem.

"You tell your wife to leave my son alone."

"I don't understand."

"You tell your wife to leave my son alone. I don't know how many other men she's after but if I catch her near my boy again I'll scratch her eyes out."

"I don't . . ." She had exhausted her strength and he closed the door calling: "Melissa, Melissa." Why didn't she answer? Why didn't she answer? He heard her climbing the stairs and he followed. The door stood open and she sat at her dressing table with her face in her hands. He felt the blood of murder

run in his veins and as, in desire, he sometimes seemed to feel
her body beneath his hands before he had touched her, now
he seemed to feel her throat, its cords and muscles, as he put
out her life. He was shaking. He came up behind her, put his
hands around her neck and when she screamed he strangled
the scream but then some fear of Hell rose in him and he threw
her onto the floor and went out.

26

What had happened; what had happened to Moses Wapshot?
He was the better-looking, the brighter, the more natural of
the two men and yet in his early thirties he had aged as if the
crises of his time had been much harsher on a simple and impetu-
ous nature like his than on Coverly, who had that long neck,
that disgusting habit of cracking his knuckles and who suffered
seizures of melancholy and petulance.

Moses arrived suddenly in Talifer one Saturday morning, un-
announced. He found his brother washing windows. A mythology
that would penetrate with some light the density of the relationship between brothers seems to stop with Cain and Abel and
perhaps this is as it should be. The utter delight with which
Coverly and Moses greeted one another was seasoned unself-
consciously with mayhem. Moses smiled scornfully at his brother's window-washing rags. Coverly noticed that Moses' face was
red and swollen. Moses carried a walking stick with a silver handle. As soon as he got into the house he unscrewed the handle
and poured himself a martini from the stock. "It holds a pint,"
he said calmly. "Wouldn't Father have liked one?" He drank
his gin that early in the day as if the memory of his father and
so many other stalwarts had exempted him, as a Wapshot, from
the problems of abstemiousness and self-discipline. "I'm on my
way to San Francisco," he explained. "I thought I'd drop in.

There's a plane out at five. Melissa and the boy are *fine*. They're just bully."

He said this boisterously and with force for like Coverly—like Melissa—he had developed an adroitness at believing that what had happened had not happened, that what was happening was not happening and that which might happen was impossible. The mystery of Honora was their first concern. Coverly had telephoned St. Botolphs but no one answered. His letters to Honora had been returned. Moses had felt that her letters about the holly tree might have concealed the fact that she was sick but how could this fit in with the fact that she had broken some law? Coverly might have shown his brother the computation center or let him see the gantry line through his binoculars but instead he drove Moses to the ruined farm and they walked there in the woods. It was a fine winter's day in that part of the world and Coverly brought to its brightness and space considerable moodiness. The orchard still bore some crooked fruit and the sound and fragrance of windfalls seemed to him as ancient a piece of the world as its oceans. Paradise must (he thought) have smelled of windfalls. A few dead leaves coursed along the wind, reminding Coverly of the energies that drive the seasons. Watching the leaves drawn down and along he felt in himself an arousal of aspiration and misgiving. Moses appeared to be concerned principally with his thirst. When they had walked for a little while he suggested that they find a liquor store. As they were going back to the car there seemed to be an abort on the gantry line. There was a loud explosion from that direction and then there were signs that an air alert had been sounded. No planes could be seen in the blue sky but they could be heard roaring like that most innocent of roarings when a sea shell is held by some old man to the ear of a child.

They went back to the car and drove to a liquor store in the outskirts but the place was shut. A sign hung in the glass window: "This store is closed so that our employees can be with their families." Now sporadic and senseless panic sometimes swept Talifer. A handful of men and women would lose their hopefulness and retire to their shelters to pray and get drunk; but this seemed no more significant to Coverly than the Adventists of his childhood who would now and then dress in sheets, climb Parson's Hill and wait for the resurrection of the dead and the life of the world to come. Total disaster seemed to be some part of the universal imagination. They drove on toward the shopping center and found a liquor store that was open. Moses said that he needed cash and the proprietor of the store, on Coverly's endorsement, cashed a check for a hundred dollars. When they got back to the house Moses filled up his walking stick and settled down for some serious drinking. At four Coverly drove his brother to the commercial airport and said good-by to him at the main entrance; a farewell that seemed to be for both of them a violent mixture of love and combativeness.

Three days later the liquor store called to say that Moses' check had bounced. Coverly stopped there and covered it with a check of his own. On Thursday a motel near the airport called. "I saw your name in the phone book," the stranger said, "and it's such a funny name I thought you might be related. There's a man out here named Moses Wapshot. He's been here since Saturday and just by counting the empties I would guess he's drinking about two quarts a day. He hasn't made a nuisance of himself or nothing but unless he's pouring the stuff down the sink he's heading for trouble. I thought you ought to know if he was a member of your family." Coverly said he would be right out and he drove to the motel but when he got there Moses had gone.

27

It is doubtful that Emile had ever loved Melissa, had ever experienced a genuine impulse of love for anyone but himself and the ghost of his father. He thought now and then of Melissa, always concluding that he was blameless; that whatever suffering she endured was no responsibility of his. He killed some time after he was fired from Narobi's and presently went to work at the new supermarket on the hill—the one with a steeple. He was employed nominally as a stock boy but when Mr. Freeley, the manager, took him on, he explained that he would have another mission. The market had then been open two months but business was poor and the housewives of the village, like indulged children, were capricious and sometimes ill-tempered from the lack in their lives of the tonic forces of longing and need. Mr. Freeley had seen them storm his doors on opening day and take away the fresh orchid corsage that was given to each customer, but when the flowers were all gone he had seen them return with something like heartlessness to their old friends, the Grand Union and the A & P. They swarmed like locusts, exhausting his below-cost specials and buying the rest of their groceries somewhere else. His market, he thought, was a thing of splendor. The broad glass doors opened at a beam of light onto a museum of victuals—galleries and galleries of canned goods, heaps of frozen poultry and, over by the fish department, a little lighthouse above a tank of sea water in which lobsters swam. The air was full of music and soft lights. There were diversions for the children and delicacies for the gourmet but nobody—almost nobody—ever came his way.

The store was one of a chain and the capriciousness of the spoiled housewives had been calculated by the statisticians in the central office. The ladies were incapable of fidelity and could be counted upon, sooner or later, to find their idle way into Mr. Freeley's museum. One only had to wait and keep the place resplendent. But the ladies delayed longer than the statisticians had expected and Mr. Freeley was finally given an exploitation package. On Easter Eve a thousand plastic eggs were to be hidden in the grass of the village. All of them contained certificates redeemable at the store for a dozen country-fresh eggs. Twenty of them contained certificates redeemable for a two-ounce bottle of costly French perfume. Ten of them contained certificates redeemable for an outboard motor and five of them—golden ones—were good for a three-week, all-expense vacation for two at a luxury hotel in Madrid, Paris, London, Venice or Rome. The response was terrific and the store filled up with customers. They reasoned that the eggs would be hidden by someone who worked at the store and they intended to find out which clerk it was. "It has been our experience," Mr. Freeley read in the explanatory literature, "that there is among the housewives in any community a large number who will stop at nothing to ascertain the identity of the egg-hiders and the probable position of the eggs. This has led in some instances to an astonishing display of immorality." It was Emile that Mr. Freeley hired to hide the eggs. Had he checked with Narobi's he wouldn't have hired Emile at all but he thought the boy's face clear and even virtuous. He told Emile the details in his office. He had been given a chart explaining where the eggs were to be hidden. They were to be hidden between two and three on the morning of Easter. Emile would be paid above his salary a stipend of twenty-five dollars and in order to insure secrecy Mr. Freeley would not speak to him again until Easter Eve. In the meantime Emile would stamp cans.

The store closed at six on Easter Eve. The last potted lily had been sold, but some housewives still lingered in the museum galleries, trying to tempt from the stock boys the secret of the eggs. At quarter after six the doors were locked. At half-past six the lights were turned off and Mr. Freeley was alone in the office with the eggs. He took the chart out of the safe and studied it. A few minutes later Emile came up the stairs. Everyone else had gone home. Mr. Freeley showed him the treasure and gave him the chart. His plan was to store the eggs in the back of Emile's car. He would be waiting on the sidewalk in front of Emile's house at two in the morning and they would begin their mission from there. Before they took the crates of eggs down from Mr. Freeley's office they made a careful examination of the waste bins and empty cartons at the back of the store to make sure that no housewife had concealed herself there. The eggs filled the luggage compartment and back seat of Emile's car. It was dusk when they began their work and dark when they had finished. They shook hands in a pleasant atmosphere of conspiracy and parted. Emile drove home cautiously as if the eggs at his back were fragile as well as valuable. The power of felicity and excitement they contained seemed palpable. There was an old garage behind the house and he put the car in here and padlocked the door. He was excited and a little oppressed by the fear that something might go wrong. The secret was not out but neither was it perfectly concealed. He knew that there were at least ten people at the store who, through a process of elimination, had come to suspect that he might be in charge of the treasure and he had had to deal with their questioning.

Mrs. Cranmer, having decided that Melissa had preyed on her son's innocence, had resumed her peaceable life with Emile. In spite of her age and the sorrows she had borne Mrs. Cranmer was still able to engage herself in friendship as passionately as a schoolgirl. She was easily slighted and easily elated by the neglect or attention of her neighbors. She had recently made a new friend in Remsen Park—the low-cost development—and talked with her on the telephone much of the time. She was talking on the telephone when Emile came in. Emile read the paper while he waited for his mother to finish her conversation. Mr. Freeley's exploitation specialists had taken the back page of the paper and the copy was inflammatory. There were pictures of the five European cities and an assurance that all you had to do was to look in your grass in the morning and you would be on your way.

They ate supper in the kitchen. When the dishes were washed Mrs. Cranmer got back on the telephone. Now she was talking about the eggs and Emile guessed that many conversations in the village that night would be on this subject. It had not occurred to Mrs. Cranmer that her son might be chosen and he was grateful for this. After supper he watched television. At about nine o'clock he heard a dog barking. He went across the hall to his room and looked out of the window but there was no one by the garage. At half-past ten he went to bed.

Mr. Freeley felt very happy that evening. The store had begun to prosper and he felt that the trips to Madrid, Paris, London, Rome and Venice that would soon be hidden in the dewy grass were the result of his own generosity, his own abundant good nature. Kissing his wife in the kitchen he thought that she was as desirable as she had been when he married her many years ago; or if she was not that, she had at least kept abreast of the changes time and age had worked in him. He desired her ardently and happily and looked at the clock to see how long he must wait before they would be alone. There was a roast in the oven and she moved out of his embrace to baste it and then again to set the table, draw the baby's bath and pick up the toys, and as he watched her go about these necessary tasks he saw the wanness of fatigue come into her face and realized that by the time she had washed the dishes, ironed the pajamas, sung the lullabies and heard the prayers she might not have the strength to respond to his passionate caresses. This conflict in generative energies left him uncomfortable and after supper he took a walk.

The sky was dark and low but even if it rained, he thought, it would be better for his purposes than a bright moon. He walked out of his neighborhood into Parthenia and thought guiltily of how few eggs would be hidden here. Supermarkets and other changes had left the stores mostly deserted. Filth was written on the walls and in one of the store windows, beyond the FOR RENT sign, was a display of funeral wreaths made of dry moss and false boxwood. One of these was shaped like a valentine heart and had a banner that said "Mother and Father" draped across its ventricles. This was Water Street, the demesne of the hoods. He saw three hoods standing in a doorway ahead of him and thought they looked familiar.

A week earlier Mr. Freeley had gone to the Easter Assembly at the high school to hear his daughter sing. He had come in late and stood at the back of the auditorium near the door, waiting like any other parent for the appearance of his child. His daughter, although she had no special gifts that he knew of, had been chosen to sing a solo. It was unfortunate that he had come in too late to find a seat. Standing near him at the door was a group of local hoods, whose whispering and shuffling made it difficult for him to give all his attention to the children's singing. The hoods seemed uncommitted to the performance. They kept slipping in and out the door and he thought how uncommitted they were to anything. They did not play games, they did not study, they did not skate on the ice pond or dance in the gymnasium but they menacingly circled all these activities, always in some doorway or on some threshold, in and out of the light as they were this evening.

Then the pianist began to hammer out the music for his daughter's solo and he saw the girl step shyly from the ranks of the chorus to the front of the stage. At the same time one of the hoods left his shadowy position at the door and joined a girl who was standing in front of Mr. Freeley. They blocked the view of his daughter. He moved to the left and then to the right, but the hood and his girl were always in the way and he only had a glimpse of his child. He had a good view of the hood and his maneuvers with the girl. He saw him put an arm around her shoulders. He heard him whispering into her ear. Then to the music of "I Know That My Redeemer Liveth" he saw him slip his hand into the front of her dress. Mr. Freeley seized the boy and the girl roughly by the shoulders and thrust them apart, saying so loudly that his daughter looked out at the disturbance: "Cut it out or take it out. This is no place for that kind of thing." He was shaking with rage and to keep himself from hitting the youth in the face he walked out of the auditorium and onto the schoolhouse steps.

He lit a cigarette with difficulty. He was so deeply disturbed that he wondered if what was really bothering him was not fear for his daughter. He was sure that he had been enraged as a father and a citizen at the unsuitability of what he had just been a witness to during an Easter hymn in a building that belonged, at least in spirit, to the innocent. When his cigarette had burned down he went back into the auditorium. The hoods stood aside to let him pass and he thought he had never experienced such an emanation of naked hatred as came from them toward him.

The hoods in the doorway on Water Street had the same suspenseful attitudes, showed the same choice of half-lights, and he felt a revolting strangeness toward them as if they had not come from another class or neighborhood but had come hurtling down from an evil planet. As he approached them he saw they were passing around a whisky bottle. He could not reproach them for lawlessness and depravity. Lawlessness and depravity were their aspirations. He smelled whisky as he passed the doorway and then he was struck on the back of the head and instantly lost consciousness.

Emile's alarm woke him at half-past one. While he was shaving a gust of wind slammed the door of his room and woke his mother. Waked so suddenly she sounded heavy and her voice like the voice of a much older woman. "Emile. You sick?"

"No, Mum," he said. "It's all right."

"You sick? You in trouble, dear? Those frozen crab cakes— did they make you sick?"

"No, Mum," he said. "It's nothing."

"You sick?" she asked, still heavily, and then she cleared her voice and seemed at the same moment to clear her mind. "Emile!" she exclaimed. "It's the eggs."

"I have to go now, Mum," he said. "It's nothing serious. I'll be back before breakfast."

"Oh, it's the eggs, isn't it?"

He could hear the bed creak as she sat up and put her feet on the floor, but he got by the door of her room before she reached it and went down the stairs. "I'll be back before breakfast," he called. "I'll tell you about it then." He felt for the chart in his pocket and let himself out the front door.

The stars were shining. It was much too early in the year for there to be anything blooming but a few clumps of snowdrops and the only wild flowers were the speckled skunk cabbages in the hollow but there was in the air a soft fragrance of earth as fine as roses and he stopped to fill his lungs and his head with it. The world seemed fine in the street light and the starlight and young, too, even in its shabbiness, as if the fate of the place had only just begun to be told. The earth, covered lightly with leaves, moss, garlic grass and early clover, was waiting for his treasure.

When there was no sign of Mr. Freeley at quarter after two he began to worry. It was so still that he could have heard a car in the far distance and he heard nothing. He wanted help on his mission, he did not want to do it alone, but at twenty minutes past two he decided that he would have to. He unlocked the garage doors, which, poorly hung, scraped loudly in the gravel. He looked in the back seat. His hoard was safe. When he backed the old car out onto the road the only light burning in the neighborhood was in his mother's parlor. He was too excited to imagine the mischief she might be up to and she was up to plenty. She had her new friend in Remsen Park on the telephone. "Emile's just gone out to hide the eggs," she said. "He just left. I don't know but I've got a feeling he's going to hide them in the Delos Circle neighborhood. I mean wouldn't it be just like Mr. Freeley to give everything to those rich snobs and forget his friends in Remsen Park? Wouldn't it be just like him?"

In another two hours, Emile thought, as he shifted from reverse into low, his mission would be accomplished and, this close to success, he saw how heavily the responsibility had weighed on his mind. A light was burning in a house at the corner but it was a small, narrow window, closely curtained, and he guessed that it was a bathroom. As he watched the light went out. From the top of Turner Street near the golf links he could see all over the village—see how perfect and reassuring the darkness was and how deeply the place slept, and the thought of so many men, women, children and dogs wandering through their labyrinthine dreams made him smile. He stood at the headlights of his car, reading the instructions. Eight eggs at the corner of Delwood Avenue and Alberta Street, three eggs on Alberta Street, ten eggs at the junction of Delos Circle and Chestnut Lane.

The Hazzards lived at the corner of Delwood Avenue and Alberta Street. Mrs. Hazzard was awake. She had waked from a bad dream at about two and was sitting at the open window, smoking. She was thinking about the eggs—about those that contained warrants for travel—and wondering if any would be hidden on Alberta Street. She wanted to see Europe. There was more envy than longing in her feeling. It was not so much that she wanted to see the world as that she wanted to see what other people had seen. When she read in the paper that Venice was sinking into the sea and that the leaning tower of Pisa was due to collapse, what she felt was not sadness at the disappearance of these wonders but a sharp bitterness at the image of Venice vanishing beneath the waves before she, Laura Hazzard, had seen it. She also felt that she was singularly well equipped to appreciate the pleasures of travel. It was her kind of thing. When friends and relations returned from Europe with their photographs and souvenirs she listened to their accounts of travel with the feeling that her impressions would have been more vivid, her souvenirs and photographs would have been more beautiful and that she would have fitted more gracefully into a gondola. But there were some tender sentiments mixed with her envy. Travel was linked in her mind to the magnificence and pathos of love; it would be like a revelation of the affections. She had sensed, in love, a sky much deeper than the blue sky of the Northern Hemisphere; more spacious rooms and stairways, arches, domes, all the paraphernalia of the enormous past. She was thinking of this when she saw a car come around the corner and stop. She recognized Emile and watched him begin to hide his eggs in the grass. This whole sequence of events— the bad dream that waked her, her thoughts as she sat at the open window and the sudden arrival of the young man in the starlight—seemed to her marvelous and in her excitement she called down to him from the window.

Despair swept over Emile when he heard her voice. How, short of wringing her neck, could he undo the fact that she had seen him at his secret task? "Shhh," he said, looking up at the window, but she had gone and in a minute she opened the door and ran out barefoot and in her nightgown. "Oh, Emile, you know I think I was meant to find one," she said. "I couldn't sleep and I was just sitting at the window when you came along. I have to have one of the gold ones, Emile! Give me one of the gold ones."

'It's supposed to be a secret, Mrs. Hazzard," Emile whispered. "Nobody's supposed to know. You're not supposed to look for them until morning. You have to go back into your house now. You go on back to bed."

"What do you think I am, Emile?" she asked. "You think I'm a little girl or something? You give me a golden egg and I'll go back to bed but I won't move until you do."

"You'll spoil everything, Mrs. Hazzard. I won't hide any more eggs until you go back into your house."

"You give me a golden egg, you give me one of those golden eggs or I'll help myself."

Mrs. Hazzard's voice waked old Mrs. Kramer who lived next door. Instantly alert, she installed her teeth, stepped into her slippers and went to the window. She understood the meaning of the scene at once. She went to the telephone and called her daughter, Helen Pincher, who lived three blocks away on Millwood Street. Helen woke from a deep sleep and mistook the telephone for the alarm clock. She tried to stop the ringing, shook the clock and finally turned on the light before she realized that it was the telephone. "Helen, it's Mother," the old woman said. "They're hiding the Easter eggs. Right in front of my house. I can see them out of my window. Get over here!"

The ringing of the bell had not waked Mr. Pincher but the light and the last of the conversation did. He saw his wife put down the phone and run out of the room. For the last month or so Mr. Pincher had been alarmed by his wife's conduct. She had overdrawn the checking account three times, she had run out of gasoline three times in the same week, she had forgotten to wear stockings to the Gripsers' wedding, she had lost her snake bracelet and she had ruined his good leather hunting jacket by putting it into the washing machine. Each time she had said: "I must be going out of my mind." When he heard footsteps outside and looked out of the window and saw that she was running down the front walk in her nightgown he was convinced that she really had become irrational. He got into his bathrobe but he couldn't find any slippers and so he ran barefoot out of the house after her. She had a lead of a block or more and he called loudly: "Helen, Helen, come back, dear. Come home, dear." He woke the Barnstables, the Melchers, the Fitzroys and the DeHovens.

Emile got back into his car. Mrs. Hazzard tried to open the other door and get in but it was locked. He tried to start the car but he was nervous and the motor flooded. Then into the beam of his headlights came Helen Pincher, running. Her nightgown was transparent and the curlers in her hair looked like a crown. Her mother was hanging out of the window, urging her on. "That's them, Helen, there they are!" Behind her, her husband shouted: "Come back, darling, come back, sweetheart."

Emile got the car started just as Helen reached it and she put her head in at the window. "I want the one for Paris, Emile," she said.

Emile put the car into gear and as he began slowly to let out the clutch Mr. Pincher joined them shouting: "Stop that car, you damned fool. She's sick." Now in the beam of his headlights Emile saw the approach of a dozen or more women in nightgowns. They all appeared to be wearing crowns. He continued to move the car slowly forward but some of the women stood directly in his way and he had to stop twice to avoid harming them. During one of these stops Mrs. DeHoven let the air out of one of his rear tires.

Emile felt the car settle. He knew what had happened but he went on moving slowly. The deflated tire slumped against the shoe and he could not get up much speed but he thought he might outstrip his pursuers. Alberta Street at that point went steeply downhill for perhaps half a mile. On the left was a large tract of empty land. The owner (old Mrs. Kramer) was asking ten thousand an acre and the property hadn't moved. It had gone to deep grass and scrub wood and on every wild cherry and sumac tree there was nailed the name and telephone number of some real estate agent. Emile thought that if he got to Delos Circle he might be in the clear. He speeded up going downhill, but just as his headlights reached Delos Circle he saw the housewives of Remsen Park, thirty or forty of them, most of them wearing long robes and what appeared to be massive crowns. He swung the car sharply to the left, bumped over the curb and the sidewalk into the unsold house lots and drove straight to the far boundary of the property. He was trapped but he still had some time at his disposal. He cut the motor and the lights, ran around to the back and opened the luggage compartment and began to pitch the eggs off into the deep grass. He had a good wing and by heaving the eggs far away from him he was able to divert the advancing crowd. His arm got lame before long and then he began to take the egg crates and dump their contents into the grass. He disposed of all but one before the women reached him and he straightened up to see them, so like angels in their nightclothes, and hear their soft cries of longing and excitement. Then with a single egg in his pocket— a golden one—he cut back through the woods.

The pain of the blow that had stunned Mr. Freeley drew him back into consciousness. His head felt broken. He found himself lashed by wire to a post in a cellar. He shook with cold and saw that he had nothing on but his underpants. At first he thought he had lost his mind but the centralizing force of pain in his head gave a terrible vividness and reality to his circumstances. He was a big man, his body carpeted with the brindle hair of middle age. The wires that bound him cut deeply into his fleshy arms and his hands were numb. Suddenly he roared for help but there was no reply. He had been robbed and beaten and now he was trapped and helpless in some place that seemed to be underground. The outrageousness of the situation—and panic—made him feel that his brain was cracking open and when he trembled the wire cut his skin. Then he heard footsteps and voices upstairs, the voices of the hoods. They came, one by one, into the cellar. It was the same three. There was the leader, then there was one with a fat face and then a thin, pale one with long hair.

"Chicken," the leader said, looking at him.

"What do you want from me?" Mr. Freeley said. "You have my money. Was it because of that girl at the high school?"

"I don't know nothing about no girl at no high school," the leader said. "I just don't like your looks, chicken, that's all. What's the matter, chicken? Why you shaking so? You afraid we're going to torture you with matches and all?" He struck a match and held it close to Mr. Freeley's skin but he didn't burn him. "Look at chicken. Chicken's afraid of dying. That's why I don't like your looks, chicken. Jesus, listen to chicken roar."

Mr. Freeley roared. The floor tipped first to the left, then to the right and he lost consciousness again. Then he felt that he was being touched. He was being cut down. He could feel the loosening of the wires and the rush of blood back into his arms. He would have fallen but someone caught him and supported him. It was the pale one with the long, oily hair. He led Mr. Freeley over to the corner where there was an old automobile seat and he fell onto it.

"Where are the others?" he asked.

"They gone," the boy said. "They got scared when you blacked out."

"You?"

"I'm scared all the time."

"What do you want?"

"Nothing now. It's just like he said. He don't like your looks. You want some water?"

"Yes."

The boy got some water and held the glass to his lips.

"When can I go?"

"Go," the boy said. "Your suit's upstairs. It didn't fit nobody. Harry took your watch. I didn't take nothing. Good-bye now."

He swung out of the door and Mr. Freeley heard him run

lightly up some stairs. He felt his head wound and then he felt his arms and legs. Everything seemed to be sound and he went feebly up the stairs. His suit was by the door and when he got outside he saw that he was in an abandoned roadhouse at the edge of town.

Mr. Freeley walked home. So did Emile but they took different routes. Emile cut through some back yards to Turner Street and started up the hill. The scene was apocalyptic. Forsaken children could be heard crying in empty houses and most of the doors stood open in the dawn as if Gabriel's long trumpet had sounded. At the top of Turner Street he cut over onto the golf links, climbed to the highest fairway and sat down, waiting for the day. He felt tired, happy, humorous and relieved of his responsibility and of a much heavier burden. Something had happened. Something had changed. Like everyone else who reads the newspapers he had come to hold in his mind a fear that some drunken corporal might incinerate the planet and to hold in another part of his mind the most passionate longings for a peaceful life among his generations. In spite of his youth he had breathed in this concept of general infirmity. He seemed at times to listen to the planet's heartbeat as if the earth were a melancholy hypochondriac, possessed of great strength and beauty and with them an incurable presentiment of sudden and meaningless death. Now the moment of danger seemed past, and he felt joyfully that the illustrious and peaceful works of man would go on forever. He could not describe his feelings, he could not describe the dawn, he could not even describe the hooting of a train that he heard in the distance or the shape of the tree under which he sat. He could only watch and admire the vast barrel of night fill up to its last shelf and crevice with the fair light of day and all the birds singing in the trees like a band of angels whistling to their hounds.

On his way home he stopped at Melissa's and put the golden egg for Rome on her lawn.

Part Three

28

For someone so old, born and raised in a distant world, Honora's familiarity with the photographs of the monuments of Rome made at one level her entry into the city a sort of homecoming. A large, brown picture of Hadrian's Tomb had hung in her bedroom when she was a child. Waiting for sleep, suffering and recovering from illnesses, its drum-shaped form and rampant angel had taken a solid place in her reveries. In the back hall there had been a picture of the Bridge of Angels and two large photographs of the Imperial Forum had been handed backward, room to room, until they ended up in the cook's quarters. Thus, some of Rome was very familiar. But what did one do in Rome? One saw the Pope. Honora asked at the American Express office how this could be arranged. They were very helpful, respecting her age, and sent her on to a priest at the American college. The priest was courteous and interested. An audience could be arranged. She would receive her invitation within twenty-four hours of the appointment. She was to wear dark clothes and a hat and if she wanted to have some medals blessed he could recommend a shop—he gave her an address—where there was a fine assortment of religious medals sold at a 20 percent discount.

He explained, tactfully, that while the Holy Father spoke English, he spoke the language more fluently than he understood it and that should he forget to bless her medals, she could consider them blessed by his presence. Honora was, of course, opposed to the use of medals but she had plenty of friends who would value a blessed medal and she bought a stock. Returning one evening to her *pensione* she was handed a card from the

Vatican, announcing her audience for ten the next morning. She rose early and dressed. She took a taxi to the Vatican, where a man in immaculate evening dress asked for her name and her card. He pronounced her name "Whamshang." He asked her please to remove her gloves. His English was thickly accented and she did not understand. It took some explaining to make clear to her that one did not wear gloves in the presence of the Holy Father. He took her up a flight of stairs. She had to stop twice to rest her legs and get her wind. They waited in an anteroom for half an hour. It was after eleven when a second equerry opened some double doors and ushered her into an enormous *salone,* where she saw the Holy Father standing by his throne. She kissed his ring and sat in a chair that was proffered by a second equerry. He held, she noticed, a salver in his hands in which there were several checks. It had not crossed her mind that she would be expected to make a contribution to the Church during her audience and she put a few lire onto the salver. She was not shy but she felt herself to be in the presence of holiness, the essence of a magnificently organized power, and she regarded the Pope with genuine awe.

"How many children have you, Madame?" he asked.

"Oh, I don't have any children," she said, speaking loudly. "Where is your home?"

"I come from St. Botolphs," she said. "It's a little village. I don't suppose you've ever heard of it."

"San Bartolomeo?" the Holy Father asked with interest.

"No," she said, "Botolphs."

"San Bartolomeo di Farno," the Pope said, "di Savigliano, Bartolomeo il Apostolo, Il Lepero, Bartolomeo Capitanio, Bartolomeo degli Amidei."

"Botolphs," she repeated, halfheartedly. Then suddenly she asked, "Have you ever seen the Eastern United States in the autumn, Holy Father?" He smiled and seemed interested but he said nothing. "Oh, it's a glorious sight," she exclaimed. "I don't suppose there's anything else like it in the world. It's like a harvest of gold and yellow. Of course the leaves are worthless and I've gotten so old and lame that I have to pay someone to rake and burn them for me but my they are beautiful and they give such an impression of wealth—oh, I don't mean anything mercenary—but everywhere you look you see golden trees, gold everywhere."

"I would like to bless your family," the Pope said.

"Thank you."

She bowed her head. He spoke the blessing in Latin and when she felt sure that it was ended she loudly said *Amen.* The interview ended, an equerry took her down and she passed the Swiss Guards and returned to the colonnade.

Melissa and Honora didn't meet. Melissa lived on the Aventine with her son and a *donna di servizio* and worked on a sound stage near the Piazza del Popolo, dubbing Italian spectacles into English. She was the voice of Mary Magdalen, she was Delilah, she was the favorite of Hercules; but she had the Roman Blues. These are no more virulent than the New York Blues or the Paris Blues but they have a complexion of their own and like any other form of emotional nausea they can, when they are in force, make such commonplace sights as a dead mouse in a trap seem apocalyptic. If homesickness was involved, it was not, for Melissa, a clear string of images evoking the pathos, the sweetness and the vigor of American life. She did not long to canoe on the Delaware once more or to hear, once more, harmonica music on the dusky banks of the Susquehanna. Walking down the Corso her blues were the blues of not being able to understand the simplest remark and the chagrin of being swindled. It was the Campidoglio on a rainy day, with a guide trailing her around and around the statue of Marcus Aurelius, complaining about the season and the business. It was a winter rain so cold that she felt for the host of naked gods and heroes on the rooftops without even a fig leaf to protect them from the wet. It was the damps of the Forum, the chill in the seventeenth-century stairwells and the forlorn kitchens of Rome with their butcher's marble, their fly-specked walls and their stained pictures of the Holy Virgin hung above a leaky gas ring. It was

autumn in a European city with war forever in the air; it was
the withering of those clumps of flowers that grow in the highest
orifices of Aurelian's Wall, those clusters of hay and grass that
sprout up between the very toes of the saints and angels who
stand around the domes of Roman churches. It was that room
on the Capitoline where the Roman portrait busts are stacked
up; but instead of feeling some essence or shade of Imperial
power she was reminded of that branch of her family that had
gone north to Wisconsin to raise wheat. There seemed to be
Aunt Barbara and Uncle Spencer and cousins Alice, Homer, Ran-
dall and James. They had the same clear features, the same thick
hair, the same look of thoughtfulness, fortitude and worry. Their
royal wives were helpmates—and they sat in their marble thrones
as if the pies were in the oven and they were waiting for their
men to return from the fields. She tried to walk through the
streets looking alert and hurried—caught up in the tragedy of
modern European history—as most of the people on the street
seemed to be, but the sweetness of her smile made it clear that
she was not a Roman. She walked in the Borghese Gardens
feeling the weight of habit a woman her age or any other age
carries from one country to another; habits of eating, drinking,
dress, rest, anxiety, hope and, in her case, the fear of death.
The light in the gardens seemed to illuminate the bulkiness of
her equipment, as if the whole scene, and the distant hills, had
been set up for someone who traveled with less. She walked
by the moss-choked fountains and the leaves were falling among
the marble heroes; heroes with aviators' caps, heroes with beards,
heroes with laurels and ascots and cutaways and heroes whose
marble faces time and weather had singled out capriciously for
disfigurement. Troubled and uneasy, she walked and walked,
taking some pleasure in that tranquillity that falls with the shade
from great trees onto the shoulders of man. She watched an
owl fly out of a ruin. At a turning in the path she smelled marigolds. The garden was full of lovers, very sweet with one another
and candid about their pleasures, and she watched a couple kiss-

ing by a fountain. Then suddenly the man sat down on a bench and took a pebble out of his shoe. Whatever the significance of this was, Melissa realized that she wanted to get out of Rome and she took a train to the islands that night.

29

Emile was out of work for most of the summer and in the fall his mother's brother Harry came to visit them while he attended a convention in New York. He was a pleasant, heavy man who ran a ship-provisioning business in Toledo. He could, through his influence as a provisioner, get Emile a place as an unlicensed hand on one of the ships that plied the seaway to Rotterdam or Naples and Emile agreed to the plan at once. When Uncle Harry returned to Toledo he wrote to say that Emile could sail as a deck hand on the S.S. *Janet Runckle* at the end of the week.

Emile bought his bus ticket to Toledo at a travel agency in Parthenia, said good-bye to his mother and went on into New York. The bus was scheduled to leave at nine that night but by eight o'clock there were more than a dozen passengers on the waiting platform. These were travelers and you could tell it by their finery, their shy looks and their new bags. Every people seems to have some site, some battlefield, tomb or cathedral where their national essence and purpose is most exposed, and the railroad stations, airports, bus stops and piers of his country seemed to be the scenery where his kind found their greatness. They were dressed, most of them, as if their destination were some sumptuary judgment seat. Their shoes pinched, their gloves were stiff, their headgear was top-heavy, but this nicety in dress seemed to suggest that the ancient legends of travel— Theseus and the Minotaur—were still, however faintly, remembered by them. Their eyes were utterly undefended, as if an exchanged glance between two miscreants would plunge them both into an erotic abyss, and they kept their looks to themselves, their bags, the paving or the unlighted sign above the platform. At twenty minutes to nine the sign was lighted—it said TOLEDO— and they stirred, got to their feet, pressed forward, their faces filled with light as if a curtain had just risen on a new life, a paradise of urgency and beauty, although it rose in fact on the Jersey marshes, the all-night restaurants, the plains of Ohio and some troubled dreams. The windows of the bus were tinted green and driving out of the city all the street lights burned greenly as if the whole world were a park.

He slept well and woke at dawn. They spent the day crossing Ohio. The green windowglass made the landscape baneful, as if the sun had grown cold and these were the last hours of life on the planet, and in this strange light people went on hitchhiking, mowing fields and selling used cars. Late in the day they came to the outskirts of Toledo but he might have been coming home to Parthenia. There were hamburger stands and places where you could buy fresh vegetables and used-car lots with strings of lights and a dog-and-cat hospital and a woman in a bathing suit pushing a gasoline lawn mower and a pregnant woman hanging out her wash and the elms and the maples were the same, he noticed, and Queen Anne's lace grew in the fields and you couldn't tell until you got to the center of the city whether you were in Parthenia or Toledo.

The other passengers scattered and Emile stood on a corner with his suitcase. The air, he thought, had a grassy smell. Perhaps this was from the surrounding farms or the lake. The street lights burned and the store windows were lighted but there was still a rosy light from the setting sun and he felt that excitement he always experienced in the ball park when, during the fourth or fifth inning of a double-header, they would turn on the lights while the sky was still blue. It was not cold at all but he shivered as if at this hour and in this flat country there were some subtle rawness in the air. He asked a policeman for directions to the Union Hall. It was a long walk. The daylight had risen off the buildings and up out of the sky and he walked in the light from store fronts, restaurants and bars. The Union Hall when he got there seemed empty, a place with green walls and an oiled floor and benches for waiting. A man behind a window took his thirty-dollar fee and said that his uncle had made the arrangements. They would board the ship that night and sail whenever the loading was completed. He sat down on one of the benches and waited for the crew to come in.

The first to come was the cook, a short man in a brown business suit, who hailed his friend behind the window and introduced himself to Emile. His skin was sallow, his nose was broken and unset. That was the first thing you noticed, that and the monkey light in his eye. It was the broken nose that dominated his face, the widespread nares that made the shrewd light in his eye seem simian, mischievous at times and at times as reflective as the eyes of any cold monkey in a Sunday afternoon zoo. "You look just like a fellow shipped out with us last year," he said. "Paff was his name. He got a scholarship in some university and left the sea. You look just like him."

Emile was happy to resemble someone who had gotten a scholarship to college. Some of the stranger's intelligence seemed to rub off on his shoulders. The rest of the crew began to straggle in and one by one they told him how much he looked like Paff. The first mate was a young man who knocked his cap to the back of his head like a ballplayer and who seemed cheerful, aggressive but not at all bellicose. The second mate was an old man with a thin mustache and a threadbare uniform who took a photograph of his daughter out of his wallet and showed it to Emile. The picture showed a girl in ballet costume, posed on the roof of a tenement. Then the cabin steward joined Emile and the cook. He was a young man with that identifiable gentility that is bred in the turf huts of Nebraska; a mode of elegance that is formed in utter despair. There were thirty-five in all. The last to come was a dark-skinned man carrying a bar bell.

Taxis took them out of the city. Emile sat in front with the driver and the cook, trying to make out Toledo. There were lights, buildings, a river in the distance, and there must have been a beach nearby because many of the people in the opposite lanes of traffic wore bathing suits. Emile felt with intense discomfort that he had not made his presence in Toledo a reality; that he had left the better part of himself in Parthenia. They crossed railroad tracks and went into a dark neighborhood lit by gas-cracking plants, with here and there a saloon on a corner. They stopped at a gate where a man in uniform sent them on at the sight of the cook and then they were in a wilderness until at a turn in the road they came into a broad circle of light and an uproar of engine noise where the S.S. *Janet Runckle* was being loaded in a night world independent of the fact that the sun had set on the banks of Lake Erie two or three hours ago and where, like the music of some romantic agony, the noise of cranes, winches, ore-loaders, fork lifts, donkey engines, hopper cars and boat whistles filled the air.

The passengers came aboard at midnight. The first was an old man with his wife or daughter. He climbed the long gangway directly but the woman with him seemed afraid. It was finally suggested that she take off her high-heel shoes and with a deck hand in front and one behind she was eased up the gangway. The next to come was a man with his wife and three children. One of the children was crying. The last to come was a young man carrying a guitar. At four Emile went on duty and hosed down the decks with the rest of the watch. He wore Paff's water-proofs. The captain ordered a tug for five but when the tug was delayed he put two men overside in the bosun's chair and warped the ship out into the channel with lines and winches. They blew their stack in the dawn and Emile wished on the morning star for a safe voyage.

The morning watch hosed down the decks and washed the superstructure and deckhouse with soap and water. The after-noon watch chipped paint. The work was easy and the company was cheerful but the food was terrible. It was the worst food Emile had ever eaten. There were powdered eggs for breakfast, greasy meat and potatoes for dinner and cheese and cold cuts every night. Emile was hungry all the time and his hunger took on the scope of some profound misunderstanding between the world and himself. The plate of cheese and cold cuts that he faced each evening seemed to represent, like a sacrament, stupidity and indifference. His needs, his aspirations and his time of life were all misunderstood and cheese and cold cuts exacerbated the fact. He left the galley in anger one evening and went back to the stern. Simon joined him there; Simon was the one with the bar bell. "This *Runckle,*" Simon said. "She's famous all over the world for bad chow."

"I'm hungry," Emile said.

"I'm skipping ship in Naples," Simon said. "I got four hundred dollars in travel checks. You come with me."

"I'm hungry," Emile said.

"There's this American restaurant in Naples," Simon said. "Roast beef, mashed potatoes. You can even get a club sandwich. You come with me."

"Where," Emile asked, "where will we go?"

"Ladros," Simon said. "There's this beauty contest I'm going to be in. The way I figure it is, you got just so many chances and I know one thing, I got my looks. I'm very good-looking. It's the only thing I got and I better cash in on it before it's too late. In Ladros you can pick up two, three thousand dollars in this contest."

"You're crazy," Emile said.

"Well, there's no doubt about the fact that I'm vain," Simon said. "I'm a very vain man. I never go by a mirror without looking at myself and thinking there goes a very good-looking man. Never. But you come with me. We'll go to this restaurant. Apple pie. Hamburgers."

"Blueberry pie's my favorite," Emile said. "After that lemon meringue. Then apricot."

Emile saw the Azores glumly across a plate of cheese and cold cuts. Gibraltar was meat loaf. He ate bloated spaghetti sailing down the coast of Spain and when they docked early one morning in Naples he felt, in spite of his indifference to Simon's ambitions, that he had no choice. They left the *Runckle* in the middle of the morning and went to an American restaurant where Emile put away two plates of ham and eggs and a club sandwich and felt like himself for the first time since leaving Toledo. They took an afternoon boat in a choppy sea to Ladros. Simon got seasick. The contest headquarters was in a café in the main *piazza* and although Simon's face was green the first thing he did was to enroll and pay his entry fee. They got cots in a dormitory near the port where twenty-five or thirty other contestants were boarding. Simon worked conscientiously on his muscle-building. He oiled and sunned himself and wore, like the others, something called a slip, a sort of codpiece. He rented a boat and exercised in this during the mornings. After his siesta he worked out with the bar bells. Emile, wearing voluminous American trunks, rowed with him in the morning and spent a pleasant time swimming off the rocks.

It was very hot and Ladros was crowded but the sea had a color he had never seen before and there was something in the air, a suspension of conscience, that made the white beaches and the dark seas of his own country seem censorious and re- mote. He seemed, in crossing the Bay of Naples, to have lost his scruples. The contest was on Saturday and on Friday Simon came down with a bad attack of food poisoning. Emile bought him some medicine in a pharmacy but he was up most of the night and was too weak to get out of bed in the morning. Emile felt for him deeply and wished it were in his power to help. He had wasted his savings and if his sole ambition was ridiculous could he be blamed? Simon asked Emile to take his place and in the end he agreed. It was the brute power of boredom that forced his decision. He had nothing else to do. He got into his bathing trunks, put on Simon's numeral and went up to the *piazza* at a little after four. The hot, bright sunlight could still be seen at the foot of the street but the square was in shade. There was a long wait. Presently a boatload of English tourists came in and filled up the tables at the edge of the square and then, in numerical order, the procession started.

He didn't want to seem sullen, that after all would have been unfair to Simon, but he did want to seem disengaged, to make clear that this was not his idea, not what he wanted. He didn't look at the faces below him but stared at an advertisement for San Pellegrini mineral water on a wall beyond the café. What would his mother have thought, his uncle, the ghost of his father? Where was the dark house in Parthenia where he had lived? When he had crossed the *piazza* he waited around with the others and then was led into the café by the proprietor and didn't realize until then that there were only ten and that he was one of the winners.

It was getting dark by then, deepening into the grape-colored sky that more than anything else made him feel not unpleasantly far from home. Now the *piazza* was crowded. The ten men stood at the bar drinking coffee and wine, held together by the bond of a common experience and a questionable victory and alienated by the barriers of language. Emile stood between a Frenchman and an Egyptian and the best he could do was to speak a little crude Italian and smile hopefully but fatuously to prove that he was friendly and self-possessed. As it grew darker and darker in the *piazza*, as the light of day faded and as they stood under the bare lights of the café that had been arranged sensibly and economically to light the work of the bartenders and to flatter no one, they might, but for their lack of clothing, have been a group of workmen, clerks or jurors, stopping for a drink on their way back to wherever their lives were centered, to wherever they were awaited and wanted. Emile did not understand what would happen next and he asked the proprietor in dumb show to explain. The explanation was long and it was a long time before Emile understood that they, the ten winners, would now be auctioned off to the crowd in the *piazza.* "But I'm an American," Emile said. "We don't believe in that!"

"Niente, niente," the judge said gently and explained to Emile that if he didn't want to be sold he was free to go. In his own country Emile would have gone home indignantly but he was

not in his own country and inquisitiveness or something deeper
held him there. He was shocked to think that unfamiliar surroundings, lights and circumstances might influence his morals.
To reinforce his character he tried to recall the streets of Parthenia but they were worlds away. Could it be true that his character
was partly formed from rooms, streets, chairs and tables? Was
his morality influenced by landscapes and kinds of food? Had
he been unable to take his personality, his sense of good and
evil, across the Bay of Naples?

In the *piazza* a band began to play and from behind the café
a few mortars were fired off. Then the *padrone* opened the door
and called to a man named Ivan, who smiled at his companions
and went out onto the terrace where there was a block on which
he stood. He seemed to acquiesce gracefully to this turn of events.
Emile went out onto the terrace and stood in the shelter of an
acacia tree. The bidding began lightheartedly, it seemed a joke,
but as the bidding increased he realized that the young man's
skin was up for sale. The bidding rose quickly to a hundred
and fifty thousand lire; but then it came in slowly and the stir
in the crowd was erotic. Ivan seemed impassive but the beating
of his heart could be seen. Was this sin, Emile wondered, and
if it was, why should it seem so deeply expressive of everyone
there? Here was the sale of the utmost delights of the flesh,
its racking forgetfulness. Here were the caves and the fine skies
of venery, the palaces and stairways, the thunder and the lightning, the great king and the drowned sailor, and from the voices
of the bidders it seemed that they had never wanted anything
else. The bidding stopped at two hundred and fifty thousand
lire and Ivan stepped off the block and walked into the dark
where someone, Emile couldn't see who, had been waiting with
a car. He heard the motor start and saw the headlights shine
on the ruined walls as they drove off.

An Egyptian named Ahab came next but something was wrong.
He smiled too knowledgeably, seemed much too ready to be
sold and to perform what was expected of him and was knocked
down at fifty thousand lire in a few minutes. A man called Paolo

re-established the atmosphere of sexuality and the bids, as they had been for Ivan, came in slowly and hoarsely. Then a man named Pierre climbed onto the block and there was some delay before the bidding began at all.

Something had gone wrong. The bloom was off him. He had drunk too much wine or was too tired and now he stood on the block like a stick. His slip was cut scant enough to show his pubic hair and his pose was vaguely classical—the hips canted and one hand curved against his thigh—classical and immemorial as if he had appeared repeatedly in the nightmares of men. Here was the face of love without a face, a voice, a scent, a memory, here was a rub and a tumble without the sandy grain of a personality, here was a reminder of all the foolishness, vengefulness and lewdness in love and he seemed to excite, in the depraved crowd, a stubborn love of decency. They would sooner look at the prices on the menu than at him. His look was sly and wicked, he was more openly lascivious than the others but no one seemed to care. There was some subtle change in the atmosphere of the place. Ten thousand. Twelve thousand. Then the bidding stopped. This was the worst of all for Emile to see. Ivan had sold himself to God knows whom, a face in the dark, but it seemed more shameful and more sinful that Pierre, who was willing to perform the sacred and mysterious rites for the least sacred rewards, was wanted by no one and that for all his readiness to sin he might, in the end, have to spend a quiet night in the dormitory counting sheep. Something was wrong, some promise, however obscene, was broken and Emile sweated in shame for his companion, for to lust and to be unwanted seemed to be the grossest indecency. In the end Pierre was knocked down for twenty thousand lire. The *padrone* turned to Emile to ask if he wanted to reconsider his decision and in an intoxication of pride, a determination to prove that what had happened to Pierre could not happen to him, he went forward and stood on the block looking out boldly at the lights in the *piazza* as if he had in this way managed to come face to face with the world.

The bidding was spirited enough and he was knocked down

for a hundred thousand lire. He stepped off the platform and walked through the tables to where a woman was waiting. It was Melissa.

She drove him up into the hills and through the gates of a villa where he could hear the loud noise of a fountain and nightingales singing in the trees and where he discovered that he had not brought his sense of good and evil across the bay. This eruption of his senses, this severance from the burdens of his life, was so complete that he seemed to fly, to swim, to live and die independently of all the well-known facts, that he seemed violently to destroy and renew himself, demolish and rebuild his spirit on some high sensual plane that was unbound from the earth and its calendar.

There was a pool in the garden where they swam and they ate their meals on a terrace. With her this time he never seemed to achieve consciousness; or perhaps he had discovered a new level of consciousness. There were six black dogs around the place who watched them and the servants came and went with trays of food and liquor. He had no idea of the passage of time but he guessed he had been there a week or ten days when she said one morning that she had to drive down to Ladros on an errand but that she would be back before lunch.

She hadn't returned by two and he ate his lunch alone on the terrace. When the maids had cleared the table they went upstairs to take their siesta. The whole valley was still. He lay on the grass by the pool, waiting for her to return. He felt drugged by an acuteness of sexual sensation and like the absence of a drug her delayed return left him in pain. The black dogs lay in the grass around him. Two of the dogs kept bringing sticks for him to throw. Their demands were insistent and tedious. Every few minutes they would drop a stick at his feet and if he didn't throw it at once they would howl for his attention. He heard a car in the road and thought that in another five minutes she would be with him but the car continued on to a villa farther up the cliff. He dove into the pool and swam the length of it, but as he pulled himself out of the cold water into the hot sun this contact only made his need for her seem keener. The flowers in the garden seemed aphrodisiac and even the blue of the sky like some part of love. He swam the length of the pool again and lay on the grass in a shady part of the garden where the dogs joined him and the retrievers howled for him to throw sticks.

He wondered what she was doing in Ladros. The cook bought the wine and the food and there was, he thought, nothing she needed. Her inability to resist his touch and his looks made him wonder if she could resist the touch or the look of any other man and if she was not now climbing some staircase with a stranger with hairy forearms. The degree of his pleasure in her immersion in sensuality was the exact degree of his jealousy. He couldn't credit her with any vision of constancy; and he went on throwing sticks for the dogs.

He went on throwing sticks as if some clear duty were involved, as if their welfare and amusement were on his conscience. But why? He had not liked them or disliked them. His feeling was substantial enough to be traced. He did, it appeared, feel some obligation to the dogs. There was some mutuality here as if in the past he had been a dog, dependent upon the caprices of a stranger in a garden, or as if in the future he might be transformed into a dog asking to be let in out of the rain. There were obligations and rewards, it seemed, for the patience with which he threw sticks. But where was she? Why was she not now with him? He tried to imagine her on some innocent errand but he couldn't. Then he sat up suddenly in anger and pain and the dogs sat up to watch. Their golden eyes and the whining of the retrievers made him angrier and he climbed the stairs to the *salone* and poured himself a drink but he left the door open and the dogs followed him in and sat around him on their haunches as he stood at the bar as if they expected him to speak with them. The house was still; the maids would be sleeping. Then his rage at her propinquity, her uselessness, her corruption shook him and the gaze of the animals only seemed more questing, as if this hour were speeding toward a climax they well knew; as if he were traveling toward some critical instant that involved them all; as if their dumbness and his lust, jealousy and anger were converging. He ran up the stairs and dressed. It was an hour's walk to the village but he didn't expect her car to pass him because he was convinced by then that when she did return it would be with another lover and he would have been transformed into a dog. But when she did pass him and stopped and when he saw that there were groceries in the back of the car, his moral indignation collapsed. He went back with her to the villa and returned to Rome with her at the end of the week.

30

Returning to her *pensione* one morning Honora found Norman Johnson waiting for her in the lobby. "Oh, Miss Wapshot," he said, "oh, it's so good to see you. It's so good to see anybody who can talk English. I was told that all these people studied English in school but most of the ones I've seen don't speak anything but Italian. Can we sit down here?" He opened his briefcase and showed her the order for her extradition, a copy of the criminal indictment passed down by the circuit court in Travertine and an order for the confiscation of all her property; but with so much documented power in his hands he seemed shamefaced and it was she who felt sorry for him. "Don't you worry," she said, touching him lightly on the knee. "Don't you worry about me. It's all my fault. It was just that I was so afraid of the poor farm. I've been afraid of the poor farm all my life. Even when I was a little girl. When Mrs. Bretaigne used to take me motoring to see the autumn foliage I used to close my eyes when we passed the poor farm, I was so afraid of it. But now I'm homesick and I want to go back. I'll go down to the bank and get my money and we'll go home in one of those flying machines."

They walked together to the American Express office, not as a jailer and a culprit but as dear friends. He waited downstairs while she closed her account and she joined him, carrying a large bundle of twenty-thousand-lire notes. "I'll get a taxi," he said. "You can't walk through the streets like that. You'll be robbed." They stepped out into the Piazza di Spagna.

It was a bright winter's day. At Fregene the catamarans would be up on rollers, the bathhouses shut, the light on the olives a sad light, the *zuppa di pesce* signs fallen or hanging from a single nail. The swallows were gone. In Rome it was hot in the sun, cold in the shade, the soft, bright light heightening the curious tidewater look of that old and crowded city as if, sometime in the past, the Tiber had risen over its banks—a flood of dark water—and stained the buildings and churches up to their pediments, leaving the limestone above still pale and still, this late in the year, overgrown at every cranny with thick tufts of grass and capers that looked so like pubic hair that they gave to the celebrated square an antic look. Americans wandered away from the office reading the news from home-sweet-home. Most of the news appeared to be humorous since most of them, from time to time, would smile. They walked, unlike the Italians, as if they accommodated their step to some remembered and explicit terrain—a tennis court, a beach, a plowed field—and seemed set apart by an air of total unpreparedness for change, for death, for the passage of time itself. There were perhaps a hundred and fifty people in the square when Honora entered it and glanced up at the sky. A Danish tourist was photographing his wife on the Spanish Steps. An American sailor was dousing his head in the fountain. There were fresh flowers on the monument to the Virgin. The air smelled of coffee and marigolds. Sixteen German tourists were drinking coffee in a café across the street. 11:18 A.M.

Honora was approached by a barefoot beggar in a torn green dress who held a baby. She gave her a lira note. She gave one to a man in a striped apron, to a little boy in a white coat carrying a tray of coffee, to a good-looking tart holding her coat closed at the throat, to a stooped woman wearing a hat shaped like a

wastebasket, to three German priests in crimson, to three Jesuits
in black with lavender piping, to five barefoot Franciscans, to
six nuns, to three young women in the black, sleazy uniforms
worn by the maids of Rome, to a clerk from one of the souvenir
shops, to a hairdresser, a barber, a pimp, three clerks, their
fingers stained with lavender government office ink; to one dis-
possessed marquesa, her ragged handbag stuffed with photographs of lost villas, lost houses, lost horses, lost dogs; to a
violinist, a tuba player and a cellist on their way to the rehearsal
hall on the Via Athenee; to a pickpocket, a seminarian, an antique
dealer, a thief, a fool, an idler, a Sicilian looking for work, a
carabiniere off duty, a cook, a nursemaid, an American novelist,
a waiter from the Inglese, a Negro drummer, a medical-supply
salesman and three florists. There was not a hint of charity in
her giving. The good her money might do would never cross
her mind. The impulse to scatter her money was as deep as
her love of fire and she sought, selfishly, an intoxicating sensation
of cleanliness, lightness and usefulness. Money was filth and this
was her ablution.

By this time the roofs of the square were black with people.
A clerk from the express office climbed out the window, slid
down the awning and dropped to the sidewalk at Honora's feet.
Bystanders stood knee deep in the water of the fountain. Then
some mounted *carabinieri* came up the Via Condotti and Honora
turned and climbed the stairs while the voices of thousands
blessed her in the name of The Father, The Son and The Holy
Ghost, world without end.

31

Coverly's security clearance was renewed pending Cameron's
return from New Delhi but Brunner had gone to England and
Coverly had no way of knowing when the old man would come
back. Then, through some irreversible and confused bureaucratic

process, Coverly was served a ten-day eviction notice by the government housing office. His feelings were mixed. Their life in Talifer seemed over, if it could ever have been said to have begun. He could easily find work as a preprogrammer somewhere else and the thought of leaving Talifer seemed to Betsey like the promise of a new life. At about this time he received a wire from St. Botolphs. COME AT ONCE. This unprecedented directness from his old cousin alarmed him and he packed and left. He arrived there late the next afternoon. The day was rainy but as they approached the sea the rain turned to snow. The fall of snow whitened the bare trees and the slums beside the tracks and gave them, so Coverly thought, a pathos and beauty that they would have at no other time in their history. All this whiteness made him lighthearted. When he got off the train Mr. Jowett was nowhere around and the station had been abandoned. He saw no one to wave to in the windows of the Viaduct House; no one in the feed store. Crossing the green he was stopped by a procession of men and women leaving the parish house of Christ Church. They were eight and they walked two by two. All the men but one, who was bareheaded, wore stocking caps. He guessed that there had been a tea, a lecture, some charitable gesture, and that these were the inmates of the poor farm. One of them, an angular man, seemed mad or foolish and was muttering: "Repent, repent, your day is at hand. Angel voices have told me how to make myself pleasing to the Lord. . . ." "Hushup, hushup, Henry Saunders," said a large Negress who walked at his side. "You just hushup until we get into the bus." A bus was parked at the curb with HUTCHENS INSTITUTE FOR THE BLIND painted on its side. Coverly watched a driver help them in and then walked on up Boat Street.

A nurse opened Honora's door. She gave Coverly a knowing smile as if she had heard a great deal about him and had already formed an unfavorable opinion. "She's been waiting for you," she whispered. "The poor thing's been waiting for you all day." There was no reason for reproach. Coverly had wired his old cousin and she knew exactly when he would arrive. "I'll be in the kitchen," the nurse said and went down the hall. The house was dirty and cold. The walls, plain as he remembered them, were now covered with a paper printed in black latticing and dark red roses. He opened one of the double doors into the living room and thought at first that she was dead.

She slept in a shabby wing chair. During the months since he had seen her she had lost her corpulence. She was terribly wasted. She had been robust—hardy, as she would have said— and now she was frail. Her leonine face and the childish placement of her feet were all that was not changed. She slept on and he looked around the room which, like the hallway, seemed neglected. Here was dust, cobwebs and flowered wallpaper. The curtains were gone and he could see the light snow through the high windows. Then she woke.

"Oh, Coverly."

"Cousin Honora." He kissed her and sat on a stool by her chair.

"I'm so glad you got here, dear, I'm so glad you came."

"I'm glad to be here."

"You know what I did, Coverly? I went to Europe. I didn't pay my tax and Judge Beasely, that old fool, said they'd throw me in jail so I went to Europe."

"Did you have a good time?"

"Remember the tomato fights?" Honora asked, and he wondered if she had lost her mind.

"Yes."

"After the frost I used to let you and the others come into my tomato patch and have tomato fights. When you'd thrown all the tomatoes you used to pick up the calling cards the cows had left and throw those." That this redoubtable old woman should call a steaming pile of cow manure a calling card was a reminder of the eccentric niceties of the village. "Well, when you'd thrown all the calling cards and all the tomatoes you used to be quite a mess," Honora said, "but if anyone asked you if you'd had a good time I expect you'd say yes. That's the way I feel about my trip."

"I see," said Coverly.

"I've changed," Honora asked, "you can see that I've changed, can't you?" There was some lightness, some hopefulness, even some pleading in her voice as if he might say persuasively that she hadn't changed at all and she could then stamp out into the garden and rake a few leaves before the snow covered them.

"Yes."

"Yes, I suppose I have. I've lost a lot of weight. But I *feel* much better." This was bellicose. "However, I don't go out now because I've noticed that people don't like to see me. It makes them sad. I see it in their eyes. I am like an angel of death."

"Oh, no, Honora," Coverly said.

"Oh, yes, I am. Why shouldn't I be? I'm dying."

"Oh, no," Coverly said.

"I'm dying, Coverly, and I know it and I want to die."

"You shouldn't say that, Honora."

"And why shouldn't I?"

"Because life is a gift, a mysterious gift," he said feebly in spite of the weight the words had for him.

"Well," she explained, "you must be going to church a great deal these days."

"I sometimes do," he said.

"High or low?" she asked.

"Low."

"Your family," she said, "was always high."

This was harsh, flat, that old contrariness upon which she had counted more than anything else to express herself, but now she seemed too feeble to keep it up. She followed his eyes to the ugly wallpaper and said: "I see you've noticed my roses."

"Yes."

"Well, I'm afraid they're a mistake but when I came home I called Mr. Tanner and asked him to bring me over some wallpaper with roses on it to remind me of the summer." Stooped and leaning forward in her chair, she raised her head, her eyes, and gave the roses a terribly haggard look. "I get awfully tired of looking at them," she said, "but it's too late to change."

Coverly looked up at the wall, at her mistake, and noticed

that the flowers were not the true colors and shapes of roses at all. The buds were phallic and the blooms themselves looked like some carnivorous plant, some petaled fly-catcher with a gaping throat. If they had been meant to remind her of the roses that bloomed in the summer they must have failed. They seemed like a darkness, a corruption, and he wondered if she hadn't chosen them to correspond with her own sense of this time of life.

"Will you please get me some whisky, Coverly," she said. "It's in the pantry. I don't dare ask *her*." Honora nodded her head toward the back of the house where the nurse must be sitting. Then she screened her mouth with her left hand, presumably to direct her voice away from the door, but when she spoke it was in such a vituperative hiss that it must have carried down the hall. "She *drinks*," Honora hissed, rolling her eyes wildly toward the kitchen in case Coverly should have missed the point.

Coverly was surprised to have his old cousin ask for whisky. She used to take a drink at the family parties but always with the most vocal misgivings and reservations as if a single highball might stretch her out unconscious on the floor, or still worse, lead her to dance a jig on a table. Coverly went through the dining room to the pantry. The two changes he had noticed, disrepair and an obsession with roses, were continued here. The walls were covered with dark-throated roses and the table was ringed and scored under a thick layer of dust. There was, in the lap of one of the chairs, a broken leg and arm. The place was out of hand but if she was dying, as she had said, she seemed, like a snail or nautilus, to be approaching the grave in the carapace of her own house, projecting her dimness of sight and her loss of memory in cobwebs and ashes.

"Can I do anything for you, Mr. Wapshot?" This was the nurse. She sat in a chair by the sink, empty-handed.

"I'm looking for some whisky."

"It's in the jelly closet. There isn't any ice but she doesn't like ice in her drinks."

There was plenty of whisky. There was a half-case of bourbon and at least a case of empty bottles scattered helter-skelter on the floor. This was completely mysterious. Had the nurse ordered in these cases of whisky and swigged them alone in the kitchen?

"How long have you been working for Miss Wapshot?" Coverly asked.

"Oh, I'm not working for her," the nurse said. "I just came in today to improve appearances. She thought you'd worry if you found her alone so she asked me to come in and make things look nice."

"Is she alone all the time now?"

"She is when she wants to be. Oh, there's plenty of people who'll come over and make her a cup of tea but she won't let them in. She wants to be alone. She doesn't eat anything any more. She just drinks."

Coverly looked more closely at the nurse to see if, as Honora had claimed, she was drunk and meant to shift her vices onto the old woman.

"Does the doctor know about this?" Coverly asked.

"The doctor. Ha. She won't let the doctor into the house. She's killing herself. That's what she's doing. She's trying to kill herself. She knows that the doctor wants to operate on her and she's afraid of the knife."

She spoke with perfect pitilessness as if she were the knife's advocate, its priestess, and Honora the apostate. So that was it; and what could he do? His time in the kitchen was running out. If he stayed any longer she would become suspicious. It was unthinkable that he would return and charge her with the fraudulence of the nurse and the empty whisky bottles. She would deny it all flatly and would, what's more, be deeply wounded for he would have rudely broken the rules of that antic game in which their relationship was contained.

He went back through the pantry and the dining room, re-minded by its disrepair of death, as a plain fact with which she seemed to be grappling boldly. He remembered walking down from the beach at Cascada with a bagful of black clams on his back. What does the sea sound like? Lions mostly, manifest destiny, the dealing of some final card hand, the aces as big as headstones. Boom, it says. And what did all his pious introspection on metamorphosis amount to? He thought he saw on the beach the change from one form of life to another. The sea grass dies, dries, flies like a swallow on the wind and that angry-looking tourist will make a lamp base out of the piece of driftwood he carries. The line of last night's heavy sea is marked with malachite and amethyst, the beach is scored with the same lines as the sky; one seemed to stand in some fulcrum of change, here was the barrier, here as the wave fell was the line between one life and another, but would any of this keep him from squealing for mercy when his time came?

"Thank you, dear." She drank thirstily and gave him a narrow look. "Is she *drunk?*"

"I don't think so," Coverly said.

"She conceals it. I want you to promise me three things, Coverly."

"Yes."

"I want you to promise me that if I should lose consciousness you will not have me moved to the hospital. I wish to die in this house."

"I promise."

"I want you to promise that when I'm gone you won't worry about me. My life is over and I know it. I've done everything I was meant to do and a great deal I was not meant to do. Everything will be confiscated, of course, but Mr. Johnson won't do this until January. I've asked some nice people here for Christmas dinner and I want you to be here and make them welcome. Maggie will do the cooking. Promise."

"I promise."

"And then I want you to promise me, to promise me that . . . Oh, there was something else," she said, "but I can't remember what it was. Now I think I'll lie down for a little while."

"Can I help you?"

"Yes. You can help me over to the sofa and then you can

read to me. I like to be read to these days. Oh, remember how
I used to read to you when you were sick? I used to read you
David Copperfield and we would both cry so that I couldn't go
on. Remember how we used to cry, Coverly, you and I?"

The fullness of feeling in this recollection refreshed her voice
and seemed to send it back through time until it sounded for
a moment like the voice of a girl. He helped her out of the
chair and led her over to the old horsehair sofa, where she lay
down and let him cover her with a rug. "My book is on the
table," she said. "I'm reading *The Count of Monte Cristo* again.
Chapter twenty-two." When she was settled he found her book
and began to read.

His recollection of her reading to him was not an image, it
was a sensation. He could not recall her tears while she sat by
his bed but he could recall the violent and confused emotions
she left behind her when she went away. Now he read uneasily
and he wondered why. She had read to him when he was a
sick child; now he read to her as she lay dying. The cycle was
obvious enough, but why should he feel that she, as she lay
on the sofa, utterly helpless and infirm, had the power to weave
spells that could ensnare him? He had never had anything from
her but generosity and kindness, so why should he perform this
simple service uneasily? He admired the book, he loved the old
woman and no room on earth was so familiar as this, so why
should he feel that he had stepped innocently into some snare
involving a fraudulent nurse, a case of whisky and an old book?
Halfway through the chapter she fell asleep and he stopped reading. A little later the nurse came to the door wearing a black
hat and with a black coat over her uniform. "I have to go,"
she whispered. "I have to cook supper for my family." Coverly
nodded and listened to her footsteps pass into the back of the
house and then the closing of the door.

He went to the long and dirty window to see the snow. There
was some yellow light at the horizon, not lemony, not confined
to its color, the light of a lantern, a lanthorne, a longthorne,

the shine of light on paper, something that reminded him of childhood and its garden parties, isolated now by the lateness of the hour and the season.

"Coverly?" she asked, but she spoke in her sleep. He went back to his chair. He saw how terribly emaciated she was but he liked to think that this had not changed the force of her spirit. She had not only lived independently, she seemed at times to have evolved her own culture. There was nothing palliative in her approach to death. Her rites were bold, singular and arcane. The gloom and disrepair of her beloved house, the fraudulent nurse, the gaping roses—she seemed to have arranged them all around her satisfactorily as an earlier people had confidently supplied themselves, while dying, with enough food and wine for a long voyage.

"Coverly!" She woke suddenly, lifting her head off the pillow. "Yes."

"Coverly. I just saw the gates of Heaven!"

"What were they like, Honora, what were they like?"

"Oh, I couldn't say, I couldn't describe anything like that, they were so beautiful, but I saw them, Coverly, oh, I saw them." She sat up radiantly and dried her tears. "Oh, they were so beautiful. There were the gates and hosts of angels with colored wings and I saw them. Wasn't that nice?"

"Yes, Honora."

"Now get me some more whisky."

He went lightheartedly through the dark rooms, as happy as if he had shared her vision, and made some drinks, consoled to think that she would not, after all, ever die. She would stop breathing and be buried in the family lot but the greenness of her image, in his memory, would not change and she would be among them always in their decisions. She would, long after she was dust, move freely through his dreams, she would punish his and his brother's wickedness with guilt, reward their good works with lightness of heart, pass judgment on their friends and lovers even while her headstone bloomed with moss and her coffin was canted and jockeyed by the winter frosts. The goodness and evil in the old woman were imperishable. He carried her drink back through the darkness and put another log on the fire. She said nothing more but he filled her glass twice.

He called Dr. Greenough at half-past six. The doctor was having his supper but he came about an hour later and pronounced her dead of starvation.

So they wouldn't all come back to a place that was changed and strange and Coverly was the only member of the family at her funeral. He had no way of finding Moses, and Betsey was busy closing up the house in Talifer. Melissa had disappeared and the last we see of her is on a bus returning from one of the suburbs to the city of Rome. It is nearly Christmas but there are not many signs of this. Either Emile or his barber has cultivated a lock of hair that hangs over his forehead, giving him a look that is arch, boyish and a little stupid. He seems a little drunk and is, of course hungry. Melissa's hair is dyed red. One result of living with someone so much younger—and they are living together—is to have made her manner girlish. She has developed a habit of shrugging her shoulders and resettling her head, this way and that. She is not one of those expatriates who are ashamed to speak English. Her voice is musical, genteel, and it carries up and down the bus. "I know you're hungry, darling," she says, "I *know* that but it's really not my fault. As I understood it they had invited us to lunch. I *distinctly* recall that she asked us for lunch. What I suppose happened was that after she had invited us to lunch the Parlapianos asked *them* to lunch and they decided to jettison us; put us off with a drink. I noticed that the table wasn't set when we came in. I *knew* something was wrong then. It would have been much pleasanter if she'd telephoned and canceled the engagement. That would have been rude enough but to have us come all the way out there expecting lunch and then to tell us that they were engaged is one of the rudest things I've ever heard of. All we can do is to forget it, forget it, it's just something else to be forgotten. As soon as we get back to Rome I'll do the shopping and cook you some lunch. . . ."

And so she does. She goes to the Supra-Marketto Americano on the Via Delle Sagiturius. Here she disengages one wagon with a light ringing of metal from a chain of hundreds and begins to push her way through the walls of American food. Grieving, bewildered by the blows life has dealt her, this is some solace, this is the path she takes. Her face is pale. A stray curl hangs against her cheek. Tears make the light in her eyes a glassy light but the market is crowded and she is not the first nor the last woman in the history of the place to buy her groceries with wet cheeks. She moves indifferently with the alien crowd as if these were the brooks and channels of her day. No willow grows aslant this stream of men and women and yet it is Ophelia that she most resembles, gathering her fantastic garland not of crow-flower, nettles and long purples, but of salt, pepper, Bab-o, Klee-nex, frozen codfish balls, lamb patties, hamburger, bread, butter, dressing, an American comic book for her son and for herself a bunch of carnations. She chants, like Ophelia, snatches of old tunes. "Winstons taste *good* like a cigarette should. Mr. Clean, Mr. *Clean,*" and when her coronet or fantastic garland seems completed she pays her bill and carries her trophies away, no less dignified a figure of grief than any other.

32

Betsey and Binxey arrived the day before Christmas and Coverly went down to the station to meet the train. "I'm so tired," Betsey said, "I'm just so tired I could *die.*" "Was the train trip bad, sugarluve?" Coverly asked. "Bad," said Betsey, "bad. Just don't speak to me about it, that's all. I don't see why we have to come all the way down here to have Christmas anyhow. We might just as well have gone to Florida. I've never been to Florida in my whole life."

"I promised Honora that we'd have Christmas here."

"But you told me she was dead, dead and buried."

"I promised." For a moment he felt helpless before this incompatibility; felt as if his blood had been transmuted by anger or despair into something syrupy and effervescent, like Coca-Cola. It was unthinkable that he should break his promise to the old woman, it was some part of his dignity, and yet he could see clearly that it was unthinkable to Betsey that he should trouble himself. Coverly walked beside his wife with the slight crouch of a losing sexual combatant, while Betsey stood more erectly, held her head more sternly, seemed to seize on every crumb of self-esteem that he dropped. Coverly had done what he could to get the house in order. He had lighted fires, decorated a tree and put presents under it for his son and his wife. "I have to put Binxey to bed," Betsey said indignantly. "I don't guess there's any hot water for a bath, is there? Come on, Binxey, come on upstairs with Mummy. I'm just so tired I could *die.*"

After supper Coverly waited for the carol singers but they had either given up this ceremony or taken Boat Street off their route. At half-past ten the bells of Christ Church began to ring and he put on a coat and walked out to the green. The ringing of the bells stopped as he approached the door. He was preceded by three women, all of them unknown to him. They seemed not together and they were all three past middle age. The first wore a drum-shaped hat, covered with metal disks from which the street lights flashed with the brilliance of some advertising lure. Buy Ginger-Fluff? Texadrol? Fulpruff Tires? He looked into her face for the text but there was nothing there but the text of marriage, childbirth, some delight and some dismay. The other two wore similar hats. He waited until they had entered before he went in and found that they four were the only worshipers on Christmas Eve.

He went to a pew way forward, genuflected with a loud creaking of his kneebones and said his prayers, immersed in the immemorial and Episcopal smell of ancient rains. Mr. Applegate came in without his cassock and lighted the candles. He returned to the altar a moment later, carrying the Host. "Almighty God," he intoned, "unto Whom all hearts are open, all desires known and from Whom no secrets are hid, cleanse the thoughts of our hearts with the inspiration of Thy holy spirit. . . ."

The resonance of the Mass moved into that gloomy place on Christmas Eve with the magnificence of an Elizabethan procession. Perorative clauses spread out after the main supplication or confession in breadth and glory and the muttered responses seemed embroidered in crimson and gold. On it would move, Coverly thought, through the Lamb of God, the Gloria and the Benediction until the last Amen shut like a door on this verbal pomp. But then he sensed something strange and wrong. Mr. Applegate's speech was theatrical but what was more noticeable was a pose of suavity, a bored and haughty approach to the holy words for which Cranmer had burned. As he turned to the altar to pray Coverly saw him sway and grab at the lace for support. Was he sick? Was he feeble? The woman with the lights in her hat turned to Coverly and hissed: "He's drunk again." He was. He spoke the Mass with scorn and contumely, as if his besottedness were a form of wisdom. He lurched around the altar, got the general confession mixed up with the order for morning prayer and kept saying: "Christ have mercy upon us. Let us pray," until it seemed that he was stuck. There is no point in the formalities of Holy Communion where, in the case of such a disaster, the communicants can intervene and there was nothing to do but watch him flounder through to the end. Suddenly he threw his arms wide, fell to his knees and exclaimed: "Let us pray for all those killed or cruelly wounded on thruways, expressways, freeways and turnpikes. Let us pray for all those burned to death in faulty plane-landings, mid-air collisions and mountainside crashes. Let us pray for all those wounded by rotary lawn mowers, chain saws, electric hedge clippers and other power tools. Let us pray for all alcoholics measuring out the days that the Lord hath made in ounces, pints and fifths." Here he sobbed loudly. "Let us pray for the lecherous and the impure. . . ." Led by the woman with the flashing hat, the other worshipers left before this prayer was finished and

Coverly was left alone to support Mr. Applegate with his Amen. He got through the rest of it, divested himself, extinguished his candles and hurried back to his gin bottle, hidden among the vestments, and Coverly walked back to Boat Street. The telephone was ringing.

"Coverly, Coverly, this is Hank Moore over at the Viaduct House. I know it's none of my business but I thought maybe you were wondering where your brother was and he's over here. He's got the widow Wilston with him. I don't want to put my nose in nobody else's business but I just thought you might like to know where he was."

It was Christmas Eve at the Viaduct House but the scene upstairs was flagrantly pagan. This was no sacred grove and the only sound of running water came from a leaking tap but Moses the satyr leered through the smoky air at his bacchante. Mrs. Wilston's curls were disheveled, her face was red, her smile was the rapt and wanton smile of forgetfulness and she held a lovely glass of lovely bourbon in her right hand. Her jowls—the first note of pendulousness to be massively reiterated by her breasts— were very meaty. "Now you listen to me, Moses Wapshot," she said, "you just listen to me. You Wapshots always thought you were bettern everybody else but I wanna tell you, I wanna tell you, I can't remember what I wanna tell you." She laughed. She had lost the power of consecutive thought and with it all the stings and pains of living. She waked and yet she dreamed. Moses, naked as any satyr, smacked his lips and left his chair. His walk was lumbering, bellicose and a little haunted. It was on the one hand pugnacious and had on the other the lightness, the fleetness, the hint of stealth of a man who is stepping out of a liquor store after having paid for a quart of gin with an unsubstantiated check. He made his way to her, smacked her wetly in several places and gathered her up in his arms. She sighed and lolled in his embrace. He started for the bed with his jolly burden. He weaved to the right, recouped his balance and weaved to the right again. Then he was going; he was going; he was gone. Thump. The whole Viaduct House reverberated to the crash and then there was an awful stillness. He lay athwart her, his cheek against the carpet, which had a pleasant, dusty smell like the woods in autumn. Oh, where was his dog, his gun, his simple joy in life! She, still lying in a heap, was the first to speak. She spoke without anger or impatience. She smiled. "Let's have another drink," she said. Then Coverly opened the door. "Come home, Moses," he said. "Come home, brother. It's Christmas Eve."

Christmas Day in the morning, when Coverly woke and romanced Betsey, was dazzling. The frost on the window-glass, shaped like shrapnel, distilled and amplified the light. Maggie came early and opened the furnace drafts and presently hot air and coal gas began to pour out of the registers. Binxey emptied his stocking and unwrapped the presents that Coverly had bought for him and they all had breakfast in the warm kitchen off a wooden table that was as slick and porous as hand soap. The kitchen was not a dark room but the power of light on the new snow outside made it seem cavernous.

Moses woke in a crushing paroxysm of anxiety, the keenest melancholy. The brilliance of light, the birth of Christ, all seemed to him like some fatuous shell game invented to dupe a fool like his brother while he saw straight through into the nothingness of things. The damage he had done to his nerves and his memory was less painful than a sense he suffered of approaching disaster, some pitiless fatality that would break him without making itself known. His hands had begun to shake and in another fifteen minutes he would begin to sweat. This was the agony of death, with the difference that he knew the way to life everlasting. It was in the bottles of bourbon Honora had left in the jelly closet. He thought of bourbon while he shaved and dressed but when he went down to the kitchen and found them sitting at the table there he saw them not as the members of his family but as cruel obstacles, standing between himself and the alpine landscapes in a bottle of sour mash. The coffee and orange juice that Maggie gave him seemed innocuous and nauseating. How could he get them out of the room? If he had only thought to buy some presents and left them under the tree, he might have been alone for a minute. "Jelly," he exclaimed, "I want some jelly for my toast." He went into the closet and shut the door.

Going through the dining room after breakfast Coverly saw that Maggie had set the table for twelve guests and he wondered who they would be. Honora had always had a large table at Christmas. After Thanksgiving she would begin, in public places—trains, buses and waiting rooms—to look around for those faces that bore the inexpungeable mark of loneliness and invite them to her house for Christmas dinner. Intuition and practice had made her discerning and she could single out her prey unerringly and yet, knowing as she did how the passion of loneliness runs through the lives of all men, she was oftener rebuffed than accepted by strangers who, she saw, as they turned away from her, would sooner spend their holiday in a bare room than admit to her or even to themselves that they lacked a host of friends and relations and a groaning board. Wayward pride had been her adversary, and a formidable one, but the wish to fill up her table seemed, like her love of fires and her disinterest in money, aboriginal, and she had once gone up to the railroad station waiting room on Christmas morning and corraled the strays who were warming themselves there at the coal stove.

Coverly cleared the walks after breakfast. The loud ringing of his shovel on the paving had a singular and a foolish charm, as if this rude music, this simple task, evoked the spirit of Leander in a happier role than he had seemed damned to play out in the wreckage of the old house on River Street. The blinding light on the snow seemed to ring again and again around the boundaries of the village like the vibrations of a rubbed water glass, but even that early in the day the brilliance of the light could be seen to shift, to be the lights of one of the shortest days of the year.

The Bretaignes and the Dummers came in at eleven. Maggie gave them sherry and raspberry shrub. There was such a hard and mischievous light in Moses' eye by this time that they did not stay for long. Some time after noon Coverly was standing at a window when he saw the yellow bus he had seen on the night he returned. There was the same driver, the same passengers and the legend HUTCHENS INSTITUTE FOR THE BLIND. The bus stopped in front of the house and Coverly ran down the stairs, leaving the hall door open. "Wapshot?" the driver asked. "Yes," said Coverly. "Well, here's the company for your Christmas dinner," said the driver. "They told me to pick them up at three." "Won't you come in?" asked Coverly. "Oh, no, thanks, no," the driver said. "I got stomach trouble and all I want is a bowl of soup. I'll get something in the village. Turkey and all that. It makes me sick. You'll have to show them up the steps though. I'll give you a hand."

Coverly opened the door and said to the Negress he had seen on the green: "Merry Christmas. I'm Coverly Wapshot. We're very happy to have you here." "Merry Christmas, Merry Christmas," she said while from a portable radio she carried a chorus of hundreds sang "Adeste Fideles." "There are seven steps," Coverly said, "and then one more into the house." The woman took his arm with the trust of custom and helplessness and lifted her face to the brilliance of the sky. "I can see a little light," she said. "Just a little. It must be bright out there." "Yes, it is," said Coverly. "Five, six, seven." *"Joyeux Noël,"* said Moses, bowing from the waist. "May I take your wraps?" "No, thank you, no, thank you," the woman said. "I took a chill in the auto and I'll keep them on until I warm up." Moses led her into the parlor while the driver brought up the angular prophet, who was saying: "Have mercy upon us, have mercy upon us, most merciful Father; grant us Thy peace." "Hushup, hushup, Henry Saunders," said the Negress. "You spoil everybody's party." Her radio sang "Silent Night."

There were eight in all. The men wore stocking caps that seemed to have been pulled down over their ears with impatience and severity by the hands of some attendant who was anxious to get off and enjoy his own Christmas dinner. When Coverly and Betsey had got them all seated in the parlor Coverly looked

around for the wisdom of Honora's choice and thought that
these eight blind guests would know most about the raw material
of human kindness. Waiting for unseen strangers to help them
through the traffic, judging the gentle from the self-righteous
by a touch, suffering the indifference of those who so fear con-
spicuousness that they would not help the helpless, counting
on kindness at every turn, they seemed to bring with them a
landscape whose darkness exceeded in intensity the brilliance
of that day. A blow had been leveled at their sight but this seemed
not to be an infirmity but a heightened insight, as if aboriginal
man had been blind and this was some part of an ancient, human
condition; and they brought with them into the parlor the mysteries of the night. They seemed to be advocates for those in
pain; for the taste of misery as fulsome as rapture, for the losers,
the goners, the flops, for those who dream in terms of missed
things—planes, trains, boats and opportunities—who see on waking the empty tarmac, the empty waiting room, the water in
the empty slip, rank as Love's Tunnel when the ship is sailed;
for all those who fear death. They sat there quietly, patiently,
shyly, until Maggie came to the door and said: "Dinner is served
and if you don't come and get it now everything will be cold."
One by one they led the blind down the brightness of the hall
into the dining room.

So that is all and now it is time to go. It is autumn here in
St. Botolphs where I have been living and how swiftly the season
comes on! At dawn I hear the sound of geese, this thrilling
cranky noise, hoarse as the whistling of the old B & M freights.
I put the dinghy into the shed and take up the tennis court
tapes. The light has lost its summery components and is penetrating and clear; the sky seems to have receded without any
loss of brilliance. Traffic at the airports is heavy and my nomadic
people have got into their slacks and haircurlers and are on
the move once more. The sense of life as a migration seems
to have reached even into this provincial backwater. Mrs. Bretaigne has hung a blue plastic swimming pool out on her clothes-

line to dry. A lady in Travertine has found a corpse in her mint bed. In the burial ground where Honora and Leander lie, there is a carpet of green, drawn like a smile over the tumultuous conversion to dust. I pack my bags and go for a last swim in the river. I love this water and its shores; love it absurdly as if I could marry the view and take it home to bed with me. The whistle on the table-silver factory blows at four and the herring gulls in the blue sky sound like demented laying hens.

This late in the year the Williamses still drive down to Travertine for a swim in that dark and nutritious sea and after supper Mrs. Williams goes to the telephone and says to the operator: "Good evening, Althea. Will you please ring Mr. Wagner's ice-cream store." Mr. Wagner recommends his coffee and delivers a quart a few minutes later on a bicycle that rings and rattles so in the autumn dusk that it seems to be strung with bells. They play a little whist, kiss one another good night and go to sleep to dream. Mr. Williams, racked by the earth-shaking, back-breaking, binding, grinding need for love, dreams that he holds in his arms the Chinese waitress who works in the Pergola Restaurant in Travertine. Mrs. Williams, sleepless, sends up to heaven a string of winsome prayers like little clouds of colored smoke. Mrs. Bretaigne dreams that she is in a strange village at three in the morning ringing the doorbell of a frame house. She is looking, it seems, for her laundry, but the stranger who opens the door cries suddenly: "Oh, I thought it was Francis, I thought Francis had come home!" Mr. Bretaigne dreams that he is fishing for trout in a stream whose stones are arranged as coherently as those in any ruin and have as profound a sense of the past as the streets and basilicas of some ancient place. Mrs. Dummer dreams that she sails down one of the explicit waterways of sleep, while Mr. Dummer, at her side, climbs the Matterhorn. Jack Brattle dreams of a lawn without quack grass, a driveway without weeds, a garden without aphids, cutworm or black spot and an orchard without tent caterpillars. His mother, in the next room, dreams that she is being crowned by the governor of Massachusetts and the state traffic commissioner for the unprecedented scrupulousness with which she has observed the speed limits, traffic lights and stop signs. She wears long white robes and thousands applaud her virtue. The crown is surprisingly heavy.

Some time after midnight there is a thunderstorm and the last I see of the village is in the light of these explosions, knowing how harshly time will bear down on this ingenuous place. Lightning plays around the steeple of Christ Church, that symbol of our engulfing struggle with good and evil, and I repeat those words that were found in Leander's wallet after he drowned: "Let us consider that the soul of a man is immortal, able to endure every sort of good and every sort of evil." A cavernous structure of sound, a sort of abyss in the stillness of the provincial night, opens along the whole length of heaven and the wooden roof under which I stand amplifies the noise of rain. I will never come back, and if I do there will be nothing left, there will be nothing left but the headstones to record what has happened; there will really be nothing at all.